KT-161-522

WHITE MARS

WHITE MARS

Or, The Mind Set Free
A 21st-Century Utopia

BRIAN W. ALDISS

in collaboration with

ROGER PENROSE

LITTLE, BROWN AND COMPANY

A *Little, Brown* Book

First published in Great Britain in 1999
by Little, Brown and Company

Copyright © Brian W. Aldiss and Roger Penrose 1999

Legal advisor: Laurence Lustgarten

The moral right of the authors has been asserted.

*All characters in this publication are fictitious
and any resemblance to real persons, living or dead,
is purely coincidental.*

All rights reserved.
No part of this publication may be reproduced,
stored in a retrieval system, or transmitted, in any
form or by any means, without the prior
permission in writing of the publisher, nor be
otherwise circulated in any form of binding or
cover other than that in which it is published and
without a similar condition including this
condition being imposed on the subsequent purchaser.

A CIP catalogue record for this book
is available from the British Library.

ISBN 0 316 85243 0

Typeset by Palimpsest Book Production Limited,
Polmont, Stirlingshire
Printed and bound in Great Britain by
Clays Ltd, St Ives plc

Little, Brown and Company (UK)
Brettenham House
Lancaster Place
London WC2E 7EN

Dedicated to the Warden and Fellows
of
Green College, Oxford

This people is 500 miles from Utopia eastward
Sir Thomas More, *Utopia*

We are getting to the end of visioning
The impossible within this universe,
Such as that better whiles may follow worse,
And that our race may mend by reasoning
Thomas Hardy, *We Are Getting To The End*

Contents

On this day, Leo Anstruther decided he would walk to the
jetport because he believed in being unpredictable. I went
with him, carrying his notecase. Two bodyguards walked
behind us, following at a short distance.

We wound our way down narrow back streets. Anstruther
walked with his hands clasped behind his back, seemingly
deep in thought. This was a part of his island he rarely
visited; it held few charms for him. It was poverty alley. The
narrow houses had been sub-divided in many cases, so that
their occupants had overflowed into the streets to pursue their
livelihoods. Vulcanisers, toy-makers, shoemakers, kite-sellers,
junk-dealers, chandlers, fishermen and sellers of foodstuffs –
all obstructed the freeway with their various businesses.

I knew Anstruther had a concealed contempt for these
unfortunates. These people, no matter how hard they
worked, would never improve their lot. They had no vision.
He often said it. Anstruther was the man of vision.

He paused abruptly in a crowded square, looking about
him at the shabby tenements on all sides.

'It's not just the poor who help the poor, as the absurd
saying has it,' he said, addressing me although he looked
elsewhere, 'but the poor who exploit the poor. They rent
out their sordid rooms at extortionate rates to other families, inflicting misery on their own families for the sake of
a few extra shekels.'

I agreed. 'It's not a perfect world.' It was my job to
agree.

Among the dreary muddle of commerce, a bright stall

stood out. An elderly man dressed in jeans and a khaki shirt stood behind a small table on which were stacked jars of preserved fruit, together with mangoes, blackcurrants, pineapples and cherries, as well as a handful of fresh vegetables.

'All home-grown and pure, señor. Buy and try!' cried the old man as Anstruther paused.

Observing Anstruther's scepticism, he quoted a special low price per jar for his jams.

'We eat only factory food,' I told him. He ignored me and continued to address Anstruther.

'See my garden, master, how pure and sweet it is.' The old man gestured to the wrought-iron gate at his back. 'Here's where my produce comes from. From the earth itself, not from a factory.'

Anstruther glanced at the phone-watch on his wrist.

'Garden!' he said with contempt. Then he laughed. 'Why not? Come on, Moreton.' He liked to be unpredictable. He gestured to the bodyguards to stay alert by the stall. On a sudden decision, he pushed through the gate and entered the old fellow's garden. He slammed the gate behind us. It would give the security men something to think about.

An elderly woman was sitting on an upturned tub, sorting peppers into a pot. A sweet-smelling jasmine on an overhead trellis shaded her from direct sunlight. She looked up in startlement, then gave Anstruther and me a pleasant smile.

'Buenos dias, masters. You've come to look about our little paradise, of that I'm certain. Don't be shy, now.'

As she spoke, she rose, straightened her back and approached us. Beneath the wrinkles she had a pleasant round face, and though fragile with age stood alertly upright. She wiped her hands on an old beige apron tied about her waist and gave us something like a bow.

'Paradise, you say! It's a narrow paradise you have here, woman.' Anstruther was looking down its length, which was circumscribed by tile-topped walls.

'Narrow but long, and enough for the likes of Andy

2

and me, master. We have what we require, and do not covet more.'

Anstruther gave his short bark of laughter. 'Why not covet more, woman? You'd live better with more.'

'We should not live better by coveting more, merely more discontentedly, sir.'

She proceeded to show her visitors the garden. The enclosing walls became concealed behind climbers and vines.

Their way led with seeming randomness among flowering bushes and little shady arbours under blossom trees. The paths were narrow, so that they brushed by red and green peppers, a manioc patch and clumps of lavender and rosemary, which gave off pleasant scents as they were touched. Vegetables grew higgledy-piggledy with other plants. The hubbub of the streets was subdued by a murmur that came from bees blundering among flowers and the twitter of birds overhead.

The woman's commentary was sporadic. 'I can't abide seeing bare earth. This bit of ground here I planted with comfrey as a child, and you see how it's flourished ever since. It's good for the purity of the blood.'

Anstruther flicked away a bee that flew too near his face. 'All this must cost you something in fertiliser, woman.'

She smiled up at him. 'No, no, señor. We're too poor for that kind of unwise outlay. Human water and human waste products are all the fertilising we require in our little property.'

'You're not on proper drainage? Are you on the Ambient?'

'What's that, the Ambient?'

'Universal electronic communication system. You've never heard of it? The American bio-electronic net?'

'We are too hard-up for such a thing, sir, you must understand. Nor do we require it for our kind of modest living. Would it add to our contentment? Not a jot. What the rest of the world does is no business of ours.' She searched his face for some kind of approval. He in his turn

3

studied her old worn countenance, brown and wrinkled, from which brown eyes stared.

'You say you're content?' He spoke incredulously, as though the idea was new to him.

She gave no answer, continuing to gaze at him with an expression between contempt and curiosity, as if Anstruther had arrived from another planet.

Resenting her probing regard, he turned and commenced to walk back the way we had come.

'You aren't accustomed to gardens, I perceive, señor.' There was pride in her voice. 'Do you shut yourself in rooms, then? We don't ask for much. For us, ours is a little paradise, don't you see? The soil's so rich in worms, that's the secret. We're almost self-sufficient here, Andy and me. We don't ask for much.'

He said, half joking, 'But you enjoy moralising. As we all do.'

'I only tell you the truth, sir, since you invited yourself in here.'

'I was curious to see how you people lived,' he told her. 'Today, I'm off to discuss the future of the planet Mars – which you've probably never heard of.'

She had heard of Mars. She considered it uninteresting, since there was no life there.

'No worms, eh, my good woman? Couldn't you do something better with your life than growing vegetables in your own excreta?'

She followed us up the winding path, brushing away a tendril of honeysuckle from her face, amused and explaining, 'It's healthy, my good sir, you see. They call it recycling. I've lived in this garden nigh on seventy years and I want nothing else. This little plot was my mother's idea. She said, "Cultivate your garden. Don't disturb the work of the worms. Be content with your lot." And that's what Andy and I have done. We don't wish for Mars. The vegetables and fruits we sell keep us going well enough. We're vegetarian, you see. You two gentlemen aren't from the council, are you?'

4

Something in the tone of her voice stung Anstruther.

'No. Certainly not. So you've simply done what your mother told you all the years of your life! Did you never have any ideas of your own? What does your husband make of you being stuck here for seventy years, just grubbing in the soil?'

'Andy is my brother, master, if you refer to him. And we've been perfectly happy and harmed no one. Nor been impolite to anyone . . .'

We had regained the tiny paved area by the gate. We could smell the fragrance of the thyme, growing in the cracks between the paving stones, crushed underfoot. The two looked at each other in mutual distrust. Anstruther was a tall, solidly built man, who dominated the fragile little woman before him.

He saw she was angry. I feared he might destroy all her contentment with an expression of his irritation at her narrow-mindedness. He held the words back.

'Well, it's a pretty garden you have,' he said. 'Very pretty. I'm glad to have seen it.'

She was pleased by the compliment. 'Perhaps there might be gardens like this on Mars one day,' she suggested, with a certain slyness.

'Not very likely.'

'Perhaps you would like some beans to take away with you?'

'I carry no money.'

'No, no, I mean as a gift. They might improve your temperament after all that factory food you eat.'

'Don't be disgusting. Eat your beans yourself.'

He turned and gestured to me to open the gate. His two security men were waiting for him outside.

Anstruther's jet took us to the UN building. Members of the United Nationalities rarely met in person. They conferred over the Ambient, and only on special occasions were they bodily present; this was such an occasion, when the future of the planet Mars was to be decided. For this reason, the United Nationalities building was small, and not particularly imposing, although in fact it was larger than it needed to be, to satisfy the egos of its members.

On my Ambient I called Legalassist on the third level and gained entry to their department while Anstruther fraternised with other delegates below.

A Euripides screened me various files on EUPACUS, the international consortium whose component nations – the European Union, the Pacific Rim nations, and the United States – all had a claim on Mars.

Flicking to a file on the legal history of Antarctica, I saw that a similar situation had once existed there. Twelve nations had all laid claim to a slice of the White Continent. In December 1959 representatives of these nations had drawn up an Antarctic Treaty, which came into effect in June 1961. The treaty represented a remarkable step forward for reason and international cooperation. Territorial disputes were suspended, all military activities banned, and the Antarctic became a Continent for Science.

I took print-outs of relevant details. They might prove useful in the forthcoming debate. What the twentieth century had managed, we could certainly better, and on a grander scale, in our century.

In the ground-floor reception rooms, I found my boss consorting with Korean, Japanese, Chinese and Malay diplomats, all members of interested Pacrim countries. Anstruther was improving his shining image. A great amount of smiling by activating the zygomatic muscle went on, as is customary during such encounters.

When the session gong sounded, I accompanied Anstruther into the Great Hall, where we took our assigned places. Once I was seated at a desk in the row behind him, I passed him the Legalassist prints. Unpredictable as ever, he barely glanced at them.

'Today's the time for oratory, not facts,' he said. His voice was remote. He was psyching himself up for the debate.

When all delegates were assembled and quiet prevailed

6

in the hall, the General Secretary made his announcement: 'This is the General Assembly of the United Nationalities, meeting on 23 June 2041, to determine the future status of Planet Mars.'

The first speaker was called.

Svetlana Yulichieva of Russia was eloquent. She said that the manned landing on Mars marked a new page, if not a new volume, in the history of mankind. All nationalities rejoiced in the success of the Mars mission, despite the tragic loss of their captain. The way of the future was now clear. More landings must be financed, and preparations be made to terraform Mars, so that it could be properly colonised and used as a base for further exploration of the outer solar system. She suggested that Mars come under UN jurisdiction.

The Latvian delegate was eloquent. He agreed with Yulichieva's sentiments and said that the space-going nations must be congratulated on the enterprise they had shown. The loss of Captain Tracy was regretted, but must not be allowed to impede further progress. Was not, he asked rhetorically, the opening-up of a new world part of a human dream, the dream of going forth to conquer space, as envisioned in many fictions, book and film, in which mankind went forward boldly, overcoming everything hostile which stood in its way, occupying planet after planet? The beginning of the eventual encompassing of the galaxy had begun. The terraforming of Mars must assume top priority.

The Argentinian delegate, Maria Porua, begged to disagree. She spoke at length of the hideous costs of an enterprise such as terraforming, the success of which was not guaranteed. Recent disappointments, such as the failure of the hypercollider on the Moon – the brainchild of a Nobel Prize winner – must act as a caution. There were terrestrial problems enough, on which the enormous investments required for any extraterrestrial adventure could more profitably be spent.

Tobias Bengtson, the delegate for Sweden, scorned the last speaker's response to a magnificent leap into an expanding future. He reminded the assembly of the words of Konstantin Tsiolkovsky, the great Russian aeronautical engineer, who had said that Earth was the cradle of mankind, but that mankind could not remain for ever in the cradle. 'This great nineteenth-century visionary woke up the human race to its destiny in space. The dream has grown more real, more accurate, more pressing, as the years have progressed. A glorious prospect must not be allowed to slip away. A few deaths, a little expense, along the way must not deflect the nationalities from achieving our destiny, the conquest of all solar space, from the planet Mercury right out to the heliopause. Only then will the dreams of our forefathers – and our mothers – be fulfilled.'

Other speakers rose, many arguing that terraforming was a necessity. Why go to Mars if not to create more living space? Some warned that Mars would become a United States dependency, others that a ruling was required, otherwise competing nations would use Mars not as living space, but as a battlefield.

'I am going to talk practicalities,' said a delegate from the Netherlands. 'I have listened to a lot of airy-fairy talk here today. The reality is that we have now acquired this entire little planet of waste land. What are we to do with it? It's no good for anything.' He thumped the desk for emphasis. 'Who'd want to live there? You can't grow anything on it. But we can dump our dangerous nuclear waste on Mars. It would be safe there. You can build a mountain of waste by one of the poles – it might even make the place look a bit more interesting.'

It was Leo Anstruther's turn to speak. The antagonism generated against the previous delegate's speech gave him the opportunity to put his argument forward. He walked deliberately to the rostrum, where he scrutinised the assembly before speaking.

'Do you have to act out the dreams of your mothers and fathers?' he asked. 'If we had always done so, would we not still be sitting in a jungle in the middle of Africa, going in fear of the tribe in the next tree? EUPACUS – and not simply NASA – has achieved a great feat of organisation and engineering, for which we sincerely congratulate them. But this arrival of a crew of men and women on the Red Planet must have nothing to do with conquest. Nor should we turn the place into a rubbish dump. Have we lost our reverence for the universe about us?'

My boss went on to say that he had nothing but contempt for people who merely sat at home. But going forward did not mean merely proliferation; proliferation was already bringing ruin to Earth. Everyone had to be clear that to repeat our errors on other planets was not progress. It more closely resembled rabbits overrunning a valuable field of wheat. Now was our chance to prove that we had progressed in Realms of Reason, as well as in Terms of Technology.

What, after all, he asked, were these dreams of conquest that mankind was supposed to approve? Were they not violent and xenophobic? We had not to permit ourselves to live a fiction about other fictions. To attempt to fulfil them was to take a downward path at the very moment an upward path opened before us, to crown our century.

The old ethos of the nineteenth and twentieth centuries had been crude and bloody, and had brought about untold misery. It had to be abandoned, and here was a God-given chance to abandon it. He disapproved of that too readily used metaphor that said 'a new page in history had been turned'. Now was the time to throw away that old history book, and to begin anew as a putative interplanetary race. Delegates had to consider dispassionately whether to embark on a new mode of existence, or to repeat the often bloody mistakes of yesterday. 'All environments are sacrosanct,' Anstruther declared. 'The planet Mars is a sacrosanct environment and must be treated as such. It has not existed untouched for millions of years only to be reduced to one of Earth's tawdry suburbs today. My strong recommendation is that Mars be preserved, as the Antarctic has been preserved for many years, as a place of wonder and meditation, a symbol of our future guardianship of the entire solar system – a planet for science, a White Mars.'

The General Secretary declared a break for lunch.

The German delegate, Thomas Gunther, came up to Anstruther, glass in hand. He nodded cordially to us both.

'You have a fine style of rhetoric, Leo,' he said. 'I am on your side against the mad terraformers, although I don't quite manage to think of Mars as in any way sacred, as you imply. After all, it is just a dead world – not a single old temple there. Not even an old grave, or a few bones.'

'No worms either, Thomas, I'm led to believe.'

'According to latest reports, there's no life on it of any kind, and maybe never has been. "Martians" are just one of those myths we have lumbered ourselves with. We need no more silly nonsense of that kind.'

He smiled teasingly at Anstruther, as if challenging him to disagree. When Anstruther made no answer, Gunther developed his line of argument. The safe arrival of men on the Red Planet could be traced back to the German astronomer, Johannes Kepler, who – in the midst of the madness of the Thirty Years War – formulated the laws of planetary motion. Kepler was one of those men who, rather like Anstruther, defied the assumptions of others.

To declare for the first time that the orbit of a planet was an ellipse, with the sun situated at one focus, was a brave statement with far-reaching consequences. Similarly, what was decided on this day, in the hall of the UN, would have far-reaching consequences, for good or ill. Brave statements were required once more.

Gunther said his strong prompting was not to vex the delegates with talk of the sanctity of Mars. Since much – everything, indeed – was owed to science, then the planet must be kept for science. Sow in the minds of delegates the doubt whether the long elaborate processes of terraforming could succeed. Terraforming so far existed only in laboratory experiments. It was originally an idea cooked up by a science fiction writer. It would be foolhardy to try it out on a whole planet – particularly the one planet easily accessible to mankind.

'You could quote,' Gunther said, 'the words of a Frenchman, Henri de Chatelier, who in 1888 spoke of the principle of opposition in any natural system to further change. Mars itself would resist terraforming if any organisation was rash enough to try it.'

He advised Anstruther to stick with the slogan 'White Mars'. The simple common mind, which he deplored as much as Anstruther, would wish something to be done with Mars. Very well. Then what should be done was to dedicate the planet to science and allow only scientists on its surface – its admittedly unprepossessing surface. People should not be allowed to do their worst there, building their hideous office blocks and car parks and fast-food stalls. They must be stopped, as they had been prevented from invading the Antarctic. He and Anstruther must fight together to preserve Mars for science. He believed there was a delegate from California who thought as they did.

After all, he concluded, there were experiments that could be conducted only on that world.

'What experiments do you mean?' Anstruther enquired.

At this, Gunther hesitated. 'You will think me self-interested when I speak. That is not the case. I seize on my example because it comes readily to mind. Perhaps we might go out on a balcony, since there are those near us anxious to overhear what we say. Take a samosa with you. I assure you they are delicious.'

'My secretary always accompanies me, Thomas.'

'As you like.' He threw me a suspicious glance.

The two men went out on the nearest balcony, and I followed them. The balcony overlooked beautiful Lake Louise, the pellucid waters of which seemed to lend colour to the sky.

'No doubt you know what I mean by "the Omega Smudge"?' Gunther said. 'It's the elusive final ghost of a particle. When it's known – all's known! As I presume you

11

are aware, I am the president of a bank that, together with the Korean Investment Corporation, financed a search for the Gamma Smudge on Luna, following the postulate of the Chin Lim Chung-Dreiser Hawkwood formulation.' He bit into his samosa and talked round a mouthful.

'It was thought that the lunar vacuum would provide ideal conditions for research. Unfortunately, the fools were already busy up there, erecting their hotels and supermarkets and buggy parks and drilling for this and that. As you know, they have now almost finished construction on a subway designed to carry busybodies back and forth to their nasty little offices and eateries.

'At great expense, we built our ring – our superconducting search ring. Useless!'

'You did not find your smudge, I hear.'

'It is not to be found on the Moon. The drilling and the subway vibration have driven it off. Certainly experts argue about whether that was so – but experts will argue about anything. It has still to be discovered.' Gunther went on to explain that the high-energy detection of the Beta Smudge nearly two decades ago had merely disclosed a further something, a mess of resonances – another smudge. Gunther's bank was prepared to fund a different sort of research, to pin down a hidden symmetry monopole.

'And if you find it?' Anstruther asked, not concealing his scepticism.

'Then the world is changed . . . And I'll have changed it!' Gunther puffed out his chest and clenched his hands. 'Leo, the Americans and the Russians have tried to find this particle, and others, without success. It has an almost mystical importance. This elusive little gizmo so far remains little more than an hypothesis, but it is believed to be responsible for assigning mass to all other kinds of particle in the universe. Can you imagine its importance?'

'We're talking about a destroyer of worlds?'

Gunther gestured dismissively. 'In the wrong hands, yes, I suppose so. But in the right hands this elusive smudge will provide ultimate power, power to travel right across the galaxy at speeds exceeding the speed of light.'

Anstruther snorted to show he regarded such talk as ridiculous.

'Well, that's all hypothetical and I'm no expert,' said Gunther, defensively, and went on, laying emphasis on his words. 'I am not yet ruined and I wish for this quest to be continued. It can be continued only on Mars. I know I can raise the money. We can find the Omega Smudge there, and transcend Einstein's equations – if we fight today to keep Mars free of the terraformers.'

Anstruther gave me a glance, as if to show that he was aware of Gunther's bluster. All he asked, coolly, was, 'What in practical terms do you have against terraforming?'

'Our search needs silence – absence of vibration. Mars is the only silent place left in the habitable universe, my friend!'

When the bell rang for the afternoon session, the delegates trooped back to their places in a more sober mood than previously. The delegate for Nicaragua gave voice to a general uncertainty.

'We are required to pronounce judgement on the future of Mars. But can "judgement" possibly be a proper description for what will conclude our discussions? Are we not just seeking to relieve ourselves of a situation of moral complexity? How can we judge wisely on what is almost entirely an unknown? Let us therefore decide that Mars is sacrosanct, if only for a while. I suggest that it comes under UN jurisdiction, and that the UN forbids any reckless developments on that planet – at least until we have made doubly sure that no life exists there.'

Thomas Gunther rose to support this plea.

'Mars must come under UN jurisdiction, as the delegate from Nicaragua says. Any other decision would be a disgrace. The story of colonisation must not be repeated, with its dismal chapters of land devastation and exploitation of workers. Anyone who ventures to Mars must

13

be assured that his rights are guaranteed right here. By maintaining the Red Planet for science, we shall give the world notice that the days of land-grabbing are finally over.

'We want a White Mars.

'This is not an economic decision but a moral one. Some delegates will remember the bitter arguments that raged when we were deciding to move the international dateline from the Pacific to the middle of the Atlantic. That was a development dictated purely by financial interests, for mere convenience of trade between the Republic of California and their partners of the Pacrim. We must now make a more serious decision, in which financial interest plays no part.

'If we are to explore the entire solar system and beyond, then this first step along the way must be marked by favourable omens and wise decisions. We must proceed with due humility and caution, forgetting the damaging fantasies of yesterday.

'I beg you to set aside a whole folklore of interplanetary conquest and to vote for the preservation of Mars – White Mars, as Mr Leo Anstruther has called it. By so doing, we shall speak for knowledge, for wisdom, as opposed to avarice.' Gunther nodded in a friendly way to Anstruther as he strode from the podium.

Other speakers went to the podium to have their say, but now, increasingly, the emphasis was on how and why the Red Planet should be governed.

The sun was setting over the great milky lake beyond the conference hall when the final vote was taken. The General Secretary announced that the UN Department for the Preservation of Mars would be set up, and the White Mars Treaty executed.

Taking Thomas Gunther aside, the Secretary asked casually if Anstruther should be appointed head of the department.

'I would strongly advise against it,' Gunther said. 'The man is too unpredictable.'

2

My eyes had not been trained to see such a panorama. I was disoriented, like my entire physical body depended on my sight. Closing my eyes, I became aware of another source of strangeness. I was standing on solid ground, but I had lost pounds in weight.

Bracing myself, I tried to take account of our surroundings. Beyond the suited figures of my friends lay a world of solitude, infinite and tumbled, with nothing on which the gaze could rest. My mind, checking for something familiar, ran through a number of fantasy landscapes, from Dis to Barsoom, without relief. Grim? Oh yes, it was grim – but marvellously complex, built like a diabolical artist's construct. I was looking at something wonderfully unknown, indigestible, hitherto inaccessible. And I was among the first to take it all in!

And suddenly I found myself flushing. Like a blow to the heart came the thought: But I am of a species more extraordinary than anything else there ever was.

One day all this desolation would be turned into a fertile world much like Earth.

We broke from our trance. Our first task was to unload the body of Captain Tracy from our vehicle and place it in its body bag on the Martian surface. Although he was in his late thirties, Guy Tracy had seemed to be the fittest among us, but the acceleration and later deceleration had brought on the heart attack that killed him before we landed.

This death in Mars's orbit had seemed like a bad omen for the mission, but, as we laid his body down among the rocks of the regolith, a glassy effect flared into the sky as if in welcome. Low, almost beyond the visible, it was, we figured later, an aurora. Charged particles from the sun were interacting with molecules of the thin atmosphere trapped in Mars's slight magnetic field. The ghostly phenomenon seemed to flutter almost at shoulder level. It faded and was gone as we stepped back from the body bag. For a planet receiving sunlight equivalent to only some 40 per cent of Earth's generous ration, the little illumination show was encouraging.

Calls from base broke into our solemn thoughts. We were reluctant to talk back to Earth. They challenged us to say what had gone wrong.

'You have to be here to understand. You have to have made the journey. You have to experience Mars in its majesty to know that to try to alter – to terraform – this ancient place would be wrong. A terrible mistake. Not just for Mars. For us. For all mankind.'

There was a long pained argument. It takes forty minutes for a signal to traverse the distance between Earth and Mars and back – and between experiences. Night came on, sweeping over the plain. The stars glittered overhead.

We waited. We tried to explain.

Base ordered us to continue with our duties.

We said – everything was recorded – 'It is our duty to tell you that humanity's arrival on another planet marks a turning point in our history. We should not alter this planet. We must try to alter ourselves.'

Forty minutes passed. We waited uneasily.

'What do you mean by this talk? Why are you going moral on us?'

After some discussion, we replied, 'There has to be a better way forward.'

After forty minutes, a different voice from base. 'What in hell are you going on about up there? Have you all gone crazy?'

'We said you wouldn't understand.' And we closed the link and went to our bunks. Not a sound disturbed our sleep.

16

Our salaries, like our training, came from the EUPACUS combine. I knew and trusted their engineering skills. Of their intentions I was less sure. To win the Mars tender, the consortium had agreed merely to run all travel arrangements for ten years and to organise expeditions. I was well aware that they intended to begin the long process of terraforming by the back door, so to speak. Their hidden intentions were to turn Mars into saleable real estate; profitability depended on it. So I was told.

EUPACUS was contracted to run all ground operations on Mars, and could prevent unwanted curiosity there. Their investors would be eager to get their money back with interest, without being too concerned with how it was done. I woke with a firm determination to defy the stockholders.

Like everyone else, our crew had seen and been seduced by computer-generated pictures of EUPACUS-format Mars. Domes and greenhouses were laid out in neat array. Factories were set up for the task of extracting oxygen from the Martian rock. Nuclear suns blazed in the blue sky. In no time, bronzed men in T-shirts stepped forth among green fields, or climbed into bubble cars and drove furiously among Martian mountains already turning green.

Standing amid that magnificent desolation, the salesman's dream fizzled out like a punctured balloon.

We had landed almost on the equator, in the south-western corner of Amazonis Planitia, to the west of the high Tharsis Shield. Our parent ship acted as communication relay satellite, so that we could travel and keep in touch with one another. Highly necessary on a world where the horizon – supposing the terrain to be flat, which it mostly was not – was only 25 miles away. In its areosynchronous orbit, travelling 17,065 kilometres above ground, the ship appeared stationary to us, a reassuring sight when so much was strange.

But before we began our surveying we had to erect our geodesic dome to support a one-millimetre-thick dome fabric. We had been weakened by the months of flight, despite in-board exercise. This weakness turned the building of the dome into a major task, impeded as we were by our space-suits. Night was upon us before we were half finished. We had to retreat back into the module, to wait for morning.

When morning came, out we went again, determined not to let the structure beat us. We needed the dome. It would afford protection against the deepest cold and dust storms. We could exercise here and offload into it some of the machinery that made life in the module maddeningly cramped. Of course, as yet we had no means of filling it with breathable air at a tolerable pressure, even after we made it airtight. Since the dome had to go up, up it eventually went. When the last girders were bolted together and the last tie of the plastic lining secured – why, we needed no more exercise . . .

Our brief was to explore a few kilometres of the planet. Its enormous land area was as great in extent as Earth's, if not quite as various. It had plains, escarpments, riverbeds, vast canyons greater than anything terrestrial and extinct volcanoes – none of them traversed by human beings. We activated the TV cameras, and climbed aboard the two methane-powered buggies, to head eastward.

The intensity of that experience will always remain with me. While folks back home might see nothing on their screens but a kind of broken desert, that journey for us carried a strong emotional charge. It was as if we had travelled back in time, to a period before life had begun in the universe. Everything lay waiting, still, latent, piercing. None of us spoke. We were experiencing a different version of reality – a reality somehow menacing but calming. It was like being under the thunderous eye of God.

As we climbed, the regolith became less rocky. We might have been traversing the palm of an old man's withered hand. On either side were dried gulleys, forming intricate veins, and small impact craters, evidence of the bombardment of this world from space. We stopped periodically, taking up samples of rock and soil and storing them in an outer compartment for examination later, always marking the micro-environment from which they came. Since the ground temperature was sixty degrees below, we had little expectation of finding even a micro-organism.

Our progress became slower as the slope became steeper. We were now within sight of the flanks of the massive Tharsis Shield. August, lugubrious, it dominated the way ahead. It would be the subject of a later and better equipped exploration. Once we had caught sight of the graceful dome of Olympus Mons – a volcano long extinct – we turned the vehicles about and went back to base.

For the first kilometre of the return journey, the dust we had disturbed still hung in the thin atmosphere.

The laboratory was in my charge. By sundown, I had begun to test the first rock samples. The gas chromatograph mass spectrometer gave no indication of life. Part disappointed, part relieved, I went to join the others in the canteen for supper.

We were a strangely silent group. We knew something memorable had happened in the history of mankind and wanted to digest the meaning of the occasion. Drilling equipment had been set up in the dome before our excursion. A computer beeping summoned us to judge results. Water had been discovered 1.2 kilometres below ground level. Upon analysis, it was found to be relatively pure and inert. No traces of micro-organisms.

We rejoiced. With a water supply, living on Mars was now practicable. But the way lay open for terraforming.

Cang Hai's Account

3

The EUPACUS Deal: The Rotten Door

Should the citizens of the United States, for example, be answerable solely to Martian law when on Mars? Eventual answer: Yes. Mars is not a colony, but an independent world.

This was the sensible legal decision that became the foundation stone for the Deed of Independence that governs our lives on Mars and will stand as exemplar for all the other worlds we inhabit in times to come.

One of the greatest achievements of the last century was the establishing of preliminary planetary surveys. Less acknowledged was a system of workable international law.

From the start, weapons were prohibited here. Smoking is necessarily prohibited, not only as a pollutant but as a needless consumer of oxygen. Only low-grade alcohols are allowed. Habit-forming drugs are unknown. An independent judicial system was soon established. Certain categories of science are encouraged. We owe everything to science.

Under these laws and the laws of nature, we have built our community.

When I think back to this early time just now, I find consolation there. My daughter, Alpha Jefferies – now Alpha Jefferies Greenway – left Mars last year to live on a planet she had never known. I fear for her on that alien globe, although she now has a contract-husband to protect her.

She told me once, when we were still in communication, that Earth is the world of life. My image of it is as a world of death – of starvation, genocides, murders, and many horrors from which our world here does not suffer.

My arguments with my dear lost daughter have caused me to look again at those first years on Mars, when there was an excitement about being on a strange world and we were not entirely free of Earth-generated myths regarding ancient life on Mars, of finding old land-locked canals leading nowhere, or great lost palaces in the deserts, or the tombs of the last Lords of Syrtis! Well, that's all juvenile romanticism, part of the fecundity of human imagination, which sought to populate an empty world. And that is what still thrills me – this great empty world in which we live!

I will introduce myself. I am the adopted daughter of the great Tom Jefferies. I first knew life in the crowded city of Chengdu in China, where I was trained as a teacher of handicapped children. After five years of teaching in the Number Three Disability School, I felt a longing to try another planet. I applied for work on a UN work scheme and was accepted.

For my community service, I served for a year as kennel-maid at a dog-breeding station in Manchuria, where life was extremely hard. I passed the behavioural tests to become a fully fledged YEA. After all the preliminaries, including the two-week MIC – or Martian Inculcation Course – I was permitted to board the EUPACUS ship to Mars, together with two friends, on an ORT, an Opposition Return Trip.

What excitement! What dread!

Although I had anticipated that Mars itself would be bleak, I had not imagined life in the domes, which, by the time I arrived, was unexpectedly colourful. As a reminder of the semi-Oriental composition of Marvelos, the travel bureau subsidiary of EUPACUS which freighted everyone to Mars and back, brilliant lanterns were hung among the simple apartment blocks. Tank-walls of living fish stood everywhere. Flowering trees (originating from

21

Prunus autumnalis subhirtella) were planted along avenues. And what I liked best were the genetically adapted macaws and parrots that cast a scatter of colour as they flew free, and sang with sweet voices instead of croaking.

Apart from this pleasant sound, the domes were reasonably quiet, since the small jojo ('jump-on-jump-off') electric buses taking people about made little noise.

As I grew to know the settlement better, I found this colourful sector was just the 'tourist spot'. Beyond it lay the rather grimmer Permanents Sector, austere and undecorated, lying behind P. Lowell Street.

All this was enclosed, of course, under domes and spicules. Outside lay an airless planet of rumpled rock. My spine tingled just to look out at it.

Not that this view was featureless. To the west lay the rumpled extent of Amazonis Planitia, on the eastern edge of which we were situated. The domes had been built squarely on the 155th latitude, 18 degrees north of the equator. The site was sheltered from ferocious winds, which had built the yardangs to westward.

Our shelter loomed to the east of us, to the immense bulk of Olympus Mons, the cliff-like edges of whose skirts were only some 295 kilometres away. Its seamed slopes were lit every evening by the dull sun.

The Pavonis Observatory began immediately to give brilliant results. Studies of the gas giants became transformed almost into a new branch of astrophysics. Research into earlier temporalities and proto-temporalities was enlarging an understanding of the birth of the universe. Probes launched from the Martian surface had brought back iron-hard samples of ammonia-methane mix from Pluto containing impurities suggesting that the distant planet had its origins beyond the solar system.

A meteorite watch station became operative.

Thomas Gunther's Omega Smudge detector was being established when I made my first trip outside. The tube was under construction. I heard it said that clever lawyers were bending the proscriptions on doing science under Martian law in order to permit a larger ring to be built if needed.

However that was, the research unit, established half a kilometre from the domes (Areopolis as it now is), came under the control of the authoritarian particle physicist, Dreiser Hawkwood.

Because of its later significance, I must report a conversation that took place some time in those early days. It was recorded, as were most discussions in the first years, and now resides in the Martian Archive. Maybe similar conversations took place elsewhere. They assumed importance in the light of later discoveries.

Four scientists in the Pavonis Observatory, perched high on the Tharsis Shield, were talking. The deepest voice was identifiable as that of Dreiser Hawkwood himself. He was a bulky man with an unfashionable moustache and a gloomy expression.

'When we were driving up here,' a woman said, 'I kept thinking I saw white objects like tongues slicking away underground, fast as an oyster goes down a gullet. Tell me I was dreaming.'

'We've established there is no life on Mars. So you were dreaming,' said a colleague.

'Then I was dreaming too,' said another. 'I also saw those white things sticking up, disappearing as we approached. It seemed so unlikely I didn't care to say anything.'

'Could they be worms?'

'What, without topsoil?' Dreiser Hawkwood asked. His deep voice is easily identifiable. He laughed, and his colleagues laughed obediently with him. 'We shall find a natural geological explanation for them in time. They may be a form of stalagmite.'

The fourth member of the group did not contribute to this conversation. He was sitting somewhat distant from his friends, staring out of the canteen window at Olympus Mons, only a few kilometres away.

'Must get together an expedition to look at that weird volcano,' he said. 'The largest feature on the planet and we make little of it.'

Olympus Mons was about 550 kilometres across. It rose to 25 kilometres above the Mars datum, in consequence of which it could be seen from Earth even in the days of terrestrial telescopes. It rated as one of the most remarkable objects in the solar system.

Despite the interest of the scientists, increased demand for oxygen and water severely limited exploration work. Fuel for vehicular exploration consumed more oxygen. It was to be some while before Olympus Mons was investigated – or really entered our consciousness to any extent.

I'm not accustomed to being an historian. Why have I set myself this task? Because I was there on that occasion when Tom Jefferies stood up and declared, 'I'm going to kick down a rotten door. I'm going to let light in on human society. I'm going to make us live what we dream of being – great and wise people, cicumspect, daring, inventive, loving, just. People we deserve to be. All we have to dare to do is throw away the old and difficult and embrace what's new and difficult and wonderful!'

I'm getting ahead of myself, so I'd better describe how it was in the early days on the Red Planet.

I want to set down all the difficulties and limitations we, the first people on an alien planet, experienced – and all our hopes.

EUPACUS got us there, EUPACUS set up all the dimensions of travel. Whatever went wrong later, you have to admit they never lost a ship, or a life, in transit on the YEA and DOP shippings.

You certainly stayed close to nature on Mars, or the Eternal Verities, as a friend of mine called them. Oxygen and water supplies were fairly constant preoccupations.

Water was rationed to 3.5 kilograms per person per day. Communal laundering drank up another 3 kilograms per head per day. Everyone enjoyed a fair share of the supply; in consequence there were few serious complaints. Spartan though this rationing may sound, it compared quite favourably with the water situation on Earth. There, with its slowly rising population, industrial demands on fresh water had increased to the point where all water everywhere was metered and as expensive as engine fuels of medium grade. This effectively limited the economically stressed half of the terrestrial population to something less than the Martian allocation.

The need to conserve everything led to our system of communal meals. We all sat down together at table in two shifts, and were leisurely about our frugal meals, eking out food with conversation. Sometimes one of the company would read to us during the evening meal – but that came later.

At first I was shy about sitting among all those strange faces, amid the hubbub. Some of the people there I would later get to be friends with (not Mary Fangold, though), such as Hal Kissorian, Youssef Choihosla, Belle Rivers, funny Crispin Barcunda – oh, and many others.

But by luck I chanced to sit next to a pretty bright-faced YEA person. Her shock of curly dark brown locks was quite unlike my own straight black hair. She overcame my shyness, and obviously treated the whole business of being on a strange planet as a wonderful adventure. Her name was Kathi Skadmorr.

'I've been so lucky,' she told me. 'I just came from a poor family in Hobart, the capital city of Tasmania. I was one of five children.'

This shocked me. It was not permitted to have five children where I came from.

She said, 'I served my year at Darwin, working for IWR, International Water Resources. I learned much about the strange properties of water, how the solid state is lighter than the liquid state, how with capillary action it seems to defy gravity, how it conducts light . . .' She broke off and laughed. 'It's boring for you to hear all this.'

25

'No, not at all. I'm just amazed you wanted to talk to me.'

She looked at me long and carefully. 'We all have important roles to play here. The world has narrowed down. I'm sure your role will be important. You must make it so. I intend to make mine so.'

'But you're so pretty.'

'I'm not going to let that stop me.' And she gave a captivating chuckle.

As almost everyone of that first Martian population agreed, to survive on Mars close cooperation was a necessity. The individual ego had to submit to the needs of the whole body of people.

Continual television reports from Mars brought to the attention of the Downstairs world (as we came to call Earth) the fairness of Martian governance and our egalitarian society. It contrasted markedly with terrestrial injustice and inequality.

I don't want to talk about my own troubles, but I had been rather upset by the voyage from Earth, so much so that I had been referred to a psychurgist, a woman called Helen Panorios.

Helen had a dim little cabin on one of the outer spicules where she saw patients. She was a heavily built lady with dyed purple hair. I never saw her wearing anything other than an enfolding black overall-suit. A mild woman she was, who did seem genuinely interested in my problems.

As I explained to her, the six-month journey in cryosleep had terrified me. I had been detached from my life and seemed unable to reconnect with my ego. It was something to do with my personality.

'Some people hate the experience; some enjoy it as a kind of spiritual adventure. It can be seen as a sort of death, but it is a death from which you reawaken – sometimes with a new insight into yourself.' That's what she kept telling me. Basically she was saying that most people accepted

26

cryosleep as a new experience. Just coming to Mars, being on Mars, was a new experience.

I had come to hate the very name EUPACUS. The thought of undergoing that same annihilation getting home again to Earth scared me rigid. There had to be a better way of making that journey across millions of miles of space – or *matrix* as the new more correct term had it. Interstellar matrix teemed with radiations and particles, so that to naked experience 'space' had come to have a Victorian ring about it.

Travel between Earth and Mars was on the increase, or at least it had been before the disaster. Marvelos was hard pressed to meet the demand. Space vehicles were manufactured in terrestrial orbit under licence. Practically every industrialised nation of Earth was involved in their manufacture, if only in making pillows for the coffin-cots. The space vehicles, each with elaborate back-up facilities, were billion-dollar items. Shareholders were reluctant to invest in more rapid development. Takeovers and mergers of companies were happening all the time under the EUPACUS roof.

Helen talked me through the entire process of a voyage.

The consortium's ferry ships carried us passengers up from Earth to the interplanetaries, which parked in orbit about Earth and Luna. I was queasy from the start, even with a g-snort in me. I'm really not a good traveller. Then we passed into the interplanetary passenger ships, popularly known as 'fridge wagons'. You never forget the curious smell in a fridge wagon. I believe they start right away with some sort of airborne anaesthetic circulating.

'I didn't care for the way the compartments were so like refrigerated coffins,' I told Helen. Even before the wagon released from orbit, you were going rapidly into that dark nowhere of cryosleep as bodily functions slowed. That was terror for me . . .

'You were primed beforehand, Cang Hai, dear,' said Helen. 'You know well the economics of that journey back at that stage of development. Taking passengers in

27

cryosleep obviates the need for the ships to carry food and water. Little air is needed. Fuel and expense are saved. Otherwise, well, no trip . . .'

I relived the rush upwards from Earth. For most people, the spirit of adventure overcame any feelings of sickness, though not for me. Two hundred and fifty-six kilometres up, the barrel shape of the fridge wagon loomed, riding in its orbit. It had looked small, then it was enormous. Its registration number was painted large on its hull.

You have to admit it was a neat manoeuvre, considering the speed at which both bodies were travelling. With hardly a jar, they locked. I did then dare, before entering the wagon, to take a last look out at the Earth we were leaving. Fridge waggons have no ports.

I had to cry a little. Helen tenderly placed a hand on my shoulder, like the mother I never had, saying nothing. I was leaving behind my Other, back in Chengdu. Nobody would understand that.

Once in that strange-smelling interior, dense with low murmurs of various machines, we were guided to a small apartment, a locker room really. There one undressed with a neuter android in attendance, stowed away one's few belongings, and took a radiation shower. It was like preparing for a gas chamber. Advised by the android, you now had to lock your bare feet into wall-grooves and clasp the rungs in the curving wall above head level. The compartment now swung and travelled to a vacant coffin-cell. Music played. The aria 'Above my feet the roses speak . . .' from Delaport's opera *Supertoys*.

Then you were somehow motionless and monitors uncoiled like snakes. Tiny feeds attached themselves to your body. Before the wagon left orbit, your body temperature was approaching that of frozen meat. You might as well have been dead. You were dead.

I did a bit of screaming in front of Helen Panorios. Gradually I seemed to get better.

We worked through the disorientation of rousing back

to life in Mars orbit, speeding above all that varied tumble of rock and desert and old broken land.

'You certainly have to welcome new experience to get that far!' I said at one point.

When disaster struck, those who welcomed new experience were certainly well prepared for anything. Which was an important factor in influencing what happened to us all.

Helen rather liked to lecture me. She called it 'establishing a context'. Marvelos organised two types of visit to Mars, one when Earth and Mars were in conjunction, (called the CRT, the Conjunction Return Trip), one when they were in opposition (called the ORT, the Opposition Return trip).

Outward bound both trips took half a year. It was inevitable that those trips had to be passed in cryosleep.

Perhaps it's worth reminding people that by 'year' I always mean Earth year. Earth imposed its year on Mars thinking much as the Christian calendar had been imposed over most of Earth's nations, whether Christian or not. We will come to the rest of the Martian calendar and our clocks later.

The difficulty lay in the provision of return journeys. Helen grew quite excited about this. She showed me slides. While the return leg of an ORT took an uncomfortable year, the CRT took only half a year, no longer than the trip outwards. The snag was that the ORT required a stay of only thirty days on Mars, which was generally regarded as a pretty ideal time period, whereas the CRT entailed a stay of over a year and a half.

I was booked for an ORT, and found I couldn't face the mere thought of it. Helen had booked on a CRT. Her time away from Earth was going to be eighteen times longer than mine. Although I remained in touch with my Other in Chengdu, I could not have faced such a long stretch away. Now I found I could not face the long year in cryosleep.

Of course everyone who came to Mars had made these decisions. Despite such obstacles, the number of applications for flights increased month by month, as those returning reported on what for most was the great emotional experience of their lifetime.

The UN and EUPACUS between them agreed on the legal limits of those permitted to visit Mars. Their probity had to be proved. So it had fallen out that those who came to Mars arrived either as YEAs or as DOPs.

The arrangements for a Mars visit were long and complex. As EUPACUS grew, it became more and more bureaucratic, even obfuscatory. But the rule was quickly established that only these two categories of persons ever came to Mars, and then only under certain conditions. (This excluded the cadre needed for Martian services.)

The main category of person was a Young Enlightened Adult (YEA). This was my category, and Kathi Skadmorr's. Provision was also made for – the Taiwanese established this term – Distinguished Older Persons (DOPs). Tom Jefferies was a DOP.

Once these visitors reached Mars – I'm talking now about how it was back in the 2060s – she or he had to undergo a week's revival and acclimatisation (the unpopular R&A routine). Maybe they also saw a psychurgist. R&A took place in the Reception House, as it was then called, a combined hospital and nursing home run by Mary Fangold, with whom I did not get along. This was in Amazonis. Later other RHs were set up elsewhere.

'In the hospital,' Helen reminded me, 'you were given physiotherapy in order to counteract any possible bone and tissue loss and to assist in the recovery of full health. Why did you not accept the offer of psychurgy there and then?'

This was when I had to admit to her that I was different.

'How different?'

'Just – different.' I did not wish to be explicit, which was perhaps a mistake.

30

If you were unversed in history, you might wonder that anyone endured all these demanding travel conditions. The fact is that, given the chance to travel, people will endure almost any amount of discomfort and danger to get to a new place. Such has been the case throughout the history of mankind.

Also you must remember that an epoch was drawing to a close on Earth. There was no longer the promise of material abundance that once had prevailed. Not through exploration, conquest, or technological development. The human race had proved itself a cloud of locusts, refusing to curb their procreative and acquisitive habits. They had sucked most of the goodness from the globe and its waters. The easier days of the twentieth century, with individual surface travel readily available, were finished.

So for the young, us YEAs, harsh Martian conditions were seen as a challenge and an invitation. The experience of being on Mars, of identifying with it, was seen as worth all the time spent in community work and matrix travel.

But somehow, with me . . . well, it was different. I guess I just took longer to adjust. It was something to do with my personality.

We have the testimony of an early Mars visitor, Maria Gaia Augusta (age twenty-three) on video. Her report says: 'Oh, the experience must not be missed. I have ambitions to be a travel writer. I spent my YEA community service in the outback of Australia, seeding and tending new forest areas, and was glad to have a change.

'At the back of my mind was a decision to gather material on Mars for knocking copy. I mean, Mars was to me like just a shadowy stone in the sky. I couldn't see the attraction – apart from curiosity. But when I got there – well, it was another world, quite another world. Another life, if you like.

'You know what the surface of Mars is? Loneliness made solid, rock solid.

'Course, there were restrictions, but they were part of the

31

deal. I loved all the fancy-shaped domes they're setting up in Amazonis Planitia. In the desert, in fact. They put you in the mood of some Arabian Nights fantasy. You get to thinking, "Well, look at the frugal life the Arabs used to lead. I can do that." And you do.

'I did the compulsory aerobic classes during my R&A period after we had landed, and got to enjoy them. I had been a bit overweight. Aerobics is weird in lighter gravity. Fun. I met a very sweet guy in the classes, Renato, a San Franciscan. We got along fine.

'We enjoyed sex in that light gravity and maybe invented a few positions not in the Kama Sutra. Mars is going to be left behind in a few years' time, when we settle the moons of Jupiter. Sex will really be something out there, in real low gravity! Meantime, Mars is the best thing we got in that respect.

'Me and Renato got on the list for a four-body expedition beyond the domes. Four-bodies were then the standard package. I know it's different now. Two-bodies were considered too dangerous, in case one body got ill or something. Not that there are all that many illnesses on Mars, but you never know.

'We didn't go madly far, just to the Margarite Sinus, towards the equator, because of fuel restrictions, but that was enough. Of course, every little four-body had to have a scientific component – the buggy was like a small lab, complete with cameras and electrolysis equipment and I don't know what-all. Radio, of course, to keep us oriented, and listen out for dust storms. We were exploring the canyons in Margarite and we came on a great wall of rock, rubbed smooth by the wind. Me and Renato were seized with a mad idea. We slipped into suits – you have to wear suits – atmosphere there was about 10 millibars, compared to 1,000 millibars back on Earth. Any case, you couldn't breathe it. We got these paints from the buggy store, climbed outside and began to decorate the rock surface. The other couple joined in. There we were, actually alone on the open surface. Wild!

'And we painted a lovely luminous Mars dragon, flying up to the stars. We worked till nightfall, just using red, green and gold colours. To finish off, we had to turn on the buggy headlights. There was a sort of – well, I almost said religious feeling about what we were doing. It was like we were aborigines, making a sacred kind of hieroglyph.

'When we got back to base, we showed photos of the dragon around and nearly started a panic. Some people thought it was the work of autochthonous Martians! Quite impossible, of course, but some folk are incurably superstitious.

'No, I lapped up my time on Mars. It was a life apart. A formative experience. I longed to be out there alone, or alone with Renato, but that wasn't considered safe until my last month there. Just to be out in the desert at night, in a breather-tent, it's beyond description. You're alone in the cosmos. The stars come down and practically touch you. You just feel they should come right in and penetrate your flesh . . .

'It's contradictory. You're entirely isolated – you could be the only person who ever lived, ever – and yet you are an intense part of everything. You know you're – what's the word? – well, somehow you're an integral part of the universe. You are its consciousness.

'Like being the seeing eye of this incalculably vast thingme out there . . .

'I say it's contradictory. What I mean is the perception feels contradictory, because you've never experienced it before. You'll never forget it, either. It's a tattoo on your soul, sort of . . .

'Oh, sure, there were things I missed out there. Things I did without but didn't miss, and things I missed. What things? Oh, I missed trees. I missed trees quite badly at first.

'But my life has changed since I was there. I can never go again but I'll never ever forget it. I try to live a better life because of it.

That's no joke in the muddle we're in here, downstairs on Earth.'
END TAPE.

The 'fancy-shaped domes' to which Maria Gaia Augusta refers are the linked spicules, constructed from a small number of repetitive sections, which formed the basis of what was eventually to become Mars City or Areopolis. The monotony of this structure was relieved by conjoined tetrahedral structures, rather similar to those erected in the north of Siberia a few years previously.

From orbit, this sprawling structure, white-painted against the tawny Martian regolith, made a striking pattern.

4

Broken Deals, Broken Legs

Looking back, I see how silly I was in my early days – silly and shy. I worked in the biogas chamber unit, and practically took refuge there. Everyone else seemed so clever. Kathi was clever. Why did she seek out my company?

Her interest at this time was in politics, about which she talked endlessly. Placements within the YEA and DOP brackets were systematically arranged through the Mars Department, under Secretary Thomas Gunther. Kathi had a particular dislike of Gunther, saying he was radically corrupt.

Whether that was true or not – many people praised Gunther – there was always bad feeling over the placements. Who was accepted or not as a YEA was open to local manipulation. I thought the system worked pretty well, enabling as many people as possible to visit the Red Planet. The United States insisted that matrix travel (the term 'space travel' had become old-fashioned) was a democratic right.

Kathi's main complaint concerned the whole business of selection as a YEA. To qualify within the 16–28 years age bracket we had to undergo a rigorous Genetic and Superficial Health Test as well as a GIQ Exam. The General Intelligence was supposedly free from cultural and sexual bias and intended to establish the emotional stability of the examinee. Kathi was one-eighth Aborigine, and swore this was held against her at the Sydney board.

'I came up against a filthy little man who gave me the

final interview. Do you know what he said? Only my granting him sexual favours would get me through! Can you imagine?'

I hardly dared ask what she had done.

She tossed her hair back. 'What the hell do you think? I wasn't going to let him stop me. I let him screw me. Next day my boyfriend broke both his stinking legs in his back yard . . .'

By far the greatest percentage of YEAs had no means by which to cover the exorbitant costs of interplanetary travel. Nor was financial payment allowed – although Kathi said this too could be arranged if you were one of the Megarich. Funding poured through the UN Matrix Tax to EUPACUS. Gunther was pocketing a 'whole river' of this money, according to Kathi. I had seen pix of Gunther and thought he looked nice.

Having passed their exams, the young educated adults were allocated to stations in which to spend a year of community service. Some got lucky, some lived like slaves, as I did. Some laboured on newly established fish farms in Scapa Flow, or the anchovy nurseries off the west coast of South America. Some served in the great new bird ranges of the taiga, or in satellite manufactories, 2,000 miles above Earth. Some were sent to Luna to work on the underground systems as technicians. Kathi was lucky and went to Darwin and the Water Resources.

'And sitting there like a fat pig in a strawberry bed was Herby Cootsmith, a Megarich, squatting on his investments, gradually buying up all Darwin,' Kathi said.

As a group, the YEAs were mistrustful of the socio-economic systems from which they emerged. They hated the disparity between the poor, with their harsh conditions and short lives, and the Megarich, whose existences were projected to extend over two centuries. Life for the Megarich, Kathi declared, misquoting Hobbes, was 'nasty, brutish, and long'.

It was estimated that 500 people owned 89 per cent of the world's wealth. Most of them belonged in the

Megarich category, being able to pay for the antithanatotic treatments.

After your year's community service, you had to pass the various behavioural tests. Then you were qualified for the Mars trip.

'How did you manage?' Kathi asked.

I hesitated, then thought I might as well tell her. 'A rich protector came forward with a bribe.'

Kathi Skadmorr gave a harsh cackle. 'So we're both here under false pretences! And I wonder how many others – YEAs and DOPs?! Don't you just long for a decent society, without lies and corruptions?'

It came as a surprise to me to discover that Tom Jefferies and his wife Antonia – both of them DOPs – had also used a bribe to get to Mars. That I shall have to tell about in a minute, and to describe Antonia's death.

Antonia died so many years ago. Yet I can still conjure up her fine, well-bred face. And I wonder how different history would have been if she had not died.

The DOPs were reckoned to have served their communities; otherwise, they would hardly be Distinguished. As Older Persons, they did not have to undergo the GIQ examination. However, the Gen & S Health test was particularly rigorous, at least in theory, in order to avoid illness en route, that long, spiralling, burdensome route to the neighbouring planet. In some cases, behavioural tests were also applied.

DOP passages were generally paid for by some form of government grant from their own communities. In the eighteenth century, Dr Johnson told Boswell that he wished to see the Great Wall of China: 'You would do what would be of importance in raising your children to eminence ... They would be at all times regarded as the children of a man who had gone to view the Wall of China. I am serious, sir.' To have visited Mars brought a similar mark of distinction – conferred, it was felt, on whole communities as well as on the man or woman who had gone to Mars and returned home to them.

One of the excitements of being on Mars was that one occasionally met a famous DOP, not necessarily a scientist, perhaps a sculptor such as Benazir Bahudur, a literary figure such as John Homer Bateson, or a philosopher such as Thomas Jefferies. Or my special friend, Kathi Skadmoor.

I first saw Tom Jefferies from afar, looking sorrowful and remote, but I held the popular misconception that all philosophers looked like that. He was an elegant man, sparse of hair, with a pleasing open face. He was in his late forties. A vibrancy about him I found very attractive.

So I was immediately drawn to him, as were many others. While I was drawn, I did not dare speak to him. Would I have spoken, had I known how our paths would intertwine? Perhaps it is an impossible question – but we were destined to face plenty of those . . .

Many scientists went to Mars under the DOP rubric, among them the celebrated computer mathematician, Arnold Poulsen, and the particle physicist I have already mentioned, Dreiser Hawkwood. A percentage of those who had travelled on the conjunction flight became acclimatised to Mars and, because the work and lighter gravity there were congenial to them, stayed on. It should be added that many YEAs stayed on for similar reasons – or simply because they could not face another period of cryogenic sleep for the return journey.

From 2059 onwards, as interplanetary travel became almost a norm, every Martian visitor was compelled by law to bring with him a quota of liquid hydrogen (much as earlier generations of air travellers had carried duty-free bottles of alcohol about with them!). The hydrogen was used in reactions to yield methane for refuelling purposes.

Another factor powered the movement in the direction of Mars. Competition to exist in modest comfort on the home planet grew ever more intense. To gratify its desire for profit and then more profit, capitalism had required economies of abundance, plus economies of scarcity into whose markets its entrepreneurs could inflitrate. Now, under this guiding but predatory spirit, there existed only the voracious developed world and a few bankrupt states, mainly in Africa and Central Asia. Increased industrialisation, bringing with it global overheating and expensive fresh water, made life increasingly difficult and corrupted the competence of democracies. Prisons filled. Stomachs went empty.

While there were many who deplored this state of affairs, they were as powerless to alter it as to stop an express train.

Now a number of them had an alternative.

The Martian community developed its own ethos. Being itself poor in most things, it proclaimed an espousal of the poor, downtrodden and unintelligent. More practically, it fostered a welcoming of the estrangement that Mars brought, a passion for science, a care for the idea of community.

Most Martians had discarded their gods along with the terrestrial worship of money. They were thus able to develop a religious sense of life, unwarped by any paternalistic reverences. Always at their elbows was the universe with its cold equations; living just above the subsistence level, the Martians sought to understand those equations. It was hoped that the tracing of the Smudge would resolve many problems, philosophical as well as scientific.

We lived under stringent laws on Mars, laws to which every visitor was immediately introduced. The underground water source would not last for ever. While it did last, a proportion of it underwent the electrolysis process to supply us with necessary oxygen to breathe. Buffer gases were more difficult to come by, although argon and nitrogen were filched from the thin atmosphere. The pressure in the domes was maintained at 5.5 psi.

It will be appreciated that these vital arrangements absorbed much electricity. Technicians were always alert for ways of extending our resources. To begin with they relied on heat-exchange pumps as generators, and photovoltaic cells.

I have to tell myself that I am a serious person, interested in serious matters. I will not speak of my increasing affection for Kathi Skadmorr, who after all is a marginal person like me, or my admiration for Tom Jefferies, who is a central person unlike me. Instead, I will talk about worms.

In one Amazonis laboratory was a precious Martian possession – 'the farm', a wit called it. Dreiser Hawkwood had introduced it; his side interest was biochemistry. The farm was contained in a box two metres square and a metre and a half deep. In it was rich top soil from the Calcutta Botanical Gardens, expensively imported by courtesy of Thomas Gunther and his EUPACUS associates. In the box grew a small weigela and a sambucus. Below, in the soil, were worms of the perichaeta species, working away and throwing up their castings.

The metabolism of the worms had been accelerated. Their digestion and ejection of soil was rapid. They worked at dragging down the leaves fallen from the plants, thus enriching the soil with vegetable and microbial life. The enriched soil was to be set in a bed inside one of the domes to provide the first 'natural'-grown vegetables. The tilth would eventually cover acres of specially prepared regolith, breaking it down under greenhouse domes into arable land.

From this modest beginning in the farm, great things were to come. It is doubtful if Mars would ever have become more than marginally habitable without that lowly and despised creature, the earthworm, which Charles Darwin regarded so highly, not dreaming that it would one day transform an alien planet as it had transformed Earth itself.

This new agricultural revolution, intended to supplement

the food grown in chemical vats, was assisted by work carried out high above the Martian crust.

Mars has two small satellites that chase across the sky, Swift and Laputa. Early astronomers had bestowed on these two small bodies the unbecoming names of Phobos and Diemos. Swift unwearyingly rises and sets twice in a Martian day. Landings have been made on both satellites. On Swift have been found metallic fragments, presumably the remains of an unsuccessful twentieth-century Russian mission.

Working from a small base on Swift, a series of large PIRs – polymer inflatable reflectors – was set in orbit about Mars to reflect much needed sunlight to the surface. The PIRs are cheap, and easily destroyed by space debris, but equally easily replaced.

The PIRs can be seen in daylight or at night, when they shine brightly unless undergoing occasional eclipse.

It will be deduced from these developments that, despite all the protests, Mars was slowly and inevitably being drawn nearer to terraforming.

Despite all the regulations, the pressure to live brought this change about.

The observatory built on Tharsis Shield near Olympus Mons continued to yield results. The meteorite watch station became operative. The new branch of astrophysics studying the gas giants was officially named jovionics. The telescopes of the observatory tracked many asteroids. Dedication to research was a feature of the scientific atmosphere on Mars. There was little to distract the scientists, as the asteroid-watchers sought to prove the small bodies were the remains of a planet that, before being torn apart by forces of gravity, occupied an orbit between Mars and Jupiter.

Studies of magneto-gravitic irregularities revealed a remarkably high gravity reading for the region near Olympus Mons. I discovered that Kathi was interested in this. No such anomaly existed on Earth, she claimed. She was reading many scientific papers on her Ambient, and told me she believed there was a connection between magneto-gravitic influences and consciousness, so that at present she was looking for a dimensionless quality, but I did not understand her.

When I questioned this connection she believed in, she explained patiently that there were electric and magnetic fields. Whereas electric charges were the direct sources of electric fields, as far as was known there were no equivalent magnetic charges – that is to say, no magnetic monopoles. The influence of hidden-symmetry monopoles on consciousness was subtle and elusive – or appeared to be so as yet. The sophistry underlying the apparently simple laws of the physical universe, the exceptional qualities of many elementary particles, might lead one to suspect the universe of possessing a teleological character.

She was continuing the explanation when I had to admit I could follow her no further.

With a sympathetic smile, Kathi nodded her head and said, 'Who can?!'

She became inquisitive about my beloved Other in Chengdu. Feeling sorry I had mentioned her, I was not very forthcoming. Later, I saw she was interested in the question of consciousness; the existence of my Other, so simple to me, seemed to raise complex questions in her mind.

There seemed little for biochemists and xenobiologists to do once it was agreed that Mars held no life and that its early life forms – archebacteria and so forth – had perished many millions of years before mankind appeared on Earth.

The heliopause, with its strange turbulences, was studied. While Mars was regarded as a completely dead world, indications of life on Ganymede, one of the moons of Jupiter already mentioned, were observed by new instruments.

But I am getting ahead of our history again. Things were well enough for the Martian-terrestrial relationship, until the disaster occurred that changed the situation, entirely and for ever.

5

You need to remember how complex and ill judged terrestrial affairs were up to this period.

Among the harsh pleasures of Mars were many negative ones. I was particularly glad to escape the constant surveillance to which we had been subject. On Earth crime rates were such that every city, every road, every apartment house and condominium and almost every room in those buildings was watched day and night by the glass eyes of security cameras. The sellers of masks profited accordingly, and crime thrived. Oppression and blackmail prospered even more.

The mansion of Thomas Gunther was well equipped with surveillance devices, including those of the latest type. The camgun for instance, would fire yards of adhesive at any visitor to the building whose characteristics were not held in its computer.

Not all forms of crime yielded to inspection. Fraud and corruption could take place in broad daylight, with smiles to outface any camera. Smiles had been worn like masks in the upper echelons of the EUPACUS consortium.

The collapse of the entire enterprise began with a seemingly small event in 2066. A senior clerk in the tall ivory-white tower in Seoul that was the main EUPACUS building was caught embezzling.

The clerk was sacked. No charges were brought against him. He was found dead in his apartment two days later. Possibly it was suicide, possibly murder. But an electronic message was released, triggered by the stoppage

43

of the clerk's electronic heart, to be received at the North American Supreme Court of Justice. It led the court to uncover a massive misappropriation of funds by EUPACUS directors. In comparison the clerk's misdemeanours were nugatory.

A cabal of senior executives was involved. Five arrests were immediately made, although all managed mysteriously to escape custody and were not recaptured.

Investigators visiting a vice-chairman's residence on Niihau Island, in the Hawaiian chain, were met by gunfire. A two-day battle ensued. In the bombed-out ruin of the palace were found disks incriminating directors of the consortium: tax evasion on a massive scale, bribing of lawyers, intimidation of staff and, in one instance, a case of murder. The affairs of EUPACUS were put on hold.

EUPACUS offices were closed, sealed off for judicial investigation. All flights were halted, all ships grounded. Mars was effectively cut off. Suddenly the distance between the two planets seemed enormous.

Our feelings were mixed. Along with alarm went a sort of pleasure that we had been severed from the contemptible affairs of Earth for a while.

We did not understand at first how long that while was to be. Earth's finances were entangled with the vast EUPACUS enterprise. One by one, banks and then whole economies went bust.

Japan's Minister of Exterior Finance, Kasada Kasole, committed suicide. Four hundred billion yen of bad debts were revealed, hidden outside the complex framework of EUPACUS accounts. The debts stemmed from tobashi trading; that is, moving a client's losses to other companies so that they do not have to be reported. Chiefly involved was the Korean banking system, which had invested heavily in its own right in EUPACUS.

An equities analyst said that the Korean *won*, closely linked to the Japanese economic system, was now standing against the US dollar at 'about a million and falling'.

Recession set in, from which the EU was particularly

slow to recover, as its individual members were forced, one by one, to close shop.

All round the globe were companies and manufactures that had relied on or invested in EUPACUS business. Many were already in debt because of delayed payments. The closure of EUPACUS Securities led to a collapse of the world banking system.

Shares fell to just over one quarter of their 2047 peak. Property values followed, leaving the PABS – Pacrim Accountancy and Banking System – with substantial bad debts and asset write-offs. The IFF was unable to muster a credible rescue package.

The deflationary impact was already being felt in North America. The situation, said one US official, was deteriorating dramatically as Asian speculators were selling off their huge holdings of US financial assets in order to try and meet their obligations nearer home. 'The US home market is going into meltdown,' an official said.

Only a month after this remark, the world's economy was in meltdown.

We sat on our remote planet and watched these proceedings with a horrified fascination. Bad went to worse, and worse to worse again. There came the day when terrestrial television went dead. And we were truly alone.

A fish stinks from the head. I'm told it's an old Turkish proverb. Despite the rigorous checks that had been set up by the UN, bad conditions and poor pay had made workers in the Marvelos Health Registration Department just as open to bribery as those at the top of the vast organisation.

So it was that Antonia Jefferies and her husband Tom were able to pass the Gen & S Health Test and travel to Mars on a CRT trip just under four years before EUPACUS collapsed, and the world economy with it.

Antonia suffered from a cancer of the pancreas, on which she had refused to have nanosurgery; it was a long while before I discovered why. Nevertheless, the gallant woman

45

was determined to set foot on the Red Planet before she became too ill to travel. Her interest was in the Smudge experiment, which she saw as an extreme example of the interlinkage between science and human life, for good or bad.

She was a historian. Her boovideo, *The Kepler Effect*, had been a bestseller. Tom Jefferies had moved from employment as a theoretical physicist specialising in monopole research to what he called Practical Philosophy. His new profession brought him fame and the soubriquet the 'Rich Man's Tom Paine'.

Tom was in his early fifties. His wife was forty-eight. They had no children. He had married Antonia only after the cancer, then in her pancreas, had been diagnosed. The diagnosis had been in 2052.

Roused from cryosleep, disembarking from their ship, the Jefferies went to the R&A Clinic. Her cancer had not slept on the voyage. The diagnosis by Mary Fangold revealed that she was very ill. Tom told me later that Fangold was 'an angel', but was not able to provide a cure.

At Antonia's request, Tom drove her in a buggy to the Tharsis Shield. They sat at nightfall with remoteness all about them – in Tom's words, 'with that singing quality which absolute isolation has' – as Earth rose above the horizon, a distant star. There Antonia died, lying and gasping out her life in her husband's arms.

'Thank you for everything,' she said. Those were her last words.

He buried his face on her shoulder. 'You are my everything, my darling wife.'

Tom Jefferies had to return to base when his oxygen was running low. A memorial service was held before Antonia's body was slipped into one of the biogas chambers. I saw her go. At that service, Tom vowed he would never leave the planet where his wife had died. He would dedicate himself instead to the stability of the Martian community.

In fact, he all but gave up his research work in order to serve the community. Tom Jefferies came to the fore when EUPACUS collapsed and connections between Earth and Mars failed. It is amazing what the will of one man can achieve.

I can see this must include some personal history, as well as the story of the development of Mars. I arrived on the same fridge wagon as did the Jefferies, and came to know both Tom and Antonia slightly in the R&A Hospital. Kathi was helping out as a nurse and invited me in. Antonia's ivory-white face was so fine, so intelligent, it was impossible not to want to be near her. Tom was quite a large man, but elegant, as I have said.

What is more difficult to tell is what set him apart from everyone else. His manner was less severe than well controlled. He showed great determination for the cause in which he believed, yet softened it with humour, which sprang from an innate modesty. He was not above self-mockery. In his speech, he adopted the manner of a plain man, yet what he said was often unexpected. Under the calm surface, he was quite a complex person.

To give an example. At one time I happened to sit near to him at a communal meal, when I overheard a scrap of his conversation. This was shortly after his wife had died. Ben Borrow, his neighbour at table, had said something about 'soul' – I know not in what context. He butted in on what Tom was saying about the dimension and temporality of the universe being compatible with a human scale, remarking with a tinge of scorn, 'I want to talk about your soul, Tom, and all you'll talk about is the damned universe.'

To which Tom said, 'But we can train ourselves to listen to two tunes at once, Ben.'

Challenged to explain what exactly he meant, Tom gave as an example the view of Earth as seen from Mars. It was merely a dim star, often lost against the background of stars. It was clear to us that Earth was not the centre of the universe as was supposed for many centuries.

'But this is not to say that mankind is a meaningless accident,' he said. 'Indeed, our existence seems to depend on a number of strange cosmic coincidences involving the exothermic nuclear reactions that generate the heavier elements. Those elements are eventually utilised to build living things. As you know, we are all constructed from such elements – dead star matter.' He looked about him to see that we understood what he was saying. 'This is proof of our intimate relationship with the cosmos itself.

'Of course, this creative process takes time. About ten billion years, in fact. Since we're in an expanding universe, it follows that its size is a function of its age. So why is the observable universe fifteen billion light years in extent? Because it is fifteen billion years old.

'It seems unlikely, bearing these facts in mind, that life could have evolved elsewhere much earlier than it did on Earth. There are no Elder Gods.

'So why have we come into existence? Possibly because we are an integral part of the design plan of the universe. Not accidental. Not irrelevant!

'Each one of us is insignificant in him or her self. But as a species . . . Well, perhaps we should reconsider what a universe is, what it means. Without itself being conscious, it may need a consciousness fully to exist.

'By coming to Mars, we may be enacting the first minute step of a vast process. Whether we are up to seeing the process through, well . . .'

'Quite, quite,' agreed Ben, hastily. 'Mmm. Well . . . Let's see . . .'

That was one of the things which set the wonderful Tom Jefferies apart. He could always hear two opposed tunes playing and make harmony from them, possibly because he had trained himself to think of unimaginably distant futures.

Of course I attended Antonia's memorial service. I was full of grief – hers was the first death on Mars, and a man wrote an elegy on it.

At the time of the EUPACUS collapse, when we found we were stuck on the Red Planet, all hell broke loose. There was rioting, and I was witness to one incident that Tom quelled with a quick answer.

An idiot was trying to incite violence, shouting out that they must destroy the domes. 'We've been lied to. Our lives have been stolen. What they call civilisation is just a sham, a stinking sham. There's no truth – it's all a lie. Burn the place down and have done, it's all a big lie. Everything's a lie!'

Tom stood up, saying loudly, 'But if that were true, then it would be a lie.'

Silence. Then strained laughter. The crowd stood about uneasily. The orator disappeared. The domes were not destroyed.

It must be admitted, I was in despair; I was really scared of being stuck on Mars for any length of time. I took a buggy from the buggy rank without authorisation and made off into the steeps of Tharsis to hide myself away, to commune with myself, to adjust. Although I spoke with my Other, she was a nothing, a green weed floating under water. When night was coming on, I parked myself on the edge of a gully and watched darkness gather, comforted in a way by its remorseless advance, as death had advanced on Antonia.

Whatever you do, I thought to myself, the darkness is always encroaching.

A wind rose. A dust storm brewed up from nowhere. Sudden gusts slammed against my vehicle. It seemed to stagger. Then it was falling over and over, down the gully. I struck my head on a support and became unconscious, although curiously aware all the while.

In that trance-like state, the person with whom I was closest came to stand by me. She sat in a room with a wide window overlooking the Pearl River and unbound her piled dark hair. This she shook out in a dark shower, to show that she knew of my ill fortune and grieved for me.

In her hands she held a silver carp, the meaning of

which I did not understand. The carp swam from her grasp, through the pure air.

When my senses returned I was confusedly aware of a pain and a light. The pain came from my right leg – or was it coming from the pinpoint of light glaring at me over a shoulder of Tharsis? Waves of pain prevented me from thinking coherently.

Eventually I managed to drag myself up. Then I realised that the light I had seen was Saturn, shining low over the rock. The buggy lay on its side against a cliff. By good fortune, it had not cracked open during the drop, or I would have died from lack of oxygen while senseless.

Yet I might as well have been dead. My trip having been unauthorised, I had no radio with which to summon help. Nor had I a suit in which to attempt to extricate myself. Could I have climbed into a suit? That was doubtful with my ruined leg. I could do nothing but crouch there, waiting to die.

But the Martians look after their own. They had instituted a search once the buggy had been reported missing. When the dust storm died, they were out in strength.

I became hazily aware of a noise overhead. A man was scraping the dust away from a side window and looking down at me. I could not recognise his face, and fainted away.

When I roused, I was in a hospital bed, in the Reception House, coming round from anaesthesia. A handsome but stern woman bent over me. Gently brushing my forehead with her hand, she said, 'You see, it was irrational to take out an unauthorised buggy, wasn't it?' Those were the first words Mary Fangold ever said to me.

Only later did I find that my shattered right leg had been removed and a synthetic limb grown in its place.

Now I understood the meaning of the silver carp that my dear friend had shown me in a dream. It swam away from her to indicate that one could live well without legs.

Tom Jefferies came to visit me every day. It was he who had discovered me, trapped in my stolen buggy.

50

Perhaps he felt he had been given my life to compensate for the loss of Antonia's. I loved him platonically. It was like a fairy tale. I clung to him. I could not let him out of my sight; he was to me the father and mother I had never had.

When I was out of hospital, I besought him and besought him, as a man of destiny, to let me love him and look after him. So I became his adopted daughter, Cang Hai Jefferies.

And all this time – little though I realised it – Tom was planning a constitution for utopia, and holding discussions with people every day.

Testimony of Tom Jefferies

6

A Non-Zero Future!

Stranded on Mars! Although I wished only to mourn the death of Antonia, some force within me insisted that I should turn to the future and face the challenge of existence on a Mars isolated for an indefinite period.

This necessity became more urgent when we were confronted by a wave of suicides. There were those whose spirit was not strong enough to face this challenge. Whereas I saw it as an opportunity. Perhaps it was curiosity that drove me on.

Taking command, I ordered that there should be only one memorial service for all suicides, which numbered thirty-one, the majority of them single men in their thirties. I viewed the act of despair with some contempt and saw to it that the memorial service was kept short. At its conclusion the corpses were consigned to the biogas chambers below ground.

'Now we are free to build our future constructively,' I declared. 'Our future lies in operating as a unit. If we fail to cooperate – zero future!'

The strange airless landscapes beyond our domes had only a remote relationship with our existences; our task was to make good what was inside, not outside, the domes. And since I had taken command – though not without opposition – a grand plan developed slowly in my mind: a plan to transform our society, and hence humanity itself.

I called people together. I wanted to address them direct and not through the Ambient.

'I'm going to kick down a rotten door. I'm going to let light in on human society. I need your help to do it.' That's what I said. 'I'm going to make us live as we dream of being – great and wise people, circumspect, daring, inventive, loving, just. The people we deserve to be.

'All we have to do is dare to throw away the old and difficult crooked ways and leap towards the new and difficult and wonderful!'

I was determined that the collapse of EUPACUS and our subsequent isolation on Mars – for however long that might be – should not be viewed negatively. After the considerable sacrifices everyone had made to reach the Red Planet, we had to struggle to exist, to prove something. With the death of my beloved wife, I decided I would never leave Mars, but remain here all my days, finally to mingle my spirit with hers.

Ambient was already in place. Working with other technicians, we extended it so that everyone had a station. I now sent out a nine-point questionnaire, enquiring into which features of terrestrial life we who were temporarily stranded on Mars were most pleased to escape. I asked for a philosophical approach to the question; such factors as bad housing, uncertain climatic conditions, etc., were to be taken for granted.

Instead of isolating myself with any period of mourning, I set about analysing the responses I received. Remarkably, 91 per cent of the domes' inhabitants answered my questionnaire.

Enlisting the assistance of able organisers, I announced that there would be a meeting to discuss the ways in which we might govern ourselves happily, in justice and truth. All Martian citizens were invited to attend.

At this momentous meeting, a great crowd assembled in our grandest meeting-place, Hindenburg Hall. I took the chair, with the distinguished scientist, Dreiser Hawkwood, at my right hand.

'There is only one way in which we can survive the

crisis of isolation,' I said. 'We must cooperate as never before. We do not know how long we will have to stay on Mars with our limited resources. It will be sensible to anticipate a long stay before world finances and the pieces of EUPACUS are put together again. We must make the best of this opportunity to work together as a species.

'Do not let us regard ourselves as victims. We are proud representatives of the human race who have been granted an unique chance to enter into an unprecedented degree of cooperation. We shall make ourselves and our society anew – to turn a new page in human history, as befits the new circumstances in which we find ourselves.'

Dreiser Hawkwood rose. 'On behalf of the scientific community, I welcome Tom Jefferies's approach. We must work as a unit, setting aside nationality and self-interest. Without attributing intention to what looks like blind chance, we may be given this opportunity to put ourselves to a test, to see what miracles unity can work.

'The humble lichen you see on boulders or stonework back home can flourish in the most inhospitable environments. Lichen is a symbiosis between an alga and a fungus. We might regard that as an inspiring example of cooperation. On this boulder, on which we are temporarily stranded, we will also survive.

'Remember that our survival is necessary for more than personal reasons, important though those are. We scientists are here to press forward with the Smudge Project, in which much finance and effort has been invested. A positive result will influence the way in which we comprehend our universe. For a successful outcome, here too we need unity and what we used to call good old team work . . .'

Heartened by Hawkwood's support, I went on to say, 'In our misfortune we can see great good fortune. We are in a position to try something new, revolutionary. We have here a population equivalent to that of ancient Athens in numbers – and in intellect about equal – and in knowledge much greater. We are therefore ideally placed to establish a small republic for ourselves, banning those elements of existence we dislike, as far as that is possible, and enshrining the good in a constitution upon which all can agree. That way we can flourish. Otherwise, we fall into chaos. Chaos or new order? Let's talk about it.'

As I spoke, I heard murmurs of dissent from the audience. Among the visiting YEAs were many who cared nothing for the Smudge Project and regarded Hawkwood as a career man.

A Jamaican TV star, by name Vance Alysha, one of the YEAs, spoke for many when he rose and said, 'This Smudge Project is typical of the way science has become the tool of the rich. It's all abstract nowadays. There was a time when scientific, or let's say technological, advance brought the poor many advantages. It made life easier – you know, motorbikes, motor cars, refrigerators, radio, of course, and the television. All that was practical, and benefited the poor all over the world. Now it's all abstract, and increases the gulf between rich and poor – certainly in the Caribbean, where I come from. Life becomes harder all the time for our people.'

There were murmurs of approval from the hall. Dreiser asked, 'Is it an abstraction that such ills as cancer and Alzheimer's disease are now curable? We cannot predict exactly what the Smudge will bring, but certainly we would not be here on Mars without investment in the research.'

At this point a young dark-eyed woman stood up and said, in clear tones, 'Some may view our being stranded here as a misfortune. They should think again. I would like to point out that our being here, living in the first community away from Earth and Luna, comes as the end result of many kinds of science and knowledge accumulated throughout the centuries – science both abstract and practical.

'We're fooling ourselves if we don't grasp this opportunity to learn new things.'

As she sat down, Hawkwood leaned forward and asked her what sort of things she imagined we should learn.

She stood up again. 'Consciousness. Our faulty consciousness. How does it come about? Is it affected perhaps by magneto-gravitic forces? In the lighter gravity of Mars, will our consciousness improve, enlarge? I don't know.' She gave an apologetic laugh. 'You're the scientist, Dr Hawkwood, not I.' She sat down, looking abashed at having spoken out.

'May I ask your name?' This from Hawkwood.

'Yes. My name is Kathi Skadmorr and I come from Hobart in Tasmania. I worked in Water Resources in Darwin for my community year.'

He nodded and gave me a significant look.

Assembled in the Hindenburg Hall were almost all the men, women, and children on the planet. Since there were insufficient chairs to seat everyone, boxes and benches were drawn up. When everyone was as comfortable as could be, the discussion proper began.

It was interrupted almost at once by a commotion from the rear door, and female cries for us to wait a minute.

In came three overalled women from Communications, bringing with them lights and video cameras.

The leader, Suung Saybin, showed herself to be a perceptive woman. She had thought of something that had not occurred to the rest of us. 'Allow us to set up our equipment,' she said. 'This may prove an historic occasion, which must be recorded for others to study.'

The scene was lit, she gave the sign, we began our discussion.

Almost immediately a group of six masked men charged the platform. Both Dreiser and I were roughly siezed.

One of the masked men shouted, 'We don't need discussion. These men are criminals! This dome remains EUPACUS territory. They have no right to speak. We are in charge here until EUPACUS returns—'

But they were mistaken in naming EUPACUS so boldly. It had turned into a hated name, the name of failure, the label for those who had isolated us. Half the hall rose en masse and marched forward. Had any of the masked intruders been armed – but guns were forbidden on Mars – there would have been shooting at this point. Instead, a fight ensued, in which the intruders were easily overpowered and Dreiser and I released.

How were the masked men to be punished? All proved to be EUPACUS technicians in charge of landing operations, refuelling or repairs. They were not popular. I sent for six pairs of handcuffs, and had them cuffed around metal pillars for six hours, with their masks removed.

'Is that all their punishment?' asked one of my rescuers.

'Absolutely. They will not reoffend. They suddenly lost their authority. They are only disoriented by the new situation, as we are. Now everyone can have a look at them. That will be shame enough.'

One of my attackers shouted that I was a fascist.

'You are the fascist,' I said. 'You wanted to rule by force. I want to use persuasion – to bring about a just and decent society here, not a mob.'

He challenged me to define just and decent.

I told him I would not define what the words meant just then, particularly since I had never experienced a just and decent society. Nevertheless, I hoped that we would work together to form a society based on those principles. We all knew what just and decent meant in practice, even if we did not define them with precision. And I hoped that in a few months we would recognise them as prevailing in Mars City.

The man listened closely to this, pausing before he spoke.

'My name, sir, is Stephens, Beaumont Stephens, known as "Beau". I will assist your endeavours if you will free me from these handcuffs.'

I told him that he must serve his punishment. Then he would be welcome to help me.

Our forum found a powerful supporter in Mary Fangold, the woman who ran the Reception House. She was a neat, rather severe-looking woman in her late thirties, of

Mediterranean cast, with dark hair cut short, and striking dark blue eyes. I had developed a strong liking for her through her kindness to Antonia in the latter's last days.

'If we are to survive here as a society, then everyone must be given a chance to be part of that society.' Her voice, while far from shrill, held a ring of conviction. I was to find that indeed she was a woman with a strong will. 'On Earth, as we all know, millions of people are thrown on the scrap heap. They're unemployed, degraded, rendered useless, while the rich and Megarich employ androids. These wasteful creatures are the new enemies of the poor – as well as being inefficient.

'It's no good talking about a just society. First of all, we must ensure that everyone works, and is kept busy at a job that suits her or his intellect.'

'What job is that?' someone shouted.

Mary Fangold replied coolly, 'My Reception House must become our hospital. I need enlarged premises, more wards, more equipment of all kinds. Come and see me tomorrow.'

While I had anticipated that many of us would harbour negative responses, even feeling suicidal, about being stranded on Mars, I had not expected so many clearly stated objections to everyday existence on Earth. These the forum wished to discuss first of all, as bugbears to be disposed of.

These bugbears came roughly under five heads, we finally decided. The first four were Mistaken Historicism, Transcendics, Market Domination and Popular Subscription, all of which made existence more difficult than it need be for the multitudinous occupants of our green mother planet. Fifthly, there was the older problem of the rich and the poor, the Haves and Have Nots, a problem of heightened intensity since a long-living Megarich class had developed.

When it came my turn to sum up the debate, which continued for some days, I had this to say (I'm checking here with the records):

'Some issues on Earth are much discussed, or at least make the headlines. They consist in the main of crime, education, abortion, sex, climate, and maybe a few other issues of more local interest. These issues could be fairly easily dealt with, if the will were there.

'For instance, education could be improved if the teaching profession were paid more and better respected. That would happen if children and their futures were the subject of more active general concern. And, if that were the case, then crime rates would fall, since it is the disappointed and angry child who becomes the adult lawbreaker. And so on.

'Unfortunately, a dumbing-down of culture has precluded the general consideration of five issues about which you have expressed unhappiness. They are far less easy to deal with, being more nebulous. Perhaps they are difficult to discern in the general hubbub of competing voices and anxieties. The six thousand of us assembled here must seize on the time and chance we have been given to consider and, if possible, to eliminate these issues.

'I will take these issues, which do not mirror our needs for a decent society and are impediments to such a society, one by one, although they are interrelated.

'Mistaken Historicism is a clumsy label for the problems of squaring a global culture with varied local traditions. The problems spring perhaps from conflating human history with evolutionary development. We are prone to conceive of deep cultural differences as merely an episode on the way to a universal consensus – a developmental phase, let's say, to an homogenous civilisation. Our expectation is that these various local traditions will die out and the global population become homogenised. This idea is patronising, and will not hold water much longer, as the days of Euro-Caucasian hegemony draw to a close.

'For example, we cannot expect the quarter of the terrestrial population that speaks a Chinese language to convert to English instead. Nor can we expect those whose faith is in Mohammed to turn into churchgoers of the Methodist persuasion. The Chinese and the Muslims may fly by airplanes manufactured in the United States for at least a few decades longer: that does not alter their inward beliefs in the superiority of their own traditions one whit.

'We observe the tenacity of tradition even within the European Union. A Swede may spend all his working life in Trieste, designing parts for the fridge wagons; he may speak fluent Italian and enjoy the local pasta; he may holiday on the beaches of Rimini. But, when it comes time to retire, he returns to Sweden, buys a bungalow in the archipelago, and behaves as if he had never left home. He soon forgets how to speak Italian.

'Our traditional roots are valuable to us. We may argue whether or not they should be, but the fact remains that they are. Nor are the arguments against them always valid.

'For instance, such roots are supposedly the cause of war. True, certainly they have been in the past. There were the Crusades, the Opium Wars against China, and so on and so forth. But modern wars, when they happen, are most frequently not between different civilisations but are waged among the same civilisations, as were the terrible wars in Europe between 1914 and 1918 and 1939 and 1945.

'The mistaken assumption that cultural differences are going to disappear and a single civilisation will prevail, perhaps in the manner of Mr H.G. Wells's Modern Utopia, has precluded constructive intellectual thought on ways to ease friction between cultures which are, in fact, permanent and rather obdurate features of the world in which we have to live. The sorry tale of the conflict between Israel and Palestine is a recent example of the ill effects of Mistaken Historicism.

'If we could drop our Mistaken Historicism, we might establish more effective international buffers for intercultural relationships.'

At this point there was an important intervention by a small sharp-featured man with scanty white hair. He rose and introduced himself as Charles Bondi, a worker on the

Smudge Project, whom we already knew was one of the prime movers of the scientific project.

'While I take your point about linguistic differences and religious differences and so forth,' he said, in a pleasant husky voice, 'these are all global items we have learned to put up with, and to some extent overcome. I believe it might be claimed that cultural differences are dying out, at least where it matters, in public relations. Certainly there is evidence of a fairly general wish to help them die out, or else we would have no revived United Nationalities.

'You could argue, indeed, that Mistaken Historicism was mistaken but is no longer. Don't we see a convergence in prevailing attitudes of materialism, for instance, in East and West – and all points in between? What we want is a new idea, something that overrides cultural difference. I believe that the revelations that the detection of a Smudge phenomenon will grant us could be that transforming idea.'

'We'll discuss that question when a Smudge has been identified,' I said.

'Smudge interception is vastly more likely than utopia,' Bondi said, sharply. I thought it wiser not to answer, and continued with my list.

'We come next to Transcendics. I use the term rather loosely, not in the Kantian sense, but to mean the transcendence of humanity over everything else on the globe. Perhaps anthropocentrism would be a better word. Despite the growth of geophysiology, people by and large value things only as they are useful for human purposes. The rhinoceros, to take an obvious example, was hunted to extinction within the last forty years, simply because its horn was valued as an aphrodisiac. This splendid creature was killed off for an erroneous notion.

'But more widely we still use our seas as cesspits and our globe as a doormat. We take and take and consume and consume. We have a belief that we are able to adapt to any adverse change, and can survive and triumph, in spite of all the diseases that rage among us – in many cases diseases we have provoked through our ruination of the balance of nature. For instance when that vegetarian grazing animal, the cow, was fed meat and offal, bovine spongiform encephalitis infected herds and spread to the perpetrators of the crime.

'The myth of man's superiority over all other forms of life is, I'm bound to say, propagated by the Judaic and Christian religions. The truth is that the globe would thrive without human beings. If our kind was wiped from the earth, it would heal over in no time and it would be as if we had never been . . .'

At this point, reflection on the miseries we had created for ourselves on the beautiful terrestrial globe overcame me. I cried aloud in protest at my own words, knowing in my heart that, though we must make the best of our opportunities on Mars, Mars would never be the lovely place that Earth was, or had been.

Perhaps I should interrupt my narrative here to say that the hall in which we held our public discussions was dominated by a blow-up of one of the most extraordinary photographs of the Technological Age. Towering over us in black and white was a shot taken in 1937 of an enormous firework display. When the Nazi airship the *Hindenburg* was about to attach itself to a mooring mast, having flown across the Atlantic to the United States, its hydrogen tanks exploded and the great zeppelin burst into flame.

That beautiful, terrifying picture, of the gigantic structure sinking to the ground, may seem like the wrong signal to those who had crossed a far greater distance of space than had the ill-fated airship. Yet it held inspiration. It showed the fallibility of man's technological schemes and reminded us of evil nationalist aspirations while remaining a grand Promethean image. We spoke under this magnificent Janus-faced symbol.

But, for a moment, I was unable to speak.

*　　*　　*

Seeing my distress, Hal Kissorian, a statisticial demographer and one of the stranded YEAs, spoke up cheerfully.

'We all have complaints against our mother planet, Tom, much though we love it. But we have to learn things anew, to suit our new circumstances here. Do not be afraid to speak out.

'Let me offer you and all of us some comfort. I have been looking into the computer records, and have discovered that only fifteen per cent of us Martians here assembled are the first-borns in their families. The great majority of us are later-born sons and daughters.'

There was some laughter at the apparent irrelevance of this finding.

Kissorian himself laughed so that his unruly hair flopped over his brow. He was a cheerful, rather wanton-looking, young fellow. 'We laugh. We are being traditional. Yet the fact is that over a great range of scientific discoveries and social upheavals which have changed mankind's view of itself, the effects of familial birth order have played their part.'

At calls for examples, Kissorian instanced Copernicus, William Harvey, discoverer of the circulation of the blood, William Godwin with *An Enquiry Concerning Political Justice*, Florence Nightingale, 'The Lady with the Lamp', the great Charles Darwin, Alfred Wallace, Marx, Lenin, Dreiser Hawkwood, and many others, all later-born progeny.

A DOP I recognised as John Homer Bateson, the retired principal of an American university, agreed. 'Francis Bacon, Lord Verulam, makes more or less the same point,' he said, leaning forward and clutching the chair back in front of him with a skeletal hand, 'in one of his essays or counsels. He says that, among children, the eldest are respected and the youngest become wantons. That's the term he uses – wantons! But in between are offspring who are pretty well neglected, and they prove themselves to be the best of the bunch.'

63

This observation was delivered with such majesty that it incurred a number of boos.

Whereupon the retired principal remarked that dumbing-down had already settled itself on Mars.

'Anything can be proved by statistics,' someone called to Kissorian.

'My claim will demonstrate its validity here by our general contrary traits and our wish to change the world,' Kissorian replied, unperturbed.

'Our wish is to unite and change this small world,' I rejoined, and went on with my catalogue of the five partially concealed causes of global unhappiness.

'Our preconceived concept of mankind as master of all things prevents us from establishing sound institutions – institutions that might serve to provide worldwide restraints against the sort of depredations of which we have talked. Were it not for our anthropocentrism, we would long ago have established a law, observed by all, against the pollution of the oceans, the desecration of the land, and the destruction of the ozone layer.

'The myth that we can do anything with anything we like causes much misery, from the upsetting of climates onwards. As you all know, had we acted under that mistaken belief, Mars would now be flooded with CFC gases in an attempt to terraform it, had it not been for a good man as General Secretary of the UN and his few far-sighted supporters.

'Transcendics I regard as embodying something destructive in the character of mankind. For instance, the lust to obliterate old things, from buildings to traditions, which make for stability and contentment. Terraforming is just one instance of that intention. Yet new things have no rich meaning for us unless they can be seen to develop from the old. Existence should be a continuity.

'While I am no believer, I see the role of the Church – and its architecture – in communities as a stabilising, unifying factor. Yet from within the Church itself has emerged a retranslation of Bible and prayer into so-called plain language – a dumbing-down that destroys the old sense of mystery, reverence and tradition. We need those elements. Their loss brings a further challenge to family life.'

'Forget family life!' came a voice.

'Yeah, let's forget oxygen,' came a speedy rejoinder from my new supporter, Beau Stephens.

For some minutes an argument raged about the value of family life. I said nothing; I did not entirely know where I stood on the question; mine had been a strange upbringing. I held what I considered an old-fashioned view: that at the centre of 'family life' was the woman who must bring forth a new generation, and both she and her children needed such protection as a male could give. Undoubtedly, the time would come when the womb was superseded. Then, I supposed, family life would fade away, would become a thing of the past.

After a while, I called for order and returned to my list of discontents.

'Let's move on to the third stumbling block to content-ment, Market Domination – another little item we have escaped here on Mars. We have all felt, since we came here, the relief of having no traffic with money. It feels strange at first, doesn't it?

'Money, finance, has come increasingly to dominate every facet of life on Earth, particularly the lives of those people who have least, who are at the bottom of a wasps' nest of economics. How can we claim that all men are equal when on every level inequalities exist?

'It became a shibboleth in the twentieth century that maximum economic growth would resolve human prob-lems. Earning power outweighed social need, as the quest for greater profit failed to count the cost in civilised living.

'One way in which this happened was in the dismantling of welfare provisions, such as health care, pensions, child benefit, unemployment allowances.'

Mary Fangold interrupted. She stood tall and proud.

'Tom, I have been thankful to live on Mars, having to watch terrestrial affairs go from bad to worse. Perhaps the people there don't notice the decline. The dismantling of welfare provisions of which you speak has deepened a well of worldwide poverty. One result is an increase in many infectious diseases.

'We all know smallpox returned with the pandemic of about ten years ago. Cholera is rampant in the Pacrim countries. Many contagious diseases once thought all but vanished early in the century have returned. Fortunately those diseases do not reach Mars.'

'Sit down then!' someone shouted.

Mary looked towards the interruption. 'Bad manners evidently have travelled. I am making a reasonable point and will not be deflected.

'I would like everyone here to realise how fortunate we are. The encouraging medical statistics put out by terrestrial authorities are often drawn from the Megarich class, who of course have their own private hospitals, and whose orderly records make them easy subjects for study.

'There is at present a serious outbreak of multiple drug resistance, notably of VRE, or vancomycin-resistant-enterococci, particularly in the ICUs in public hospitals. This is caused in part by the overemployment of antibiotics, while the synthesis of new and effective antibiotics has been falling off. Many thousands of people are dying as a result. Hundreds of thousands. Intensive Care Units are breaking down everywhere on Earth.

'A cordon sanitaire exists between Earth and Mars. Because of the long journey time, anyone who happens to be carrying VRE or any virus or infective disease – not, alas, cancer, or any malfunctioning cellular illness' – here she glanced sympathetically at me – 'will have recovered from the disease or have died from it. People do die in their cryogenic caskets en route, you know. Perhaps that statement surprises you. We try to keep it quiet.

'So all you YEAs and DOPs, do not wish the journey to take a shorter time. We are fairly safe from terrestrial disease. And that, to my mind, counts for more on the plus side than these dreary negatives we are listening to.'

For her speech Fangold was applauded. She gave me a glance, half apology, half smile, as she sat down.

I could only agree about the dreary negatives, and called a break for lunch.

As usual, we all sat at long communal tables. We were served with vegetable soup, so-called, followed by a synthetic salami stew, accompanied by bread and margarine.

Discussion ran up and down the table. Several voices were raised in anger. Aktau Badawi asked me what I was going to say about Market Domination. 'Is this about multinationals?'

'Not really. We all know about the biggest of the lot, EUPACUS, which has stranded us here.

'Downstairs, on Earth, work became an overriding imperative for those in whom poverty and unemployment had not become ingrained. The family mealtime, often rather better than what we are getting now, where families talked and argued and laughed and ate in a mannerly way together, fell victim to the work ethic at an early stage. Fast food was often eaten while preparing to leave for work, at work, or in the streets. There was no mingling of the generations, such as we have here in Amazonis Planitia, no conversation. At least we have that,' I said, pushing my plate aside.

'If jobs were not available locally, then the worker must go elsewhere. In the United States of America, this was no great hardship; it was already a pretty rootless society, and the various states made provision for people to move from one state to another. Elsewhere, the hunt for jobs can mean exile – sometimes years of exile.'

Aktau Badawi said, in his halting English, 'My family is from Iran. My father has a big family. He has no employ. His brother – his own brother – was his enemy. He travels far to get a job in the Humifridge plant in Trieste, on a distant sea, where they make some units for the fridge

67

wagons. After a two-year, we never hear from him. Never again. So I must care for my brothers.

'I am like Kissorian has said, second brother. I go north. I work in Denmark. Is many thousand kilometres from my dear home. I see that Denmark is a decent country, with many fair laws. But I live in one room. What can I do? For I send all my monies to home.

'Then I do not hear from them. Maybe they all get killed. I cannot tell, despite I write the authorities. My heart breaks. Also my temper. So I rather do the community year in Uganda in Africa. Then I come here, to Mars. Here I hope for fairness. And maybe a girl to love me.'

He hung his head, embarrassed to have spoken so openly. May Porter, a technician from the observatory, sitting next to him, patted his arm.

'Labour markets require high mobility, no doubt of that,' she said. 'Careers can count very low in human values.'

'Human values?!' exclaimed Badawi. 'I don't know its meaning until I listen today to the discussions. I wish for human values very much.'

'Another thing,' said Suung Saybin. 'Food warehouses dominate cities because, once a machinery of supply is established, it is hard to stop. Small shops are forced out by competition. Their closure leads to social disorder and the malfunction of cities. The bigger the city, the worse this effect.'

A little Dravidian whose name I never learned broke in here, saying, 'There is always the excuse given by pharmaceutical manufacturers. They profit greatly from the sale of fertilisers and pesticides that further decimate wildlife, including the birds. My country now has no birds. These horrible companies claim that improved crop yields are necessary. This is one of their lies. World food production is more than sufficient to feed a second planet! There are 1.5 billion hungry people in the world of today, many of them personally known to me. Their problem is not so much the lack of food as lack of the income with which to purchase food already available elsewhere.'

Dick Harrison agreed. 'Don't by this imagine we're talking only of starving India, or of Central Asia, forever unable to grow its own food. The most technologically advanced state, the United States, has forty million people on the breadline – forty million, in the world's largest producer of food! I should know. I came from New Jersey to Mars to get a good meal . . .'

After the laughter died, I continued.

'The all consuming machinery of greater and greater production entails deregulation of worker safety laws and health provisions. In our lifetimes we have seen economic competition increasing between states. They must grow monstrous to survive, as trees grow to eclipse a neighbour with their shade. So bad capitalist states drive out good, as we see in South America. Greater profits, greater general discomfort.'

At this point, I was unwilling to continue, but my audience waited in silence and expectancy.

'Come on, let's hear the worst,' Willa Mendanadum, the slender young mentatropist from Java, called down the table.

'Okay. The three concealed discomforts we have mentioned occasion much of the unhappiness suffered by terrestrial populations. They form the undercurrents behind the headlines. Where remedies are applied only to the headline troubles – capital punishment for murder, private insurance for accident, abortion for unwanted babies – they do little good. They merely increase the burdens of life.

'Why are they not thrown out and deeper causes attended to?

'The answer lies in Popular Subscription, our fourth impediment.'

'Now we're getting to it,' said Willa. Someone hushed her.

'What it means, Popular Subscription?' asked Aktau Badawi.

'We are conditioned to subscribe to the myths of the age. We hardly question the adage that fine feathers make fine birds, or that young offenders should be shut up in prisons for a number of years until they are confirmed in misery and anger. When witch-hunts were the thing, we believed in witches or, if we did not believe, we did not like to speak out, for fear of making ourselves silly or unpopular.

'That fear is real enough, as we see in the instances of rare individuals who dare to speak out against unscrupulous practices in giant pharmaceutical companies or national airlines. Their lives are rapidly made impossible.

'It is Popular Subscription that permits the three other mistaken conceptions we've mentioned to beggar our lives.'

'This is no new perception, by the way, Tom,' came the supercilious voice of John Homer Bateson. 'The learned Samuel Johnson remarked long ago that the greatest part of mankind had no other reason for their opinions than that they were in fashion.'

I nodded in his direction. 'The fifth of our bugbears is, simply, the prevalence of Haves and Have Nots – of the gulf between rich and poor. It has always existed on Earth. Perhaps it always will exist there. Now we have the new long-lived Megarich class, living behind its golden barricades.

'But here – why, on Mars we start anew! We're all in the same boat. We have no money. We're all dirt poor and must live at subsistence level. Rejoice that we have escaped from a deep-rooted evil – as deeply rooted as the diseases of which Mary Fangold has spoken.

'We six thousand Crusoes are cut adrift from these miseries – and other miseries you can probably think of. Our lives have been drastically simplified. We can simplify them still further by maintaining a forum here, wherein we shall endeavour to extirpate these errors of perception from our society.

'With a little team work, we can and we will build a perfect and just society. The scientists will do their work. As for the rest of us – why, we have nothing better to do!'

7

Under the Skin

Needless to say, my summing up of mankind's problems did not go undisputed.

At one juncture I was challenged to say what was the point of my lengthy disquisition. I responded, 'We are listing some of the preconceptions of which we must rid our minds. There are others to come. While we are here – while we have the chance – I want us to change, change for our own sweet sakes. We have been slaves to the past. We must become people of the long future. We must set the human mind free. Only then can we achieve the greatest things.'

'Such as what?' a YEA called.

'Once you have set your mind free, I will tell you!'

Willa Mendanadum ignored this vital point. She summed up the opposition.

'These hidden stumbling blocks to mankind's happiness are interesting in their way, but are academic to our present discussion. If we wish to find a means to govern ourselves here, happily and justly, then we must forget about what they are up to on Earth.

'Besides, there are worse and more immediate impediments to our happiness than the ones you mention. If you take my own country, Indonesia, as an example, there you can see a general rule in operation, that big decisions are always made by well-fed people. The well-fed control the ill-fed, and it is in their interest to keep it that way.'

Amid general laughter, as we acknowledged the force of this truism, someone intervened to say, 'Then we can make fair decisions here, because we are all ill-fed.'

Another important statement was made by May Porter, who said, 'I like the word justice. I dislike the word happiness, always have done. It has a namby-pamby taste in my mouth. It was unfortunate that the American Declaration of Independence included that phrase about the pursuit of happiness being an inalienable right. It has led to a Disneyfied culture that evades the serious meaning – the gravitas, if you like – of existence. We should not speak of maximising happiness, but rather of minimising suffering. I seem to recall from my college days that Aristotle spoke of happiness as being only in accordance with excellence.

'It makes sense to strive for excellence. That is an attainable goal, bringing its own contentment. To strive for happiness leads to promiscuity, fast food, and misery.'

Laughter and general clapping greeted this statement.

As a break from all this debate, which I was not alone in finding exhausting, I did the morning rounds with Arnold Poulsen, the domes' chief computer technician, after the day's communal t'ai chi session.

Poulsen was one of the early arrivals on Mars. I regarded him with interest. He was of ectomorphic build, with a slight stoop. A flowing mop of pale yellowish hair was swept back from a high brow. Although his face was lined, he seemed neither young nor old. He spoke in a high tenor. His gestures were slow, rather vague; or perhaps they might be construed as thoughtful. I found myself impressed by him.

We walked among the machines. Poulsen casually checked readings here and there. These machines maintained atmospheric pressure within the domes, and monitored air content, signalling if CO_2 or moisture levels climbed unacceptably high.

'They are perfectly reliable, my computers. They perform miracles of analysis in microseconds which would otherwise take us years – possibly centuries,' Poulsen said. 'Yet they don't know they're on Mars!'

'If you tell them – what then?'

He gave a high-pitched snort. 'They would be about as emotionally moved as the sands of Mars . . . These machines can compute but not create. They have no imagination. Nor have we yet created a program for imagination,' he added thoughtfully. 'It is because of their lack of imagination that we are able completely to rely on them.'

They could arrive swiftly at the solution of any problem set for them, but had no notion what to do with the solution. They never argued among themselves. They were perfectly happy, conforming to Aristotle's ancient dictum, as quoted by May Porter, that happiness was activity in accordance with excellence – whereas I felt myself that morning to be baffled and cloudy.

Should I not have allowed myself to mourn in solitude the death of my beloved Antonia, rather than embark on the substitute activity of instigating a suitable Martian way of life?

Against one wall of the computer room stood three androids. The computers would activate them when necessary. They were sent out every morning to polish the surfaces of the photovoltaic plates on which we relied for electricity. They had completed their task for the morning to stand there like butlers, mindlessly awaiting fresh orders.

I remarked on them to Poulsen. 'Androids? A waste of energy and materials,' he said. 'We had to discover how to create a mechanical that could walk with reasonable grace on two legs – thus emulating one of mankind's earliest achievements! – but once we've done it . . .'

Pausing, he stood confronting one of the figures. 'You see, Tom, they give off no CPS, no CPS. Like the dead . . . Do you realise how greatly we humans depend on each other's signals of life? It emanates from our basic consciousness. A sort of mental nutrition, you might say.'

73

I shook my head. 'Sorry, Arnold, you've lost me. What is a CPS?'

Poulsen looked at me suspiciously, to see if I was joking. 'Well, you give one off. So do I. CPS is Clear Physical Signal. We can now pick up CPSs on what we call a savvyometer. Try it on these androids: zilch!'

When I asked him what the androids were here for, he told me they had been intended to maintain the integrity of the air-tight structures in which we lived. 'But I will not trust them. In theory they're on lease from EUPACUS. You see, Tom, they're biotech androids, with integrated organic and inorganic components. I ordered BIA Mark XI – the Euripedes. The EUPACUS agent swindled us and sent these Euclids, Mark VIII, obsolete rubbish. I wouldn't entrust our lives to a mindless thing, would you?'

The androids regarded us with their pleasant sexless faces.

Turning to one of the androids, Poulsen asked it, 'Where are you, Bravo?'

The android replied without hesitation, 'I am on the planet Mars, mean distance from the Sun, 1.523691 AUs.'

'I see. And how do you feel about being on Mars as opposed to Earth?'

The android answered, 'The mean distance of Mars from the Sun is 1.523691 AUs. Earth's mean distance is 1 AU.'

'Feel. I said feel. Do you think life's dangerous on Mars?'

'Dangerous things are life-threatening. Plagues, for instance. Or an earthquake. An earthquake can be very dangerous. There are no earthquakes on Mars. So Mars lacks danger.'

'Sleep mode,' Poulsen ordered, snapping his fingers. As we turned away, he said, 'You see what I mean? These androids have halitosis instead of CPS. They create hydroxils. I rate certain plants higher than these androids – plants mop up airborne hydroxil radicals and protect us from sick-building syndrome . . .'

When I asked which plants he recommended, Poulsen

said that it was necessary to maintain a clean atmospheric environment. Ozone emissions from electronic systems mixed with the chemicals humans gave off to form what he called 'sass' – sick air soups. Mary Fangold's hospital was handling too many cases of sore throats and irritated eyes for comfort. Selected plants were the things to swallow up the harmful sass.

'What can we do to ease the problem?' I asked.

Poulsen replied that he was getting suitable plants into the domes. A consciousness-raising exercise would be the rechristening of streets and alleys with plant names. K.S. Robinson Avenue could become Poinsettia, and K. Tsiolkovski Place Philodendron.

'Come on,' I said. 'Who could pronounce Philodendron?' We both chuckled.

Using my Ambient, I spoke to the YEA from Hobart, Kathi Skadmorr. Her manner was defensive. She looked straight at me and said, 'I happened to be viewing Professor Hawkwood's *Living Without Knowing It*.'

'I'm sorry to have interrupted you. What do you make of his theory of the coming of consciousness?'

Without replying to my question, she said, 'I love learning – particularly hard unquestionable science. Only it is difficult to know what is actually unquestionable. I have so much to take in.'

'There are good technical vids about Mars. I can give you references.'

'So where is the dateline on Mars? Has that been established?'

'We have yet to place it. The question is not important yet.'

'It will be, though. If God wills it.'

I gave a laugh. 'God hasn't got much to do with it.'

I thought I detected contempt in her voice when she replied, 'I was speaking loosely. I suppose I meant some higher consciousness, which might well seem like a god to us, mightn't it?'

'Okay, but what higher consciousness? Where? We have no proof of any such thing.'

'Proof!' she echoed contemptuously. 'Of course you can't feel it if you close your mind to it. We're awash here with electromagnetic radiation, but you don't sense it. We're also awash with each other's CPS signals, isn't that so? Maybe consciousness, a greater consciousness – supposing that here on Mars – oh, forget it. Why are you logging me?'

The question somehow embarrassed me. I said, 'I was interested in the way you spoke up in our debates. I wondered if I could help in any way?'

'I know you have been of great help to Cang Hai. But thanks, Dr Jefferies, I must help myself, and stop myself being so ignorant.'

Before she switched off, a ghost of a sweet smile appeared on her face.

A mystery woman, I said to myself, feeling vexed. Mysterious and spikey.

At one time, a woman called Elsa Lamont, a slip of a person with dyed-blonde hair cut short, came to my office, accompanied by a sullen-looking man I recognised as Dick Harrison. I had marked him out as a possible trouble-maker, although on this occasion he was civil enough.

Lamont came to the point immediately. She said that my talk of terrestrial discomforts had ignored consumerism. It was well known that consumerism was responsible for much greed and injustice. She had worked for a big advertising agency with world-wide affiliations, and had been responsible for a successful campaign to sell the public Sunlite Roofs, at one time very fashionable, though scarcely necessary.

She explained that their TV commercials had been aimed at everyone, although only 20 per cent of viewers could afford such a distinctive luxury item. However the remaining 80 per cent, knowing they could never afford such a roof, respected and envied the 20 per cent, while the 20 per cent understood this very well and felt their status increased by the clever commercial.

Behind Lamont lay a period of art training. She woke one morning realising she disliked the nature of her advertising job, which was to make people feel greedy or ashamed, so she left the agency and worked to become a YEA and visit an ad-free world. Now she asked, would not people on Mars miss commercials, which had become almost an art form?

We talked this over. She argued that we needed commercials to dramatise the concept of unity. She had been trained as an orthogonist at art school, and using orthogonal projection she could create figures on the walkways that would appear to be erect – amusing figures, dancing, walking, holding hands.

At this point she introduced Dick Harrison, saying that he had studied art and would assist her.

It seemed to me that the idea had possibilities. If anyone volunteered to do anything, it was sensible to let them try. She was given Bova Boulevard to experiment on. Soon she and Harrison had covered the street with amusing Chirico-like figures, without faces, dancing, jumping, cheering. From a distance, they did seem to stand up from the horizontal.

It was clever. But no pedestrian could bring themselves to walk on the figures, which meant the boulevard was virtually closed. It was clever, but it was a failure.

However I liked Elsa Lamont's energy and ideas, and later appointed her to be secretary of Adminex.

Dick Harrison's future was less distinguished.

In the space we used for our debating hall, many people were already assembled, discussing, arguing or laughing among themselves.

The subject that arose from the chatter and had to be formally addressed was how we should govern ourselves. Beau Stephens, who had long been released from his pillar together with his associates, suggested that he should be in command. His argument was that he remained a EUPACUS official and, when EUPACUS returned in strength, he would have to hand over affairs in an orderly and accountable manner.

Amid boos, his bid was turned down.

An argument broke out. The YEA faction did much shouting. Finally the tall bearded Muslim with whom I had already spoken, Aktau Badawi, rose to speak. He was born in the holy city of Qom, as he reminded us. It seemed that already his English was improving. Later I found that he was taking lessons from a fellow Muslim, Youssef Choihosla.

Badawi said that shouting was never to be trusted. In the Muslim faith there was a saying: 'Do not walk on the Earth in insolence'. By and large, the Muslim nations rejected the present way of getting to any other planet; he was here only because he had been elected as a DOP. But he would not walk on Mars in insolence. He was content to be governed, if he could be governed wisely, by people who did not shout. But, he asked, how could they be governed if there was no money? If there was no money, then no taxes could be raised. Hence there could be no government.

A thoughtful silence fell. This point had not been made before.

I said that we needed an ad hoc government. It need only rule for a transitional period, until our new way of life was established. It would quietly wither away when everyone had 'got the message'.

What did I mean by that? I was asked.

'All must understand that our limitations hold within them great possibilities for constructive life modes. We are operating in a radically new psychological calculus.'

Rather to my surprise, this was accepted. Then came the question of what the government should be called. After a number of suggestions, some ribald, we settled for 'Administration Executive', or Adminex for short.

We talked about the question of incentives. Not everyone

could be expected to work for good will alone. Something had to replace money by way of incentive.

Not on that momentous day but later, when Adminex held its first meeting, we drew up a rough schedule. Men and women could not be idle. To flavour the pot, incentives were necessary, at least at first. The degree of participation in work for the common good would be rewarded by so many square yards of floor living space. Status could be enhanced. Plants had scarcity value, and would serve as rewards for minor effort.

A common Teaching Experience should be established. We had already seen how separation from the mother planet downstairs had engendered a general wish to stand back and consider the trajectory of one's own life. Personal life could itself be improved – which was surely one of the aims of a just and decent society.

Benazir Bahudur, the sculptor and teacher, spoke up shyly. 'Excuse me, but for our own protection we must establish clear prescriptions. Such as the rules governing water consumption. Increase of personal water consumption must not be on offer as a reward for anything; it would lead only to quarrels and corruption.

'All the same, my suggestion is that we women require a larger water ration than men because of our periods. Men and women are not the same, whatever is claimed. Washing is sometimes a priority with us.

'With none of the terrestrial laws in effect, and no money in circulation, education could play a greater role, provided education was itself overhauled. It must include current information. For instance, how much water exactly remains on this terrible planet.'

As I was to learn later, this vital question of water resources was already being investigated by the science unit. Involved in these investigations was our lady from Hobart, Kathi Skadmorr. I had noted Dreiser Hawkwood's interest in her. He too had spoken to her by Ambient, and received a better reception than I had done.

Dreiser had offered to coach her in science – in what

he was now calling 'Martian science'. When he questioned her about her work with International Water Resources, Kathi had told him she had been employed at one time in Sarawak. I later turned up the record and heard her voice.

'My bosses sent me to Sarawak, where work was being done on the caves in Mulu National Park.'

'What are these caves?' Dreiser asked.

'You don't know them? Shame on you. They are vast. Great chains of interconnected caves. Over 150 kilometres have been explored. The Malaysians who own that part of the world are piping water to Japan.'

'What was your role in the project?'

'I was considered expendable. I did the dangerous bit. I did the scuba work, swimming down hitherto unexplored submerged passageways. With faulty equipment. Little they cared.'

Dreiser gave a snort. 'You do see yourself as a victim, don't you, Ms Skadmorr?'

She replied sharply. 'I'm Kathi. That's how I'm called. You must have some knowledge of the mysterious workings of the authoritarian mind.

'Anyhow, the fact is that I loved that work. The caves formed a wonderful hidden environment, extensive, beautiful, cathedrals in rock, with the water – sometimes still, sometimes racing – as their bloodstream. It was like being inside the Earth's brain. So you'd expect it to be dangerous. What's your interest in all this, anyhow?'

He said, 'I want to help you. Come and live in the science unit.'

'I've had male help before. It always carries a price tag.' She raised her hands to her face to cover a naughty grin.

'Not this time, Kathi. There's no money here, so no price tags. I'll send a vehicle for you.'

'If I come to your unit, I want to walk. I need to feel the presence of Mars.'

The first I knew of all this was when Kathi paid me a personal visit. Her claws were not in evidence. She needed my support. She was eager to see science in action and wished to go to the science unit but also to remain a member of the domes and retain her cabin with us.

She had far more eyelashes, above and below her eyes, than most women. I agreed to her request without even consulting the other members of Adminex.

'Wouldn't it be simpler for you to remain in the science unit?'

'I have friends here, believe it or not.'

She went. Although I do not wish to get ahead of my narrative, it makes sense to set down here what happened when Kathi came under Dreiser's wing.

Our overhead satellite had revealed what looked like entrances to caves in the vast stretches of the Valles Marineris, a kind of Rift Valley. This formidable feature stretches across the Martian equator for a total of some 34,500 square kilometres, almost a quarter of the surface of Mars, so that one sector can be in daylight while the rest is in night. For this reason, ferocious winds scour the valley.

Marineris is like no physical feature on Earth. It is 100 kilometres wide in places and up to 7 kilometres deep. Mists roll down its length at daybreak. It is not a good place to be.

This enormous rift was probably caused by graben events, when the relatively brittle crust fractured. Analysis shows that lakes had once existed along the base of Marineris.

So Hawkwood decided that what seemed like cave entrances would be worth inspecting. He hoped to find reservoirs of underground water. This was in the third month of 2064. However, when assembling his expedition, he found he could muster only one speleologist, a nervous young low-temperature physicist called Chad Chester. To Dreiser's way of thinking, Kathi Skadmorr was much the more foolhardy of the two.

Two buggies containing six people as well as equipment and supplies made the difficult journey overland. Dreiser had insisted on being present. He could strike up no conversation with the Hobart woman, who had retreated into an all-embracing silence.

Kathi stared unspeaking at the Marscape. She had known not dissimilar landscapes back home, long ago. Her intuition was that the very antiquity of these empty vistas had rendered them sacred, as she told me later. She experienced a longing to jump out and paint religious symbols on the boulders they passed.

At last they gained the comparatively smooth floor of the great rift valley. Its high wall towered above them. Of the cliff on the far side they could see nothing; it was lost in distance.

They made slow progress against a strong wind and, when they came to the first three caves, found them blind. The fourth they were able to enter further. Kathi and Chester wore scuba gear. Chester had allowed Kathi to go ahead. Her headlamp showed that the passage was going to narrow rapidly. Suddenly, the floor beneath her caved in and she fell. She disappeared from sight of the others. They cried with alarm before advancing cautiously on the hole.

Kathi was sprawling 2 metres below. 'I'm okay,' she said. 'It was a false floor. Things get more interesting here. Come on down, Chad.'

She stood up and went ahead without waiting for the others.

The rock in her path was tumbled and treacherous. She climbed down with the roof overhead narrowing, until she was moving within a chimney and in danger of snagging her suit. She called up to the rest of the expedition not to follow, else she would have been struck by falling rock.

At last she reached the end of the chimney. Slipping amid scree, she was able to stand again – to find herself in a large cave, which she described over the radio as the size of a cottage – 'contemptible by the dimensions of caves in the Mulu Park area'.

The floor of the cave contained a small pool of ice.

The rest of the team cheered when they heard of this.

Skirting the ice, Kathi explored the cave and reached a narrow cleft at the far end. Squeezing through it, she entered a small dark hole. She was forced to crawl on hands and knees to cross it, where she found a kind of natural staircase, leading down. This she reported to Dreiser.

'Take care, damn it,' he said.

The staircase widened. She squeezed past a boulder and found herself in a larger cavern, in cross-section resembling a half-open clam. The roof was scalloped elaborately, as if by hand, the ancient product of swirling water. And the floor of this cavern held a pool of water, unfrozen. She lobbed a small rock into it. Ripples flowed to the sides in perfect circles.

Her heart was beating fast. She knew she was the first person ever to see extensive water in its free state on the Red Planet.

She waded into it. The ripples stirred by her entry caused light patterns to play on the roof above.

The water came up to her breasts and no further. She plunged and swam below the surface. Her light revealed a dark plug hole on the stony bed. She swam vertically down it, to find herself in a chimney with smooth sides. As it narrowed, she had to push against the sides rather than swim. The fit became tighter and tighter. She could not turn to go back. Her light failed.

The team were calling her on the radio. She did not reply. She could hear her own labouring breath. She squeezed forward with great effort, her arms stretched out in front of her.

The tube seemed to go on for ever as she moved, head down. She thought there was a dim light ahead, or else her sight was failing.

She found herself shooting from the tube like a cork from a bottle. She was floundering upward in a milky sea. Her head emerged into the open. Breathing heavily, she managed to haul herself on to a dry ledge. She was in some sort of a natural underground reservoir. The ceiling was only 2 feet above her. She thought, 'What if it rains?' But that thought came from back in Sarawak, where even a distant shower of rain might cause water levels to rise dramatically and drown an unwary speleologist. On Mars there was no danger of rain.

As her pulse steadied, she stared across the phosphorescent pool, whose depth she estimated to be at least 12 metres. Kathi knew that humble classes of aquatic animals emitted light without heat. But was there not also a mere chemical phosphorescence? Had she stumbled on the first traces of Martian life? She could not tell. But lying on the shelf of rock, unsure of how she would ever emerge again to the surface, she told herself that she was detecting a Martian consciousness. She looked about in the dimness: there was nothing, only the solemn slap of water against rock, reflected and magnified by the low roof overhead. Was she not in the very throat of the monster?

She lay completely still, switching off her radio to listen, there, at least a kilometre beneath the suface of the planet. If it had a heart, she was now a part of it.

The situation was somewhat to her liking.

When she switched on her radio, the babble of humanity came to her. They were going to rescue her. Chad was possibly in an adjacent chamber. She was to stay put. Was she okay?

Without deigning to answer that, she reported that the temperature reading was 2 degrees above zero Celsius and that she had taken a water sample. She still had a reserve of 3.6 hours of air. Sure, she would stay where she was. And she would keep the radio on.

She lay on the ledge, perfectly relaxed. After a while she swam in the phosphorescent reservoir. At one corner, water fell from the roof in a slow drip, every drop measuring out a minute.

Raising herself in the water, her fingers detected a crevice in the rock overhead. Hauling herself up, she found she could thrust her arm into a niche. With this leverage she could also wedge a foot in the niche, and so cling, dripping, above the water. By slow exploration, she was able to ease herself into the rock. She cursed the lack of light, and cursed her failed headlight. Inch by painful inch, she dragged herself through the broken rock fissures. She was in total darkness, apart from an occasional glint of falling water drops. She struck her head on rock.

The one way forward was to twist over on her back and propel herself by hands and feet. She worked like that for ten minutes, sweating inside her suit. Then she was able to get on to her hands and knees.

Gingerly she stood up. Hands stretched before her, she took a step forward. Something crackled beneath the flippers of her suit. She felt and brought up a fragment of ice. In so doing, she clipped her headlamp against rock. Feeling forward, she came on sharp rock everywhere. She stood in the darkness, nonplussed. When she stretched her arms out sideways, she touched rock on either side. As far as she could determine, she was trapped in a narrow fissure. In the pitch dark, the fallen rocks were too dangerous to negotiate. So she stood there, unable to move.

At length, with what seemed to her like unutterable slyness, the dimmest of lights began to glow. Slowly the illumination brightened. Coming from a distant point, it showed Kathi that she was indeed standing in the merest crack between two rough shoulders of rock. The floor of this crack was littered with debris. She recognised a vadose passage, formed by a flow of water cutting into the rock.

She summoned up all her courage. With her awe came a cold excitement. She was convinced that she had intruded into a lofty consciousness and that some part of it – whether physical or mental – was now approaching her. Her upbringing had accustomed her to sacred places. Now she must face the wrath or at best the curiosity of something, some ancient unknown thing. She felt her lower jaw tremble as the light increased. There was nowhere she could run to.

The light became a dazzle.

'Oh, there you are! Why did you rush off like that?' said

Chad Chester, in an annoyed voice. 'You could have been in deep shit.'

She was back in the buggy, sipping hot coffdrink. Dreiser put an arm protectively about her shoulders. 'You gave us all quite a scare.'

'Why wasn't your lousy headlamp maintained? You're as bad as the slavedrivers in Sarawak.'

'At least we have established the existence of subterranean water, thanks to you,' he said comfortably.

8

The Saccharine/Strychnine Drip

Meanwhile our humdrum lives in the domes were continuing, but I at least was filled with optimism regarding our plans, which ripened day by day.

Adminex circulated our findings on the Ambient and published them on impounded EUPACUS printers. We emphasised that people must be clear on what was acceptable. We invited suggestions for guiding principles.

We suggested a common meeting for discussion in Hindenburg every morning, which anyone might attend.

We placed a high priority on tolerance and the cultivation of empathy.

We concluded by saying, What Cannot be Avoided Must Be Endured.

I received a message back on my Ambient link, saying, 'Be practical, will you? We need more toilets, boss. What cannot be endured must be avoided.' I recognised Beau Stephens's voice.

In those days, I became too busy to think about myself. There was much to organise. Yet some things organised themselves. Among them, sport and music.

I was jo-joing back from the new hospital wing when I saw the freshly invented game of skyball being played in the sports arena. I stopped to watch. Aktau Badawi was with me.

Skyball was a team game played with two balls the size of footballs. One ball, painted blue, was half filled with helium so that, when kicked into the air, its descent was slow. Play could continue only when the blue ball was in

87

the air. Grouping and positioning went on while it was descending. The blue ball could not be handled, unlike the other ball, which was brown.

'Thankfully, we are too old to play, Tom,' said Aktau.

A young man turned from the watching crowd and offered to explain the subtleties of the game to us.

We laughingly said we did not wish to know. We would never play.

'Nor would I,' the man said, 'but I in fact invented the blue ball in honour of our lighter gravity. My name is Guenz Kanli, and I wish to speak to you about another innovation I have in mind.'

He fell in with us and we walked back to my office.

Guenz Kanli had a curious physiognomy. The flesh of his face seemed not to fit well over his skull, which came to a peak at the rear. This strange-looking man came from Kazakstan in Central Asia. He was a YEA who, at twenty years of age, had fallen in love with the desolation of the Martian landscape. His eyes were bloodshot, his cheeks so mottled with tiny veins they resembled an indecipherable map.

He lived at the top of one of our spicules, which gave him a good outlook on the Martian surface. He described it in eloquent terms.

'It's all so variable. The wispy clouds take strange forms. You could watch them all day. There are fogs, and I have seen tiny snow falls – or maybe frost it was. The desert can be white or grey or almost black, or brown, or even bright orange in the sun.

'Then there are many kinds of dust storm, from little dust devils to massive storms like avalanches.

'None of this can we touch. It's like a form of music to me. You teach people to look inward on themselves, Tom Jefferies. Maybe looking outward is good too.

'We need more of a special music. It exists already, part sad, part joyful.

'If I may, I will take you to hear the wonderful Beza this evening.'

Guenz Kanli was enthusiastic to a remarkable degree, which was perhaps what commended him to me in the first place. I dreaded that a mood of irreversible depression would descend on us if the ships did not soon return.

That evening, we went to hear Beza play.

I was seized with Guenz's idea, although I never entirely saw the connection, as he did, between Beza's gipsy music and the Martian landscape.

There was always music playing somewhere in the domes – classical, jazz, popular, or something in between. But, from that evening on, one of our favourite musicians was Beza, an old Romanian gypsy. I persuaded the leading YEAs to listen – Kissorian, May Porter, Suung Saybin, and others. They were taken by it, and from then on Beza was in fashion.

Beza had been elected as DOP – rather against his wish, we gathered – by a remote community in the Transylvanian highlands.

To see Beza during the day, sitting miserable and round-shouldered at the Mars Bar or a café table, wearing his floppy off-white tunic, you would wonder what such a poor old fellow was doing on Mars. But when he took up his violin and began to play – *bashavav*, to play the fiddle – his real stature became apparent.

His dark eyes gleamed through his lank grey hair, his stance was that of a youngster, and the music he played – well, I can only say that it was magic, and so compelling that men ceased their conversation with women to listen. Guenz sometimes took up his fiddle too and played counterpoint.

With the fiddle at his chin and his bow dancing, Beza could play all night. His music was drawn from a deep well of the past, like wine flowing from centuries of slavery and wandering, rising from the pit of the brain, from the fibres of the body. These tunes were what is meant when music is said to be the first of all human arts.

A time dawned when Guenz's theory that this was the

true music of Mars became real to me. I wondered how it had come into being before Mars had ever been thought of as a place for habitation.

After I had listened to Beza I would lie in bed, wide awake, trying to recreate his music in my head. It always eluded me. A slow sad *lassu*, with its notes long drawn out, would be followed by a sprightly *friss*, light and airy as a stroll along an avenue, which then broke into the wild exhilaration of the *czardas*. Then, quite suddenly, sorrow again, driving into the heart.

I must admit I learned these foreign terms from Guenz, or from Beza himself. But Beza was a silent man. His fiddle spoke for him.

Beza's music was so popular that it became subject to plagiarism. In a small classical quintet was an ambitious Nigerian, Dayo Obantuji. He played the violin adequately, and the quintet was a success, perhaps because Dayo was something of a show-off. He liked to leap to his feet to play solos and generally appear energetic.

The quintet became less popular while Beza's music was still the rage.

Dayo was also a composer. He introduced a piece, a rather elegant sonata in B flat major, which he christened 'The Musician'.

After 'The Musician' had been played several times, Guenz became suspicious. He made a public denunciation of the fact that much of the sonata, transposed into another key and with altered tempo, was based on a piece that Beza played.

Dayo strongly denied the accusation.

When Beza was brought into an improvised court as a witness in this case of plagarism, he would only laugh and say, 'Let the boy take this theme. It is not mine. It hangs in the air. Let him play with it – he can only make it worse.'

There the matter was dropped. But 'The Musician' was not played again.

Instead Dayo came to me and complained that he was the victim of racism. Why had this unfair charge been brought, if not because he was black? I pointed out that although Beza was himself of a minority – indeed a minority of one – he was almost the most popular man in Mars City. I said I felt strongly that racism had no place on the planet. We were all Martians now. Dayo must be mistaken.

Angrily, Dayo asserted that I was denying what was obvious. He had been disgraced by the accusation. His name had not been properly cleared. He was the victim of injustice.

A long argument ensued. Finally Guenz was brought in. He also denied prejudice. He had found an echo of Beza's music in Dayo's piece. It was hardly surprising, but there it was. However, he had been convinced that the similarity was accidental, so powerful was Beza's influence. He was content to believe that Dayo's name had been cleared. And he apologised graciously, if rather playfully, for having made the charge in the first place.

Dayo again asserted he had been victimised. He burst into angry tears.

'Oh dear, the blue ball is in the air again,' said Guenz.

Then Dayo changed tack. He admitted that he had stolen the theme from Beza's music, having been unable to get it out of his head.

'I admit it. I'm guilty as hell. You lot are guilty too. Okay, you show no racial prejudice against Beza and the Orientals, but you are prejudiced against us blacks. You secretly don't believe we're good for anything, though you'll never admit it. I'm quite a good musician, but still I'm a black musician, not just a musician. Isn't that the case?

'My compositions were not appreciated. Not until I took that Romanian tune and transcribed it. Didn't Brahms do the same sort of thing? What's wrong with it? I altered it, made it my own, didn't I? But just because I was black, you picked on me.'

'Perhaps the mistake was,' said Guenz, mildly, 'not to

label the piece "Romanian Rhapsody" – to acknowledge the borrowing. Then you'd have been praised for your cleverness.'

But Dayo insisted that he would merely have been accused of stealing.

'I meant no harm. I only wished to raise my status. But if you're black you're always in trouble, whichever way you turn.'

He went off in dejection.

Tom and Guenz looked at each other in dismay.

Then Guenz broke into a laugh. 'It's you whites who are to blame for everything, including getting us here,' he said.

'My instinct is to legislate. But what could legislation do in a case like this? How might one word it? Can I ask you, Guenz, do you feel yourself racially discriminated against, as a Central Asian?'

'It has sometimes proved to be an advantage, because it had some slight novelty value. That's worn off. There was a time when people were suspicious of my foreignness, but that is in-built, a survival trait. I was equally suspicious of you whites. Still am, to a degree.'

They discussed whether they had any extra in-built discrimination against the Nigerian, Dayo. Had they expected him to 'get away' with something? Had the dismal past history of white victimisation of blacks anything to do with it? Was there a superstitious mistrust of 'black' as a colour, as there might be of lefthandedness?

These were questions they could not answer. They had to conclude it might be the case. Certainly, they would be wary if a traditional green Martian appeared in their midst.

They could only hope that such atavistic responses would die away as rational men of all colours mixed.

We could only hope that the colour question would fade away, united as we were by a common concern regarding survival and in perfecting our society. However, the matter was to arise again later, and in a more serious case.

*   *   *

During this period, I consulted with many people, delegating duties where it was possible to do so. Many people also came to my office to deliver advice or complaint. One of these visitors was a rather lacklustre-looking young YEA scientist. He announced himself as Chad Chester.

'Maybe you know my name as the guy who went down into the water caves off Marineris with Kathi Skadmorr. I guess I didn't make a great showing compared with her.'

'Not many of us do. What can I do for you?'

Chad explained that he had listened to my lecture on the five obstacles to contentment on Earth. He noted that at one point I had referred to the slogan, 'All men are equal'. He was sure this saying embodied a mistaken assumption; he never thought of himself as equal to Kathi, for example. That experience in the caves had led him to put down his thoughts on paper. He felt that 'All men are equal' should not be used in any utopian declaration we might make, for reasons he had tried to argue.

When he had gone I set Chad's paper aside. I looked at it two days later.

His argument was that the very saying was self-denying, since it mentioned only men and not women. It was meaningless to pretend that men and women were equal; they were certainly similar in many ways, but the divergence between them made the question of being equal (except possibly in law) irrelevant. Furthermore, the diversity of the genetic code meant a different inheritance of capacities even within a family.

'All men are equal' held an implication that all could compete equally; that also was untrue. A musician may have no capacity for business. A nuclear physicist may be unable to build a bridge. And so forth, for several pages.

He suggested that a better slogan would be, 'All men and women must be allowed equal opportunities to fulfil their lives.'

I liked the idea, although it had not the economy, the

93

snap, of the original it replaced. I wondered about 'All dudes are different.'

Any such sloganeering boiled down to one thing. It was important to have maximum latitude to express ourselves within the necessarily confining rules of our new society. Someone mentioned the dragon that earlier YEAs had painted on the rock face; they emphasised the way in which it had caused alarm, being unexpected. Yet creativity must continue to produce the unexpected or the community would perish. Although latitude was needed, it was generally accepted that our society had to operate within prescribed rules.

Creativity we needed, but not stupidity and ignorance.

We had begun to discuss education when a slightly built and handsome young woman with dark hair came forward. She poured out from the pockets of her overalls on to a central table a number of gleaming objects, various in shape.

'Before you speak of any orderly society, you'd better be aware,' she said, 'that Mars is already occupied by a higher form of life. They carved these beautiful objects and then, evidently dissatisfied with them, cast them away.'

The room was in an uproar. Everyone was eager to examine the exquisite shapes, seemingly made of glass. Some appeared to be roughly shaped translucent models of small elephants, snails, labias and phalluses, puppy dogs, hippopotami, boulders, coproliths, and hedgehogs. All were bright and pleasant to the touch.

The faces of those who picked up the objects were full of alarm. Always at the back of our minds had been the suspicion that the yet almost unexplored planet might somehow, against all reason, harbour life.

The young woman allowed the drama of the situation she had created to sink in before saying, loudly, 'I'm an areologist. I've been working alone in the uplands for a week. Don't worry! These are pieces of rock crystal, chemical formula SiO_2. They're just translucent quartz, created by nature.'

A howl mingled with dismay and approbation rose.

The young woman said with a laugh, 'Oh, I thought I'd just give you a scare while you were making up all these rules to live by.'

I persuaded her to sit by me while the crowd reassembled. She was lively and restless. Her name was Sharon Singh, she told me. She was half-English, half-Indian, and had spent much of her young life in the terrestrial tropics.

'You can't find Mars particularly congenial,' I remarked.

She gave a wriggle. 'Oh, it's an adventure. Unlike you, I do not intend to live here for ever. Besides, there are many idle and eager men here who enjoy a little romance. That's one of the real meanings of life, isn't it? Mine is a romantic nature . . .' She flashed a smile at me, then regarded me more seriously. 'What are you thinking?'

I could not tell her, saying instead, 'I was thinking that we can sell these pretty rock crystal objects for souvenirs when matrix traffic resumes.'

Sharon Singh uttered a rather scornful laugh, momentarily showing her pretty white teeth. 'Some things are not for sale!' She gave her wriggle again.

That night, I could not sleep. The smile, those dark eyes fringed by dense lashes, the carelessness, the wriggle – they filled my mind. All my serious contemplations were gone, together with my resolves. I thought – well, I thought that I would follow Sharon Singh to Earth, and gladly, if need be. That I would give anything for a night with her in my arms.

In order to sublimate my desire for Sharon Singh, I made a point of talking personally to as many men and women as possible, sounding out their opinions and gathering an impression of their feelings towards our situation and the practicalities of living decently.

My quantcomp rang as I was going down K.S. Robinson. A woman's voice requested an appointment. In another half-hour, I found myself confronting Willa Mendanadum and her large companion, Vera White. I saw them in my small office. With Vera in her large flowing lilac robes, the room was pretty full.

Willa had a commanding voice, Vera a tiny one.

'As you will no doubt be aware, Vera and I are mentatropists,' said Willa. 'While we support your wish to form a utopian society, we have to tell you that such is an impossibility.'

'How so?' I asked, not best pleased by her haughty manner.

'Because of the contradictory nature of mankind in general and individuals in particular. We think we desire order and calm, but the autonomous nervous system requires some disorder and excitement.'

'Is it not exciting enough just to be on Mars?'

She said sternly, 'Why, certainly not. We don't even have the catharsis of S&V movies to watch.'

Seeing my slight puzzlement, Vera said in her high voice, 'Sex and Violence, Mr Jefferies, Sex and Violence.' She spread "violence" out into its three component syllables.

'So you consider utopia a hopeless project?'

'Unless . . .'

'Unless?' Vera White drew herself up to her full girth. 'A full course of mentatropy for all personnel.'

'Including all the scientists,' added Willa in her deepest tone.

They departed in full sail when I thanked them for their offer and said Adminex would consider it.

Kissorian came in and exclaimed that I looked taken aback. 'I've just met some mentatropists,' I said.

He laughed. 'Oh, the Willa-Vera Composite!' And so they became known.

We did not forget – at least in those early days – that we constituted a mere pimple on the face of Mars, that grim and dusty planet that remained there, uncompromising, aloof. Despite the reinforcements of modern science, our position was best described as precarious.

The static nature of the world on which we found ourselves weighed heavily on many minds, especially those of delicate sensibility. The surface of Mars had remained stable, immovable, dead, throughout eons of its history. Compared with its restless neighbour from which we had come, Mars's tectonic history was one of locked immobility. It was a world without oceans or mountain chains, its most prominent feature being the Tharsis Shield, that peculiar gravitic anomaly, together with the unique feature of Olympus Mons.

Emerging from the hectic affairs of the third planet, many people viewed this long continued stillness with horror. For them it was as if they had become locked into one of the tombs in Egypt's Valley of the Kings. This obsessive form of isolation became known as areophobia.

A group of young psychurgists was called before Adminex to deal with the worst afflicted cases. Some of them had earlier reproached me for the thirty-one suicides, saying their services, had they been called into action, would have saved the precious lives. I found among them an enormous respect for the Willa-Vera Composite; clearly the mentatropy duo were not the figures of fun I had taken them for. Psychurgy itself had developed from a combination of the old psychotherapy and more recent genome research; whereas mentatropy, embodying a new understanding of the brain and consciousness, was a much more hands-on approach to mental problems.

The psychurgists reported that sufferers from areophobia endured a conflict of ideas: with a fear of total isolation went a terror that something living but alien would make its sudden appearance. It was a new version of the stress of the unknown, which disappeared after counselling – and, of course, after a reassurance that Mars was a dead world, without the possibility of life.

For this fear of alien beings I felt that Mr H.G. Wells and his followers were much to blame. The point I attempted to make was that Mars's role in human thought had been benevolent and scientific – in a word, rational.

To this end, I persuaded Charles Bondi to give an address. Although he regarded my attempts to regulate society as a waste of time, he responded readily enough to deliver an exposition of Mars's place in humanity's progressive thought.

His speech concluded: 'The great Johannes Kepler's study of the orbital motions of the body on which we find ourselves yielded the three laws of planetary motion. Space travel has come to be based on Kepler's laws. The name of Kepler will always remain honoured for those brilliant calculations, as well as for his wish to reduce to sense what had previously been muddle.

'If we are to remain long enough on Mars, our eccentric friend here, Thomas Jefferies, will try to perform a feat equivalent in sociological terms to Kepler's, reducing to regulation what has always been a tangle of conflicting patterns of behaviour from which, to my mind, creativity has sprung.'

Bondi could not resist that final dig at me.

Yes, ours was an ambitious task. I saw, as he did not, that it could be accomplished because we were a small population, and one which, as it happened, had been self-selected for its social awareness.

During one debate the Ukrainian Muslim YEA named Youssef Choihosla rose and declared that we were all wasting our time. He said that whatever rules of conduct we drew up, even those to which we had readily given universal consent, we would break; such was the nature of mankind.

He was continuing in this vein when a woman of distinguished appearance spoke up to ask him cuttingly if he considered we should have no rules?

Choihosla paused. And if we were to have rules, pursued the woman, pressing home her advantage and looking increasingly majestic, was it not wise to discover what the best rules were and then try to abide by them?

The Ukrainian became defensive. He had spent his year of community service, he claimed, working in an asylum for the mentally deranged in Sarajevo. He had experienced terrible things there. He believed as a result that what Carl Jung called 'the shadow' would always manifest itself. It was therefore useless to hope to establish even a mockery of a utopia. You could not pump morality into a system to which it was not indigenous. (A year or two later, interestingly, he would put forward a much more positive viewpoint.)

Several voices attempted to answer him. The woman who had previously spoken quelled them with her clear firm tones. Her name was Belle Rivers. She was the head-mistress in charge of the cadre children, semi-permanently stationed on Mars.

'Why is there a need for laws, you ask? Are laws not present in all societies, to guard against human "shadows"? As scientific people, we are aware that the human body is a museum of its phylogenetic history. Our psyches too are immensely old; their roots lie in times before we could claim the name of human. Only our individual minds belong to ontology, and they are transient. It is the creatures – our archetypes, Jung calls them – that reside in the unconscious, like your shadow, which act as prompts to the behaviour of the human species.

'The archetypes live in an inner world, where the pulse of time throbs at a drowsy pace, scarcely heeding the birth and death of individuals. Their nature is strange: when they broke into the conscious minds of your patients in Sarajevo, they undoubtedly would have precipitated psychosis. Your psychurgists will tell you as much.

'But we moderns know these things. The archetypes have been familiar to us for more than a century. Instead of fearing them, of trying to repress them, we should come to terms with them. That means coming to terms with ourselves.

'I believe that we must draw up our rules firmly and without fear, in acknowledgement of our conscious wishes. I also regard it as healthy that we acknowledge our unconscious wishes.

'I therefore propose that every seventh day be given

over to bacchanalia, when ordinary rules of conduct are suspended.'

My glance went at once to the bench where Sharon Singh lounged. She was gazing serenely at the roof, the long fingers of one hand tapping gently on the rail of her seat. She was calm while much shouting and calls for order continued round her.

An old unkempt man rose to speak. He had once been Governor of the Seychelles; his name was Crispin Barcunda. We had spoken often. I enjoyed his quiet sense of humour. When he laughed a gold tooth sparkled briefly like a secret signal.

'This charming lady puts forward a perfectly workable idea,' he said, attempting to smooth down his mop of white hair. 'Why not have the odd bacchanalia now and again? No one on Earth need know. We're private, here on Mars, aren't we?'

This suggestion was put forward in a droll manner so that people laughed. Crispin continued more seriously. 'It is curious, is it not, that before we have established our laws, there should be what sounds like rather a popular proposal to abolish them every seventh day? However welcome the throwing off of restraints, dangers follow from it . . . Is the day after one of these bacchanalias to be declared a mopping-up day? A bandaging-of-broken-heads day? A day of broken vows and tears and quarrels?'

Immediately, people were standing up and shouting. A cry of 'Don't try to legislate our sex lives' was widely taken up.

Crispin Barcunda appeared unmoved. When the noise died slightly, he spoke again.

'Since we are getting out of hand, I will attempt to read to you, to calm you all down.'

While he was speaking, Barcunda produced from the pocket of his overalls a worn leather-bound book.

As he opened it, he said, 'I brought this book with me on the journey here, in case I woke up when we were only three months out from Earth and needed something to read. It is written by a man I greatly admire, Alfred Russell Wallace, one of those later-borns our friend Hal Kissorian mentioned in his remarkable contribution the other day.

'Wallace's book, by the way, is called *The Malay Archipelago*. I believe it has something valuable to offer us on Mars.'

Barcunda proceeded to read: '"I have lived with communities of savages in South America and in the East, who have no laws or law courts but the public opinion of the village freely expressed. Each man scrupulously respects the rights of his fellow, and any infraction of those rights rarely or never takes place. In such a community, all are nearly equal. There are none of those wide distinctions, of education and ignorance, wealth and poverty, master and servant, which are the product of our civilisation; there is none of that wide-spread division of labour, which, while it increases wealth, produces also conflicting interests; there is not that severe competition and struggle for existence, or for wealth, which the dense population of civilized countries inevitably creates.

'"All incitements to great crimes are thus wanting, and petty ones are repressed, partly by the influence of public opinion, but chiefly by that natural sense of justice and of his neighbour's right which seems to be, in some degree, inherent in every race of man."'

Snapping the book shut, Barcunda said, 'Mr Chairman, my vote is that we have but one law: Thou shalt not compete!'

A YEA immediately shouted, 'That's all very well for you DOPs. We young men have to compete – there aren't enough women for all of us!'

Again I looked towards Sharon Singh.

She was examining her nails, as if remote from intellectual discussion.

After the session closed, I talked with Barcunda. We had a coffdrink together. His pleasant personality came across very clearly. I said that it was unfortunate we were not in as favourable a position as Wallace's savages.

He replied that our situations were surprisingly similar, sunshine deficiency apart.

Our work was not labour, our food was adequate, and we had few possessions.

And we had a benefit the savages of Wallace's East could not lay claim to, which was the novelty of our situation: we were in a learning experience, isolated millions of miles from Earth.

'It is vitally important that we retain our good sense and good humour, and draw up an agenda for a just life quickly. We cannot secure total agreement, because the pleasure of some people is to disagree. What we require is a majority vote – and our agenda must not be seen to be drawn up merely by DOPs. That would give the young bucks among the YEAs an opportunity to challenge authority. They can't go out into the jungle to wrestle with lions and gorillas to prove their manhood: they'd wrestle with us instead.'

He gestured and pulled a savage face face to demonstrate his point.

'You can't say I'm a very dictatorial chairman.'

'I can't. But maybe they can. Take a day off, Tom. Hand over the chair to a young trouble-maker. Kissorian might be a good candidate, besides having such a fun name.'

'Kissorian goes by favour, eh?'

Looking at me poker-faced, Crispin said that he wanted legislation to improve the Martian brand of ersatz coffee. 'Tom, joking apart, we are so fortunate as to have the bad luck to be stuck on Mars! We both see the survival of humanity on a planet on which we were not born as an extraordinary, a revolutionary, step.

'I must say I listened to your five bugbears with some impatience. I wanted you to get to the bugbear we have clearly escaped from: the entire systematic portrayal of sexuality and violence as desirable and of overwhelming importance. We no longer have these things pouring like running water from our television and Ambient screens. I fancy that deprived of this saccharine/strychnine drip, we can only improve morally.'

* * *

At the next meeting of Adminex (as always, televised for intercom and Ambient), we discussed this aspect of life: the constant projection of violence and sexual licence on media that imitated life. Both Kissorian and Barcunda were coopted on to the team. It was agreed – in some cases with reluctance – that most of us had been indoctrinated by the constant representation of personal assult and promiscuity on various screens, so as to accept such matters as an important part of life, or at least as a more dominant component of our subconscious minds than we were willing to admit to. In Barcunda's elegant formulation: 'If a man has an itch, he will scratch it, even when talking philosophy.'

Without pictorial representations of a gun and sex culture, there seemed a good chance that society might become less aggressive.

But Kissorian disagreed. 'Sex is one thing, and violence quite another. Barcunda compounds them into one toxic dose by talking of the saccharine/strychnine drip. I agree that it's really no loss that we do not have these activities depicted on TV here, but, believe me, we need sex. What else do we have? Everything else is in short supply. We certainly need sex. You speak as if there were something unnatural about it.'

Barcunda protested that he was not against sex, only constant and unnecessary depictions of its various activities.

'It's a private thing,' he said, leaning across the table. 'Showing it on the screen transforms a private thing into a public, a political, act. And so it muddies the deep waters of the spirit.'

Kissorian looked down his nose. 'You DOPs had better realise that for the amount of screwing that goes on you'd think we were on Venus.'

Kathi Skadmorr's activities as a speleologist had made her the hero of the hour. It was suggested at the end of the meeting that I should coopt her on to the Adminex, if only to make that body more popular. I agreed, but was not eager to have another confrontation with her on Ambient.

We continued our discussion of Crispin Barcunda's saccharine/strychnine drip privately. One of the fundamental questions was whether love and sexuality would become more enjoyable if they retreated into being private things? Without constant representation visually in the media, would not a certain precious intimacy be restored to the act? But how to bring this thing about without censorship: that is, to influence public opinion so that ordinary persons who wished to do so could rid themselves of the poisonous drip, as they had in previous ages rid themselves of the enjoyments of cock-fighting, slavery and tobacco-smoking?

Crispin said, 'You want to advance towards the betterment of mankind? Maybe it can be done, maybe not! But let's have a try, Tom. After all, it gives our lives here an objective. Betterment means a break with the past – chop, like that! – not just a continuation of it, as would have been the case had the terraformers and realtors had their way. Maybe we can do it. But I'd be against any suspicion that sexuality and eroticism was not in itself one of mankind's blessings. The older I get, and the more difficult sex gets, the more I become convinced it holds the meaning of any valued life.'

I could but agree. 'We must try to influence minds. It is important – and not just for our little outpost here. We're not going to be isolated for ever. Once EUPACUS or its successors have been reassembled, once the world economy has picked up, ships are going to be operating again.

'By that time, we must have our mini-utopia up and running. Just to be a shining example to Earth, to which most of us wish to return.'

'Then maybe on Earth, as in good old Wallace's island community, the ideal might be reached, where each man

104

scrupulously regards the rights of his fellow man.' As he spoke, Crispin gazed earnestly and short-sightedly into my eyes. 'Like not shooting him or fucking his wife.'

He was a good man. Talking with him, I was convinced we could become a better, happier, humanity – without the pathetic need of saccharine/strychnine drips.

'Now you'd better go and coopt Skadmorr,' he said. 'She'll lower the average age of Adminex by a few years!'

I was up early next morning. Runners and the semi-flighted were already about in the streets, exercising. Although we had yet to solve the question of the Martian date line, we had solved the problem of dividing up the days and weeks. Mars's axial rotation makes its day only sixty-nine minutes longer than Earth's day. In the time of EUPACUS, an extra 'hour' of sixty-nine minutes had been inserted to follow the hour of two in the morning. This was the 'X' hour. The other hours conformed to the terrestrial twenty-four.

The innovation of the 'X' hour meant that at first terrestrial watches had to be adjusted every day, until an ingenious young technician, Bill Abramson, made his reputation by inserting what he called 'the "X" trigger,' which suspended the momentum of watches and clocks for sixty-nine minutes every night, after which they continued working normally as before.

Since an hour is basically the way we measure our progress through the day, there were few complaints at this somewhat ad hoc arrangement. But it did mean that human activity restarted fairly early in the day.

Taking in the scene around me, I could only appreciate the change from the city on Earth I had left, with its gigantic byzantine structures housing thousands of people, walled in like bees in their cells with Ambient connections supplying many of their needs, the façades of these structures awash with pornographic images once sun had set. Below those great ragged skylines, below the coiling avenues, lived the impromptus, subsisting on the city's grime, anaesthetised by the free porntrips overhead.

But here, under our low ceilings, was a more hygienic world, where coloured plastic ducts were running in parallel or diverging overhead, with jazzy patterns in rubber tiles below our feet and stylised lighting. Birds flew and called among the plant clusters at every intersection. It was at once more abstract and more human in scale than terrestrial cities. I recalled an exhibition I had attended in my home city hall of the paintings of an old twentieth-century artist, Hubert Rogers. Those visions of the future that had so inspired me as a young man were here realised. I recalled them with pleasure as I hopped on a jo-jo bus.

So it was just before six o'clock that I called on Mary Fangold at the hospital for a coffee. I liked to talk over events with this reasonable and attractive woman – and incidentally to visit my adopted daughter, whose implanted leg was now almost completely regenerated.

The first person I encountered was Kathi Skadmorr. She was striding out of the gym with a towel round her neck, looking the picture of health.

'Hi! I was watching your discussion of the prevalence of violent and sexual material. I thought you were talking sense for once.' She spoke in a friendly way, regarding me through those dark, lash-frilled eyes of hers. 'What we usually do in private should remain private. Ain't that what you were saying? It's pretty simple really.'

'Bringing about the change is a problem, though. That's not simple.'

'How about telling people to keep it quiet?'

'It's better to get people's consent rather than just telling them.'

'You could tell them, then get their consent. Remember the old saying, Tom: Once you get folk by the balls, their hearts and minds will follow.' She giggled.

'So what are you doing here, so early in the morning?'

'I came over from the science unit to see Cang Hai. Then I did an hour's work-out. Are you visiting your daughter?'

'Um, yes. Yes, I am.'

She then asked me what I made of Cang Hai's Other,

her mental friend in Chengdu. I had to admit I had really not considered it. Her Other did not impinge on my life.

'Nor apparently does your daughter,' she said with a return to her earlier asperity. 'She really loves you, you know that? I believe she has an unusual kind of consciousness, as I have. Her Other may be a kind of detached reflection of her own psyche. Or it may be a little encapsulated psyche within her own psyche, like a – a kind of cyst within her soul. I'm studying it.'

At this juncture, Mary appeared. She was direct as usual and told us to enter her office for coffee and a talk. 'But it had better be a brief talk. Say twenty minutes at most. I have a lot to do today.'

As we sat down, I asked Kathi if her unusual kind of consciousness was also a 'cyst within her soul'. I used her phrase.

'My consciousness embraces an external. It embraces Mars. It's all to do with the life force. I'm a mystic, believe it or not. I've been down into the gullet, or maybe the vagina, of this planet, into its bladder. I have nothing but contempt for those thirty or however many it was who committed suicide here. They were prats. Good that they died! We don't want people like that. We want people who are able to live beyond their own narrow lives.'

'They were all victims, cut off from their families,' Mary Fangold said.

'They didn't do their families much good by killing themselves, did they?'

She crossed her long legs and sipped at the mug of coffdrink Mary had brought. Almost to herself, she said, 'I thirst for what Tom proposed – the mind set free!'

Mary and I started to talk together, but Kathi cut us short, speaking eagerly. 'You should get rid of all this flaunting of sex, as you say. Sex is just a recreation, after all, sometimes good, sometimes not so good. Nothing to be obsessed about. Once you get it out of the way you can fill everyone's minds with real valuable things, mental occupations. Without TV or the other distractions, we can be educated in science in all its branches. We must learn more, all of us. It's urgent. "Civilisation is a race between education and catastrophe" – you remember that saying? Education throughout life. Wouldn't that be wonderful?'

Somehow I did not take that opportunity to invite her to join Adminex. I felt she might be too disruptive. However Kissorian asked her a few weeks later. Kathi turned down the offer, saying she was not a committee person. That we could well believe.

Kissorian had a piece of gossip too. He said Kathi was having a love affair – 'frequently in the sack', was his way of putting it – with Beau Stephens. We thought about that. Beau at this time showed little ambition, and was working on the jo-jos.

I realise that I have made little mention in this record of Cang Hai, who had attached herself to me. Certainly she is devoted, and it is hard not to return affection when it is offered without condition. She became increasingly useful to me, and was no fool.

Of course she was no substitute for Antonia.

Cang Hai's Account

9

Improving the Individual

In hospital I learned to walk with my artificial leg. At first it had no feeling; cartilage growth was slow. Now the nerves were growing back and connecting, giving a not unpleasant fizzy sensation. When I was allowed out of hospital for an hour at a time, I took a stroll through the domes, feeling my muscle tone rapidly return.

Attempts had been made to brighten the atmosphere of our enforced home while I had been out of action. The jo-jo buses were being repainted in bright colours; some were decorated with fantastic figures, such as the 'Mars dragon'.

Glass division walls were tanks containing living fish, gliding like sunlit spaceships in their narrow prisons. The flowering trees recently planted along the main avenues were doing well. More Astroturf had been planted. Between the trees flitted macaws and parrots, bright of plumage, genetically adapted to sing sweetly.

I liked the birds, knowing they had been cloned.

Inspired by these improvements, I tried to brighten Tom's spartan quarters.

When I was fit enough to rejoin my fellows, I found more confidence in myself, perhaps as a result of my friendship with Kathi.

So a year passed, and still we remained isolated on Mars.

Our society was composed as follows. There were

412 non-visitors or cadre (all those who were conducting scientific experiments, technicians, 'carers', managers, and others employed permanently on Mars before the EUPACUS crash), together with their children. This number comprised 196 women, 170 men and 46 children, ranging in age from a few months to fifteen years old, plus 62 babies under six months. Of the 2,025 DOPs, 1,405 were men and 620 women, and of the 3,420 YEAs, 2,071 were men and 1,349 women. A visiting inspection team consisted of 9 medics (5 women and 4 men) and 30 flight technicians (28 men and 2 women).

Thus the total population of Mars in AD 2064 was 5,958.

To which it must be added that two carers, two DOP women and 361 of the YEA women (about one-quarter of them) were pregnant. The population of the planet was, in other words, due to increase by about 6 per cent within the next six months.

This caused some alarm and much discussion. Blame went flying about, mainly from the DOPs, although as a group they were not entirely blameless. A pharmacist came forward to admit that the pharmacy, which was housed in the R&A hospital, had run out of anti-conception pills, having been unprepared for the EUPACUS crash and the cessation of regular supplies of pharmaceuticals.

After this revelation some DOPs suggested that young people use restraint in their sexual lives. The suggestion was not well received, not least because many couples had discovered that sex held an additional piquancy and that an act of intercourse could be sustained for longer, in the lighter Martian gravity. Nevertheless worries were expressed concerning the extra demands on water and oxygen supplies that the babies would exert.

I tried to commune with my shaded half in Chengdu. My message was: 'Once more, the spectre of overpopulation is raising its head – on an almost empty planet!' It was puzzling to receive in return an image of a barren moorland covered in what seemed to be a layer of snow.

As I tried to peer at this snow cover, it resolved itself into a great white flock of geese. The geese bestirred themselves and took to the air. They flew round and round in tight formation, their wings making a noise like the beating of a leather gong. The ground had disappeared beneath them.

It was all beautiful enough, but not particularly helpful.

Tom and I took a walk one evening, and were discussing the population question. A strip of sidewalk along the street was covered with an Astroturf that mimicked growth and was periodically trimmed. This was Spider Plant Alley, renamed after the plants that mopped up hydroxyls, much as Poulsen had said. Throughout the domes, plants were pervading the place.

I particularly liked Spider Plant at the evening hour. It was then that the quantcomp that controlled our ambient atmospheric conditions turned lighting low and cut temperatures by 5 degrees for the night. A slight breeze rustled the plants – a tender natural sound, even if controlled by human agency.

As I hung on Tom's arm, I asked him when he was going to regulate primary sexual behaviour.

He replied that anyone who attempted such regulation would meet with disaster, that sexuality was a vital and pervasive part of our corporeal existence. While other facets of that existence were denied us on Mars, it was only to be expected that sexual activity should intensify.

'You also have to understand, dear daughter, that sexual pleasure is good in itself – a harmless and life-enhancing pleasure.' He looked down at me with a half-smile. 'Why else has it excited so many elders to control it throughout the ages? Of course, beyond the sexual act lie potential ethical problems. With those we can perhaps deal. I mean – well, the consequences of the sexual act, babies, diseases and all those rash promises to love for ever when lust is like fire to the straw i' the blood, as Hamlet says.'

We walked on before I added, 'Or, of course, whether both parties give their consent to the merging of their bodies.'

I thought of how I was always reluctant to give that consent. Had I, by becoming Tom's adopted daughter, somehow managed to avoid giving that consent yet again? I did not know myself. Though I lived in an info-rich environment, my inner motivations remained unknown to me.

'You are justifying sex simply because it's enjoyable?' I asked.

'No, no. Sex justifies itself simply because it's enjoyable. Sometimes it can even seem like an end in itself.'

Silence fell between us, until Tom said – I thought with some reluctance – 'My father spent all his inherited wealth on a medical clinic in a foreign land. I was brought up there. When I was repatriated at the age of fifteen, both my parents were dead. I was utterly estranged, and put under the nominal care of my Aunt Letitia.' He stopped, so that we stood there in the semi-dark. I held his hand.

'I fell in love with my cousin, Diana – "Diana, huntress chaste and fair", the poet says. Luckily, this Diana was fair and unchaste. I was cold, withdrawn – traumatised, I suppose. Diana was a little older than I, eager to experience the joys of sexual union. I cannot express the rapture of that first kiss, when our lips met. That kiss was my courageous act, my reaching out to another person.'

'Is that what it needs? Courage?'

He ignored me. 'Within hours we were naked together, exploring each others' bodies, and then making love – under the sun, under the moon, even, once, in the rain. The delirium of innocent joy I felt . . . Ah, her eyes, her hair, her thighs, her perfume – how they possessed me! . . . I'm sorry, Cang, this must be distasteful to you. I'll just say that beyond all sensual pleasure lies a sense of a new and undiscovered life.

'No, I'm a dry old stick now, but I'd be a monster if I tried to deny such pleasures to our fellow denizens . . .'

I was feeling cold and suggested we went inside.

'People still think you're some kind of a dictator,' I said, with more spite in my tone than I had intended.

Tom replied that he imagined he was rather a laughing stock. Idealists were always a butt for humour. Fortunately, he had no ambition, only hope. Enough hope, he said, lightly, to fill a zeppelin. He repeated, enough hope . . .

Yet in his mouth that last word held a dying fall.

That night, when alone, I wept. I could not stop.

I wept mostly for myself, but also for humanity, so possessed by their reproductive organs. Our Martian population was slave to unwritten ancient law, multiplying as it saw fit. That pleasure of which my Tom spoke always came with responsibilities.

At least the R&A hospital could prepare for an outburst of maternity, its original duties being in abeyance. There were no new intakes of visitors to be acclimatised. One ward was converted into a new maternity unit, all brightly lit and antiseptic, in which births could be conducted with conveyor-belt efficiency.

Everywhere, there was industry. Existing buildings were converted to new uses. The synthesising kitchens were extended. Factories were established for the synthesis of cloth for clothing. All talents were seized upon for diverse works. During the day the noise of hammering and drilling was to be heard. We would endeavour to be comfortable, however temporary our stay.

There was music in the domes. Not all terrestrial music was to our taste, and composers like Beza were sought to compose Martian music – whatever that might be!

The more far-sighted of us looked ahead to a more distant future. Among these was Tom. Whether or not he really had hope, he and his committee pressed ahead with his plans to involve everyone in everyone else's welfare. They engrossed him; sometimes I felt he had no personal life.

He declared that it was a matter of expedience that the education of young children should be given priority. There I was able to assist him to some extent.

Several committees were elected to formulate with others their hopes and endeavours for a better society. They held colloquia, which began in itinerant fashion, the more appealing ones becoming permanent features of our life. Sometimes they were met with impatience or hostility, although it was generally conceded that conditions in the domes might get rapidly worse unless they were rapidly improved. Improvement was something we strove for.

Emerson's remark long ago that people preened themselves on improvements in society, yet no one individual improved, lay at the basis of many endeavours. The mutuality required for a just society implied that we must hope to improve the individual, to fortify him; otherwise any improvements would merely enhance the status of the powerful and lower that of the less powerful, and we would be back with the suppressions so prevalent on Earth.

Somewhere in the individual life must lie the salvation of whole societies, or else all was lost.

Hard as I tried, I found it difficult to study. If only I could learn more, I told myself, Tom would love me more. Many a time, I would simply sit in a café and listen to the music that filled the place. Kathi Skadmorr and I had many conversations. For her, learning seemed easy. She worked with Dreiser Hawkwood and found him, she said, a little overpowering. I thought privately that anyone Kathi found overpowering was worth a great deal of respect.

She had become absorbed in studying Olympus Mons. At times, the great volcanic cone seemed to fill her thought. She had submitted a carefully reasoned paper to Dreiser on the Ambient, suggesting a name change. Olympus was a 'fuddy-duddy' name. She had found a better name for it when talking with an Ecuadorian scientist, Georges Souto. He had told her of an extinct volcano in Ecuador, the top of which, he said, because of the oblate spheroidal nature of Earth, was the point furthest from the centre of the Earth. In fact, it was 2,150 metres further from that centre than Everest, commonly assumed to be the highest point on Earth.

The sophistry of this argument greatly amused Kathi. When she learned that this defunct volcano was named Chimborazo, meaning the 'Watchtower of the Universe', she campaigned for Olympus Mons to be renamed Chimborazo. The campaign was a failure at first, and Dreiser, she said, was annoyed with her for talking nonsense.

Shortly after this, she studied satellite photographs of the Tharsis Shield, and observed – so she claimed – tumbled and churned regolith on the far side of Olympus, as if something had been burrowing there. When she pointed this out to Dreiser, he told her not to waste his time, or she would be sent back to the domes.

Many of the pressures extant on Earth – or Downstairs, as had become the fashionable term for our mother planet – had been relieved by our exile Upstairs. The intense pressure of commercialism had been lifted. So had many of the provocations of racism; here, we were all in the same boat, rather than in many jostling boats.

In particular, money, the gangrene of the political system, had been removed from play, although admittedly a sort of credit scheme existed, whereby payments were postponed until we were hypothetically returned Downstairs.

After a year or so, this credit scheme had taken sick and died, primarily because we found we could manage without it, and secondarily because we ceased to believe in it.

It was deemed futile to approach any individual with ambitious schemes if he or she was miserable. Many people missed or worried about their families Downstairs. Once our communication cards ran out, there was no renewing them, and the terrestrial telecom station was closed down – another feature of the EUPACUS fiasco. Counselling was provided, and the psychurgical group was kept busy. Also effective in healing was the community spirit that had arisen, and a renewed sense of adventure. We lived in a new place, within a new context, the 'different psychological calculus'.

One of our colloquia became engaged in the art of making new music: primarily a capella singing, which we raised to high standards. We had brought in home-made and revolutionary musical instruments. The 'Martian Meritorio' was established in time as our great success. But I still remember with affection our solo voices raised in song – in specially written song.

No bird flies in the abyss
    Its bright plumage failing
No eye lights in the dark
    Its sight unavailing
The air carries no spark
    Only this –
    Only this
Where sunlight lies ailing –
Our human hopes sailing
    In humankind's ark

The improvement of the individual was pursued in such sessions as body-mind-posture, conducted at first by Ben Borrow, a disciple of the energetic Belle Rivers. Borrow was a little undersized man, full of energy, as easily roused to anger as to raucous laughter. He drove and inspired his attendees to believe, as he did, that the secret of a good life lurked in how one stood, sat and walked in the light gravity.

Perhaps because the bleak surroundings led our thoughts that way, our Art of Imagination colloquium was always successful. Swift and Laputa, those two satellites, first dreamed of by an Irish dean, that chased regularly above our heads, were used to connect the reality of our lives with the greater reality of which we were a transitory part.

A way of knowing ourselves was to relate our lived

experience with the flow of language, thought and concepts surrounding us, by which the mundane could be reimagined. 'Know thyself' was an exortation requiring, above all, imagination. In this department, the Willa-Vera Composite, one so whippetlike, the other so much like a doughnut, proved invaluable.

Hard work along these lines produced some extraordinary artistries, not least the four-panel continuous loop video abstract entitled 'Dawning Diagram' which, with its mystery and majesty, affected all who watched it. Human things writhed into shape from the molecular, rose, ran, flowered in bursts of what could have been sun, could have been rain, might have been basalt, died, bathed in reproductive dawns. In another quarter of the screen an old Tiresias read in a vellum-bound volume, tirelessly turning the same page.

Everything happened simultaneously, in an instant of time.

The aim of the Art of Imagination colloquium was to revive in adults that innocent imagination lost with childhood (although children also enjoyed the programme and gave much to it).

'I know the Sun isn't necessarily square. I just like it better that way.' This remark by an eight-year-old, as comment on his strange painting, *Me and My Universe*, was later embodied in a large multimedia canvas hung at the entrance of the Art of Imagination Department (previously Immigration).

There were those who attended this colloquium who were initially unable to seize on the fact that they were alive and on Mars. So obnubilated were their imaginations they could not grasp the wonder of reality. They needed a metaphorical sense to be restored to them. In many cases, it was restored.

Then they rejoiced and congratulated themselves that they were Upstairs.

To our regret, the scientists in the main kept to their own

quarters, a short distance from the domes. It was not that they were aloof. They claimed to be too busy with research.

I accompanied Tom to the station when he went to talk privately with Dreiser Hawkwood. A woman who announced herself as Dreiser's personal assistant asked us to wait in a small anteroom. We could hear Dreiser growling in his office. Tom was impatient until we were admitted to his presence by this same assistant.

Dreiser Hawkwood was a darkly semi-handsome man, with the look of one who has bitten deep into the apple of the Tree of Knowledge. Indeed, I thought, noticing that his teeth protruded slightly under his moustache, he might have snagged them on its core. He was much preoccupied with the fact that the paper substitute was running out.

'Predictions are for amusement only,' he said. 'When computers came into general use, there was a prediction that paper would be a thing of the past. Far from it. High-tech weaponry systems, for instance, require plenty of documentation. US Navy cruisers used to go to sea loaded with twenty-eight tonnes of manuals. Enough to sink a battleship!'

He jerked his head towards the overloaded bookshelves behind him, from which manuals threatened to spill.

Tom asked him what he was working on.

'Poulsen and I are trying to rejig the programme that controls all our internal weather. It's wasteful of energy and we could use the computer power for better things.'

He continued with a technical exposition of how the current programme might be revised, which I did not follow. The two men talked for some while. The scientists were still expecting to find a HIGMO.

Regarding the science quarters rather as an outpost, I was astonished to see how well the room we were in was furnished, with real chairs rather than the collapsible ones used in the domes. Symphonic music played at a low level; I thought I recognised Penderecki. On the walls were star charts, an animated reproduction of a late-period Kandinsky and a cut-away diagram of an American-made MP500 sub-machine gun.

The personal assistant had her own desk in one corner of the room. She was blonde and in her thirties, wearing a green dress rather than our fairly standard coveralls.

At the sight of that dress I was overcome with jealousy. I recognised it as made from cloth of the old kind, which wore out, and so was expensive, almost exclusive. The rest of us wore costumes fabricated from Now (the acronym of Non-Ovine Wool), which never wore out. Now clothes fitted our bodies, being made of a semi-sentient synthetic that renewed itself, given a brush occasionally with fluid. Now clothes were cheap. But that dress . . .

When she caught my gaze, the personal assistant flashed a smile. She moved restlessly about the room, shifting paper and mugs, while I sat mutely by Tom's side.

Tom said, 'Dreiser, I came over to ask for your presence and support at our debates. But I have something more serious to talk about. What are these white strips that rise from the regolith and slick back into it? Are they living things?' He referred to the tongues (as I thought of them) we had encountered on our way over to the unit. 'Or is this a system you have installed?'

'You think they are living?' asked Dreiser, looking hard at Tom.

'What else, if they are not a part of your systems?'

'I thought you had established that there was no life on Mars.'

'You know the situation. We've found no life. But these strips aren't a mere geological manifestation.'

Hawkwood said nothing. He looked at me as if willing me to speak. I said nothing.

He pushed his chair back, rose, and went over to a locker on the far side of the room. Tom studiously looked at the ceiling. I noticed Dreiser pat the bottom of his assistant as he passed her. She gave a smug little smile.

He returned with a hologram of some of the tongues, which Tom studied.

'This tells me very little,' he said. 'Are they a life form, or part of one, or what?'

Dreiser merely shrugged.

Tom said that he had never expected to find life on Mars, or anywhere else; the path of evolution from mere chemicals to intelligence required too many special conditions.

'My student, Skadmorr, seems to believe we're being haunted by a disembodied consciousness or something similar,' Dreiser remarked. 'Aborigine people know about such matters, don't they?'

'Kathi's not an Aborigine,' I said.

Tom took what he regarded as an optimistic view, that the development of cosmic awareness in humankind marked an unrepeatable evolutionary pattern; humankind was the sole repository of higher consciousness in the galaxy. Our future destiny was to go out and disperse, to become the eye and mind of the universe. Why not? The universe was strange enough for such things to happen.

Dreiser remained taciturn and stroked his moustache.

'Hence my hopes of building a just society here,' said Tom. 'We have to improve our behaviour before we go out into the stars.'

'Well, we don't quite know what we've got here,' replied Hawkwood, after a pause, seemingly ignoring Tom's remark. He thumped the hologram. 'With regard to this phenomenon, at least it appears not to be hostile.'

'It? You mean they?'

'No, I mean it. The strips work as a team. I wish to god we were better armed. Oxyacetelyne welders are about our most formidable weapon . . .'

As we started the drive back to the domes, Tom said, 'Uncommunicative bastard.' He became unusually silent. He broke that silence to say, 'We'd better keep quiet about these strips until the scientists find out more about them. We don't want to alarm people unnecessarily.'

He gave me a grim and searching look.

'Why are scientists so secretive?' I asked.

He shook his head without replying.

10

Some malcontents rejected everything offered them in the way of enlightenment, so impatient were they to return to Earth. They formed an action group, led by two brothers of mixed nationality, Abel and Jarvis Feneloni. Abel was the more powerful of the two, a brawny games player who had done his community service in an engineering department on Luna. Jarvis fancied himself as an amateur politician. Their family had lived on an Hawaiian island, where Jarvis had been one of a vulcanism team.

Expeditions outside the domes to the surface of Mars were strictly limited, in order to conserve oxygen and water. The Fenelonis, however, had a plan. One noontime, they, and four other men, broke the rules and rode out in a commandeered buggy. With them they took cylinders of hydrogen from a locked store.

A certain amount of hardware littered the area of Amazonis near the domes. Among the litter stood a small EUPACUS ferry, the 'Clarke Connector', abandoned when the giant international confederation had collapsed.

The action group set about refuelling the ferry. In a nearby heated prefab shed stood a Zubrin Reactor, still in working order despite the taxing variations in Martian temperatures. It soon began operating at 400° Celsius. Atmospheric carbon dioxide plus the stolen hydrogen began to generate methane and oxygen. The RWGS reaction kicked in. Carbon dioxide and hydrogen, plus catalyst, yielded carbon monoxide and water, this part of the operation being maintained by the excess energy of the operation. The water was immediately electrolysed to produce more oxygen, which would burn the methane in a rocket engine.

The group connected hoses from the Zubrin to the ferry. The refuelling process began.

As the group of six men sheltered in the buggy, waiting for the tanks to fill, an argument broke out between the Feneloni brothers, in which the other men became involved. Each man had a pack of food with him. The plan was that when they reached the interplanetary vessel orbiting overhead, all except Abel would climb into cryogenic lockers and sleep out the journey home. Abel would fly the craft for a week, lock it into an elliptical course for Earth, allow the automatics to take over, and then go cryogenic himself. He would be the first to awaken when the craft was a week's flight away from Earth, and would take over from the guidance systems.

Abel had shown great confidence during the planning stage, carrying the others with him. Now his younger brother asked, hesitantly, if Abel had taken into account the fact that methane had a lower propellant force than conventional fuel.

'We'll compute that once we're aboard the fridge wagon,' Abel said. 'You're not getting chicken, are you?'

'That's not an answer, Abel,' said one of the other men, Dick Harrison. 'You've set yourself up as the man with the answers regarding the flight home. So why not answer your brother straight?'

'Don't start bitching, Dick. We've got to be up in that fridge wagon before they come and get us. The on-board computer will do the necessary calculations.' He drummed his fingers on the dash, sighing heavily.

They sat there, glaring at each other, in the faint shadow of the ferry.

'You're getting jumpy, not me,' said Jarvis.

'Shut your face, kid.'

'I'll ask you another elementary question,' said Dick. 'Are Mars and Earth at present in opposition or conjunction? Best time to do the trip is when they're in conjunction, isn't it?'

'Will you please shut the fuck up and prepare to board the ferry?'

'You mean you don't bloody know?' Jarvis said. 'You told us the timing had to be right, and you don't bloody know?'

A quarrel developed. Abel invited his brother to stay bottled up on Mars if he was so jittery. Jarvis said he would not trust his brother to navigate a fridge wagon if he could not answer a simple question.

'You're a titox – always were!' Abel roared. 'Always were! Get out and stay out! We don't need you.'

Without another word, Jarvis climbed from the buggy and stood there helplessly, breathing heavily in his atmosphere suit. After a minute, Dick Harrison climbed down and joined him.

'It's all going wrong,' was all he said. The two men stood there. They watched as Abel and the others left the buggy and went towards the now refuelled ferry. As the men climbed aboard, Jarvis ran over and thrust his food pack into his brother's hands.

'You'll need this, Abel. Good luck! My love to our family!'

His brother scowled. 'You rotten little titox,' was all he said. He swung the pack on to his free shoulder and disappeared into the ferry. The hatch closed behind him.

Jarvis Feneloni and Dick Harrison climbed into the shelter of the buggy. They waited until the ferry lifted off into the drab skies before starting the engine and heading back to the domes. Neither of them said a word.

Abel Feneloni's exploit and the departure of the fridge wagon from its parking orbit caused a stir for a day or two. Jarvis put the best gloss he could on the escape, claiming that his brother would present their case to the UN, and rescue for all of them would soon be at hand.

Time went by. Nothing more was heard of the rocket. No one knew if it reached Earth. The matter was eventually forgotten. As patients in hospital become so involved in the activities of their ward that they wish to hear no news of

124

the outside world, so the new Martians were preoccupied with their own affairs. If that's a fair parallel!

Lotteries for this and that took place all the time. I was fortunate enough to win a trip out to the science unit. Ten of us travelled out in a buggybus. The sun was comparatively bright, and the PIRs shone like a diamond necklace in the throat of the sky.

Talk died away as we headed northwards and the settlement of domes was lost below the near horizon. We drove along a dried gulch that served as a road. There was something about the unyielding rock, something about the absence of the most meagre sign of any living thing, that was awesome. Nothing stirred, except the dust we churned up as we passed. It was slow to settle, as if it too was under a spell.

This broken place lay defenceless under its thin atmosphere. It was cold and fragile, open to bombardment by meteors and any other space debris. All about us, fragments of primordial exploded stars lay strewn.

'Mars resembles a tomb, a museum,' said the woman I was travelling next to. 'With every day that passes, I long to get back to Earth, don't you?'

'Perhaps.' I didn't want to disappoint her. But I realised I had almost forgotten what living on Earth was like. I did remember what a struggle it had been.

I thought again, as I looked out of my window, that even this progerial areoscape held – in Tom's startling phrase – that 'divine aspect of things' which was like a secret little melody, perhaps heard differently by everyone susceptible to it.

I managed to terrify myself by wondering what it would be like to be deaf to that little tune. How bearable would Mars be then?

I was grateful to him for naming, and so bringing to my conscious mind, that powerful mediator of all experience. All the same, I disliked the drab pink of the low-ceilinged sky.

*   *   *

The tall antennae and the high-perching solar panels of the Smudge laboratory and offices showed ahead. It was only a five-minute drive from Mars City (as we sometimes laughingly called our congregation of domes). We drew nearer. The people in the front seats of the bus started to point excitedly.

At first I thought paper had been strewn near the unit. It crossed my mind that these white tongues were plants – something perhaps like the first snowdrops of a new spring. Then I remembered that Tom and I had seen these inexplicable things on our visit to Dreiser Hawkwood. As we drew close to them they slicked out of sight and disappeared into the parched crusts of regolith.

'Life? It must be a form of life . . .' So the buzz went round.

A garage door opened in the side of the building. We drove in. The door closed and atmosphere hissed into the place. When a gong chimed, it was safe to leave the buggy. The air tasted chill and metallic.

We passed into a small reception hall, where we were briefly greeted by Arnold Poulsen. As chief computer technician, Poulsen was an important man, answerable only to Hawkwood and seldom appearing in public. I studied him, since Tom had spoken highly of him. He stood before us in a wispy way, uttering conventional words of greeting, looking pleasant enough, but forgetting to smile. Then he disappeared with evident relief, his social moment finished.

We were served a coffdrink while one of the particle physicists, a Scandinavian called Jon Thorgeson, youthful but with a deeply lined face, spoke to us. He was more communicative than Poulsen, whom he vaguely resembled, being ectomorphic and seemingly of no particular age.

Did he recognise me from my previous visit? Certainly he came over and said hello to me in the friendliest way.

Thorgeson briefed us on what we were going to see. In fact, he admitted, we could see very little. The science institution comprised two sorts of people. One was a somewhat monastic unit, where male and female scientists thought about what they were doing or what they might do, free from pressures to produce – in particular the pressure to produce 'Big Science'. The other unit comprised people actually doing the science. This latter unit was still adjusting the equipment that, it was hoped, might eventually detect Rosewall's postulated Omega Smudge.

As we were being shown around, Thorgeson explained that their researches were aimed at tackling the mystery of mass in the universe. Rosewall had made an impressive case for the existence of something called a HIGMO, a hidden-symmetry gravitational monopole. The team was running a pilot project at present, on a relatively small ring, since the density of HIGMOs in the universe remained as yet unknown. The ring lay at the rear of the science unit, under a protective shield, we were told.

One of the crowd asked the obvious question of why all this equipment and this team of scientists were shipped to Mars at such enormous expense.

Thorgeson looked offended. 'It was Rosewell's perception that you needed no expensive super-collider, just a large ring-shaped tube filled with appropriate superfluid. Whenever a HIGMO passes through this ring, its passage will be detected as a kind of glitch appearing in the superfluid. Any sort of violent activity outside the tube would ruin the experiment.'

I found myself asking how HIGMOs could manage to pass through the ring. He seemed to look hard at me before answering, so that I felt silly.

'Young lady, HIGMOs can pass clean through Mars without disturbing a thing, or anyone being any the worse for it.'

Someone else asked, 'Why not build this ring on the Moon?'

'The Moon – we're too late for that! Tourist activities, mining activity, the new transcore subway . . . The whole satellite shakes like a vibrator in a wasps' nest.'

Turning his gaze on me, he asked, 'You understand this?'

I nodded. 'That's why you're out here. No wasps' nests.'

'Full marks.' He came and shook my hand, which made me very uncomfortable. 'That's why we're out here. It's fruitless to pursue the Smudge on Earth or on Luna. Far too much racket. The Omega Smudge is a shy beast.' He chuckled.

'And if you capture this Smudge, what then?' asked one of the group, Helen Panorios, the YEA woman with dyed purple hair and dark complexion.

'It holds the key to many things. In particular, it will tell us just how the microverse relates to the macroverse, giving us the precise parameters for the dividing line between the small-scale quantum world of atoms and fundamental particles, and the larger-scale classical world of specks of dust upwards to galaxies and so on. I take the view of current 'hard science' that these parameters should also tell us how the exterior universe relates to human consciousness. The detailed properties of the universe seem to be deeply related to the very existence of conscious observers – observers maybe like humans, maybe a more effective species which will supersede us. If so, then consciousness is not accidental, but integral. At last we'll have a clear understanding of all existence.'

'So you hope,' ventured a sceptical voice.

'So we hope. When the ships come back and we can obtain more material, we expect to build a superfluid ring right around the planet. Then we'll see.'

'Now we see through a glass darkly . . .' said Helen, admiringly.

'We don't quote the Bible much here but, yes, more or less.'

A man who had already asked a question enquired rather sneeringly, 'What exactly is this key between the large and small you mention? Isn't human consciousness just a manifestation of the action of the quantputers in our heads?'

'That may well be true in principle, but we can't proceed without knowing some important physical parameters more exactly, most particularly what's labelled the HIGMO q-factor, whose value is completely unknown at present – let's call it "the missing-link of physics".'

'So what what happens when you find it? Will the universe come to an end?'

Jon Thorgeson laughed to the extent of exciting the deep lines in his cheeks. He said that life for the majority of people might go on as usual. But even if the universe did end – well, he said, to make a wild guess, the probability was that there were plenty of other universes growing, as he put it, on the same stem. Mathematics indicated as much.

He came to a halt in the middle of a corridor, and our group halted with him and gathered round as he talked.

'As you know, stars keep going by exothermic fusion of hydrogen into helium-4. When the core hydrogen is almost used up, gravitational contraction starts. The consequent rise in temperature permits the burning of helium. In our universe, nucleosynthesis of all the heavier elements is achieved by this continued process of fuel exhaustion, leading to contraction, leading to higher central temperatures, leading to a new source of fuel for the sustaining nuclear energy.

'But in our universe there are what in lay terms we may call strange anomalies in this process. For instance, unless nucleosynthesis proceeded resonantly, the yield of carbon would be negligible. By a further anomaly, it happens that the carbon produced is not consumed in a further reaction. So we live in a universe with plentiful carbon and, as you know, carbon is a basic element for our kind of life.

'I wouldn't like my boss to hear me saying this, but – who knows? – in a neighbouring universe, these strange anomalies may not occur. It might be entirely life-free, without observers. Or maybe life takes another course and is, say, silicon-based. Such possibilities will become clearer if we can get the tabs on our Smudge.'

One of our group asked if it would be possible for us to enter another universe, or for something from another universe to enter ours.

The lines on Thorgeson's face deepened in amusement. 'There we venture into the realms of science fiction. I can't comment on that.'

At the end of our tour, I managed to speak to Thorgeson face to face. I told him that many of the people in the domes, particularly the YEAs, were interested in science but did not understand what the particle physicists were working at. Indeed, the scientific team were regarded as being rather secretive.

Lowering his voice, he said that there was dissension in the scientific ranks. The issues were complex. Many men and women on the team did not see the Omega Smudge as worth pursuing, and favoured more practical concerns, such as establishing a really efficient comet- and meteor-surveillance system. On the other hand . . . Here he paused.

When I prompted him to continue, he said that practical goals were for people without vision – clever people, but those without vision.

'Was Kepler being practical when, in the middle of a war, he sat down and computed the orbits of planets? Certainly not. Yet those planetary laws of his have eventually brought us here. That's pure science. The Smudge is pure science. I'm not very pure myself' – said with a sly laughing glance at me – 'but I support pure science.'

Since I understood those sly glances, I asked him boldly if he would visit the domes and lecture us on the subject?

'Want to come and have a drink with me and talk it over?'

'I have to keep with my group. Sorry.'

'Too bad. You're an attractive lady. Korean, are you? We're a bit short of adjuncts to living over here. Monastic is what we are.'

'Then leave your monastery and lecture us on particle physics.'

'You might find it rather dull,' he said. Then he smiled. 'It's a good idea. I'll see what I can do. I'll be in touch.'

At that stage, I did not realise how prophetic those words were.

We were waiting in the reception area for our buggybus to finish recharging. I started talking to the technician on duty, and asked her about the small white tongues we had seen outside the building.

'Oh, the Watchers? I can show you them on the monitors, if you like.'

I went behind her desk to take a look at the surveillance system. It clearly showed the white tongues, unmoving outside.

The technician flicked from screen to screen. The tongues surrounded the establishment. Behind them, Olympus Mons could be seen distantly, dominating its region.

'You get a clearer idea of them when I switch over to infrared,' said the technician, so doing.

I exclaimed in alarm. The tongues were no longer tongues. They reminded me, much more formidably, of gravestones I had seen in an old churchyard, tall and unmoving. They formed almost a solid wall about the establishment. It seemed they were covered in a kind of oily, scaly skin of a dull green colour. I asked if they were going to break in.

'They're quite harmless. They don't interfere. We think they're observing. They don't get in anyone's way.'

As we looked, a maintenance engineer came into view on the screens, suited up and shouldering welding equipment. As if to confirm the duty technician's words, the Watchers flicked back into the regolith and were gone, offering him no impediment. He moved out of view and the tongues at once returned.

I could not help feeling cold fear running through my body.

131

'So there is life on Mars,' I said.

'But not necessarily Martian life,' the technician said. 'Sit down for a minute, pet. You look terribly pale. I'm only joking. There's no life on Mars. We all know that.'

But jokes frequently hold bitter kernels of truth. Knowledge of the Watchers spread and caused alarm. But custom dulls the edge of many things. Whether alive or not, they made no hostile moves. We became used to their presence and finally ignored them.

After my return from Thorgeson and company, I told Kathi over the Ambient how impressed I was by Thorgeson's intellect. She asked what he had said.

I tried to explain that he had claimed the consciousness of humanity, or of a species that might supersede us, was – what had he said? – an integral function of the universe.

She laughed scornfully. 'Who do you think he got that idea from?' she asked.

After a silence, she said, 'If we cannot behave in a better and more utopian way, then we deserve to be superseded, don't you think?'

I changed the subject and spoke about the tongues surrounding the science unit.

'Don't worry,' she said lightly. 'We shall find out their function in good time. Do you know about quantum state-reduction? No? I'm reading up about it now. It's the collapse of the wave function, such as Schrödinger's cat – you know all about Schrödinger's cat, Cang Hai?'

'Of course I've heard of it.'

'Well then, the collapse of the wave function resolves the problem of that poor hypothetical quantum-superposed moggie. It becomes either a dead cat or a live cat, instead of being in a quantum superposition of both a dead and an alive cat.'

'I see . . . Is that better or worse for the cat?'

She scowled at me. 'Don't try to be funny, dear. Such

132

quantum superpositions occur in the electron displacements in a quantcomp. The definitive experiments conducted by Heitelman early this century made it clear that state-reduction actually takes place when it is the internal gravitational influences that become significant. You see where this leads us?'

I shook my head. 'I'm afraid I don't, Kathi.'

'I'm working on it, babe!' With a cheery wave of its hand her image faded from view.

Sitting there vexed, I tried to understand what she was saying. The gravitational link puzzled me. On inspiration, I decided to Ambient Jon Thorgeson in the science unit.

An unfamiliar face came up in the globe. 'Hi! I'm Jimmy Gonzales Dust, Jon's buddy. We're training for the marathon and he's busy on the running machine. Can I help? He's spoken to me about you. He thinks you're cute.'

'Oh . . . Does he? Do you know anything about the – what do you call it? The gravitational . . . no . . . The magneto-gravitic anomaly? Have you any information about it?'

He looked hard at me. 'We call it the M-gravitic anomaly.' He asked me why I was worrying. I said I didn't really know. I was trying to learn some science.

Jimmy hesitated. 'Keep this to yourself if I give you a shot from the upsat. There's been a slight shift in the anomaly.'

The photograph he released came through the slot.

I stared at it. It was an aerial view of the Tharsis Shield from 60 miles up. The outline of Olympus Mons – or Chimborazo, to use Kathi's name – could clearly be seen. Across the shot someone had scrawled with marker pen G – WSW + 0.13°.

Why and how, I asked myself, should the anomaly have shifted? Why in that direction – in effect towards Arizonis Planitia and our position?

As I stared at the photo, I noticed furrowed regolith to the east of the skirts of Olympus. Kathi had pointed this furrowing out to me earlier. Now it seemed the furrowing was rather more extensive. I could not understand what it meant. In the end, I returned to my studies, not very pleased with myself. Cute? Me?!

The domes had become a great hive of talk. There were silent sessions by way of compensation. Sports periods were relatively quiet. Other colloquia concentrated on silence, and were conducted by the wooden tongue of a pair of clappers. Silence, meditation, walking in circles, sitting, all reinforced at once a sense of communality and individuality. Those who concentrated on these buddhistic exercises reported lowered cholesterol levels and a greater intensity of life.

Much later, these colloquia became the basis of Amazonis University.

Fornication evenings were a popular success. Masked partners met each other for karezza and oral arts under skilled tutors. Lying together without movement, they practiced inhalation, visual saturation and maryanning. Breath control as a technique for increasing pleasure was emphasised.

Breath control formed the entire subject of another colloquium. In a low-lit studio, practitioners sat in the lotus position and controlled ingoing and outgoing breaths while concentrating on the *hara*. Mounting concentrations of carbon dioxide in the blood led to periods of timeless 'awayness' which, when achieved, were always regarded as of momentous value, leading to a fuller understanding of self.

This opening up of consciousness without the use of harmful drugs became highly regarded in our society, so that the breathing colloquium had to be supplemented by classes in pranayama. At first, pranayama was seen as exotic and 'non-Western', but, with the growing awareness that we were in fact no longer Western, pranayama became regarded as a Martian discipline.

Whether or not this concentration on the breath, entering

by the nose, leaving by the mouth, was to be accounted for by our awareness that every molecule of oxygen had to be engineered, this discipline, in which over 55 per cent of our adults soon persevered, exerted a considerable calming effect, so that to the remoter regions of the mind the prospect of a tranquil and happy life no longer seemed unfamiliar.

'A better life needs no distraction . . .'

In all the colloquia, which rapidly established themselves, the relationship between teacher and taught was less sharp than usual. No one had a professional reputation to uphold; it was not unknown for a teacher to exclaim to a bright pupil, 'Look, you know more about this than I – please take my place, I'll take yours.'

Old hierarchies were dissolving: even as Tom had predicted, the human mind was becoming free.

At all this great activity I looked in amazement. To repair the damage done to my body I studied pranayama, becoming more aware of Eastern influence in our society. I wondered if this was really the case, or did I, with my Eastern inheritance, merely wish it to be so?

I asked this question of Tom. Perhaps we had grown closer over the past year. Tom said, 'I cannot answer your question today. Let's try tomorrow.'

On the morrow, when we met with Belle Rivers again for another discussion of what education should consist, he looked amused and said, 'Has your question been answered overnight?'

Playing along with this zen approach, I replied, 'No religion has a monopoly on wisdom.'

At this he yawned and pretended to be bored. He said he believed, though without sure foundation, that there had been a time when the West, the little West which then called itself Christendom, had been a home of mysticism. Come the Renaissance, people forgot constant prayer, loving instead the riches and excitements of the world about them. They had given themselves up to the worldly things

135

and even neglected to love, first others, then themselves. Now it was possible that in our reduced circumstances we might learn to love ourselves again with a renewed mysticism.

'And love God?' I asked.

'God is the great cul de sac in the sky.'

'Only to those with spiritual myopia,' Belle said, with a trace of irritation.

I couldn't resist teasing Tom – a tease in which there was some flattery – telling him he was the new mystic, come to guide us.

'Don't get that notion in your head, my dear Cang Hai, or try to put it in mine. I cannot guide since I don't know where we are going.'

But he offered me, chuckling, a story of a holy man who finally gave up calling on Allah because Allah never spoke in return, never said to the man, 'Here am I.' Whereupon a prophet appeared to the holy man in a vision, hot foot from Allah. What the prophet reported Allah as saying was this: 'Was it not I who summoned thee to my service? Was it not I who engaged thee with my name? Was not thy call of "Allah!" my "Here am I"?'

I said I was pleased that Tom had a mystical as well as a practical side, to which he answered that he clung to a fragment of mysticism, hoping to be practical. That practicality might permit our grandchildren to espouse the contentment of real mysticism.

I thought about this for a long time. It seemed to me that he denied belief in God, and yet clung to a shred of it.

Tom admitted it might be so, since we were all full of contradictions. But whether or not there was a god outside, there was a god within us; in consequence he believed in the power of solitary prayer, as a clarifier, a magnifying glass, for the mind.

'At least, so I believe today,' he said teasingly. 'My dear Cang Hai, we all have two hemispheres to our brains. Can we not carry two different tunes at the same time? Do you not wish to be silent in order to listen to them?'

While we were talking in this abstract fashion, our

friends were making love and more children were being conceived. Too many would threaten the precarious balance of our existence. To find Tom planning for two generations ahead made me impatient.

'We must deal with our immediate difficulties first, not add to them. This random procreation threatens our very existence. Why do you not issue a caution against unbridled sexuality?'

'For several good reasons, Cang Hai,' he said. 'The foremost of which is that any such caution would be useless. Besides, if I, a DOP, issued it, it would be widely – and maybe rightly – regarded as an edict flung across the generation gap.'

I laughed – 'Don't be afraid of that. You are older, you know better! Don't you?' – for I saw his hesitation.

'No, to be honest I don't know better. Sexual temptation does not necessarily fade with age. It's merely that the ease with which one can give in to it disappears!' He laughed. 'You see, our generations have become too preoccupied with sexuality. You know what Barcunda said.

'Our relationships with natural things withered and died in the streets. We no longer tend our gardens – or sleep under the stars, unless we are down-and-outs. We think stale city thoughts, removed from nature. All we have to relate to is each other. That's unnatural; we should be responding to agencies outside ourselves. The quest for ever more sexual satisfaction runs against true contentment. Against love, joy and peace, and the ability to help others.'

'Ah, those "agencies outside ourselves" . . . Yes . . .'

We sat silently for a while.

At last I said, 'It is sometimes difficult for us to speak our minds. Perhaps it's because I have reverence for you that I agree with what you say. Yet not only that . . . I have not found great pleasure in sex, with either men or women. Is that something lacking in me? I seem to have no – warmth? I love, but only platonically, I'm ashamed to admit.'

Tom put his large hand on mine.

'You need feel no shame. We are brought up in a culture where those who seek solitude or chastity are made to think of themselves as unwell – fit subjects for new sciences like psychurgy and mentascopism – almost beyond the pale of society. It was not always so and it will not be so again. Once, men who sought solitude were revered. These matters are not necessarily genetic but a question of upbringing.'

After a pause, he said, 'And your upbringing, Cang Hai. Where are you in Kissorian's scheme of things – a later-born, I'd guess?'

'No, Tom, dear. I am a dupe.' Looking searchingly at him, I was surprised he did not immediately understand.

'A dupe?'

'A clone, to use the old-fashioned term. I know there's a prejudice against dupes, but since our difference doesn't show externally we are not persecuted. My counterpart lives in China, in Chengdu. We are sometimes in psychic touch with one another. But I do not believe that case affects my attitude to sexuality. As a matter of fact, I spend much time in communication with those archetypes of which you say someone spoke in the debate. I believe I am in touch with myself, though I'm vexed by mysterious inner promptings. Those promptings brought me to Mars – and to you.'

'I am grateful, then, for those inner promptings,' he said, giving me a grave smile. 'So you are that rare creature, not born of direct sexual union . . .'

I told him I knew of at least a dozen other dupes with us on Mars.

With a sudden intuition, Tom asked if Kathi was also a dupe. I said it was not so; was he interested in her?

He chose to ignore this. Dropping his gaze, he said, 'My destiny seems to be as an organiser. I'm doomed to be a talker, while in my heart of hearts, that remote place, I believe silence to be a greater thing.'

'But not the silence, surely, that has prevailed on Mars for centuries?'

138

His face took on a ponderous expression I had observed previously. He stared down at the floor. 'That's true. That's a dead silence. We shall have to cure it in the end . . . Life has to be the enemy of such tomb-like silence.'

Smiling apologetically, he dismissed me.

I regretted not telling him that Kathi did not find Mars's silence a dead silence; she claimed that it could be heard if only we attuned ourselves to it. But she and I had no authority. After all, Tom was a famous and successful man, and who was I? Although I relished his attention, and his kindly looks, he had said nothing about his personal history since the evening on Spider Plant when he had spoken of his first love. Did he regret confiding in me? Could I bear any more of the same?

This is not intended to be a record of my personal feelings. Yet I must admit here that I often thought about that fortunate girl who, Tom had told me, was the youthful Tom's first lover. I could imagine everything about her.

Even while I practised my breathing exercises – even then, I found myself thinking of her. And of young Tom. And of the two of them, locked together with rain bathing their naked bodies.

This is not really a record of history. I never told anyone this before. But unexpectedly I started thinking that Tom Jefferies did not care for me at all. I felt so bad. I secretly thought I was beautiful and my body was lovely, even if he never noticed, even if no one noticed. Except Jon, who thought I was cute.

Kathi Skadmorr came over from the science unit with some discs of an old jazz man called Sydney Bechet and some laboratory-distilled alcohol. She was spending the night with her lover, Beau Stephens, and invited me to drink with them.

After some drinks, I asked Beau if he thought I was pretty.

'In an Oriental way,' he said.

I told him that was a stupid remark and meant nothing.

'Of course you're pretty, darling,' said Kathi. Suddenly, she jumped up, put her arms round me, and kissed me on the mouth.

It went to my head like the drink. A track then playing was a number called 'I Only Have Eyes For You'. I had never heard it before. It was good. I began to peel off my Nows and dance. Just for the fun of it. And my new leg looked fine and worked beautifully.

When I was down to my bra and panties it occurred to me not to go further. But the two of them were cheering and looking excited, so off they came. My breasts were so nice and firm – I was proud of them. I flung my clothes at Beau. What did he do? He caught my panties and buried his face in them. Kathi just laughed.

With the track ending, I suddenly felt ashamed. I had shown so much crotch. I ran into the bathroom and hid. Kathi came to soothe me down. I was crying. She sang softly, 'I don't know if we're in a garden, Or in a crowded rendezvous.' And I felt awful next morning.

I never told anyone about this before.

'We must take the most tender care,' Tom said, when the Adminex was discussing education, 'of our youngsters, so that they do not think of themselves negatively as exiles from earth. Education must mean equipping a child to live in wisdom and contentment – contentment with itself first of all. We need a new word for a new thing, a word that means awareness, understanding . . .'

'There's the Chinese word juewu. It implies awareness, comprehension,' I suggested.

'Juewu, juewu . . .' He tried it on his tongue. 'It has something of a jewel about it, whereas education smells of dusty classrooms. I can almost hear children going to their first playschool at the age of three, chirruping jewey-woo jewey-woo . . .'

The word was adopted by the group.

We then fell to discussing what activities those early chirrupers should engage in.

Sharon Singh was certain that young children most enjoyed music and verse with strong rhymes; rhythm, clapping, she said, was the beginning of counting, counting of mathematics, and mathematics of science.

Mary Fangold remarked that in the discussions in Plato's *Republic* some time is spent wondering which metrical feet are best to express meanness or madness or evil, and which ones grace. The speakers conclude that music engenders a love of beauty.

I ventured to say that 'beauty' had become a rather suspect, or at least a specialised, word.

Tom agreed that it had accumulated some embarrassments; yet we still understood that it had something to do with rightness and truth. It was hard to define except by parallels; certainly the right music at the right time was a benison. Better even than the art of speaking with grace, was employing a rich vocabulary – which was rarely the mark of an empty head.

And with the music had to go activity, dancing and such like. This was a way in which juewu helped to unite mind and body.

But we agreed that, while good teaching was important, it could be achieved only by good teachers. As yet no method had been established for guaranteeing good teachers, beyond the simple expedient of training and paying well, though not lavishly.

'But once the system is established,' Tom said, 'then our well-taught children will make the best teachers. Patience, love and empathy are more valuable than knowledge.'

The next stage was the regularisation of educational curricula for various ages.

We wanted our first generation of Martian children to understand the unity and interconnectedness of all life on Earth.

We also wished them to understand themselves better

than any generations had done before. Phylogeny was a required subject, for only from this could grow knowledge of one's self.

Ambient and computer skills were already being taught, together with history, geophysiology, music, painting, world literature, mathematics. There would be personality sessions, wherein children could discuss any problems brewing; difficult situations could be dealt with swiftly and compassionately.

Tom appeared pleased with the work. Almost as an afterthought he suggested that the entire scheme should be shown to Belle Rivers, who had spoken on the subject of archetypes during our debates and was in charge of teaching cadre children.

Belle Rivers was slender and elegant, with a certain grandeur to her. She carried her head slightly to one side, as if listening to something the rest of us were unable to hear. She was about forty years old, perhaps more.

Tom opened the conversation by apologising for altering her curriculum. Altered circumstances demanded it. He said that he hoped the revised syllabus, a copy of which we had printed out, would please her.

Without responding, Rivers read through the syllabus. She set it down on a desk, saying, 'I see you do not wish religion to be taught.'

'That is correct.'

'We have had to train our children for future careers. Nevertheless we always take care to include world religions in our curriculum. Do you not believe that God prevails as much on Mars as on Earth?'

'Or as little. We cannot leave it to any god to remedy in future those things he or she has failed to remedy in the past. We must attempt a remedy ourselves.'

'That's rather arrogant, isn't it?' She appeared less offended than contemptuous.

'I trust not. We are merely amused by ancient Greek tales of gods and goddesses interfering directly in the affairs

142

of humanity. Such beliefs are outdated. We must try to laugh at any belief that imaginary, omnipotent gods will remedy our deficiencies. We must try to do such things for ourselves, if that is possible.'

'Oh? And if it proves impossible?'

'We do not know it will be impossible until we have tried, Belle.'

'That may be true. But why not enlist God in your enterprise? I seem to recall that the great utopian, Sir Thomas More, made certain that the children of his utopia were brought up in the faith and given full religious instruction.'

'The sixteenth century thought differently about such matters. More was a good man living in a circumscribed world. We must go by the advanced thought of our own time. All utopias have their sell-by dates, you know.'

'And your utopia has dropped any sense of the divine aspect of things.'

Tom offered a chair to Belle Rivers and invited her to be seated. His manner became apologetic. He said he realised that he had made a mistake in having Adminex draw up a new syllabus without consulting her in the first place. It must seem to her that he had usurped her powers, although that had been far from his intention. He had been too hasty; there was much still needing attention.

However, she would notice that her ideas had been taken into consideration. Phylogeny was on the timetable for even small children, wherein the make-up of human consciousness and her understanding concerning archetypes could be considered.

She gazed frowningly into a corner of the room.

Tom shuffled somewhat before asking Belle Rivers not to believe that he was without sympathy for her religious instincts. He was himself all too conscious of the divine aspect of things. Did not everyone who was not utterly bowed down by misfortune or illness, he asked, have a sense of a kind of holiness to life?

Staring hard at Belle, he became lyrical and so, I thought, possibly insincere.

143

As we moved through our lives, he continued, was there not a vein of enchantment in events, in awakening, in sleeping, in our dreams and in the power of thought? That elusive element, which the best artists, writers, musicians, scientists – even ordinary persons in ordinary jobs – experienced, that special lovely thing of which it was difficult to speak, but which gave life its magic. It might perhaps be simply the ticking of the biological clock, the joy in being alive. Whatever it was, that firefly thing, it was something of which the poet Marlowe spoke:

> One thought, one grace, one wonder, at the least
> Which into words no virtue can digest.

Listening to this speech, Belle Rivers clasped her hands on the desk in front of her and appeared to study them.

Religion, at least the Christian religion, Tom said, changed over time, abandoning the ill-tempered and savage Jehovah of the Old Testament for a more responsive faith in redemption – though it still based itself on such impossibilities as virgin birth, the resurrection of the dead and eternal life – impossibilities designed to impress the ignorant of Christ's unscientific age.

When the Omega Smudge would be detected, we should see a genuine miracle – once we understood what had been detected. (Yet would I ever understand this area of science? I made a resolve to learn still more . . .)

By going two steps forward and one step back, continued Tom, humankind since the days of Jesus Christ had scraped together some knowledge of the world, the universe and themselves. The situation now, in the late middle of the twenty-first century, was that God got in the way of understanding. God was dark matter, an impediment rather than an aid to our proper sense of the divine aspect of things. We had been forced to leave many good things behind on Earth; God should be left behind too.

The world was more wonderful without him.

Belle Rivers, continuing to regard her hands, said merely, 'It cannot be more wonderful without him, since he created it.'

Until this juncture Mary Fangold had remained silent, watching Tom and Belle with a faint smile on her lips. Tom said afterwards that Mary, the apostle of reason, knew we had fallen into human error by excluding the hard-working Belle from most of our educational plans. She felt her position to be undermined. Mary spoke up.

'The prospectus is only at the planning stage, Belle. We rely on you to continue teaching, just as the children rely on you. We wonder if you would care to include a subject such as we might call, say, Becoming Individual, in your time-table, whereby religion would form a part of it, together with archetypal behaviour and the interrelationship of conscious and sub-conscious.'

Belle regarded her suspiciously. 'That does not sound like my idea of religion.'

'Then let's say religion and reason . . .'

After a moment's silence, Belle smiled and said, 'Do not think I am trying to be difficult. Basically, your entire plan for improved learning cannot flourish without one additional factor.'

She waited for us to ask her what that factor might be. Then she explained that there were children who were always resistant to learning, who found reading and writing hard work. Others were happy and fulfilled with such things. The difference could be accounted for by the contrast between those children who were sung to and read to by their mothers and fathers from birth onwards, perhaps even before birth, when the child was still in utero, and those who were not, who were neglected.

Learning, she said, began from Day One. If that learning was associated with the happiness and security of a parent's love, then the child found no impediments to learning and to the enjoyment of education. Those children whose parents were silent or indifferent had a harder slog through life.

The basis of all that was good in life was, she declared, simply love and care, which arose from a love of Christ.

Tom rose and took her hand. 'We are in perfect agreement there, at least as far as love and care of the child are concerned,' he said. 'You have probably cited the most vital thing. There's no harm in using Christ as an exemplar. We're very happy you are the headmistress here, and in charge of learning.'

Tom's and my, in some respects, mysterious, relationship deepened. I was legally adopted as his daughter at a small ceremony; I became Cang Hai Jefferies, and lived in harmony with him. To be truthful, I mean more or less in harmony with him. It was not easy to get mentally close.

Often when my new leg troubled me – it got the twitches – I would lie in his arms. This was bliss for me; but he never attempted a sexual advance.

Our activities had become formalised. Indoor sports, plays, revues, recitations, dances and baby exhibitions (the many pregnancies had yielded our first Mars-born infants) were weekly events. Training for the first Mars marathon was in progress.

A woman of French origin, Paula Gallin, produced a dark, austere play, shot through with humour, which combined video with human actors. *My Culture*, to give it its title, was reluctantly received at first, but slowly became recognised as a master work. Most of the action took place on a flat sloping plain, the tilt of which increased slowly as the play proceeded.

My Culture played a part in turning our community into the world's first modern psychologically oriented civilisation. The setting-up of the Smudge Project grew nearer to completion by the end of 2065, despite material limitations hampering its development. Dreiser kept us informed by frequent bulletins on the Ambient. But many of us sensed that the technological culture of Earth was gradually giving way to an absorption in Being and Becoming.

Being and Becoming had a very practical focus in the

maturing of our children. It was prompted by a natural anxiety regarding the happy development of the young in a confined, largely 'indoor' world. But the comparative gloom of Mars prompted introspection and, indeed, empathy. It was noted early in our exile that most of us enjoyed unusually vivid dreams of curious content. These dreams, it was understood, put us in touch with our phylogenetic past, as if seeking or possibly offering therapeutic reassurance.

Mistaken Historicism had filled the world with the idea of progress, bringing greater pressure on greater numbers of people, the rise of megacities and the loss of pleasant communication with the self. A wise man of the twentieth century, Stephen Jay Gould, said: 'Progess is a noxious, culturally embedded, nonoperational, intractable idea that must be replaced.'

We were trying to replace it – not by going back but going forward into a realisation of our true selves, our various selves, which had experience of the evolutionary chain. Exchanging technocracy for metaphysics, in Belle's words.

My true self led me to experience pregnancy. Shortly after our much delayed adoption ceremony, I went to the hospital, where I had myself injected with some of Tom Jefferies's DNA. My womb was grateful for the benevolent gravity and I delivered my beautiful daughter Alpha without pain one day in March 2067. Tom was with me at the birth. There my baby lay in my arms, red in the face after her exertions to emerge into the world, with the most exquisite little fingers you ever saw. Alpha had dark hair and eyes as blue as Earth's summer skies. And a temperament as fair.

Unfortunately the hospital permitted me no luxury of peace. Almost as soon as I was delivered I was sent back into society. That was Fangold's doing. The move upset my child for a short while, and then she recovered.

Kathi sent me a message from the science unit. It said, 'Did you succumb to Tom or to society? Why are you pretending to yourself you are an ordinary person? Better to pretend to be extraordinary. Kathi.'

It was not very kind.

Following the birth of Alpha, I – and I hope Tom too – was in a trance of happiness. His sorrow for the death of his wife was not forgotten, but he had put it behind him; he accepted her loss as one of those sorrows inescapable from our biological existence. Although I knew that one day terrestrial ships and business would return, I always hoped that day would be far off, so that our wonderful experience of finding our real selves could continue unabated.

My cloud of contentment was increased by a slogan I passed almost every day. Outside the hairdresser's salon someone had painted VIOLENCE BEGETS VIOLENCE – PEACE BEGETS PEACE. The words might have come from my heart.

Belle Rivers seemed to increase in stature. Her Becoming Individual sessions, which parents often attended with their children, as I soon did with Alpha, were perceived to contain much wisdom, which at first appeared uncomfortably to challenge the unity of the self. The significance of archetypes playing distinct roles in our unconscious was difficult for many people to grasp at first. Gradually more and more people became absorbed in the symbolic aspects of experience.

Belle said, magisterially, 'We begin to understand how health springs from our being lived, in a sense, as well as living, and from accepting that we act out traditional roles. On Mars we shall come to require new ground rules.'

During the term of my pregnancy I used to wonder about this remark. I wanted to be different. I wanted things to be different.

I discussed this point with Ben Borrow. Ben was a smooth YEA who had done his community service on Luna and was, in his own words, 'into spirituality'. However that might be, it was noticeable that he was a devoted disciple of Belle Rivers, often closeted late with her.

'The more we feel ourselves lived, the more we can live independently.'

'The melding of opposites, spirit/matter, male/female, good/evil, brings completeness.'

'Only technology can free us from technology.'

'True spirituality can only be achieved by looking back into green distance.'

These were some of Borrow's sayings. I wrote them down.

He was intent on becoming a guru; even I could see he was also something of a creep. He had a tiny little pointed beard.

Under the tutelage of his powerful mistress, Borrow started a series of teach-ins he called Sustaining Individuality. These were well attended, and often became decidedly erotic. Rivers and Borrow taught that neurophysiological processes in the mind-body, such as dreaming, promoted the integration of limbic system dramas, thus increasing awareness and encouraging cognitive and emotive areas to merge. As there are swimmers in oceans who fear the unknown creatures somewhere below, beyond their knowledge, so there were those who feared the contents of the deeper levels of mind; they gradually lost this culturally induced phobia to enjoy a blossoming of awareness.

After one of these teach-ins I had to tell Borrow that I didn't know whether or not my awareness was blossoming. How could I tell?

'Perhaps,' he said, matching finger-tip with finger-tip in front of him, 'one might say that the aware find within themselves an ability to time-travel into the remote phylogenic past, and discover there wonderful things that give savour to reason, richness to being.

'Not least of these elements is a unity with nature and instinctive life, from which a knowledge of death is absent. Consciousness is something so complex and sensuous that no artificial intelligence could possibly emulate it. Don't you think?'

'Mmm,' I said. He hurried off, still with finger-tip touching finger-tip. It was not quite the way you put your hands together in prayer. Perhaps he wanted to indicate that he was in touch with himself.

And didn't wish to be in touch with me.

Our community became locked into this physiological-biological-philosophical type of speculation. Humanity's spiritual attainments, together with their relationship with our lowly ancestral origins, produced problems of perception. If what we perceive is an interpretation of reality, rather than reality itself, then we must examine our perceptions. That much I understand. But since it's our unconscious perceptual faculties that absorb and sort out our lifelong input of information, how does our conscious mind make them comprehensible? What does it edit out? What do they edit out between them? What vital thing are we missing?

I asked this question of May Porter, who came to give a short talk about perceptual faculties.

She said, 'Ethology has shown that all animals and insects are programmed to perceive the world in specific ways. Thus each species is locked into its perceptual umwelt. Facts are filtered for survival. Non-survival-type perceptions are rejected. An earlier mystic, Aldous Huxley, cited the case of the frog, whose perceptions cause it to see only things that move, such as insects. As soon as they stop moving, the frog ceases to see them and can look elsewhere. "What on earth would a frog's philosophy be – the metaphysics of appearance and disappearance?" Huxley asks himself.

'Similarly Western humanity values only that which moves; silence and stillness are seen as negative, rather than positive, qualities.'

I was thinking of Kathi's remarks when I asked May, 'What if there was a higher consciousness on Mars that we were not trained to perceive?'

She gave a short laugh. 'There is no higher consciousness on Mars. Only us, dear.'

These and many more understandings had a behavioural effect on our community. Certainly we became more thoughtful, if by thought we include pursuing visions. It was as if by unravelling the secrets of truly living we had come up against the tantalising conundrum of life itself, and its reasons, which were beyond biology. Single people or couples or families preferred to live alone, combining with others only on special occasions, such as a new performance of *My Culture* or a Sustaining Individuality session.

Thus most people came to live as individually as limited space would permit. As a would-be utopia, it was non-authoritarian, in distinct contrast to Plato's definition of a good place.

Nor do I imply that a sense of community was lost. We still ate together once or twice a day. It happened that many a time I caught the jo-jo bus to work with Alpha in my arms and found the whole place humming and vibrating like a hive; so many people were doing pranayama yoga on their own, uttering the eternal 'Om'.

Oh, then how happy I was! For me it was the best period of our Martian existence, too sensitive, too in-dwelling to prove permanent. I clutched my dear child in my arms and thought, 'Surely, surely Mars people will never again be as united as this!'

Since all our teach-in and community sessions were videoed, beamed to Earth, and saved, we could check on our progress towards individuality. Many of us had to chuckle at our earlier selves, our naïve questions, our uncertainty.

We were moving towards a degree of serenity when I received a nasty little shock. I caught on my globe an Ambient exchange between Belle Rivers and my beloved Tom.

She was saying, '. . . on Earth. And there's a scientist by name Jon Thorgeson. He says he wants to talk to Cang Hai. He says she suggested he might give a lecture about the Omega Smudge to us plebs. Is that okay by you?'

'Just keep her out of my hair, Belle. Let Thorgeson go ahead.'

Belle's image remained. With her head on one side, she regarded Tom. Then she asked, 'Do you know of anything odd going on in the science unit?'

'No. It's true I haven't heard from Dreiser just recently. Why do you ask?'

'Oh, simply the feeling something was in the air when I was speaking to Thorgeson. Could be the oncoming marathon, I suppose.'

By the time their images faded I was worried. What did he mean by keeping me out of his hair? He was always so good and kind. He relied on me, didn't he? It was true he had become rather grumpy recently.

Perhaps it was simply that he disliked hearing Alpha cry – such a beautiful sound! I pitied him.

The Missing Smudge

In a rotation of jobs, I was allocated to the synthetic foods department. I preferred it to the biogas department. The smells were better. Here I helped in time to develop something which resembled a Danish pastry. We always glossed over the fact that our foods were created from everyone's manure. Nevertheless, my friends teased me about it.

One of my closest friends, Kathi Skadmorr, had adopted a teasing approach to me since I had danced naked before her and her lover. She rang me unexpectedly in serious vein and invited me on a short expedition to view what she called the 'Smudge experiment'. I was always ready to learn. Although baby Alpha was so small, I left her in the care of Paula Gallin for a few hours while I joined Kathi.

Behind the science unit, Amazonis sprawled broken-hearted under a layer of dusty colour which seemed to be sometimes pink, or rose, or sometimes orange. A swan's feather of cloud vapour overhead reflected these hues.

Kathi and I had suited up before leaving the science unit. As we walked along a netted way, where latticed posts supported overhead cables, a slight agoraphobia attacked me. I clutched Kathi's hand: she was more used to open spaces than I. Yet at the same time I found something closed about the Martian outdoors. Perhaps it was the scarcity of atmosphere; or perhaps it was the indoor feeling of dust lying everywhere, dust much older than ever dimmed the surface of a table back on Earth.

To our left, the ground rose towards the heights that

would culminate in Olympus Mons. There, I caught movement out of the side of my eye. A small boulder, dislodged by the morning heat, rolled downhill a few metres, struck another rock, and became still. Again, it was a motionless world we walked through.

The horrors got at me. Was it wise to have brought Alpha into this world? Granted that it was passion rather than wisdom which fathered babies, yet I had experienced no passion. And supposing our fragile systems broke down . . . then the dread world of the unmoving would prevail over everything . . . even over my dear baby. The past would snap back into place like the lid of a coffin.

As if she had read my thought, Kathi began talking about another kind of past, the past of a scientific obsession. She said I would see the latest produce of a line of research stretching back into the previous century.

'Dreiser is teaching me the history of particle physics. It begins before this century,' she told me. 'It's a tale of reasoning and unreasonable hopes. Last century, American physicists proposed to build a giant accelerator beneath the state of Texas. The accelerator was planned to measure many kilometres in diameter. They christened it a superconducting supercollider, SSC for short. The SSC was designed to detect what they referred to as the "Higgs particle". It would cost billions of tax-payers' money, and take an enormous chunk out of the science budget.

'This was the twentieth century's idea of Big Science.' She gave a sardonic chuckle. 'US Congress kept asking why anyone would think it legitimate to believe that so much money should go in a search for a single particle. After three billion dollars had been spent, the whole project was scrapped.'

I asked why it had been thought necessary to find this Higgs particle.

'The physicists who were searching for these basic ingredients which comprise the universe argued that finding the elusive Higgs would supply them with vital answers. It would complete their picture of the fundamental units.

They were like detectives seeking the solution of a mystery.

'The mystery remains. Hence the whole purpose of the Mars Omega Project. You might say the mystery is why we are here. The more deeply we probe nature, the clearer it becomes that these basic units have to be things without mass. There's the mystery – where does mass originate? Without mass, nothing would hold together. Our bodies would disintegrate, for instance.'

I could not help asking what the Higgs particle had to do with mass. Kathi replied that it was still unclear to her, but the physicists of the time had an idea in their heads that the highly symmetrical scheme of the universe would have that symmetry spoilt according to what they termed 'spontaneous symmetry breaking'. The Higgs was tied up with that idea.

'You see, for the pure unbroken scheme with exact symmetry, it was necessary to have all particles without mass. When Higgs enters the picture, everything changes. Most particles acquire mass. The photon is a notable exception.'

'I see. The Higgs was to be a kind of magic wand. As soon as it enters the stage, "Hey presto!" mass comes along.'

'A rhymester said it in a nutshell:

The particles were lighter far than gas.
Then Higgs weighs in, and all is mass.

'Because of this rather magical property, Higgs was christened by journalists "the God particle".'

'And the physicists of that time believed that the SSC would enable them to catch a glimpse of this God.' I found I had lost most of my fears and let go of Kathi's hand.

'According to the theory current at the time,' she said, 'there had to be a certain limited range of possibilities for the mass of the Higgs. Otherwise, there would be an inconsistency with other things which had already been established by experiment. The God particle must deign

155

to live among its subjects, just as if it were an ordinary mortal massive particle.'

I had to ask her what she meant by that.

'In accord with Einstein's famous equation, $E=mc^2$, the Higgs particle, it was believed, would correspond to a certain energy. That energy was supposed to lie within the range of what the SSC would have been capable of. But – the SSC was never built, as I have told you.

'As luck would have it, a rival project was already at the planning stage. This was at the international research centre, CERN, in Geneva, Switzerland.

'The CERN project was greatly cheaper than the cancelled SSC would have been. It employed a tunnel already in use for an earlier experiment. The new project was the Large Hadron Collider, the LHC.'

I imagined a great tube, with a vanishing perspective into circular darkness.

'In the late twentieth century, the earlier experiment on the CERN site had yielded a great deal of information about leptons. But the energy used to produce leptons was not nearly enough to produce a Higgs. A lepton, by the way, is a member of the lightest family of subatomic particles, such as an electron or a muon. However, the clever group who constructed the LEP, as the tunnel was called, foresaw that it would be possible comparatively cheaply to modify their experiment, so that protons replaced the positrons and electrons of the original experiment.

'Protons, neutrons, and their anti-particles, belong to the family of more massive particles known as *hadrons*. Hence the terminology, the Large Hadron Collider.'

Kathi stopped. Then she spoke rather abstractedly. 'Imagine the drama of it! The world seemed to be on the brink of a great discovery. Would they be able to trace the Higgs through the LHC? The equipment was finally up and running in about 2005. A year later, it began to reach the kind of energy levels at which it seemed possible that they might actually detect the Higgs particle. This was at the lower end of the scale of theoretical possibilities for the

Higgs mass. So the fact that they found no clear candidate they could identify with the Higgs did not unduly worry the physicists.'

We stood in that unnatural place, staring at our boots.

'Do you think the day will come when we can understand everything?' I asked.

Kathi grunted. Without giving an answer, she continued with her account.

'There had never been any guarantee that the LHC could build to the energies required to find the elusive particle – unlike the potential of the scrapped SSC.'

'So more money was wasted . . .'

'Can you not understand that science – like civilisation, of which science is the backbone – is pieced slowly together from ambitions, mistakes, perceptions – from our faltering intelligences? Patient enquiry, that's it. One day, one day far ahead in time, we may understand everything. Even the workings of our own minds!'

I remembered something I had been taught as a child. 'But Karl Popper said that the mind could not understand itself.'

'With mirrors we may easily do what was once impossible, and see the back of our own heads. One step forward may be formed from a number of tiny increments. For example, the hunt for this elusive smudge has been facilitated by the seemingly trivial innovation of self-illuminating paper – ampaper – and 3D-paper. Their impact on scientific development has been incalculable.'

'So they did find the Higgs particle at some point?' I asked.

'By 2009, the entire energy range of conceivable relevance to the Higgs particle had been surveyed. No unambiguously identifiable Higgs was found. But what the physicists did find was at least as interesting.'

We had continued our walk. As we reached the crest of a small incline, Kathi said, 'More of this later. We are nearly there!'

Over the crest, the desolation was broken by tokens of

human activity. A group of suited men stood by three parked buggies. Their attention was directed towards a vast silvery tube, above which was suspended something which immediately reminded me of an immense saucepan lid. This lid evidently afforded protection against any slight aerial bombardment – any falling meteorite – for the tube below.

The men hailed us, and as we drew nearer to them I could see that this protective lid was of meshed reinforced plastic. Below it lay a large inflated bag from which cables trailed. In the background were sheds from which the sound of a generator came.

The importance of this installation was emphasised by a metal version of the UN flag, which was now raised on an extemporised flagpole.

Dreiser Hawkwood beckoned us on. His face behind its helmet appeared darker than ever. He briefly embraced Kathi, both of them clumsy in their suits, before shaking my hand in a perfunctory way. I was Kathi's guest, not his. Among the men in the background, I saw Jon Thorgeson, whose lecture I had postponed while I was pregnant.

Climbing on to a metal box, Dreiser raised himself above us to make a short speech.

'This is such a momentous day, I thought we might hold a small ceremony. It's to mark the occasion when, at last, the bag is completely filled. It has been a slow process. As you will know, we have had to avoid the possibility of setting up currents in the superfluid. But from this moment onwards, we are able to begin in earnest our search for the Omega Smudge.'

Pausing, he reached up to stroke his moustache but had to make do with stroking his visor instead.

'Jon and I were having an argument, although out here is not the best place for it. We were arguing about something hard to define – "consciousness". Jon's hard-line view is that consciousness emanates from the interaction of brute computation, quantum coherence, quantum entanglement, if you like, and quantum state reduction – those factors

158

which produce a CPS, a sure indicator of *mind*. Many people – and our quantputers – would agree with him. He claims that science is "nearly there" – and will arrive there before long, in these areographic wastes. Is that a fair description of your position, Jon?'

Thorgeson said, 'Approximately.'

'Kathi and I take a more radical view. We see that, indeed, there are still some minor issues to be sorted out from the details of the particle physics, primarily the Smudge parameters. They will determine all the present unknowns. However, we radicals – I prefer the term visionaries – argue that something *profound* is still missing.'

'Yes,' said Kathi. 'And we believe that magneto-gravitic fields will turn out to be part of the missing story of that profundity.'

Dreiser continued briefly in this vein, before embarking on a different topic.

'You'll all have made use of the Ng-Robinson Plot? Let's just have a thought for that vital minor innovation! It was named after its inventors, Ng being a Singaporean and Robinson British. This was East meeting West – very fruitfully. The Plot has given us a wonderful method of displaying vast quantities of quantputer-generated information. At the time when it was first employed, supercomputers were already giving place to our QPs, or quantputers, to use their full name – much faster and more versatile machines. The computer read off the mass of a particle along one axis, its lifetime along another, and the q-factor along a third, all colour-coded according to the various quantum numbers possessed by the particle in question – charge, spin, parity, etc.

'And one of the crucial features Ng-Robinson introduced is a key intensity factor which indicates the probability of the detection being a reliable one. A very sharp bright image indicates firm identification of a particle, while a fuzzy one implies there may be some considerable uncertainty as to the suggested identification of an actual particle.

'The essentials of so many lines of research, which

in earlier times would have presented great difficulties, become immediately transparent. The Ng-Robinson Plot has proved extremely valuable in experimental particle physics, because a lot of that activity consists of sniffing out tiny subtle effects from enormous amounts of almost entirely irrelevant information!

'What they expected for the Higgs would have been one sharp, bright, and very *white* spot. That's according to the conventions used in this system of colour-coding. It should have stood out clearly from a background of variously coloured spots in other places in the generally dark background of the N-R Plot. These other spots would indicate the complex array of particles of different kinds generated by the experiment. Show the vidslide, Euclid.'

At this point, an android stepped forward to project a replica of the plot. It sparkled before the small audience with its dark pointillism. It could have been mistaken for a glimpse of another universe.

Dreiser asked, 'What did they see in place of a spot? They saw a *smudge*. Just a smudge. It arose around about the right place, pretty precisely where the particle physicists had come to expect that something would be found – which would be consistent with all the other junk observed earlier. But there was no clear-cut Higgs particle – merely a great big Higgs smudge!

'And the ultimate descendant of that smudge is what we hope to capture – one day, starting from now!'

We all clapped. Even Euclid clapped.

Somehow I felt depressed.

Even when I had my babe back in my arms, a feeling of my insignificance in the scheme of things persisted. To arrange for Jon Thorgeson to come at last and give his lecture on the Omega Smudge was a welcome diversion.

Paula Gallin helped me in the early stages. She found a small lecture hall we could use. Lectures made in person had proved more vital than lectures delivered over the Ambient – though I had no suspicion regarding the way this one was going to turn out. While I had forgotten about Jon in my preoccupation with dear Alpha, he had not forgotten his promise.

'Ah, my little honeypot!' was his greeting. I made no retort because it was pleasant to see his young-old face light up at sight of me. He was followed into the ante-room by a porter trundling a large man-size crate. Once it was set down, and was stood upright, Jon thumped it.

'There's someone in here who can see what we are doing. Give me a kiss before I let him out.'

I put up my hands defensively. 'No, I don't do that sort of thing.'

'I wish you did,' he said, with a sigh. I was angry. The truth was, he was attractive after a fashion; it was just that his manner was so pushy. In a burst of confidence, he told me that he had left a Chinese lover back on Earth. I was a physical reminder to him of this lady. He longed to get back to her. He was miserable on Mars; it was for him a prison. 'Sorry to offend you,' he said, with a hangdog look.

He turned and unlatched the box the porter had brought. 'This is my visual aid,' he said, over his shoulder. The door of the box opened. A small android stepped out from its padded interior.

'Where am I?' it asked in a lifelike way.

'On Mars, you idiot.' Turning to me, Jon said, with mock-formality, 'Cang Hai, I'd like you to meet my friend, Euclid.'

'I have met him before,' I said, although no recognition was forthcoming from the android.

I offered Euclid my hand. It did not move. Nor did its well-moulded face manage more than a twitch of smile.

'It's one of Poulsen's cast-offs,' said Jon. 'I borrowed it for the occasion. It's house-trained.'

I remembered it then as one of the machines Poulsen had complained about. The android was dressed in blue overalls, much as Thorgeson was dressed. Its hair was cut to a fashionable length, unlike Jon's which was trimmed short. Its face wore a blankly pleasant expression which changed little. Jon clapped it on the shoulder.

There was something in its extreme immobility I found disconcerting. It had no presence. It gave out no CPS. It lacked body language.

Jon turned to me with a grin. 'Kathi tells me you are a mother now! Was it a virgin birth?'

'Change the conversation. It's none of your business. You didn't come here to be insulting, I hope.'

He shrugged, dismissing the topic. 'All right, you invited me over just to talk science. And when I get in that hall, I am going to talk about the continuing search for the ultimate smudge. All miseries forgotten.'

'Let's go. The audience is waiting. How long will you talk for?'

'My lecture is designed for ten-year-olds,' said Thorgeson. 'Euclid helps to hold their interest through the technical bits.' He caught my wrist. 'Do you think the audience knows anything of the past history of particle physics?' As he spoke, he slid an arm about my waist.

'I think you can count on it,' I said, disengaging myself.

'Oh, good. Then I had better not go into all that too much. How long have I got to talk?'

'Until you lose their interest. Now come on and don't be nervous.'

He was anything but nervous with me. 'Be nice to me,' he begged. 'I only came over to see you again.'

I told him not to be silly. But I was not completely annoyed.

We went into the hall, followed by the android. The audience gave us a round of applause. I introduced Thorgeson by saying that he would explain why there were so many scientists on Mars, and that he would speak of the problems they were hoping to solve. He would touch on matters affecting us all. His artificial friend, I said, would assist him.

Tom sat in the front row and nodded approval of my

162

short speech – the first I had made before such a large gathering.

Thorgeson began nervously, clearing his throat and gesticulating too much.

'As our understanding of the basic units of the universe deepens, it becomes yet clearer that these units are entities that possess no mass. There is a profound mystery here. Ordinary matter obviously possesses mass, and so do the basic particles of which matter is composed – protons, neutrons, and electrons, and also their constituent quarks and kliks. For many decades, physicists have struggled with the question: where does mass come from?

'This is a serious issue. Without mass everything would disintegrate. We'd be instantly dispersed into a flash of ethereal substance – not even mist – spreading outwards with the speed of light. Not a brilliant way to get to the nearest star.'

The feeble joke earned chuckles enough from the audience for Thorgeson to relax a little.

Euclid spoke. 'So tell us, what is the purpose of the Mars Omega Smudge Project?'

Glancing at a prepared script, Thorgeson continued, 'The Omega Smudge is what has brought us here. To explain why we call this vital smudge a smudge I should remind you of some history of particle physics last century and earlier this century.

'Euclid, do you remember the names given to the six varieties of basic subnuclear entity which was postulated last century?'

Euclid: 'Down, Up, Strange, Charm, Bottom, Top.'

'He has a faultless memory,' Thorgeson said, as another chuckle ran through the listeners.

He continued for a while, describing highlights of twentieth-century particle physics, which I was able to follow mainly because of Kathi's earlier explanations.

He was saying, '. . . the superconducting supercollider or SSC that was planned to be built under Texas was a miracle that did not quite happen. It would have cost billions and was designed to discover what was referred to as "the Higgs particle". I see that some of you DOPs remember the name, though, of course, not the excitement of the time.

'Here's an artist's impression of the proposed SSC entrance.' He showed a vidslide in 3D of an airy and imposing glass structure, topped by a geodesic dome.

Euclid: 'Why would anyone think that so much money should be spent in search of a single particle?'

'It's a good question, Euclid. In the end the US Congress dropped the project. But the physicists – why, they argued that finding the elusive "Higgs" would have supplied them with the answer to the question of what comprises the basic units of the universe.'

Euclid: 'Did they believe that in those days?'

'Well, maybe not quite. But they did regard the finding of the Higgs as vitally important in their scheme of things. Also, completing the SSC would have achieved other targets. They put all their eggs in one basket to get the collider funded. The argument became over-heated. Certain physicists assigned an almost religious quality to the Higgs, referring to it as "the God particle" – a good journalistic phrase . . .'

Euclid: 'Did they believe that in those days?'

Thorgeson looked nonplussed. 'No Euclid, that's where you say, "Why was the Higgs regarded as so important?"'

Amid sympathetic laughter, Euclid spoke. 'Why was the Higgs regarded as so important?'

At his ease now, Thorgeson said, 'I'm glad you asked me that, Euclid. It all has to do with the question of mass. You are aware that most particles of nature have mass, but the photon and graviton – the basic quanta of electromagnetism and gravitation respectively – are exceptions. Those quanta of which matter is mainly composed, the protons and neutrons or their constituent quarks, are massive particles. So also are the kliks and pseudo-kliks that compose the much less massive leptons, such as electrons and muons.'

As Thorgeson continued, referring to 'LEP', the 'LHC', and various particle physics notions such as 'lepton' and 'hadron', I found that I was beginning to lose the thread of much of what he was saying. Fortunately Kathi's earlier explanations were still useful to me, so I knew what some of the terms meant.

Then I heard Euclid saying, 'Could they use the LHC to trace the Higgs? Could they use the LHC to trace the Higgs? Could they use the LHC to trace the Higgs?'

Thorgeson thumped Euclid's back. 'You mean to say, "Could they use the LHC to trace the Higgs?" Well, they finally got the equipment working in about 2005 . . .'

I realised that Euclid was talking with Thorgeson's voice although, without inflection, it sounded almost like a foreign language. But Thorgeson had programmed it. It amused me to think that, although Thorgeson was a stalwart 'hard science' man where questions of the human mind were concerned – believing there was nothing more to human mentality than the functions of a very effective quantputer – he could not resist making fun of his creature now and again.

Kathi had once tried to explain this 'hard science' position to me. Apparently it is commonly held by today's scientists.

She told me that they are simply missing the point. She explained their view to be that human mentality results solely from those physical functions that underlie an ordinary quantputer. I'm not really familiar with these underlying principles, but Kathi did have a go at trying to explain them. Apparently quantputers, and their smaller brothers the quantcomps, act by a combination of brute force computation in the old twentieth-century sense, and a collection of quantum effects referred to as 'coherence', 'entanglement' and 'state reduction'. Although I was never clear about these terms, Kathi explained that mentatropy and CPS detectors ('savvyometers'!) are based on such effects.

Thorgeson was saying, 'The riddle of mass needed a solution. A Korean scientist by the name of Tar Il-Chosun came up with a brilliant conception that, in effect, increased the energy range of the LHC by a factor of about one hundred. As a result, by 2009 the LHC had surveyed the complete range of energies that could possibly be relevant to the Higgs mass. Frustratingly, there was nothing that could be clearly identified with the Higgs. Instead they found something else, as strange as it was interesting.'

Euclid: 'What was that?'

'Using the newly perfected Ng-Robinson Plot, they found a smudge, roughly where the Higgs particle should have appeared.'

Euclid: 'So they found the Higgs?'

'They just found a smudge. No particle.'

Euclid: 'So that's where the name Smudge came from . . .'

'Absolutely.'

Euclid: 'But if they found this smudge in 2009, why all this business of setting up an umpteen-billion-dollar project to look for it here on Mars?' (Spoken with that same bland pleasant expression on its face.)

'What excitement this smudge caused! Excitement and dissension in the ranks! This, by the way, was when the consortium we know as EUPACUS was being assembled. Since CERN was already involved, the Europeans agreed to invest massively in it. You can bet they're regretting that now!

'The first problem the smudge threw up was that, by its very nature, its appearance on the Plot merely indicated a probability of something being there. The Higgs smudge had a very faint intensity, meaning the probability of the existence of a particle corresponding to any particular position on the Plot was very slight. Yet, on the other hand, the smudge covered so large a region of the Plot that the overall probability that something was there approached certainty.

'More experiments needed. The smudge remained.

'With finances forthcoming, the Americans with Asian and European backing finally built the SHC, the Superconducting Hypercollider, of beloved memory. My father worked on it as a young man, in an engineering capacity. They constructed this monumental bit of Big Science not in Texas, but straddling the states of Utah and Nevada.'

He projected a vidslide of an artist's cutaway of the great tube, burrowing under desert.

'And when they got the SHC working – darned if it didn't come out with the same results as previously! Seems a lot of dough had gone down the drain for nothing, one more time! The sought-after smudge remained just a smudge ... At that, it was a smudge on an entirely theoretical construct, the Ng-Robinson Plot. No actual Higgs particle could be pin-pointed. Yet, you see, the overall probability that something was there amounted to certainty.'

Euclid: 'No actual particle could continue to produce just an unresolvable smudge on the Plot?'

'Quite right, Euclid. They had a first-class mystery on their hands. And there, just when it gets exciting, we're going to take a break for ten minutes.'

Applause broke out as I led Jon into an anteroom. We left Euclid on the platform, standing facing the audience with his customary pleasant blank expression.

Thorgeson shut the door behind us and came towards me saying, 'I'm doing all this for you, my little Asian honeypot!'

He wrapped an arm round my waist, pulled me close, and kissed my lips.

I gave a small shriek of surprise. Asian honeypot indeed! He did not release me, but showered compliments on me, saying he had adored me ever since he had set eyes on me in the science unit. I did not mind the compliments. When he started to kiss me again, and I felt the warmth of his body against me, I found myself returning them.

I rejoiced when his tongue slipped into my mouth. I was becoming quite enthusiastic when the door opened and Tom and some others came in to congratulate Thorgeson on his exposition. This was one time when I felt really mad at Tom.

Back we marched into the hall. Thorgeson seemed quite

calm. I was trembling. He had been about to grab my breasts under my clothes, and I could not decide how I would feel about that. I was furious with the situation. It was all I could do to sit there and listen to him. How should I deal with him when the lecture was over – with that Euclid looking on, too?

However, I now saw a new kind of passion in Jon – not a physical passion but an intellectual one, as he took over from Euclid and spoke of the next epoch of scientific discovery.

'Euclid and I were talking about the smudge mystery,' he said when the audience had settled down. 'I will skip some years of confusion and frustration and speak about the year 2024. That was the year when there were two breakthroughs, one experimental, one theoretical.

'The experimental breakthrough came when SHC got up to full power, far beyond anything originally planned for the unbuilt SSC, using a further innovation contributed by the Indonesian physicist, Jim Kopamtim. Lo and behold at far greater energies than were achieved previously, another smudge was found!

'So the Higgs smudge had to be rechristened the alpha-smudge, while the new one went by the name of beta-smudge.

'The theoretical breakthrough – well, I should say it came a while before the SHC observations. A brilliant young Chinese mathematician, Chin Lim Chung, achieved a completely reformulated theoretical basis for particle physics as it stood at the time. Miss Chin introduced some highly sophisticated new mathematical ideas. She showed how a permanent smudge could indeed come about on the Ng-Robinson Plot, *but* the culprit could not possibly be a particle in any ordinary sense.

'It was a new kind of entity entirely. So from henceforth it was simply referred to as a *smudge*.

'Soon after the SHC announcement, Chin Lim Chung, working in conjunction with our own Dreiser Hawkwood, figured out that the alpha and beta smudges had to belong to a whole sequence of smudges, at higher and higher energies. It was clear that until this sequence was known as a whole, there was going to be no solution to the mystery of mass.

'Mother Teresa! It was as though we had discovered a row of galaxies on our doorstep!' As if he could not stop himself, he added, 'The remarkable Miss Chin is still alive and working. I happen to know her daughter.'

Something in Jon's manner, in his very body language, suggested to me that this lady must have been his Chinese lover, back on Earth.

Euclid: 'You cannot forever go on building bigger and bigger machines. So why did not the physicists just give up on the mystery?'

'Well, we don't give up easily.' He shot me a glance as he said this. 'It was hoped that once the gamma-smudge was found, then the mystery of mass could be resolved after all.'

Euclid. 'So they built an even bigger super-duper collider, did they? Where this time? Siberia?'

'On the Moon.'

He showed a vidslide of a gleaming section of tube crawling across the Mare Imbrium.

'A collider that formed a ring completely round the lunar surface. Alas for ambition! The Luna project turned out to be a total failure, at least with regard to finding the gamma-smudge. It did produce some data, relatively minor but useful. But no new smudge.'

Euclid: 'A costly mistake, wasn't it? Why did it fail?'

'The bill all merged into Lunar expenses, when the Moon was the flavour of the year, in the late 2030s. After a host of teething troubles, the Luna Collider appeared to do more or less what it was intended to do.

'I guess the final disaster rested with nature herself. She just didn't come up with a smudge – not even with the fantastic energy range available to a collider of that size.'

Euclid: 'Why didn't that kill off the whole idea? But you

are about to tell us that after that disaster, funding was found to start all over again *here* – on Mars?'

'Politics came into it. The fact that Mars was a UN protectorate made it tempting. Also, there is the precept that even pure science, however expensive it may seem, pays off in the unforeseen end. Consider the case of genetically mutated crops, and how they have contributed to human longevity. Some people are willing to pay for ever-widening horizons, for freeing the human mind from old shibboleths.

'And there were two further chunks of scientific progress to encourage them – and another different kind of development which had been brewing away for some while earlier.'

Euclid: 'They were?'

'Even last century, a number of theoreticians had realised that the enigma of mass could not be resolved at the energy levels relevant to the Higgs. Why? Well, the very concept of mass is all tied up with gravitation. Gravitation . . . Let me give you an analogy, Euclid.

'Another long-standing "mystery" in particle physics is the mystery of electrical charge. It's a mystery of a sort let's say, although a good number of physicists would claim they understand why electric charge comes about.

'The trouble is that although there are good reasons why electric charge always comes in whole-number multiples of one basic charge – which is one twelfth of the charge of an electron – there's no real understanding why the basic charge has the particular value it happens to have.

'I should say there was a time, late last century, when this basic value was believed to be one third of the electron's charge. Before that it was held to be the electron's charge itself. But the one-third value is the quark charge, and it was still thought that quarks were fundamental. Only after Henry M'Bokoko's theory of leptons and pseudo-leptons was it realised there were yet more elementary entities. Things called kliks and pseudo-kliks underlay these particles in the same way quarks underlie the hadrons.

'These kliks, pseudo-kliks and quarks, taken together, gave rise to the basic one-twelfth charge that we know today. A diagram will make that clear.'

He flashed a vidslide in the air. It hung before the audience, a skeletal Rubik's cube in three dimensions.

'Now, there are certain fundamental "natural units" for the universe – the units Nature herself uses to measure things in the universe. Sometimes these are called Planck units, after the German physicist who formulated them in the early years of last century.

'You see how one finding builds on the previous one. That's part of the fascination which keeps scientists working. In terms of these units, the basic value of the electric charge turns out to be the number 0.007, or thereabouts. This number has never been properly explained. So we don't, even yet, properly understand electric charge. There is, indeed, still a charge mystery. End of analogy!'

Euclid, unblinkingly: 'So what follows?'

'The point about the mass mystery – a point made by a few physicists even as long ago as last century – was that no one would seriously attempt to find a fundamental solution to the charge mystery without bringing the electric field into consideration. Electric charge is the source of the electric field. In the same way, so the argument went, it made little sense trying to solve the mystery of mass without bringing in the gravitational field. Mass is, of course, the source of the gravitational field.

'And yet, you see, the original hopes of resolving the mystery of mass in terms of finding the Higgs particle made absolutely no reference to gravitation.'

Euclid: 'What do you make of all this?'

'It was really a whole bag of wishful thinking. You see, Euclid, finding the Higgs particle was considered just about within the capabilities of the physicists of the time. So, if a solution to the mystery of mass could be found that way – why, then it would have been pretty well within their grasp.

'But if the issue of the role of gravity had to be seriously faced – there would not have been a hope in Hell of their finding an answer to the origin of mass experimentally. They were looking for God with a candle!

'The energy required would have been what we call the Planck energy – which is larger than the Higgs energy by a factor of at least – well, if we said a few thousand million million, we wouldn't be far out.

'Put it this way. Even a collider the length of the Earth's orbit would not have been enough.' His young-old face broke into a broad grin at the thought of it.

Euclid: 'Yet you tell us that they still did not give up. Why is that?'

'As I told you, it was all wishful thinking. They believed that finding the Higgs would be enough. Anyhow, science often proceeds by being over-optimistic. It's a way in which things do eventually get done. Eventually.

'So although the mass mystery remains unsolved, we now think our project here could well be close to doing so.'

Euclid: 'More over-optimism?'

'No, this time the case is pretty convincing. The thing is that we are now really facing up to the Planck energy problem.'

Euclid: 'I may be only an android, but as far as I know our experiment does not involve a collider of anything like that length. Or any collider at all.'

Jon released a 3D projection of something like a dark matrix motorway into the lecture room. He let it hang there as he spoke. On that infinite road, smudges shot off endlessly into distance. A cloud of other coloured spots sped after them.

'We're looking at a VR projection of a succession of different smudges, alpha-, beta-, gamma-, delta-smudges. Artist's impression only, of course. You're right, we have no collider on Mars. I've said there were a couple of encouraging breakthroughs. Those breakthroughs make our Mars project possible.

'First breakthrough. The realisation that there was no point in working through this whole gamut of smudges, at greater and greater energy levels, the list continuing for ever.'

He switched off the projection. The scatter of smudges died in their tracks.

The Icelandic physicist, Iki Bengtsoen, showed that when Einstein's theory of gravitation – already confirmed to an unprecedented degree of accuracy – was appropriately incorporated into the Chin-Hawkwood smudge theory, it became obvious that the energies of all the different smudges, alpha, beta, gamma and so on, did not just increase indefinitely, sans limit, but converged on the Planck energy limit.

'You see what this implies? All would be resolved if just a single experiment could be devised to explore the "ultimate" smudge, that limiting smudge, where all the lower energy smudges are supposed to converge. It's this putative ultimate smudge we call the *Omega Smudge*.'

Euclid. 'So we have got to it at last.' He maintained an expression of goodwill. 'But maybe you can explain how an experiment out here, on Mars, can be of particular use in finding this Flying Dutchman of a smudge – supposing it to exist at all.'

'That's where our other breakthrough comes in. Harrison Rosewall argued convincingly that a completely different kind of detector could be used to find this Omega Smudge, supposing it to exist at all.

'This involves the phenomenon known as "hidden symmetry".'

Euclid: 'And what might that be?'

Jon stood gazing at the low ceiling, as if seeking inspiration. Then he said, 'Every part of the explanation takes us deeper. These facts should have been part of everyone's education, rather than learning about past wars and histories of ancient nations. Well, I don't want to go into details, Euclid, but a hidden symmetry is a sort of theoretical symmetry which is dual in a certain sense, to a more manifest symmetry than might exist in theory. The idea goes back to some hypotheses popular late last century, although at that time the correct context for the hidden-symmetry idea was not found.

'What was important for Rosewall's scheme was that there can be things called monopoles associated with hidden-symmetry fields.

'A magnetic monopole would be a particle that has only a magnetic north pole or south pole assigned to it. As you know, an ordinary ferroperm magnet has a north pole at one end and a south pole at the other. Neither north nor south poles exist singly.

'But the great twentieth-century physicist, Paul Dirac, showed that the charge values had to be integer multiples of *something*. If you could find even a single example of a separate north or south pole, then – as we have since discovered to be the case – all electric charges would have to come in whole-number multiples of a basic charge.

'So, a number of years later, experimenters set to work to find such magnetic monopoles. If just one was found, then a major part of the mystery of electric charge would be solved. One group of experimenters even argued that the most likely place to find these things would be inside *oysters*. Of which, as we know, there's a considerable shortage on Mars.'

Euclid: 'Any luck?'

'No. No one has ever found a magnetic monopole, even to this day. But, in Rosewall's case, the hidden symmetry refers to a dual on the gravitational field. Rosewall made an impressive case that a hidden-symmetry gravitational monopole – known as a HIGMO – *ought* actually to exist. In fact there is a solution to the Einstein gravitational equations – found in the early 1960s, I believe – which describes the classical version of this monopole.

'This was Rosewall's brainwave. He realised that if you built a large ring-shaped tube, filled with an appropriate superfluid – argon 36 is what we use, under reduced pressure – then whenever a HIGMO passed through the ring, it would be detectable – just barely detectable – as a kind of "glitch" appearing in the superfluid.'

A voice from the audience asked, 'Why argon 36 and not 40?'

'Proton and neutron numbers are equal in argon 36, which underlies the reason for its remarkable superfluidity under reduced pressure. A technical advantage is the low pressure of the Martian atmosphere. Fortunately, argon 36 is not radioactive. Okay?'

At this point, he projected a vidslide of a scene I recognised. There lay the massive inflated tube, protected by its lid. There stood Dreiser, delivering his little speech. I had been a part of that historic scene!

'Obviously, this is a large-scale but delicate experiment. No other disturbances of any kind must affect the superfluid in the tube. You have to do the best you can to shield the superfluid from external vibrations, because any significant outside activity is liable to ruin the experiment.

'No place on Earth is going to be remotely quiet enough for such an experiment. Never mind human activity, the magma under Earth's crust is itself active, like a giant tummy rumbling. Earth is an excitable planet.'

Euclid: 'What about Luna?'

'The Moon proved no longer possible. Too much tourist activity and mining was already taking place. Maybe forty years ago the Moon could still have been used, but not now, certainly not since they began building the transcore subway.

'But Mars . . . Mars is ideal for the Omega Smudge experiment. No moving tectonic plates, vulcanism dead . . . That is, it's ideal provided that human activity is kept down to present levels.'

Euclid: 'No terraforming?'

Thorgeson laughed. 'The UN did a trade-off. No terraforming for a few years. The hidden agenda was that this would give a breathing space for the Omega Smudge experiment. The gun at our heads is that we have to get results.'

At this there were rumblings from the audience, and an angry voice called, 'So how long is "a few years"? Tell us!'

After a moment's pause, Thorgeson said, 'There was to be a stand-off of thirty years – four years from now – before they began to bombard the Martian surface with CFC gases, to start the warming-up process. This was the deal pushed through by Thomas Gunther.'

This statement provoked angry interjections from the audience. Thorgeson calmed things down with a wave of his hand.

'Obviously the collapse of EUPACUS has altered all such arrangements.

'The experiment we're now getting under way involves only a relatively small ring, sixty kilometres in diameter. Will we discover any HIGMOs? That depends on the HIGMO density in the universe, of which there are only estimates so far. We need results. Otherwise – who knows – the terraformers take over, the CFC gases rain down . . .'

'Get on with it, then!' came a shout from the audience, followed by roars of support.

Thorgeson said, 'The terrestrial economy is still in melt-down. Don't worry.

'Our present experiment is basically a pilot project, partly to test out how we work in adverse conditions. Maybe we can manage with this. If not, we hope to build a superfluid ring around the entire planet.'

'Another way of ruining Mars!' yelled a voice.

'We need to solve the problem at last. With the planet ringed, the answer to the vexed question of mass will finally be answered. Maybe Mars was formed precisely to enable us to find that solution.'

'Victorianism!' came a cry from a now restive audience.

Thorgeson answered this cry directly. 'Okay, tell me what else is Mars good for? You invited me here. Listen to what I have to say. I'll take sensible questions afterwards. Till then, keep quiet, please.'

As if to back him up, Euclid spoke. 'Say why it is so important to solve the mystery of mass. If a few physicists satisfy their curiosity in this respect, what good does that do ordinary people?'

'It is always difficult to justify curiosity-driven research in terms of its ultimate benefit to society. We can't tell ahead of time. Nevertheless the effect of such research, which seems entirely abstract to the lay person, can be tremendous. An obvious example is Alan Turing's analysis of theoretical computing machines done in the 1930s. It changed the world in which we live. We are on Mars because of it.'

Euclid: 'You must have some idea as to the value of this immensely costly research in areas other than particle physics.'

'Smudge research will have an important impact on other areas of physics and astrophysics. After all, it is concerned with the deepest issues of the very building bricks of the universe, the particles of which we are all composed, and their constituent elements.

'A full understanding of mass may lead to matrix-drives that will carry us to the heart of our galaxy.

'It's concerned, too, with gravitation and with the nature of matrix and time. It relates in a vital way to the under-standing of the big bang origin of the universe, and thus to deep philosophical questions. The whole mystery of where the universe comes from and of what the universe is composed – this is what smudge research ultimately involves.'

The same angry voice from the audience now interposed to say, 'Self-justification is no justification.'

I saw anger in Thorgeson's eyes, but he answered in a controlled manner one could not but admire.

'You might ask how any of this really affects society, although the matter remains of great interest to any intelligent person. Well, society might also be deeply affected for a different type of reason. This relates to a third breakthrough, which occurred at about the same time, having to do with the very nature of the human mind – or the *soul*, as some unscientific people put it.

'In the early years of this century, the development of electronic into quantum computers encouraged the already

177

widely held view that *mind* was just something that developed when sufficient powerful and effective computations took place. Chess, finally even the oriental game of Go, succumbed to the brutal but speedy computations of these devices.

'Yet no matter how effective these machines were, it was always obvious that they possessed no minds. They couldn't even be called intelligent in any ordinary sense of that word. Something essential was missing.

'With the development of the quantputer about 2023, distinct new physical features were incorporated, using basic quantum-mechanical principles. We have evidence that the human brain itself operates using these same principles. Thus, it is likely that we have in a quantputer all the essentials of human mentality. As yet, we are still short of knowing all the needed physical parameters.

'In 2039, definitive experiments carried out in France established that there is a CPS, a clear physical signal, emanating from conscious entities alone, and not from non-conscious entities like our present-day quantputers.'

Thorgeson paused to let this sink in before adding, with some emphasis, 'We have to improve the quantputer. When we have all the physical parameters – which the smudge should supply – then we shall be able to construct a quantputer that will actually emit a CPS. In other words, it will have consciousness.'

The audience remained unsettled, with voices still calling that Mars was not a laboratory.

John Homer Bateson rose from his seat and spoke, arms folded protectively across his chest. 'Professor Thorgeson, I am embarrassed to admit that I lost the thread of your involved argument when you began talking about mind. Whatever mind is. Have you not strayed from your proper subject? And is this not the way of physicists – to usurp ground properly the territory of philosophers?'

'I have not moved from my original topic,' Thorgeson said quietly. But another quiet voice in the audience, that of Crispin Barcunda, said, 'At least on Mars we have escaped the powers of the GenEng Institute, busy sculpting Megarich personalities and dupes and living rump steaks. While you guys here stay away from the biological sciences and stick to physics—'

'What's your question, Crispin?' I asked, insulted by his connecting dupes with living rump steaks.

'Is not the most pressing matter that now confronts us the possible connection between mind and your proposed smudge ring?'

'That's what we hope to find out,' Thorgeson said.

Other voices started calling. I told them to be silent and allow the lecture to continue.

At this point, Ben Borrow stood up, raising his hand to be seen. 'As a philosopher, I must ask what is to be gained by this search for the Omega Smudge? Is it not *that* which, by your own admission, has brought us to this wretched planet and caused the complete disruption of our lives?'

I answered before Thorgeson could.

'Why should you talk about the disruption of our lives? Why not the extension of our lives? Aren't we privileged to be here? Can't we by will power adapt our attitudes to enjoy our unique position?'

He looked startled by my attack, but rallied smartly, saying, 'We are of the Earth and belong there. It's the breast and source of our life and our happiness, Cang Hai.'

'Happiness? Is happiness all you want? What a pathetic thing! Hasn't the cult of the quest for happiness been a major cause of misery in the Western world for almost two centuries?'

'I didn't say—'

But I would not let him continue. 'The quest for scientific truth – is that not a far nobler thing than mere self-gratification? Please sit down and allow the lecture to continue.'

Thorgeson shot me a grateful look – although he was soon to teach me a horrid lesson in self-gratification. He came boldly to the front of the dais, to stand with hands on hips, confronting his hecklers.

179

'Look, everything in the universe depends on the fundamental laws that govern particles. All of chemistry, all of biology, all of engineering, every human – and inhuman – action – all of them ultimately depend on the laws of particle physics. Can't you understand that?'

The audience continued to be noisy. Thorgeson pressed on.

'Most of those laws are already known. The one major thing we do not yet know is where mass comes from. Once we know the Omega Smudge parameters – which will be fixed as soon as we have sufficient HIGMO data, then we will basically know *everything* – at least in principle. Isn't that important enough to put a bit of money into, just in itself? It's philistinism to ask for further justification.'

'Not if you're stuck here for years,' called someone from the audience, provoking laughter. Thorgeson spoke determinedly over it.

'It happens that some people in the early days of setting up the Mars experiment thought there was another justification for it. These people believed that there has to be *more* to the human mind than what they refer to as "just quantputing". They reckoned that finding HIGMOs would lead us to a "mysterious something" which would provide a better understanding of human consciousness. Maybe I should use the term "soul" again here.' He gave a brief contemptuous laugh. 'There are still some people – even some important people on the project, who shall be nameless – who continue to pursue this sort of notion. A load of nonsense in my opinion.'

He spoke more calmly now, and retired behind his podium to talk rather airily.

'There's no such thing as "soul". It's a medieval concept. Our brains are just very elaborate quantputers. Maybe we do still have to tune a few parameters a bit better, but that's basically all there is to it. Even Euclid would have a mind if he had been constructed with greater sophistication and better tuned parameters. But you can see he has a long way to go – haven't you, Euclid?'

Euclid: 'But I think I have a mind. A different kind of mind, perhaps. Maybe after a few more years, research will detect . . .'

'The only kind of minds *so far* we have direct reason to believe in are possessed by humans and animals, since they alone give the clear physical signal which shows up positively in the French experiment.'

Euclid: 'You are being anthropocentric and trying to prove you are better than I.'

'I am better than you, Euclid. I can switch you off.'

'Well, what has all this to do with smudges?'

'The mind is a product of the brain, our physical brains, so that mind depends on the physics of our brains. We need to know that physics just a little better. As we shall do when the Omega Smudge reveals all. Shall we soon be able to reproduce mind artificially? Smudge is clearly central to these questions.

'Here I need to retire to relax my throat for five minutes. I shall return to answer your questions.'

He motioned me to follow him, and he, I and Euclid trooped off the platform to general applause.

His performance had converted me from mistrust to admiration. 'A brilliant exposition,' I said, as we went into the rest room. 'You must have enlarged the understanding of—'

'Those fools out there!' he exclaimed. As he spoke, he turned the lock in the door behind his back. 'What did they understand? It was all gobbledy-gook to them. They show no inclination to learn. I'm not going back. I came over here to see you, you minx, and now I'm going to have you!' As he spoke, he was tearing off his overall. His face entirely altered from one of philosophical contemplation to a mask of lust and determination, its lines working angrily.

Never had I seen a man change so rapidly. I dreaded to think what thoughts he had been storing up in his mind during his long disquisition.

'Look, Jon, let's just talk—'

'You're going to be my payment—'

181

He tore from his pants the instrument with which he intended to rape me. I regarded it with interest. It differed from a dog's pizzle, mainly in having a padded bulb at the top for comfort during the penetration. This must have been, I thought, an evolutionary development tending towards producing better relationships between the sexes. Nevertheless, although I admired the design, I could not conceive of having it in my body.

Or not without a lot of consideration.

Making some absurd compliments about it, I took hold of the thing and began to stroke it. Thorgeson's 'No, no, no,' turned quickly to 'Oh oh oh,' as I hastened my strokes. I moved aside as he ejaculated on the floor.

All the while this embarrassing episode was taking place, Euclid stood there, smiling his blank smile. I ran past him, unlocked the door, and rushed into the passage.

12

The Watchtower of the Universe

The Martian marathon was organised by a group of young scientists working on Operation Smudge. They had set an ingenious 6-kilometre course through the domes, parts of which involved them leaping from the roofs of four-storey buildings, equipped with wings to provide semi-flight in the light gravity.

The marathon was regarded as an excuse for fun. Beza and Dayo had teamed up to provide a little razmataz music. Over 700 young people, men and women, together with a smattering of oldsters, were entered in the race.

Many appeared in fancy dress. The Maria Augusta dragon was present, with several small offspring. A bespectacled and bewigged Flat Mars Society showed up. Many little and large green men, complete with antennae, were running alongside green semi-naked goddesses, jostled by other bizarre life forms.

Everyone not in the race turned out to watch. The music played. It proved an exciting occasion. First prize was a multi-legged dragon trophy, created in stone and painted by our sculptor, Benazir Bahudur, with less elaborate versions for runners who came second and third.

The winner was the particle physicist Jimmy Gonzales Dust. He finished in 1,154 seconds. He was young and good-looking, with a rather cheeky air about him; he was very quick with his answers. At a modest banquet held in his honour, he was reported to have made a remarkable speech. Feeling somewhat dizzy, I did not attend.

Jimmy said that he had once believed that the process of terraforming the planet should have been undertaken from the start of our tenure of Mars. There could be no ethical objection to such work, since there was no life on Mars that would suffer in the process.

He went on to say that the duration of life on Earth was finite. The Sun in senescence would expand until it consumed Earth and the inner planets. Long before that, Earth would have become untenable as an abode of life and the human race would have had to move on or perish.

He claimed that other ports of call – the phrase was Jimmy's – awaited. In particular, he pointed out, it was common knowledge that the satellites of Jupiter had much to offer. Whereas the hop from Earth to Mars was a mere 0.5 astronomical units on average, a much greater leap was required to reach those Jovian satellites – a leap of 3.5 AUs. Once humanity grew away from the corruption that dogged great enterprises to devise a better mode of propulsion than the chemical fuel presently used – or not being actually used, he added, to laughter – this leap would be less formidable and would prove to be nothing compared with that leap that would surely have to be made one day, the leap to the stars themselves.

Such a leap, he continued, would be undertaken within a century. Meanwhile a great engineering project, such as that which would be required to endow Mars with a breathable atmosphere at tolerable atmospheric pressure and within acceptable temperature tolerances, would attract the populations of Earth. It would provide the inspiration to look outward and to grasp that factor which, apparently, many found insurmountable – namely that, with labour equivalent to the labour which had gone to make Earth habitable for multitudes of species, many varieties of bodies could be provided with pleasant dwelling places.

Eventually, like a flock of migratory birds, terrestrial species would have to leave an exhausted Earth and fly elsewhere. Their first resting points could well be on those moons of Jupiter, Ganymede and Callisto in particular. They would have the vast water resources of Europa to draw upon, and their extraordinary celestial scenery to marvel at. Thus technology would help to achieve the apotheosis of humanity.

At this point, someone interrupted the speech, shouting, 'This is all political rhetoric!'

It is never wise to barrack a popular young hero. The banqueters booed, while Jimmy said, smilingly, 'That certainly wasn't a politic remark,' and continued with his talk.

However, he said, his ambition to see Mars terraformed – often referred to as a first step towards humanity's becoming a star-dwelling race – had been based on a mistaken assumption, about which he wished to enlighten his audience, he hoped without alarming them.

Certainly, he had some disturbing news.

'For many years, people believed Mars to be inhabited,' he said. 'The quasi-scientific opinions of Percival Lovell, author of *Mars as an Abode of Life*, encouraged interest in the idea, which had been founded on the erroneous assumption that Mars was a more ancient planet than Earth. Improved astronomical equipment, and visits by probes, had swept all such speculation away. Finally, with manned landings, the point had been conceded. There was no life on Mars.

'Millions of years earlier, some archebacteria developed. Conditions deteriorated. They died out. Since then, everyone believed, Mars had been destitute of life. Destitute for millions of years.'

Jimmy paused, to confront the seriousness of what he was about to say.

'That is not the case. In fact, for millions of years there has been life on this planet. You will know of the white tongues which surround our laboratories. They are neither vegetable nor mineral. Nor are they independent objects. We have reason to believe they are the sensory perceptors of an enormous – animal? Being, let's call it.

'You will be aware of the M-gravitic anomaly associated with the Tharsis Shield. That anomaly is caused by a being so large it is visible even through terrestrial telescopes. We know it as Olympus Mons.

'Olympus Mons is not a geological object. Olympus Mons is a sentient being of unique kind.'

Immediately chaos erupted in the hall. Shouts of 'It can't be!' mingled with cries of 'I told you so!' When calm was restored, Jimmy resumed, smiling rather a guilty smile, pleased by the shock he had engendered.

'My fellow scientists in this room will confirm what I say. This immense being, some seven hundred kilometres across, is a master of camouflage. Or else it's a huge kind of barnacle. Its shell resembles the surrounding terrain, much as a chameleon takes on the colour of its background. Its time-sense must be very different from ours, since it has sat where it is now, without moving, for many centuries.

'Under its protective shell is organic life.'

He gave a nervous laugh.

'Terraforming would harm it. We are, ladies and gentlemen, sharing this planet with an amazingly large barnacle!'

The learned John Homer Bateson, leaning nearby against a pillar, hands in his robe, said, 'An amazingly large barnacle! The mind is inclined to boggle somewhat. Well, well . . . Was it not Isocrates who called man the measure of all things? Such Ptolemaic thinking needs revision. Clearly it is this mollusc that is the measure of all things.'

Others present pressed forward with anxious questions.

Jimmy sought to give some reassurance.

'We can only speculate as to where the being came from, or where it might be going. Is it friend or enemy? We can't tell as yet.'

'You mad scientists!' Crispin Barcunda was heard to exclaim. 'What might this thing do if disturbed – if, say, we had started the terraforming process, with attendant atmospheric and chthonic upheavals?'

186

Jimmy spread his hands. 'Olympus has its exteroceptors trained on us. All we can say is that it has, as yet, made no hostile move.'

Even the special performance of *Mine? Theirs?*, revised once again by Paula Gallin, was ill attended after this disconcerting news.

Speculation concerning Olympus, as it became known, continued on all levels. Much discussion concerned whether it might be regarded as malevolent or benevolent. Did this strange being consider that it owned Mars, in which case it might well regard humans as parasitic intruders? Or was it merely some unexpected variety of celestial jellyfish, without intention?

More alarm was caused when Jimmy Dust and his fellow scientists revealed that they had secured as a specimen one of the white tongues – had, in fact, hacked it off. Its complex cellular organisation had convinced them that, whatever Olympus was, it enjoyed sensory perception. Some reassurance was afforded by the fact that it had not retaliated against this attack on its exteroceptors. But perhaps it was merely biding its time.

I did not at this juncture realise how unwell I was. However, I had sufficient energy to call Dreiser Hawkwood on the Ambient. I demanded to know why the news that Olympus Mons was a living entity had been released to us in such a casual manner, by Jimmy Dust, the marathon winner. I asked if some kind of dangerous joke was being played on us. I raved on. I even said it had been firmly established that there was no life on Mars.

Dreiser listened patiently. He then said, 'We chose to make the announcement as informally as possible, hoping not to alarm people. You will find the strategy is largely successful. People will cluck like hens and then get on with their day-to-day business. And you, Tom, I trust, will regain your customary good humour.'

It was the meek answer that increases wrath. 'You told

187

me when we spoke about Olympus that it was in no sense alive.'

'I never said that.'

'When we were preparing to address the assembly over a year ago, did you or did you not tell me there was no life on Mars?'

'No. I may have said we had found no life on Mars. Olympus was so big that it escaped our notice . . .' He chuckled. 'I may have said we should expect Martian life to be very different from life Downstairs. So it proves.'

'You're trying to tell me that this monstrous thing has just flopped out of the skies from space, or from another universe?'

'I might try to tell you many things, Tom, if you were fit to listen. I merely tell you this for now – that Olympus is entirely indigenous to Mars.'

When I asked how it was that he had made this discovery, rather late in our second year of isolation on Mars, Dreiser replied that a study of satellite photographs had convinced him there was some movement in the region.

'To whom did you first communicate this knowledge?'

He hesitated. 'Tom, there are two things you should know. Firstly, we owe this perception – a perception I will admit I resisted at first – to the young genius you turned up, Kathi Skadmorr. What a clever young woman she is, what a quick brain!'

'Okay, Dreiser. And the second thing?'

'This object that Kathi insists on calling the "Watch-tower of the Universe" is definitely on the move. And it's moving in our direction, slow but sure. More news later. Goodbye.'

He signed off. I felt mortified that I had spoken so ill advisedly, and that the conversation had been recorded.

I went to lie down.

The physicists proposed sending an investigative expedition to Olympus. They were told to wait. Caution was to be the order of the day. Olympus might have a slower time sense than biological beings and could be planning a counterattack, so any close approach might imperil human lives.

I held private discussions with Jimmy Dust and his scientific colleagues, including the young man who maintained that cephalopods possessed intelligence.

'Human nature being what it is, the wish to believe in something bigger than themselves comes naturally to people,' one of the women said. 'But we need to discourage the idea already circulating in some quarters that Olympus is a god. As far as our limited knowledge goes, it's just a huge lump of rather inert organic material.'

'Yet we call it Olympus – traditionally the home of the gods.'

'That's just a semantic quibble. Our guess is that this being is of low intelligence, being rupicolous.'

'Eh? What's rupicolous?'

'Means it lives off rocks. Not a bright thing to do.'

'How so? At least there's a generous supply of rock around right here . . .'

The discussion broke up without coming to any conclusion.

Adminex invited Hawkwood to come to the Hindenburg Hall and address an assembled crowd on the subject of Olympus. In particular we wished him to clarify its nature.

He agreed as long as his talk took the form of an interview. If I would ask the questions. I agreed. When we had both prepared for the talk, an assembly was called.

Since the occasion was so important, children were permitted to be present. In they streamed, carrying their tammies – tammies that had been fed and cosseted before their entry.

Dreiser arrived in style. He was prompt. He came with a retinue of four, the wispy Poulsen, another scientist, a blonde personal assistant whom we had met, as Cang Hai reminded me, in Dreiser's office, and a fourth member whom I hardly recognised at first. Gone were her thick and curly chestnut locks. Her hair was now black, straight, and cut short. It was Kathi Skadmorr. When she shook my hand and smiled, I knew that smile.

The retinue settled themselves in the front seats, while Dreiser and I sat under the great photograph of the flaming zeppelin, in the dazzle of Suung Saybin's lighting.

Dreiser began by saying that he wished to inform everyone of the little he knew concerning the nature of the life form called Olympus. He reminded us that Olympus had maintained its present existence for far longer than terrestrial telescopes had been around to be trained on Mars. It was an object, a life form, of immense antiquity, almost as ancient as the rocks to which it clung.

To remind us of its size, he zapped before the audience a 3D vidslide showing Olympus in profile, with a dawn light on its higher reaches, while its tall serrated skirts remained in a dusky red twilight. Its vast span covered 600 kilometres of ground.

'There it is, waiting for we know not what, amid ancient cratered topography over three billion years old.'

A shot of Earth's Mount Everest was superimposed over Olympus. It showed as the merest pimple below the central caldera.

'As you see,' said Dreiser, 'Olympus is unusually large for a volcano. For a life form it defies the imagination.'

An uneasy hush fell on the audience.

I remarked that Mars had previously been ruled out as an abode of life.

But this, Dreiser argued, was merely a reference to the many studies that had been conducted of soil and rock samples, of the analysis of the atmosphere, and of drillings made down into the crust. None had revealed any evidence for Martian life of any kind – even when allowances were made for the fact that life here might be completely different from life on Earth.

It was still difficult, I said, not to think of Olympus as simply an extraordinarily large volcano among other Martian volcanoes, admittedly of smaller size, such as

Elysium, Arsia and Pavonis. Or were they also the cara-paces of living beings?

He thought not. 'Reproduction is a basic evolutionary function. Nevertheless it seems that Olympus has not spawned. Maybe it is a hermaphrodite. Maybe it simply lacks a partner.'

We would come to what it resembled later, Dreiser said. He wished to state that he had no quarrel with all the previous research centring on the quest for life. Those conclusions were definitive. Olympus was unique.

At this juncture, Dreiser said, he believed that the spot-light should shine on his associate, who had first brought the movements of Olympus to scientific notice. Those movements were so unprecedented that at first they were not credited. In introducing Kathi Skadmorr, he knew she was already celebrated as the YEA who had courageously gone down into the throat of the Valles Marineris and found considerable underground reservoirs of water.

Kathi now came to the dais and spoke without preamble, almost before the clapping had finished. 'I'm campaigning to call Olympus Mons by a more vital name. It was christened in ignorance, long ago. I propose rechristening it, in the light of our new-found knowledge, Chimborazo, which means the "Watchtower of the Universe". So far my campaign has only one member, but I'm still hoping.

'We don't as yet know what we have here. Okay, Chimborazo moves, but whole mountains have been known to move. So movement does not necessarily mean life. Here's where we detected movement.'

She zapped a vidslide taken from the satcam, showing the tumbled regolith on Chimborazo's westerly side, and continued to speak.

'The broken regolith shows where our friend upped stumps and began to move. We secured one of those elusive white tongues you will all have seen. They are in fact inorganic, but with organic nerves and feelers lacing them. It seems not all tongues are identical, and that they serve different functions.

191

'Our hypothesis at present is that the tongues, more scientifically termed exteroceptors and proprioceptors, were once digestive organs, and that they have been modified over the eons. Not only do they provide nourishment to Chimborazo: they also function as rudimentary detectors. Thus, you see, they provide evidence that Chimborazo is not only a massive life form: it is also a life form with some kind of intelligence.

'Now I will hand over to Tom and Dreiser again.' She did not leave the dais, but took a seat next to me.

After thanking Kathi, I asked Dreiser where this monstrous thing had come from? From outer space? The Oort Cloud?

Not at all. 'Olympus Mons,' said Dreiser, then hesitated. 'Very well then, Chimboranzo—'

Kathi immediately interrupted, saying, 'It's Chimborazo, Dreiser!'

He gave a grunt and grinned at her. 'Chimborazo is entirely indigenous. Nor is there anything uncanny about it. Our belief is that it is the result of a curious form of evolution – curious, that is, from the point of view of one accustomed to thinking in terrestrial terms. Curious – but by no means irrational.'

But if this life form actually evolved on Mars, as Dreiser claimed, there would surely be evidence of other life in the atmosphere, I said. Not only in the atmosphere, but in the rocks and regolith. 'Evolution', after all, implied 'natural selection', so there must have been other forms of life with which this monstrous Olympus organism had been in competition. I remarked that it would be silly to turn our backs on Darwin's findings, since natural selection was now a well-established principle.

Dreiser had adopted a slouching posture, as if scarcely interested in the topic we were discussing. Now he sat up and looked at me with a direct stare.

'I am not disputing those principles, Tom. Far from it. But it is all too easy to fall into the way of thinking that how natural selection has operated in the main on Earth is its only method. Conditions here are vastly different from those Downstairs. Which is not to say that Darwin's perceptions do not still apply.'

Of course conditions differed, I agreed. But I could not see how his Olympus could have extinguished all other life forms on the planet, simply by sitting there like a great lump, all in one place.

'For some while we thought exactly as you do. I have to say it is a limited point of view. Mounting evidence that Olympus is a living thing has made us change our opinions, our rather parochial earthly opinions. In fact, evolution on Earth itself has not been entirely "Nature red in tooth and claw". I could name many examples of cooperation between species that have led to vital evolutionary advantage. I stress that: cooperation, not competition.'

I supposed he was thinking of man and his long relationship with the dog.

'Unfortunately we did not bring our loyal friend the dog here with us, more's the pity. We will certainly need him when we travel towards the stars to face unforeseen challenges. We did bring all the bacteria in our stomachs, without which we could not survive. That's a handy example of a symbiotic relationship.'

What could that have to do, I asked, with his Olympian organism wiping out the rest of Martian life?

'That is not my argument. Not at all. There are many examples where symbiosis has played a vital role in evolution. Let's take lichens. Two differing organisms got together, a fungus and an alga, to form the unbeatable lichen, the hardiest of terrestrial life forms. Lichens are the first to move in after a volcanic eruption has wiped a mountainside clean. Even we, resourceful humankind, depend on our bacteria, just as swarming microlife depends on us.'

We had found no lichen-like organisms on Mars, I argued, and asked where that left us.

'Hang on. I'm not finished. I have some even more apposite examples of cooperation. There were times in the evolution of life on Earth when symbiotic relations have been absolutely vital.

'Take the eukaryotic cell. This is the kind of cell of which all ordinary plants and all animals are composed. It's a cell that contains a distinct nucleus within which chromosomes carry genetic material. It has long been established that the first eukaryotic cells came about by the union of two other more primitive types of organism, the earlier prokaryotic cell and a kind of spirochete. The development of all multicellular plants and animals – and humans – stems from this union.

'Incidentally, on the subject of life, you might ask yourself how likely – what are the odds – of such a coincidence happening elsewhere in our galaxy. Long odds, I'd say.'

Although I was in agreement with this statement, I got Dreiser back on track again by asking what all this had to do with Olympus's extinction of the rest of Martian life.

'No, no, you have the wrong picture in your head still, Tom. That's not what happened here, as we envisage it. There was no extinction.'

He paused before continuing, perhaps considering how to explain most clearly.

'With the very different conditions on Mars, the balance of advantage in evolutionary processes was also different. Even on Earth, two types of evolutionary pressure have been important. We have become accustomed to considering the idea of competition as being the more important. This may be because Darwin's splendid perceptions were launched in 1859 into a highly competitive capitalist society.

'In the competition scenario, the different species battle it out, and the "fittest" are, on the whole, the ones that survive. But the cooperative element in evolution has sometimes proved important – vital, you might say – as we've seen in the instances of symbiotic development I have already mentioned.

194

'On Earth, competitive aspects of evolution have rather dominated the cooperative elements in our consideration. Our enforced social competitiveness has led us in that direction. We tend to think that the competitive element predominates, although in fact the entire terrestrial biomass works in unconscious cooperative ways to create a favourable environment for itself.

'These cooperative processes stem from the early days when life first crept from sea to the land. Initially both land and atmosphere were hostile to life of any kind, and various symbiotic relationships had to be adopted. Otherwise life could not have survived. But gradually, as conditions on Earth became more favourable, competitive elements began to assert themselves. We now see – or think we see – the competitive elements dominating the cooperative elements.'

Somewhere in the audience, a tammy began to chirp and was hushed. I asked Hawkwood if evolution had taken a different course on Mars.

'Possibilities for life here differ considerably from Earth, as we have said. Conditions have never been other than harsh. Now they weigh heavily against life. We have low atmospheric pressure, almost zero oxygen content, abnormally dry conditions. But basic natural laws always applied.

'In the case of evolution, cooperation had a distinct edge over competition. In the early days of Mars's history, conditions more closely resembled Earth's. But gradually oxygen became bonded into the rocks while water vapour leaked away. As conditions became more and more adverse, cooperation among the indigenous life forms won out over competition.

'The enormous diversity of life forms, such as we find on Earth, never had a chance to develop here. Evolution on Mars was forced into a combining together of life. All forms eventually huddled together for protection against adverse Martian conditions. It was the ultimate Martian strategy.'

They huddled together, I suggested, under what we have always thought was a volcano, Olympus Mons. Why should they have chosen that particular shape?

'A cone shape is economical of material. And since the life forms were not going to be particularly mobile, they chose a defence readily adopted by countless of Earth's creatures – they opted for camouflage. Camouflage against what we can't tell; nor, I suppose, could they. But their instincts are readily understandable. In fact, the shell is just that, a shell made from keratin and clay – very tough and durable.'

It would keep heat in, I suggested.

'Yes, and fairly large meteorites out.'

A child's voice from the audience asked, 'What are the people like under the shell, Dreiser?'

'They aren't people in our sense of the word,' Dreiser replied. 'The use of keratin as a binder in the shell suggests hair, nails, horns, hooves, feathers . . .'

At the words 'hooves, feathers . . .' a frisson ran through the audience like the rustling of great wings.

Dreiser continued. 'Olympus Mons – sorry, Kathi, Chimborazo – has grown gradually into the vast volcano shape we know today. The creatures under it must be still surviving, perhaps even thriving, since Olympus is now in a growth phase. It extends very slowly, we think upwards. But our surveys indicate an expansion of something like 1.1 centimetres every other decade.'

So how did it feed?

'Its exteroceptors suck nourishment and moisture from the rocks.

'As you have heard from Kathi here, Chimborazo is executing a slow horizontal movement. It advances at the rate of a few metres every Martian year.'

At the exclamations from his audience, Dreiser looked gravely ahead of him. He spoke next with emphasis.

'This advance began only when these domes and the science unit were established. Chimborazo is probably attracted by a heat source.'

'You mean it's advancing on us?' cried a nervous voice from the floor.

'Although its forward movement is much faster than its growth rate, it is still no speedster by terrestrial standards. A snail runs like a cheetah by comparison. We're all quite safe. It will take nearly a million years to drag itself here at present rate of progress.'

'I'm packing my bags now,' came a voice from the floor amid general laughter.

Vouchsafing the remark a wintery smile, Dreiser continued, 'We monitored the horizontal movement first. You may imagine our incredulity. We did not immediately realise we were dealing with a living thing – undoubtedly the biggest living thing within the solar system.

'We did not connect it at first with those white exteroceptors, which flick so quickly out of sight. They are the creature's sensors, and of complex function. Not eyes exactly. But they appear to be sensitive to electromagnetic signals of various wavelengths. The multitude of them together is probably used to build up a picture of sorts. They retract at any unexpected signal, which caused us problems in getting a clear picture of them to start with.'

A subdued voice asked a question from the audience. Dreiser needed it repeated: 'I can't believe what you're telling us. How can that enormous thing possibly be alive?'

Kathi answered sharply. 'You must improve your perceptions. If it can think, Chimborazo is probably asking itself how a small feeble bipedal thing like you could possibly be alive – not to mention intelligent.'

The questioner sank back in her chair.

'You can perhaps imagine our shock when we discovered that Chimborazo was advancing towards our research unit. Nothing can stop its approach,' Kathi said. 'Unless we make some sort of conscious appeal to it . . .'

I asked if Dreiser thought that Olympus had a mind anything like ours.

'The balance of opinion is that it has a mind radically different from ours. So Kathi has half persuaded us. A mind compounded of a multitude of little minds. Thought may be greatly slowed down by comparison with our time-scales.

'Yes, I have to say it may well have awareness, intelligence. We have detected a fluttery CPS – the clear physical signal that is the signature of mind. It may tick over slowly by our standards, but speed of thought isn't everything.'

'Now you're being anthropomorphic!' said a voice from the floor.

'It is one of the functions of intelligence to respond discriminatingly to the events that come within its scope. Which is what Olympus seems to be doing. Its response to mankind's arrival here is to move towards us. Whether this can be construed as hostile or friendly, or merely as a reaction to a heat source, we have yet to decide. It has decided!'

He paused for thought. 'It may well have consciousness. Consciousness is not necessarily the gift solely of earthly beings such as ourselves.

'In our discussions here, I have noticed the frequency with which ancient authorities are appealed to, from Aristotle and Plato onwards – to Count Basie, I may say. This is because our consciousness has a collective element. "No voice is ever lost," if I may take my turn at quoting. Our consciousness has been enriched by the minds of those good men who lived in the past. Perhaps you may regard this as a mental evolutionary principle of cooperation in action.

'Consciousness is unlike any other phenomenon, compounded of many elements and apparent contradictions along the quantum-mechanical level. In the close quarters engendered by its shell, the huddled creatures of Olympus would probably have developed a form of consciousness.

'I will also venture the suggestion that here in our cramped quarters we could be developing a new step forward in human consciousness, represented by the word "utopian". A thinking alike for the common good . . .

'If that is so – and I hope it may be so – it will mean the

198

fading away of individualism. This is what has happened with our friend Chimborazo, if I guess correctly. It has become a single creature consisting of the symbiotic union of all indigenous Martian life.'

Came a shout from the audience. 'What gives you the idea that this weird mind is good?'

Dreiser responded thoughtfully. 'I repeat that individualism had no chance on Mars. To survive, this entity evolved a collective mind. It has therefore learned control . . . But we can only speculate upon all this. With awe. With reverence.'

Here Kathi chipped in to say, 'It may seem to us slow and ponderous, but why should we not believe it to be superior to our own fragmented minds?'

After the talk, Helen Panorios came up to Dreiser and asked, timidly, why Olympus had camouflaged itself as a volcano.

'Olympus lies among other volcanoes. So it can become pretty well lost in the crowd.'

'Yes, sir, but what has it camouflaged itself against?'

Dreiser regarded her steadily before replying. 'We can only suppose – although this is terrestrial thinking – that it feared some great and terrible predator.'

'Space-born?'

'Very probably space-born. Matrix-born . . .'

From this occasion onwards, Dreiser and I spent more time together, discussing this extraordinary phenomenon. Sometimes he would call in Kathi Skadmorr. Sometimes I called in Youssef Choihosla, who professed an empathy with Olympus.

One of the first questions I asked Dreiser was, 'Are you now going to abandon your search for the Omega Smudge?'

He stroked his moustache as if it was his pet, gave me an old-fashioned look, and replied with a question, 'Are you going to abandon your plans for a utopian society?'

So we understood each other. Ordinary work had to continue.

But it continued under the shadow of that enormous life form that unceasingly inched its way towards us. Despite warnings to the contrary, the four of us drove out one calm day to inspect Olympus at close quarters. Crossing the parched terrain, we began to climb, bumping over parallel fracture lines. Kathi, in the rear seat with Choihosla, seemed particularly nervous, and clutched Choihosla's large hand.

When I jokingly made some remark to her about her nervousness, she replied, 'You might do well to be nervous, Tom. We are crossing Chimborazo's holy ground. Can't you feel that?'

The terrain became steeper and more broken. Dreiser drove slowly. The exteroceptors were all about us. They seemed thicker here, more reluctant to slide back into the frozen regolith. The buggy dropped to a mere crawl. Dreiser flicked his headlights on and off to clear the track. 'God, for a gun!' he muttered. We were all tense. No one spoke.

We surmounted a bluff, and there the rim of it was, protruding above ground level like a cliff. We stopped. 'Do we get out?' I asked. But Kathi was already climbing from the vehicle. She walked slowly towards Chimborazo.

I got out and followed. Dreiser and Choihosla followed me. Suited up, we could hear no external sound.

Even near to, Olympus closely resembled a natural feature, its flanks being terraced in a roughly concentric pattern. There were imitations of flowlines, channels and levees, as well as lines of craters that might or might not be imitations of the real things. We could by no means see all of its 700-kilometre diameter. Even the caldera was hardly visible, though a small cloud of steam hovered above it. Whether as a volcano or a living organism, it seemed impossible to comprehend.

In its presence I felt the hair at the back of my neck prickle. I simply stood and stared, trying to come to terms with it. Dreiser and Choihosla were busy with instruments, noting with satisfaction that there was no radiation reading, receiving a CPS.

'Of course there's a CPS,' said Kathi. 'Do you really need instruments to tell you that? How's the back of your neck, for instance?'

Braver than we were, she climbed up on to the shell and lay flat upon it, her little rump in the air. It was as if – but I brushed aside the thought – she desired sexual intercourse with it.

After a while, she returned and joined us. 'You can feel a vibration,' she said. She returned to the buggy and sat, arms folded across her chest, head down.

Cang Hai's Account

13

At this period, I used to like to go with my baby daughter to a small café on P. Lowell called the Oort Crowd. The talk there was all about Chimborazo. The threat from outside seemed to have drawn people together and the café was more crowded than ever.

My Ambient was choked with messages from Thorgeson, which alternated between apologies, supplications, abuse and endearments. I preferred café life, as did Alpha.

Although I did not wish to be impolite, I eventually sent Thorgeson a message: 'Go to hell, you and your ventriloquist's dummy!' At the same time, I found some sheets on the Ambient network and tried to gain a better understanding of particle physics. I was making little progress, and called Kathi, asking if I might see her.

'I'm busy, Cang Hai, sorry. We have problems.'

Trying to keep the disappointment from my voice, I asked her what the problems were.

'Oh, you wouldn't understand. There's some trouble with the smudge ring. Stray vortices in the superfluid. We're getting spurious effects. Sorry, must go. Meeting coming up. Love to Alpha.' And she was gone.

Possibly this was what my Other in Chengdu had warned me about. I had been walking up a mountain with a king – or at least a man with a crown on his head. The air was so pure. We listened to bird song. Another man came along. He too had something on his head. Or perhaps it was a mask. I wanted him to join us. He smiled beautifully, before starting to run at a great pace up the mountain ahead of us. Then I saw a lake.

The manager of the Oort Crowd was Bevis Paskin Peters. He had taken over a department of the old Marvelos travel bureau. He ran the café very casually, being a part-time dress designer – the planet's first. Peters was rather a heavy man, with a sullen set to his features that disappeared when he smiled at you. In those moments, he looked amazingly handsome.

However, Peters was not the reason I went to the Oort Crowd. Nor was Peters often there, leaving the running of the café to an assistant, a fair-haired wisp of a lad. I went because Alpha loved to watch the cephalopods. The front wall of the café consisted of a thin aquarium in which the little cephalopods lived, jetting their way about the tank like comets.

A YEA marine biologist had become so attached to his pets that he had brought two pairs with him to Mars. Convinced of their intelligence, he had built them a computer-operated maze. The maze, built from multi-coloured perspex, occupied the tank. Its passageways and dead ends altered automatically every day. The cephalopods multiplied and had to be culled, so the Oort often had real calamari on the menu. Ten of the creatures lived in the tank, and seemed to take pleasure in threading their way about the maze.

Alpha sat contentedly for hours, watching. Her particular admiration was for the way in which the squid changed body colour as they glided through the coloured passageways.

We were there one day – I was chatting to some other mothers – when in came Peters with a dark-skinned man I did not know, together with the famous Paula Gallin.

She scooped up Alpha, who knew her well, and kissed her passionately, calling endearments and making Alpha give her beautiful chuckle. The two men, meanwhile, were putting a cassette into a player at the rear of the bar.

Then Paula demanded the attention of the café's clientele.

'I just want you all to take a look at a piece of film. A sneak preview of my next production, okay? It won't take a minute. Okay, guys.'

The mirror behind the bar opaqued and there were figures moving and talking. They were in a long hall, filmed in longshot. All was movement. A man and a woman were talking in the crowd, talking and quarrelling. In the main, they avoided each other's gaze, shooting angry glances now and then. As they continued walking but their voices grew louder, the crowd about them froze into immobility.

The man said, 'Look, all I do I do for you.'

'You don't. You do it for yourself,' said the woman.

'You're the selfish one. Why are you always attacking me?'

'I don't attack you, you liar. I was just asking you why—'

'You were distinctly interrogating me,' he said, breaking into her sentence. 'You're always on at me.'

'I simply had a small suggestion to make, but you would not listen. You never listen.'

'I've already heard what you have to say.' He was red in the face now.

'I do everything for you. What do you do for me?'

His manner changed entirely. 'I do nothing for you, do I?' He appeared completely crestfallen. The woman turned her head angrily away.

The film cut, the mirror returned.

Paula laughed with a rich kind of gurgle. 'Okay, folks, now which of those two characters do you think was in the wrong, or was most wrong?'

We gave our opinions, the few of us sitting in the café. Some thought the man was feeling guilty about a misdemeanour. Others thought the woman was a nagger. Most of the speakers took sides. I said that they had got themselves into the kind of situation where both parties were wrong; they needed to stop quarrelling and try to find agreement, if necessary calling in a third party.

'Gee, you're an enlightened bunch,' said Paula, joshingly. 'Now tell me what you make of the woman's last remark, "I do everything for you; what do you do for me?"'

So we chewed it over, we café-goers, while Paula cooed over Alpha. We were more or less in agreement that the woman's statement was destructive in itself. We disagreed about whether it was made more awful by being the truth or a vicious lie. Nor could we agree about the man's response: was it a sullen repudiation of her remark or a wretched admission of the truth?

'That's enough,' Paula said, sharply. 'Thanks. Bevis, Vance . . .'

What we did not realise was that the mirror behind the bar was a two-way mirror. Later, we saw an edited version of ourselves in Paula's new filmplay, *Mine? Theirs?* Since we never knew what the filmed pair were quarrelling about, our judgements seemed facile. It was one of Paula's rather unpleasant tricks.

Perhaps that habit of hers caused the tragedy that was to follow – a tragedy that for a while eclipsed our preoccupation with Chimborazo.

Paula had a beautiful and strong face with marked features – a forceful jaw, in particular, and a beaky nose; her features were very unlike my rather ambiguous ones. Although she often took and discarded lovers, her real interests, or so it seemed to me, were directed elsewhere. Her predatory and creative mind wished to ingest the experiences of other people, and by so doing widen her own dimensions. Perhaps she had a driving need to resolve her own tensions.

Her clothes were designed by Bevis Paskin Peters. She rejected the customary unisex Now overalls, so Peters became the planet's first popular costume designer. He evolved a classical line imaginatively in keeping with the shortage of materials. The other man in Paula's ménage à trois was called Vance Aylsha. He was a technician and rather a genius, according to report. He also looked after the little cephalopods in the café aquarium.

At times Paula could be large and florid. At other periods she appeared smaller, perhaps when she was actually working in her studio and unconscious of her own persona. I cannot say I liked her much. She was bigger than I, and unpredictable.

Nevertheless I was quite frequently in her company because she adored – or at least was fascinated by the growth experience of – Alpha. She would cease her work, towards which she was otherwise obsessive, to play for two hours at a stretch with Alpha. There was nothing Alpha liked better.

Nor was there much I liked better than to see these two intellects, the mature and the awakening, meeting in quizzes and tricks and mock deceptions and sheer nonsenses. I was aware of the antiquity of these games and that awareness added to my happiness.

How starkly the lovely energies of the three of us, the warmth of our bodies, contrasted with the frozen world outside, making it more thrilling to be there!

It was not all plain sailing; with such an outgoing character, arguments were always springing up. I had made some remark in praise of Tom Jefferies, whereupon Paula said, cuttingly, 'You should stay away from that creep.'

When I protested that Tom was a courageous and altruistic man, Paula gave this reply.

'Not at all. He's a creep. Of course he loves his plan. He wants us all to conform to it. He wants us all to be better people. That's because he doesn't like us much. Maybe he's scared of us – no, not of you, Cang Hai, but you're another sexless little thing, aren't you?'

'I'm certainly not sexless. Nor is Tom.'

'But you don't have sex, do you?' She laughed. 'You need awakening. Come to bed with me and I'll show you what you're missing.'

Although I did not take up her offer, it was from lack of courage rather than from virtue. I saw why her two current men lusted for her.

I saw how her interest, as expressed in her plays, was in

people rather than theories of behaviour. She liked chaos. It answered a dangerous element in her make-up.

At the time of which I am speaking, Paula Gallin was working on *Mine? Theirs?* She spent her days cutting, editing, morphing, swearing. I was witness to her outbreaks of anger against her male friends, whom she found necessary even as they broke her concentration. Creativity was by now better understood and better respected, but I went to the Ambient stand to look at the words of an old savant, Doctor Storr, whose work on the dynamics of creation remained of value.

Doctor Storr says that a child who has a parent who ill treats him but on whom he is nevertheless dependent will regularly deny the 'bad' aspects of the parent and repress his own hatred, perhaps by developing some symptom such as nail-biting or hair-pulling. These activities show the displacement of repressed aggression and its turning against the self.

'It seems likely, however,' the doctor continues, 'that there is another way of dealing with incompatibles and opposites within the mind, provided one is sufficiently robust to stand the tension; and this is the way adopted by creative people. One characteristic of creative people is just this ability to tolerate dissonance. They see problems that others do not see; and do not attempt to deny their existence. Ultimately the problem may be solved, and a new whole made out of what was previously incompatible, but it is the creative person's tolerance of the discomfort of dissonance that makes the new solution possible.

'The process is easy to see in the case of scientific discovery. Something very similar may be going on in the case of the production of works of art. I have discussed the quest for identity characteristic of at least some creative artists, and suggested that, if this is a particular need for such people, as it seems to be, it is connected with an attempt to reconcile incompatibles or opposites in the mind. This is, of course, intimately connected with the problem of identity; for identity, or rather the sense of one's own identity, is a sense of unity, consistency and wholeness.

'One cannot have a sense of one's continuous being if one is always conscious of two or more souls warring within one breast. In the case of Tolstoy, the ascetic and the sensualist were never reconciled; but one aspect of his creative existence was certainly an attempt to bring this about.'

I was surprised. For the first time I saw that the doctor's statement, true as far as it went, did not encompass the contrasts and conflicts built into the mind by blind evolutionary development – the phylogenetic, as opposed to the ontogenetic, brain.

To employ the doctor's rather poetic phraseology, there would always be the two souls warring within one breast; this was what gave to *Homo sapiens sapiens* our restless drive to develop further; it was part of the general creativity we were attempting to harness. We were now developing into a phylogenetic-conscious society, accepting and coming to terms with our inbuilt contradictions, revealing the 'natural' human.

Paula's drama on which she was working, *Mine? Theirs?*, was precisely about the interplay between the two kinds of conflict, the ancient generic and the personal.

I considered these intellectual ideas but, even when practising my pranayama, I taunted myself with the thought of what it would be like to be in bed with Paula, with her dark tempestuous body against mine. These images crept in upon my meditation . . .

At this juncture Vance Alysha and Bevis Paskin Peters were the two rivals for Paula's love. Both were men of spirit and worked on the computer simulations necessary for episodes in Paula's drama. Alysha was Caribbean; he had been a star on television in his native Jamaica, and remained proud of it. Peters had won a prize for paranimation at the age of six; he was vain and had a quick temper. And he was said to dress privately in his own flamboyant women's costumes.

An argument arose between the two men over the interpretation of a turn in Paula's narrative: was a certain character's decision to retreat into the wilds a brave or a cowardly act? This developed into a quarrel over which of them best satisfied Paula's sexual needs. Happily, Alpha and I were not present.

They fell on the floor, wrestling with and punching each other. Peters seized on a length of computer cable and wrapped it round Alysha's neck. Paula entered the workshop at this point and screamed for Peters to stop. He did not stop. Although Alysha struggled, he was choked to death.

Mars City had no police as such. Paula called for the guards – those men who maintained the integrity of our structures. They hauled Peters away, unresisting. Since there was nothing like a prison on Mars, they shut Peters in their office, where he sat and wept, overcome by what he had done.

The guards summoned Tom. Tom and Guenz called our legal forum together to discuss the case. It assembled under the blow-up of the incandescent Hindenburg.

We were silent, rather sullen this time. Everyone was miserable in their own way. I sat at the rear with other onlookers, holding Alpha, next to a grim Paula. She shed no tear, but her face was ashen. I put a comforting arm round her waist, but she shrugged it off.

Thinking back to that time, I am surprised that we had faced no such crisis before. There had been animosities and quarrels, certainly, but all had been settled peaceably. Without the aggravation of money or those inhibitions of marriage so wrapped up in old-fashioned notions of property, the levels of discontent had been considerably lowered.

Jarvis Feneloni was one who spoke up for Peters's execution. Since the sallow-complexioned young man had attempted to leave Mars with his brother – nothing more had ever been heard of Abel and his ship – he had gained something of a reputation by being unruly. 'We have no doubt the man is guilty. He confesses to the crime. We have nowhere to imprison him. In any case, the traditional punishment for murder is death. Why muck about? We must execute Peters. Let's discuss how that should be done.'

'His confession lessens the case against him, while his remorse is his own punishment,' Tom responded. 'How exactly do you suggest we should kill him? By the methods he used on Alysha? By throwing him out on the Martian surface? By cutting off his head or his oxygen? We have no more right to kill than he. All methods of deliberate killing are distasteful to civilised men.'

'Well, I'm not civilised! We must set an example, take strong measures. This is our first case of murder, particularly the murder of a—' He stopped himself. We guessed what he was about to say. Instead Feneloni finished lamely, 'Particularly the murder of one so young. We must set an example, so that it does not happen again. And we must build a prison.'

Tom replied that he agreed an example must be set. But they had to set that example for themselves. If a family has a boy who misbehaves, punishment will probably make him worse; the family must seek to discover what makes him misbehave and remedy it. They will in all probability find that they themselves are in some way at fault. Far from punishing Peters, the assembly should try to see what provoked him to violence.

'Sex, of course,' said Feneloni, with a laugh. 'Look no further. It's sex. Why are your sympathies with the murderer, not his victim?'

Guenz responded, eyes twinkling. 'I fear, Jarvis, that sympathy with Peters's victim can do the victim little good.'

'Okay then, try to discover what motives Peters had, other than sexual jealousy. Then we hang him. Both phases of the operation to be done in public.'

Tom said that could not be permitted, else all would be implicated in a second death. Peters must submit to a private course of mentatropy.

Then, said Jarvis, legislation had to be drawn up. Were they to deal with crimes of passion as a special subject, subject to special measures?

Interruptions from the floor continued for many minutes. 'We want no deaths here!' Choihosla shouted.

Someone claimed that freedom could not be legislated for. He was answered by another voice that said that they were not free, were indeed isolated far from their home ground, but had founded a contented society; fulfilment need not depend on freedom at all.

At this, there was uproar. A woman claimed that their 'happy society' was breaking up. It had been at its best one of de Tocqueville's 'voluntary associations', viable only while everyone subscribed.

But like de Tocqueville's, another voice replied, it depended on hierarchy. Perhaps all this time, they'd been living under the wrong hierarchy. Laughter followed this remark, and the temperature cooled.

So soon after the disgrace of Dayo, no one in the court dared suggest there was a racial element in Alysha's murder. Perhaps there wasn't, although such suspicions circulated on the Ambient. But who could prove a negative? Better to sweep the whole notion under the carpet.

Bill Abramson rose to suggest that they had paid too much attention to building a good society and not enough to lobbying Earth to rescue them and restore them to their own planet. What if the subterranean fossil water gave out? It was to their credit that a sort of mediating structure had been established, permitting them to live orderly lives; but perhaps they forgot on what an uncompromising basis that order was built. For himself, with a family at home in Israel, he prayed every night that Earth would send ships.

'Pray there'll be no more murders,' called a voice from the rear.

Paula and I had been listening in silence to all this. She

now rose, and brought the debate back to the subject, saying in a quiet voice, 'You lay no blame on me, the cause of the men's quarrel. But I also must share the guilt. I liked to have the men vying for me with each other. It satisfied my egotism – and other senses as well. I'm greedy for life, as Peters is and Alysha was. But frankly I'd rather be hanged than have some fool shrink prying into my past life. My past is my property as much as my breath.'

Tom asked if Paula was trying to alienate the forum's sympathy. 'You might think differently about hanging if you were actually on trial for such a hideous crime. A course of mentatropy must be Peters's sentence. It can but have a better effect on him than a hanging . . .'

A vote was taken on what Peters's punishment should be. The audience was four to one against his execution.

Jarvis Feneloni bowed to Tom, who declared the court adjourned. Jarvis's manner throughout had been courteous. But I caught a look of hatred as he made his salutation to Tom. He had ambitions for himself as well as for justice, and did not like to be bested in argument.

As usual, the debate was filmed. No one gave a thought to how it would be received on Earth.

14

'Public Hangman Wanted'

Tom was unwell after the Peters debate. He became with-drawn and easily irritated. His answers were brief. I wanted to take him up into the Lushan Mountains in China, to fresh air and solitude. It was the first time I had longed for Earth, with its sensuous landscapes.

When I said this to him, he told me – quite politely – to go away.

I took to painting the mountains in watercolour, to amuse myself as well as Alpha. I talked to her about the mountains, the mists in early morning, and the beautiful clouds, the temples looking out over precipices. All this, as it later transpired, was a mistake; it planted a seed of longing in her mind.

My counterpart in Chengdu sent me a beautiful sexual fantasy, in which a ship somehow enfolded me. We flew through the blue air and I was its engine.

One day we received a message on our Ambient terminal, as did everyone else on Mars. The harsh voice of Jarvis Feneloni spoke:

Friends,

We have amused ourselves too long with the foolish utopian schemes of our elders. By beaming all our debates to Earth, the terrestrials become sedated. They see no reason to hurry and rescue us. Our broadcasts must cease forthwith.

I am not alone in being bored by VR representations of beaches, seas and palm trees. I want the real thing again. I can't live without my home and family.

If we broadcast once more, it should be only to

send strongly worded demands to terrestrial powers to come and get us out of this dump.

Otherwise, I predict mayhem here.

Feneloni

'I must speak to everyone,' Tom said.

'You are not well,' said Guenz. 'If I may, I will address them. I believe I am a fluent speaker.'

He did so. Tom seemed relieved to have the duty taken from him. Guenz said that there were times when everyone was tired of the hardships they endured.

Nevertheless, those hardships were endured communally. It was that which made them bearable, even ennobling.

But the hardships were an essential. There was an old Latin saying he remembered from his university days, *Sine efflictione nulla salus* – 'Without suffering, no salvation.' They were reaching towards salvation, in an unprecedented attempt to build what he might call, to use an old Chinese term 'a spiritual civilisation'.

'All of us are a part of this challenging task. The weaker-minded among us are fortunate in being able to enjoy VR simulations of an easier life, of palm trees and golden beaches. For the rest of us, our unreal reality is enough, and the building of a just society reward enough.

'I will tell you something I believe with all my heart. That when the ships finally return here, and those of us who wish to leave go back to Earth, we shall never forget this momentous time, this brave time, when we struggled with ourselves to create a better way of social existence – and triumphed. And we shall never again find such happiness as we have here, so far from the Sun.'

There was some applause for what many regarded as a final peroration. But, delighted by his success as an orator, Guenz puffed out his cheeks until their capillaries began to resemble an imaginary map of the planet, and started again.

'Some of us don't dream hard enough. Some of us think

they don't need a utopia. But it's inevitable. It has already been born—'

From the front row, Jarvis Feneloni rose to interrupt. 'And is already threatened by that monstrous barnacle—'

From the rear of the hall a violin sounded. Guenz's rhetoric and Feneloni's interruption alike were swept away on a torrent of Baza's music.

Many were the suggestions of how punishment should be meted out, both in the present case of Peters and in any possible future cases. For a while the idea of penitential suits was popular; stocks were suggested, but the humiliation of a wrongdoer, it was decided, only increased his animus against society.

Confinement with civilised treatment won the day, the malefactor to meet with a mentatropist every day, and with a number of ordinary people once a week for conversation, topics to be confined to everyday events and not directed against the prisoner.

Those who protested that such treatment was too lenient and would encourage crime were reminded that the abolition of public hangings had met with similar outcry. The civilised decision that had been reached was one on which all could pride themselves.

After this debate, Bill Abramson circulated a message on the Ambient. He appeared, saying, 'The case of Peters, with his mild punishment, gratifies our liberal instincts but represents a case of cognitive dissonance, the disjunction between reality and one's ideas. Such is usually the case with utopianists.

'Since we are not free of terrestrial vices, we must adhere to terrestrial laws in these matters. Peters committed murder. His pretence of penitence is immaterial. Murderers were traditionally put to death. Peters should be put to death.

'Despite the collapse of financial infrastructures on our home planet, it cannot be long before ships arrive here to return us to our families. Nevertheless, let us suppose we have to remain here for another year. Or even, if we suppose ships set out now, half a year. In that time, I calculate that something like five hundred extra mouths will have to be fed. That is the result of our unchecked population growth, and unchecked promiscuity. But our food output cannot very greatly increase. So at some point in the future we shall face starvation, or else possibly our precious reservoir of water will dry up.

'Those who increase their numbers promiscuously are a threat to our small community. I propose that they also should be punished – if not with death, then with a jail sentence and isolation in prison. To my mind, a prison is more urgently needed than utopia.

'Thank you for listening to me. I require no cheap abuse in return, but will gladly receive constructive suggestions.'

The Adminex made an immediate response. They built a gallows on Bova Boulevard and appended to it a large notice: PUBLIC HANGMAN WANTED.

Downstairs, on Earth, a queue for the job would have formed. But in our small enlightened community, no one wished to be branded a hangman. So Bill Abramson was answered.

A committee of three interviewed the senior mentatropists, the Willa-Vera Composite. The Composite marched into the meeting loaded down with equipment. Mendanadum was in white, White was in lilac. They proceeded to demonstrate how every area of the brain had been precisely mapped, and how mind-body connections had been established over recent decades. In consequence, nanoneuro-surgery was proving its worth.

With the aid of the quantcomp, the mentatropist could despatch 'remotes' to explore the entire structure of the brain and nervous system. Vera spoke enthusiastically of the 'wired neurons' that served this purpose.

'These synthetic neurons send back a receivable signal,

and can be programmed to trigger the release of chemicals that store memory. We guide the wired neurons to reach the appropriate synapse. We don't really expect you to comprehend the science behind our science – which may seem like magic to the uninformed – but Willa and I assure you that our work is a mingling of technical ability and sheer artistry.

'Indeed, we are somewhat taken aback that you find it necessary to question our abilities. You have received our CVs, after all.'

The Composite was engaged for the task of remedying Bevis Paskin Peters.

Nevertheless, the mentatropy of Peters, conducted by the Willa-Vera Composite, was a slow business, continuing over many months.

I was permitted to be present at their first session.

The remotes travelled slowly forward, downward. Neurons glowed and died on the monitor like small security lights as they ventured onward, probing various cytoarchitectonic areas. To the remotes, every neuron marking a local circuit was like a single star, while about them macroscopic systems resembled entire galaxies, dense with suns and dark matter.

Something that resembled light flickered away from their progress.

The remotes journeyed through the hemispheres of the cerebrum, some diverting to the diencephalon, a collection of nuclei below the hemispheres, into the thalamus and hypothalamus. Other remotes entered regions of the limbic system and putamen. Still others toured in the cerebral cortex, the blanketing mantle of the cerebrum, a massive and complex constellation of synaptic activity, by one system of measurement a mere 3 millimetres thick.

It was these latter remotes that detected an area of disturbed neurotransmitters. They moved into the region and began to activate the groupings involved. Here they entered the large-scale quantum coherences that are essential to the generation of consciousness.

On the screens where the neuroscientists, Willa and Vera, watched, pictures and actions became evident. The skill of the women lay in interpreting the pictures as the remotes fired adjacent synapses.

'Slightly viridian,' said Willa.

'Needs fewer fibres,' said Vera. They had their own slang for what they did. 'We're getting coherency.'

Specific tightly interconnected groups of neurons acted coherently as a single unit. The validity of these groupings was sustained by a coherent quantum-mechanical process, like that of a superconductor or superfluid.

With tuning, the fibres sank back to form a huge black anatomy, its head hardly visible. Screaming cream things wavered in the background. A pudding cowered in a puddle.

Home life of Bevis Paskin Peters, aged three. Perception, as someone had said, was all. The sun was square and permeated by fish.

The Composite caught a signal from a remote homing in on the amygdala. They checked its programme. Here, deep in the limbic brain, wavered a primitive recollection. It had remained there, undiminished by time, since electrical resistance diminishes to zero in the HTC structures located there, much like the similar high temperature superconductors in our electrical cables.

Although a good theoretical understanding of ordinary superconductivity had been established halfway through the previous century, a proper understanding of HTCs had to wait until the early years of the twenty-first. This understanding had been put to important use in the new brain sciences. The neuron probe began to participate in the collective quantum state, showing a blur on the mentatropy screen which refined itself into an interpretable picture.

Pressures created an oval viewing like a squeezed lemon. Again a monster male, shouting and raving in deeper than viridian, the waves of anger misshaping it. The monster loomed over a limp white worm. Pale in pink the helpless something fluttered what might have been a hand.

The two separate remote fleets activated their groupings. The effects of quantum entanglement began to manifest themselves. The patient's anciently stored pain became now.

A door of jelly slammed and wiped the oval all away.

'He resents us,' murmured Willa. 'We'll rest him and try again.'

It took expertise, but Willa-Vera interpreted the code to recognise in the white worm the being that would later grow to become the huge black body, the parent.

'Father dominant,' muttered Vera. 'Son wishing to be father?'

I could contain myself no longer but said I hardly understood what was going on.

'Basically, it's fairly simple,' said the fragile Willa Mendanadum, standing on tiptoe in her eagerness to explain. 'Our remotes are travelling in areas where the effects of quantum state-reduction first become important. That's where a quantum superposition actually becomes one of the classical alternatives. In fact, it appears that the entire phenomenon of consciousness is activated only when certain such quantum-coherent states begin to resolve into these classical alternatives.'

'But I don't know what you mean by classical alternatives!' I wailed.

'Oh, that's simple too,' Vera White said, with a knowing smile at her partner. 'Imagine the nebulous borderline between the quantum and classical levels of physical activity, right? This has to do with the measurement problem of quantum mechanics: why is it that when we measure a quantum system we get one answer or another – the classical alternatives – instead of a quantum superposition of alternatives, which are an inherent part of the quantum-mechanical description of nature?'

I shook my head, feeling foolish.

'Well, you see, when an observer steps in, the rules

219

change. The standard quantum-mechanical procedures are interfered with! So what effect does the observer have? Why, quantum state-reduction comes in, and one thing or another happens, as Willa has said.'

She turned to her little partner. 'Ready for another probe? Try coordinates between D60 and – let's open E75.'

They peered into their spec-monitors. Behind them, paralysed but aware, strapped on the couch while the picoprobes toured his brain, lay Peters, screaming without sound.

Mentatropy, which would eventually hunt down his terrors and weaknesses and eradicate them, was not an easy option.

Neuroscience was a subject of popular satire; but, no other workable system of remedy presenting itself, since nobody was prepared to turn themselves into hangman or jailer, the mentatropists continued their work.

So gradually the dispute regarding the treatment of criminals died down, as other matters arose to be considered.

Signals were still being sent to Earth Control, the technical centre, and to the UN, both on roughly Feneloni's suggested lines. The response was evasive. The ramifications of EUPACUS's collapse had bitten deep into the socio-political structure of the planet. Until the recession was over, all matrix operations had been suspended. So we were told.

Now an extra body of advisers congregated about Tom, who continued to be unwell. Supporters included Val Kissorian and Sharon Singh, the woman who had found the rock crystal. I must confess I was jealous of the way in which Tom so clearly doted on her. Sharon was an amiable but shallow personality.

Of the new questions arising, the most pressing concerned the education of children.

Following the murder of Alysha, the Oort Crowd closed

down and the cephalopods disappeared. I ceased to associate with Paula Gallin, who was not much to be seen.

A crowd of us used to go to the Captain Nemo to sit around and talk in the evenings, while sipping coffdrinks.

Generally the talk was about Chimborazo. When I could bear Kathi's silence no longer, I called her on my Ambient.

'So what's new, Kathi? Why don't I hear from you? Are we not friends any more?'

'Friends for ever, Cang Hai – however long that may be,' she said in her best sarcastic tone. 'Just to prove it, I will tell you a secret. Don't go spreading it around, eh?'

'What is it? Are you in love with someone else?'

'Yes, with that great alien intellect on our doorstep, ninny! You know what? We have discovered that it is accelerating towards us!'

'What?' I was shocked.

'It's making much faster progress, babe! It's accelerating at such a rate that it could even collide with the science unit in a year or two . . .'

'Kathi! What does this mean? How awful!'

'And I'm luring it on!' She screamed with laughter and closed down. Her face sank into oblivion.

I managed to keep quiet about Kathi's news, although I wondered if Tom had been told. I sat in the Nemo with Alpha on my knee as if nothing had happened.

One day Belle Rivers appeared, accompanied by Crispin Barcunda, carrying several pages downloaded from her Ambient which she spread before us. Belle was her usual majestic self, rock crystal beads jangling down to the waist of her long dress. Crispin was diminished beside her, lightly though he carried his age. We noticed with what old-fashioned courtesy he behaved towards Belle. He sported a long, floppy white moustache and his eyes at least were full of life as he smiled at the company.

'Crispin and I have become firm friends,' Belle said, cocking her head to one side. 'Between us we encompass

221

much experience of dealing with difficult people. I wish to get away from the concept of good and bad persons, and to speak of difficult people. I know the difficult ones as children, Crispin as adults, when he was Governor of the Seychelles. We have a plan for decreasing the difficulties experienced by difficult people, which we wish to present to you.'

'We have to talk about this plan,' said Crispin. 'Maybe it will never get further than talk, since it requires many years for its fruition and we may not have that long.'

'Well, now, it all sounds very mysterious,' said Tom, in rather grumpy fashion.

'On the contrary, Tom,' said the old man, laughing. 'Like all good radical plans for mankind's happiness, it contains nothing that most sensible people don't already know.'

Belle began to talk. She said that her educational regime was now running smoothly. It included, as yet informally, the education of parents in the pleasure of being parents, of reading to and listening to their progeny. The Becoming Individual classes she had established received a good response from the children. She had been interested to perceive – here she shot a stern glance at Tom – how most children had what she called 'a religious sense of life'.

'No one denies that,' Tom interrupted. 'It's the divine aspect of things, Belle – what you have called the phylogenic aspect of things. Your charges have but recently evolved from the molecular state of being. Of course they are full of wonder. I'm delighted you give it expression.'

She nodded and continued. She loved her children and was concerned that the best possible teaching might not help them prevail in the rough and tumble of terrestrial life (assuming they ever returned to Earth, as she personally did not intend to do). There had been much discussion about punishment for crime; the right conclusion had been reached – that care and consultation were more effective than punishment. She wanted Crispin to talk for a moment about the bad situation on Earth.

222

15

Java Joe's Story

Crispin Barcunda spoke. 'As Governor of the Seychelles, I was plagued by petty crime. Muggings, theft, aggression against tourists, hot-rodding, break-ins and murder, which sprang from these sometimes rather petty incidents. And we had drug barons and their victims. Often the crimes were drug- or alcohol-related.

'In short, the Seychelles was a paradigm in small of the rest of the world. Except it was a tropical paradise . . .

'Only I didn't see it as a paradise, I can tell you. Fast as we locked the little buggers up, others sprang to take their place. Our prisons were pretty savage places, sordid, old-fashioned, with frequent floggings of delinquents for deterrent effect.

'Only we know floggings don't deter. They just keep the middle classes happy. Of the little buggers they make big buggers with a grudge against society. I will tell you how we changed all that.

'It says a great deal for the human race that goodness survives even in the worst places of confinement. Among faces that bear the expressions of rats and snakes, cold, merciless, vindictive, you meet faces that beam decency and kindness.

'Such a good face belonged to a prisoner called Java Joe. Maybe he had another name, but I never heard it. Just an ordinary black man who happened to be released from a jail sentence on the day I made a very popular speech. I had addressed my audience in Victoria town square by our famous clock tower, exhorting *them* to value themselves and turn from crime. I had called them, I blush to say, the noblest creatures of the universe.

223

'As I was resting up from this hypocrisy, this ex-prisoner, Java Joe, was shown into my presence. He was perfectly polite. He even made himself obsequious. Yet he carried himself with pride. He had come, he said, especially from Crome Island to hear me speak. I asked him if prison had reformed him.

'His answer was simple. Delivered without reproach, it was simply, "Hell's for punishment, not reformation, isn't it?"'

Crispin tugged the ends of his moustache in order to contain a smile.

'Java Joe had come to me with a suggestion, he said. He told me he had read a remarkable old book when he was held in solitary confinement in prison. Java Joe emphasised that he was not a fussy man, but the state of what he called "the bogs" in the prison was a disgrace, planned and intended to humiliate all who had to use them. He repeated this latter phrase. This made a passage in this old book he was able to read all the more impressive.

'"What was the book?" I asked him.

'Joe was uncertain whether it was a history or a fiction. Maybe he did not understand the difference between the two types of writing, which is little enough, I grant you. Part of the book concerned the building of an ideal house, called Crome.

'The architect of Crome, Joe told me, was concerned with the proper placing of his privies. By which he meant, in plain English, sir, begging my pardon, the bogs. And here Java Joe began to quote verbatim from the book: "His guiding principle in arranging the sanitation of a house was to secure that the greatest possible distance should separate the privy from the sewage arrangements. Hence it followed inevitably that the privies were to be placed at the top of the house, being connected by vertical shafts with pits or channels in the ground."

'Java Joe eyed me closely to make sure I understood this elaborate language from the ancient book. Seeing I appeared to do so, he continued to quote: "It must not be thought that Sir Ferdinando (the architect, sir, you see) was moved only by material and merely sanitary considerations; for the placing of his privies in an exalted position he had also certain excellent spiritual reasons. For, he argues, the necessities of nature are so base and brutish that in obeying them we are apt to forget that we are the noblest creatures of the universe." '

'"Are you trying to be satirical at my expense?" I roared. But plainly he was not. He explained that to counteract these degrading effects, the author of the strange book advised that the privies in every house should be nearest to heaven, that there should be windows opening on heaven, that the chamber should be comfortable and that there should be a supply of good books and comics on hand to testify to the nobilty of the human soul.

'"Why vex me with this recitation?" I demanded. "Is it not more appropriate that the privies in our prisons should be down in the bowels of the earth?"

'Java Joe explained to me that he had thought much about this wonderful place, Crome, while passing his motions. He saw it all as a metaphor – although he did not know that particular word. From this vision of the good house his suggestion had evolved. Here he paused, searching my face with that good-natured gaze of his. I prompted him to go on.

'"Us shits," he said, "should be kept separate as far as possible from the sewers of your prisons. We've never been far from their stink in all our lives. We should be placed in a good place with a view of heaven. Then we might be able to stop being shits." '

Crispin looked about him to see what effect his story was having before he went on. 'Was there anything in what Java Joe said? Maybe there was more sense than in all the rhetoric of my speech in the town square. I decided to act.

'We had an empty island or two in the Seychelles group. To the north was Booby Island, a pleasant place with a small stream on it. What was to be lost? I had it renamed

225

Crome Island and shipped a hundred of my criminals there, to live in daylight rather than darkness.

'What a howl went up from the respectable middle classes! That men should enjoy themselves in pleasant conditions was no punishment for crime. This experiment would kill the tourist trade. It would cost too much. And so on . . .'

'Let's get to the end of the tale, Crispin,' said Tom, with some impatience. 'Obviously the experiment wasn't a failure, or you would not be telling us about it.'

Crispin nodded cordially, saying merely, 'We can learn from failure as well as success.'

'Come on then, Crispin,' said Sharon. 'Tell us what happened to your criminals. I bet they all swam away to freedom!'

'They were marooned on an island round which fierce currents ran, and could not escape, my dear. They dug themselves latrines, they built a communal cookhouse, they built houses. All using just local materials. They fished and grew maize. They sat about and smoked and talked. They were prisoners – but they were also men. They regained their self-respect. A supply ship protected by armed guards called once a week at Crome Island, but no one escaped.

'And after their sentence was served, very very few reoffended. They had done what I could not manage to do, and reformed themselves.'

'What about Java Joe?' I asked.

Crispin chuckled. 'He went to live voluntarily on the island; the convicts christened him King Crome.'

At this juncture Paula Gallin came and sat down at a nearby table, escorted by Ben Borrow. They were deep in conversation but, after they had ordered two sunglows, began taking an interest in our discussion, which certainly was not private.

'We hope,' said Belle, 'to follow that example Crispin has offered. Earth is a planet full of prisons. It must never happen here. At one time, in a brief period of enlightenment, the British government permitted me to teach reading and writing to prisoners. The majority of people in prison, I found, were young bewildered men. They were ignorant and brutalised, two elements the penal system encouraged. Many had been brought up without a family. They had mostly been "in care". They were truants from school, fly boys. Most of them hid deep misery under a hard shell.

'In a word, the prisons – not only the one in which I worked – were filled by the products of poverty, unemployment, underprivilege and depression. The politicians were locking up the victims of sociopolitical crimes.'

'Excuse me, you surely go too far there,' said Hal Kissorian. 'We are mistaken in expecting politicians to remedy matters that are beyond political scope. That there are the rich and successful and the poor and unsuccessful, and every shade in between, is surely a natural and ineradicable phenomenon.'

I saw he glanced at Sharon for approval of his little speech. She gave him an encouraging wink.

Belle became so stern that her beads shook. 'There is the case of nurture as well as genetic inheritance. Prison and punishment do not reconcile these unfortunate and malevolent youths with society. Quite the reverse. They leave prison only to reoffend more expertly. Of course I am speaking only of the reformable majority. A different case can perhaps be made for the mad and the really dangerous.

'It is when we come to consider the state of affairs beyond the prison walls that we see how unenlightened we have become. Judges are now constrained by their governments to deliver fixed sentences of a number of years for various crimes. Mandatory sentencing deprives the judges of administering justice according to the facts of the case. Thus both sides of the law become machine-like. Quantputers might as well take over, as no doubt they shortly will.

'How did mandatory sentencing become the rule? Firstly,

227

because it speeded up the legal process, much as the banishing of juries has done. Then, later, it simplified the introduction of computerisation, to cut costs.

'All this because of the rise in crime. More and more people become imprisoned, and in consequence more violent and skilled in violence. Of course, the real crimemongers escape the law, as seems to be the case with the swindlers within EUPACUS. Our isolation here lasts so long because, to my mind, the law cannot indict the culprits.

'Most governments attempt to solve the increasing crime rate by building more prisons. They can't adopt Crispin's scheme of marooning them on a desert island to create their own society—'

'As we are marooned here—' Kissorian interjected.

'—so they continue to build prisons whose one objective is to maintain security, not to re-educate or train the inmates in various trades. So I'll come to my point at last.

'All that is being done is worse than useless. Criminals are the activists of unjust societies. Our Dayo's relatively innocent scam with his musical composition was a case in point; he strove merely to become equal, no more than that, in what he feels is a society unjustly prejudiced gainst his kind. Behind every young thug there are several depressed people, usually women, living out their short lives, battered and afraid and probably slow-witted. Undernourished certainly. And certainly harmless, within the meaning of the word. Hopeless, too. The cure for crime is not punishment but its reverse, love, caritas . . .

'We need a revolution that no politician would countenance – fundamental changes in society, with really good education for our children from the earliest age onwards. With a rebuilding of family life and the arts and pleasures of citizenship. Community work was a good start towards a caring society, but it did not go far enough.

'The civilised countries must increase taxes and invest extra revenues in rebuilding slums and lives, and listening to those who have had no say. In a very few years, I guarantee, the exorbitant cost of crime prevention would be diminished. A better and happier and more equable culture would result. And it would be found to be self-sustaining.'

Sharon clapped her pretty hands. 'It's wonderful. I can see it already.'

But Kissorian asked, 'What happens to the abortion issue in this happier world of yours?'

It was Crispin who answered. 'An unwanted child tends to retain his unwanted feeling all his life. Of course, that may turn him into a philosopher. It's more likely he will turn to rape or arson or become the driving force of a security company, wielding a big stick.'

'So you're pro-abortion?'

Belle said quietly, 'For reasons I hope we've made clear, we're pro-life. Which means at this stage of existence that we reserve the right of women to control their own bodies and to abort if they are driven to take such a grave step.'

'Then say it,' interposed Grenz Kanli. 'You're pro-abortion.'

'We're pro-abortion. Yes,' said Belle, adding, 'until both men and women learn to control their sexual urges.'

I saw Sharon returning Kissorian's glance. She gave a sly smile. There, I thought, was another kind of happiness that could not be legislated for. I could not help liking her a little – and envying her at the same time.

Turning from her companion, Ben, Paula at the next table entered the discussion. Belle's remark about people curbing their sexual urges had made her restless.

'Haven't you people forgotten about mothers?' she asked. 'You know, the people who actually bring forth babies from their goddamn wombs into the world? Since it's a result of sexual activity, I suppose you've forgotten about mothers.'

'We've not—' Belle began, but Paula overrode her.

'You don't need all this bureaucracy if you honour mothers as they should be honoured, treat them properly, favour them in society. Start thinking about actual people rather than legislation.'

'We are thinking about people. We're thinking about children,' said Belle, sharply. 'If you have nothing better to contribute to the discussion, I'd advise you to keep silent.'

'Yes, yes, yes . . . If anyone doesn't think your way, they'd better shut up. That's your way of thinking, isn't it?'

'I was thinking,' said Belle, coldly, 'more of your recent abortion. That is a pretty clear indication of your precious regard for motherhood.'

Paula looked absolutely astounded. Belle turned her back on her and asked me, 'How's Alpha getting on, my dear?'

I could not answer. Paula rose and marched out of the café. As she went she clicked her fingers. Ben Borrow stood up, gave us an apologetic glance, and followed Paula.

Only afterwards, when I talked to Kissorian and Sharon about this spat, did I understand the emotions that provoked it. The reason was simple. Belle stepped out of her normal rather magisterial role because she was jealous. Ben Borrow had been her protégé. She was furious to see that he had taken up with Paula. He had said nothing. His mere presence was enough to irritate Belle.

I reflected on my ineptness at reading motives.

After more discussion, and more coffdrink, Belle calmed down enough to return to the conversation.

She said, 'For some centuries, the civilised nations, so-called, have had health-care services. Time and again, those services failed, in the main through underfunding. The essence of our scheme involves continuity – that an underprivileged child should have a helper to whom he can always turn, who indeed meets up with him over a cup of something once a week.'

'We call this the C&S system, and it can run throughout life if necessary,' said Crispin. 'C&S – Care and Share. Always someone there to share problems and talk to.'

Kissorian laughed. 'Isn't that what husbands and wives do, for heaven's sake? Your C&S is a kind of sexless marriage, isn't it?'

'No, it's sexless parenting,' Crispin said sharply.

'I had as difficult a childhood as you can imagine, and I could never have tolerated any stranger's shoulder to cry on.'

'Just stop and think about that, Kissorian,' Belle said. 'Suppose there had been not strangers but a steady friend, always there to turn to . . .'

'I'd have stolen his wallet!'

'But with our C&S system in operation, your childhood would not have been so difficult, and so you would not have felt that compensatory need to steal a wallet. You can't be glad you had such a difficult childhood?'

He smiled, directing half of that gleam towards Sharon. 'Oh yes, I can. Now that it's over. Because it is an integral part of my life, it formed my character, and I learned from it.'

Silence fell while we digested what had been said.

At length Tom spoke. 'You have some concrete proposals, Belle and Crispin. They're certainly sane and benevolent in intention, although how any terrestrial politicians can be strong enough, enlightened enough—'

Belle interrupted. 'We have a singular advantage here, Tom. No politicians!'

'At least, not in the accepted sense,' added Crispin, with a smile.

'We enter this plan into our constitution here, and enact it as far as is possible – in the hope that Earth may take it up later. Example sometimes wins converts.' Belle turned her regard suddenly on me. 'And what does our silent and watchful Miss Cang Hai make of all this?'

I saw in her expression ambition and hostility, which were quickly wiped away by a mask of patience; the confusion of human senses is such I remained unsure whether I had read her correctly, or was projecting my own misgivings.

'It's benevolent but cumbersome to operate,' I told her. 'Who would you find willing to take on these burdens of assisting the young, perhaps often in opposition to the natural parents?'

231

'People are surprisingly willing to assist when they see a worthwhile enterprise. Their lives would also be enriched.' She added firmly, 'For a civilised society, there is no other way.'

I paused, wondering if I cared to contradict this forceful woman. 'There is another way. The way of medicine. Simple supervision of a child's hormone levels – oestrogen, testosterone, serotonin – is better than many a sermon.'

As if the thought had just occurred to her, Sharon said, leaping in, 'And what if all this well-meaning stuff did not work? What if the kids still offended?'

Without hesitation, Belle Rivers said, 'They would be beaten before witnesses. Where kindness fails, punishment must be available.'

Sharon screamed with laughter, displaying the inside of her mouth like a tulip suddenly opening.

'Would that do them good?'

Crispin said, 'At least it relieves the frustrated feelings of the teachers . . .'

'So be it,' Tom said. 'Let's take it to the forum of the people and try to gain support for your plan. We'll see what our friend Feneloni has to say to it.'

All this while, the days and weeks and months of our lives were eroding away. As we entered on the third year of our isolation on Mars, I had to speak to Tom about the news of Olympus's accelerated progress towards the science unit.

'I know,' said Tom. 'Dreiser told me.' He sat there with his head in his hands and said not another word.

16

Life is Like This and This . . .

My head was extremely bad. I did not attend the discussion when Belle Rivers stood beneath the blazing Hindenburg and argued her case for continuous education. As expected, it was opposed by Feneloni. Cang Hai and Guenz and the others reported the essence of the meeting.

After Belle and Crispin had outlined their plan, there was general applause. Several people rose and affirmed that the upbringing and care of children held the secret of a better society. One of the scientists quoted Socrates as saying that only the considered life was really worth living, and that consideration had to be nurtured in the young to sustain them throughout life.

Feneloni thought differently. The whole Rivers scheme was unworkable, in his opinion, and deserved to be unworkable. It was against human experience. It was wet nursing of the worst order. He became vehement. All living things had to find their own way in life. They succeeded or they failed. Rivers's plan, in trying to guarantee there were no failures, guaranteed there would be no successes.

Was she not aware, he asked, of the tragic sense of life? All of the world's great dramas hinged upon error or failure in an otherwise noble or noble-minded person. He cited Sophocles ('already mentioned'), Shakespeare and Ibsen as masters of this art form, which purged us with pity. Tragedy was an integral part of human society, tragedy was necessary, tragedy increased our understanding.

And at this point, someone laughed. It was the murderer, Peters, under mentatropy, who to many remained an outcast.

Others idly joined in the laughter. Feneloni looked confused and sat down, muttering that people who took him for a fool would soon find they were wrong.

It was agreed that the 'Rivers plan' should be implemented, and allowed to run for a test period. The universe was too young for an emphasis to be laid on tragedy.

Volunteers were called for. They would be vetted and asked for their qualifications.

As usual, the proceedings were recorded, and the decisions arrived at entered on our computers.

My state of mind was low. Although we seemed to be making progress, I feared some malignant force from within might burst like a cancer into the open and render our plans and hopes useless. Outside, beyond our spicules, beyond our community of 6,000 biological entities, was the great indifferent matrix, a confusion of particles inimical to humanity.

And there was Olympus, monstrous and enigmatic. It was never far from our thoughts. Like life itself, it seemed imponderable, its laboured progress somehow a paradigm of the approach of illness.

It was in this glum mood I looked in on the C of E, the Committee of Evil, holding its weekly meeting. The rather comical title had been dreamed up by Suung Saybin, but the purpose was serious enough: to try and determine the nature and cause of evil, with a view to its regulation. 'Perhaps the humour lies in the fact that they haven't a hope,' I thought to myself. Maybe the committee was just another way in which people kept themselves amused.

Suung Saybin remained as chair and Elsa Lamont, she of the orthogonal figures and an Adminex official, as secretary. Otherwise, members of the panel changed from month to month. As I entered, John Homer Bateson rose to his feet.

'The previous speaker wastes our time,' he declared. 'We cannot eradicate evil by religion, or even control it, as history shows. All history is a demonstration of the workings of evil. Like Thomas Hardy's Immanent Will, "it weaves unconsciously as heretofore, eternal artistries of circumstance". Nor will reason work. Reason is frequently the ally of wrong-doing.

'Here we are, stuck on this little dried-up orange of a planet, and we plan to banish this monster? Why, we're in its clutches! What are the component parts, the limbs, the testicles, of evil? Greed, ambition, aggression, fear, power . . . All these elements were integral to the very nature of EUPACUS, the conglomerate that dumped us here.

'What impossibly naïve view do you have of the nations that stranded us? The United States is by no means the worst of them. But it seeks to extend its empire into space – apologies, matrix. All the grand designs we may have about exploring this matrix mean nothing to the absconding financiers who backed matrix exploration. All this talk of utopia – it means nothing, absolutely nothing, to the greedy men in power. Power, money, greed – if you kicked out the present set of slimebags, why, more slimebags would fill the breach.

'I'll tell you a story. It's really a parable, but you'd distrust that term.'

'You have five minutes, John,' interposed Suung Saybin.

Ignoring her, Bateson continued, 'A man was stranded alone on a planet that was otherwise uninhabited. He lived the blameless life of a hermit, befriending bats, rats, slugs, spiders – anything that amused him. That way, you attain sainthood, don't you? One day, a vessel came down from space – pardon me, from the matrix – to rescue him. A grand sparkling ship, from which emerged a man in a golden space suit with long wavy blond hair and a manly tan, bearing a large picnic hamper.

'"I'm your saviour," he exclaimed, embracing the hermit.

235

'The hermit got a good grip on the man's throat and strangled him. Now he owned the spaceship. And the picnic basket.

'What, I ask you, were his motives? Hatred of intrusion on his privacy, hunger, envy of the golden suit, aversion to this intruder's display of hubris, greed to possess the ship, ambition to enjoy power himself? Or all these things? Or had solitude driven him mad?

'You cannot resolve these questions – and I have offered you a simple textbook case. The promptings to evil are in all of us. Evil is not a single entity, but a many-splendoured thing. You're wasting your time here if you think otherwise.'

I crept from the room.

Being unable to take lunch, I went to a remote upper gallery in search of solitude. Fond though I was of Cang Hai, I hoped to avoid her endless chatter. But there I happened upon my adopted daughter, sitting with her child playing at her feet. Alpha ran to me. I hugged her and kissed her cheeks. Cang Hai, meanwhile, picked up her sheets and assumed a pose whereby I was to take it she had been studying them.

'I'm surprised to see you up here, Tom. How are you?'

'Fine. And you?'

'Trying to learn some science. I'm trying to understand about superfluids. Apparently they are called Bose-Einstein condensates.'

Alpha said, 'Mummy looks out the window.'

'Yes. I believe that's what Dreiser's ring contains.'

'I said, Mummy looks out of the window most of the time!' screamed Alpha.

'You can certainly learn science there,' I said. Under the endless panoply of stars, dark matter and particles, the Martian landscape rolled its dunescape away into the distance, unvarious, unchanging, and baked or frozen by turns. The thought came, What harm in trying to turn it into a garden?

'Is something troubling you?' I asked.

'No.' Then, 'I try to study here, alone with Alpha. I'm glad, always glad, to see you.' Then, 'Those lustful hounds I had to work with in Manchuria ... No ... Only the ambiguities of this research.' She tapped her 3D sheets. 'Even light behaving like both waves and particles. It's hard to grasp!'

'We're subject to the dissolution of absolutes. Our life here is a bit ambiguous ... Perhaps that's why we question everything. But that's not what's wrong?'

After a pause, during which she took her child on to her knee: 'I told you about Jon Thorgeson. He stays in my mind, making me unhappy. Or my behaviour does.'

'He was impertinent.'

'I don't mean that. I mean ... he wanted me. He was not unpleasant, physically. Why didn't I – you know, let him get on with it? Why does that sort of thing not attract me? Is it that I'm ... ? Well, I don't know. It's absurd to be a puzzle to yourself, isn't it?'

'Mumma, let's play, please, please, Mumma,' said the child, looking into Cang Hai's face.

Whatever her failings, Cang Hai, a cloned person, possessed plenty of maternal instinct. As mother and daughter cosseted each other, I continued to gaze out at the world we had inherited – we, who must find a reason for this Martian testing ground, we, the creatures who had only recently learned to walk upright, who had harnessed fire not much more than a million years ago, who had emerged from various forgotten creatures – and who must be the forerunners of myriads more various peoples – oh yes, it was apparent why sex so dominated our thoughts ... But there my reverie was broken by the child's laughter.

I thought, as I turned back to this nervous, perceptive little person I loved – ah, but not one quarter as much as I had loved my Antonia! – how the Martian landscape was to me, as Charles Darwin had the phrase in one of his letters, not a landscape but 'a most strange assemblage of ideas'.

237

I said, 'It doesn't have to be either/or, daughter. We have moved into a mode of both/and understanding.'

'I mean,' she said boldly, 'am I a saint, a prude, or a lesbian?'

'Don't force a decision. You are young. Be clear that you consist of your confused self. But in the case of that impositioning Thorgeson, you evaded a case of rape as any woman might have done, had she a cool enough head.'

'And a warm enough hand!' Suddenly, she laughed, and squeezed Alpha. 'Had I not done so, I would be pregnant now. But no man is going to terraform me until I say so.'

Why did her words make me happy? Were they designed to do so? Weren't the human mind and human courage great things? I kissed her and her daughter.

That afternoon we underwent one of our periodic discussions regarding money. Certainly one element distinguishing the texture of Martian life from life Downstairs was that we carried no credit cards. Some people wanted to bring the credit system back, saying it made them feel more like functioning humans. Against that, our economists on Adminex argued that where there was no ownership of property it was impossible to fix prices.

We had an electronic points system up and running. It worked through the Ambient. The unit was called a credit. To launch the system, our 'bank' – once a cash till in the Marvelos offices – allocated everyone a hypothetical 1,000 credits, somewhat like the dummy money we were given at the start of a game of Monopoly. These credits could be drawn on at any time.

On the whole, prices of what few things there were to acquire for personal use remained trifling. A cup of coffdrink, for instance, was two credits, moonglow and sunglow were three. In practice it made the system hardly worth bothering with. So the money element withered away. We found we could get along happily without it.

No one drew wages or paid taxes.

A reckoning will come when – if ever! – the rockets

return from Downstairs. But, after all, we own the planet, thanks to the UN constitution, and so can sort the matter out without too much friction.

One evening, Cang Hai was on her way to see a dupe friend of hers living above the We Mend Everything post, in the recesses of the old cadre building. The lane was deserted. Of a sudden, a door ahead of her was flung open and three masked men rushed out. Cang Hai had barely turned to run before they slammed into her, seized her and dragged her into a bare room, a store of some kind.

She heard the door being locked as they tied her to a chair. A bright light was shone into her eyes. She could scarcely make out the outline of her attackers for its dazzle.

She heard their breathing and was afraid.

'Right, girl, don't be frightened. We only want to talk to you,' said a voice that Cang Hai recognised as Feneloni's. 'We are not planning to do anything unpleasant, as we could easily do, such as raping you or pulling off that artificial leg of yours.' Someone behind the light chuckled.

'The time to talk was during the forum,' she said, but could hardly bring the words out from her trembling lips.

'Now then, just you listen to us. We've had enough yacking from your lot. You and your pal Jefferies. This shit about the Rivers plan and utopia has got to stop. It's nothing but a time-waster. How are you going to improve people – people stuck on Mars? It's crap! We're going to die here if we just sit around yakking.'

'Let me have a go at her. She's a tasty little dish,' said one of the hidden men.

'In a minute,' said Feneloni. 'She's a wimp, doesn't much like sex. Maybe you could teach her.' They laughed. She begged them not to touch her. Feneloni replied, 'Look, we're trying to scare some sense into you. Get real! Stop all this pissing about. Stop beaming these stupid sessions of yours back to Earth, as if everything here was okay. It's not okay. My brother's ship was lost, worse luck, or he'd have done something about us being stuck here.

'We need to get back to real life. We should be staging scenes of riot, carnage, starvation. We have to force the hand of the UN. Get a ship up here, get us out of this mess. You understand that?'

'Yes,' she said. 'Yes, of course. But—'

'So you go back to Jefferies and tell him to keep his namby-pamby mouth shut from now on, or you're going to suffer damage, you and your kid. You understand?'

'Let's have a little fun with her,' said one of the men. 'So she takes us seriously . . .'

'Don't think about it,' Feneloni ordered.

The door burst open. Two security guards ran in, armed with torches and truncheons. The store had been designed as a dry goods warehouse and was covered by functioning security cameras, a factor Feneloni had disregarded. Directly he saw the men he shouted to the others to follow and rushed the intruders. The guards kicked his legs from under him and pinned him to the floor as he fell. The other two men burst out of the door and ran for it down the passageway.

Once Feneloni was tied up, the security men went over to Cang Hai and released her from the chair. She collapsed with shock. They phoned me. I arrived and helped her back to our quarters. After a shower she fell asleep, to wake in the morning recovered, at least in part.

Now the question arose of what to do with Feneloni. I went to see him. He was being held in his quarters on Tharsis Street, and looked as sullen as one might expect.

I asked him what he had to say for himself.

'You're the talker.'

I stood looking at him, saying nothing, trying to master my anger.

Finally he burst out in a torrent of words, saying that he had intended no harm, but could not get a proper hearing for his view, which everyone shared, that everyone hated my guts, that he was only acting on behalf of all, who wished to get back to normal life on Earth and not waste their time on 'this miserable stone'. All he wanted was a decent life again . . .

'So is your idea of a decent life to capture and threaten an innocent woman – to threaten to rape her and tear off her leg? You're a coward and a brute, Feneloni, no less a coward and a brute because you do this on Mars rather than Earth. Isn't it to guard against your kind that we try to set up decent rules to live by under our difficult conditions?'

'Look, we were only scaring the girl.'

'And were you in control of the situation? Violence of any kind releases baser instincts. Right now I'd like to beat your brains out, but we've tried to set up laws against that kind of thing. What the hell are we going to do about you? A course of mentatropy?'

He hunched his shoulders and hung his head.

I waited. 'Well?'

After a long silence, he said, 'Not mentatropy . . . I'm not the brute you take me for. There's plenty worse than me. I don't have your powers of speech. That doesn't mean I don't suffer. Why should we be ruled over by those with better powers of speech?'

I had no wish to talk with him, but forced myself to answer.

'In every society so far there have been top dogs and underdogs. The question is how we here can make the gulf between them as narrow and as flexible as possible. Would you rather be ruled by those who have – as you put it – "better powers of speech", or those who have the greater brute strength?'

He stared at the ground. After a pause he said, in a low voice, 'It's a stupid question. All men are supposed to be equal, but if they aren't heard then they aren't equal.'

'You were heard and dismissed. I could give you an example of a man with great powers of speech – the academic called John Homer Bateson, who is laughed off whenever he addresses the audience. We know that all men are not equal, although it befits a government of any kind to attempt to behave as if they were.'

'But you're trying to establish your little government here, instead of busting a bracket to get us back to Earth.'

'Don't be ridiculous, man. What leverage have we with Earth in its present state? Nothing's going to get us home until the repercussions of the EUPACUS disaster clear up. Meanwhile we must do our best to live like humans.'

The alternatives were clear enough to me. Not to Feneloni. He said that all our committees and forums were a waste of time.

'I'm not entering into a debate with you, Feneloni. Not only am I determined to establish a fair society, but I expect the intellectual exercise involved to protect us from violence and unrest.

'Any scum determined to promote violence and unrest must be isolated, as if they had an infectious disease.'

'No such thing as justice,' he muttered, and hung his head again.

I waited. I was curious about the way his mind worked; I knew there was good in him.

After a silence, he said, 'It's all right for you. Some of us have families back on Earth. Kids.'

I gave him no reply, only wishing I could claim as much.

Feneloni looked up angrily. 'Why don't you speak, since you're so good at it?'

'You cannot be allowed to attack a young woman and go unpunished. Tomorrow we will hold a court to decide what that punishment should be. Probably a course of mentatropy. You will be allowed to speak in your defence.'

Turning on my heel, I left him. Afterwards I wished I had said that to be eloquent was not necessarily a virtue; but it implied orderly thought and, perhaps more than that, wide experience and knowledge. But such, of course, was the reward of privilege, if only genetic privilege. My own troubled boyhood came back to me.

We made no attempt to track down Feneloni's associates, hoping that without a leader they would not reoffend.

So it proved. Nevertheless we knew they were there, ready for violence should the opportunity arise.

Cang Hai was nervous after her experience.

'Tom, this is the second time I've been threatened with rape! What is it about me . . . ?'

We talked it over and over. Ben Borrow came and let her talk it out of her system, as far as that was possible.

One evening, she said to me, 'We know there are such men on Earth. Why should we be surprised to find them here, except that you and I are such innocents?'

It surprised me that she should think me an innocent, but I made no comment on that. 'They will submit to the rules of society as long as it suits them.'

'I don't know. Perhaps there's an undercurrent of violence here we are blind to. Just as you and I are blind to the great amount of busy sexual activity going on. How is it that we enjoy debate more than sexual intercourse? Are we exceptions to the rule?'

I was stung by what she had said; I had assumed that my sexually active life had faded away during my period of mourning for my dead wife. As for Cang Hai, she clearly needed indoctrination into the pleasures of sex. That night, when the domes lay under their usual suspirations that passed for silence, and Laputa and Swift slid across the sky outside, I undressed and went to Cang Hai's bed.

She sat up angrily. She told me she did not wish me to try and prove anything. That was not love.

'Don't be silly. Let me in! We may as well have some pleasure.'

'Go away! I'm having a period. You're too old. I'm not prepared for anything like this. Why didn't you warn me? You're taking advantage of me.' She kicked out at my legs.

Having been sent away, I lay in the dark in my own bed,

wakeful, listening to the great machine that gave us life, breathing, breathing.

What had her real motives been, what mine?

How badly the human race needed a period of quiet, for reflection, and to become acquainted with its deepest motives . . .

After only brief discussion, we decided that Feneloni should be confined to the store room to which he had taken Cang Hai. The door should be strengthened. He should speak to no one, although he would be permitted the statutory one conversation with visitors. He should have three meals a day. A television monitor would be permitted, on which he could follow the events of the day in the domes. He should be incarcerated for two weeks, and then questioned again, to be set free if he had come to any better conclusion about himself.

If not, then mentatropy was to be applied.

In order to hasten Cang Hai's return to her normal state of equilibrium, and to allow me some relief from the burdens of organisation, which seemed to be exacting a toll on my health, the two of us sat in on some of Alpha's nursery classes.

Their Social Skills class began with a song:

> Folk of many creeds and nations
> Travelled in realms of thought,
> Made their computations,
> Forged from steel and flame
> Ships of no earthly sort –
> > Leaving earthly port –
> So strangers to Red Planet came.

The song ran though several verses. The children sang lustily, with enjoyment. It was noticeable that the girls concentrated on the music. Some of the boys were secretly prodding each other and making faces.

Afterwards I asked Alpha what she thought of the song, which sounded rather laboured to my ears.

'We like it,' Alpha said. 'It's a good song, about us.'

'What do you like about it?'

'"Ships of no earthly sort" – that's really hot. What does it mean, do you suppose?'

The teacher, the sculptor Benazir Bahudur, kept the two sexes in the same classroom but segregated. 'It's a difference in the genes,' she explained. 'The boys have more difficulty in learning social skills, as you know. The girls are more intuitive. We think the boys need the girls in the room, to be given a glimpse of an alternative way of behaving. You will see the difference when we get to the games. But first we have a Natural History Slot. Are you ready, kids?'

Benazir was a slightly built woman. Her leisurely movements suggested a certain weariness, but when the full regard of her deep-set eyes was turned on you, an impression of drive and energy was received.

A screen lit on the wall. Insect noises could be heard. A brilliant landscape was revealed, the landscape of East Africa. The viewpoint moved rapidly towards a fine stand of trees.

'They're acacia trees,' said Benazir.

Young saplings grew here, as well as mature trees with their corded bark. Benazir gave the children an explanation of what trees were and how they had developed. As she was explaining how grazing animals threatened the very existence of trees of all kinds, the viewpoint snuggled into the shade of a particular tree as if it would nest there. The children were silent, wondering.

A branch served as a highway for ants. The creatures were busy patrolling the whole tree. The camera followed them down to the ground and up to the fragrant blossoms of the acacia.

'I'm glad we don't have those little things up here, miss,' said one of the girls.

'Ants are clever little creatures,' Benazir replied. 'They

have good social organisation. They guard the acacias from enemies – from herbivores and other insects. In return, the trees give them shelter. You wouldn't want to climb that tree, would you? Why is that?'

'Because you'd get stung/attacked/bitten/eaten alive,' came gleeful answers from various parts of the room.

A thoughtful-looking boy asked, 'What about the tree having sex? How can bees get to the flowers if they are attacked by these creepy little things?'

Benazir explained that the young acacia flowers, which smell very sweet, put out a chemical signal to keep the soldier ants away, so allowing the bees to pollinate them.

'What do the flowers smell like, exactly?' the boy asked.

Cang Hai and I debated privately if such glimpses of life on Earth would not start the children wondering about what they were missing. When we put this point to Benazir, she said that her charges had to be prepared for their return to Earth. She fed them with these shots of knowledge before they went out to play.

The children's games had been cleverly adapted to encourage the boys without discouraging the girls. Skipping and counting games were played 'outside', on the Astroturf. The differences between the temperaments of boys and girls became clear when Alpha volunteered to tell everyone a story.

Her story was about a little mummy animal (evidently a mole), who lived with her tiny family under the Astroturf. She told her children to behave and, if they were good, they would get extra cups of tealem, their favourite drink. They all went to bed in little plastic beakers and slept well till morning. The End.

Scornfully, a boy called Morry took up Alpha's tale. The mummy animal was going off to get some groceries. She popped her head up above the ground just as the machine that trimmed the Astroturf was whizzing along. Zummmm! It cut off her head, which went flying with a trail of blood like a comet into someone's shoe!

'Oh no, it didn't at all!' shrieked Alpha angrily.

'Well, let's see how likely these events really are,' said Benazir, smiling at both sides.

'Her head did not come off,' said Alpha firmly. 'More likely it was Morry's head.'

Unable to sustain verbal argument, Morry stuck his tongue out at her.

Benazir said nothing more, but began to dance in front of her pupils. Her steps were slow, teasingly cautious, her hand gestures elaborate, as if they said, 'Look, dear children, life is like this and this, and so much to be enjoyed that no quarrels are required . . .'

As Cang Hai and I walked back to our apartment, we discussed what kind of future citizens of utopia these children would make. We decided that the anti-social phase the children were going through would not be sustained; and we hoped the element of fantasy and imagination would remain. We realised how important were the skills of mothers, fathers and teachers.

Back in our apartment, I was forced to lie down. I slept for a while.

17

The Birth Room

Despite recurring dizzy spells – and advice from Cang Hai and Guenz and others to consult a doctor – I continued to work steadily with the team to finalise our utopian plans.

Guenz protested that it was useless work if Olympus could rouse up and destroy our little settlement at any time. Mary Fangold replied that it was not reasonable to sit about waiting for a disaster that might never happen. She used a phrase we had heard several times before – almost the motto of the Mars colony – 'You gotta keep on keeping on'.

Dreiser Hawkwood and Charles Bondi set up a secure Ambient group with Kathi Skadmorr, Youssef Choihosla and me. We discussed, at Dreiser's direction, the question of whether Earth should be informed of Olympus's movements.

We studied the latest comsat photographs. 'As you can see,' Dreiser said, 'its rate of progress is increasing, even though it is crossing rough territory.'

'It has withdrawn its exteroceptors from around this unit,' Kathi remarked. 'One deduction is that it requires them elsewhere to act as under-regolith paddles. Hence the abrupt acceleration.'

Bondi was busy measuring. 'Using the churned regolith as the base line, Chimborazo has covered ninety-five or ninety-six metres in the last Earth year. This is an extraordinary rate of acceleration. If it could maintain this acceleration rate – pretty ridiculous, in my opinion – its prow would strike the unit – let's see, well, hmm, it still has nearly three hundred kilometres to go, so . . . well, we would have plenty of time – four years at the very least, even on that reckoning.'

'Four years!' I echoed.

Interrupting, Choihosla asked if Chimborazo left excreta behind on its trail.

'Don't be silly,' Kathi exclaimed. 'It is a self-contained unit, can't waste anything. It'll have excreta-eaters in under that shell.'

'The point of my question is – do we inform Downstairs or not? I'd like your answer, Tom,' said Dreiser. 'This doesn't have to go to Adminex. We five must say yea or nay.'

'They probably have the Darwin fixed on Mars,' I said. 'So they'll see this thing's hoof marks.'

'Maybe they have not maintained their telescope since the breakdown,' Dreiser said. 'Or, if they have, they may not be too quick to evaluate the implications of the tumbled regolith. What I mean to say is, they may just reckon we triggered a landslide of some magnitude.'

'We should inform Downstairs that "the volcano" has shifted,' said Kathi. 'No other comment. We certainly don't inform them that we think Chimborazo has life, never mind intelligence. Otherwise they'd probably nuke the place – xenophobia being what it is.'

So that was agreed on, after more discussion.

Bondi said, wryly, 'You can't predict what they'll do down there. They may simply conclude we've gone mad.'

'They probably think that already,' I said.

A thousand questions poured through my mind that night, sometimes merging with phantasmagoric strands of dream. My mind was like a rat in a maze, being both rat and maze.

At the 'X' hour of night, I climbed from my bed and walked about the limited confines of my room. The question arose in my consciousness: Why was it that, in all the infinitude of matrix, mankind built itself these tiny hutches in which to exist?

I longed to talk with someone. I longed to have Antonia again by my side, to enjoy her company and her counsel. As tears began to roll down my cheeks – I could not check them, though she had been gone now for three years – my Ambient sounded its soft horn.

The face of Kathi Skadmorr floated in the globe.

'I knew you were awake, Tom. I had to speak to you. The universe is cold tonight.'

'One can be lonely, locked in a crowd.' It was as if we exchanged passwords.

'However we may aspire to loneliness, we can't be as lonely as . . . you know, that pet of ours out there. Its very being preys on my mind. It's a case for weeping.'

Guiltily, I wiped away my tears. 'Kathi, it's an immense vegetable thing. Despite its CPS, we don't know that it has anything paralleling our form of intelligence. How do we know it didn't grow silently in vegetable state – a sort of fungus, well nigh immune to external influence.'

She was silent, sitting with downcast eyes. 'You appreciate the curious parallel between it and us. We live as it does, under a dome . . .' Seeing she was thinking something out, I said nothing. I liked her face and her sensibility in my globe. For once, she was not being prickly; that too I liked. We certainly were parked in a lonely part of the universe.

Looking up smartly, she said, 'Tom, I admire you and your gallant attempt to make us all better people. Of course it won't work. I am an example of why it won't work – I was born with an obstinate temper.'

'No, no. Something may have made you obstinate. You're . . . you're just the sort of person we need in utopia. Someone who can think and . . . feel . . .'

As if I had not spoken, she said – she was looking into a dark corner of her room – 'Oh, Chimborazo is conscious right enough. I feel it. I felt it when we were there, right by it. I feel it now.'

'We got a CPS, certainly. But . . . I fear that if there is a

250

mentality at work under its shell, then human understanding has to change. It must change.' I stared down at the digits on my watch, ever flickering the seconds of life away. 'If there is life on Earth's neighbour, then the universe must be a great hive of wildly diverse life. As if intelligence was the natural aim and purpose of the universe.'

'Yes, if consciousness is not simply a local anomaly. But that is too anthropocentric, isn't it? I came on such ideas too recently to know. Me with my Abo background.' Some of her old scorn sounded in her voice. And then, as if in contradiction, her thought took off. She said about this thing on our doorstep that perhaps in its solitude, in its stony centuries of meditation under its camouflaging shell, it had come to comprehend universals that had never even impinged on human skulls. The human race had always been driven by a few imperatives – hunger, sex, power – and lived by diversity; maybe – just maybe – the unity of this huge thing was proof of a vastly greater strength of understanding . . .'

She sighed. 'Beau's here with me, Tom. He's sleeping. He does not feel Chimborazo's presence as I do. Oh, we're so limited . . . Maybe its unity is proof of a greater understanding. Something gained through the chilly expanses of time – what we comprehend as time, anyway – until it has reached perfect knowledge and wisdom. Does that sound like wishful thinking?' She laughed at herself.

'Suppose it was like that, Kathi. Would we be able to converse with it? Communicate? Or would its understandings put it for ever beyond our conceptual reach? "What we comprehend as time" – there's an example . . . So it's to us a kind of god – totally without interest in anything outside itself.'

'I wouldn't be too sure of that . . .'

She put her hands to her cheeks in a gesture I had seen her use before. 'It's that time of night when imaginations run away with themselves. Could be it's just a freak mollusc, stranded on a failed planet that long since yielded up its

251

essence . . . Tom, go to sleep! I wish I were there to talk to you, closely . . .'

Her face faded and was gone.

I could not sleep. The conversation lingered in my mind. My head ached; I felt stifled.

I staggered out of my chamber in search of company, and barged without knocking into Choihosla's apartment.

Youssef Choihosla was kneeling on a small mat, his forehead to the floor. A dim lamp stood nearby.

I halted in the doorway. Choihosla looked up with a brow of thunder. He began a stream of abuse, biting it off when he recognised me.

'Tom? You look ghastly! Come in, come in. What's up? It's "X" hour.'

He rose as I entered. I said, 'You were in the midst of prayer. I'm sorry to break in.'

'Allah is great. He will forgive an interruption. Come and sit down.'

I sat weakly and he brought his great bulk close and also sat, hands on knees. I spoke of my confusion of mind, brought about by the thought of the unknown life form not far away from us. He confessed that his prayer – 'largely wordless' – had been seeking reassurance for the same reason.

We talked for a long while, merely speculating.

My curiosity got the better of me. I saw an electronic gadget with a small screen, at present blank, lying on the floor by Choihosla's prayer mat, and asked him what it was.

He hesitated, then picked it up and presented it to me for my inspection.

Pressing a button, I set golden bodies in motion on the screen, while figures jerked across the lower section of it.

This was a Muslim ephemeris. It calculated the positions, not only of the Sun, the Moon, Earth and Mars, but also of Mecca, throughout the year. It enabled Choihosla to pray towards the holy city when the revolutions of Earth

252

brought Mecca to a point facing towards Amazonis, where our structures were situated. Choihosla explained that it was considered poor theology to pray when Mecca was on the other side of Earth's globe, facing away from Mars.

'Well, it's ingenious,' I remarked. He hefted the little calculator in the palm of his hand. 'You buy these ephemerises for a few cents in the bazaars,' he said, offhandedly. 'Of course, it's a Western invention . . .'

Seeing the puzzlement in my eyes, he said, 'You wonder about my faith – maybe how I persist in it? Don't you need something bigger than yourself in life?'

I pointed in what I imagined to be the direction of Olympus Mons.

'It's out there,' I said.

Monstrous things apart, we came to realise nothing could be achieved without decent living conditions. The thinness of the atmosphere of Mars rendered us susceptible to meteoritic bombardment, as we had been well aware. We now set about extending our quarters by excavation, creating a new subterranean level where the apartments had rooms larger than those in our previous quarters. These apartments had balconies and galleries; the bricks we fabricated were glazed in various colours, while genetically altered plants – in particular creepers – were planted and flourished under artificial light. Rooms were decorated in various bright colours and afforded better opportunities for solitude.

I found a glowing message waiting on my Ambient. When I punched Receive, Charles Bondi's voice came to me, full of controlled anger: 'Jefferies, what are you people doing over there? Why do you think our research unit was positioned on Mars? It was because we required complete silence and no vibrations, wasn't it? Our foundation represents the whole reason for habitation on this planet. Your drillings are threatening our search for the Omega Smudge. We're getting strange readings. I have to tell you that all drillings and excavations must cease at once. Immediately. Please acknowledge that this has been done.'

I froze his face. Studying it, I did not see the aggression implied by his words.

My reply was brief. 'Charles, I am sorry we upset your solitude. But so far your researches have produced nothing. Meanwhile we have to live. This is why our spicules were sited at a distance from your foundation. We shall be finished within a few days. I have no intention of failing to complete what will be new much required living quarters, and I invite you to inspect them when you have recovered from your annoyance.'

He sent a one-word reply, 'Luddite!' Then we heard no more of the matter. While marvelling at scientific arrogance, I saw its necessity and urged the workers to press on as speedily as possible, to get the vibration over and done with.

As the plans for our utopia came nearer to realisation, so discussions on the employment and containment of power became more urgent. In what sort of context would an autocratic temperament like Bondi's be content? How could the admirable restlessness of enquiry be satisfied by a utopian calm? How could our utopia maintain both stability and change? These were some of the questions that confronted us.

We debated the nature of power and the striving for power. Eventually it was Choihosla who suggested that we should question our concept of power itself.

He began by asking us a riddle. Who is it who holds most power of life and death over another?

Answers from the floor included an executioner, an army sergeant in the heat of battle, a murderer, the chief of a savage tribe, the launcher of nuclear missiles, and (mischievously) a scientist.

Choihosla shook his head. 'The answer is – a mother over her newborn child. Bear that in mind while I speak to you.'

254

He said he realised his proposals would be anathema to all whose brains had been, as he put it, 'dissolved by the Western way of life'. But a little thought was needed on the matter and that thought must be directed to overturning accepted ideas of power as an opportunity for gain.

The various presidents, monarchs and dictators who wielded power Downstairs were not to be emulated Upstairs. All of them sought to accumulate wealth for themselves. The citizens under them also sought to accumulate wealth for themselves. We, fortunately, had no wealth. Nevertheless we would need a leader, a man or a woman, to whom all questions of justice could eventually be referred. He suggested this person should assume the title of Prime Architect. The title was neutral as regards gender, and it correctly implied that something constructive was going on.

But the conception of power as a force that enabled an individual to gain more than was his or her due had to be discarded. Power had to derive from the determination to achieve and maintain a well-organised society. Since this determination would be reinforced by the hope – however illusory – of achieving the perfectability of humanity, it would follow that the powerless would not be harmed by power, any more than a child is harmed by the mother's power over him. Indeed, the linkages of power, from officials to parents, to children, to pets, would share by example the unifying hope of a general well-being. Both child and mother benefit by the maternal wielding of power.

At this point, Cang Hai said, 'You are trying to bring back Confucianism!'

'Not so,' replied Choihosla. 'Confucianism was too rigid and limited, although it contained many enlightened ideas. But these days we hear much about "human rights" and too little about human responsibilities. In our utopia, responsibility carries with it satisfaction and a better chance for benevolence.'

'So what is your revised nature of power to be?' someone asked.

'No, no.' He shook his heavy head, as if regretting he had spoken in the first place. 'How can I say? I don't seek to change the nature of power – that's ridiculous. Only our attitude to power. Power in itself is a neutral thing; it's the use of it that must be changed from malevolent to benevolent. By thought, by empathy. I am sure it can be done. Then power will provide a chance to increase everyone's well-being. Given a society already positive in aspect, that will be the greatest satisfaction. Both Prime Architect and citizen will benefit by what I might call a maternal wielding of power.'

He was a big clumsy man. He looked oddly humble as he finished speaking and folded his massive arms across his chest.

After a meditative silence all round, Crispin said, quietly, 'You are wanting human nature to change.'

'But not all human nature,' Choihosla replied. 'Some of us already hold the concept of power-as-greed in contempt. And I think you are one of them, Mr Barcunda!'

While the excavations for our extension were in progress, I was busier than ever. Fortunately, our secretary, the silent Elsa Lamont, arranged my appointments and saw that I kept them. She and Suung Saybin dealt personally with all those applying for rooms in the new building.

Unexpectedly, one evening, working late at night when we should both of us have been relaxing, Elsa turned to me and said, 'In my love affairs, I have always been the one who was loved.'

I was startled, since I had not associated the rather drab-looking Elsa with affairs of the heart or the body. For me, she was just an ex-commercial artist with a head for figures.

'Why are the figures I paint faceless? Tom, I realise I am not capable of deep love. It's unfair to my partners, isn't it?'

Since my eyebrows were already raised, I could only think to ask, 'What has prompted this reflection, Elsa?'

She had been thinking about Choihosla's redefinition of power. Mothers loved deeply, yes, she said. But perhaps for those who were unable to love deeply, power was the next best thing. Perhaps power was a kind of corruption of the reproductive process.

'I can see that the need to be free to reproduce can lead to all kinds of power struggle . . .' I began.

Elsa repeated the words slowly, as if they were a mantra, '"I can see that the need to be free to reproduce can lead to all kinds of power struggle . . ." That's true throughout nature, isn't it? We have to hope that we can unite to prove Choihosla's statement holds some truth.' Then without pause, she added, 'A delegation of women has booked a forum in Hindenburg Hall tomorrow, 10 p.m. They wish to talk about better ways – more congenial ways, I suppose – of giving birth. Can you be there?'

'Um . . . you're not trying to tell me you're pregnant, are you, Elsa?'

Perhaps a pallid smile crossed her face. 'Certainly not,' she said. 'If only I were pregnant with the truth . . .'

She turned back to her work. And then said, 'Could be I prefer detachment, rather than letting go and returning the love of my lovers. Does that give me more power?'

It sounded like a weakness to me, but I cautiously treated her question as rhetorical.

Prompt at ten next morning, a delegation of women met under the giant Hindenburg mural.

The Greek woman, Helen Panorios, spoke on behalf of the group. She placed her hands on her hips and stood without gesture as she spoke.

'We make a demand that may at first seem strange to most of you. Please hear us out. We women require a special apartment in the new extension. It need not be too large, as long as it is properly equipped. We wish to call it the Birth Room, and for no men ever to be allowed inside it. It will be sacred to the processes of birth.'

She was interrupted by Mary Fangold, the hospital personnel manager. 'Excuse me. Of course I have heard this notion circulating. It is a ridiculous duplication of work that our hospital's maternity branch already carries out effectively. We have a splendid record of natal care. Mothers are up and out a day after parturition, without complications. I oppose this so-called "Birth Room" on the grounds that it is unreasonable and a slur against the reputation of our hospital.'

Helen Panorios barely moved a muscle.

'It is your cooperation, not your opposition we hope for, Mary. You condemn your system by your own words. You see, the hospital still carries out production-line methods – mothers in one day, out the next. Just as if we were machines, and babies to be turned out like – like so many hats. It's all so old-fashioned and against nature.'

Another woman joined in in support. 'We have spent so much time talking about the upbringing and education of our children without looking at the vital matter of their first few hours in this world. This period is when the bonding process between mother and child must take place.

'The bustle of our hospital is not conducive to that process, and may indeed be in part the cause of negligent mothers and disruptive children. The Birth Room will change all that.'

Crispin asked, 'Is this a way of cutting out the fathers?'

'Not at all,' said Helen. 'But there is always, rightly, a mystery about birth. Men should not be witnesses to it. Oh, I know that sounds like a retrograde step. It has been the fashion for men to be present at bornings, and indeed often enough male doctors have supervised the delivery. But fashions change. We wish to try something different.

'In fact, the Birth Room is an old forgotten idea. It's a place for female consolation for the rigours of childbearing. Women will be able to come and go in the Room. They can rest there whether pregnant or not. Female midwives will attend the accouchement. More importantly, mothers will be able to stay there after the birth, to be

258

idle, to suckle their child, to chat with other women. No men at all.

'No men until a week after the birth. Women must have their province. Somehow, in our struggle for equality we have lost some of the desirable privileges we once enjoyed in previous times.

'You must allow us to regain this small privilege. You will soon discover that large advantages in behaviour flow from it.'

'And what are husbands supposed to do?' I asked.

Helen's solemn face broke into a smile. 'Oh, husbands will do what they always do. Enjoy their clubs and one another's company, hobnob, have their own private places. Look, let us try out the Birth Room idea for a year. We are confident it will work well and serve the whole community.'

A Birth Room was built in the subterranean extension, despite male complaints. There women, and not only the pregnant ones, met to socialise. Men were totally excluded. After giving birth, woman and baby remained together in peace, warmth and subdued light for at least a week, or longer if they felt it necessary. When they emerged, to present the husband with his new child, a little ceremony called Reunion developed, with company, cakes and kisses. The cakes were synthetic, the kisses real enough.

The Birth Room soon became an accepted part of social life, and a respected feature of the comforts of the new extension.

18

The Debate on Sex and Marriage

Weeks turned into months, and months into another year. There were many who, despite the misfortune of their confinement on Mars, regarded our society as a fair and just one. I, on the other hand, came to see utopia as a condition of becoming, a glow in the distance, a journey for which human limitations precluded an end. Yet there were comforting indications of improvement in our lot.

Kissorian and Sharon were among the first to take advantage of the greater scope for solitude afforded by the subterranean extensions. Their marriage was celebrated to the joy of many (and the envy of some), and they retired for a while from public life.

At the same time, the men who worked on the Smudge Project were experiencing new difficulties. One of the positive results of the recognition of Chimborazo as a life form was a closer union between scientists and non-scientists. Most of the gallant 6,000 realised that ours was one of the great scientific ages, and took pride in sharing its news. So we all felt involved when Dreiser announced that there was a minor glitch in the superfluid. At last, a signal had been received that was interpreted as the passage of a HIGMO through the ring.

Dreiser said that the Mars operation was coming to fruition as planned.

'When we have found just two more HIGMOs, or even one more, we shall finally have an approach towards an estimate of the crucial parameters of the Omega Smudge.'

'How long do we have to wait?' someone asked.

'Depends. We must be patient. Even ten or fifteen more

HIGMOs will begin to give us fairly accurate values for these parameters. Various controversial issues will be settled once and for all, among other important things.' He glanced sidelong at Kathi Skadmorr, as if saying 'Don't rock the boat', when her face now came up on the Ambient.

'We should just say there are some minor anomalies about the glitch detected in the superfluid,' she said. 'Maybe we have a signal representing a HIGMO passing through the ring, maybe not. Some of us have a few worries about that. So we are waiting for the second HIGMO. As Dreiser says, we must be patient.'

But a second HIGMO was indicated only two days later.

'Well, it does seem a little fishy,' said Dreiser. 'The ring has only been in full working order for a year. I'm talking terrestrial years now, as though we were no more aware than our androids that we are on another planet.' He gave a dry chuckle. 'A year till we get a signal, then a second so soon.'

'Can't they come in groups?' I asked.

He seemed to ignore the question, muttering to someone beyond lens range. Turning to face his audience again, he said, 'There's something particularly odd about the signature of this second glitch. It's not the form we expected. You see, there's a gradual oscillatory build-up instead of the anticipated almost clean "step-function" you'd expect from a HIGMO. You have to appreciate that the first glitch took us unawares. Full details of its profile were not obtained.

'We'll keep you posted.'

So we had to get on with our lives. The betterment of conditions brought about by the development of Lower Ground, as we called it, improved everyone's morale. But, as with many improvements, these would not guarantee lasting contentment. I had taken a liking to Dayo Obantuji, the anxious young Nigerian, who showed great interest in our circumstances. We often discussed the developments of

Lower Ground. Having abandoned musical composition, Dayo proved adept at devising decorative tile patterns, bursting with life and colour, to adorn the main corridor.

But I said to him, 'If we look back to the metropolises of the nineteenth century, we see filthy cities. In New York and Paris and London, filth and grit and stench were permanent features of life. These cities – London in particular – were coal-oriented. There was coal everywhere, coal dumped down chutes in the street, coal dragged upstairs, coal spilt and burned in a million grates, grimy smoke, cinders and ash strewn here and there.

'The exudations of coal mingled with the droppings of the horses that dragged the coal carts through the streets and pulled all kinds of carriages and cabs. The whole place was a microclimate of filth. The twentieth century saw vast improvements. Coal was banished, smokeless zones were introduced. The noisome fogs of London became a thing of the past. Electric heating developed into central heating and air-conditioning. Solar-heating panels replaced chimneys. Animals disappeared from the streets, to be replaced by automobiles, which – at least until they multiplied beyond tolerance and were banished from our cities – brought a decided improvement to urban life.

'And was the new comfort and ease of the home, reinforced by vacuum-cleaners and other devices that made homes more hygienic, considered utopian? Not at all. The improvements came in gradually and, once there, were taken for granted.'

'I wish they could have been taken for granted where I came from,' said Dayo. 'Our governments never had the interests of the people at heart.'

'To greater or lesser extent,' I said, 'that is the characteristic of all governments. It happened that in Western countries an educated population had a strong enough voice to regulate or become government. That educated class also accumulated the capital to invest in sustained improvement, which has in itself promoted more improvement, often in unanticipated spheres.

262

'To give an instance of the sort of thing I'm thinking of, back in the 1930s, in the fairly early days of motoring, an ordinary family found that a small car was within its price range; they could buy what was called, in those bygone days, "the freedom of the road".

'Crude though methods of contraception were in those days, the family then had a choice: another baby or a Baby Austin? Another mouth to feed or a T-model Ford? By opting for the car, they lowered population growth rates, which improved family living standards and encouraged the liberation of women.'

Dayo looked moody. 'In Nigeria it is scarcely possible to speak of the liberation of women. Yet when I think how intelligent my mother was – far more clever than my father . . .' Looking at the floor, he added, 'I wish I was dead when I think how I behaved to her – learned behaviour, of course . . . Now she's gone and it's too late to make amends.'

Because I was afflicted by a migraine, Belle Rivers and Crispin Barcunda conducted the debate on sex and marriage. The motion was opposed by John Homer Bateson and Beau Stephens.

Bateson began in his most flowery manner: 'To look back over the history of matrimony is to recoil from the cruelty of it. Love between a man and a woman hardly enters into the picture. It all comes down to a question of property and dowry and enslavement, either and most probably of the woman by the man, or of the man by the woman. As a woman by name Greer or Green said last century, "For a woman to effect any amelioration in her condition, she must refuse to marry."

'I would say too for a man to attain the detachment that wisdom brings, he also must refuse to marry. He must quell the lust to possess, which lies at the base of this question. The woman, until recently, was legally bound to give up everything, her freedom, even her name, while the man was supposed to give up his freedom of choice and to apply himself, sooner or later, to the expense of the rearing of the children he conceived on his wife.

'Thus, while the word "wedding" may cause some excitement in some breasts, somewhat like the word "mealtime", the excitement is evanescent as the true nature of marriage dawns on the wedded pair. They must then contrive somehow to love their demanding offspring, who, it is fair to say, are most unlikely to requite that love by reciprocal affection or gratitude.

'We have already made what to my mind is overdue provision for children here – not to mention their careless addition to our population. Let them go – as the saying used to be – "on the parish", into the care of Belle Rivers and her professional carers. Let there continue to be the usual conjunction of overheated bodies, men with women, women with women, and men with men. But let us not consider the continuance on Mars of matrimony in any shape or form. We are imprisoned enough as it is.'

Bateson sat down and Crispin took the stand. 'The genial Oliver Goldsmith remarked that a man who married and brought up his family did more service to the community than he who remained single and complained about the growing population. The outburst of misogyny we have just heard takes no account of love. I know it's a word that covers a multitude of sins as well as virtues, but if we weigh love against its opposite, hatred, then we see how easily love wins.

'True, marriage once involved property. That's history. In any case, Upstairs here we have no property beyond our persons. Now we marry to make public our commitment to each other, and to ensure, as far as that is possible, the stability of our lives for the enhancement of our children's most tender years.

'If we do not want children, then we need not marry, but must take precautions until lust gives out and we forsake our partner for another.

'How satisfactory that is, I leave you to judge, but it would be folly to legislate against it. Is free love a prescription for contentment? I remind you of the old joke I heard in the Seychelles long ago. "Remember, no matter how pretty the next girl is who comes along, somewhere in her background there's a guy who got sick of her shit and nonsense."' He showed his gold tooth in a wide grin, before adding, 'And that goes for the other sex as well, ladies . . .

'I can tell you now that I believe, on the other hand, that there is something ennobling about marriage and constancy, and that those qualities should be encouraged in our constitution. So convinced of their virtue am I that I'm proud to say Belle and I – despite some difference in our ages – intend to marry soon.' He burst out laughing with joy, gesturing gallantly towards Belle.

Belle immediately rose to her feet. She was seen to blush. 'Oh, that was meant to be a secret!' she cried, between tears and laughter herself. He put his arms round her and they clung together.

I wished that Kissorian and Sharon could have been present, but we had not seen them for a while. 'After this display, we're bound to win,' Cang Hai whispered to me.

But Beau Stephens now rose, frowning. 'Friends, this is a disgraceful spectacle, carefully rehearsed, no doubt, to persuade us to vote with our hearts instead of our heads. If these two rather ageing people are emotionally involved with each other, it is better it should be kept secret than acted out before us in this embarrassing charade.

'The case against marriage is that it is out-of-date and has become merely an opportunity for display and sentiment. Present-day ethics are against the whole idea. After the party's over, and the gifts mauled about and complained of, before the confetti's trampled into the mud of the pavement, most couples get divorced, only to indulge in legal wrangles that may continue for some years.

'That's when we see that marriage is simply about property and lust. It shows no care for any children. It's dishonest – another bad old custom that must go, if only to impoverish the lawyers.

'You seem fond of quoting, so I'll give you a quote from Nietzsche, whose *Also Sprach Zarathustra* I read in my university days. As far as I recall, Nietzsche takes a spiritual view. He says that you should first be mature enough to face the challenge of marriage, so that marriage can enable you both to grow. You should have children who will profit by your spirituality, to become greater than you are. He calls marriage the will of two people to create a someone who is more than those who created it.

'This is a rigorous view of marriage, I know, but, as a child of divorced parents who hated each other, I took stock of Nietzsche's words. The gross side of marriage has killed it as an institution.

'What we propose should be written into our constitution is that marriage is forbidden. No more marriages. Instead, an unbreakable contract to produce and rear children. Demanding, yes, but with it will come benefits and support from the state.

'This unbreakable contract may be signed and sealed by any two people determined to devote themselves to creating the brilliant and loving kind of child Belle Rivers thinks can be produced by an impractical rank on rank of shrinks. The new contract cannot be broken by divorce. Divorce is also forbidden. So it will be respected by one and all. Outside of that contract, free love can prevail, much as it does now – but with severe penalties for any couple producing unwanted babies.'

Stephens sat down in a dense silence as the forum chewed over what he had said.

Crispin slowly rose to his feet. 'Beau has been talking about breeding, not marriage. Just because his – or rather, Nietzsche's – ideas are admirable in their way, that doesn't make them practical. They're too extreme. We could not tolerate being locked for ever into a twosome that had proved to have lost its original inspiration, or to have found no other inspiration. To grow as Beau suggests, we must be free. We offer no such draconian answer as Beau proposes, to a question that has defeated

266

wiser heads than ours.' He sighed, and continued more slowly.

'But we do know that a marriage is as good as the society in which it flourishes – or fails . . . It may be that when our just society is fully established the ancient ways of getting married – and of getting divorced where necessary – will prove to be adequate. How adequate they are must depend not on laws, which can be broken, but on the people who try to abide by them.

'Marriage remains a lawful and honourable custom. We must just try to love better, and for that we shall have the assistance of our improved society.'

He sat down, looking rather dejected. There was a moment's silence. Then a wave of applause broke out.

At this period, I felt dizzy and sick and little able to carry on with my work. I seemed to hear curious sounds, somewhat between the bleat of a goat and the cry of a gull. Even the presence of other people became burdensome.

There was an upper gallery, little frequented, which I sought out, and where I could sit in peace, gazing out at the Martian lithosphere. From this viewpoint, looking westward, I could see the sparsely fractured plain, where the fractures ran in parallel, as if ruled with a ruler. These lines had been there – at least by human standards – for ever! Time had frozen them. Only the play or withdrawal of the Sun's light changed. At one time of day, I caught from this vantage point the glint of the Sun on a section of the ring of the Smudge Project.

Visiting the gallery on the day following the marriage debate, I found someone already present. The discovery was the more unwelcome because the man lounging there was John Homer Bateson, who had displayed such misanthropy in his speech.

It was too late to turn back. Bateson acknowledged my presence with a nod. He began to speak without preliminaries, perhaps fearing I might bring up the topic of the recent debate.

'I take it that you do not subscribe to this popular notion

that Olympus Mons is a living thing? Why is it that poor suffering humanity cannot bear to think itself alone in the universe, but must be continually inventing alternative life forms, from gods to cartoon characters?

'Make no mistake, Jefferies, however industriously you busy yourself with schemes for a just society, which can never come about, constituting as it does merely another Judeo-Christian illusion, we are all going to die here on Mars.'

I reminded him that we were looking for a new and better way to live – on which score I remained optimistic.

He sighed at such a vulgar display of hope. 'You speak like that, yet I can see you're sick. I'm sorry – but you have merely to gaze from this window to perceive that this is a dead planet, a planet of death, and that we live suspended in a kind of limbo, severed from everything that makes existence meaningful.'

'This is a planet of life, as we have discovered – where life has survived against tremendous odds, just as we intend to do.'

He pulled his nose, indicating doubt. 'You refer, I assume, to Olympus? You can forget that – a piece of impossible science invented by impossible scientists enamoured of a young Aborigine woman.'

'Ships will be returning here soon,' I responded. 'The busy world of terrestrial necessity will break in on us. Then we shall regard this period – of exile, if you like – as a time of respite, when we were able to consider our lives and our destinies. Isn't that why we DOPs and YEAs came here? An unconsidered life is a wasted life.'

'Oh, please!' He gave a dry chuckle. 'You'll be telling me next that an unconsidered universe is a wasted universe.'

'That may indeed prove to be the case.' I felt I had scored a point, but he ignored it in pursuit of his gloomy thought.

'I fear that our destiny is to die here. Not that it matters greatly. But why can we not accept our fate with Senecan dignity? Why do we have to follow the scientists and imagine that that extinct volcano somewhere out there, out in that airless there, is a chunk of life, of consciousness, even?'

'Why, there is evidence—'

'My dear Jefferies, there's always evidence. I beg you not to afflict me with evidence! There's evidence for Atlantis and for Noah's flood and for fairies and for unidentified flying objects, and for a thousand impossibilities . . . Are not these absurd beliefs merely unwitting admissions that our own consciousness is so circumscribed we desire to extend it through other means? Weren't the gods of the original Greek Olympus one such example, cooked up, as it were, to explain the inexplicable? I suspect that the universe, and the universes surrounding it, are really very simply comprehended, had we wit enough to manage the task.'

'We have wit enough. Our ascendancy over past centuries shows it.'

'You think so? What a comfortable lack of humility you do exhibit, Jefferies! I know you seek to do good, but heaven preserve us from those who mean well. Charles Darwin, a sensible man, admitted that the minds of mankind had evolved – if I recall his words correctly – from a mind as low as that of the lowest animal.'

Attempting a laugh, I said, 'The operative word there is evolved. The sum is continually ever greater than its parts. Give us credit, we are trying to exceed our limitations and to comprehend the universe. We'll get there one day.'

'I do not share your optimism. We have made no progress in our understanding of that curious continuity that we term life and death since – well, let's say, to be specific, because specificity is generally conceded to be desirable – since the Venerable Bede wrote his *Ecclesiastical History* some time in the seventh century. I trust you are familiar with this work?'

'No. I've not heard of the book.'

'The news has been slow to reach you, n'est ce pas? Let me quote, from my all too fallible memory, the Venerable

Bede's reflections on those grand questions we have been discussing. He says something to this effect. "When compared with the stretch of time unknown to us, O king, the present life of men on Earth is like the flight of a solitary sparrow through the hall where you and your companions sit in winter. Entering by one high window and leaving by another, while it is inside the hastening bird is safe from the wintery storm. But this brief moment of calm is over in a moment. It returns to the winter whence it came, vanishing for ever from your sight. Such too is man's life. Of what follows, of what went before, we are utterly ignorant."'

Sighing, I told Bateson I must return to my work.

As I walked away, he called to me, so that I turned back.

'You know what the temperature is out there, Jefferies?' He indicated the surface of Mars with a pale fluttering hand. 'I understand it's round about minus 76 degrees Celsius. Even colder than a dead body in its earthly grave! Nothing mankind could do would warm that ground up to comfortable temperate zone temperatures, eh? Do you imagine any great work of art, any musical composition, was ever created at minus 76 Celsius?'

'We must set a precedent, John,' I told him.

I left him alone on the upper gallery, gazing at the bleached landscape outside.

19

The R&A Hospital

On the following day, when I was resting, Dayo came to visit me again. He tried to persuade me to see what 'the computer people', as he called them, were doing. I could not resist his blandishments for ever, and got myself up.

Going with him to the control room, I found that Dayo was popular there too. He had been learning to work on the big quantputer with the mainly American contingent who staffed the machines. The striking patterns on his tiles for the Lower Ground had been devised using it.

The mainframe had originally been programmed to handle the running of the Martian outpost – its humidity, atmospheric pressure, chemical contents, temperature levels and so forth. Now all these factors were being handled by a single rejigged laptop quantputer.

I was astonished, but the bearded Steve Rollins, the man in charge of the programme under Arnold Poulsen, explained they had evolved a formula whereby interrelated factors could all be grouped under one easily computable formula. Our survival and comfort were being controlled by the laptop. The change-over had taken place at the 'X' hour, during a night some five months previously. No one had noticed a shade of difference, while the big mainframe had been freed for more ambitious things.

And what things! I had wondered why the control staff took so little interest in our forums and the utopian society. Here was the answer: they had been otherwise engaged.

At Dayo's prompting, Steve showed me the programme they were running. He spoke in an easy drawl.

'You may think this is unorthodox use of equipment,'

Steve said, stroking his whiskers with a gesture he had and grinning at me. 'But as that great old musician, Count Basie, said, "You just gotta keep on keeping on". If you regard science as a duel with nature, you must never drop your guard. Stuck here on this Ayers Rock in the sky, we must keep on keeping on or we stagnate. Guess you know that.'

'Guess I do.'

'As a kid I used to play a game called Sim Galaxy on my old computer. It produced simulations of real phenomena, from people to planetary systems. If you kept at it long enough, fighting entropy and natural disasters, it was possible to get to rule over a populated galaxy.'

Steve said that his team had adapted a more modest version of the game, into which they had fed all the quantputer records, sedulously kept, of every person and event on Mars. The simulation had become more and more accurate as the programme was refined. Every detail of our Mars habitation, every detail of each person in the habitation, was precisely represented in the simulation. They called the programme Sim White Mars.

We watched on a widescreen monitor. There people lived and moved and had their being. Our small Martian world was totally emulated; the one item missing was Olympus, a being as yet incomputable.

I fought against the suspicion that this was not a true emulation but a trick, until Steve mentioned casually that they were using a new modified quantputer that computed faster, fuzzier, than the old conventional quantputer – certainly than any of the quantcomps people carry around with them.

The scale of the thing made me feel dizzy. Dayo was immediately at hand, fetching me a stool.

In full colour, recognisable people went about their business, around the settlement and in the laboratory. They seemed to move in real time.

The scene flipped to a schoolroom, where Belle Rivers was talking with a jeuwu class of ten children. Steve moved a pointer on to Belle, touched a key, and at once a scroll of characteristics came up: Belle's birth date and place, her entire CV and many other details. They flashed on the screen and were gone at another touch of a key.

'We call these simulated objects and people emulations, they are so precise,' said Steve. 'To them, their world is perfectly real. They sure think and act like real.'

'But they are mere electronic images. They can't be said to think.'

Steve laughed. 'Guess they don't realise they're just a sequence of numbers and colours in a computer, if that's what you mean.' He added, in lower key, 'How often do we realise we're also just a sequence in another key?'

I said nothing.

The people on screen were now gathering in the main thoroughfare. This was recognisably the day the third marathon was held. There were the runners, many with false wings attached to them. There were the officials who ran the race. There were the crowds.

A whistle blew and the runners started forward, struggling for space, so closely were they packed, even as they had done weeks previously.

'All this takes real heavy puting power, even using the quantputer,' Steve said. 'That's why we are running some weeks behind real time. We're working on that problem.' The runners began to trot, jostling closely for position. 'I guess we'll catch up eventually.'

'Want to bet on who will win?' Dayo asked mischievously.

'You see this is a kind of rerun of the marathon,' Steve said. 'And now, I just tap on a couple of keys . . .'

He did so. The screen was filled with phantom creatures, grey skeletons with strange pumping spindles instead of legs, naked domes for heads, their teeth large and bared. The inhuman things pressed onwards, soundless, joyless . . . The Race of Death, I thought.

'We got the X-ray stuff off the hospital,' Steve said. 'It's spare diagnostic equipment . . .'

The skeletons streamed on, with ghostly grey buildings as background, racing through their silent transparent world.

Steve tapped his keyboard once more and the world on the screen became again the one we recognised as ours.

With a flash of humour, he said, 'You have your utopia, Tom. This is our baby. How do you like it?'

'But in the wrong hands . . .' I began. A feeling of nausea silenced me.

Dayo took my arm. 'I want you to watch yourself as an emulation, Tom. Please, Steve . . .'

Steve touched a couple of keys on his keyboard. The scene changed. An office block along the marathon course came into focus. Moving through the window, the emulation picked out a man and two women, standing close together, watching the runners pass their building. I recognised Cang Hai, Mary Fangold and myself.

My emulation clutched his head and went to the back of the room to sit on a sofa. Cang Hai came over to it and stood there in silence, looking down at its – my – bowed head. After a moment, I stirred myself, smiled weakly at Cang Hai, rose, and returned to the window to watch the runners.

'I don't remember doing that,' I said.

'The CV, Steve,' Dayo prompted.

The key. My details, my birth date and place, my CV. Momentarily my skeletal self was there, grey, drained of all but emptiness, long bony fingers clutching at my ostrich egg of skull. Then: 'Diagnosis: Suffers from untreated brain tumour'. Only later did it occur to me that had I died then, my emulation would have continued to live, at least for a while.

I found Steve gazing at me and stroking his beard. 'You better get yourself looked after, chum,' was all he said.

The old R&A hospital was greatly enlarged in order to cope with its new general functions. Entry was through an airlock, the hospital atmosphere being self-contained against external emergencies and slightly richer in oxygen than in the domes in order to promote feelings of well-being. Extensive new wards had been built and a nanotechnology centre added, where cell repair machines were housed.

I must confess to feeling nervous as I entered the doors. I was greeted warmly by the hospital personnel manager, Mary Fangold.

As we shook hands, her dark blue eyes scrutinised me with more than professional interest.

'You're in good hands here, Tom Jefferies,' she said. 'We are all admirers of your utopian vision, which is carried out in our hospital as far as is possible. I hope to take care of you personally. We are treating only a few persistent sore-throat and eye cases at present.

'We regard those who are ill and enter here less as patients than as teachers who bring with them an opportunity for us to study and repair illness. Our progress is less towards health than towards rationality, which brings health.'

When I remarked that, despite her kind sentiments, the old, the ageing, would become a burden, she denied it. No, she said, the burdens of old age had been greatly exaggerated in former times. The old and experienced, the DOPs, cost very little. On Earth, many of them had savings that they gradually released after retirement on travel and suchlike. Thus they contributed to society and the economy. Their demands were much fewer than were those of the young.

I asked her if she was keen to return to Earth, to practise there.

She smiled, almost pityingly. Not at all, was her answer. 'The elements in the formula have been reduced here to a manageable level.'

She was determined to remain on Mars in her interesting experimental situation, free of many diseases which plagued Earth, helping to bring about a utopian phase of human life. For her money, we could remain cut off for good! Were not working and learning the great pleasures for anyone of rational intelligence?

She and a nurse conducted me to a ward-lounge, where we sat over coffdrink gazing out of windows that showed simulated views of beach, palm trees and blue ocean, where windsurfers rode the breakers.

Continuing her discourse, Mary said that it was the young who were expensive. Child benefits, constant super-vision and education, health care, the devastations of drink and drugs, and – at least on Earth – crime, all formed major items in any nation's financial regimen of expenditure. Contrary to the general consensus that children were a blessing, she maintained they were rather a curse; not only were they an expense, but they forced their parents to participate in a second childhood while rearing them. She regarded this as an irrational waste of years of young adulthood.

'It's true,' I answered, 'that most crime on Earth is committed by the young. Whereas, if I recall the statistic correctly, the over-seventies account for only 1.3 per cent of all arrests.'

'Yes. Mainly for dangerous driving, the occupational hazard of the age! Happily, we do not have that problem on Mars.'

We laughed together. But her laughter was rather abstrac-ted. She began thinking aloud. Belle Rivers's jeuwu did not carry matters far enough. Although Mary had nothing against children per se, she would like to see them removed from their parents at birth, to be reared in institutions where every care would be lavished on them; protected from the amateurishness and eccentricity – if not downright indifference – of their parents, they would grow up much more reasonably. She repeated this phrase in a thoughtful manner. Much more reasonably . . .

Knowing that Mary Fangold had been disappointed by the establishment of the Birth Room, I asked her how she regarded the matter now.

'As a rational person, I accept the Birth Room as an

experiment. I do not oppose the Birth Room. Indeed, I permit my midwives to go there when summoned. However, its function is undoubtedly divisive. The division between the sexes is increased. The role of the father is curtailed.'

'Do you not think that the important mother-baby bond is strengthened by the Birth Room procedures? Are we not right to encourage birthing to become a ceremony? The role of the father is enhanced by the celebration when he is again united with his wife?'

'Ah, now, there you should say husband rather than father. Men favour the husbandly role above that of a father. I will speak plainly to you. The one reason why I did not oppose the Birth Room is that the new mother is given a week's freedom from the importunings of the male. You perhaps would not credit how many men insist on sexual union again, immediately after their wives have delivered, when their vaginas are still in a tender state. The regulations of the Birth Room protect them from that humiliating pain.'

'You must see the worst of human nature in hospital.'

'The worst and the best. We see lust, yes, and fear – and courage. The spectrum of human nature.' After a pause, she added, 'We still have women who prefer to come here to hospital to give birth, and have their husbands with them.'

'But increasingly fewer as time goes by, I imagine?'

'We shall see about that.' Her lips tightened and she turned to summon a nurse.

After a while, Mary said she had a vision of what life could be. For her, Olympus the Living Being (as she phrased it) was an inspiration. Its age must surely be a guarantee of its wisdom, its eons of isolation a promoter of thought. I questioned that. 'Eons of isolation? I would think they might as easily promote madness. Could you endure being alone for long?'

Her glance was humorous and questioning. 'You're really alone, Tom, aren't you? What may be good for the vast living being may not be so good for you . . .'

She would like to see a society where the young were supported financially until their eighteenth birthday, in order to 'find themselves', as she put it. Only then would they be put to work for the good of the society that had nourished them.

At the other end of the scale the compulsory retirement of men and women at the age of seventy-five would be abolished. Molecular technology had reached a point where the curse of Alzheimer's disease had been banished and both sexes lived healthily well into their early hundreds – barring accidents. It was expected that the class known as the Megarich would live for two centuries. Meditech, she said, had accomplished much of recent decades, although the time when humans lived for 500 years – an opportunity to learn true wisdom, she said – was still far in the future. Say twenty years ahead, given the peace they enjoyed on Mars. Longevity would become inheritable.

When I asked her what pleasure there would be in a lifespan of 500 years, Mary regarded me curiously.

'You tease me, Tom! You of all people, to ask that! Why, given five centuries, you would be able fully to enjoy and appreciate your own intelligence, with which you are naturally endowed. Growing out of the baser emotions, you would achieve true rationality and experience the pleasures of untroubled intellect. You would live to see the perfection of the world to which you had contributed so much. You'd become, would you not, an authority on it?'

I asked playfully, 'The baser emotions? Which are they?'

As she leaned towards me to fit a light harness on my head, I caught a breath of her perfume. It surprised me.

'I don't mean love, if that's what you imply. Love can be ennobling. You pay too little heed to your emotional needs, Tom, do you understand?' Her deep blue eyes looked into mine.

While this discussion was taking place, the nurse was busy securing a cable to my wrist, making sure that it fitted comfortably where a tiny needle entered a vein. The other end of the cable ran to a computer console where a technician sat, his back to me. It in turn was linked with the nanotank.

'What is happening in surgical advance,' Mary was saying, 'is essentially in line with your reforming principles. The technology has developed because of a gradual change in public attitudes. Notably, the dissociation of the acceptance of pain from surgery, which began with the discovery of ether anaesthesia halfway through the nineteenth century. You, similarly, wish to separate the association of aggression from society, if I understand you aright.'

Before I could agree or disagree Mary rushed on to say that, as we talked, the computer was analysing the findings of the nanobots that had penetrated my system to check on the concentration of salts, sugars and ATP in the renegade cells of my brain – to, in short, perform a biopsy. The quantputer would order them to redirect the energies of malignant cells, or else to eliminate them.

'So the words pain and knife no longer—' I began. But a curious light was streaming in from I knew not where. I could not trace its source. Perhaps it was a flower, temporarily obscuring my view, as if I were a bee entering it for honey, for pollen, burrowing, burrowing, among the white waves of petals, endless white waves, festive but somehow deadly. With them, a dull scent, an unreal buzzing, the two of them interfused.

As if new senses had roused themselves . . . In the middle of them, a dull orange-tinted stain that moved, weeping through puny mouths as it sucked its way onward. But the holy rollers were pressing forward, extinguishing it to the sound of – sound of what? Trumpets? Honey? Geraniums? It was so fast I could not tell.

Then the light and sound were gone, only the endlessness of white waves remaining, churning over in a great ocean of confused thought. Antonia's face? Her nearness? Mary's lips, eyes? A sense of great loss . . .

'—spring to mind,' I finished. I felt as weak as if I had

been away on a long swim. I could hardly focus on those violet-coloured eyes looking into mine.

'It's all over,' said Mary Fangold, kindly, stroking my hand. 'The nanobots have removed your tumour. Now you will be well again. But you must rest awhile. I have a neat little ward waiting for you, next to my apartment.'

She came to me quietly at the first hour of the night, when the sigh of air circulation fell to a whisper. Her lips had been reddened. Her hair lay about her shoulders. Her pale breasts showed through a semi-transparent nightdress. She stood by my bedside, asking if I slept, knowing well the answer.

'Time for a little physiotherapy,' she murmured.

I sat up. 'Come in with me, Mary.'

Slipping her garment from her body, she stood there naked. I kissed the bush of dark hair on her mons veneris, and pulled her into the bed. There we were in joy, all night, our limbs interlocked, hers and mine. At times it seemed to us that we were back on the great fecund Earth, rolling on its course with its ever changing mantle of blue skies and cloud and its restless oceans.

I remained in hospital for a week, indifferent to what was happening elsewhere. Every night, at the first hour, Mary came to me. We sated ourselves with each other. By day she was again the rational, professional person I had known until then, until the revelation of her lovely body.

During my recuperation period, Cang Hai visited me, accompanied by her precocious child, Alpha. And many other visitors, Youssef Choihosla among them.

On one visit, finding that I looked perfectly well, Cang Hai ventured to ask me why it was that my late wife had not undergone nanosurgery for her cancer. I was mortified to feel that I had ceased, or almost ceased, to mourn the death of Antonia.

'My distrust of religion springs in part from this. Antonia was a Christian Scientist all her life. She was brought up in her parents' creed. She held that her cancer could be

healed by prayer. Nothing would persuade her otherwise.

'I could not force her,' I said. 'She had every right to her
beliefs, however fatal.'

A tear trickled from under the neat epicanthic fold of
Cang Hai's eye. 'You surely can't believe that still, Tom.'
But I believed I caught her thinking, even as she wiped the
tear away, that some good had come from my dear wife's
death, whereby I had sublimated grief by striving to change
society.

Little Alpha liked to be told stories of bikers and their
gang warfare in the days before I was born. In the underprivileged part of the world where my boyhood had been
spent, it was sometimes possible to obtain a magazine
entitled *Biker Wars*, which I had greatly relished at the
time.

As I was telling the child one such story, we were
interrupted by a tiny cry, something between the bleat
of a goat and the shrill of a gull.

''Scuse me, unkie,' said the child. 'My little Yah-Yah
needs attention.'

She brought forth from the basket she was carrying what
appeared to be a small cage. It contained a kind of big-eyed
red animal. Alpha showed it to me when she had attended
to its needs. So I had my first close look at a tammy.

'Crispin gave it to me,' she said, with pride.

The men and women in the fire prevention force had
been rendered virtually unemployed by the success of the
Sim White Mars operation. Rather than remain idle they
had cannibalised some of their equipment, making an
improved version of a toy that had enjoyed a vogue on
Earth many decades previously.

In Alpha's cage was a small VR pet. It was born and
it grew, constantly needing feeding, cleaning and loving
care from the child who owned it. If neglected, the pet
could die or 'escape' from its cage. In adolescence, it
became rather rebellious and needed tactful handling. Con-
veniently, at this age a pet of the opposite sex entered

the cage. With some guidance from the small owner, the two pets could mate and eventually bring forth another generation of pet.

Time inside the VR cage had been speeded up. The lifespan of a pet was rarely more than twenty-eight days. The far-sighted leader of the fire prevention team had designed the computer pets as a learning toy. When I eventually spoke to this lady, she said, 'Belle Rivers recognises that the children need love. She is less ready to recognise that children also need to give love, to own love-objects, something other than human, to help in developing their own personalities. Kids with tammies will grow up into caring adults – and have fun meanwhile.'

It was far-sighted, but not far-sighted enough. Every kid wanted a tammy. The domes were maddened by the moans, howls and chirps of a wide range of the VR pets. Concerts and plays were ruined by the incessant demands of the toys in the audience. Eventually, tammies had to be banned from such occasions, although this meant that children excluded themselves, lest their charges perished . . . I hated imposing bans, but the government of behaviour was an inescapable part of civilised society.

Tammies next became banned at mealtimes, so that children might associate properly with adults. Adminex had in mind here a passage from Thomas More's *Utopia*, in which he says, 'During meals, the elders engage in decent conversation with the young, omitting topics sad and unpleasant. They do not monopolise the conversation for they freely hear what the young have to say. The young are encouraged to talk in order to give proof of the talents which show themselves more easily during meals.'

This was not always successful. The elders sometimes grew tired of childish prattle. The atmosphere was always soothed by music – not Beza's music, but something much more anaemic, suited to our austere diet.

20

A Collective Mind

I managed to drag myself away from the raptures of Mary Fangold and her delicious physiotherapy. Although I was back in the busy world, finding a juster society slowly developing, act by act, I wished to give Mary a present.

Seeking out Sharon Singh, I asked to see her collection of rock crystal pieces. She displayed them for me, meanwhile gazing up at my face from under her dark fringe of hair. Among the many shapes, I chose one that, in its finely detailed folds, closely resembled a vagina.

Giving it to me, Sharon said, 'Isn't it curious that the cold pressures of Mars should create such a hot little thing?'

She gave a tinkling laugh.

Olympus – now more frequently referred to as Chimborazo; Kathi Skadmorr had won that argument – had taken hold of people's imaginations. Discussion groups met regularly to chew over the riddle. It was a subject for argument in public and across the Ambient.

Most Ambient users found it hard to accept that Chimborazo could be conscious. They were daunted by the thought of that great solitary intellect sitting permanently upon a planet that had become hostile to life. What was it waiting for? was a frequently asked question.

Certainly not a bombardment by CFC gas, was one answer.

The parallel between Chimborazo's shelter for collaborating species and our own situation in the domes was quickly seized on. Fondness replaced fear as a response to its existence.

283

Dreiser's remark about a stack of thoughts 23 kilometres high kept returning to me. Also there was the speculation about what one might encounter if one prized up the protective shell and looked – went? was drawn? – inside.

I believe that Hawkwood's interview was a great persuasive force in the establishment of our utopian constitution.

One interesting theory I heard discussed on my return to society was that Chimborazo's power of consciousness was far greater than we had suspected. Its attention had become directed across the gulfs of matrix to where it sensed other minor flames of consciousness. It had kept the minds of terrestrials busied with ambitions to visit Mars in order to lure them to provide it with company.

These were speculations without much ground in fact. However, when I contacted Dreiser and Kathi, I found that they too were in the midst of a welter of troubled speculation. Their new findings presented us with new problems. I moved Adminex to call a meeting in Hindenburg Hall at once.

A whole phalanx of scientists attended. The meeting was crowded. Children were welcomed. Their tammies had to be left behind.

Dreiser began speaking without preamble. 'We have a confusion of opinions here. You have every right to hear them. In some cases they amount to serious disputes between us.

'The fact is that, over the last week, we have observed no less than twenty-seven glitches in the superfluid of the ring. The interpretation of these phenomena is unclear as yet. When examined closely, the build-up to these glitches has a curious and complicated structure. Most of us have therefore reached the conclusion that the glitches are not caused by HIGMOs after all.

'The question then is: What does cause them?

'I am going to ask Jon Thorgeson to give his point of view.'

Thorgeson rose. As when he had spoken in public before, he began nervously but soon got into his stride.

'I don't really expect you non-scientists to understand all the nuances of the situation. Maybe you've heard before that there is something going wrong in the ring. There may be stray vortices in the superfluid which lead to spurious effects. I believe that to be the case. It is the obvious explanation.

'Before we go any further, or develop any crazy ideas, we have to turn off the refrigeration units so that the superfluid can return to its normal fluid state. Okay, so then we examine the tube thoroughly and clean it. That is a meticulous job. Then we switch the refrigeration on again, turning it up very very slowly, so that no vortices can develop.

'It's just lousy luck that this procedure will take about a year. By that time the ships will be back, I don't doubt – and their vibrations would spoil everything. We have to take that chance.

'To be honest, I have a suspicion that the irresponsible excavations of your Lower Ground may be the cause of everything . . .'

He sat down and folded his arms across his chest.

While he was talking I noticed Kathi shaking her head in mute disagreement, but it was Charles Bondi who spoke next, in flat denial of the last speaker.

'I'm sorry, but that's all arrant nonsense. Vortices in the superfluid are well understood. They would produce quite different effects from the patterns we have observed. You need only simple calculations to see that it is so.

'Besides which, we have no spare year to play around in. We must find a solution for today. Leo Anstruther made the plea for White Mars, but somehow he was ruled out as Administrator of the UN Department for the Preservation of Mars. When the ships return they will probably be obsessed once more with the idea of terraforming Mars. It makes our situation an urgent one.'

A YEA technician rose and said, 'We don't want to let a plea of urgency destroy understanding. I'd say we should haul off and wait to see what comes next. I mean, what the ring comes up with. Seems we have run out of HIGMOs this week. We should keep watch on next week.'

Georges Souto spoke next. 'I'm largely in agreement with the last speaker. For one thing, we don't know what exactly is going on Downstairs. Maybe they've turned their back on the whole notion of matrix travel. Maybe they're never coming back. Think of that!'

That the audience was thinking of it was apparent from the general exclamation that went up at Souto's words.

Souto continued. 'It could be that the conventional hypothesis that HIGMOs were distributed randomly and uniformly throughout the universe is just plain wrong. Our findings imply that the distribution of HIGMO encounters with the ring may be extremely clumped. The explanation for seeing all these HIGMOs together in such a short space of time is simply that we're passing through a HIGMO shower, okay?'

Even as he spread wide his hands in explanation, someone shouted out that he was talking nonsense.

Suung Saybin spoke from the audience. 'Could all these glitches that you're worrying about be caused by one and the same HIGMO being trapped in Mars's gravitational field, so that it oscillates back and forth in the ring?'

'That's not possible,' Souto answered and was echoed by several other voices.

'All right, smartarses, it was just a suggestion,' said Saybin tartly.

Dreiser said, 'Just to make it clear, I can show you what we actually saw in our screens.'

A large 3vid hung in the air above the dais, as Dreiser projected it. The image was as severe as a text-book diagram. It showed, against the fuzzy grey background, a colourless blur that wavered before shooting up a step halfway along, then continuing on a straight horizontal course.

'The phase is the vertical,' Dreiser explained. 'The horizontal is time. In this case, it's something like 0.5 of a nanosecond from one side of the screen to the other. The

286

step up is 4π. As you see, the signal is not at all clear. But the step function makes it plain that something passed through the ring from above to below. Otherwise the step would have been down by the same 4π. The oscillation before the step becomes more complex throughout our series of glitches.'

A silence fell over the proceedings.

The image faded from overhead.

Kathi spoke quietly from her seat, without getting up. 'So you're all off track. Forget the HIGMO question. The glitches are being caused by Chimborazo itself.'

Laughter came from some scientists as well as the audience.

'Chimborazo is causing the glitches,' repeated Kathi, as if the statement was made more understandable by being recast.

This time the laughter was more mocking.

'Let's hear what the lady's case is,' Dreiser interjected. 'Give her a chance. What's on your mind, Kathi?'

She flashed him a grateful look before standing to say, 'Arnold Poulsen is experimenting to see whether his 16-hertz sound oscillations will cause people to be more conciliatory towards each other. As yet, he has nothing conclusive.

'Over the last few months, however, I have become convinced that we are experiencing a genuine improvement in personal relations. I notice the difference even in myself.' At this there was brief laughter.

'I've become equally convinced that this has nothing to do with Arnold's experiment. Or, for that matter – sorry, Tom – with the utopia effect. No, it's Chimborazo working on us, the Watchtower of the Universe.' She paused to let this sink in, confronting her audience with arms akimbo.

'We know there is a powerful consciousness in that being. We get a CPS, and this has now been confirmed on an ordinary savvyometer, which we modified to accommodate an extremely low frequency range. Our rapidly advancing friend has plenty of awareness right enough!'

She paused as we all took a deep breath at that.

287

'We know too – or we think we do – that Chimborazo is a symbiotic and epiphytic being; all its component life forms have learned to cooperate rather than compete. That strong cohesive influence appears to work satisfactorily.

'I do not think it would be at all surprising if this "influence", whatever it is, has had its effect on our own human conscious behaviour. We know that quantum effects can hold over great distances. Quantum entanglements between photons have been observed to stretch over a hundred thousand kilometres at least. Probably there is no limit.'

'Sounds to me like fifteenth-century mysticism,' remarked Thorgeson. '*The Will of God*.'

'Well,' Kathi said challengingly, in something like her old style, 'so what does that prove? Not all fifteenth-century mystics were fools!'

Dreiser, ignoring this exchange, said to Kathi. 'You talk about your Chimborazo – if I'm forced to use that label – having a powerful consciousness. Would you care to clarify that for us?'

Several of the men sitting behind him showed signs of discontent. They evidently did not like the respect Dreiser – the great Dreiser Hawkwood – paid this newcomer.

Once he had given Kathi the floor, she went happily on.

'Well, we still aren't sure about consciousness. It's a riddle awaiting solution. The CPS device is simply a passive detector, much as a geiger counter used to register radioactivity. It does not in any way alter consciousness. It registers the presence of consciousness by the effect of consciousness on a quantum state-reduction phenomenon – let's say on some coherent quantum superposition involving a large number of calcium ions.

'What we do know is that consciousness in an entity can detectably affect the reduction of a quantum state, and can be affected by it. That's how a mentatrope works, after all. The quantum superposition in a mentatrope is influenced by the presence of consciousness as well as

288

influencing consciousness. So it's not at all unreasonable that consciousness might affect the quantum coherence in our superfluid ring.'

Willa Mendanadum spoke from the audience. 'Excuse me, Kathi, but a mentatrope contains no superfluid. The quantum superposition is between different calcium ion displacements. It's much the same as the superpositions of electron displacements in a quantputer.'

'I'm aware of that,' Kathi replied. 'But no quantputer gives a reading on a mentatrope. The organisation of calcium ions in a mentatrope is of a completely different character from that in a quantputer – much more like the superfluid in our ring, where the total mass involved begins to be significant.'

Willa was adamant. Her slight figure seemed to vibrate with scorn. 'Sorry, Kathi, I know you're bidding fair to be a guru and all that, but there is absolutely no evidence of any similarity between this ring and a mentatrope. The scale's completely different, for one thing. The geometry is different. The materials are different. The purposes are different.'

'But—'

'Let me finish, please. I must make the point that there is absolutely no evidence that the proximity of a conscious human being has any effect whatsoever on the functioning of the ring. In fact, as I understand it, the argon 36 in the ring's superfluid is geared specifically to detect the monopole gravitational effects of a HIGMO – not of a brainwave!'

Kathi seemed unmoved. She said, 'We don't know what the appropriate quantum superposition parameters are for Chimborazo. Chimborazo is built on an entirely different scale from us humans. Very possibly it has the ability to tune its own internal mental activities so as to relate specifically to the ring.'

'Absurd!' exclaimed Jimmy Gonzales Dust from the back row of boffins.

She turned to him, saying mildly, 'Absurd, is it? For an

289

alien intellect twenty-five kilometres high? How dare we presume to suggest its limitations?'

'But you are speculating wildly,' Jimmy protested.

'I'd say that at this juncture, a little wild speculation is in order,' Dreiser said. 'Continue, Kathi.'

'My speculation is based on fact, by the way,' Kathi said, with something of her old tartness in her voice. I remembered her fondness for correcting those who were basically on her side. What her relationship was with Dreiser was difficult to guess. 'We know that a mentatrope works, but not why. The discovery of the Reynaud-Damien effect was an accident. The implication was that consciousness has a subtle influence on the reduction of a quantum state.'

'I don't accept that, Kathi,' Jimmy said, cutting in. 'However, one result of the French guys' researches was the development of a CPS detector.'

Her eyes flashed irritation, but she said with disarming mildness, 'And the CPS detector led to the development of the mentatrope for psychiatric purposes. Thanks for your contribution, Jimmy. At least we do know that a mentatrope has something in common with the ring. In each case the important element is a quantum state-reduction phenomenon. I've looked into the history of the subject. You people, like Jimmy here, are too sunk in ring-technology to remember where it all comes from.'

Jimmy broke in indignantly. 'We all know about quantum state-reduction. That was sorted out early this century with the definitive Walter Heitelman experiment.'

Kathi studied him for a moment, gave a brief nod, smiled, and said, changing tack, 'And there were some ideas put forth last century, suggesting various possible connections between consciousness and quantum state-reduction. They all petered out because of lack of experimental confirmation, in most cases because of a direct conflict with observation. But the general idea itself still remains, at least in principle. There were heated discussions in the scientific literature, most of it forgotten.

'I'd say that if you put these ideas together – bearing

290

in mind that the glitches in the ring are indeed state-reduction effects – there's a plausible case for a connection between the ring glitches we've recorded and Chimborazo's consciousness.'

Thorgeson gave a curt laugh. 'You'll be telling us next that the ring will reveal "a soul".'

'Souls are even harder to define than consciousness. But, after all – why not?'

Clapping his hands, Dreiser interposed. 'The next obvious move is to perform a mentatropic examination of the ring. I agree with Kathi that these glitches we've been observing imply that the Watcher of the Universe has already transferred some "consciousness effects" to the ring. We must find out if that is the case.

'And, by the way, this notion that the ring is "pregnant" or "getting ready to conceive" is just a silly joke – which Jimmy probably started!

'We do not yet understand the powers of Chimborazo. We have discussed this endlessly, and think the life form is probably benign and even defensive. Its collective mind may be immensely powerful. Maybe it could wipe out all our minds with one blast of directed thought; but shelled animals are generally pacific, if terrestrial examples are anything to go by.' He paused to let this sink in.

'One explanation for its camouflage may be that it long ago sensed other consciousnesses on Earth – even across the great matrix distances separating the two planets – and was fearful. Despite its great bulk, it concealed itself as best it could.'

Someone in the audience asked what Dreiser would do if it was found that the ring was acquiring elements of consciousness.

He stroked his little moustache thoughtfully before answering. 'If that does turn out to be the case, we'll have to rethink the whole Smudge experiment. To turn off the refrigeration would be tantamount to murder. Or, let's say, abortion . . . It might also be dangerous with Chimborazo towering above us! It's a dilemma . . .

'The ring would no longer be a viable tool in the search for the Omega Smudge. The UN authorities, supposing they still exist, would not be happy about that. On the other hand, we would stand on the brink of another great discovery. We would be on the way to understanding what consciousness is all about – what causes it, sustains it . . .'

Kathi had a word to add. 'Just to respond to Charles Bondi's earlier remark. Of course, if the ring were to be kept going, there could never be any terraforming permitted . . .'

My thoughts were so overwhelmed by speculation that I could not sleep. I was walking down East Spider (late Dyson Street) in dim-out, when the unexpected happened. Two masked men jumped from the shadows, armed with either pick helves or baseball bats or similar weapons.

'This is for you, you bloody titox, for ruining religion and normal human life!' one shouted as they pitched into me. I managed to strike one of them in the face. The other caught me a blow across the base of my skull. I fell.

I seemed to fall for ever.

When I roused, I was in the hospital again, being wheeled along a corridor. I tried to speak but could not.

Cang Hai and Alpha were waiting for me. Alpha was sitting on the floor, watching her mother bounce a ball again and again against the wall. I saw how Cang was still something of a child, using the excuse of her daughter to play childishly. She stopped the bouncing rather guiltily, scooped Alpha up in her arms, and approached me.

'My dear little daughter,' I tried to say.

'You need rest, Tom, dear. You'll be okay and we'll be here.'

Mary Fangold came briskly along, said hello to Alpha and directed my carriage into a small room, talking meanwhile, ignoring Cang Hai. The room became full of tiny specks of light, towards which I seemed to float.

With an effort I roused, to see Cang Hai close by. A spark of anger showed in her eyes. She said, determinedly and loudly, 'Anyhow, as I was saying, my Other in Chengdu told me of a dream. An orchestra was playing—'

'Perhaps we'd better leave Mr Jefferies alone just now,' said Mary, sweetly. 'He needs quiet. He will be fully restored in a day or so.'

'I'll go soon enough, thank you. You could use that symphony orchestra as a symbol of cooperative evolution. Many men and women, all with differing lives and problems, and many different instruments – they manage to sublimate their individualities to make beautiful harmony. But in this dream, they were playing in a field and eating a meal at the same time. Don't ask me how.'

'Would you like a shower, Mr Jefferies?' Mary asked. I gestured to her to let Cang Hai rattle on for a moment.

'And you see, Tom, I thought about the first ever restaurant – no doubt it was outdoors – which opened in China centuries ago. It was a cooperative act making for happiness. You had to trust strangers enough to eat with them. And you had to eat food cooked by a cook who maybe you couldn't see, trusting that it was not poisoned . . . Wasn't that restaurant a huge step forward in social evolution . . . ?'

'Really, thank you, I think we've had enough of your dreams, dear,' said Mary Fangold.

'Who's this rude lady, Mumma?' Alpha asked.

'Nobody really, my chick,' said Cang Hai and marched indignantly from the room.

I managed to say goodbye after she had gone. My head was clearing. Mary looked sternly down at me and said, 'You're delivered into my care again, Tom!' She suppressed a joyous laugh, pressing her fingers to her lips. 'I hope all this irrational chatter did not disturb you. Your adopted daughter seems to have the notion that she is in touch with someone in – where was it? Chengdu?'

'I too have my doubts about her phantom friend. But it makes her rather lonely life happier.'

Wheeling me forward, she tapped my name into the registry. 'Mmm, same ward as before . . .'

She gave me a winning smile. 'There I have to disagree with you. We must try to banish the irrational from our lives. You have fallen victim to the irrational. We need so much to be governed by reason. Most of your gallant efforts are directed towards that end.'

She wagged her finger at me. 'You really mustn't make private exceptions. That's not the right route to a perfect world.

'But there, it's not for me to lecture you!'

The attack on me had shattered a vertebra at the top of my spine. The nanobots replaced it with an artificially grown bone-substitute. But a nerve had been damaged that, it appeared, was beyond repair, at least within the limited resources of our hospital.

I stayed for ten days, in that ward I had so recently left, to enjoy once more Mary's pleasant brand of physiotherapy. I lived for those hours when we were in bed together.

Perhaps all ideas of utopia were based on that sort of closeness. In the dark I thought of George Orwell's dystopia, *Nineteen Eighty-Four*. Orwell set forth there his idea of utopia: a shabby room, in which he could be alone with a girl . . .

Mary looked seriously at me. 'When your assailants are captured, I have drugs in my pharmaceutical armoury that will ensure they never do anything thuggish again . . .' She nodded reassuringly. 'As we agree, we want no prisons here. As my captive, you naturally want me to keep you happy.'

'Passionately I want it,' I said. We kissed then, passionately.

I practised walking with my arm on a nurse's arm. My balance was always to be uncertain; from then on, I found it convenient to walk with a stick.

I rested one further day in hospital. As I was leaving its doors, Mary bid me farewell. 'Go and continue your excellent work, my dear Tom. Do not trouble your mind by seeking revenge on those who attacked you. Their reason failed them. They must fear a rational society; but their kind are already becoming obsolete.'

'I'm not so sure of that, Mary. What kind are we?'

Laughing, she clucked in a motherly way and squeezed my arm. She was her professional self, and on duty.

Suddenly she embraced me. 'I love you, Tom! Forgive me. You're our prophet! We shall soon live,' she said, 'into an epoch of pure reason.'

I thought, as I hobbled back to Cang Hai with my stick, of that wonderful satire of Jonathan Swift's, popularly known as *Gulliver's Travels*, and of the fourth book where Gulliver journeys among the cold, uninteresting, indifferent children of reason, the Houyhnhnms.

If our carefully planned new way of life bred such a species, we would be entering on chilly and sunless territory.

Where would Mary's love be in those days?

Yet would not that rather bloodless life of reason be better than the world of the bludgeon, the old unregenerate world, continually ravaged by war and its degradations in one region or another? My father, whose altruism I had inherited, had left his home country to serve as a doctor in the eastern Adriatic, among the poor in the coastal town of Splon. There he set up a clinic. In that clinic, he treated all alike, Catholic, Orthodox or Protestant.

My father believed that the West, with its spirit of enquiry, was moving towards an age of reason, however faltering was its progress.

In Splon I passed many years of my boyhood, unaffected by the poverty surrounding us, ranging free in the mountains behind the town. My elder sister, Patricia, was my great friend and ally, a big-hearted girl with an insatiable curiosity about nature. We used to swim through the currents of our stretch of sea to gain a small island called Isplan. Here Pat and I used to pretend to be shipwrecked, as if in prodromoic rehearsal for being stranded on another planet.

Civil war broke out in the country when I was nine years old, in 2024. My father and mother refused to leave with other foreign nationals. They were blind to danger, seeing it as their duty to stay and serve the innocent people of Splon. However, they sent Pat away to safety, to live with an aunt. For a while, I missed her greatly.

Civil war is a cancer. The innocent people of Splon took sides and began to kill and torture each other. Their pretext was that they were being treated unfairly and demanded only social justice, but behind this veneer of reasonable argument, calculated to dull their consciences and win them sympathy abroad, lay a mindless cruelty, a wish to destroy those whose religious beliefs they did not share.

They set about destroying not merely the vulnerable living bodies of their former neighbours, the new enemies, but their enemies' homes as well, together with anything of historic or aesthetic worth.

The bridge over the River Splo was one of the few examples of local architecture worthy of preservation. Built by the Ottomans five centuries earlier, it had featured on the holiday brochures distributed by the tourist office. People came from all over the world to enjoy the graceful parabola of Splon's old bridge.

As tanks gathered in the mountains behind the town, as an ancient warship appeared offshore, as mortars and artillery were dug in along the road to town, that famous Splo Bridge was available for target practice. It fell soon, its rubble and dust cascading into the Splo.

The enemy made no attempt to enter the town. Their soldiers loitered smoking and boozing some metres down the road. They laid cowardly siege to Splon, setting about destroying it, not for any strategic purpose but merely because they had hatred and shells to spare.

Anyone trying to escape from Splon was liable to capture. As prisoners, they suffered barbaric torture. Women were raped and mutilated. Children were raped and used as target practice.

Occasionally, one such captive, broken, was allowed to crawl back to Splon to give a report on these barbarities, in order that the fear and tension of the starving inhabitants might be increased. Often such survivors died in my father's little surgery, beyond his aid.

The great organisations of the Western world stood back and watched dismayed at the slaughter on their TV screens. In truth they were puzzled as to how to quell civil war, where the will to fight and die was so strong and the reason for the struggle so hard to comprehend.

During that year of siege we lived for the most part in cellars. Sanitation was improvised. Food was scarce. I would venture out with my friend Milos under cover of darkness to fish off the harbour wall. More than once hidden snipers fired at us, so that we had to crawl to safety.

Starvation came early to Splon, followed by disease. To bury the dead in the rocky soil, exposed to snipers on all sides, was not easy – a hasty business at best. I spent some days away from the town, lying in long grass, trying to kill a rabbit with a stone from a catapult. Once, when I returned, triumphant, with a dead animal for the pot, it was to find my mother dying of cholera. My sorrow and guilt haunt me still.

I can never forget my father's cries of misery and remorse. He howled like a dog over mother's dead body.

Exhaustion set in among the struggling factions. The war finally petered out. Days came when no shells were fired at us.

A party of the enemy arrived in a truck, waving white flags, to announce an armistice. The leader of the party was a smartly uniformed captain, wearing incongruous white gloves. Quite a young man, but already bemedalled.

It was the chance our men had waited for. They rushed the truck. They set upon the soldiers with rifles and knives and bayonets, and carved up the party, all but the captain, into bloody pieces. They rubbed the face of one man into the broken glass from the vehicle's windscreen. They set fire to the truck. I stood in the broken street, watching the massacre, enjoying it, thrilling to the screams of those about to die. It was like a movie, like one of my Biker stories.

The captain was dragged into a burned-out factory down the road. He was stripped of his gloves and his uniform, made naked. Some of Splon's women were allowed – or encouraged – to hack off his testicles and penis and ram them into his mouth. They beat him to death with iron bars.

I was curious to see what was going on in the burned-out factory. A man stopped me from entering. Other boys got in. They told me about the atrocity afterwards.

Next day, a Red Cross truck rolled into town. My father and I were evacuated. My father had lost his will to live, dying in his sleep some weeks later. That was in a hospital in the German city of Mannheim.

While I was laid low in hospital these past memories returned vividly to mind. I was forced to relive them as I had rarely done before. In fear of the horrors of that awful period, I recognised my strong desire for a better ordered society, and for a time and place where reason reigned secure.

Mary and I sat up in bed. She listened sympathetically as I told my tale. Tears, pure and clear, escaped from her eyes and ran down her cheeks.

Perhaps the riddle of Olympus had brought on my horrors. The mood under that vast carapace could be one of regret, rage even, at the way the life forms had had to imprison themselves in order to survive as the old free life died. A billion years of rage and regret . . . ?

Several visitors came while I was recovering. They included Benazir Bahudur, the silent teacher of children.

She said, 'Until you recover fully your ability to move,

dear Tom, I will dance for you to remind you of movement.'

She danced a dance very similar to the one I had watched once before. In her long skirt, with her bare arms, she performed her dance of step and gesture, as supple and subtle as deep water. Life is like this and this. There is so much to be enjoyed . . .

It was beautiful and immensely touching. 'You manage to dance without music,' I said.

'Oh, I hear the music very clearly. It comes through my feet, not my ears.'

Another welcome visitor was Kathi Skadmorr. She slouched in wearing her Now overalls and perched on the end of the bed, smiling. 'So this is where utopias end – in a hospital bed!'

'Some begin here. You do a lot of thinking. I was thinking of dystopias. Presumably you think about quantum physics and consciousness all the time . . .'

She frowned. 'Don't be silly, Tom. I also think a lot about sex, although I never perform it. In fact, I spend much time sitting in the lotus position staring at a blank white wall. That's something I learned from you lot. It seems to help. And I also recall "I saw a new heaven and a new Earth: for the first heaven and the first Earth were passed away." Isn't that what you Christians say?'

'I'm not a Christian, Kathi, and doubt whether the guy who wrote those words was either.'

She leaned forward. 'Of course I am fascinated by scientific theory – but only because I would like to get beyond it. The blank white wall is a marvellous thing. It looks at me. It asks me why I exist. It asks me what my conscious mind is doing. Why it's doing it. It asks if there are whole subjects the scientists of our day cannot touch. Maybe daren't touch.'

I asked her if she meant the paranormal.

'Oh, the way you use that label. Tom, dearest, my hero, your adopted daughter whom you so neglect – she has inexplicable, paranormal, experiences all the time.

They're part of her normal life. Nobody can account for them. We need to reconceptualise our thought, as you have reconceptualised society. Stop clinging to frigid reason.

'Chimborazo is a million times stranger than Cang Hai's world, yet we think we can account for it within science, can accommodate it within our perceptual *Umwelt*. Yet all the time it's performing miracles. Turning a sack of superfluid into a conscious entity . . . That's a miracle worthy of Jesus Christ. Yet Dreiser doesn't turn a hair of his moustache . . .

'Anyhow, I must be going. I just called to bring you this little present.' From a pocket of her overalls she produced a photocube. In it a complex coil slowly revolved, its strands studded with seedlike dots. I held it up to the light and asked her what it was.

'They've analysed one of the exteroceptors they hacked off Chimborazo. This is just an enlarged snippet of its version of a DNA structure. You see how greatly it is more complex than human DNA? Four strands needed to hold its inheritance. The doubled double helix.'

When I was up and about I went to see Choihosla again, this time taking the trouble to knock at his door. We talked these matters over. I even ventured to speculate whether mankind was experiencing a million years of regret that it had achieved consciousness, with the burdens that accompanied it.

'We all suffer on occasions from the dark soul of the night,' he said.

'You mean the dark night of the soul, Youssef.'

'No, no. Look outside! I mean the dark soul of the night.'

Was it the old quirky sage, George Bernard Shaw, who had said that utopia had been achieved only on paper? Perhaps it had been achieved too in Steve Rollins's simulation. The people in his quantputer went about their business without feeling, without any sense of tomorrow, being subject to Steve's team's supervision. Not a sparrow fell without proper computation.

An enviable state?

It was time to get to work again.

I called the advisers of Adminex to me. The date was the first day of Month Ten, 2071.

'Hello!' Dayo said, seeing me with my stick for the first time. 'What's happened to you?'

'The human condition,' I told him.

It was necessary to set about drawing up a constitution for our community. We needed to have the best possible way of life memorialised and, as far as might be, made clear to all.

The Adminex meeting was well attended. Clearly the external threat – if threat it was – from Chimborazo had served to excite our intelligence, if not to unite us. Only once before had so many people attended our forums, when Dreiser had addressed us. They gathered under the doomed Hindenburg and sat there quietly. By now, I thought with affection, I knew all of their faces and most of their names, these creatures of a human Olympus.

A late arrival at our discussion was Arnold Poulsen, who came by jo-jo car. It was a long while since I had seen him; he so rarely entered our forums. He sat now, his hands clasped between his knees, his long pale hair straggling about his face, saying nothing, contributing nothing but his presence.

Because I had been away I knew that things had moved on, and I anticipated argument and opposition. But even Feneloni seemed to have undergone a change of mind.

Speaking slowly, he said, 'I must put aside my reservations regarding your creation of a better and just society. I felt the wisdom of your judgement while I was shut away, and it seems to have had its bearing on my change of mind. While it's true I long to get back to Earth, that's no reason to create difficulties here. I can't exactly bring myself to back you, but I won't oppose you.'

We shook hands. Our listeners applauded briefly.

Crispin Barcunda was present with Belle Rivers. She was looking younger and dressing differently, although she still strung herself about with rock crystal beads. It was noticeable how affectionately she and Crispin regarded each other.

'Well, well, Tom Jefferies, you will turn us yet into a pack of coenobitic monks,' Crispin said, in his usual jocular fashion. 'But your declaration of utopia, or whatever you call it, must not be padded out with your prejudices. If you recall the passage I quoted, to the benefit of everyone, from the good Alfred Wallace's *Malay Archipelago*, he states that a natural sense of justice seems to be inherent in every man.

'That may not be quite the case. Perhaps it was stated merely in the fire of Victorian optimism – a fire that has long since burned itself out. However, Belle and I believe that a natural sense of religion is inherent in every man. Sometimes it's unrealised until trouble comes. Then people start believing all over again in the power of prayer.

'The little nondenominational church we set up has been well attended ever since we learned about Olympus – Chimborazo, I mean – and its movements.

'We are well aware that you are against religion and the concept of God. However, our teaching experience convinces us that religion is an evolutionary instinct, and should be allowed in your utopia – to which we are otherwise prepared to subscribe. We need you, as chief law-giver, to realise there must be laws that go against your wishes, as there will be some laws contrary to everyone's wishes. Otherwise there will be no reality, and the laws will fail.'

Belle now turned the power of her regard on me and reinforced what Crispin had said. 'Tom, our children need guidance on religion, as they do on sex and other matters. It's useless to deny something exists just because you don't like it, as we once denied there was life on Mars because it made us feel a bit safer. You have seen and heard the kids

302

with their tammies – a nuisance to us maybe, but seemingly necessary to them. You must listen too to the squeaks of the godly.

'If we are to live rational lives, then we must accept that there are certain existential matters beyond our understanding – for the present at least, and maybe always and for ever.

'It is certainly no perversion to feel a reverence for life, for the miracle of it, for the world and for the universe. Doesn't the discovery of Chimborazo increase our wonder? Into such reverence the idea of God slips easily. Our minds are not quantputers. They work in contradictory ways at one and the same time. It's for this reason we sometimes seem at odds with ourselves.'

While listening intently I nevertheless noticed at this moment a fleeting smile on the face of Poulsen, who had sat motionless, not shifting his position, making no comment.

Belle was continuing. 'Those most vehement against established religion are often proved to be those most attracted to its comforts. We exist at the heart of a complexity for which any human laws we promulgate must seem flimsy, even transitory.

'There was a time when it was bold to take up an anti-religious stance. That time is past. Now we see that religion has played an integral role in our evolution. It has been a worldwide phenomenon for many centuries, and—'

At which point Dayo broke in, sawing the air with one hand, saying, 'Look, Missis Belle, slavery too was a worldwide phenomenon for many centuries. It still exists Downstairs! Millions of people were snatched from West Africa to serve the white races in the New World – twenty-five million people snatched from East Africa by Islamic traders in one century alone. I have the figures!

'Slavery isn't done away with yet. Always it's the rich and powerful against the poor and powerless! That doesn't mean to say we don't need to banish slavery – or religion. Or that these terrible things are good, just because they're old, does it? Antiquity is no excuse. We're trying to reform these horrible blemishes on existence.'

Dayo received a round of applause. A look of delight filled his face. He could not stop beaming.

Belle gave Dayo a nod and a tigerish smile, while seeming to continue her monologue uninterruptedly.

'Life for all generations, more particularly in the dim and distant past, has been filled with injustice, fear, injury, illness and death. God is a consolation, a mediator, a judge, a stern father, a supreme power, ordering what seems like disorder. For many, God – or the gods – are a daily necessity, an extra dimension.

'We like, in our Christian inheritance, to think that God made us in His image. It's more certain that we made Him in our image.

'And where does that image live? Beyond matrix, beyond time, beyond space-time. Was it intuition that dreamed up such a place, which scientists now believe might exist?'

'You make,' I replied, 'religion sound like a unitary matter. In its many sects, in fact, it has proved divisive throughout Earth's history, a perennial cause of war and bloodshed.'

'But we are creating Mars's history now,' said Crispin, smiling and allowing a glimpse of his gold tooth, while Belle, scowling radiantly, said, 'Tom, let me quote a phrase Oliver Cromwell once used: "I beseech you, in the bowels of Christ, think it possible you may be mistaken!"'

I let myself be persuaded by their eloquence. 'As long as you don't start sacrificing goats,' I said.

'Heavens,' Crispin said. 'Just show me a Martian goat!'

The discussion then turned to other subjects, on which agreement was reached with unique ease, and – with everyone's assistance – Adminex accordingly drew up and put on record our laws.

As Arnold Poulsen was about to depart as silently as he had come, I caught his sleeve and asked him what he made of the debate.

'Despite wide divergence of opinion, you were agreeable together, and so able to come to an agreeable conclusion. Did you not find that a little unexpected?' He brushed his hair back from his forehead and scrutinised me narrowly.

'Arnold, you are being oblique. What are you saying?'

'From my childhood,' he said, in his high voice, 'I recall a phrase expressing unanimity: "Their hearts beat as one". Perhaps you agree that seemed to be the state of affairs here just now. Even Feneloni was amenable to a point . . .'

'Supposing it to be so, what follows?'

He paused, clutching his mouth in a momentary gesture, as if to prevent what it would say. 'Tom, we have difficulties enough here, Upstairs. You have difficulties enough, trying to resolve the ambiguities of human conduct by sweet reason.'

'Well?'

Smiling, he sat down again and, with a gesture, invited me to sit by him as the hall was clearing. He then proceeded to remind me of the extract from Wallace's *Malay Archipelago* that Crispin Barcunda – 'very usefully', as Poulsen put it – had read to the company. Poulsen had thought about the passage for a long while. Why should a community of people, those islanders characterised by Wallace as 'savages', live freely without all the quarrels that afflicted the Western world? Without, indeed, the struggle for existence? Such utopianism could not be achieved by intellect and reason alone.

Was there an underlying physical reason for the unity of these so-called savages? Arnold said he had set his quantputer to analysing the known factors. Results indicated that the communities Wallace referred to were small, in size not unlike our stranded Martian community. It was not impossible to suppose – and here, he said, he had consulted the hospital authorities, including Mary Fangold – that one effect of isolation and proximity was that heartbeats synchronised, just as women sleeping in dormitories all menstruated at the same time of the month.

On Mars we presented a case of all hearts beating as one.

The result of which was an unconscious sense of unity, even unanimity.

Poulsen had established a small research group within the scientific community. Kathi had referred to it. To be brief, the group had decided that an oscillating wave of some kind might serve as a sort of drumbeat to assist synchronisation. In the end, adapting some of Mary Fangold's spare equipment, they had produced and broadcast a soundwave below audibility levels. That is to say, they had filled the domes with an infrasound drumbeat below a frequency of 16 hertz.

'You tried this experiment without consulting anyone?' I demanded.

'We consulted each other.' He spoke in the light, rather amused tone into which he frequently slipped. 'We knew there would be protests from the generality, as there always are when anything new is introduced.'

'But what was the result of your experiment?'

Arnold Poulsen laid a thin hand on my shoulder, saying, 'Oh, we've been running the beat for six days now. You saw the benevolent results in our discussion. All hearts beat as one. Science has delivered your utopia to you, Tom . . . The human mind has been set free.'

I didn't believe him. Nor did I argue with him.

Later, when I was lying with Mary, I told her of what Poulsen claimed to have done, for his pride in scientific ingenuity had irritated me. 'To claim that an oscillating wave brought about our utopia, instead of our own endeavours – why, you might as well claim that God did it . . .'

She was silent. Then she said, almost in a whisper, 'I don't want to sound unreasonable, but perhaps all those things conspired together . . .'

I kissed her lips: it was a better course than argument.

Further Memoir by Cang Hai

21

Utopia

Dear Tom has been dead now for twenty years. He died at the youthful age of sixty-seven. I zeep these words in what would be midway through 2102 by the old calendar.

A statue to Tom stands at the entrance of the Strangers Hall of Aeropolis in Amazonis Planitia. It depicts him in an absurdly triumphalist pose. I never saw him stand like that. Tom Jefferies was a modest man. He regarded himself as ordinary.

But perhaps the legend below his name is correct:

Prime Architect of Mars –
2015–2082
The Man Who Made Utopia Part of Our Real World.

Did Tom love me? I know he loved Mary Fangold. They never married. Marriage had gone out of fashion. But they were In Liaison as the new rationalism has it.

Do I miss him? Probably I do. I did not remain on Mars. In my old age I have decided to move further out, to lighter gravities.

My daughter Alpha went to seek out those Lushan Mountains I painted for her when she was a child. But I find I am an independent animal, as long as I retain contact with my Other. So our lives unfold.

On the occasion when Tom's just society was announced and its constitution read aloud, everyone was in a mood for rejoicing. We truly knew we had made a human advance.

Our proceedings, together with the celebrations that followed, were recorded as usual and, as usual, broadcast to Earth.

One incident of that day is vividly recalled. I had not seen my friends, Hal Kissorian and Sharon Singh, for some while – not, in fact, since their marriage – and longed for their company to make my happiness complete.

I rang their bell and was admitted. Both of them greeted me warmly. They were scantily dressed. As they embraced me, I smelt sweet and heavy odours about the room. We talked about all that was happening – or rather, I talked. I talked about Chimborazo and about the wonderful sense of social completeness we had managed to build. They regarded me with fixed smiles on their faces. I belatedly realised that the topics held little interest for them.

On the wall behind the sofa on which they sat was a hand-painted mural. I recognised a blue-skinned Krishna with his flute. Krishna was plump, his figure rather rounded in a girlish way, his eyes large and sparkling. Around him lounged pink ladies in diaphanous gowns, holding flower buds or tweaking one of the god's oily locks scarcely contained by his crown. They all gazed with lascivious approval at his immense mauve erection.

'Well, that enough of my affairs,' I said. 'What have you two been doing?'

Both Kissorian and Sharon burst into joyous laughter. 'Shall we show you?' asked Sharon.

I came away with that curious mixture of shame and envy that people of the mind feel for people of the flesh.

It was then I decided I was a solitary person. With a numb heart, it is easy to behave like a true utopian.

By the fifth year after the collapse of EUPACUS our society had settled on an even keel. All our various disciplines had taken root and were beginning to blossom. The Birth Room was a thriving institution. We had found room for diverse personalities to live together peacefully.

At that time, I visited the Birth Room frequently. I

miss it now such things do not exist. I went not only for companionship but to enjoy the transformation in women's personalities from their personae among men when they entered there. They became simpler and more direct, perhaps I should say unguarded, when they escaped from male regard.

Many were the arguments there about a possible return to Downstairs. By no means all women wanted it. Life Upstairs, although austere, was far less abrasive than it had been on Earth. Certainly child-rearing was easier, while the new generation of children seemed brighter and more companionable, despite their tammies.

Received wisdom was traded.

'Earth has decided to leave us here.'

'Let Downstairs get on with its affairs while we get on with ours.'

'They've forgotten all about us.'

Such remarks, often heard, were made with varying tones of optimism or gloom.

Olympus was moving steadily nearer. Observation showed, alarmingly, that its rate of progression was ever increasing. Various attempts to communicate with it failed. Willa and Vera, the mentatropists, had driven to the site, where they picked up a CPS, followed by a scrambled signal. The signal was intensively studied, but years passed before it was understood.

It was in that fifth year of our exile that Meteor Watch reported an object approaching Mars at a considerable velocity. Everyone was alarmed. But the speed of the object decreased. Eventually, a capsule shot from it, extruded a helichute, and landed a few kilometres north of the domes. An expedition set out immediately to investigate it.

The capsule bore a large symbol, TUIS, painted on its side. When transported into the domes and opened up, it was found to contain various medical supplies, scientific equipment, and a veritable store of foodstuffs, many of the names of which we had all but forgotten.

The supplies were accompanied by a plaque that read, 'With the Admiration of the Terrestrial Utopian International Society'. We wondered at the title, which indicated that the times were changing Downstairs.

Early in our sixth year, which is to say six terrestrial years on the calendar to which we clung, notching up days like Crusoe on his island, the outer rim of Chimborazo appeared over the horizon, to be clearly viewed from both domes and science unit. Its leading edge seemed now to be approaching at a rate that was hard to credit – at least 500 metres a day. It was easy to imagine its paddles beating furiously through the underlying regolith. However, the speed of movement did not represent the motion of Chimborazo as a whole. Chimborazo's scope encompassed more and more of the Martian surface, tumbling in our direction – a terrifying wave of regolith ploughed up before its prow.

Willa-Vera announced they would soon decode the signals they had recorded: Chimborazo's 'voice' fluctuated up and down the electromagnetic spectrum, and might be comprehended more as music than actual speech. They would have everything interpreted in a year or possibly two.

Their well-publicised conviction was that, after many centuries of meditation, this towering mentality – a mentality dwarfing Everest – had become a virtual god in wisdom. Once its mode of communication was understood, Chimborazo's immaterialism and transcendent qualities would set humankind upon a fresher and more vital path than could at present be visualised.

We would then move forward into 'an ultimate reality'.

I would certainly welcome a reality beyond my present day-to-day life . . .

It was six years and 100 Martian days since the economic collapse that had swept EUPACUS away, carrying the terrestrial infrastructure with it. A manned ship arrived within Mars matrix and went into orbit about the planet. The visitor appeared enormous, resembling, some said, St

310

Paul's Cathedral turned upside-down. We marvelled at it as if we were peasants.

Another age had dawned in the history of matrixflight. This strange object proved to be a ship powered by nuclear fusion. The epoch of wasteful chemical rockets was dead.

'What – what kind of rocket is that, for God's sake?' exclaimed a young YEA.

It was John Homer Bateson who replied, and even he sounded impressed, 'I would suggest that rockets are now as obsolete as the bathysphere.'

'What in hell is a bathysphere?' was the response.

A ferry floated down from this new marvel. Witnesses remarked that in the gentleness of its descent it was like a giant metal leaf. Our isolation was now ended . . .

Much jubilation broke out in the domes. Of a sudden, the prospect of green meadows, golden beaches and blue oceans became almost overwhelmingly desirable. We looked eagerly to see the faces of our rescuers from Downstairs.

Three unsmiling men confronted us. Marching into the domes, they announced that the Premier of the UK had taken over the assets of the failed EUPACUS consortium. They were the legal inheritors of all EUPACUS property. A EUPACUS ship had been stolen five years previously; its pilot, one Abel Feneloni, together with his accomplices on the ship, had been arrested. The ship was badly damaged when crash-landing in the north of Canada.

In his defence, continued the newcomers, Feneloni had claimed he was sent in the stolen ship under direct orders from the so-called government of Mars. A considerable stack of dollars was therefore owed by Mars to the government of the UK. Until this outstanding bill was paid, no free flights back to Earth were going to be allowed.

So we were quickly given the opportunity to relearn the value of money, and that some people lived by it.

Tom stepped forward. 'We do not use money here.'

'Then you do not use our ship.'

The three terrestrials were invited to a consultation

311

meeting. They refused, saying there was no necessity for consultation. All they required was settlement of an unpaid debt. They were clumsy in their spacesuits and we easily overpowered them.

To our disgust we found they wore guns under their suits. These were the first guns ever seen on Mars, our White Mars. We imprisoned them, took over their ship and signalled the UN on Earth.

We stressed that guns were not permitted on Mars; their importation therefore constituted an illegal act. Nor did we accept responsibility for the actions of Abel Feneloni; we regarded him as an outlaw. The UK had no entitlement to try and extract monies from us for Feneloni's crimes.

To ameliorate this confrontational tone, we declared that we possessed a discovery beyond price that, as utopians, we were prepared to share with everyone.

Clearly, much had changed on Earth during our absence. The United Koreas had become a great power, but were at odds with the UN – and with the rest of the planet. The response we received was favourable to us. The matter of the stolen ship remained to be resolved. Meanwhile our three captives had to be convinced that they were in the wrong and released, pending trial; and as many people as wished to return to Earth were immediately to embark on the waiting ship. They would be welcome Downstairs.

It was done. Many of our people crowded aboard the great orbiting ship – in particular, those who had children.

I wept when saying farewell to my friends.

I cannot tell here the histories of those who returned Downstairs. Some adjusted to the hectic heavy-gravity globe. Some became happy and settled. Some struggled in a world grown unfamiliar – and, of those, some prospered while others sank into failure.

Sharon Singh and Hal Kissorian parted company. Perhaps their involvement with each other had been too intense to endure. Kissorian became a great utopianist, and held a responsible position in government in Greater Scandinavia. Sharon Singh emigrated to Mercury and joined the FAD rebels in the Fighters Against Dictatorship struggle for Mercurian utopia.

The fact remains that when our Martians stepped out from the rescue ship into the dazzling draughty light of their mother planet, they were greeted like heroes. Receptions were held for them in many of the world's great cities. Several of them found themselves to be famous, their faces well known, even their speeches memorised.

Dreiser Hawkwood was the star of this select group. TUIS, the Terrestrial Utopian International Society, which had sent provisions to Mars, had gained power in several places, and in some countries had become the de facto government. They saw to it that Dreiser's achievements were widely recognised.

The explanation for this widespread acceptance was not far to seek. Leo Anstruther had become the founder of TUIS. Against the interdictions of many powers, his society had recorded all our transmissions from Mars and beamed them via satellite round the world. At that time, the world – humbled, uncertain – had been in the mood to listen, watch and learn.

Ramifications of the EUPACUS collapse had brought the capitalist system into disrepute and, in some cases, had demolished it entirely. The tentacles of corruption had reached out to involve famous figures in both East and West. Complex legal proceedings were still grinding through the law courts of California, Germany, China, Japan, Indonesia and elsewhere.

Climate, that unacknowledged legislator in the history of mankind, was a contributory cause of the marked change in political thinking. The overheating of the globe had brought hazardous weather and great oceanic turbulences. New York, London and Amsterdam, together with many another low-lying city, had been invaded by ocean. These cities were now practically deserted, crumbling under the force of the tides. Climatic change had ruined

313

many an economy and revived others, the United Koreas among them.

Into this unsettled situation the possibility of building a free and just society had infiltrated. The example of the Martian exiles proved more attractive than we could have imagined.

Planet Earth, we found, was now largely a Han planet. Which is to say that modes of Chinese Pacific thought prevailed, as more confrontational Western modes of thought had dominated in the previous century.

Yearning for a better life had always been latent in society. Now came a renaissance. One of its effects was the establishment of Huochuans in many global centres. Huochuan was a Chinese word for cargo vessel; the name caught on for travelling institutes, which drifted from city to city with a freight of learning and wisdom. One whole section of a Huochuan was devoted to a huiyan, literally 'minds that perceive both past and future', now applied to life-story-storage systems.

As nationality came to play a less active role in human affairs, the concept of age-grouping, with activities suitable for each age, became predominant. Divisions such as YEAS and DOPS were influential in this shift in thinking. It proved to be the thirty-something group that received most benefit from Huochuan teaching.

Huochuans promoted a system of two-way communications. Those whose lives had taken a wrong turning could receive consultation and/or counselling. A method developed whereby long-bygone conversations could be recalled verbatim and improved. Anyone had opportunities to reconsider their lives and alter career or direction if insight demanded it.

In payment the beneficiary contributed to the huiyan by depositing a vid, document or disk, recording their inward and outward lives. In this way, the Huochuans accumulated a grand compendium of the experiences of generations in a kind of psychic genetic inheritance. For

314

the first time in human history, attention was paid to the individual life – to all individual lives – 'this odd diversity of pain and joy', as an old folk song has it.

Such huiyan records served as a style of general entertainment/enlightenment (called tuokongs), much in the way of some serious TV programmes of the twentieth century.

With the proliferation of genetically altered vegetables and fruits, the eating of meat became a thing of the past in many regions. Domesticated animals became a rarity, although cats, dogs and songbirds were almost venerated, as were the semi-domesticated reindeer of far northern lands. Here and there, gates of zoo cages were flung open and their occupants set free.

People lived differently. They thought differently. Their cities were now contained; they kept in contact with one another by Ambient, much as ships at sea had once kept in touch by radio satellite. The old system of M-roads fell into decay. Beyond city walls, the wilderness was allowed to return. There, as on Mars, a degree of solitude could be enjoyed.

'The Utopians!' It became a magical word. While a percentage of those returning from Mars fell prey to terrestrial diseases, the virus of utopian thinking spread. I am told that, in the great hall of the Unified World (as the reconstituted United Nationalities is called) stands a row of bronze busts of those of us who made history. There in effigy is Dreiser Hawkwood, there is Tom Jefferies, of course, and Kathi Skadmoor and Arnold Poulsen. And I am there too!

If future generations enquire why I, my humble little self, should stand there with the great, there is a reason. For I it was who went out with Kathi and Dreiser to confront Chimborazo when it gave birth.

The inspiration to do this came to me in a waking dream from my earthly Other. I was walking somewhere in a kind of desert called Crapout – though how I knew its name I have no idea – with another person, maybe male, maybe female, when a strange manifestation filled the sky.

It appeared like the cloud of an explosion, very alarmingly. I sheltered my companion in my arms, and was unafraid. A noise of trumpets sounded when, from the great threatening cloud, something beautiful appeared. I can't describe it. Not an angel, no. More like a – well, a winged octopus, a pretty winged octopus, trailing streamers. It seemed to glance down at me with much kindness, so that I woke crying.

I gathered my courage and called Kathi. She spoke to Dreiser. We suited up and went out on the surface. Chimborazo was immense; the furrow of regolith it ploughed before itself was close to the science unit. The Smudge ring was covered in a layer of grit.

Chimborazo towered over us, ridged and immeasurable. A fearful wind blew. I remember the date. It was the second day of Month One of the year 2072.

Then came the noise, a call of some kind, like bugles and cellos combined.

The three of us stood our ground. The mighty thing reared up. We had a glimpse of pronged exteroceptors and a kind of mucus curtain. From the curtain shot a pale stalk, perhaps like an elephant's trunk, withered in appearance, with a mouth and labia, moist, at its end. This strange protrusion penetrated the ring.

Again the trumpet note of triumph. I gripped Kathi's hand. Liquid surged. Dreiser said faintly, 'Amniotic fluid!'

The enormous creature seemed to back away and settle down. It became motionless.

On the churned regolith lay a thing resembling a small boulder. I went forward and lifted it with ease. It was comparatively light. As I carried it in my arms into the science unit, the thing began to open up.

After billions of years, Chimborazo had managed to reproduce itself, pumping both male and female cells into the receptive fluid . . .

*   *   *

316

So the great yearning for utopia spread on Earth. It brought about revolution first of all in Europe, that fertile ground of so many past upheavals. Was it Chimborazo's influence that made us unite as one, as never before? Be that as it may, we must believe we achieved utopia of our own volition. We must believe in free will and the strength of will.

Now my daughter Alpha lives far away from me, while I myself am even further from Earth than Mars is. She has a man and a child, so her life is fruitful and, I suppose, happy. I will never see her again, or embrace her, or kiss her little daughter.

At least it is a consolation to know she will enjoy the promises of what to me is the inaccessible future.

Note

By Beta Greenway, Daughter of Alpha Jefferies

I am a Jovian. I live a life of pattern. My actions are premeditated. I am pleased to contribute to this report.

Since the Jovian moons carried little or no emotional freight for human beings, they were not treated with the scruples Mars had once enjoyed.

Monitor probes, accompanied by a freighter, arrived by the turn of the century at what Galileo Galilei originally termed 'the Medician stars', our four sizeable moons. A base was established on Ganymede while the other satellites, in particular Io and Europa, were surveyed by machinonauts.

Ganymede was made habitable by bioengineered plant-insect stock. These ephemeral life forms had been despatched in unmanned probes, to soft-land here and prepare it for human life. They clothed it in their corpses before we arrived. Such advances were not possible in the early days of Mars landings.

Our first ugly prefabricated buildings have long since been devoured and regurgitated to form our spinlifters.

Life is pleasant here. I find much scientific research to keep me occupied, and am compiling an Amb entitled *Pluto As an Abode of Life*. Although the sun is distant, we enjoy the brilliant spectacle of Jupiter in our skies, together with the swarming variety of other moons to inspire us and tempt our thoughts ever outwards, into further and better transformations of human life.

The quest for knowledge continues.

Indeed, such work continues beyond the solar system, beyond the Oort Cloud. There, beneath the light of stars, a Cheeth-Rosewall is coming into operation. This Chheeth-Rosewall is immeasurably larger than the failed miniature HIGMO detector constructed on Mars a century ago.

The ring has a diameter of about the same extent as one of Saturn's outer rings, with a cross-section of just a few millimetres. The volume of superfluid is therefore not too large. However, we expect to detect a HIGMO at last.

HIGMO density is a good deal less than anticipated. However, the research has acquired vital importance: as generally agreed, it will yield important truths about the nature of *consciousness* – as well as solving the riddle of mass.

Once we can control these things, we shall be able to project our minds across the universe. And what we shall there encounter, who can say?

I have no communication with the person who was my mother. She lives on Iapetus, out by Saturn. But I will zeep this note to her for her mother's record of ancient times. Frankly, the thought of womb-birth amuses me. How clumsy and inefficient it was, and how inconvenient for womankind! We do not have families.

Our Jovian generations are now all of extra-uterine extraction, apart from the subbermans. E-u techniques have enabled us to combine pseuplant life into our genes; when our lungs breathe out, our foliagics breathe in; what the foliagics emit, we breathe in.

Thus we are almost entirely independent of atmosphere suits for long periods. We are a mathematical people. By the end of their first year, infants can calculate the orbits of most matrix bodies we observe orbiting about us.

Having trained Chimborazo to spawn, we now have small Chimbos with us everywhere. We benefit from their acute diagnostic powers. Indeed, it can be claimed that human and Chimbos form a symbiotic species.

Together, we and Chimbos are planning to voyage out into the universe, far beyond the heliopause. We hope to call it to account. Because we are utopians, we can do this. One can proudly say that the human race, risen from lowly and irrational forms, with a mind, in Darwin's words, once as low as that of the lowest animal, has at last become REASONABLE.

Appendix by Dr Laurence Lustgarten

The United Nationalities Charter for the Settlement of Mars

The peoples of the Earth, represented through the United Nationalities, do hereby make provision for the human settlement of our sister planet, Mars, consistent with respect for its equal status with the nations of Earth within the solar system.

The United Nationalities, recognising the fragility of the Martian environment and acutely conscious of our present ignorance of the capability of its ecosystem to sustain physical incursion and change, hereby agrees:

Art. I: All nations comprising the United Nationalities do individually and collectively disclaim any territorial rights of ownership or control over any portion of the planet Mars or its airspace. Equally they bind themselves to reject any such claims that may in future be asserted by any political entity on the planet Earth.

Art. II: Mars shall be governed by the United Nationalities as a trusteeship, held in trust for the entire population of Earth. It shall be treated as a single entity, and never sub-divided and subject to different regimes. The environment of Mars shall be regarded as sacrosanct; any large-scale projects that threaten its individual character shall be prohibited, at least until such time as the entire globe has been scientifically explored and studied.

Art. III: In light of the severe limitations on its ability to sustain the intrusion of an alien civilisation, human settlement of Mars shall be strictly limited in numbers and subject to qualifications by the United Nationalities. While it is accepted that member states may select exclusively their own nationals for their share of any settlement quota, they shall observe the principles of non-discrimination on grounds of race, colour, sex and religious or political opinion in their selection.

Art. IV: All questions of economic or other relations with the settlement established on Mars shall be conducted with the delegates of the United Nationalities, who shall be ever mindful of their trusteeship obligations.

Art.V: Mars shall be used for peaceful purposes only. All activities of a military nature, such as the establishment of bases or fortifications, or the testing of any type of weapons, are absolutely prohibited. Serious scientific projects that find the Martian environment advantageous to their researches are not prohibited.

Art VI: The disposal of waste products generated on Earth, of any kind, is absolutely prohibited. The exiling of criminal elements from Earth to Mars is also prohibited.

Art. VII: The United Nationalities shall appoint observers whose function is to ensure compliance with the foregoing provisions. The observers shall enjoy full freedom of access at all times to any installation or structure established on Mars.

How It All Began

APIUM: Association for the Protection and Integrity of an Unspoilt Mars

Plans are already afoot to send human beings to Mars. Behind these exciting possibilities lies a less worthy objective: an assumption that the Red Planet can be turned into something resembling a colony, an inferior Earth. This operation would extend prevailing dystopian tendencies into the next century.

Planets are environments with their own integrity. Any vast engineering schemes would be invasive. The end result could only be to turn Mars into a dreary suburb, imitating the less attractive features of terrestrial cities. A military-industrial complex would probably rule over it.

APIUM stands for humanity's right to walk on Mars, and is against its rape and ruination. Mars must become a UN protectorate, and be treated as a 'planet for science', much as the Antarctic has been preserved – at least to a great extent – as unspoilt white wilderness. We are for a WHITE MARS!

Mars should remain as a kind of Ayers Rock in the sky. It must be made visitable to ordinary men and women (the travel costs to be met by community service at home). Its solitudes will be preserved for silence and meditation and honeymooning. From Mars, traditionally the God of War, a myth of peace will spread back to Earth, supplanting the myth of energy/power/exploitation that has so darkened the twentieth century.

APIUM believes that great good will come to both planets if we have the courage to sustain a WHITE MARS.

Brian W. Aldiss
President, APIUM
Pamphlet distributed January 1997
Green College, Oxford, England

323

MIT

Mairi Topham

KT-161-819

Double Cross

www.**rbooks**.co.uk

By Malorie Blackman and published
by Doubleday/Corgi Books:

The Noughts & Crosses sequence
NOUGHTS & CROSSES
KNIFE EDGE
CHECKMATE
DOUBLE CROSS

A.N.T.I.D.O.T.E.
DANGEROUS REALITY
DEAD GORGEOUS
HACKER
PIG-HEART BOY
THE DEADLY DARE MYSTERIES
THE STUFF OF NIGHTMARES
THIEF!

UNHEARD VOICES
(An anthology of short stories and poems,
collected by Malorie Blackman)

For junior readers, published by Corgi Yearling Books:
CLOUD BUSTING
OPERATION GADGETMAN!
WHIZZIWIG and WHIZZIWIG RETURNS

**For beginner readers, published
by Corgi Pups/Young Corgi Books:**
JACK SWEETTOOTH
SNOW DOG
SPACE RACE
THE MONSTER CRISP-GUZZLER

Audio editions available on CDs
NOUGHTS & CROSSES
KNIFE EDGE
CHECKMATE
DOUBLE CROSS

www.malorieblackman.co.uk
www.myspace.com/malorieblackman

Praise for the *Noughts & Crosses* sequence:

Noughts & Crosses

'Packs some powerful political punches to
which readers will undoubtedly respond. But Blackman
never compromises the story, which is dramatic,
moving and brave' *Guardian*

'A sad, bleak, brutal novel that promotes
empathy and understanding of the history of civil
rights as it inverts truths about racial injustice . . .
But this is also a novel about love, and inspires
the reader to wish for a world that is not divided
by colour or class' *Sunday Times*

'A book which will linger in the mind long after
it has been read and which will challenge children to
think again and again about the clichés and stereotypes
with which they are presented' *Observer*

Knife Edge

'Devastatingly powerful' *Guardian*

'A powerful story of race and prejudice' *Sunday Times*

'Supercharged' *Scottish Sunday Herald*

Checkmate

'Thought-provoking brilliance' *Funday Times*

'Another emotional hard-hitter . . . bluntly told and
ingeniously constructed' *Sunday Times*

'Complex but beautifully crafted . . . dramatic, intensely
moving . . . it truly ensnares the reader' *Carousel*

MALORIE BLACKMAN

Double Cross

DOUBLEDAY

DOUBLE CROSS
A DOUBLEDAY BOOK 978 0 385 61551 8
TRADE PAPERBACK 978 0 385 61552 5

Published in Great Britain by Doubleday,
an imprint of Random House Children's Books
A Random House Group Company

This edition published 2008

9 10 8

Copyright © Oneta Malorie Blackman, 2008

The right of Malorie Blackman to be identified as the author of this work has
been asserted in accordance with the Copyright, Designs and Patents Act 1988.

All rights reserved. No part of this publication may be reproduced, stored in a retrieval
system, or transmitted in any form or by any means, electronic, mechanical, photocopying,
recording or otherwise, without the prior permission of the publishers.

The Random House Group Limited supports the Forest Stewardship Council (FSC), the
leading international forest certification organization. All our titles that are printed on
Greenpeace-approved FSC-certified paper carry the FSC logo. Our paper procurement
policy can be found at www.rbooks.co.uk/environment.

Mixed Sources
Product group from well-managed
forests and other controlled sources
www.fsc.org Cert no. TT-COC-2139
© 1996 Forest Stewardship Council

Set in Sabon

RANDOM HOUSE CHILDREN'S BOOKS
61–63 Uxbridge Road, London W5 5SA

www.kidsatrandomhouse.co.uk
www.rbooks.co.uk

Addresses for companies within The Random House Group Limited can be found at:
www.randomhouse.co.uk/offices.htm

THE RANDOM HOUSE GROUP Limited Reg. No. 954009

A CIP catalogue record for this book is available from the British Library.

Printed and bound in Great Britain
by CPI Mackays, Chatham ME5 8TD

For Neil and Lizzy,

Mum and Wendy – with love.

And big thanks to Annie and Sue – what would I do without you?

Lizzy, this is the book you asked me for. Sort of!

*'The mere imparting of information is
not education. Above all things, the effort must
result in making a man think for himself . . .*

*When you control a man's thinking you
do not have to worry about his actions.
You do not have to tell him not to stand
here or go yonder. He will find his
"proper place" and will stay in it.'*

Carter G. Woodson

---

*'. . . What would he do,
Had he the motive and the cue for passion
That I have?'*

Hamlet – Act II, Scene II

Prologue

The Glock 23 felt heavy and seductively comfortable in my hand. The pearl stock, warmed by my body heat, fitted snugly against my palm. I now held McAuley's custom-made semi automatic.

A real, honest-to-God gun in my hand.

A proper killing machine.

Or was that me? Where did I stop and the gun start? I really couldn't tell any more.

Now what?

McAuley lay on the floor, the previous torrent of blood that had been gushing from his nose now reduced to a trickle. His once crisp, white designer suit and matching designer shirt lay twisted in an ungainly manner around him. The random splashes of red on McAuley's suit resembled an abstract painting. I stared into one particular bloodstain in the middle of McAuley's chest.

'It's more like a Rorschach ink blot than a painting,' I thought inanely.

It reminded me of my own face in skewed profile.

Now what?

McAuley's blond hair hung like day-old spaghetti around his face. It was streaked with random red high-lights which occasionally dripped onto his shoulders. Red highlights donated involuntarily by McAuley's last victim. The assorted blood splatters on his jacket alone would fill at least a couple of chapters in a forensic science textbook. I wondered whether the SOCO – scene-of-crime-officer – lucky enough to be assigned to McAuley's body would be an art-lover?

I glanced towards the office door. The heavy, arrhythmic banging on it was beginning to get to me. The noise vibrated straight through my head, making it hard to think. Making a slow fist with my free hand, I dug my short nails as deeply as I could into my palms. I had to resist the temptation to let the frenetic drumming on the door dictate the pace of my thinking.

Think, Tobey. Think.

There had to be a way out of this.

But even as the thought pushed its way into conscious-ness, I knew I was deluding myself. Turn and face the truth.

Time had run out.

'Durbridge, dig yourself a grave and crawl into it 'cause you are *dead*. D'you hear me?'

I aimed a kick between McAuley's legs and allowed myself a small, satisfied smile as the blood-spattered scumbag howled, curling up like the letter C. Small pleasures. There was nothing and no one in McAuley's office to stop me getting a few kicks in. And if I was going to die . . . The smile faded from my face as I watched McAuley writhe on the floor.

At the sound of their boss's roar of pain, McAuley's men pounded even harder on the office door. Luckily for me, McAuley's paranoia had seen to it that the door was solid, reinforced hardwood. It would hold for a while, but even that door couldn't indefinitely withstand the kind of punishment McAuley's thugs were dishing out. I reckoned I only had a couple of minutes before it gave way completely and then the door wouldn't be the only thing in trouble.

Could I do it? Could I really go through with this?

Hell, yes.

There was a time, less than six weeks and over a lifetime ago, when I'd thought a person could only sink so low. Sooner or later, you went down just as far as you could and after that, the only direction was up. But, just as loving Callie had shown me that Heaven had no roof, hating McAuley and the Dowds had taught me that Hell had no basement.

McAuley started to laugh. Even though his hands were cupped around his groin and he was still curled up, he found this funny. Creepy McAuley, the hard man. My finger stroked at the trigger. White fire blazed through my veins instead of blood, burning away all thought, all feeling. All fear. I had a gun in my hand, like a syringe pumping one hundred per cent pure, unadulterated adrenalin straight into my heart.

The frustrated hammering on the door was growing more insistent.

'You're dead, Durbridge,' McAuley said again, 'and there's nothing you can do about it.'

I pushed the gun barrel against the older man's head, drawing small circles around his temple. McAuley froze.

'Then that makes two of us, you bastard,' I stated softly. 'That makes two of us.'

SIX WEEKS
EARLIER

The Rise . . .

'Tobey, I was er . . . thinking that maybe you and me could . . . er . . . you know, go to the pictures or go for a . . . er . . . you know, a meal or something this weekend?'

Godsake! Couldn't she get through one sentence, just one sentence, without sticking umpteen 'er's and 'you know's in it first?

'I can't, Misty. I'm already going out.' I turned back to my graphic novel – a humorous fantasy that was better than I had thought it would be when I'd borrowed it from the library.

'Oh? Where're you going?'

'Out.' I frowned, not bothering to look up from my book.

'For the whole weekend?'

'Yes.'

'Out where?'

I turned in my chair to look at her. Misty tossed back her brunette hair with blonde highlights in a peculiarly unnatural move that had obviously been practised to death in front of her bedroom mirror.

'Out where?' Misty asked again.

This girl was stomping on my last nerve now. She'd

been asking me out all term and I'd always found some reason to turn her down. Couldn't she take a hint? Miss I'm-too-sexy-for-myself leaned closer in to me, so close that I had to pull back or she'd've been kissing my neck.

'I'm going out with my family. We're visiting relatives,' I improvised.

I'm too nice, that's my trouble, I thought sourly. Why on earth didn't I just tell her that I wasn't interested in a date or anything else for that matter? For one thing, hugging her would be like trying to cuddle a chopstick. I liked curves. And even if I did fancy her – which I didn't – there was no way I'd ever get it on with an ex-girlfriend of my mate, Dan. That was a definite no.

'Maybe the er . . . erm . . . following Saturday, then? We could maybe . . . er . . . go out then if you'd like?' said Misty.

Rearrange this sentence: hell – freezes – over – when.

The classroom door swung open and Callie Rose strolled into the room. She stopped momentarily when she saw who was sitting in her chair. Scowling, she strode over to Misty.

'D'you mind?' Callie asked.

'I'm talking to Tobey.'

'Not from my chair, you're not,' Callie shot back.

'Er . . . can't you find somewhere else to sit until the lesson starts?' Misty wheedled.

Uh-oh! I held my breath. Callie let her rucksack slip from her hand to the floor as her eyes narrowed. She was one nanosecond away from moving up to Kick-arse Condition 1.

'Misty, you need to get up off my chair,' Callie said softly.

'I'd shift if I were you,' I advised Misty.

Much as I found the thought of a cat-fight over me appealing, I didn't fancy Callie getting into trouble and then giving me grief for what was left of the term.

Misty huffed and stood up. 'Callie, I'm going to remember this.'

'Remember it. Take a photo. Break out your camcorder. I don't give a rat's bum. Just move.' Callie stepped aside so that Misty could squeeze by, before flopping down into her now vacant seat.

'Damn cheek!' Callie carried on muttering under her breath as she dug into her bag for the history books required for our first lesson. She turned to look at Misty, who was now back in her own chair.

'If looks could kill, I'd be seriously ill,' Callie said as she turned to me, annoyance vying with amusement to colour her eyes more hazel than brown. Every time she was upset or angry, her eyes literally turned greener. It was one of the many things about her that got me going. She had the most expressive eyes I'd ever seen. Chameleon-like, they changed colour to reflect her every mood.

'Every time I want to sit down next to you or be within half a kilometre of you, I can't move without tripping over that girl first. What's up with that?'

I sucked in my cheeks in an effort not to chortle. One snicker and Callie would bite my head off. I tried for a nonchalant shrug.

'So what did Miss Foggy want this time?' Callie asked.

'Why d'you insist on calling her Miss Foggy?' I laughed.

I know it was mean, but 'Miss Foggy' really suited Misty.

'That's her name, isn't it? Besides, I'm not the one who chose to name her after a type of weather, and if the shoe fits . . .' Callie said pointedly. 'And you haven't answered my question.'

'She was inviting me out this weekend,' I replied.

I watched keenly for her reaction.

She shook her head. 'Damn! Misty's got it bad.'

'Are you jealous?' I asked hopefully.

Callie's eyebrows shot up so far and so fast, she got an instant face-lift. 'Are you kidding? I just think it's pitiful. She's been chucking herself at you all term and you haven't exactly been rushing to catch her, have you? In fact, most of the time you just fold your arms and let her drop on her face over and over again. You'd think she'd have got the message by now.'

'So you are green-eyed.' I grinned.

'Tobey, I don't know what you're taking, but you need to get yourself to rehab – quick, fast and in a hurry.'

'My girl is jealous.' My grin broadened. 'It's OK, Callie Rose. There'll never be anyone for me but you.'

'Go dip your head,' Callie told me.

'I mean it.' I crossed both my hands over my heart and adopted a ridiculously soppy expression. 'I give my heart . . . to you.' I mimed placing it carefully on the table in front of her. Glowering, Callie picked up her pen and mimed stabbing my heart on the table over and over again.

I burst out laughing, but had to smother it as Mr Lancer, the history teacher, entered the room. Callie started muttering all kinds of dire threats and promises under her breath the way she always did when I got under her skin.

And I loved it. It was music to my ears.

Callie quickly suppressed a laugh as the buzzer sounded for the end of the lesson. I'd spent the last fifty minutes passing her silly notes and making *sotto voce* remarks about Mr Lancer's newly bald head with its deep groove down the middle. It now resembled a certain part of the male anatomy and there was no way I could let that pass without comment. Callie had been in smothered fits of the giggles throughout most of the lesson. I loved making Callie laugh. God knows, she'd done little enough of that since her nana died in the Isis Hotel bomb blast. Callie was reaching for her rucksack on the floor and I'd barely made it to my feet when we had company.

Lucas frickin' Cheshie.

Misty wasn't the only one who couldn't take a hint. OK, so I still wasn't quite sure what to call my friendship with Callie, but I knew what Lucas and Callie weren't — and that was an item. She wasn't Lucas's girlfriend any more, so why did he persist in sniffing around her? Being older than us, he wasn't even in our class. But he must've seen Callie through the classroom window — and now here he was, lingering like an eggy fart. Smarmy git.

Completely ignoring me, Lucas said softly, 'Hi, Callie Rose, how are you?'

Callie's smile faded. She was instantly wary. I was grateful for that, if nothing else.

'I'm fine, Lucas. How are you?'

'Missing you.' Lucas smiled.

Callie searched for something to say, but unable to find

anything, she merely shrugged. I glared at Lucas, but he wasn't going to give me the satisfaction of acknowledging my presence.

'Ignore me all you want, but if you think I'm leaving you alone with Callie . . .' I projected my hostility towards him through narrowed eyes.

'I'm so glad to see you smiling again, Callie Rose. I'm glad you're getting over the bereavement in your family,' said Lucas.

The light in Callie's eyes vanished, as if a great, dark cloud had swept across the face of the sun. Callie's grandmother had died two months before, but Callie wasn't over it. Sometimes I wondered if she'd ever be truly over it.

'And you were so close to your nana Jasmine, weren't you?' Lucas continued.

I glanced at Callie before turning back to Lucas. A Cyclops with a pencil in his eye could see that Callie was getting upset. Lucas would have to be stupid not to see the effect his words were having. And Lucas was a lot of things, but stupid wasn't one of them.

Callie said nothing.

'Callie Rose, if you ever need to talk about your grandmother and how she died or anything, then I'm here for you. OK?' Lucas smiled. 'I just want you to know that I'm your friend. I'll always be your friend. If you need anything from me you only have to ask.'

Dismayed, I turned to Callie again. With a few well-chosen words, Lucas had not only knocked Callie to the ground, but then danced all over her. Her face took on the haunted, hunted look she always wore when thinking about Nana Jasmine. Her eyes glistened green with the tears she desperately tried to hold back. Callie hated for anyone to see her cry. My hands clenched into fists at my side. I had to hold myself rigid to refrain from smacking Lucas a sizeable one.

Lucas put his hand under Callie's chin to slowly raise her head. He was still ignoring me. 'Just think about what I said. I mean every word.' He smiled again, then sauntered off to join the rest of his crew waiting in the doorway for him.

Callie and I were alone in the classroom. I chewed on the inside of my bottom lip. What to say? What to do? I was so useless at this kind of thing.

'Callie . . .' I turned to her in time to see the solitary tear balanced on her lower eyelashes splash onto her cheek.

'Callie, don't listen to him. He was being a git,' I began furiously.

Puzzled, Callie turned to me, her eyes still shimmering. 'He was just trying to be kind.'

'Kind, my arse. He did that deliberately . . .'

'Tobey, what's wrong with you?' Callie whispered. 'You know what, I can't cope with this now.'

'Callie, can't you see what Lucas was up to? He was . . .'

But I was talking to myself. Callie was out the door, leaving me in the classroom.

Alone.

BOMB BLAST VICTIM IDENTIFIED AS JASMINE HADLEY

Jasmine Hadley was yesterday finally identified as one of the victims of the bomb blast at the Isis Hotel. The former wife of Kamal Hadley, ex-MP, was killed five days ago, but it has taken this long to make a positive identification. A source working for the forensic science division of the police force stated, 'The damage to her body was so severe that a combination of dental records and DNA testing had to be used to conclusively identify the victim.' One other unidentified Nought male was also killed in the hotel explosion. The police are making strenuous efforts to establish the identity of this Nought in an effort to ascertain his connection, if any, to the blast. This latest outrage is suspected to be the work of the Liberation Militia, although as yet no one has claimed responsibility. Jasmine Hadley's ex-husband, Kamal Hadley, whose party crashed so ignominiously in the general election held last week, was unavailable for comment.

Try as I might, I just couldn't let go of that newspaper clipping. It was either in my hand or in my head. And it never left my heart. Nana Jasmine's photo shone out alongside the article about her death. I recognized the photo. It was the one with Nana in the middle, my mum and me on her right and Aunt Minerva, Uncle Zuri and cousin Taj on her left. It was at least ten years old and in it Nana looked so happy, so proud. I'd asked Nana about the photo once. I'd only been five or six at the time, so to be honest, I couldn't remember that much about it. And what's more I didn't think the photo was all that, but Nana kept a framed copy on the night table beside her bed, a framed copy on her piano and a smaller version of the same photo in her purse. Taj looked like he'd just finished picking or was just about to pick his nose, Mum appeared a bit fed up and Aunt Minerva was looking at Uncle Zuri instead of straight at the camera. But Nana didn't care.

'I have my whole family beside me,' she told me when I asked her about it. 'That's what makes it so special.' Then she added wistfully, 'The only one missing was your dad, Callum.'

But for the article, they'd chopped off the rest of us,

showing only Nana. The worn, folded seams of the newspaper clipping in my hand had made the paper as fragile as a cobweb, but that didn't stop me from re-reading it. Every day.

Every. Damn. Day.

I tried to imagine what had gone wrong. Had Nana Jasmine tried to return the bomb to Uncle Jude? Is that what happened? Did she go to his hotel to throw it in his face? Did it go off accidentally? Did Uncle Jude detonate it deliberately? Did Nana Jasmine try to run and hide? Was there a struggle? Did they fight over it? If so, then Nana Jasmine wouldn't have stood a chance. She took my bomb and, knowing her as I did, she would've relished handing it back to Uncle Jude. But there's no way she could have known just how dangerous Uncle Jude was. The bomb got him − but it got Nana Jasmine too. How did I even begin to forgive myself for that?

Uncle Jude and Nana Jasmine were dead because of me.

Because of my bomb.

I'd made the thing, put it together with rage and hatred in equal measure. I look back on my life of a few months ago and it's like being a voyeur in someone else's twisted mind. I look into my memories and see the thoughts and actions of a stranger, but a stranger with my face.

'Nana Jasmine, I'm so sorry . . .'

Sorry. Such a ridiculous, inadequate word.

Sorry.

I despised that word.

I buried my face in my hands. I didn't want to see or be seen. At times like this, I just wanted to crawl away and find a place to hide from the world. Hide from myself.

Was there any such place? I would've given everything I owned to find it.

Little moments of forgetfulness. I guess that is all I can hope for now. Tiny fragments of moments when I can forget how my nana died. Sometimes I'll be cooking with Mum and she'll smile at me, or I'll be arguing with Nana Meggie and she'll huff at me, or I'll be doing my homework with Tobey and he'll deliberately wind me up, and in those wonderful, amazing moments, I forget. But such times are few and far apart.

I couldn't even blame Uncle Jude for what had happened. Not really. My uncle was a soldier. A terrorist. A sad, angry, bitter man. Since his death, I'd learned so much about him and the things he'd done. The Internet and my local library had provided all the details I could ever need. I wish I'd taken the time to find out more about him when he was alive. Tobey tried to warn me, so did Lucas, but I wouldn't listen. I thought that Uncle Jude was the only one who understood me, the only one who was honest with me. How could I have got everything so wrong? I'm obviously not very perceptive. And the pitiful thing is that, until Uncle Jude's death, I thought I could tell everything about a person within three glances. God, I was such a fool.

All those lies Uncle Jude told me. All that hatred filling him to overflowing. Hatred that he couldn't wait to pour into me. And I let him. And even though I'd made the bomb at his instigation, that still didn't help when I thought about the way he'd died. Him and my nana . . .

One of the first things this new government did when they came into power a couple of months ago was abolish capital punishment – for good this time, I think. It was abolished over sixty years ago, then brought back five years before I was born after a public referendum indicated that the majority of people in this country wanted Liberation Militia terrorists and those convicted of serious crimes to be executed. This current government claimed that extreme circumstances made for bad laws – like the reintroduction of capital punishment and imprisonment without trial. But part of me just wants to walk into the nearest police station, give myself up and take whatever is coming to me. And if this country still had capital punishment then even better.

'Nana, I wish you could hear me. D'you hate me? You can't hate me any more than I hate myself. I never meant for you to get hurt. I swear that was never my intention. My head was all over the place then. I didn't know who I was or where I belonged. I do now. But I never wanted that knowledge to come at the cost of your life. Mum keeps saying that I mustn't blame myself – it was all down to Jude. But I'm not stupid. Nana, I'm so sorry.'

'Callie Rose, didn't you hear me calling you for dinner?' Mum stood in the doorway, her hands on her hips. 'We're all waiting for you downstairs.'

'Is Nathan here?' I asked, folding up the newspaper article again and placing it in the drawer of my bedside table.

Mum's hands fell to her sides as she walked further into the room. I heard her sigh softly.

'Yes, he is. I invited him for dinner. Callie, d'you . . . d'you mind about Nathan and me? We haven't really had a chance to talk about him since . . . since your Nana died.'

'I don't mind at all, Mum,' I said honestly. 'In fact, I'm glad that you've got someone.'

Mum scrutinized my face, as if trying to gauge how many of my words were true. I met her gaze without flinching or even blinking. I meant every one.

'Something's bothering you about me and Nathan, though,' she said slowly.

I had to smile. Mum was so astute when it came to reading my expressions, far more astute than I had ever given her credit for.

'I was just thinking . . . what about you and Sonny?' I couldn't help asking.

Sonny was Mum's old boyfriend. The only trouble was, he was still in love with her and trying to win her back, even though Mum had told him she was going to marry Nathan.

'Sonny and I were the past. Nathan and I are the present.'

'Does Sonny know that?'

'I've told him often enough over the last few weeks.' Mum sighed again. 'It's time for all of us to move on. I can't live in the past. I won't.'

Was Mum trying to convince me – or herself?

'Mum, are you and Nathan going to get married, or live together or what?'

'I don't know. We talked about getting married, but we might have to put our plans on hold,' Mum admitted. 'Nathan's business isn't doing too well and he's now thinking it might be better to wait.'

'And how d'you feel about that?'

'I think he's right. I . . . we don't want to rush into anything.'

'Mum, Nathan loves you, so why hang about?' I said. 'Life is too short.'

'I guess so,' Mum said faintly.

Was that doubt I heard in Mum's voice? It certainly sounded like it. I wasn't quite sure I got Mum and Nathan's relationship. It seemed to be an affair more of the head than the heart, at least on Mum's part. Sometimes, when she thought no one was watching, a sombre, thoughtful look clouded her eyes, and in those moments, I knew she was thinking about my dad. Once I'd been ashamed that my dad was Callum McGregor, a hanged terrorist. Not any more. And now that I knew just how much Mum and Dad had loved each other, I wasn't surprised that Mum found it hard to give her whole heart to anyone else. It gave me a strange feeling to know that my dad loved Mum and me so much, had sacrificed so much for us, even before I was born. A strange, warm, comforting, sad feeling.

Mum and I both stood in a brooding silence, until Mum opened her arms. I immediately stepped into her embrace. We hugged. Mum stroked my hair. Loving moments turned into peaceful minutes.

On my sixteenth birthday, I was reconciled with my mum. And I lost my nana. It wasn't fair. It just wasn't fair. For a while, after Nana's death, I was so scared that my new relationship with my mum wouldn't last, that things would go back to the way they used to be between us, but thankfully, that hadn't happened. Oh, we'd had the odd hiccup and a couple of shouting matches, but Mum always allowed me to cool off and then she'd come and hug me and tell me that she loved me and my anger would burn away like early morning summer mist. I don't know how I would've coped with Nana Jasmine's death if it hadn't been for Mum. Tobey and Nana Meggie let me know they were there for me, but Mum had never left my side. At Nana Jasmine's funeral she'd held my hand throughout the service to let me know that I wasn't alone. And not once did Mum throw it back in my face that I'd made the bomb that killed Nana Jasmine. Not once. With each smile, each hug, every stroke of my hair she kept trying to tell me that she'd forgiven me. But how could I accept Mum's forgiveness when I knew I'd never forgive myself?

'I love you very much, Callie Rose. You do know that, don't you? And there is nothing on this earth or beyond that could ever change that,' Mum said softly.

I found that so hard to believe, but Mum's face was an open book as she looked at me.

'D'you promise?' I whispered.

Mum smiled. 'Cross my heart.'

'Mum, I love you.'

Mum hugged me harder at that. And I wished . . . I wished so much that Nana Jasmine was still around to see it.

three. Tobey

'Raoul, you blanker, get up!' Dan put his hands to his mouth and yelled so hard, my head started ringing.

'Godsake, Dan! My frickin' eardrums.'

'Sorry,' Dan said with a grin.

I sniffed around his shoulders before recoiling. 'Damn, Dan! Your pits are howling!'

Dan raised his arm to sniff at his armpits. He looked like a bird covering its head with its wing.

'Oh yeah, you're right!' he said, surprised.

I pushed his arm back down before he gassed everyone on the pitch. 'You do know that armpits can be washed, don't you?'

'I forgot to put on some deodorant today.' Dan grinned.

I mean, Godsake!

Our Monday evening football match was well under way. The July evening was still bright and uncomfortably hot. Within minutes of running around, my shirt was sticking to my armpits and my back. Dan and I were on opposing teams, both on the wing, supposedly marking each other. But mostly we were talking. We watched patiently as once again pain stopped play. Raoul was *still* rolling on the ground, clutching his lower leg like he was in a death scene in some bad straight-to-DVD movie.

The Wasteland, where we were playing (or Meadowview Park, as the local authority had it listed on their website), wasn't as busy as usual. Only enough guys had turned up for a seven-a-side football match, hence the reason I was playing. With a full complement of players I was usually relegated to one of the park benches. The Wasteland was a flat patch of rectangular land, with a children's adventure playground at one end and a flower garden enclosed by knee-high blunt railings at the other. Except the flower garden hadn't had any flowers in it for close to two decades, according to my mum. The criss-cross paths of concrete were now used by roller-bladers, skate-boarders and trick cyclists. Anyone using the park for any wheeled activity did so at their own peril – so the numerous signs posted around the place stated. I often wondered if that included pushing baby buggies and pulling shopping trolleys? Closer to the garden than the adventure playground was the football pitch, surrounded on all sides by rusting wire-mesh fencing. It wasn't much, but it was ours. And the football pitch was kept clean of dog crap and clear of litter. All the footballers in the neighbourhood saw to that.

Raoul finally stood up and shook out his leg. About time! The ball was kicked to me and I displayed semi-adequate skills by getting rid of it asap – and to someone on my own side too, which made a change.

'So what d'you reckon?' Dan flashed his new watch about a centimetre away from my nose, twisting his forearm this way and that. It was so close I couldn't see it properly. Was he trying to poke out one of my eyeballs with the thing or what? And eau-de-stinky-pits was repeatedly punching at my nose again.

'The watch?' Dan prompted. 'What d'you think?'

'Does it shoot down low-flying aircraft?' I asked, taking a quick step back.

Dan pursed his lips. 'Not that it says in the manual.'

'Does it contain the nano-technology to drain a subdural haematoma?'

'That's the next model up from this one.'

'Then it tells the time, the same as my cheap effort,' I said.

'Yeah, but mine looks good and cost more than everything you have in your bedroom and then some.'

'Could you lower your arm before you kill me?' I pleaded.

Dan took pity on me and did as I asked.

'Your watch, did you buy it or acquire it?'

'I bought it, you blanker. And I have the receipt and sales certificate to prove it.' Dan frowned. 'You sound just like a Cross copper.'

I held up my hands. 'Hey, it's no skin off my nose where you got it from.'

'Well, I bought it with cash money, made from earning a living rather than dossing at school like some people I could mention.' Dan's frown lessened only slightly.

'And is it accurate?'

'Of course. It's guaranteed to lose only one second every hundred years.'

For the kind of money Dan must've forked out for his watch, it shouldn't lose any time at all – ever. And surely it did more than just turn two strips of arrow-shaped metal

through three hundred and sixty degrees periodically?
'So what else does it do?' I asked.

'Nothing else. It's not some digital toy out of a cracker,' said Dan, preening. 'This is pure class.'

'But all it does is tell the time,' I repeated.

'Damn, Tobey. How are we friends? You don't have a clue,' Dan said, exasperated.

'It's a lovely watch, Dan,' I sighed. 'If I ever get married, it'll be to your watch.'

'Feel free to bugger off and die at any time.' Dan scowled.

I grinned. 'Only if you'll bury me with your watch over my heart.'

'Tobey . . .'

'OK, OK. I'll shut up now.'

Dan gave a reluctant smile. He was still annoyed at my lack of open fawning appreciation for his watch, but he'd get over it. I glanced over to the sidelines, wondering which of the girls standing there was Dan's latest girlfriend.

'How's your love life?' I asked.

'Non-existent, thank God!' Dan's reply was heartfelt.

'How's your sex life?'

Dan sighed. 'Non-existent, unfortunately. Talking of sex . . .' His eyes lit up. 'How's Callie Rose?'

Damn! I should've seen that coming. 'Dan, don't start.'

'What?' said Dan, acting the innocent. 'I'm just asking if you two are still an item?'

'We are,' I said firmly.

''Cause if you're not,' Dan continued as if I hadn't spoken, 'I wouldn't mind some of that. She's extra fit – for a Cross.'

'Callie isn't a Cross.'

'She ain't one of us either,' said Dan.

'Then what is she?' I asked, annoyed.

'Extra fit – I already told you.'

We stood in silence for a while. Why had I been so quick to deny that Callie was a Cross? Maybe because I still couldn't quite believe she'd chosen me over Lucas. I couldn't help wondering if she'd wake up one morning and realize . . . realize that she could do better.

'Tobey, chill. I was only messing with your head a bit.'

'I know. Remind me to pay you back for that later,' I replied.

If only I had the money for watches and bracelets and all the things Callie deserved. If only . . . I took hold of Dan's arm to give his watch a proper look.

'That is one cool watch, though,' I admitted.

'You could afford a watch like this too, you know. And more besides,' said Dan.

'You know my job only pays minimum wage.' I shrugged. My Saturday job of almost a year was roughly twenty per cent selling mobile phones and eighty per cent listening to customers whinge. It just about paid for my school stationery and a few textbooks, and that was it. 'So at that rate I should be able to afford a watch like yours in about – what? Five or six years?'

'Selling mobile phones isn't the only game in town,' Dan said pointedly.

'It's the only game I'm interested in playing,' I replied.

'Aren't you tired of having nothing?'

And that was just it. Because I *was* tired of having no money. All the things I could do, all the things I could *be* if I had money kept slipping into my head like mental gate-crashers.

'You could just make deliveries like me,' Dan continued. 'Dropping off a package here, picking up a parcel there.'

For the first time, I started to listen. 'I don't know . . .' I began.

Sensing hesitation like a shark sensing blood, Dan pounced. 'Tobey, it's easy money. Think of all the things you could do if you were holding folding. You could save up to get out of this place for a start.'

'Is that what you're doing?' I couldn't help but ask.

'Nah. If I had your brains, then maybe. But it's this or do something like take food orders and nothing else for the rest of my life. And guess what, that don't appeal. But with your smarts, Tobey, in two years you could be anything you wanted 'cause you'd have the cash to do it.'

Packages . . . deliveries . . . Dan made it sound so innocuous. So very easy.

'Who d'you deliver these packages to?' I asked.

'The people who need them or want them or should have them.'

'And who d'you deliver these packages for?' As if I couldn't guess. 'Cause it sure as hell wasn't the post office.

Dan smiled. 'Does it matter? I pick up the packages and the addresses that each one should be taken to and that's all I know or care about. Tobey, think of the money you could make. I'm tired of having your broke arse trailing behind me all the time.'

Waving the two most eloquent fingers on each hand in his direction, I thought about what he'd said.

If I had money, Callie and me . . .

I cut the thought off at the pockets. I couldn't start thinking that way. I'd go mad if I started thinking that way.

But after all, it was just deliveries.

The odd parcel delivery couldn't hurt.

Unless I got caught . . .

I shook my head, trying to dislodge all visions of cascading money. 'I don't think so, Dan. I just want to go to school and keep my head down.'

'School.' Dan snorted derisively. 'I hope your school isn't going to make you forget who you are.'

Inside, I went very still. 'And what is that exactly?'

'You're a Nought, Tobey. And going to your fancy school isn't going to change that.'

'I wouldn't want school to change that.'

'Some of our friends already think you've sold out. It's up to you to prove that you haven't,' Dan told me.

Sold out? What the—?

'I don't have to prove a damned thing, Dan.'

'Hey.' Dan raised a placating hand. 'I'm only telling you what some of our friends are saying about you.'

Friends? My eyes narrowed as I thought of my so-called friends.

Dan stepped back from the look on my face. 'I'm just saying, you have to be careful that your brain doesn't get smart at the expense of your head getting stupid.'

'Wanting to do something with my life isn't selling out,' I said, banking down my resentment with difficulty. 'Wanting something more than all this isn't selling out.'

'Tell that to Raoul and—'

'No, I'm telling it to you. That crap doesn't even make it to ignorant. Going to school so I can think for myself, so I can make something of myself, is selling out now, is it? We don't need the Crosses to keep us down with that kind of thinking. We'll do it to ourselves.'

Dan took another step back. 'Listen, I was just—'

'The next time Raoul or anyone else starts spouting that bollocks, you send them to me to say it to my face,' I said furiously. 'I'm going to go to school and keep my head down until I can get out of Meadowview and that's all there is to it.'

'Tobey, wake up. That's not even an option,' Dan stated. 'And McAuley can protect you. He's great, almost like a dad to me. Besides which, he's one of us.'

One of us . . .

McAuley was a gangster, pure and not so simple. But his being a Nought was enough mitigation as far as Dan was concerned. McAuley fancied himself as a Nought kingpin. He took his cut of every crooked deal that went down in Meadowview – that's if the Dowd family didn't get in first. The Dowds were the Cross family who ran all the illegal activities in Meadowview that McAuley didn't already have his grubby hands on. Or maybe it was the other way around. Who could tell? They both offered protection to any lowlife who pledged allegiance. Bottom-feeding Noughts tended to join McAuley. Scumbag Crosses joined forces with the Dowds. Criminal fraternity segregation.

A while ago some Nought hooli called Jordy Carson tried to take on the Dowds. He vanished like a fart in the wind. And waiting in the wings to take his place was his second-in-command, Alex McAuley. Everyone said McAuley had learned from his old boss's mistakes. McAuley had no intention of 'disappearing'. So he made sure everyone knew his name and his game. Trouble was, McAuley was even worse than Carson. I guess that for the Dowds and McAuley there was plenty of misery around for everyone to make a profit. Those of us who had to live in Meadowview – the poorer Crosses and us Noughts with a whole heap of not much – saw to that. One of us? Yeah, right.

'The point is, the no-man's-land you want to live on doesn't exist, not for either of us,' Dan continued. 'If you don't pick a side soon, you'll be nowhere.'

'Yeah, but Nowhere looks like a peaceful place to be – especially around here,' I said.

'Nowhere will get you dead,' said Dan. 'On the inside you'll be protected, you'll have back up. McAuley looks after his own. What d'you have at the moment?'

'I have you, Dan.' I smiled.

'Very funny.'

'I know you'll always have my back.'

'Don't rely on that, Tobey,' Dan said quietly.

My smile faded. Dan and I regarded each other.

'Oi, you two! This ain't a chat show,' Liam, the captain of my side, yelled out. 'Kick the damned ball.'

Dan and I both made a show of getting back in the game, but although my body ran around the Wasteland trying to look useful, my head was elsewhere. When pain stopped play again, I stood slightly behind Dan as we both waited for the game to restart and the ball to head our way.

I couldn't help thinking about what he had said.

I felt like I'd been asleep and had just been kicked awake. I'd always assumed that Dan would have my back and vice versa. But Dan running errands for McAuley had evidently changed all that. I'd blinked and missed it. Hell, I'd blinked and my world was suddenly a lot more complicated.

Years ago, I thought that getting into Heathcroft High School was it, the be-all and end-all of my existence. I'd thought that all I needed to do was keep my head down and my grades up to make it through. After school, I'd go to university and at the end of all that, I'd be something big in the financial markets. I had it all figured out. I wanted a job that'd make me tons of money. But that was stuff for the future. I'd forgotten that I still needed to make it through the here and now first. The present was filled to overflowing with McAuley and the Dowds and needing to belong to a gang just to be able to walk the streets. The present was all about friends who had your back and turning away from those who didn't. The present was hard work, not to mention dangerous.

I realized Dan had been right about one thing.

The no-man's-land I was clinging to wasn't firm ground at all, but quicksand.

four. Tobey

At school the next day, Dan's words kept ringing in my head. I walked home alone because Callie had a singing lesson after school, and I still couldn't forget what Dan had said. I'd barely shut the front door before my sister Jessica emerged from the living room. She was wearing faded jeans and a long-sleeved red T-shirt that was now more faded pink than any other colour. Her light-brown hair shot out in gelled spikes around her head. Her lips were already pinned back into a mocking smile. My heart sank. I knew what that look meant. I took off my school jacket and tossed it over the banister.

'How come you're not at work?' I frowned.

'It's my day off,' Jessica replied. 'What's with that face?'

'I'm having a bad day, Jessica. So back off.'

'How about we meditate together?' my sister suggested.

And the sad thing was, she was serious. She's into all that hippy-dippy, transcendental, rental-mental bollocks. Or at least, she was this fortnight. A month ago kick boxing had been the way to cure all of society's ills. And the month before that it'd been colour therapy. Apparently the reason I was so permanently irritable was because I wore too much blue and ate too much red and brown.

I walked past her towards the kitchen. 'Jess, I'm not in the mood for your nonsense this evening, I'm really not.'

'Tobey, what you need to do is submerge yourself in Lake You,' said Jess, following me. 'Get to know your true self . . .'

Lake You . . . Godsake!

'Jessica, get away from me,' I said.

'What's the matter, Tobey? Girlfriend giving you trouble?'

'Feel free to drop dead at any time.'

'Ooh! Sounds like you didn't get any under or over the clothes action today,' Jessica laughed.

I glared at her, but from the huge, moronic grin on my sister's face, she still didn't get the message. It took a lot to bring Jess down.

'Just how far have you two gone anyway?' she asked.

I went over to the fridge. If I ignored her, maybe she'd take the unsubtle hint and bog off.

'Come on, Tobey. Tell all. Inquiring minds want to know,' Jessica teased.

I opened the fridge door. 'Jess, what can I get you? Orange juice? Lemonade? Your own business?'

'Your business *is* my business,' Jessica informed me.

I grabbed a can of ginger beer and pushed past her.

'Tetchy!' Jessica called after me. 'Someone isn't getting any.'

Godsake! This was all I needed. First Dan. Now my sister.

'Jessica, go away,' I told her.

'Definitely not getting any,' Jessica called after me.

I headed out into the hall just as the front doorbell sounded. Being closest, I opened the door.

'Hi, Tobey. Ready to work on our history project?'

I frowned, moving out of Callie's way as she swept past me. I sniffed silently. Callie was wearing the cinnamon-spice perfume I'd given her last Crossmas. She never wore anything else now. Damn, but I loved the way she smelled.

'I thought you didn't want to do it until tomorrow.' I frowned. 'And what happened to your singing lesson?'

'Mr Seacole is ill today so my lesson was cancelled. I tried to find you at lunch time to tell you, but you were wearing your cloak of invisibility.' Callie graced me with an accusatory stare. 'I just got home and Nathan is round *again*, and he and Mum are making cow eyes at each other, so it was stay at home and be sick down my blouse or come and see you.'

'I take it I only just won?'

'It *was* close,' Callie agreed with a smile.

Callie wore her dark-brown hair tied back in her usual plaited ponytail. She'd changed out of her school uniform and into denim jeans and a light-pink, tight pink, long-sleeved T-shirt. A figure-hugging, curve-clinging, light-pink, tight pink, long-sleeved T-shirt. Dark-blue sandals showed off her unpainted toenails. She was five feet seven and most of it seemed to consist of legs. Legs and boobs. I forced myself to focus on Callie's face before she decked me. She started up the stairs to my bedroom.

'You got our history notes?' she asked, turning back to me.

I dug out my memory stick from my trouser pocket and waved it at her. I didn't go anywhere without it. 'It's all on here.'

'Hi, Callie. You OK?'

'I'm fine thanks, Jessica.' Callie smiled at my sister. 'Tobey and I are doing our history project together.'

'Enjoy,' said Jessica. 'Just remember to keep the bedroom door open and at least one foot on the floor at all times.'

'Ha frickin' ha,' I called out as I followed Callie up the stairs.

Jessica cracked up laughing. She really thought she was funny. My sister was older than me by only eighteen months and although she worked part-time as a hair-dresser, she still lived at home. On her wages, she'd be at home until she was a pensioner. I wasn't going to settle for that. No way.

There'd come a day when I'd have money dripping out of cupboards. I'd promised myself that from the time I started at Heathcroft. Success was all a matter of mental atti-tude. And I had the right stuff. I was going to be rich – by any means necessary. Any legal means, of course. No way was I going to make my money with the shadow of prison hanging over my head. At least the shadow of the noose had now been permanently removed. And about time too.

Callie turned at the top of the stairs to grin at me. I was well aware of how much me and my sister amused her. But Jessica knew exactly what to say to wind me up. Especially when she teased me about Callie. Actually, now I come to think about it, only when she teased me about Callie.

Once we reached my bedroom, I must admit, I closed my bedroom door a little louder than was absolutely necessary. I was more than a little annoyed at my sister's dense comments. What if Jessica's teasing put Callie off coming to my room at all?

'Tobey, should I strip off and lie on the bed?' Callie asked. 'That'd really give your sister something to tease you about!'

'Yes, please.' I grinned. If only.

'You wish,' Callie scoffed.

Yeah, I did actually.

'I can dream, can't I?' I gave a mock sigh.

I took off my school shirt and put on a clean white T-shirt pulled out of my wardrobe. Thanks, Mum! I decided to leave my school trousers where they were, on my body. I wasn't in the mood to listen to Callie tease me about my 'skinny uncooked chicken legs', as she kept calling them. I sat at my tiny desk, connecting my memory stick to the family computer, which stayed in my room as I used it the most.

'Tobey, all joking aside, why don't you tell your sister we're just friends?' Callie stated.

I glanced away so that Callie couldn't see my face. 'I've tried, but she didn't believe me.'

'I've told Jess more than once that you don't think of me as anything but a pain in the neck, but she didn't believe me either. I wonder why?' Callie frowned, sitting down on my bed. She glanced at her watch. 'How long d'you reckon today?'

'I give her three minutes.' I sighed, for real this time. 'And counting.'

'Nah. I reckon seven minutes, fifteen seconds,' said Callie. 'Your sister will want to wait until she thinks we're really into something before she bursts through the door.'

'You're wrong. Two or three minutes at the most. Any longer and she'll be afraid she's missing something.'

'What has she heard about you that I haven't?' Callie frowned. 'Bit of a fast lover, are you?'

Careful, Tobey . . .

'I've never had any complaints,' I replied.

Callie regarded me, a strange expression on her face before she turned away to trace the lightning-fork pattern on my duvet. 'Well, we're not all as easily pleased as Misty.'

Misty? What on earth did this have to do with Misty? More to the point, what did it take to please Callie? Had Lucas already given her some idea about that? Our conversation was spiralling away from me dangerously. Nothing I said now would come out right, so better to say nothing.

Callie stood up and headed for my desk. 'Let's see all this cool stuff you've come up with for our project then.'

I tried to access the files on the memory stick, but the computer didn't even recognize that a memory stick was connected. After trying twice more, I tried to access it directly via the operating system. Weird symbols and hieroglyphics scrolled across my screen.

'Tobey, where are my files?' Callie's voice was low, her question rhetorical. She could see as well as I could what had happened to her files.

'This isn't my fault,' I said quickly. 'I only bought this thing last month. It's supposed to be state of the art.'

'State of the another-word-beginning-with-A more like,' Callie said in disgust. 'Tobey, I really don't want to have to do all my sections again.'

'Didn't you take a backup of your notes?' I said.

'Not the latest version, no. I changed some stuff at school before loading it onto your memory stick, then I deleted the files afterwards. And what about all the film clips you added and the other stuff you said you did at school? Are they gone too?'

I nodded. 'I'll just have to do it all again. Don't worry, it'll only take me a couple of hours.' I tried to reassure Callie, knowing full well I'd lost a lot more than two days' work. It would take ages to add all the graphics and re-edit all the film clips I'd included in our presentation. Godsake!

'What happened to your memory key? Did you microwave it or something?'

'Or something.' I pulled the wretched thing out of the USB port and scowled down at it.

'Take it back to the shop you bought it from and get a refund,' said Callie.

I nodded, not holding out much hope. I had no idea where I'd put the receipt. I returned the memory stick to my pocket, mightily cheesed off. Maybe the shop would exchange it without the receipt as I didn't want my money back.

Callie headed back to my bed. 'Well, we can still carry on with the rest of our report. And I'll update my sections when I get back home.' She glanced at her watch as she sat down. 'If your sister is about to burst in on us, you'd better come over here and sit next to me. After all, you wouldn't want to disappoint her.'

I did as requested. I sat so close that our arms and thighs were squashed against each other. I could feel Callie's body heat warming me through my clothes.

'What d'you smell of?' I asked, sniffing at her neck.

'Why? Is it minging?' Callie sniffed at her wrist doubtfully. I suppose she had the same perfume I'd given her on her wrists as well. And of course she didn't reek. She smelled lovely.

'You smell of biscuits,' I told her.

Callie's eyebrows shot up. 'Thanks.'

'That's a compliment.'

Looking deeply unimpressed, Callie said, 'Tobey, a few words of advice. Don't tell Misty or any of your other girlfriends that they smell of biscuits. Tell them they smell of flowers, that they smell sexy, erotic, exotic, good enough to eat even, but not that they smell of biscuits.'

'But I like biscuits,' I protested.

'Is this another of your wind ups?' Callie said suspiciously.

I grinned at her, deciding that no answer would be the best answer in this case. I really did love the way Callie smelled and she smelled of biscuits, but I suspected if I pressed the issue, she'd go home and flush the rest of my Crossmas present to her down the loo.

Callie sighed and lay back on her elbows. I wished she wouldn't do that. It made her boobs stick out even more. Once again I had to force myself to concentrate on the area above Callie's shoulders.

'Fancy watching a film once we've finished our homework?' Callie asked.

I was instantly on my guard. 'What kind of film?'

'*Angie's Mystery* is on at nine o'clock,' Callie suggested.

'What's that?'

'It's a contemporary social drama set in—'

'Never mind where it's set. No.' The words 'social drama' were all I needed to hear to make up my mind on that one.

'Or there's *Lovelorn* on at the same time on Channel—'

'Hell, no! If it's got "love" in the title, I'm gone,' I told her straight. 'Can't we watch an action or a horror film?'

'What if I told you *Lovelorn* is an action musical.'

An action musical? Yeah, right.

'Nice try!'

Callie sighed. 'What's wrong with a romantic drama?'

'Callie, I'm not watching some drippy film that's all angst and sickly sweet sentimentality so you can sit there sighing and sniffing next to me,' I said. 'No way.'

'There's nothing wrong with the odd cathartic cry,' Callie informed me. 'I learned that when Nana Jasmine died.'

'Well, I wouldn't know,' I replied.

Callie tilted her head as she regarded me. 'No, you wouldn't,' she agreed. 'Didn't you cry when your dad left?'

'Nope.' I wasn't going to cry over that. It wasn't like he hadn't run out on us before. And if he ever came back, he was bound to do a runner again. Crying over him would be like crying because the sun rose each morning.

'When was the last time you cried?' Callie asked with a frown.

'Years and years ago,' I said truthfully.

'There's nothing wrong with crying. Sometimes it's the only thing that makes things better.'

'I'm not even sure I know how any more.' Crying wasn't me. 'Can we change the subject please?'

Callie sighed, but did as I asked. 'So what d'you reckon your sister's excuse for bursting in on us will be this time?'

I shrugged. 'Who knows? Getting back one of her magazines?'

'Hunting down her college homework?' said Callie.

Like I'd keep any of her wigs or hairdressing stuff in my room. Jess went to hairdressing college just one day a week, but the stuff she brought home was pushing me and Mum out of the house.

'How about checking up on Cuddles, my pet snake . . . ?' I suggested.

'Despite the fact that Cuddles died over five years ago,' Callie pointed out wryly.

'Ah, but Jessica can commune with friendly spirits,' I reminded her. 'Snakes included.'

'Your sister is a woman of many talents.'

'If only that included minding her own—'

The door was flung open, its hinges protesting with a severe creak.

'I hope I'm not disturbing you two. Did you call me, Callie?' said Jessica. 'I thought I heard you call me.'

Callie and I exchanged a look. I didn't even have to glance down at my watch.

'I win,' I said softly.

'I did call you actually,' said Callie. 'I'm just about to make mad, passionate love to your brother and I wondered if you'd like to watch?'

'Ugh! Callie, I thought you had better taste.' Jessica's face contorted at the thought.

'Nope. I love the way Tobey and I get down and dirty. Watch us, Jessica. You might learn something.'

Callie pulled at the back of my T-shirt, almost strangling me in the process. I fell backwards before my Adam's apple was cut in two. Callie pounced. That's the only word for it. She pounced. Before I could blink, her lips were on mine and her tongue was darting into my mouth. And damn, it felt good. I wrapped my arms around her and pulled her closer.

'That is so gross.' Jessica's voice barely registered. 'I'm outta here. You two have moved beyond sad into pitiful.'

I was vaguely aware of my bedroom door being slammed shut, but I didn't care. I pulled Callie closer still. Blood was rushing round my body, then to one particular part of my body. Callie smelled good, tasted great and felt even better. It took a few seconds to realize that Callie was trying to push away from me. I reluctantly let her go.

'We can stop now,' Callie told me, her warm breath fanning over my face. 'Your sister has gone.'

Sod my sister.

'Let's hope that cures her of her nosiness. For some reason Jessica didn't fancy the idea of watching you get your leg over.' Callie laughed.

'Godsake, Callie. Even I'm grossed out by that idea.' My lips twisted at the thought.

Callie sat up abruptly. Her smile had vanished. 'Making love with me would gross you out? Thanks a lot.'

I stared at her, then sat up myself. 'I meant . . . that's not what I meant. I meant about my sister being present.'

Callie's head tilted to one side. 'It's OK, Tobey. I get it. I'm not Misty.'

Was she nuts?

'I don't want you to be Misty. God forbid.'

Callie shrugged. She dug into her school rucksack and took out a couple of books. I sighed inwardly. She didn't believe me. Or was she winding me up as payback for earlier? Because if so, she was doing a first-class job. Usually I was streets ahead of her when it came to teasing, but over the last few months, the scales had been tipping in the other direction. She got to me like no one else.

'Callie, there's nothing going on between me and Misty,' I said.

'If you say so.' Callie still didn't look me in the eye.

'I do. And it means a lot to me that you believe that.'

'Why?'

'It just does,' I said, trying and failing to keep the impatience out of my voice. 'OK?'

'OK,' replied Callie. 'Ready to work on our school project now?'

Well, if she wanted to concentrate on homework, then I could too. Two could play that game.

'Now, about the Second World War – what point of view d'you want to write our newspaper article from? The POV of us winners or the losers?' Callie asked.

'I don't mind,' I said. 'You choose.'

'Which is what you always say whenever I ask you to make a decision,' said Callie, the faintest trace of irritation creeping into her voice. 'If you made an actual decision for yourself, would you get a nosebleed, or maybe a brain aneurysm?'

'What's wrong now?' I asked, exasperated.

Callie contemplated me, her head tilting to one side again. 'Tobey, what are we? Apart from uncomplicated?'

'We're friends,' I replied at once. 'We're good friends. Aren't we?' What was Callie getting at?

Callie nodded. 'I guess so.'

'Don't you know?'

'I'm waiting for you to figure it out, so you can tell me,' said Callie.

'What does that mean?'

'I'm waiting for you to figure that one out as well.' Callie smiled. 'Let's get on with our homework.'

Sometimes I don't understand Callie. At all.

I'm a reasonably smart guy, but I just don't get her.

Damn, but she's complicated.

five. Callie

Sometimes I don't understand Tobey. At all.

He's the smartest guy I know, but he just doesn't get it.

Damn, but he's dense.

six. Tobey

'Tobey, you still haven't told me about your careers meeting. How did it go?' asked Mum.

'Fine.' I grinned, putting down my glass of orange juice. 'Mrs Paxton was really encouraging. She reckons any university in the country will take me with the grades I can achieve if I don't let my work slip. And she's personally going to write my university reference.'

Mum smiled faintly at my enthusiasm, but I couldn't help it. Both Mrs Paxton, our head, and Mr Brooking, the school careers advisor, had basically told me that the world was mine, as long as I was prepared to keep working for it. It didn't matter what Dan and some of my friends outside of school said: I was going to go to university. Every time I thought of my future, it made me smile. And nothing and no one was going to hold me back or even break my stride.

My family were all sitting down having breakfast together, which was kind of rare as Mum's a nurse at Mercy Community Hospital, so she worked shifts. Jessica was still half asleep and picking at her fried egg and bacon. My plate was almost empty and I was eyeing Jessica's egg. If she wasn't going to eat it then I had room left in my stomach, as long as the egg wasn't cold. But if I took too much interest in Jess's breakfast, she'd gobble it up and swallow it down just to spite me.

'Mum, it's actually going to happen.' My smile widened.

'Hopefully,' said Mum.

'Not hopefully. It's gonna happen,' I amended. 'I'm going to university.'

Mum just shrugged.

'To do what?' asked Jessica.

'Something that'll make me a lot of money like an Economics or a Maths degree or maybe Business Studies with Information Technology,' I replied.

'That'll make you money?' Jessica said sceptically.

'Working with money makes money,' I said. 'Everyone knows that.'

'Don't you want to do a degree because you're interested in the subject rather than for the money you'll make at the end of it?' asked Jess.

'I'm being practical.'

'What would you do if you didn't have to worry about a job at the end of it?' my sister asked.

'I dunno.' I'd never really thought about that as it wasn't going to happen. 'Maybe Politics or Law. Something like that.'

'Tobey, don't set your heart on university,' Mum said gently. 'I can't afford three or four years' worth of fees, not on top of what I have to fork out to Jessica's college. I just don't have the money.'

'I know, Mum. Don't worry, I've got it all worked out. I'll take out a student loan to cover the tuition fees. And I'll start saving the money I earn from every holiday job I have from now on.'

'It's not just tuition fees,' Mum warned. 'You'll have to pay rent and bills and buy books and food.'

'University is for the rich or those prepared to be in debt until they're middle-aged. It's just another way of keeping us Noughts down,' Jess added.

'Isn't it more of a poor-versus-rich thing?' I frowned.

'Please,' Mum groaned. 'No politics at the breakfast table. It's too early.'

Going to university had always struck me as more of a social class thing than a race thing. As long as I wasn't going to one of those snooty, snotty 'historical' universities where they interviewed you first to ascertain your family's bank balance and social standing, what was the problem? If I got good grades in my end-of-school exams and I paid the tuition fees, surely that was enough for most universities and they wouldn't care that I was white? Mrs Paxton reckoned I had the right stuff to get into any university in the country. So, enough. I wasn't going to give voice to my doubts or argue the point. I was in too much of a good mood.

'Jess has a point, though,' said Mum. 'I mean, is that what you really want? To be in debt until your hair turns grey?'

'That's why, after university, I'm going to get a job that makes a lot of money so I can pay off the loan faster,' I said.

My good mood was rapidly evaporating. Mum and Jessica were only trying to make sure that I knew what I was letting myself in for, but they were both beginning to jump up and down on my nerves.

'Why d'you want to go to university anyway?' Jessica sniffed.

'Because I can,' I snapped. 'Because less than twenty years ago, a Nought going to university was unheard of, unless they were super rich. Because that door is open and all I have to do is walk through it.'

'For all the good it'll do you,' Jessica muttered.

'And that right there is why you'll be doing the same job in the same place for the same wage in thirty years' time.' I glared at her. 'Your attitude is why you'll always fail.'

'Thanks a lot,' Jess said indignantly.

'Does the truth hurt?' I asked with just a modicum of spite.

'Tobey, that's enough,' Mum admonished me.

'She started it,' I said childishly.

I sipped at my coffee, glaring at my sister. She gave as good as she got.

'So, Jess, how's college?' Mum asked, trying to draw her attention.

'Too much writing,' said Jess. 'Why on earth do I have to write essays on hair textures and nutrition and the structure of hair follicles? I want to cut and style hair, not lecture on it.'

'You do get to cut hair as well though, don't you?' Mum sounded worried.

Jessica wasn't keen on writing. Never had been.

'Yeah, but not enough,' my sister sighed. 'The four essays we had to do this year plus my exam next week count for sixty per cent of the total end-of-year mark.' Her eyes clouded over. Something was wrong . . .

'How d'you get the other forty per cent?' I asked.

'Practical work at my work placement and one practical assignment in front of my tutor,' said Jess.

'What's the pass mark for this year then?' I frowned.

'Seventy per cent.'

'And what happens if you fail?' I asked.

'She leaves college and gets a full-time job,' Mum answered before Jessica had the chance.

'They let you redo the year again as long as you pay the fees,' Jessica said, studying the peeling and chipped veneer on our table.

'No, Jess. If you fail this year, no more college,' said Mum sternly.

'How many of this year's essays have you done?' I asked.

'What is this? Some kind of inquisition?' Jessica exploded. 'I've done my essays. OK? I really want to be a hairdresser. I'm not about to mess that up.'

'Well, excuse me whilst I just run round the kitchen after my head.' I scowled. 'I was only asking.'

'When's your final exam, Jessica?' asked Mum, casting me a warning look.

'Next Thursday,' Jess replied, moderating her tone only slightly.

Mum glared at me. I got the message.

'I'm sorry, Jess,' I said reluctantly. I hated saying sorry to my sister. 'I didn't mean to upset you.'

Jessica shook her head slowly. 'It's all right for you, Tobey. You've never failed at anything in your life. God help you the first time you do fail, because you won't be able to handle it.'

'Then I won't fail.' I shrugged.

'And it's that simple, is it?'

'Yeah.'

I downed the rest of my orange juice and took my empty plate and glass to the sink. My appetite for more was gone.

seven. Tobey

The summer morning was already blindingly bright and blazing hot with a promise of a lot more sunshine to come. A heat haze rose up from the pavement, creating a muddled urban mirage of shimmering skyscapes and flickering, glistening buildings. To be honest, I was already sick of the heat. Roll on autumn. I pulled the strap of my rucksack further up my arm to rest upon my shoulder. The thing was heavy and uncomfortable and made me walk with my whole body tilted to one side. But that wasn't why I was in a bad mood.

Breakfast with Mum and Jessica had been bad enough. But then Callie had let me down. She must've decided to walk to school by herself today, in spite of telling me last night that she'd knock for me. I was so used to going to school with Callie that when it didn't happen, it felt strange, like I'd set foot out of my house and forgotten something vital.

But I shouldn't have been surprised. More often than

not these days, Callie was a silent companion. Since her nana had died, she'd changed. According to the newspaper reports, some anonymous Nought guy had died in the explosion as well. The authorities didn't seem to be straining themselves to establish his identity. Or maybe it'd been reported on page thirty-odd of the dead guy's local newspaper and hadn't managed to make it any further up the 'does-anyone-give-a-damn?' scale.

What had happened in that hotel the day Jasmine Hadley died? Was she really so unlucky as to be in the wrong place at the wrong time? Was life really that arbitrary? It would appear so.

An executive jet-black WMW – known as 'white man's wheels' – pulled up alongside me, its back window gliding down in expensive silence.

'Tobey Durbridge, isn't it?'

I stepped back, pulling my rucksack closer to my side. The WMW before me was almost limousine-like in its proportions. It had to be custom-made. The alloy hubcaps had been polished to a high shine and I could see my distorted reflection in them. I took another step back, as did my reflection. We both had the same idea.

A Nought man's face moved into view. I recognized him at once. Alex McAuley. Aka Creepy McAuley (only ever said behind his back) or Softly McAuley (occasionally said to his face by close friends only) because he could be kicking your head in and he'd never once raise his voice. No one – as far as I knew – had ever heard him shout. He didn't need to. His dark-grey suit covered a middleweight boxer's physique. He was still in shape, even though he was in his mid thirties. He wore his blond hair swept back off his face. His light-brown eyebrows framed hard, ice-blue eyes. The single yellow diamond stud he wore in his left ear twinkled like a giggle in the morning sunlight. He smiled at me, pulling back thin lips over perfect, high-price, sparkling white teeth. I fought my natural instinct to take another step back or, better still, do a runner. It wouldn't do any good anyway. I saw the silhouette of another Nought man in the back seat of the car next to McAuley. Between them was a state-of-the-art laptop, McAuley's no doubt, with a memory stick attached. The driver and the guy in the passenger seat were also looking at me. McAuley's car was full. The rumours were true. He never, ever travelled alone.

I answered the expectant look on his face. 'Hello, Mr McAuley.'

'Ah. So you know me?' he replied, his tone soft and lilting.

I didn't bother responding to that one. If he needed his ego stroked he'd have to find someone else to do it for him.

'I've been hearing a lot about you, Tobey Durbridge,' he said.

My heart flipped like a pancake. Didn't like the sound of that. Not one little bit.

McAuley raised his eyebrows when I failed to reply. 'Aren't you going to ask me what I've heard?'

I shook my head.

'You're not the least bit curious?'

'If it's bad, it'll crush my ego, in which case I'd rather not hear it. And if it's good, it'll make my head swell, in which case I'd better not hear it.'

McAuley considered me. I was pinned by his gaze like a lepidopterist's butterfly. 'Curiosity moves us forward,' he said.

Around McAuley, curiosity could also move you under – buried two metres under, to be precise – but I decided to keep that to myself.

'You know when to keep your mouth shut, don't you?' McAuley smiled, even though there was nothing to smile about. Mind you, if I'd forked out the kind of money he must've spent on all those porcelain veneers, I'd show them off too. 'Tobey, how would you like to work for me? I could always use a smart boy like you.'

I'd rather have my toenails extracted one by one without benefit of a general anaesthetic, but McAuley was just the man to make that happen.

'Well? I asked you a question, Tobias.' McAuley's eyebrows began to knit together and, if anything, his voice grew quieter.

'I'm still at school, sir.'

'I have little jobs that need doing over the odd weekend and a couple of evenings a month – nothing onerous. And I'm very generous, as you'll find out.'

I'm a fish and he's the fisherman and he's got his hook in my mouth. My silence will let him reel me in. Say something, Tobey. Godsake! Speak.

'I'd rather not, sir,' I replied quietly.

Inside McAuley's car, his crew began to laugh.

'You're very polite, aren't you? "I'm still at school, sir."
"I'd rather not, sir,"' McAuley mimicked. 'Three bags
full, sir.'

A single line of sweat trickled down from my left
temple in front of my ear, but I didn't dare wipe it away.
My heart was a punching bag being viciously pummelled
over and over.

'Tobey, you don't want to say no to me,' McAuley said
softly. 'I don't like that word. I mean, I *really* don't like
that word.'

A children's book. A first reader. My photo, legs pumping,
terror on my face. See Tobey run. Run, Tobey, run.

I stood still, my feet glued to my shoes, my shoes glued
to the pavement. My useless frickin' body. Adrenalin
coursed through me. Fight or flight? I couldn't do either.
Useless.

'I'm a good man to work for, Tobey.'

Why can't I just slide away on McAuley's oily
smile?

'I'm a loyal friend and I look after my own. Ask anyone
who works for me. Ask your friend Dan. But I think
you'll find I'm also a—'

'Tobey! How come you didn't wait for me?'

Callie's voice reached me before she did. That girl had
the ability to go from mute to surround sound in less than
a second. She trotted up to me, to stand between me and
McAuley.

'You were supposed to wait for me, toe-rag. Thanks for
making me run after you. Now I'm all sweaty.'

I pulled at her arm and stepped in front of her.

'What's wrong?' Callie frowned.

My eyes were still on McAuley. His gaze swept over Callie then back to me.

'This your girlfriend then, Tobey?' he asked. 'She's very pretty.'

'No. We're just . . . we walk to school together, that's all,' I replied.

'And we'd better get going, Tobey. We're going to be so late.' Callie grabbed my arm and pulled me after her. I had to trot to keep up. I trailed in her wake, forcing myself not to turn round and look into McAuley's glacier-cold eyes. Half a minute later, his black limo slid past us, the tinted windows now up. Callie and I carried on jogging until the car turned the corner. Callie let go of my arm and dropped her rucksack to the pavement, trying to drag air back into her lungs in rushed gasps.

'Tobey, are you OK?'

'Yeah.' I shrugged.

'You left without me.' There was no mistaking the accusation in her voice.

'I thought you'd already gone to school, that's why.'

'You can knock for me once in a while, you know. It doesn't always have to be me running after you. Would it have killed you to check?' Callie looked up and down the road. 'What did Creepy McAuley want?'

'He offered me a job.'

'Hellfire!' Callie turned to stare at me. 'You didn't say yes, did you?'

'I'm not entirely stupid,' I replied. 'Although saying no to that man might just be the stupidest thing I've ever done.'

'People who work for him usually end up in prison or dead,' said Callie.

Tell me something I didn't know.

'Which is why I said no, Callie.'

'D'you think he'll leave it at that?' Callie's teeth worried at her bottom lip.

I shrugged. 'Who knows? No point losing sleep over it. We'd better get going.'

I picked up Callie's rucksack and handed it to her. We walked to school without saying another word. Callie kept stealing glances at me, but I wasn't in the mood for conversation. She had known me long enough to figure that out for herself.

McAuley knew my name.

Worse than that, I was now a blip on McAuley's radar. It was hard to say which was spinning harder, my mind or my stomach.

'Tobey, you can't work for that man. You just can't.' Callie finally broke the silence between us. 'The Dowds run things around here. If they hear you're working for McAuley you won't be able to walk from your house to school without slipping.'

Slipping. The technical term for entering enemy territory. If I ever agreed to work for McAuley, it was only a matter of time before the Dowds got to hear about it, and then my house and my school and all the routes in between would mean I'd be slipping daily. That's what it was all about in Meadowview. The streets didn't belong to the government or the local authority; they'd been fought over between the Dowds and McAuley's mob. The Dowds ran practically every crooked operation on the east side of Meadowview. McAuley had carved out the west side for himself. He'd established his turf by speaking softly and ensuring that no one but himself and the few good men in his car knew where the bodies were buried. People who opposed him had the habit of 'disappearing' – including two of the Dowd family before an uneasy truce was brokered between them.

Now McAuley wanted me to work for him, even though he knew I lived on the Dowds' patch. And I didn't like what he said about asking my friend Dan for a reference. Surely Dan wasn't stupid enough to talk to McAuley about me? If McAuley didn't have any problem telling me that Dan worked for him, who else had he told? Dan only lived two streets away from me – in Dowd territory.

Damn!

How on earth was I going to extricate myself from this one? Dan might be one of my best mates, but he was stupid as a bag of rocks to get involved with McAuley. Now that I'd seen the man up close and personal, I'd have to try and persuade Dan to get out and stay out of McAuley's clutches. But most important of all, I had to make sure that McAuley kept his eyes off Callie.

Nothing bad was going to happen to Callie Rose.

Not on my watch.

eight. Callie

Tobey remained taciturn all day. It wasn't like him at all. He laughed everything off, never took anything seriously. But not today. After break, we sat together for our double science lesson, but try as I might I couldn't get him to open up to me. After the umpteenth mumbled monosyllabic response, I conceded defeat. Tobey stood over me as I put my stuff in my locker before lunch. We walked into the food hall together, but we peeled off in different directions once we'd got our lunch. I sat with Sammi and some of my other friends. Tobey sat by himself, but not for long. Some of his mates joined him, but from what I could see he still wasn't saying much. Tobey was a strange one. He didn't have many close friends, but that seemed to be by choice rather than design. He chose his friends carefully, but once he was your friend, he was your friend for life. And the mates he had were fiercely loyal in return. And I'm one of them. Every time I looked up, I caught Tobey watching me. I smiled a couple of times, but he immediately looked away.

For heaven's sake! I wanted to invite Tobey out for a meal or something the following night, but it was hard when he would barely speak to me. I mean, I didn't need three guesses to figure it out why. He was worried about

McAuley. And I couldn't say I blamed him. But why take it out on me?

McAuley was a lowlife, just like the Dowds. They climbed high up life's ladder by stockpiling the misery of others beneath them. Even the Liberation Militia were aware of their activities in Meadowview. At least, they were when I was a member. The Liberation Militia didn't bother with them over much. The L.M. considered themselves above that kind of petty wheeling and dealing. Drugs, prostitution, loan sharking, extortion – those kinds of criminal activities were left to the hag fishes, as McAuley, the Dowds and all other 'common' criminals were known within the L.M. – with the emphasis on common. The L.M. considered their cause more noble. They believed themselves to be freedom fighters. Their objective? Equal rights and equal justice for Noughts. And the means? By dispensing their own brand of justice to those they believed deserved it. And if you were innocent and got caught up, then tough luck. The world according to the L.M. The kidnap, torture and murder of the L.M.'s enemies was, in their eyes, honourable. If the government and the Cross–owned media didn't see it that way, if they chose to call the L.M. terrorists instead of freedom fighters, then so be it.

I wanted no part of any of them, not the L.M., nor the hag fishes. Never again. Uncle Jude was the worst. A hag fish masquerading as a warrior fighting for the greater good. The only greater good Uncle Jude had in his heart and his mind was getting revenge on my mother. So many things I knew now that I wished I'd known a few years ago. Even now my blood ran cold at the thought of what

I'd almost done so that Uncle Jude could have his revenge. Stupid. Stupid. Stupid.

But I'd been snatched back to sanity before I could fall irrevocably to Uncle Jude's scheme. In spite of knowing it was pointless, I still hated my uncle. And my loathing grew with each passing day. He was dead and I was still here, but it didn't make any difference. Each angry thought revolved around him. Uncle Jude was evil incarnate. He was so full of hatred that he could experience nothing else. The messages each of his senses sent to his brain were somehow transformed into one hundred per cent hate and nothing else. That was all his brain could register. When Nana Jasmine died, my uncle had died with her. I wondered about his last thoughts as the bomb he'd instructed me to make went off. That split second before his death, who had occupied his thoughts? Mum? Callum, my dad, and his brother? His family? His wasted life?

I knew it wasn't me, unless it was to curse me for fouling up his plans. I don't want to end up like him – but it's so hard. 'Cause Nana Jasmine isn't here any more. Where was the justice in that?

Mum and Aunt Minerva are going to talk to Nana Jasmine's solicitor, Mr Bharadia, again next week. They need to find out when they'll be able to hear her will and get probate, though it could be weeks still before that happens. When will it all be over?

It's taking so long because of the way Nana died and the length of time it took to prove conclusively that it really was Nana Jasmine who died in the explosion at the Isis Hotel. And then there were a number of other matters concerning her death to be sorted out first like the postmortem and the authorities releasing the body so that Mum 'and Aunt Minerva could arrange the funeral. And after the funeral, thank God for Tobey. Like Mum, he always seemed to be there when I needed company. I really don't know what I would've done without him.

I can't help wishing . . . but what's the point? Tobey is always going to treat me like the younger sister he never wanted. I'll just have to get used to it. I had hoped that maybe our kiss in his bedroom meant something to him. It meant something to me. But that's just me daydreaming. I all but held up a placard to tell him how I feel about him. I practically threw myself at him. For a moment there, when he pulled me closer, I could've sworn . . . Wishful thinking again. The best thing he could find to say about me was that I smelled of biscuits.

Biscuits! I ask you.

I was wearing the perfume he gave me last Crossmas and he thought I smelled of biscuits. I hope he didn't see how much that hurt. Biscuits . . . I'm not going to forget that one in a hurry.

It's funny, though. Even when I'm mad at him, I'm not really mad at him. Thinking of Tobey clears my head of other bitter thoughts. Thinking of him makes me smile. Maybe that's why I find myself thinking of him more and more often.

Maybe that's why . . .

nine. Tobey

'Happy birthday, Nana.' Callie kissed Meggie on the cheek and handed her a birthday card and a gift-wrapped box. At least, that's what it looked like from where I stood hovering in the doorway.

'What is it?' Meggie asked, putting the box to her ear and shaking it.

Callie teased, 'When you open it, you'll find out.'

Meggie smiled and began to carefully peel off the wrapping paper from one side of her present. Now if that'd been me, I would've just ripped the paper off. But according to Meggie, if it was removed with care, then 'the wrapping paper could have a repeat performance. Maybe several.' Godsake! It was only wrapping paper. Mind you, my current finances were such that I couldn't even afford to buy wrapping paper, never mind a present. I hadn't given Callie a present two months ago when it was her birthday and I still couldn't afford to buy her one. That really burned me. I wanted to buy Callie anything she wanted, but with what?

I looked around the sitting room, trying to find something to take my mind off the empty state of my pockets. I'd been in this room countless times before, but it never ceased to interest me how the room was a strange mix of old and new, past and present, Nought and Cross. Photos in frames lined the window sill and any available horizontal space. Photos of Meggie's family from a long time ago and another world away. Callie's Aunt Lynette occupied one photo by herself. I'd never heard anyone but Callie talk about her. Callie's aunt had died before Callie was born in some kind of road accident. Another photo on the side table showed all Meggie's children together – Lynette, Jude and Callum. They were all sitting right back on a sofa, none of their legs long enough to reach the floor. Callum couldn't've been more than two or three. It was kind of weird to think that that toddler in the photo was Callie's dad. There was a photo of Meggie and her husband Ryan together, their arms wrapped around each other as they both smiled at the camera. They looked so happy. I didn't know much about Meggie's life, but I knew she'd been through a lot and lost much – her husband Ryan and her children Lynette and Callum were now dead. It showed on every line on her face.

None of the oldies ever wanted to discuss the past, that was the trouble. Whenever I asked my mum about anything that happened more than ten years ago, she'd invariably say, 'Tobey, that was a long time ago. I can't remember.' But it seemed to me that most oldies remembered the past better than the present. They just didn't want to talk about it. Funny how Nought oldies never wanted to discuss the past and Cross oldies did nothing but. It seemed to me that the Crosses embraced their history in a way we Noughts very rarely did.

Callie's mum, Sephy, had her share of photos scattered around the room as well. Photos of her and Callie mostly.

There was one of Sephy and her older sister, Minerva, taken when they were both teenagers by the look of it. And one large photo of Callie's Nana Jasmine and Meggie sat self-consciously in the middle of the window sill. That photo was taken when they were young women. They stood side by side, arms linked as they both smiled at the camera. Every time I looked at that photo, I wondered what each of them had been thinking the precise moment the photo was taken. Callie once told me that her mum and dad, Sephy and Callum, were just kids when that photo was taken – certainly no older than nine or ten. How odd to think that two families with such different backgrounds could have their lives so intertwined.

At last Meggie got the wrapping paper off, revealing the dark-blue box underneath. I had never seen anyone take quite so long to get wrapping paper off. Meggie carefully removed the lid from the box. The surprise on her face was transformed to pure delight.

'I'm sorry it's not much,' Callie said apologetically.

'It's beautiful.' Meggie smiled at her before taking out her present. It was a gold necklace with a pendant shaped like a golden rose on a thornless stem. Callie had already shown it to me on the day she bought it, asking for my opinion.

'It's a rose from Callie Rose,' she told her nan, as if Meggie hadn't worked that bit out by now. 'It's so you'll always have something to remind you of me. You don't think that's too narcissistic, do you?'

Meggie smiled at her granddaughter. 'No, love, just unnecessary. I don't need a necklace or anything else to think of you. But thank you anyway. It's really beautiful.'

'And it won't turn your neck green,' I quipped from the door.

Meggie raised an amused eyebrow.

'Thanks for that, Tobey.' Callie scowled at me before turning back to Meggie. 'It's real gold, Nana. It's only nine carats, but it is real gold.'

'Callie, don't let Tobey wind you up, dear. It's lovely.'

'Tobey's got you something as well,' said Callie.

That was my cue to move further into the room. Reluctantly, I dug into my jacket pocket, pulling out a crumpled envelope. I handed it over, embarrassed. Meggie took hold of it and took out the birthday card. The envelope looked so manky, I wouldn't've blamed her if she'd held it gingerly by only one corner. But she didn't.

'It's a birthday card,' I mumbled, stating the obvious.

'That's very kind of you, Tobey.'

'It's not much,' I warned her as she took it out of its envelope.

Meggie looked at the expressionist vase of flowers on the front of the card and then read the words on the inside, which was more than I'd done when I bought it.

'Thank you, Tobey. It's lovely.'

The card was cheap and cheerful and had just about emptied my pockets. But Meggie was being great about it. She put it next to Callie's card on the side table.

Callie started chatting about the restaurant her mum and her nan were going to later and Meggie's face cleared as she listened. I admit I didn't contribute much to the conversation. Money was in my head again. It had to be in my head, I couldn't afford to keep it any other place.

Something had to change. I couldn't spend the next few years until I graduated from university like this.

Callie popped two lasagne meals into the microwave for us as we weren't going out to dinner with her mum and nan. We weren't invited because it was a school night. I mean, Godsake! Did I look like I went to bed before Meggie McGregor? But I wasn't going to argue. After all, it meant Callie and I could be alone together, which suited me just fine. After our meal, I asked Callie if she fancied going for a walk? The moment we stepped outside, the intense evening heat hit us like a slap round the face. We headed along our road, walking through a shock wave of rock music blaring out through the open living-room window of the house five doors along. The air smelled of chicken nuggets and bad temper. The irresistible urge to get something off my chest grew stronger with each step.

'Callie, I will get you something for your birthday. I promise.'

Callie was surprised. 'My birthday was ages ago.'

'I know. But I never got you anything.'

'It doesn't matter. I just want to forget my last birthday,' Callie said sombrely. 'Anyway, what brought that on?'

'I just . . .' I eyed the bracelet adorning her left wrist. The gold link chain set off the semi-precious lime-green stones that glinted against Callie's brown skin. It was beautiful. Just the sort of thing I'd've loved to have bought for her. Lucas and his deep pockets, no doubt.

'Tobey?' Callie prompted.

'I never got you a gift and I just wanted to let you know that I haven't forgotten. I will get you something.'

'Don't bother.' Callie shrugged.

'But I want to . . .'

'Tobey, it's no big deal. I don't want or need anything from you,' said Callie. 'At least . . . Never mind.'

'Go on. What were you going to say?'

'It doesn't matter.'

'What is it you want?'

Callie smiled. 'Let me come close to beating you at chess once in a while. That'll do.'

'Are you mad?' I replied, horror-stricken. 'Chess should be taken seriously, otherwise why bother?'

'It was just a thought.' Callie's grin broadened.

'Maybe it'll be a thought when it grows up?' I suggested.

Callie shook her head. We carried on walking.

'Are you still playing football this Sunday?' she asked.

'Yeah. You coming?'

'You mean, am I going to stand on a sweaty sideline at three on Sunday afternoon to watch you and your mates kick a ball around for ninety minutes?'

I nodded.

'I wouldn't miss it.' Callie smiled. 'See! I must really like you or something.'

We carried on walking in a companionable silence. There were all kinds of things I wanted to say, wanted to ask, but I'm useless at that kind of thing, so I did the same as usual and said nothing. I stole glances at Callie. Was she OK just walking beside me? Or did she wish she could be somewhere else? It was so hard to tell. She turned her head occasionally to catch me looking at her. Each time she'd smile like she knew something I didn't and we'd keep walking.

'Callie . . .' I began at last.

'Yes?'

'Have you . . . have you forgiven me for . . . telling you about your dad?'

I'd inadvertently revealed to Callie that her dad had been hanged as a Nought terrorist and for a long, long time afterwards she wouldn't even speak to me. It was the most miserable time of my life. After that I vowed that I'd never do anything to lose Callie's friendship again.

Callie stared at me. 'Tobey, that was a long time ago. Of course I've forgiven you. Like you said, we're friends.'

'It's just . . . I think about that day a lot. I didn't mean to hurt you.'

'I know you didn't. Let it go.'

'Easier said than done,' I sighed.

Callie nodded, her expression deadly serious. 'I know. You're not terribly good at letting things go.'

The sound of sirens split the air. And the sound was getting closer.

Callie's steps slowed. 'Sounds like we'd better head back,' she said.

Sirens were more common than birds chirping around here, especially lately. I was all for carrying on with our walk when three police cars screeched to a halt at the top of our road. Mrs Bridges was at it again. Everyone on our street knew she was dealing drugs. Punters would turn up and post money through her door, then she'd chuck the required merchandise out of a first-floor window. Her downstairs windows were barred and securely fastened, just in case some druggie fancied his or her chances. Most didn't, unless they were tired of having two working legs.

Everyone knew Mrs Bridges worked for the Dowds. Callie and I knew enough not to hang around. I took Callie's arm and practically frogmarched her back the way we'd come. For once she didn't argue.

'I hate this place,' Callie muttered from beside me. 'It never stops.'

She turned back to see what was going on. Even though the police cars were stationary, their lights were still flashing. The police were hammering away at Mrs Bridges's door. Good luck with that! Any drugs on the premises had been flushed away and were well on their way to the seaside by now. We quickened our pace away from all the banging and shouting.

'What d'you think is happening?' Callie asked.

'Who knows? What the cops would call N.H.I., no doubt.'

'N.H.I.?'

'No humans involved.'

Callie looked so profoundly shocked, I instantly regretted my cynical outburst. But I remembered the last time a Nought boy had been stabbed by another Nought around here. It was about three months ago, maybe four. I was on my way home from school when I turned a corner and saw a number of people and the flashing lights of police cars and an ambulance. Pushing my way forward, I stood rubber-necking like everyone else before we were all pushed back away from the scene. Some poor Nought boy of about my own age lay still on the ground, a slow pool of blood leaking out from beneath him. His hands were at his sides and his sightless eyes were staring straight into the sun. It was the first time I'd seen a dead body. I waited for some emotion other than sadness to kick in. What should I be feeling? Rage? Fear? Pity? Nothing stirred inside me. Taking one last look at the dead boy, I turned and walked away. I didn't run. I walked, my head down. I just wanted to get home. As I approached the street corner, I heard them before I saw them.

'So who got shot this time?' a woman's voice was asking. She might've been enquiring about the soup of the day in a restaurant for all the emotion in her voice.

'Not shot. Stabbed,' a younger male voice corrected. 'Just another kid. Some boy.'

'Noughts cleaning house again,' said the woman.

'The boy was still someone's son, someone's friend.'

'When you've been at this as long as me, you'll realize that all these Nought deaths are strictly N.H.I.,' said the woman.

'What does that mean?'

'No humans involved,' the woman replied. 'As long as it's blankers killing blankers, who cares?'

I turned the corner then. A middle-aged Cross copper was setting out cones to cordon off the road. Her younger Cross colleague looked at me, then away. It was one of those moments. They knew I'd heard them. I knew they knew. I carried on walking. N.H.I.? Was that what I was to them? Was that all I was? Something inside me began to uncoil – like something deep inside, asleep inside, was beginning to wake. I stopped walking, closed my eyes and took several long, deep breaths. Whatever had been stirring inside me settled and remained still.

It was better that way. Safer.

'Tobey, d'you think we'll ever get away from here?' asked Callie.

'I guarantee it,' I replied sombrely.

We reached my house first. I opened the door, bundled Callie inside and closed it firmly behind me.

'How can you be so sure?' asked Callie.

'Because there's no way I'm going to spend the rest of my life around here. And neither are you.'

Callie sighed. 'I wish I had your confidence.'

'I'm getting out of here, Callie. Just watch me,' I told her.

And I'm taking you with me.

ten. Callie

I loved walking to school with Tobey. He always made me laugh – when he wasn't in one of his quiet moods. And the morning was so light and bright, a promise of the day to come. The sunlight glinting on Tobey's dark-brown hair made it seem like he had occasional red highlights in it. Tobey's mum's hair was red so I suppose it was only natural that he would inherit some of her colouring. His hair used to fall in unruly waves almost to his shoulders, but at the beginning of our current school term he'd had it cut as short as I'd ever seen it. It was only two or three centimetres long now, if that, but it suited him. Made him seem older somehow. And now that his hair was shorter, it looked darker, to match his eyes. Tobey's eyes were the colour of strong coffee. But when he was angry, they grew so dark it was hard to tell where his irises ended and his pupils began. Not that there was much on this planet that could anger Tobey. He was Mr Sanguine. Tobey caught me looking at him. He smiled. I smiled back. Then I noticed something about him that hadn't registered before.

'Tobey, what's that on your chin?' I moved closer for a better look.

'It's my goatee. What d'you think?'

'That's your attempt at growing a beard?'

'A goatee.'

I shook my head. 'Tobey, I've seen more fuzz on a kiwi fruit. Lose it. It looks crap.'

'Thanks,' Tobey said sourly.

'If your best friend can't tell you the truth, then who can?' I asked. 'You look like you haven't washed your face this morning.'

'Thanks.'

I sniffed at his chin. He pulled back like he thought I was going to bite him or something. He should be so lucky!

'You smell reasonable, though,' I told him. 'Did you finally discover the meaning of life, the universe and soap?'

'You're real funny, Callie,' Tobey told me, his tone implying the exact opposite.

I smiled. 'You love me really.'

He reluctantly smiled back. 'Yeah, I adore you. Bitch!'

We both creased up laughing. Sometimes Tobey took himself a bit too seriously. And his attempt at a goatee really was wretched. We were having a good laugh, but were less than a minute away from school when all that changed. Tobey saw them before I did. I was too busy giggling at one of Tobey's silly observations about his sister's ex-boyfriend to see straight. But Tobey's accompanying laughter died on his lips and his eyes took on a hard yet wary look. I followed the direction of his gaze.

Lucas and three of his mates were standing on the steps of the school entrance, sharing a joke. I glanced between Lucas and Tobey and instantly smelled trouble. Lucas and his friends were weaving about like they didn't have a care in the world. Until Lucas spotted us. He said a few words to his crew, his eyes never leaving mine, and the laughter instantly stopped. I was too far away to hear what he said, but it had the desired effect. Lucas's friends all turned to face us, all trace of humour now gone. Tobey and I didn't alter our pace, didn't speed up, didn't slow down. Even though Tobey didn't say a word, I could sense the sudden tension in him.

I didn't understand Lucas. When he was on his own he was fine towards me. He acted like he still wanted us to be together. But when he was with his friends, it was a different story. The way they watched me and Tobey made me feel distinctly uneasy.

I broke up with Lucas soon after Nana Jasmine died. I couldn't cope with her death and Lucas as well. Being with Tobey was easy in a way that being with Lucas was not. It felt like Lucas was with me in spite of what I was, whereas Tobey couldn't care less that my dad was a Nought and my mum is a Cross. Between Lucas and me, silence was a high thorny hedge, something to be painfully overcome. But when I was with Tobey, silence embraced the two of us, pushing us together instead of driving us apart.

At first Lucas had tried to be understanding. But when I started hanging around with Tobey instead of him, our relationship changed. He was never overtly antagonistic, it wasn't that. But something about him made me . . . wary. I think if I'd been a dog, I would've held still and growled beneath my breath whenever he approached. Mum had told me that there were far more Noughts at Heathcroft School now than there ever were in her day, which was part of the reason she was happy for me to go there. And none of my friends were chosen according to their post-code or their skin colour, but I'd never seen Lucas hang out with anyone but Crosses. I guess his parents had had more of an influence over him and his thinking than either of us realized.

Steeling myself, I deliberately took hold of Tobey's hand. He instantly tried to pull away, but my grip on his hand tightened. I glared at him. He got the message and his hand faux relaxed into mine. Good thing too, or I'd never have spoken to him again. If Lucas and his friends wanted something to stare at then I was more than happy to provide it.

Tobey and I reached them. No one said a word.

'Morning, Callie,' Lucas said softly.

'Lucas,' I said, frost coating each syllable of his name. I didn't appreciate his intimidatory tactics. Not. One. Little. Bit.

'Is this "lead–a–blanker–to–school day" then?' asked Drew.

Tobey spun round to face him, pulling his hand from mine. 'Sod off, Drew,' he hissed, his hands clenched at his side.

So much for Tobey being Mr Sanguine! I was about to launch in with a few choice words of my own, but Lucas beat me to it.

'Drew, apologize,' Lucas ordered.

Drew looked at his friend like he'd lost his mind. And he wasn't the only one. I risked a swift glance at Lucas before turning my hostile glare back to the moron beside him.

'Say sorry to Durbrain?' Drew regarded Tobey with utter contempt. 'That'll be the day.'

Tobey took a step forward, as did Drew. Aaron, Yemi and Lucas moved to back up their mate. I pushed through to stand beside Tobey. He tried to step in front of me, but I sidestepped to stand beside him again. I stood with one leg slightly behind the other, taking up a strong, balanced stance, my arms at my sides, my hands poised. Thanks to Uncle Jude and his training programme for new recruits, I knew how to kick arse and take no prisoners – as Lucas and his cronies were about to find out. I assessed Aaron as the strongest of the group. He'd be the one to take out first.

'You should remember what side you belong to,' Drew told me through narrowed eyes.

'Oh, I do,' I said softly. 'And it'll always be the opposite side to you.'

'Like mother like daughter,' sneered Drew.

'What does that mean?' I asked.

'She had a thing for blankers too, didn't she?'

I was more than ready to slap Drew into a new postcode. All my previous training forgotten, I moved forward, but Tobey stepped in front of me again and Lucas moved in front of Drew. It didn't matter. Drew now had my full attention.

We were being given a wide berth by those arriving at school after us, but I was hardly aware of them. It was all about to kick off. And then Tobey, of all people, surprised the hell out of me.

'I'm not going to fight you, Lucas,' he said quietly. 'I'm not going to fight any of you. That's not what I come to school for.'

I watched in dismayed amazement as he slowly unclenched his fists.

'What's the matter, Durbrain?' Drew taunted. 'Chicken?'

'You must believe what you want to believe.' Tobey shrugged. 'Come on, Callie. Let's go inside.'

Tobey tried to take me by the arm, but I shrugged away from him. Out of the corner of my eye I could see Aaron and the others grinning disdainfully at Tobey, as if he was somewhere beneath contempt. And the studied calm I'd felt before burned away like dry paper on a bonfire. How could Tobey back down like that?

'Callie, it must be a comfort to know that Tobey Durbridge has your back,' Lucas scoffed.

I spun to face him. 'Lucas, why don't you—?'

'What is going on here?' Mrs Paxton's voice was like an icy deluge as the head emerged from the school building. She moved to stand to the side of all of us, and cast her trained eye over our still tension-filled bodies.

'Aaron, what's going on?'

'Nothing, Mrs Paxton,' Aaron mumbled, shuffling back, away from Tobey and me.

Mrs Paxton gave him a withering look before turning her attention to me and Tobey.

'Tobey?' she ordered.

Tobey looked her straight in the eye. 'Like Aaron said, there's nothing going on, Mrs Paxton.'

Mrs Paxton's lips tightened. 'All of you, go to your form rooms. At once.'

She stood aside as we trooped past her in silence. Tobey and I followed the others into school. I was still trying to work out who I was more angry at – Lucas and his friends or Tobey?

eleven. Tobey

'Why did you pull away from me?' Callie glared at me.

'What?'

'You heard.'

Well, that didn't take long. I glanced at my watch. Twenty-seven seconds into the building. I had hoped Callie would save it until we left school or, better still, till we got home. No such luck.

'It's very hard to defend the two of us with you holding one of my hands,' I told her.

'I don't need defending. I can look after myself,' Callie told me. 'And why did you back down? I wouldn't've given those gits the satisfaction.'

I shrugged. If I took on every prodigious arsehole who looked at me sideways, I'd spend my entire life with my fists clenched. I wasn't about to live like that, believing everyone was my enemy, getting my licks in first before others could touch me. That just wasn't me.

'Maybe you shouldn't be so combative,' I suggested.

The look Callie gave me would've speared right through to my vitals if I hadn't been wearing my kevlar underwear.

'Maybe you shouldn't let people walk all over you,' Callie countered.

'No one walks all over me, Callie,' I told her quietly.

The look on her face told me what she thought of that.

'There ain't one person who walks all over me,' I insisted.

Except maybe you, I added in my head.

Except probably you.

Except definitely you.

We continued to our lockers and unpacked our books for our first lesson in silence.

'I don't understand why you let them talk to you like that.' Callie shook her head.

I shrugged. 'Just because they're stupid as mud doesn't mean that I have to be.'

Callie glared at me. 'Tobey, when you throw me one of your infuriating "I'm-too-cool-for-this-earth" shrugs, I just want to kick your shins. Would you like me to teach you how to stand up for yourself? Because I'm volunteering.'

'I'm a pacifist.'

'Are you sure you don't mean another three-syllable word beginning with P?'

It took me a couple of seconds to work out what she meant.

'So I'm pathetic now, am I?'

'Tobey, what would it take for you to rise up from your laid-back, as in totally horizontal, position?' Callie was getting angrier by the second. The only way she was going to calm down was if I didn't take her seriously.

'As the Good Book says, "The meek shall inherit the Earth",' I told her, adding with a wry smile, 'With your permission, of course.'

'Tobey, it's not funny!'

My smile grew broader.

'Ugggh! Sometimes you drive me corkscrew crazy.' Callie raised her voice, causing some of those passing us to glance our way, curiosity written large across their faces. 'Don't you realize that by backing down you made that lot think that you're weak?'

'And why should I care what Lucas and his minions think of me?' I asked.

Plus I wasn't about to get kicked out of school for fighting. Mrs Paxton didn't put up with that from anyone, Nought or Cross. Getting booted out wasn't part of my five-year plan.

'You care too much about what other people think of you,' I said.

Callie's eyes carried enough mean heat to fry me where I stood. 'Don't you dare say that. I couldn't give a damn what Lucas and his cronies think of me. But I do care about being able to look at myself in the mirror.'

'Are you implying that I can't?'

Callie shook her head and returned to her locker.

'D'you think I'm weak, Callie?' I asked, no hint of a smile on my face.

Callie studied me. I wondered what she saw.

'Tell me the truth, Callie. D'you think I'm weak?'

Her answer mattered to me. Very much.

'D'you want me to be honest?' Callie asked at last.

Uh-oh! Whenever she asked that question it was because she knew I wouldn't like the answer. I nodded.

'Tobey, sometimes you look at me like you would stand beside me though any kind of rain, fire or shit storm. But sometimes, like today, I get the opposite feeling. Would the real Tobey Durbridge please stand up?'

'Is that a yes or a no?' I asked. Callie's words had scooped out a large part of my innards.

I shut my locker door and waited for her to answer. She always did that. When it was something she didn't want to say or she thought I wouldn't want to hear, she danced around her answer until I pushed. And I was pushing.

'Tobey, what would you do if someone said something derogatory about . . . us? The two of us? Together?'

Callie's face was turned up towards mine, the question mark in her head darkening her eyes and straightening her lips. What was it she wanted to hear?

'Callie, I'm not about to take on every brainless git who doesn't like the idea of the two of us together. People can say what they like.'

'I see,' she said. She turned away, but not before I saw the disappointment on her face. She muttered something. All I heard was the word 'together'. I took hold of her arm and turned her round to face me.

'Callie, what d'you want me to do? Punch out every idiot we come across?'

'No. But it'd be nice to know you've got my back.'

'I do. Don't listen to Lucas.'

Callie opened her mouth to argue just as the buzzer for assembly sounded. The harsh cacophony silenced whatever it was that she had been about to say.

'Callie Rose, I do have your back. You believe me, don't you?'

'Callie, there you are. You'll never guess what I just heard . . .' Samantha Eccles – or Sammi, as everyone called her – appeared from nowhere to link arms with Callie and drag her away.

A couple of metres further down the corridor Callie said something to Sammi, before turning back to me.

'Tobey, d'you want me to answer your question?' she asked.

I nodded. Did she really think I was weak? I was about to find out.

'The honest answer is – the jury is still out.'

She and Sammi carried on walking.

I didn't need to switch to genius mode to know that in spite of my best efforts, I'd messed up.

twelve. Callie

'Callie, are you even listening to me?' Sammi asked.

Not as such, no.

'Of course I am. Every word.'

'Yeah, right. What did I just say then?'

'Bliss is going round telling everyone how she and Lucas have a hot date this Saturday. He's taking her to the cinema and for a meal and to a party afterwards and it's going to be sooooooo divine.'

Sammi and I were the last ones to reach the athletics track. And I for one was glad to get there. Sammi had been going on about Lucas and Bliss for the last ten minutes, and to be honest, her assumption that I had to be upset was getting on my nerves. Mrs Halifax gave us a look, then tapped meaningfully at her watch, but for once she didn't have a go. The weather was over warm rather than over hot, so at least it wouldn't be like trying to exercise in an oven.

'Aren't you bothered?' Sammi whispered as we joined in with everyone else's warm-up exercises.

'Why should I be?' I frowned. Arms outstretched, I tipped over to one side then the other, stretching out my waist. What a waste of time. Compared to the physical training regimen the L.M. had put me through, this was a doddle.

'Well, you and Lucas used to be together.'

'With the emphasis on "used to be",' I pointed out. 'Lucas is free to go out with anyone he likes, though I pity his taste.'

'So it's definitely you and Tobey now, huh?'

'We'll be working on stamina today, so everyone five times around the track please,' Mrs Halifax called out.

Ignoring the groans coming from all directions, I immediately took off at a steady pace with Sammi beside me. I'd avoided her question rather nicely, I thought. Twenty steps later and Sammi was puffing like a faulty car exhaust.

'You . . .' – puff – '. . . didn't . . . answer . . . my question. Oh my God!' – wheeze – 'I'm dying!'

'Sammi, you need to exercise more and smoke less.' I frowned at her. 'Those cigarettes will kill you.'

'Answer . . . my . . . question . . .'

'What was it again?'

Sammi glared at me.

I smiled at her. 'Well, your nosiness, Tobey and I are just friends.'

'How boring,' said Sammi, disappointed.

Tell me about it!

'We shouldn't . . . have to run . . . in this heat . . .' Sammi rasped. 'This is . . . just cruel . . . and unusual . . . punishment.'

I took pity on her and eased my pace to a gentle jog, so gentle I was practically walking.

'You and Tobey . . .' – huff – 'd'you wish . . .' – puff – '. . . it was more?' Sammi asked.

I shrugged. Nana Meggie had a saying – if wishes were horses, beggars would ride. I glanced at Sammi, trying hard to keep my face neutral. I was running at about one-tenth of a kilometre an hour and Sammi was still having trouble.

'Why don't you just . . . tell him that?' Sammi coughed.

'It's not that simple,' I sighed. 'Tobey needs to figure it out for himself.'

'Oh, please. Callie, he's a guy. You'll have one foot in the grave before he catches on,' Sammi scoffed, finally getting her breath back.

'Then I'll wait.'

'You need to take him in hand, then take him to bed – not necessarily in that order,' said Sammi, winking at me.

'I don't think so.'

'I thought you liked him.'

I shrugged. 'I do. I more than like him. But that would be a bad idea.'

'Why?'

'If it doesn't work out, that's our friendship ruined. I don't want to risk that,' I admitted. 'Besides, there's no rush.'

'Except that Misty is determined to set more than just her eyes on Tobey,' said Sammi. 'So you'd better watch her – and him.'

'If Tobey really wants a girl who doesn't know a proton from a crouton, that's his business.'

'Wouldn't it bother you?'

Yes.

'No.'

'Misty says Tobey's one of the few boys in the school who knows what he's doing.'

'And the way she puts it about, she would know,' I replied with disdain.

This conversation was getting to me. I increased my pace, hoping Sammi would get too puffed out to talk so much.

'All I'm saying is' – wheeze – 'if you really like Tobey you'd better let him know and soon' – cough – 'or he's going to take what Misty keeps offering – if he hasn't already.'

'I'm not going to have sex with Tobey or any other guy just to keep him,' I argued. 'How pathetic is that. If that's what it takes then he's not worth having in the first place.'

'If you . . . say so,' wheezed Sammi doubtfully.

'I don't just say so, I *mean* so.'

I broke into a sprint which Sammi tried to match. There was no more talking as she tried to equal my pace. And she did try. But she didn't succeed. I finished my five laps with breath to spare. Sammi gave up after three, collapsed on the ground, and even Mrs Halifax's threat of a demerit slip couldn't shift her. By the time the lesson was over, I seriously wondered if Sammi was going to have a heart attack. We were back in the changing rooms getting dressed – well, most of us were. Sammi was sitting down with her head between her knees, dragging air into her burning lungs. I tied my jumper around my waist, before getting my bag out of my allocated PE locker. Glancing in the mirror, I saw my hair was all over the place. I used my fingers to unplait my ponytail, before digging out a comb. My hair reached well past my shoulder blades. During the forth-coming summer holidays I'd decided to get it cut short, more for convenience than any other reason. Plus Sammi reckoned short hair would suit the shape of my face.

'You should wear your hair loose more often,' Jennifer

Dyer, one of my Nought friends, told me. 'It really suits you like that.'

'Thanks, but—'

'Nah, it looks much better plaited up,' Maxine, another friend, interrupted. 'You look too much like a blank— I mean, you look like a Nought with your hair loose.'

The changing room went quiet. Jennifer's face was bright red. I turned to glare at Maxine. What a bitch!

'It's only hair, Maxine. And luckily for me I can wear it any way I want to,' I told her, pulling my hair back into a ponytail and re-plaiting it. I smiled at Jennifer. She returned my smile, gave Maxine a filthy look and carried on getting dressed. Maybe I'd put off cutting it for a while. Then again, maybe I wouldn't.

Sammi began to straighten up. She looked almost human again. 'Running is for horses, not people,' she complained. 'And anyone with boobs bigger than a thirty-two A should be excused from anything more strenuous than walking.'

I glanced down at my own boobs. According to Sammi's rule, I wouldn't have had one bit of serious exercise since I turned twelve.

'Callie, what's going to happen to the Isis Hotel bombing investigation now?' Talia asked, changing the subject.

My perplexed frown told her I didn't have a clue what she was talking about.

Talia dug into her bag and pulled out her mobile phone. A couple of screen taps later and one of the latest news items of the day was displayed.

The Nought man caught up in the bomb blast which killed Jasmine Hadley has finally been identified as Robert Powers, who was a guest at the Isis Hotel. With no known links to the Liberation Militia, the authorities have concluded that Robert Powers was unfortunate enough to be in the wrong place at the wrong time. Though flying glass and debris caused a number of roadside injuries, the Isis Hotel outrage claimed only two lives.

'So are the authorities no closer to finding out who planted the bomb then?' asked Talia.

'How should I know?' I raised my gaze from her phone to ask.

'There's no need to snap my head off. I was only asking.' Talia frowned.

'Sorry, it's just . . . I'm sorry,' I blustered. 'I have to go now.'

Snatching up my bag, I walked away from my friends without a backward glance. I had to get out of there. Right away from all of them. I needed to be alone. Behind me, Sammi rounded on Talia.

'What the hell is wrong with you, Talia? Callie's grandmother died in that blast. D'you really think she wants to be reminded of that every two seconds?'

I didn't wait for Talia's answer. I ran as fast as my school bag slamming against my back would allow.

Robert Powers?

Who on earth was Robert Powers?

I'd assumed that the Nought man killed with Nana

Jasmine was Uncle Jude. It had to be him. Did they find papers or a passport relating to Robert Powers on Uncle Jude's body? No, that couldn't be right. It would never have taken so long to identify him if they'd found identification papers. They must've had to reconstruct the Nought victim's jaw and teeth, and after that it was a question of finding the relevant dental records. And those records had revealed the dead man to be someone called Robert Powers. But Robert Powers and Jude McGregor had to be one and the same person. They just *had* to be. There was no other explanation.

Well, maybe just one . . .

What if it wasn't Uncle Jude who had died, but someone else? Oh, my God . . . What if some innocent man was in the wrong place at the wrong time and died because of the bomb *I* made?

And what if Uncle Jude was still alive?

thirteen. Tobey

As soon as I got home from school, I fixed myself a quick snack of scrambled eggs and beans on toast, then tried to settle down to my homework. But chemistry just wasn't lighting my fire the way it usually did. My head was too crammed with other thoughts.

Money!

Damn it! I had none and there was no prospect of any forthcoming.

Heathcroft School had provided me with a full scholarship, but just living day to day cost money. I only ever went on school day trips. My mum's pockets weren't deep enough for fortnights away skiing or singing abroad with the school choir. I'd even had to turn down the odd birthday party invitation or two because I couldn't afford to buy a decent birthday present. If only I could get the image of Dan's watch out of my head. I wasn't jealous. That wasn't it. I didn't want to own a watch like it or a designer jacket or any of that other nonsense.

I just wanted my share.

I wanted the choices, the options that money would give me.

My mobile phone roused me out of my mega-brood. Who was phoning me? I wasn't in a particularly talkative mood. But it was Dan. I took the call.

'Hi, Dan. You OK?'

'I'm fine,' Dan replied, 'but I need your help.'

'Help with what?' I frowned.

'I need to make some deliveries before eight tonight and I won't be able to do them all by myself.'

'Dan, I've already told you I'm not working for McAuley. And I don't appreciate you dropping my name to him either.'

'I didn't drop your name.'

'McAuley cornered me on the street a couple of days ago and he knew all about me.'

'Not from me, he didn't,' Dan denied.

Hmmm . . .

'Or at least . . .'

'Yes?'

'Well, I might've mentioned you in passing as a friend of mine who's cat-clever, but that's all.'

'Dan, you arse. To someone like McAuley, that's enough,' I said. 'So you can forget it. I'm not doing a damned thing for that man.'

'You wouldn't be doing it for him. You'd be doing it for me. You just need to drop off two packages for me whilst I do the other three and—'

'Which part of "no" don't you understand? The N or the O?'

'Tobey, it's just packages. You drop them off and that's it.'

'Why can't you deliver them?'

'I told you. I have to be somewhere at eight o'clock and I won't make it without your help.'

'What's in the packages?'

'I don't get told and I'm not stupid enough to ask,' Dan replied. 'It's healthier that way.'

'No frickin' way, Dan. This conversation is over.' I was about to hang up on him, but what he said next brought the phone back to my ear.

'I'll pay you. I'll give you half of what I make tonight.'

Half my brain told me to hang up anyway. But the other half turned my left hand into a magnet and wouldn't let me put down my phone.

'How much are we talking about here?' I asked at last.

The figure Dan mentioned made me catch my breath. No wonder Dan could afford designer threads and top-of-the-range watches. It would take me six months at my Saturday job to make the kind of money he was talking about.

'Come on, Tobey. It's just two packages,' Dan cajoled. He could sense that I was wavering.

Not wavering but drowning.

'Just two packages . . .'

I was on dangerous ground now. In my mind, two deliveries was already turning into a few. If all I had to do was deliver a few packages, then really, where was the harm? In fact, if I delivered a limited number of Dan's packages, think of the money I'd make. Enough to pay my university fees. Enough to live off when I was studying. Enough.

I liked the sound of that word. *Enough.*

I had to admit, the spectre of bank loans that I might never be able to pay back and debts up to my eyebrows didn't appeal massively. But there was no way I'd get to go to university otherwise. Mum just didn't have the money. And I needed to go to university like I needed to breathe. For too many Noughts and for far too long, the door to higher education had been locked, sealed and bolted. But others had given up blood, sweat and rivers of tears to kick that door open for me. How could I not walk though it? Failure just wasn't an option.

And more immediately, with the currency Dan was talking about I could buy a store-bought birthday card and a proper present for Callie. She deserved so much more than I could give her and she never once threw that fact back in my face. I still had one last year at school, plus university to get through before I could even hope to start making serious money. So where was the harm?

I mean, how long before Callie got fed up with me because I couldn't afford to take her anywhere or buy her anything? How long before money came between us? I hated money. The lack of bits of metal and paper was ruling, not to mention ruining, my life. But this . . . Dan's packages . . . Dan's world . . . this was something else again.

'It's just two packages?' I said, holding my phone like it was the enemy.

'Yeah, just two. I'll give you the easiest two,' said Dan. 'Thanks, mate. I knew you wouldn't let me down.'

'You knew more than me then,' I said sourly. 'Where are you and what time do we do this?'

'I'm outside your front door and how does now sound?'

Like the beginning of a long, slippery slope.

I sighed. 'I'll be right out.'

After a moment's thought, I took my lightweight hooded jacket out of my wardrobe and headed downstairs. 'Mum, I'm going out for a while.'

'Have you finished your homework?' Mum emerged from the sitting room to ask.

'Yeah. It's all done except chemistry and that doesn't have to be handed in until next week.'

'Where're you going?'

'Just out with Dan.'

'Where to? Another football match?'

'No. Not today. We're just going to hang out for a while. After all, it is Friday.'

'Tobey, I don't know about this . . .'

'We won't be long. A couple of hours at most,' I tried to reassure her. 'We'll probably go for a meal or something.'

'What's Dan up to these days?' Mum asked.

'Same old, same old.'

'Is he still working for the postal service?' asked Mum.

'That's right,' I replied, feeling distinctly uncomfortable.

'How come you hang around with Dan more than your other friends from school?'

That wasn't true. That was just Mum's perception 'cause she wasn't keen on Dan.

'Dan's been my friend since infant school.' I shrugged. 'Just because he didn't get into Heathcroft doesn't mean I'm going to drop him.' Besides, I didn't have to try to be something I wasn't when I was with him. At least, that's how I used to feel. I wasn't so sure any more. Now it felt like I needed to work out who I was, rather than who I wasn't. I wasn't the same Tobey I was six years ago. I'd changed. Dan hadn't.

Mum scrutinized me. 'All right, then. I'll see you later. Just . . . just keep your head down. OK? And if you see any trouble . . .'

'Walk away.' I finished Mum's mantra. 'I'll do my best.'

'Better than your best, Tobey,' she retorted. 'I don't want the police knocking on my door – for any reason. Understand?'

I nodded and headed out the door before Mum could say anything else.

Keep your head down . . .

I'd bet my next ten Saturday job pay packets that Lucas Cheshie was never told to keep his head down. I bet he was always told to do the exact opposite.

Dan wasn't lying. He stood outside my front door, bouncing impatiently from foot to foot. We immediately headed off along the street.

'Thanks, mate,' said Dan.

I nodded, ignoring the gnawing in my gut that kept telling me this was a *really* bad idea. Anything could happen.

If I got caught . . .

But all that money . . .

'Dan, I'm just helping you out because I need the money. OK? I don't intend for this to become a habit.'

Dan raised appeasing hands. 'Don't worry, blanker. I know you're just helping out a mate.' He grinned at me. 'But I really wouldn't mind your help on a few other deliveries I got lined up over the coming weeks. And at least I know I can trust you. You'd get fifty per cent of everything I make and that's more than I'd do for anyone else. Can't say fairer than that.'

'No, Dan.'

'You say no, but your empty pockets say yes. And after all, the desire for money is the most infectious disease on the planet.'

'It's not a disease I intend to catch. I need some money to tide me over and then that's it,' I told him.

'Whatever you say, Tobey.' The smug grin on his face was very eloquent.

'This is just to buy a belated birthday present for Callie,' I insisted. 'I'm not thinking beyond that at the moment.'

Dan smiled at me. We both knew that wasn't true.

fourteen. Callie

After school, I couldn't bear to face anyone so I hid away in the library for over half an hour, hoping that by then I'd be able to walk home in peace. I didn't want to be with anyone. I just wanted to be left alone, to think. I headed out of the school gates, every thought finding its way back to Uncle Jude. What if . . . ? What if he really was still alive?

'Callie Rose. Wait up.'

I turned round at the sound of my name. Lucas. I glared at him as he came running up to me, not bothering to disguise exactly what I thought of him.

'Hi, Callie,' he said diffidently.

'Hello, Lucas,' I replied. My tone could've frozen water. What did he want?

'I'm having a birthday party next week. Would you like to come?'

'Why?'

Lucas blinked in surprise at my question. 'What d'you mean?'

'Why're you inviting me?'

''Cause I'd like you to be there,' said Lucas, as if the answer was obvious.

But it wasn't, at least not to me.

'I'm not turning up at your party so you and your friends can make jokes at my expense,' I told him straight.

'We wouldn't do that.'

I raised my eyebrows.

'OK, *I* wouldn't do that. And I wouldn't let my friends do it either.'

'Yeah, I was very impressed with the way you reined them in this morning,' I said with contempt.

'I'm sorry about that,' Lucas said. 'I was just . . . I'm sorry.'

'You were just – what?' I prompted.

'I hate seeing you two together,' said Lucas. 'Tobey is trouble and you're going to get hurt.'

'What're you on about? Tobey is my friend. And my next-door neighbour. He wouldn't hurt a fly.'

'He's a Nought.'

Lucas had better not be saying what I thought he was saying. 'So?'

'Well, you're a Cross. It doesn't hurt Tobey's street cred to have everyone think of you as his girlfriend.'

I was a Cross now, was I? Funny how my status seemed to change depending on the eyes of the beholder. To Drew I was a Nought and would never be anything else. Lucas called me a Cross. Where did that leave me? On one side or the other or stuck somewhere in the middle?

'Lucas, what's your point?'

'I'm just trying to warn you to be on your guard. Tobey isn't the open book you seem to think he is.'

I shook my head, trying to figure out just what Lucas was playing at. Was it malice? Jealousy? What?

'And you know Tobey is with Misty, don't you?' Lucas

continued. 'Everyone in the school knows those two are an item.'

Well, Misty had told enough people, so that was hardly news.

'What's that got to do with me? I told you Tobey and I are just good friends,' I replied.

'The way you and I used to be "just good friends"?'

I frowned at Lucas. Where was he going with all this?

His eyes slowly narrowed. 'Or maybe Drew was right. Maybe us Crosses just aren't your thing.'

'Excuse me?'

Us Crosses? Lucas's exclusive club of which I was no longer a member? It hadn't taken much to get me kicked out.

'I guess you're more like your mother than I gave you credit for,' said Lucas.

I straightened up, trying to quash the tidal wave of hurt rising inside me. 'And that, Lucas, is why you and I together will never work,' I said quietly. 'Say what you like about Tobey, but he'd never, ever say something like that to me.'

Lucas looked genuinely remorseful, but it was far too little, much too late. He put out his hand to touch my cheek, but I flinched away from him. 'I'm sorry, Callie. That was . . . I didn't mean it.'

'Yes, you did,' I replied. 'You always make me feel like I have to constantly apologize for my mum and dad and for being who and what I am. Well, I'm not going to, not any more.'

I stepped round Lucas and this time he didn't try to stop me. A couple of steps on and I turned back. 'Lucas, you've never made me feel more than I am. But for your information, Tobey never makes me feel less. So thanks for your party invitation, but I think I'll pass.'

I headed home without another backward glance. Why did life have to be so complicated? Tears pricked at my eyes. First the news about Uncle Jude, then Lucas. What would Lucas say if he knew about my uncle? Probably think he'd had a lucky escape? Judge me as guilty by association? Or just guilty full stop?

Uncle Jude . . . Was he out there somewhere? Watching? Waiting? My uncle occupied every thought all the way home. Much as Lucas's words had hurt, Uncle Jude had the power to hurt me more. So where was he? Just waiting for the right moment to do the maximum amount of damage? He was really good at that.

Where was he?

'Hello, Ann. Is Tobey in?'

Tobey's mum shook her head. 'You've missed him by about twenty minutes. He went off somewhere with his friend Dan.'

'D'you know where?'

Ann shook her head again. 'Callie, are you OK? You look . . . out of sorts.'

My attempted smile slid right off my face. 'I'm fine. I just wanted . . . to talk to Tobey.'

'D'you want to come in and wait for him?'

I shook my head.

'He'll be back in a couple of hours if you want to come back then,' Ann told me. 'Jessica's off to a party later and I've got to go to work.'

Tobey's mum worked all kinds of unsocial hours. She was used to me coming and going in her house, just as Tobey treated my house like his second home. That's the way it had always been. Tobey's dad had gone off years before to 'find himself' and he'd stayed lost ever since. Jessica only mentioned him to curse him to hell and back. Tobey never mentioned him at all.

'If Tobey isn't in by the time you come round again, just use the spare key.' Ann lowered her voice even though there was no one around us. 'It's in its usual place.' Its usual place being under one of the plant pots in the tiny front garden.

'Thanks, Ann.'

'No problem. I'd much rather Tobey hung around with you than Dan. I don't trust Dan.'

'Why not?' I asked.

'Every time he comes into this house, he's always telling me how much everything cost — as if I didn't know already. Dan is a boy who knows the cost of everything and the value of nothing.'

I smiled faintly. I wasn't particularly keen on Dan either. Every time we met, he looked me up and down like he was working out how best to dissect me.

'If you see Tobey before I do, tell him I've left him some chilli in the fridge if he's still hungry. He just needs to heat it up. That goes for you too, Callie. Help yourself if you're hungry.'

'Thanks, I will,' I replied.

I turned round to head back home. Usually I would stand and chat with Ann, but not now, not today. Even though Tobey and I lived next door to each other, I still turned my head this way and that to see if I was being watched. Was Uncle Jude out there somewhere watching my every move? I shook my head, warning myself not to be so paranoid. It didn't help.

Usually I didn't mind coming home to an empty house – not that it happened that often. But today I did. The silence bounced off the walls and echoed around me.

I went straight up to my room. Sitting on my bed, I drew my legs up so that I could wrap my arms around them and rested my head on my knees.

Should I ask Nana Meggie when she got back home? Surely Uncle Jude would've got in touch with her by now? She was probably the only one on the planet who truly knew if Uncle Jude was alive or dead.

The bomb I'd made had killed an innocent man.

Uncle Jude could be out there, somewhere.

And if he was, nothing would be the same again.

fifteen. Tobey

Dan took me to a lockup I never realized he owned. It was secured with a combination-code padlock, opened by pressing a series of digits. Dan had to input his code three times before the thing finally clicked open. By his third frustrated try, accompanied by a lot of swearing and the muttering of several numbers, I had his code memorized –

not that I'd ever use it. So much for his security then! I walked into a small, windowless room which was a bit like a narrow garage. It smelled of damp walls and mould, like the air in the place was several months old. The only furniture was an old wooden table covered in packages and boxes of assorted sizes and shapes. The floor was strewn with rubbish, more boxes and carrier bags.

'So when did you get this place?' I asked. Thinking better of it, I raised a hand to ward off Dan's reply. 'You know what, don't tell me. I don't want to know.'

My two packages were covered in brown paper. Both were quite small. One was about the size of a bag of sugar, the other was the shape, size and weight of a pack of playing cards. Both had been wrapped to within a millimetre of their lives, with sticky tape covering the brown paper so that none of it could be peeled back to take a quick peek at what lay beneath. Dan placed both my packages in a supermarket carrier bag snatched up off the concrete floor. He gave me specific instructions.

'Guard those packages with your life. If some bastard thinks he'll take them off you, you make sure that doesn't happen. The only time that bag leaves your hand is if the cops put in an appearance. Then you drop the bag and run like the wind.'

Like I needed to be told that.

'I thought you said these packages were safe,' I said, liking this whole idea less and less with each passing second.

'I never said they were safe. That's your brain telling you what you want to hear.'

'So what's in them?' I asked again.

'I still don't know,' Dan said, a hint of exasperation in his voice. 'And asking too many questions in this line of work can get you into a whole heap of trouble.'

So whatever I was carrying, it wasn't something you'd pick up in the local supermarket. It was illegal and that meant dangerous, and dangerous meant I could end up in a youth detention centre or in prison. Or worse still, dead.

Just this once. Just this once and no more, I promise.

Please let me get away with it just this once.

Dan contemplated me.

'What?' I asked, irritated.

'D'you want some protection?' Dan asked slowly. 'Something to calm your nerves?'

'Like what?'

After giving me a scrutinizing look, Dan struggled to pick up one of the closed boxes off the floor, before dumping it on the only clear space on the table. I peered inside, then recoiled. The box was filled with mean-looking knives. I mean, double-edged, big-arsed, wicked-looking, eviscerating combat knives, switchblades, kitchen knives. In fact, every knife known to man was represented in that box.

'Godsake, Dan. What's with all the armour?'

'They're for protection.'

'Protection from which invading army?'

I couldn't believe what I was seeing. There had to be at least twenty blades in that box, maybe more. Probably more.

'Dan, are you off your nut?'

'I have to arm myself. The streets aren't safe,' he told me.

'Yeah, 'cause tossers like you can't set foot outside your house without tooling up,' I replied. 'Godsake! Why d'you need so many knives? You've only got two hands.'

'Carry one of these and no one will mess with you. D'you want one or not?' asked Dan, peeved at my lack of appreciation for his hardware.

'One what?'

'A knife? I have knives for every occasion.' Dan launched into a pseudo sales pitch. He picked up a knife at random. 'For example, this fine specimen is phosphate-treated and comes with a polymer sheath which is available in olive, camouflage and black.'

'Hell, no.'

'Tobey, I promise you, with one of these in your pocket, you'll—'

My response was heartfelt. 'No frickin' way.'

'Suit yourself.' Dan eyed me speculatively as he closed the box. 'I've got a couple of items even more effective than these knives . . .'

'Dan, don't even go there,' I warned. 'I'm not interested.'

'Suit yourself.'

'Thank you. I will,' I replied. I ran a shaky hand over my sweaty forehead. *Stop the world, I want to get off.* 'I need to get out of here. Just give me the relevant names and addresses before I see sense and change my mind,' I said.

Walk away. Walk away now, I told myself.

The answer? Not without my money. I was already thinking of it as *my* money.

★

The first stop was a forty-minute train ride out of Meadowview. The instructions Dan gave me seemed straightforward enough. Once I got off the train, I pulled up my hood, kept my head down and started walking. I thought it'd take me ten minutes max to get to my destination. Twenty-five minutes later I was only just turning into the right road. Each house in this area was detached and about a quarter of a kilometre from its neighbour – at least, that's what it felt like as I walked along. The front gardens were massive so I couldn't even begin to imagine how big the back gardens must've been. I stopped two or three houses away from my destination and looked up and down the wide, tree-lined street. Two women passed on the opposite side of the road, deep in conversation, but apart from that the road was deserted. My hood still in place, I cautiously looked up at the surrounding trees and at the tops of the lamp-posts in the vicinity. No CCTV cameras. Another glance up and down the road. I appeared to be alone.

Appeared to be . . .

Stop being paranoid, Tobey.

I headed for the designated house, trying to look a little less guilty and a little more like I had every reason to be there. My stomach was tumbling and copious beads of sweat were making my T-shirt stick uncomfortably to my back. The late evening hadn't begun to cool down yet. If anything the air had become more muggy, so that each breath was like inhaling after lifting a saucepan lid. I hated the summer.

This house was definitely upmarket. At least, it looked that way as I approached. But as I turned into the driveway, the weeds and moss sprouting up from between the paving stones were more evident. Somewhere overhead a crow cawed. I looked down at the parcel I was supposed to deliver. I guess drugs knew no boundaries and weren't confined to a single postcode or area or country come to that. One of the world's great levellers – along with love. And hate. And fear. I took another look around. It wasn't often that I made it out to the plush suburbs. Correction. I never made it out here. I tried to wrap my head around why anyone who lived here would need to haze their mind with drugs? I guess misery knew no boundaries either.

I rang the doorbell. I didn't hear any chiming inside. I pressed on it again. Silence. So I knocked as well, just in case the bell wasn't working. A baby started bawling its head off inside. Trying to ignore my racing heartbeat, I knocked on the door again, a lot harder this time. The door opened almost at once. The smell of nappies and toast hit me at once. A harassed Cross woman, in her mid-thirties, I think, answered the door. She wore white trousers and a yellow, sleeveless blouse. Her black hair was dishevelled, her onyx eyes wary.

'Yes?' she asked.

From the back of the house, the baby's crying was getting louder. She ignored it, her gaze darting nervously past me up and down the street.

'Are you Louise Resnick?'

'Who wants to know?'

'I have a package for Louise Resnick.'

'It's a little late to be delivering post, isn't it?'

I shrugged.

'Give it here then.' The woman held out her hand.

'I was instructed to only give it to the proper recipient.'

'Huh?'

'I can't give it to anyone but Louise Resnick.'

The unseen screaming baby turned up the bawling volume by quite a few decibels.

'Charlene' – the woman turned her head to scream back into the house – 'could you please do your job and stop Troy crying.' She turned back to me, her expression fraught, her eyes cold. 'I'm Louise Resnick, so pass it here,' she said impatiently.

The package stayed in my carrier bag.

'Oh, for heaven's sake,' said the woman. She picked up her designer handbag from beside the door. Annoyed, she retrieved her driver's licence and flashed it so close to my face that I had to pull my head back like a turtle. 'Happy now?' she asked.

I dug out the smaller package from my carrier bag as the woman replaced her licence and dropped the handbag onto the hardwood floor.

'Who's it from?' Louise asked suspiciously. She ran a shaky hand through her locks, making them even more untidy.

'I don't know,' I replied truthfully. 'I'm just delivering it.'

I held it out towards her. She took a half-step back, suddenly reluctant to touch it. She looked at me, trying to read my expression. I really didn't know what was in the package and it must've shown on my face because she finally stretched out her hand to take it.

'Thanks,' she murmured.

From one of the rooms behind her, the baby was now shrieking. Louise closed the door in my face without saying another word. I shrugged and turned away, heading back towards the train station. But once I reached it, I couldn't settle. I walked up and down the platform like my shoes were on fire. I made sure to keep my head down and my hood in place, just in case. The CCTV cameras placed at regular intervals along the platform would capture my jacket, jeans and trainers – and that was it. Hanging around anywhere near that woman's house was a really bad idea. I didn't know what was in the package and I didn't want to know, but every instinct I possessed screamed at me to get away, to drop my other package and run. But I couldn't. I'd agreed to help Dan and I had to see this through.

Focus on the money, Tobey, I told myself.

The train finally arrived to take me to my next port of call. Another forty-minute journey back to Meadowview and a twenty-minute bus ride later, I hopped off. This area was very different from where Louise Resnick lived. I looked around. If I ever had to draw Hell, then this was where I'd come for inspiration. Narrow streets, high-rise estates, no hint of green or any other colour except concrete grey. I'd been walking for less than five minutes when a car pulled up alongside me, matching my walking speed. The two Nought men inside, around my age or only slightly older, looked me up and down as they kerb-crawled beside me. After a swift glance at them, I looked straight ahead and carried on walking. One hand tightened around the carrier bag, the other was empty at my side. No hands in pockets. No sudden moves. No rude gestures. I forced myself not to speed up and run away or slow down either.

On the passenger's side of the car, a man with light-brown hair and dark-blue eyes looked me up and down, his expression suspicious and more. 'Which side of Meadowview d'you live on?' he asked.

'I don't,' I replied, still walking.

I skirted as close to the truth as I could get. I didn't live in Meadowview, on either side, on any side. I existed. On whose side were these two guys? Did they work for either the Dowds or McAuley? Or were they further down the pecking order than that? Did they claim ownership of a number of pages in the local map book, or just one page, or maybe just this street?

'I'm visiting a friend who lives around here,' I told them, forcing myself to look at both occupants in the car.

The man with the brown hair turned to the driver and said one word – 'Tourist.'

They drove off. The moment their car was out of sight, I stopped walking to give my heart time to stop punching my ribs. Existing was hard work. Existing wasn't much, but for the moment it was all I had.

A couple of minutes later, I reached my destination. This time it was a flat on the Chancellor Estate, a high-rise block that should've been demolished twenty years ago. Anti-social housing. I climbed up the concrete stairs, which stank of piss, vomit, disinfectant and paint, to the third floor.

Flat Eighteen was a third of the way along the walkway. I took a moment to look out over the balcony. A few people were milling about below, but no Crosses, so I was probably safe from the police. Unless they had some undercover Noughts watching me. I couldn't assume that the Noughts I saw weren't coppers. The police force was actively recruiting from 'all sections of society', as they put it in their ads. And it was working. So I had to be extra vigilant.

Careful, Tobey. You're definitely getting paranoid.

I mean, why should anyone be watching me? It's not like I'd done this before. It wasn't like I was going to be making a habit of this either.

Tobey, just deliver the package and go.

A deep breath later, I rang the doorbell. At least I didn't feel quite so close to spewing my guts out this time. The door opened after a few seconds. A man only a few years older than me opened the door. I'm tall, but he was taller. And broader. And heavier. The man wore denim jeans and a blue T-shirt beneath a black leather jacket. I wondered why he was wearing a jacket indoors, especially in this weather. Not that I was about to ask him. His designer trainers were clearly new because they were still out-of-the-box clean. His collar-length black hair was gelled back off his face and his dark-blue eyes were cold as deep, still water.

'Can I help you?'

'I'm looking for Adam Eisner.'

'That's me,' the man replied.

'Could I see some ID please?'

'Who are you?' A stillness came over the guy that instantly had me on my guard. He looked ready, willing and more than able to tip me over the balcony onto the concrete three storeys below.

'I've got a package for Adam Eisner and I've been instructed not to hand it over to anyone else.'

'And I've already told you, I'm Adam Eisner.'

'May I see some proof?'

The man's eyes narrowed. 'What's your name?'

I didn't answer.

'Who told you to deliver this so-called package?'

I didn't answer that either. Not that I could hear much over the sound of my heart trumpeting. This didn't feel right – at all. The man started to reach into his leather jacket pocket.

'Dan sent me,' I said quickly. 'I'm just helping out Dan. He's the one who told me not to give this to anyone else but Adam Eisner.'

The man's hand slowed, then stopped before emerging from his pocket, empty.

'So what's your name, kid?' asked the man.

No way was I going to answer that one.

The man unexpectedly smiled. 'You appear to have more brains than your friend Dan. So do yourself a favour, believe that I'm Adam Eisner and hand over the package.'

I did myself a favour.

Minutes later, I was out of the block of flats and heading back to the Wasteland. Dan and I had agreed to meet up there after all our deliveries had been made. When I felt sure that I was far enough away from the flats, I hopped on a bus to take me back to more familiar territory. I could've been mistaken for an owl, the way my head kept constantly turning round whilst I was on the bus. Two parcels and one evening of doing this and already I was acting like I was some kind of criminal. That said something in itself. I tried to tell myself that it was just nerves, that I was worrying over nothing, but somehow that didn't help. I obviously wasn't cut out for this line of work.

You know what? Sod this. No amount of money was worth this feeling of not being able to walk down the street without constantly checking over my shoulder. This was my first, last and only job for Dan. Ever.

When I finally got to the Wasteland, Dan was already waiting for me. He was standing on the sidelines of the football pitch. And he wasn't happy.

'Where the hell have you been?'

'Walking,' I replied.

'You should've been back thirty minutes ago.'

'Well, I'm here now.'

'Did everything go OK?' asked Dan.

That rather depends on your definition of OK, I thought.

'I delivered the packages like you asked me,' I said.

'Was Mr Eisner OK with that?' Dan swayed nervously before me like a mesmerized snake.

'Eventually,' I replied. 'He refused to show me any ID and because I'm fond of breathing, I didn't insist.'

'Tobey . . .' Dan was winding up for a rant, but I got in first.

'Don't start with me, Dan. The man was two metres tall, almost as wide, resembled a pit bull and I wasn't about to argue with him. You got a problem with that?'

'But he had black hair and was wearing a black jacket, right?'

I nodded. Dan sighed with relief.

'So where's my money?' I asked.

'When I get paid, you'll get paid,' said Dan.

I scowled at him. 'That's not what you said earlier.'

'I said you'll get half of what I make, but I won't get my money until tomorrow – or Sunday at the latest.'

I stood perfectly still and counted my heartbeats until the fire raging inside me began to dampen down. Dan kept looking away from my unblinking glare, still swaying uneasily.

'Dan, don't play me,' I warned him softly.

'I'm not,' Dan denied. 'I can't conjure money out of thin air. When I get mine, then you'll get yours.'

We both knew he'd implied otherwise. This wasn't part of our deal, not even close.

'When exactly will I get my money, Dan?' I asked.

'By the end of this weekend. Look, as we're mates, I'll pay you out of my own savings. How's that? I'll go to the bank tomorrow and get you what you're owed. Every penny. Be here at four tomorrow and I'll give it to you.'

'I work on Saturdays,' I reminded him.

'So work a half-day or call in sick,' said Dan. 'It'll be worth it.'

I regarded him without saying a word. At least if I went to work, I knew I'd get paid. If I turned up at four tomorrow afternoon and Dan was nowhere in sight, what then?

'Tobey, you'll get your money,' Dan said, exasperated. 'Trust me.'

'Why? 'Cause you've got my back?'

Now it was Dan's turn to remain silent.

'I'll see you tomorrow at four,' I sighed. 'Don't be late.'

I turned round. In my head I was already at home and stretched out on my bed.

'Tobey?' Dan began.

Wearily, I faced him. 'Yeah?'

A flush of red stole up Dan's neck and across his cheeks. If I didn't know better, I'd say he was embarrassed.

'You and I are friends, right?'

'Yeah.' At least, I used to think so.

'Well, I've gotcha. OK?'

I scrutinized Dan. His embarrassment couldn't be feigned.

'OK.' I nodded.

'I've got some more deliveries to make tomorrow if you want to double your money,' said Dan hopefully.

I frowned. So much for having my back. Only as long as I could be useful to him, by the sound of it.

'I haven't seen a single penny yet,' I replied. 'Two times nothing is still nothing.'

'Trust me.'

'No thanks, Dan. Today was enough for me. More than enough.'

'But you've seen how easy it is to make money. A couple of drop-offs here, a collection or two there. Nothing to it.'

'Nothing being the operative word. I'm not interested, Dan. Just give me the money you owe me tomorrow and we'll call it quits.'

Not wanting to prolong the argument, I headed home. I still couldn't shake the feeling that I'd just made one of the biggest mistakes of my life.

sixteen. Callie

I couldn't hide in my bedroom for the rest of my days. Was I really going to let my uncle take over my life again? I couldn't. I wouldn't. And yet I already had. Every thought, every breath I took was now wrapped around him. I sat and brooded as the hours crept by. More than once stray tears escaped to run down my face. I brushed them aside impatiently. That wasn't going to make my problem go away. But what should I do? At last I made up my mind. I took my phone out of my jacket pocket, but my index finger still hesitated before pressing the first digit.

Did I really want to do this?

What choice did I have?

I phoned Uncle Jude's private number, the mobile phone number that he gave out to very few people. But he'd given it to me when I was his soldier. When I was his puppet.

'The number you called has not been recognized,' some woman's toneless voice informed me. 'Please check and try again.'

I tried twice more, just in case I'd inadvertently or subconsciously called the wrong number, only to receive the same message. I was still alone. Mum was out with

Nathan and Nana Meggie was out with friends. I didn't want to be alone any more.

What if Uncle Jude was out there right now watching me? What was he planning? He didn't take a breath without plotting its speed and trajectory first. What did he have in store for me? Because one thing was certain: if he really was still alive, I'd be at the top of his revenge list. And Uncle Jude was a very patient man.

Maybe it was what I deserved.

Maybe it was all I deserved.

I went to my bedroom window to look out over the back of our house and our neighbours' houses. It was so still outside. A few birds swooped in the sky and the occasional plane flew in and out of view, but that was all. I went into Mum's bedroom and looked out her window. A number of people walked by over the next thirty-something minutes, Nought and Cross − but not Uncle Jude.

It didn't matter. I didn't have to see him to know he was out there. Somewhere. I wrapped my arms around myself. I was trembling. Actually trembling. Fear tore at me like some carrion bird.

Oh, Tobey, where are you?

I need you.

I need you to tell me that everything will be all right.

I need you to tell me I'm imagining things.

I need you to let me hide in your pocket. Bring me out for birthdays and holidays.

Tobey, where are you?

'Earlier today, Louise Resnick of Knockworth Park received a gruesome package. It contained the little finger taken from the left hand of a person, thought to be her husband. DNA tests are being carried out to confirm this. Louise Resnick's husband is Ross Resnick, a well-known businessman with alleged links to the Dowd family. Unconfirmed reports state that Ross Resnick has been missing for three days. It is thought that one of Mrs Resnick's three children immediately called the police once the package was opened. Louise Resnick was unavailable for comment . . .'

Ross Resnick's smiling Cross face filled the TV screen. A photograph taken when he didn't have a care in the world. I switched off the TV. The ten o'clock news was making me sick. Physically sick. Icy sweat covered my forehead. The chilli I'd just eaten was bouncing up and down in my stomach. Taking the stairs two and three at a time, I raced for the bathroom and threw up. I mean, I erupted like a volcano. I vomited so hard and for so long, I was bringing up baby food.

That package . . .

There'd been a *finger* in the package I'd delivered.

Omigod! That woman, Louise Resnick, standing at her front door, taking the package from me. Had she opened it in front of her kids? Is that what happened? Did she scream? Drop it? Cry? Did she instantly know what it was? Who the finger belonged to? I knelt on the hard, tiled bathroom floor, my hands gripping the toilet seat. I was cold. When did it get so cold? And yet, sweat was still dripping off me.

A finger. I'd delivered a finger. Frickin' Dan. I was going to kill him. That poor woman. So much for ducking the CCTV cameras in the area. What . . . what if she gave my description to the police? What if the police thought I had something to do with chopping off her husband's little finger. Oh God . . . Suppose I couldn't prove I had nothing to do with it? One package, one delivery, and I might get banged up in prison because of it. What had been in the other package? Something just as bad? I'd assumed . . . what had I assumed? Drugs, I suppose. Or maybe money. But nothing like this.

I got up on auto-pilot to wash my hands and clean my teeth. I kept thinking about the package I'd held in my hands, the package that Louise Resnick had opened, the contents that her kids had seen.

Oh hell . . .

Don't shoot me, I'm only the messenger.

Don't blame me, I'm only the delivery boy.

Don't hurt me. I'm only seventeen. I only did it for the money. I just needed some money.

Shit.

I went back to my bedroom, made sure the door was

firmly shut and hit the speed–dial icon on my phone. Dan picked up after the second ring.

'Dan, have you seen the news?' I launched straight in.

'I didn't know what was in the package. I swear I didn't,' Dan protested.

Guess he'd seen the news then.

'You must've had some idea,' I said furiously. 'Louise Resnick knows what I look like. She'll describe me to the police and they'll do a photo–fit ID or something. Once a drawing of me hits the TV and the papers, how long before someone recognizes me and tells the police who I am?'

'Hang on. You're getting a bit ahead of yourself—' Dan began.

But I wasn't having it. 'You don't want to go there, Dan. You really don't.' I was that close to losing it completely. 'You're not in the frame for this. I am.'

Pause.

'Or was that the whole point?' I asked slowly.

'What d'you mean?' I could hear the frown in Dan's voice.

'It just strikes me as strange that suddenly you can't make all your deliveries and are desperately in need of my help. Quite a coincidence that the very first thing I deliver for you could land me in prison for assault or worse.'

'You can't think I set you up?' Dan said.

'All I know is I'm suddenly in a whole world of trouble,' I replied. 'Well I'll tell you something for free, Dan. If the police come knocking, I'm not going down alone. I'm not.'

The silence between us stretched out like razor wire.

'You shouldn't make threats like that,' Dan said slowly.

'It's not a threat. It's a promise,' I told him. 'I'm going to finish school, go to university and get a decent job. My plans for the future do not include a criminal record or getting banged up for something I didn't do.'

'It won't come to that,' Dan insisted.

'Damn right it won't,' I raged. ''Cause I'm not taking the fall for either you or McAuley. Not gonna happen.'

I disconnected the call without saying goodbye. The inferno raging through me during the entire phone conversation with Dan was rapidly burning itself out. And what it left was worse. I shouldn't have said what I had. It was a bluff, full of fury and frustration but a bluff nonetheless. Because if push came to shove, I couldn't turn against my friend – and he knew that. Which meant that if things did blow up in my face, I'd be on my own. I should've listened to my instincts – after all, that's why I had them. But I'd stomped on them instead. I wouldn't make that mistake again. But it was probably already too late.

I was in deep, deep trouble.

The doorbell rang and I shot up like a rocket. Was that the police already? Maybe I could lie low and pretend no one was in. But all the lights in the house were on. Damn it. Physically shaking, I slowly made my way downstairs. Taking a deep breath, I attempted, unsuccessfully, to calm my nerves. I opened the door.

It was Callie. She took one look at me and burst into tears.

eighteen. Callie

It was hard to say who was more shocked, me or Tobey. I never – and I mean *never* cried, at least not in front of other people. But the moment I saw Tobey, the tears just spilled out of me. After staring at me, Tobey took me by the hand and practically pulled me into his house before kicking the door shut.

'What is it? What's happened?' he asked urgently.

I shook my head, desperately trying to stem my tears. I lowered my gaze. I didn't want Tobey to see into my eyes. He'd seen far too much already. It wasn't fair to expect him to fill all the frightened, empty spaces inside me, and if he knew what was happening, he'd surely try. And probably fail. But try nonetheless. Uncle Jude said tears were a luxury of the weak. I couldn't afford to be weak, not now. But I felt like a dead girl walking and that was the truth.

Tobey pulled me close and wrapped his arms around me. He didn't say anything, for which I was grateful. He just let me get all the tears out of my system. When I finally pulled away, I was deeply embarrassed and Tobey's shirt was so wet it was practically transparent. Hesitantly, I looked around.

'Jessica's out. So is my mum,' Tobey told me.

I exhaled with relief, then tried to pull myself together, without much success.

'Callie, talk to me. What's wrong?' Tobey asked.

I shook my head, not yet trusting myself to speak. Tobey took my hand and led me into his kitchen. He made me a cup of coffee, ladling in three sugars even though I never have sugar in my coffee. He pushed the hot mug into my hands, ignoring me when I shook my head.

'Drink it,' he ordered. 'You look like you need it.'

Tentatively, I took a sip, but it burned my top lip. Fresh tears filled my eyes. Not because of the coffee – it wasn't that. But now that I'd started crying, I couldn't seem to stop.

'D'you want to talk?' Tobey asked.

I nodded.

'Come on then.' And Tobey led the way upstairs to his bedroom.

nineteen. Tobey

Callie sat on my bed, her fingers lightly tracing the lightning-fork pattern on my dark-blue duvet cover. Her lips were a straight line across her face, her forehead was furrowed. She picked up her coffee from my bedside table and forced herself to drink some more. Her now hazel-coloured eyes were staring straight through my floorboards, through the foundations of the house and down into the planet's core. I opened my mouth to offer her pocket change for her thoughts, then decided against it. I didn't need to be psychic or even terribly astute to know who was on her mind. Nana Jasmine.

How long before the memory of her nana stopped slashing at her? How long before the thought of Nana Jasmine brought a smile to her eyes instead of turning them a shimmering hazel? No one deserved to die the way Jasmine Hadley did. But Callie wore the memory of her death like a hair shirt. It was an accident. Why couldn't she see that? I sighed inwardly, wishing there was some way to lessen the hurt Callie was feeling. After all, we might be something less than lovers, but at least we were something more than friends. And I hated to see Callie this way.

But then there were my own troubles. With each second I expected the police to start hammering at my door. How stupid could one person get? A world of trouble was about to descend on my head and I had no one to blame but myself. And Dan. But mainly myself. I wondered about Ross Resnick, if indeed it had been his finger in that parcel. Where was he? Was he alive or dead? No doubt Louise Resnick's present had been courtesy of Creepy McAuley. The Dowds and McAuley's lot had been trying to wipe each other out for years and the police seemed to be no closer to putting a stop to it. McAuley or the odd Dowd or two occasionally made it to court, but that's as far as it ever went. Witnesses against any of them invariably developed the strangest forms of selective amnesia, or else they just disappeared like a magician's trick. In spite of my best efforts, I was now knee-deep in something I'd fought long and hard to avoid. And if Mum found out . . .

'Tobey, are you OK?'

I sat down beside Callie. "Course. But you're not, are you?'

Callie looked at me, her eyes momentarily unfocused. A smile, fake as silicon boobs, tugged her mouth upwards. 'I'm fine now.'

'Liar,' I suggested.

A hint of a genuine smile appeared. 'What makes you think something's wrong, apart from my tears showering you earlier?'

I bit back a smile. 'Hard as it is to read your poker face, I can see something's gnawing at you.'

Even without the tears, Callie seriously believed that she could suppress her every thought and feeling, that her face was like one of those classical masks. I didn't bother pointing out the obvious. We sat in silence. A couple of times, Callie opened her mouth to speak, but no words came.

'Callie, what happened to your nana Jasmine was a tragic accident,' I ventured at last.

'You think so?' Callie whispered. She looked up at me with the saddest eyes I've ever seen.

'I know so,' I replied. 'She just had the misfortune to be in the wrong place at the wrong time.'

Callie's gaze skittered away from mine. 'I guess.'

'Callie?' There was something else going on here. I frowned. 'What aren't you telling me?'

Callie looked me in the eye, her watchful gaze never wavering. 'Tobey, d'you remember that morning we spent together on Nana Jasmine's beach, the day of the explosion at the Isis Hotel?'

Callie's birthday and the day Callie's nan died. I nodded. Of course I remembered.

'I wanted to stay on that beach with you for ever. Especially when you kissed me. I was scared to leave you.'

'Why did you then?' I asked.

Callie could no longer look at me. Her gaze bounced off my rug, my painted walls, the navy-blue curtains, anywhere but me. 'D'you remember I had a carrier bag that day?' Her voice was so quiet, I had to move closer to hear her.

I frowned. 'Vaguely.'

Silence.

'Callie . . .'

'The carrier bag had a bomb in it. The same bomb that killed Nana Jasmine.'

I stared at her. Whatever else I'd been expecting, it sure as hell wasn't that.

'Are you sure?' I regretted the inane words the moment they left my mouth. 'I mean, where did you get it from?'

'I made it. Uncle Jude taught me how and he gave me everything I needed to make it.' Callie's fingers twisted relentlessly in her lap. Head bowed, I watched as a tear dropped onto the back of her hand, quickly followed by another, and another.

Jude McGregor . . . The Jude McGregors of this world swept through life, spreading poison like weedkiller over every person who crossed their path. I placed a hand under Callie's chin, turning her face towards my own. 'Who was the target?'

'Grandpa Kamal,' Callie said at last.

I inhaled sharply. 'How did your nana . . . ?' There was no good end to that sentence, so I left it trailing.

'Somehow Nana Jasmine guessed what I was going to do. She took the bomb and went to Jude's hotel to confront him with it. They both died and it was all my fault. But now . . .'

Silence.

'Yes?'

'The Nought killed in the explosion has been identified as some man called Robert Powers. Uncle Jude wasn't killed at all. Tobey, I killed . . . I murdered an innocent man.'

I shook my head, still trying to take it all in. 'Callie, it was an accident.'

'Robert Powers is dead because of me. I'm responsible. And Uncle Jude is still out there . . . He's going to come after me. I just know it.'

I stared at her. 'You haven't heard anything from him since the bomb went off, have you?'

Callie shook her head.

'Suppose, just suppose you're right and it wasn't your uncle who was killed,' I said carefully. 'If you haven't heard from him by now, there's no reason to think he'll come after you.'

Callie sighed. 'Tobey, you don't know him. He won't stop until he's had his revenge. Look at the way he waited years before using me to get back at my mum.'

'He won't get to you, Callie, because I won't let him,' I told her.

Callie smiled faintly, but said nothing. I knew what she was thinking. Much as she might appreciate the sentiment behind my words, she didn't think I'd stand much of a chance against the likes of Jude McGregor.

'Tobey, I think . . . I'm dying inside — all over again. And I can't bear it.'

'I'm here and I won't let that happen,' I told her, my arm slipping round her shoulders. 'Callie, you're not alone, I promise.'

'That's not how it feels, in here.' Callie's finger tapped repeatedly at the place over her heart.

'Callie, don't . . .'

'What, Tobey? Don't what? "Don't say that"? "Don't feel that way"? What useless advice d'you have for me?' Callie glared at me, but I wasn't about to spout platitudes – that was my sister's speciality, not mine. I knew better.

'I'm on your side, babe,' I said softly. 'You know that.'

Callie expression slowly softened. 'I'm sorry.'

She smoothed back her long curly hair with both hands. I watched her lick her lips before she turned back to me. Moments passed as I tried my best to put into words how I felt.

'You're not the only one . . . hurting, Callie,' I said at last.

Callie regarded me, taken aback. I met her gaze unflinchingly. I didn't try to hide anything.

'What's wrong, Tobey?' she asked.

'I . . . I got stopped earlier today on Chancellor Street. Two Noughts in a car . . .'

At once Callie's expression was all concern. I didn't need to say any more. She didn't need to hear any more. She understood.

'Are you all right?'

'I'm still standing,' I said, my pathetic attempt at a joke.

'What did they want?'

'The usual. Wanted to know what side of Meadowview was my spiritual home.'

'And you said?'

'"I don't live here. I'm just visiting a friend" – unquote.'

'What did they do?' asked Callie, her unease growing rather than lessening.

'Drove off. They lost interest.'

'What on earth were you doing round the Chancellor Estate?'

'I had to see someone,' I said reluctantly.

'Tobey, are you sure you're OK?'

'They didn't touch me,' I replied, adding to make a joke of it, 'I'll strip down to my hair follicles and you can check me over very slowly if you like – just to confirm it.'

Callie raised an eyebrow. 'Thanks, but I'll take your word for it.'

We sat still. Silent seconds were batted back and forth between us.

What does it mean when you can't even admit you live in a certain place any more in case you're caught slipping?

'Something is very wrong when your postcode could be the signature on your death warrant,' I said.

'You did the right thing—'

'The cowardly thing,' I interrupted.

'The *right* thing,' Callie insisted. 'Whatever it takes to survive, Tobey. You know that. And better a lie than a knife in the gut for being in the wrong place at the wrong time. You can't afford to be stupid – none of us can.'

'I just wish . . .' I began. I didn't finish the rest. It was pointless. Wishes didn't come true, not around Meadowview.

'So do I.' Callie knew what I was trying to say without me having to say it. She shook her head. 'Every time there's a fatal stabbing or shooting and it's Noughts involved, it's in the paper for a day, if that, and the politicians say it's tragic and then it's "as you were, everyone". And the rest of the country breathes a huge sigh of relief that it didn't happen in their back yard.'

Things had changed since my mum's day. Schools could no longer openly discriminate against us Noughts and everyone had to stay in school until they were at least sixteen – Nought or Cross. OK, so the Equal Rights bill currently wending its way through Parliament wouldn't change all attitudes overnight – especially in the blinkered wrinklies over thirty. But it was a start, a step. It's just . . . it was so hard to be patient when patience was taken as a sign of weakness or, worse still, a sign of acquiescence in the status quo. Dan, Alex McAuley, the Liberation Militia and even I had grown sick and tired of being patient. We all wanted our share and we wanted it now. And if we didn't get it, if it was denied us, well, why wait? Just take. The trouble was, everyone was taking. Nought, Cross, it made no difference. When you got right down to it, it was all about territory, for everyone on the planet. If countries could fight over it, then why not individuals? What's mine is mine, what's yours is mine. All together now. Everybody sing.

I thought of Dan and his box of knives and his protestations that the streets weren't safe. There was a lot of that kind of thinking going on. That kind of thinking had turned into a self-fulfilling prophecy.

'It's not right,' Callie said, sparks in her eyes. 'Those guys in the car and the others like them, they're all hag fishes. Uncle Jude was right about that if nothing else.'

We both sat in brooding silence.

'Callie, that's not the only thing that happened today,' I admitted.

'What else?' Callie frowned.

'I did something incredibly stupid and I have a feeling it's going to come back to haunt me.'

'What did you do?'

I opened my mouth to tell her, then thought better of it. I'd got into the middle of something and now I was up to my armpits in alligators. Did I really want to drag Callie into my mess?

'I'd better not say,' I replied, turning away from her.

Now it was Callie's turn to place her hand on my chin and turn my face back towards her own. 'Was it something really bad?'

I nodded. We regarded each other.

'So one way or another we're in the same boat?' asked Callie.

I nodded again.

'What do we do about it?'

I thought about all the things I could say, but none of them seemed even remotely adequate. She looked at me. I looked at her. Neither of us said a word. We spontaneously leaned towards each other. And I kissed her. Just my lips against hers to begin with. And though she was surprised, she didn't pull away. Her hands crept up my arms to hold my shoulders. That was all I needed, to wrap my arms around her. I opened my mouth, my tongue darting out to touch her bottom lip. Callie opened her mouth immediately. My tongue slipped inside. Maybe I should've licked or nibbled her lips first. But my tongue had other ideas. And to my surprise, Callie kissed me just as intently and as intensely as I kissed her. It was just meant to be friendly kissing, two friends comfort kissing because in that moment we both desperately needed to touch and be touched. We both needed to know that for just a few moments life wasn't a journey that had to be travelled alone. But with each second it became something more.

Callie snaked her arms around my neck, her lips still on mine. I wanted Callie so much, my body was aching. One of my hands moved up from her waist to cup her breast. And she didn't pull away to tell me to stop and she didn't slap my hand away. If anything she kissed me harder, her tongue darting back and forth into my mouth. I was trying with all my might to hang onto some semblance of reason, but it was fast flying out of my bedroom window. Callie was in my room, on my bed, kissing me, touching me, her hands slipping under my shirt. My mouth was suddenly dry. I wanted her so much, but I was scared. Scared she'd stop me. Scared she wouldn't. Scared all my dreams would come true and I'd be inside her for the very first time. Scared I'd be inside any girl for the first time and I wouldn't know what to do, how to move properly or make it good for my partner. For Callie.

Were we really going to do this? We sat next to each other on the bed. Callie looked at me, but didn't smile. I needed her. I moved to kiss her again, my hands moving restlessly over her body. She pulled away from me, placing a finger over my lips. I was immediately still, all except my pounding heart and the blood sprinting around my body.

'Tobey, d'you want me?'

Was she frickin' kidding? I took her hand in mine and placed it over my erection. Answers on a postcard please!

'Wow. Is that all for me?' Callie sounded worried.

'We'll take it slow,' I assured her.

'D'you have any condoms?' she asked.

I nodded. How about five packets, hidden under my mattress! I believed in thinking ahead. Callie moved her hand lightly over my groin, sending such shock waves of electricity through me that my body pulsed like a strummed guitar string. She leaned forward for another kiss. I met her more than halfway. Our lips together, our tongues swirled around and over each other. By the time Callie reluctantly pulled away from me, I was harder than I'd ever been before.

'I've never done this before,' Callie whispered.

My eyebrows shot up. Damn, every bit of my body was up.

'How come?' I asked, surprised.

'You never wanted me before.'

I looked into Callie's brown eyes and realized she really believed that. Damn, but I should bottle this poker face and sell it on a market stall. How many nights had I lain awake wondering about Lucas and Callie when they were an item? All those sleepless nights imagining them together, doing what we were doing now.

'I thought you and Lucas . . .' I began, still not quite able to believe it.

'Never.'

I couldn't help it. A grin broke out all over my face. Snubs to you then, Lucas!

'What's so funny?' Callie frowned. 'Now that you know I didn't do it with Lucas, you're not interested any more? Is that it?'

Why did girls always have to over-think everything? Godsake!

'Of course I'm still interested,' I said, exasperated. 'Has your brain stopped working?'

'Then why . . . ?'

I kissed Callie again. I admit the first few seconds were to stop her from talking bollocks, but after that it was 'cause it felt damned good. We carried on kissing whilst we tentatively undressed each other. It was awkward and fumbling and definitely not practised, but it didn't matter. We laughed together at our mutual eager clumsiness. And that made it even better somehow, like discovering a new place together. When we were both naked we lay on my bed, just kissing and hugging and tasting and touching each other. Her boobs were hot under my hands and soft and I didn't want to stop touching them. But there were other parts of her body I wanted to touch as well. From the way my body was throbbing, I knew I couldn't hold out much longer. I stroked up and down Callie's thighs before stroking between her legs to make sure she was ready for me. I had to get out of bed and fiddle under my mattress to find just one packet of condoms, which amused Callie no end. After finally putting on a condom, which was trickier than I thought and took three attempts, I moved over Callie to lie on her, my legs between hers. We kissed and just touched each other for long, loving minutes.

'D'you really want to . . . ?' I couldn't help asking. I needed to be sure that she wanted this just as much as I did. I was never going to risk losing her again.

Callie nodded. 'But only if you do,' she teased.

My upper body supported by my extended arms, I looked into her beautiful eyes as I pushed slowly inside her. God, it felt so good – until Callie winced. I was immediately still.

'D'you want to stop?' I whispered.

Say no. Please say no.

Callie shook her head. 'Just . . . wait a bit. Let me get used to you.'

I held as still as I could for as long as I could, reciting multiplication tables and bits of the periodic table in my head to calm down. Callie started to move slowly beneath me. I used that as my signal to go further, get deeper inside her. I moved slowly, pulling out a little and pushing on, doing my best not to rush. When she grimaced for the third time, I was ready to come out of her completely. I couldn't enjoy it if she didn't. As if she sensed what I was about to do, Callie's hands moved over my bum to pull me closer to her at the same time as she arched her hips. We both gasped as I slid all the way inside her. I lay still, only kissing her then, trying to silently tell her just what she meant to me, what being with her meant to me. I rose up to look at her. Callie's eyes were closed.

'Am I hurting you?' I whispered.

'Not so much now,' Callie replied softly. 'In fact . . .'

She wriggled her hips beneath me. Lightning jolts flashed through my body again. I couldn't help but groan.

'Tobey, are we having sex or making love?' Callie asked.

It was such a girly question that I had to smile.

'What d'you think?' I whispered, before nibbling on her ear lobe.

'Feels like making love to me.' Her hands stroked over my back as our hips slowly moved together. 'Does it feel like that to you?'

'Callie, you talk too much,' I groaned.

'Aren't we supposed to talk then?'

'Your mind should be on more than just conversation,' I rose up on my arms to tell her.

'It is.'

Callie's eyes closed as I withdrew and moved slowly inside her again. The little moan of pleasure she gave then lanced through me. I hadn't expected that, that giving her pleasure would actually increase my own.

'What else is on your mind?' I murmured.

Callie opened her eyes to look straight at me. 'How much you mean to me.'

My head spun with all the words I wanted to say, the way she made me feel inside and out. My mind was all corners and cracks and crevices, and thoughts and memories of her occupied every single one. How she looked when she was pissed off with me. The way she lowered her head before giving me one of her dirty looks. The way she raised her chin before she had a good laugh. A lifetime of memories, with spaces for an eternity more. I opened my mouth, but Callie placed a finger to my lips.

'Callie, I . . .'

'No words, especially not ones you feel forced into saying.' She smiled.

No force involved or required, but I didn't speak. Our fingers laced together at our sides. Our legs twined like vines. We were so connected that I couldn't feel where I ended and she began any more. Every sense was at work and heightened. I buried my face in the crook of her neck, mouthing the words that she'd forbidden me to say. Couldn't she feel how I felt about her? Couldn't she tell what she was doing to me?

Damn it, I had to say something. Just tell her the truth.

'Callie . . .'

Her eyelids fluttered open. She had a look on her face I'd never seen before. The light in her eyes made me catch my breath. And then we couldn't stop looking at each other as we moved together.

'You and me, babe, against the world,' I whispered.

Callie smiled and hugged me closer – and the rest of the world just fell away.

twenty. Callie

Wow! I'd done it. I'd actually done it. With Tobey. Ha! If anyone had told me six months ago that my first lover would be Tobey, I would've rolled on the floor, clutching my stomach. But we did it. And it was awkward and somewhere between uncomfortable and painful to begin with and hot and sweaty and messy and so damned wonderful to conclude.

'Are you OK?' Tobey asked, once he'd come back from disposing of his condom.

'I'm fine,' I whispered. I lay next to him, my head on his shoulder, with both his arms around me. 'It's getting late.' The last thing I needed was Jessica arriving home and bursting in on us. My face grew hot just thinking about it. 'Tobey, I should go home.'

Tobey held me that much tighter. 'What d'you have planned for tomorrow?'

I shrugged. 'Not a lot. Why?'

'Dan owes me some money. I'm meeting him at four o'clock tomorrow afternoon at the Wasteland to get it. Maybe you and I could do something afterwards to celebrate.'

'What are we celebrating?'

'Well, I can get rid of my V plates for a start.' Tobey grinned. 'That's definitely worth celebrating.'

I sat up, staring at him in wide-eyed disbelief. 'But what about you and Misty?'

Tobey lay back, his arms behind his head. 'How many times do I have to tell you that I'm not the slightest bit interested in Misty before you believe me?'

'But she's going round telling everyone how wonderful you are, especially in bed,' I informed him.

'How the hell would she know?' Tobey frowned.

That lying cow! I laughed and lay down on his shoulder again. His arms were instantly around me again. That was lovely in itself, like I belonged right there and nowhere else.

'Misty is pretty, though.' I could say that now I knew Tobey wasn't secretly lusting after her.

'If you like bubble heads who weigh about as much as one pound twenty pence,' Tobey said with disdain.

I stared at him. 'Ooh! Meow! Waiter, saucer of milk for Mr Durbridge please.'

Tobey grinned ruefully. 'Well, it's true. If she ever had an original thought it would die of loneliness.'

I burst out laughing. 'Tobey, that's harsh. Remind me never to get on your wrong side.'

'You can get on any side of me you like,' Tobey said hopefully.

'Where I am now is just fine, thank you.'

We lay in peaceful silence whilst time sloped past us.

'Tobey, d'you know what you are?' I ran a finger across his lips and down his nose and along the curve of his ear before cupping his cheek.

'What?'

Tobey looked at me. If I didn't know any better, I'd say he looked . . . nervous.

I whispered, 'You are . . . my mender of broken things.'

We looked at each other then. I mean, really looked. For just a few seconds, maybe a few plus, but it was enough. Enough for my heartbeat to quicken. Enough to make me catch my breath. Enough to quell any doubts trying to surface in my head. A slow smile swept across Tobey's face. He caught hold of my hand as it fell away from his face and kissed my palm.

'What was that for?' I smiled.

'Dunno. Maybe I mistook your hand for a biscuit,' he teased. 'Besides, you girls like that kind of thing, don't you?'

I snatched back my hand. 'This girl only likes it if you mean it.'

'I mean it,' Tobey replied, no hint of a teasing smile. He had a really strange look on his face. His gaze dropped from my eyes to my lips and stayed there. I ran my tongue over my lips and then my teeth.

'What?' I asked when I couldn't stand it any longer.

'What what?' asked Tobey.

'Why're you staring at my mouth? Have I got some food stuck between my tee——?'

Tobey kissed me. Really kissed me. Soft and gentle and long and loving and passionate. It was bloody lovely. Moments turned into minutes before I finally pulled away.

'I'll take that as a no!' I said, when I got my breath back.

Tobey just smiled. I glanced at the clock on his bedside table.

'I really should go,' I said reluctantly.

'Stay just a bit longer,' Tobey whispered, kissing my forehead and nose before moving to my lips. 'I've got five whole boxes of condoms under my mattress to get through.'

'Tobey, you must be drunk!' I immediately hopped out of bed and started to get dressed.

I ask you! Not even five condoms, but five boxes. What was he like? I turned to glare at him, but instead the frustrated look on Tobey's face made me burst out laughing.

I was laughing.

I was smiling.

You know what, Uncle Jude? Sod you. I'm happy and whatever happens now, you can't take that away from me. And I'll tell you something else. There'll be no more hiding away, no more feeling sorry for myself. Those days are over.

'Thanks, Tobey,' I said, pulling my T-shirt over my head.

'For what?'

'For listening to me. For being with me.'

'You're welcome,' said Tobey, adding hopefully, 'I was joking about using up all five boxes of condoms tonight. We've got all weekend to do that.'

'Omigod! I'm shagging a sexbot,' I exclaimed, sitting down again. 'Tobey, how about we give Mr Ever-Ready a rest for tonight? Besides, I'm sore.'

Tobey was immediately at my side. 'Are you sure you're OK?'

'I'm fine, I promise. I'm sore in a good way, not a bad way,' I tried to explain.

'How does that work?' asked Tobey sceptically.

'I'm not sorry we did it,' I told him. 'In fact, just the opposite.'

Tobey smiled and we kissed again.

'But don't go boasting to your friends about the two of us – and that includes Dan,' I added fiercely when I came up for air. 'Or Mr Ever-Ready will have only his memories to keep him warm. Understand?'

'Understood.' Tobey's smile grew broader.

'I mean it, Tobey. If you say one word about this to anyone, I'll kill you.'

'OK! OK! I said I understood, didn't I?' Tobey said, exasperated. 'Damn, but you're scary when you're annoyed!'

'And don't you forget it,' I replied. 'Are you going to get dressed or not?'

Tobey finally got his bum out of bed. He dressed in silence, but every time I looked at him, he had a ridiculous grin on his face. I had to bite my cheeks to stop myself from laughing with him. If he was a peacock, his tail feathers would be open like a fan and he'd be strutting!

'We still on for tomorrow?' said Tobey.

'If you're going to meet Dan tomorrow afternoon, does that mean you're taking the day off work?'

'Yeah.'

'Tobey, the stupid thing you did today, did that have anything to do with Dan?'

'It might've done.' Tobey was at once cagey.

'Are you going to tell me what you did?'

He shook his head, his expression sombre. 'Not now. Soon.'

Much as I wanted him to confide in me, if I pushed any more, he'd clam up completely. But that did it. No way was I going to let him meet Dan by himself. If I was there, I could at least try to stop him from doing another idiotic thing. I just wished I knew what he was talking about. He'd tell me, of course, but in his own sweet time and not if I forced the issue.

'I'll go with you to the Wasteland tomorrow afternoon. Then we can talk about how to spend the rest of our evening,' I said.

'It's a date,' said Tobey. 'In fact, what're you doing tomorrow morning?'

'Nothing much. Why?'

'Wanna do nothing much with me?'

'OK,' I agreed with a smile. 'Should I just come round here then? Or d'you want to come round to mine?'

Tobey considered. 'You come round here. Your nana Meggie makes me nervous.'

Oh my goodness! Tobey had actually made a decision. I opened my mouth to rib him, but decided against it. After all, I didn't want to put him off making another one at some point!

'Why're you putting on your trainers?' I asked as I watched him fasten them.

'I'm walking you home.'

I stared at him. 'I live next door, Tobey. I think I can make it from your front door to mine without too much trouble.'

'I didn't say you couldn't. But I'm still walking you home,' Tobey insisted.

I decided not to argue. To be honest, it was kind of lovely having Tobey looking out for me. He was definitely a lover, not a fighter. In a clash against Uncle Jude or anyone else come to that, he'd be about as much use as a chocolate frying pan, but it was still sweet.

twenty-one. Tobey

'Jessica, have you moved your bed in there?' I hissed through the locked bathroom door. 'You're not the only one with a bladder, you know?'

'W-why aren't you at work?' Jessica's voice sounded strange, husky, like she was still more than half asleep.

'I've got the day off,' I said, annoyed. 'Why aren't *you* at work?'

'I'm not feeling well,' said Jessica.

'Well, could you not feel well in your own bedroom and let someone else use the bathroom please?' I mean, I was sympathetic and all that, but Godsake! My bladder was about to explode.

If Mum wasn't back from her night shift and fast asleep in her bedroom, I'd've been battering at the bathroom door by now. What on earth was Jessica doing? She'd been in there for *ages*. Being the sole guy in a house with two women was a real test of my patience. After all the girly things I'd seen over the years in our family bathroom, it was a wonder I didn't need some serious therapy.

'Jessica, I need to use the bathroom. NOW!'

'OK! OK!' There came some strange noises from inside the bathroom.

When the door finally opened I launched myself into the room whilst trying to push Jessica out at the same time. She was wearing Mum's old dressing gown, which was at least three sizes too big for her, and she had the bath towel draped over her arm.

'Where're you taking that?' I asked, pointing at the towel.

'To the laundry basket.'

'Why?'

'It's wet.'

'What am I supposed to use?'

'Get another one.'

I frowned as I took a closer look at my sister. 'Godsake, Jessica. You look rough.'

'Thanks,' she intoned, her eyes half shut.

'You look like you've been left out in the rain all day and put away wet.'

'I'm tired. OK?' She glared at me.

'Then take some vitamins and try some eye drops. You look like a vampire.'

'Bog off.' Jessica strode off back to her bedroom. She bumped into the wall twice, though, so as a dramatic gesture it kind of failed.

Frowning, I sniffed at the bathroom.

'Why does it smell of vinegar in here?' I called after my sister.

'Nail polish remover,' Jess called back before entering her room.

Godsake! Couldn't she use that stuff in her own room and not the bathroom? My bladder dictating my pace, I ran to the airing cupboard, grabbed a towel from above the hot water cylinder, and ran back to the bathroom. It was not unknown for my mum or sister to slip into the bathroom ahead of me when my back was turned. And the fact that Jessica had only just come out wouldn't stop her from trying to pop back in. I was going to have a lovely long shower, wash my hair and shave before Callie arrived. I wanted to be clean and look neat without making it look like I'd been to a lot of trouble, or any trouble at all come to that. Time to get to work on making myself irresistible.

Callie didn't turn up until mid morning. I sat in the front room, listening to my favourite rock band with the volume turned down low so as not to wake Mum. I kept glancing out of the window, watching the passers-by. The moment I saw Callie go past my window, I sprinted into the hall. I opened the door before she had her finger halfway to the doorbell.

'Mum's asleep,' I gave as the reason why I'd come to the door so quickly. But to tell the truth, Mum had nothing to do with it.

Callie was wearing a light-blue, sleeveless, V-necked T-shirt and dark-blue jeans. She wore her hair loose for a change and it fell in curly waves around her face and down past her shoulders. Her earrings were gold, reflecting her skin tone. She smiled, her eyes warm brown today. She looked so good, my stomach kinda hiccupped. Every time that happened it took me by surprise. Wasn't sure I liked it much either. It made me feel . . . exposed, like wearing trousers with no bum to them. But I had no control over the way my body reacted to her, no matter how much I tried to rationalize my feelings or find a logical explanation for what she did to me.

'How are you?' I said, opening the front door wide for her to enter.

'I'm fine,' Callie sashayed past me. I was never really sure what that word meant until that moment when she did it. Then I knew all right!

I glanced up the stairs. No sounds, but I still lowered my voice. 'Are you OK after last night?'

Callie nodded. 'I'm fine.'

'I . . . you look . . .' I stopped babbling like an idiot and leaned in to kiss her. My arms wrapped around her, her arms wrapped around me and we kissed like we had less than one minute before the world ended!

When I finally let her go, Callie laughed. 'What was that for?'

'Just saying hello.' I grinned.

'I can't wait to see how you hold a conversation then?' Callie teased. 'Any chance of a coffee?' She walked ahead of me into the kitchen. By the time I got there, she was already taking out two cups. 'You gonna have one with me?'

'Yeah, go on then.'

I put on the kettle whilst Callie spooned coffee into both cups and two sugars into mine.

'Where's your sister?' she asked.

'In her room, probably on her phone where she'll be for hours.'

'What're we going to do after our coffees?'

'What would you like to do?' I asked.

I knew what I'd like to do, but there was no way Callie would go for that with Jessica in the house.

'Can we watch a DVD?' she asked. 'And can I choose it?'

Oh hell, no!

'We can't,' I said quickly. 'We have to go and see Dan soon.'

'Not for hours yet. Please, Tobey. I fancy relaxing on the sofa and watching a film or two,' said Callie.

'But, Callie . . .'

'Please. For me . . .' She started batting her long eyelashes in my direction. 'We could cuddle up . . .'

'Oh all right then,' I said, my heart sinking at the prospect of hours spent watching soppy films. 'Damn it, Callie, I must really like you or something.'

'Or something,' Callie agreed with a wink.

twenty-two. Tobey

'So where's Dan then?' Callie asked, looking around.

'I don't know,' I replied stonily. I checked my watch. Twenty minutes past four. I must've been truly dim to believe he would show up. I'd give him five more minutes. I looked around. There was a good-natured impromptu football match going on, mostly Noughts but also some Crosses. Callie and I stood on the sidelines, half watching as we waited for my so-called friend to put in an appearance. The Wasteland was pretty crowded, even for a Saturday afternoon. I glanced at Callie, taking in her slight frown as she watched the football. She hadn't said much as we'd walked to the Wasteland. Something was definitely gnawing at her.

Callie glanced up at the sky. 'Can we not stay here too long? I think it's going to rain.'

'Thank God,' I said.

The weather over the last two weeks had been diabolical, hot as hell and twice as fierce. We were all about due for a break. That was probably why the Wasteland was so crowded, because the air had cooled down a bit. Being outside today didn't feel so much like being an insect tortured under a magnifying glass.

'How much longer do we have to stay here?' Callie asked.

'No idea.'

'When is Dan going to get here?'

'How the hell should I know?'

'Well, excuse me all over the place,' Callie snapped back.

'Sorry, babe.' I leaned in to kiss her.

'You're forgiven.' She smiled when at last our kiss ended.

'Get a room!' some git called out from the football pitch.

Callie and I shared a smile and ignored the wolf whistles and ribald comments. Apart from Dan's vanishing act, the day hadn't been too bad. In fact, it'd been on the great side of good. Callie returned to her house and brought back a DVD which was a certain-sure cure for insomnia. The thing was so slow, I swear I could feel my hair growing. So whilst she was watching it, her back pressed against my chest, her feet up on the sofa, I wrapped my arms around her and made the most of holding her tight, touching and stroking her body, nibbling on her ear and kissing her whenever the film's plot slackened – and the plot wasn't exactly drum tight.

Plus whilst Callie had been watching the film, it had given me a chance to zone out and do some serious thinking about my predicament, as well as Callie's uncle. If Jude McGregor really was alive, if somehow he'd escaped the devastation at the Isis Hotel, then I would need money to get Callie away from him. With money, Callie and I could escape to some place where her Uncle Jude would never find us. It would mean missing school and my exams, but I'd do it in a heartbeat to keep Callie safe. I wouldn't tell her of my plans just yet. I had to get enough money together first. Deliveries?

Now if Dan would just show his face, Callie and I could be off and doing. I had plans for today. An expensive meal, a film or maybe even a theatre trip to impress her and then we'd take it from there. We had the whole evening ahead of us. And we could discuss our future together when the time was right. I'd have to pick my moment carefully. I looked at Callie and realized that we had our whole lives ahead of us. Callie and I, together.

A surprisingly chilly breeze brought me back to the Wasteland. The wind ruffled my hair and tugged at my T-shirt. I glanced up. The clouds were definitely getting darker. Callie was right. Rain was coming. Though I found it hard to care about the rain, the sun or anything in between at that precise moment. Callie's gold hoop-earrings glinted, catching my eye. Not that I needed her earrings sparkling in my direction to make me look at her. She was so damned beautiful it was hard to take my eyes off her. I put my arm around her, or at least I tried to. She shied away before turning to face me.

'What's the matter?' I asked.

'Tobey, when are we going to talk about what happened last night?' Callie began, albeit reluctantly.

'Why?'

What was there to talk about? Godsake! This wasn't going to be one of those girly 'let's-analyse-the-thing-to-death' talks, was it?

Callie looked here, there and anywhere but at me. 'I know . . . I know it probably didn't mean as much to you as it did to me, but—'

Whoa!

'Where'd you get that idea?'

'Well, you didn't mention it all morning,' said Callie.

'What was I supposed to say?' I frowned. 'Great shag?'

Callie glared at me. 'See! Everything is a big joke to you.'

What was she on about?

'What're you on about?'

Was Callie deliberately trying to pick a fight? Or maybe I'd been such crap in bed, she was trying to find a way to dump me.

'Tobey, I don't regret what happened last night, really I don't. But I've been thinking all morning that maybe we shouldn't do it again, at least for a while.'

'Why?' I asked, aghast. Looks like I'd been right. I know it hadn't been the world's most polished perform-ance, but it was my first time too.

'Last night was about comfort and getting lost in each other to shut out the outside world. I just don't think that's a good enough reason to carry on . . . doing it.'

'Is that all last night meant to you?' I asked, acutely disappointed. 'A bit of comfort and a way to take your mind off your uncle?'

'Don't you dare say that,' Callie rounded on me. 'You're the one who kept crowing about not being a virgin any more. You're the one who said you did some-thing really stupid yesterday, so being with me was obvi-ously just your way of forgetting your problems for a while.'

'That's not true,' I denied.

'Isn't it? OK, Tobey, no teasing, no jokes, no evasions, just the truth. How do you feel about me?'

I opened my mouth to tell her straight, only to snap it shut again. I wanted to tell her, I really did. But certain words were very hard to retract. Once they were out, they took on a life of their own and if I said them, they might turn round and take a chunk out of my arse. Callie was watching me intently.

'This is ridiculous. You're being really stupid,' I said at last.

'Thanks,' Callie said, not attempting to mask the hurt in her voice. 'That confirms what I thought.'

'Callie, I . . .'

'Forget it, Tobey. I was drowning, you threw me a life-line, now it's over.' Callie shrugged. 'I was stupid to hope it meant any more to you than that.'

'Hi, you guys,' Dan yelled out from several metres away.

'Look, we can't discuss this here,' I told Callie. 'Once Dan gives me my money, we can go for a meal and talk about it. OK?'

'Nothing to talk about,' Callie said coldly.

Why did I suddenly feel like I was clinging onto our relationship by my fingertips? Probably because that was exactly what I was doing. It was a choice between yanking open my chest and showing Callie my heart with all the risks that involved – or losing her anyway.

'Callie, we need to talk,' I said.

'Talk or listen to you insult me some more?'

'Talk.'

Callie didn't reply.

'I'm sorry I called you stupid,' I said, exasperated. 'Can we please just go somewhere and talk? Please?'

Callie didn't answer. Instead she turned to face Dan. I did the same, feeling like I was drowning. Dan approached us, a big, beaming smile on his face.

'What's the point of having a flash watch if you still can't get anywhere on time?' I snapped when he got close enough.

'I'm here now, aren't I?' Dan couldn't see the problem. 'Hi, Callie. You're looking fine, as always.'

'Thanks, Dan.'

'I mean it. You look real fit,' he said, moving closer to her.

Annoyance began to bubble inside me like a saucepan of water heating on a cooker.

'Callie, I can take you places and buy you things that Tobey hasn't even dreamed about.' Dan's smile was an oil slick on his face as he regarded her. 'Tobey's my mate and all, but when're you going to dump the loser and go out with me?'

Callie gave me a filthy look, then turned to Dan like she was seriously considering his offer.

'You even think about making a move on Callie and I'll break every bone in your body,' I told Dan straight. 'And when you're buried, I'll dig you up to break each bone all over again.'

Dan and Callie stared at me. Then they both burst out laughing. What was so damned funny?

'Someone's got it bad,' Dan said.

Callie looked at me, a strange light twinkling in her eyes. All the ice in her expression had melted. I turned away from her so she couldn't get the full effect of the blush cooking my face.

'Now you see, Tobey,' she said softly. 'That's all you had to say!'

'I don't know what you mean,' I mumbled, deciding to ignore them both till they stopped laughing at me.

Beyond the football pitch, across the grass, a black WMW pulled up. If I hadn't known any better I would've sworn it was McAuley's car. But what would McAuley be doing at the Wasteland on a Saturday afternoon? Two suited Nought men I'd never seen before got out and ambled across the grass towards the football pitch as if they didn't have a care in the world.

'So, Callie, when did you first manage to wrap my friend around your little finger?' Dan asked, holding an imaginary microphone to her face.

'Well, Dan, it all started when I was seven years old . . .' Callie squeaked out like her lungs were full of helium.

Dan had his back to the two men, who were slowly but surely heading in our direction. Something wasn't right. I looked around. A white saloon was parked on the opposite side of the pitch. Two men got out of that car, two Crosses. They also started heading towards the football pitch. I turned back to the two Nought men walking towards us. They were talking to each other, but the prickling on the back of my neck was getting worse. The two Noughts were only a few metres away now. They reached beneath their jackets – and then all hell was let loose.

'GET DOWN!' I yelled.

But my words came too late.

twenty-three. Callie

Several loud bangs sounded, like lots of cars backfiring in quick succession. Each noise made me jump. I looked around. The whole world reduced speed to ultra slow-motion. Every colour, every sensation was heightened except . . . except all I could hear now was my heart strumming. The world was slow, my heartbeat was fast. Strange combination.

All around us, people scattered like points on a compass. I could see their mouths move, watch their frantic expressions, but still the only sound was my own heartbeat, growing ever faster. It was like a drum inside me beating its own time. What on earth was going on? I looked around. Men with guns. Men with guns on either side of the pitch, shooting at each other. And all of us in the middle.

Get down, Callie.

Drop down.

Get down. NOW.

Two Cross men had their guns drawn and were shooting past us in the direction of the road behind us. I turned just in time to see McAuley, sitting in the back of his car, the back window all the way down. Flashes flared from inside the car. Bullets? *Bullets.* My head turned this way and that. Tobey was shouting at me, his mouth moving oh so slowly, too slowly to make out the words. But he was trying to tell me something important, something urgent. That much was evident in his eyes. And he was pulling at me.

Stop pulling me.

Dan was already on the ground.

GET DOWN, CALLIE . . .

From inside his car, McAuley fired his gun. And his gun was pointing straight at us. The gun jerked in McAuley's hand. He'd fired. And again. I didn't have time to warn Tobey or push him out the way. I stepped in front of him.

twenty-four. Tobey

'Godsake, Callie. Get down.' I hit the floor, trying to pull Callie with me, but she stood stock-still in front of me, staring across the park. I scrambled in front of her, pulling harder on her arm. Furious, I looked up at her, wondering why the hell she wasn't moving. Godsake! Bullets were now whizzing around us like mosquitoes round a blood bank. Godsake . . . Callie looked down at me. And that's when my world crashed to an abrupt halt.

A dark crimson stain was spreading out over the front of Callie's sky-blue shirt. More gunshots. Something glanced off the side of Callie's head and she toppled, her body falling like a house of playing cards.

'CALLIE . . .' I threw my body over hers, trying to protect her from stray bullets. McAuley's car screeched down the road, burning rubber as it went. The two Cross men who'd made a great show of strolling across the grass towards us were now racing back to their own car. Moments later, they too screeched out of sight. Everyone ran for their lives. Dan, who'd dived down beside me at the sound of the first bullet being fired, picked himself up and bolted. Within moments there was no one left on the Wasteland except me and Callie.

I sat up, pulling Callie with me. The crimson stain was

growing bigger, covering more of Callie's shirt. There was a circular hole on the left-hand side of her shirt, just below her shoulder. Blood ran down the side of her head, from her temple past her ears.

'HELP US! SOMEONE HELP US!' I yelled out.

Callie's eyes were closed and her breath left her nose and mouth with a strange rattling sound. I looked around at all the closed windows of the flats and houses that surrounded the Wasteland on three sides.

'PLEASE. SOMEONE HELP . . .' I pulled Callie to me, rocking her back and forth in my arms as we both sat on the ground.

Digging into my trouser pocket, I brought out my phone with one hand, laying it on the ground so I could dial the emergency services for an ambulance without letting go of Callie.

'Callie, hang on,' I whispered in her ear. 'Help will soon be here. Just hang on.'

The clouds separated and sunlight bathed us, so bright I was momentarily blinded. The rattling sound Callie was making suddenly stopped. No . . . She lay limp in my arms. And her sudden silence was far, far worse. In the distance I could hear the sound of a siren. Someone somewhere must've phoned for help after all.

'Callie?' I whispered.

She lay so still, like a broken doll. My hands and clothes were covered with her blood. I hugged her to me, her cheek against mine, rocking her gently back and forth.

I've got you, Callie. I've got you. I'll never let you go. Never.

You and me, babe, against the world.

twenty-five. Tobey

The hospital corridor smelled strongly of disinfectant. Irregular beeps sounded all around me. Footsteps constantly hurried past me, but no one stopped. They wouldn't let me stay with Callie, no matter how much I pleaded. The paramedics who arrived in the ambulance didn't even want me to travel with them, but I held onto Callie's hand like we were super-glued together. Once we arrived at the hospital, Callie was whisked away to theatre. A nurse took me into a small room and asked me a number of questions about Callie's medical history, most of which I couldn't answer. I phoned Callie's mum, but she wasn't answering her mobile so I had to leave a message. I phoned Callie's home, but Meggie wasn't in either. No one was where they were supposed to be. All I could do was leave messages to say that Callie had been shot and was undergoing emergency surgery at Mercy Community Hospital. Not the sort of message I wanted to leave, but what choice did I have? I was ushered into the waiting room, which was heaving with people. There were no more available chairs so I leaned against the wall, texting my mum to let her know what had happened as I knew her phone would be switched off whilst she was working. She was somewhere in this hospital, but I didn't go looking for her. I needed to stay put so I could find out how Callie was doing the moment she was out of surgery.

Callie had been shot.

She might die.

Please don't let her die . . .

Even now I was still trying to work out what had happened. Images flashed like a series of snapshots in my head. The two Cross men in the fancy white car, they had to work for the Dowds. And McAuley and his men turning up at the Wasteland at exactly the same time, there was no way that was a mere coincidence. It hadn't kicked off in Meadowview like that in years. And now Callie was fighting for her life with a bullet in her. Maybe two. It was only just beginning to sink in.

Please don't let me lose her. Not now.

Not now . . .

Some instinct had me looking up, then around. My instincts hadn't let me down. Two officers were fast approaching, weaving their way through the others in the waiting room to get to me. They both wore suits, but I knew they were the police. One was a middle-aged Cross, the other a younger Nought, in his mid-twenties at a guess. The middle-aged Cross copper already wore a smile beneath his pencil-thin moustache. His dark eyes were watchful and shrewd. The Nought copper wore his blond hair buzz-cut. They got closer, their eyes never leaving mine. They were poised — that's the only word for it, poised — like they thought I was about to do a runner. I straightened up off the wall, then stayed perfectly still. When at last they reached me, they both stood directly in front of me. I wasn't going anywhere, even if I wanted to.

'You're the one who came in with the gunshot victim?' asked the Cross copper.

I nodded. 'Her name is Callie Hadley.'

The Cross copper extended his hand. 'I'm DI Omari Boothe. This is Sergeant Paul Kenwood.'

Warily, I shook the detective's hand. Sergeant Kenwood nodded in my direction, his blue eyes frosty, his hands staying firmly at his sides.

'What's your name, son?' asked the detective inspector, his tone even, as if he was asking for the time. Sergeant Kenwood dug out a notebook and pen from his pocket and flicked it open decisively.

'Tobey Durbridge.'

'Age?'

'Seventeen.'

'When are you eighteen?'

'In two months.' Why did he need to know that?

'Address?'

I told him.

'And the girl you came in with, you said her name is Callie Hadley?'

'Callie Rose Hadley, yes.'

'D'you know her address?'

'She lives next door to me in Johnstone Street, at number fifty-five.'

Sergeant Kenwood was scribbling furiously in his notebook, even though I hadn't said much.

'Can you tell us what happened?' asked Detective Boothe.

'I'm still not quite sure.' I shook my head. 'One moment Callie and I were watching a football match and the next moment bullets were whizzing round us like midges. It all happened so fast. A matter of seconds.'

'And where was this?'

'The pitch at the Wasteland.' I glanced at Sergeant Kenwood. He had yet to say a word. Perhaps they were playing chatty cop, silent cop.

'Who was doing the shooting?' asked the detective.

'No idea. When the bullets started flying, I was just trying to keep my head down.'

'What was Callie doing?'

'She was standing in front of me. I think . . . I think she froze.'

'How many gunshots were there in total?'

I shrugged. No idea.

'Under five? Under ten? Under fifteen?' prompted Detective Boothe.

'Maybe under ten,' I replied. 'I wasn't exactly trying to count them.'

'Did the shots all come from one direction or different directions?'

Careful, Tobey . . . I considered. 'Different directions, I think. That's why they seemed to be all around us. But I can't be sure.'

'Did you see any cars in the vicinity?'

I frowned at Detective Boothe and shook my head. 'I was watching the football match, so I wasn't paying attention to anything but that.'

'You didn't see anything?'

'No. Sorry.'

'Is Callie Hadley a friend of yours?'

'Yes,' I said warily. 'She's my girlfriend.'

Sergeant Kenwood snorted derisively at my words.

'D'you have a problem with that?' I asked belligerently.

'No. But she does, if you're the best she can do,' Sergeant Kenwood retorted. He looked at me like he wasn't looking at much. 'If that was my girlfriend lying on an operating table with a bullet or two in her, I'd want to get the bastard who did it. But all you Noughts in Meadowview have acute three-monkeys disease – see no evil, hear no evil, speak no evil.'

'All us Noughts in Meadowview have to live here when the police are nowhere around,' I replied.

'We can protect you,' said Detective Boothe quickly. 'You and your family, if that's what's worrying you.'

'I don't need protecting because I didn't see anything,' I insisted. 'I wish I had, but I didn't.'

The two coppers exchanged a look. They didn't believe a word.

'Is there anything else you can tell us about what happened?' asked the detective.

Pause.

'I—'

'Tobey? Tobey.' Callie's mum, Sephy, made a bee-line for me. 'What happened? Where's my daughter?'

'She's still in surgery,' I explained at once. 'I'm waiting to hear more.'

'You're Mrs Hadley?' asked DI Boothe, surprised.

'Miss Hadley,' Sephy corrected.

Both coppers looked Sephy up and down, before turning their speculative gaze to me.

'This boy claims that your daughter is his girlfriend,' said Sergeant Kenwood.

'She is,' Sephy dismissed. 'They've been friends for years. Could someone please tell me what's going on? Tobey, your message said Callie had been shot.'

'Your daughter was caught in the crossfire during an earlier incident,' said the detective before I could reply. 'I'm just trying to ascertain the facts from this boy, who was with your daughter at the time. But he claims he didn't see a thing.'

'Tobey?' Sephy turned to me, her eyes blazing, frown lines like train tracks marring her face.

'Don't you think I would say something if I could?' I protested.

'I don't know,' said Sephy. 'Would you?'

We regarded each other. I had to force myself not to look away. We both knew the way things worked in Meadowview.

'I need to see my daughter,' Sephy said at last, turning away from me. But not before I caught the intense disappointment clouding her eyes. It stung.

'Miss Hadley, if we could ask you one or two questions first,' insisted DI Boothe.

'Your questions will have to wait. I want to see my daughter,' Sephy insisted.

'It'll just take a minute, I assure you,' said the detective. 'Could we start by confirming your address, please?'

They led the way out of the waiting room. I could see their silhouettes through the frosted-glass window, but I was too far away to hear a word. I edged closer so that I wouldn't be across the room when Sephy came looking for me. I stood near the doorway, dreading the inevitable. After a minute or two, she came back into the waiting room, alone. My heart bounced at her approach. I knew full well what was coming.

'Tobey, I don't want any crap from you,' Sephy warned me, her voice hard with intent. 'Tell me what happened. And the truth this time.'

We regarded each other. Even though I towered over her, she still scared me to death. I admit it. Sephy was a lioness trying to protect her offspring and I was getting in her way.

'It's like I told the coppers, I hit the deck and stayed there when the bullets started flying.'

'And you didn't think to pull my daughter down with you?'

'I tried. It all happened so fast,' I said feebly.

'Did you see who did the shooting?'

I didn't reply. I couldn't lie to her, but there was no way I could answer the question either.

'Tobey, I asked you a question. Who was doing the shooting?'

Silence.

'I see,' Sephy said quietly. 'You told those police officers that Callie was your girlfriend. Did you mean a girl who just happens to be your friend or did you mean something more than that?'

'I meant both,' I replied quietly.

'But not enough of a friend for you to man up and do the right thing?'

'That's not fair—'

'Fair?' Sephy leaped on the word. 'My daughter has been shot. She could *die*. Don't you dare talk to me about "fair".'

What could I say to that? Nothing. Sephy looked me up and down, her expression bathing me with complete contempt.

'You know what? Callie can do without your so-called friendship. So why don't you go home? You're no use to anyone here. Now if you'll excuse me, I'm going to find out what's happening to my daughter.'

She was already turning round and heading out of the waiting room to find the nearest doctor or nurse. I caught up with her.

'I'll come with you.'

'No, you won't, Tobey,' Sephy turned to tell me. 'If you don't think enough of my daughter to tell the police who did this to her, then I have no use for you, and neither has Callie. Go home.'

Without waiting for my reply, Sephy strode away. After a few steps, she turned back with a look in her eyes I'd never seen before.

'Oh, and Tobey?'

'Yes?'

'You're no longer welcome in my house.' Sephy regarded me to ensure I'd got the message.

'Yes, Miss Hadley.'

The Fall . . .

twenty-six

'Tobey, can I come in?' Mum's voice was soft outside my door.

I didn't answer.

'Tobey, please.'

Silence.

I heard Mum sigh, but she respected the fact that my door was firmly closed and headed back downstairs. Mum had been knocking on my bedroom door at periodic intervals all morning – ever since she'd got in from work. How I wished she'd give up and leave me alone. I sat on the floor in the corner of my room directly opposite the door. I'd been sitting there ever since I'd arrived home the night before, with one knee drawn up, the other leg flat against the carpeted floor. In my left hand, my fingers worked at the super ball I usually kept on my desk. It was the size of a large marble and decorated with swirls of different shades of green and brown. Callie had given me the thing years ago, I can't even remember why. I hadn't moved from this corner all night, only shifting positions slightly when one leg or the other threatened to go numb. I'd never watched the dawn break before. In the middle of the night, the dark seemed so dense, it was easy to believe it would perpetually paint my room.

But the grey-blue light had pushed slowly but irrevocably against every shadow until they were all but gone.

And whilst watching the arrival of dawn, I'd been thinking. I'd been thinking a lot.

Callie's mum Sephy considered me gutless, as did the police. I wasn't about to argue with them. In spite of what Sephy had said to me the night before, I'd stayed at the hospital until Callie was out of surgery. I didn't sit with Callie's mum. She made it very clear that I wasn't wanted anywhere near her. I listened on the periphery when the surgeon finally arrived to tell us what was happening. Callie had been shot twice, once in the chest and one bullet had glanced off her temple. The bullet in her chest was out, but Callie was still in a critical condition.

'Callie has lost a lot of blood and there's considerable tissue damage, so she's not out of the woods yet. The bullet that entered her chest missed her heart by about a centimetre,' said Mr Bunch, the Cross surgeon. 'And the bullet that caught her temple caused a hairline fracture of her skull, but at least the bullet didn't penetrate. However, the next forty-eight hours will be crucial.'

'Can I see her?' I stepped forward to ask.

'She'll be unconscious for quite some time,' the surgeon warned me.

'I need to see her,' I insisted.

'No,' Sephy began. 'I don't think so . . .'

'Please, Sephy. Please.'

Sephy emphatically shook her head.

'I'll camp outside Callie's room or the ward or the hospital building if I have to until you change your mind,' I said desperately. 'Please let me see her. *Please.*'

Sephy scrutinized me for several seconds. Her gaze slid away from mine and a frown appeared across her forehead. When at last she looked at me again, she nodded, albeit reluctantly. I wondered what had made her change her mind, but I wasn't about to push my luck by asking. Mr Bunch led the way to the Intensive Care Unit. Callie was in a room by herself, the closest one to the nurses' station.

Nothing could've adequately prepared me for what I was about to see. Callie Rose was hooked up to all kinds of monitors and beeping machines. She had plastic tubing running into her mouth and an IV drip, plus a blood bag running into her arm. Her head was swathed in a bandage. Her whole body seemed so much smaller, like she'd shrunk in on herself. And all the paraphernalia around her was overwhelming. She was almost lost in the middle of it all.

I walked over to her and stroked the back of her hand which lay above the white sheets. For a long time I could do nothing but look down at her. Then I bent and whispered in her ear before kissing her forehead. I straightened up slowly, unable to take my eyes off her face. She looked fragile as crystal, like one more knock and she would irrevocably shatter.

Callie Rose, forgive me . . .

I took hold of her cold hand and held it in my own, never wanting to let it go. You see it in films and on the TV all the time. Someone's in trouble, dying, and their mum or dad or partner or best mate makes all kinds of promises and begs anyone who'll listen to swap places. Well, that's what I did. I would've swapped places with Callie quicker than a thought. But no one was listening.

She remained in the bed, hooked up to all those machines. I stood beside her, helpless.

My throat had swollen up, making it difficult for me to catch my breath.

Callie, if you can hear me, please . . .

But before I could finish my silent plea, the rhythm in the room changed. Where the monitors were beeping slow and steady before, now there was just a continuous droning hum coming from them. An alarm began to sound. Suddenly the room was full and I was shoved backwards out of the way. The pillow was whipped out from beneath Callie's head as a wave of doctors and nurses appeared from nowhere to swarm over her. And a continuous flat line continued its slide across the heart monitor. Sephy tried to get closer to her daughter, but they wouldn't let her stay either. The door was closed behind both of us. Sephy watched through the small window, her fists clenched against the pane as if she wanted to batter at it. She turned to me, her dark-brown eyes blazing.

'You . . .' she hissed. If words could kill, that one accusatory word would've butchered me where I stood. 'Who did this? *Tell me!*'

I looked through the window at the doctors and nurses still trying to resuscitate Callie, before turning back to Callie's mum. What would she do if I told her? Sephy was tough – with everything she'd been through in her life, she had to be. But she was no match for the Dowds or McAuley and his hired muscle-heads. If she went after them, which she undoubtedly would, Callie would end up an orphan . . . if Callie survived. *No. When* Callie survived. She just had to make it, and so did her mum. In that moment, I made my choice.

'I can't say 'cause I don't know.' The small words were outsized and razor-sharp in my mouth.

Sephy turned away from me. At that instant I ceased to be for her. We had nothing else to say to each other. I turned away and left the ICU and the hospital.

My grip on the super ball tightened. It wasn't like in films and games and on the TV. What had happened at the Wasteland hadn't been choreographed into chaotic elegance. No make-up person had drawn in cuts and bruises. No costume person had decided which knee of which pair of jeans needed to be torn. The bullets started flying, everyone started screaming and scattering and diving to the ground. The cuts and bruises had been all too real. Torn jeans and dirt-stained clothes had happened spontaneously. And the blood on Callie hadn't been sprayed on. It'd been pumped out. There was no one to shout: 'Cut. Great take,' or 'Let's do it again. Action.' Only now, for the first time, did I truly realize what Mum meant when she kept insisting that 'Life is not a dress rehearsal'. There were no rewrites, no retakes, no re-do icon to click on. Callie had been shot. Real life was agonizingly hard to handle. Real life was just agonizing.

I couldn't get the image of Callie lying on that hospital bed out of my head. I knew I never would. No one told me that helplessness made you feel so minuscule. At school, at work, even here in my own bedroom, I occupied very little space. Was it so wrong to want just a little bit more from life? I'd convinced myself that that was what Dan had been offering. Just a little bit more than I already had. And now everything had fallen to pieces. I stayed in my room throughout the night and most of the morning, only leaving when I needed to go to the loo. I didn't eat, I didn't sleep, I couldn't think straight. Jessica and Mum left me alone for the most part. Mum put a plate of ham sandwiches outside my door, even though I'd called out after at least ten minutes of her cajoling me to eat that I wasn't hungry. To get her off my back, I even tried one, but it was like chewing a crumpled-up page of printer paper. It didn't taste of anything and it wouldn't go down. So I spat it out into my bin and gave up. I greeted the following night lying on top of my bed, staring up at my ceiling. Closing my eyes, I waited for sleep to come and get me. But it was as if a switch had been flicked on inside my head and now my brain wouldn't stop whirling.

McAuley.

It had been McAuley's car at the Wasteland. McAuley's men had walked towards us on the football pitch. McAuley's men had shot first. And the two Cross guys who'd returned fire, they had to work for the Dowds. Was the shootout planned between them? Somehow I didn't think so. If they wanted to shoot it out, they could find somewhere better than a public park. So why had both groups turned up at the Wasteland? It didn't make sense. They weren't there to kill each other. One set of gangsters had to be there for another reason entirely. And the other lot – well they were there by either luck or design. I didn't know anything about the Dowds, except by reputation. They were ruthless and deadly when crossed, just like McAuley. All I knew about McAuley were the stories about him that were common knowledge and the things I'd learned from Dan. Had McAuley's men been after Dan? That didn't make sense. Dan had been working for McAuley for ages now. Dan and his deliveries. My luck had seriously run out from the time I agreed to . . . to . . .

Deliveries.

Ross Resnick.

I'd delivered the parcel to Ross Resnick's wife, just like Dan had asked. Was that the reason McAuley came after Dan? Because Dan should've delivered the package himself?

Or maybe . . . just maybe McAuley was after me?

Had Dan told McAuley what I'd said about not taking the fall alone if the police came knocking at my door? Was that what this was all about? Did McAuley decide I was far too dangerous to him? Godsake! I'd said a lot, but I hadn't meant it. It was just a lot of angry hot air released on the spur of the moment. I mean, as if I could take on McAuley. He had to know that I couldn't touch him. But McAuley and his men had evidently decided they needed to take care of business. McAuley'd be safe and I'd be too dead to be sorry. Was McAuley after both Dan and me? Was that the idea, to kill two birds with one stone? Or maybe I was the only one who was expendable. Either way, McAuley wanted me gone. Permanently.

That was the only explanation that made sense.

The only thing I didn't understand was how the Dowd family thugs had turned up at the same time. How did they know what McAuley had planned? There was no way they would've turned up just to save my sorry hide.

They didn't know me, and even if they did, I meant less than nothing to them.

I sought out some other more rational, reasonable explanation for what had happened – but there was none. The more I thought about McAuley coming after me, the more it seemed right.

The question was, what was I going to do about it?

As long as McAuley perceived me to be a threat, I was up shit creek with both hands and feet tied. I might as well just paint a bloody great target on my back. Is that how Dan was feeling? Where was he now? Hiding out somewhere? Or did he know he wasn't the intended target? Was he going to do a runner?

At long last, after three a.m., I finally passed out. It didn't last long. A couple of hours, according to my alarm clock. And no matter how hard I tried, I just couldn't get back to sleep.

Blood running down Callie's skin, spreading out across her blue T-shirt . . .

Blood running down the side of Callie's face . . .

Callie's eyes closing as she toppled over in front of me . . .

Gunshots like fireworks exploding all around us . . .

Those were the nightmares that forced me awake. Those were the images in my head that wouldn't leave, even with my eyes open. Especially with my eyes open. There was only one thing I could do. It was so dangerous – and not just for me but for those around me – but what choice did I have?

I had two options. I could either run and never stop, or I could get McAuley, before he got me.

Get McAuley?

Get real. Why didn't I stop all the wars on the planet and cure all diseases known to humankind whilst I was at it?

Get McAuley . . .

But I had to at least try. I owed Callie that much. He had to pay for what he'd done. And it was a simple matter of McAuley or me. What was that saying about keeping your friends close and your enemies closer? Experience was the greatest teacher. I had to get close to McAuley, convince him that I wasn't a threat.

And then it would be my turn.

There was one more week left before the school term ended. Not that it mattered. One week or one month, I just couldn't go back. My plans had to be changed completely. I had other matters to take care of now. I broke out my phone and speed-dialled. It took a good twenty seconds before my call was finally answered.

'Hi, Tobey,' said Dan before I could say a word. 'How are you? You OK? That was some shit on Saturday, yeah?'

Dan's tone was all friendly concern. It took a couple of moments before I could muster up a reply.

'Dan, I need to see you.'

'We're meeting this evening for football practice, so I'll see you then,' Dan pointed out. 'And we missed you at our football match yesterday.'

After everything that'd happened, that was all he had to say to me? My grip tightened around my mobile phone.

'You do know about Callie, don't you?'

'Yeah, I know.' Dan's voice took on a more sombre timbre. I for one was glad to hear the end of his jolly, bouncy tone. 'I'm sorry.'

Sorry . . .

So much I wanted to say. So much I couldn't.

'Where're we going to meet?' I asked quietly.

'When?'

'Now.'

'Now? But it's the arse-crack of dawn. What about football practice later? Aren't you going to come?'

'Not in the mood. I've got more important matters to deal with,' I said. 'I'll meet you in twenty outside the cinema. OK?'

'But it's not even open yet—'

'Dan, I'm not inviting you to watch a film,' I snapped. 'And by the way, did you tell McAuley what I said about grassing him up if the police came knocking?'

Silence.

'Thanks a lot.'

'You sounded like you meant it,' Dan protested. 'What was I supposed to do?'

You were supposed to have my back.

'You were supposed to know I'd never do that.'

'That's what I told Mr McAuley, I swear,' Dan rushed to explain. 'I told him it was just talk.'

I shook my head. Dan still hadn't connected all the dots. He was never very good on cause and effect.

'The cinema, Dan. Twenty minutes.' I hung up, then waited to see if he would phone me back. He didn't. It was only as I stared down at the phone on my lap that I realized with a start I was still wearing the same blood-stained shirt I'd worn at the Wasteland. Callie's blood had dried into the material, which had now stuck to my skin. And I could smell it. Why couldn't I smell it before? By the time I pulled off my shirt, I was shaking. Balling it up, I dropped it in the bin by my desk, then headed for the bathroom. I stripped off the rest of my clothes and got into the bath tub before turning on the shower. I didn't do my usual of allowing the water to run warm before I even let a toe get wet. The water was freezing, but I didn't care. It didn't matter. After a couple of minutes it was hot enough. I washed my hair and soaped my body. But it didn't matter how much or how hard I scrubbed, I could still feel Callie's blood sticking to my skin.

twenty-seven

I stepped out of the house, carefully closing the door behind me. Mum was still working nights so was fast asleep, as was my sister. Just recently, Jessica always seemed to be tired. Revising for her final exam this week, maybe? I didn't want to wake up either of them. Answering questions was not at the top of my list of priorities right now. I stepped onto the pavement when a question had me whirling around.

'Excuse me, but are you Tobey Durbridge?'

A tall, willowy Cross woman with braids falling like a waterfall round her face stood in front of me.

'Yes, I am.' I frowned.

Who was this woman? I'd never seen her before in my life.

'I understand you were with Callie Rose Hadley when she got shot?' said the woman.

'Yes, I was.' My frown deepened.

The woman's eyes lit up. 'Got one!' she called out. She brought her right hand out from behind her back. She was holding a microphone. A Nought man stepped out from behind the unmarked white van parked in front of our house. He was holding a TV camera. I stared in horror as the man came straight at me.

'Who are you?' I asked, taking a step back.

'Josie Braden. Channel Nineteen News,' said the woman as if she was delivering all I should want or need to know. 'You wouldn't believe how hard it's been to find a witness to Callie Hadley's shooting.' She turned to her colleague. 'Are we up and running, Jack?'

'In a moment,' Jack replied, checking his camera. A red light appeared at the front, like a small demon's eye unblinkingly focused on me. Jack hoisted the camera onto his shoulder and started pointing the thing at Josie.

'Three. Two. One,' Josie Braden counted down before speaking into the camera lens. 'This is Josie Braden outside Callie Rose Hadley's home in Meadowview. I'm here with Callie's neighbour Tobey Durbridge, who was with Callie Rose, Kamal Hadley's granddaughter, when she got shot.' Josie turned to face me, as did Jack's camera. 'Tobey, can you tell us what happened?'

The microphone was thrust under my chin. The red eye waited for me to speak.

I said nothing. Josie looked at me expectantly.

'Excuse me,' I said before turning round and heading off in the opposite direction.

A few steps on, I turned my head. Josie drew her hand across her neck. Jack lowered his camera. They both watched me, disappointment written in capitals on their faces. I was out of there. A medieval tongue-extractor couldn't've made me speak to the press. Hopefully she'd be the first and the last reporter to try and bother me and my family. Jess and Mum didn't know anything so what could they say? And if I said nothing then what could they report? All I could do was cross my fingers and hope against hope that my face and name didn't end up plastered across the TV or in the newspapers. It wouldn't take much more than that for McAuley to firebomb my house. The saying – there's no such thing as bad publicity? Well, that was crap. In Meadowview, there most definitely was such a thing as bad publicity. The kind of publicity that could get a person deader than a roast chicken.

'I must be mad,' Dan kept muttering. 'Mr McAuley's not going to like this . . .'

Dan had been whinging ever since we'd met up and I'd told him what I needed from him, which was an audience with McAuley. I didn't bother telling him about the reporter outside my front door. Dan was worried enough as it was. I buried my hands deeper in the pockets of my denim jacket, my hands clenched so tight, my knuckles cracked.

'You're going to get us both into big trouble,' Dan said, deeply unhappy.

'I'll explain it was my idea,' I said.

'Like Mr McAuley's going to give a damn about that.

We're both going to end up buried in concrete holding up a building somewhere at this rate.'

'How much further?' I asked, changing the subject.

'The other end of this road,' said Dan.

We'd travelled by bus for a good thirty minutes to get here, but this looked like an ordinary residential street — not the sort of place where you'd expect to find business premises. I frowned at Dan, but said nothing. We kept walking. Dan finally stopped outside an end-of-terrace house with a dark-blue door. It was nothing special. A three-up, two-down. The sort of house you'd pass a hundred times a day and never notice.

'McAuley's in there?'

Dan nodded, adding, 'This is a really bad idea. You're going to get us both killed.'

'Dan, change the tune, OK?'

'No, it's not OK. Mr McAuley doesn't like surprises.'

'He asked me to work for him, remember?'

'Yes, and you turned him down.'

'Well, I've thought better of it.'

Dan looked at me.

'What?' I asked, exasperated.

'Does this have something to do with what happened to Callie? Because Mr McAuley can sniff out bullshit at fifty paces.'

'It has nothing to do with Callie and everything to do with getting what's mine,' I replied. 'I want to make a lot of money and spend it whilst I'm still young enough to enjoy it. The shooting just woke me up to a few home truths, that's all.'

'Mr McAuley is not going to believe that.'

'Do you?'

Dan shrugged. 'It doesn't matter whether I believe it or not. It's not me you have to convince.'

'It's the truth, Dan. And if McAuley doesn't want me working for him, there's always the Dowds.'

Dan looked around fearfully. 'You don't want to joke about a thing like that. Around Mr McAuley, I wouldn't even *think* it. People have died for less.'

I gave Dan a look.

'Oh hell. I'm sorry.' Dan rushed through his apology. 'I wasn't talking about . . . I'm sorry.'

I shrugged and looked around. A black van sat outside the house. It had to belong to McAuley. The plush cream-coloured leather seats were a dead giveaway. Dan took a deep breath and headed for the front door. This was it. Once I set foot in this house, there'd be no turning back. Could I do this? Really go through with this? I could turn round and walk away and have this . . . this nothing inside me for the rest of my life. No self-respect. No pride. No Callie Rose . . . Or I could enter this house and never look back. Would McAuley believe me? Only one way to find out. Dan rang the bell three times, a pause, then twice more. The choice was made. The front door was opened by a Nought guy with light-brown, shoulder-length hair tied back in a ponytail. He wore a dark-brown suit with a crisp white shirt and was built like an army tank. If he exhaled too sharply, his clothes would fall apart around him. No way was anyone getting past him without his say-so.

'Hi, Trevor. Did you miss me?' asked Dan.

Trevor looked like he'd rip off Dan's head as soon as

look at him. I hung a few steps behind Dan and looked up and down the street. This house was the perfect disguise. No one would ever guess that McAuley's illegal activities operated out of such unassuming surroundings. He had an office for running his legitimate business in West Meadowview, on the industrial estate by the old railway bridge, but I'd put money on him visiting those premises maybe twice a year, if that. And I'd also put money on this not being the only house he used for his dodgy dealings. Very clever. Mrs Bridges at the bottom of my road dealt drugs out of her house, but she also lived there. This was a much better arrangement.

Dan waved me forward to stand next to him. 'Trevor, this is my mate, Tobey. Mr McAuley knows him.'

Mr I-Love-Steroids looked me up, down and sideways. He finally stepped aside to let us pass, but not without patting both of us down first. Godsake! What did he think I was packing? An Uzi? Dan headed into the first room on the right. A huge flat-screen TV sat on the wall like a piece of contemporary artwork. Two black leather sofas sat self-consciously facing each other on the hardwood floor. I chose to stand, as did Dan.

'So what happens now?' I asked Dan.

'We wait here until McAuley sends for us.'

A strange scraping noise sounded from overhead, like a chair being dragged across the floor. One bang and what sounded like a muffled groan later, and all was quiet.

'What was that?' I asked, pointing at the ceiling.

'Don't know – and don't want to know,' Dan replied.

I took the hint and refrained from saying anything else. After all, the room might've been wired for sound, for all

I knew. I wouldn't put anything past McAuley. My stomach twisted like an angry snake. In the history of bad ideas, this had to be the worst. There was no way this would work. But I had to do it. I had no choice. One minute turned into five before another muscle-head, bald this time, entered the room. He and Dan exchanged a cursory nod.

'All right, Byron?' Dan asked.

Byron didn't answer. He beckoned us forward. We passed through the small kitchen and out into a lean-to conservatory which held a small antique desk and two large potted plants. McAuley sat behind the desk in a huge burgundy leather high-backed chair like a king on his throne. There were two piles of papers on his left, a laptop in the middle of the desk and a cup of what smelled like fresh mint tea to the right of the laptop. Ignoring Dan, he looked directly at me.

'Tobey Durbridge . . . You're the last person I would've expected to come knocking at my door. What can I do for you?'

I took a deep breath. 'I wondered if your offer of work still stands?'

McAuley regarded me for at least half a minute. No one else in the room spoke or even moved a muscle. I forced myself to meet McAuley's gaze without flinching.

'Why're you here, Tobey?'

'For a job, sir.'

'Sir? Still so polite.' McAuley leaned forward. 'That's one of the things I like about you, Tobias Sebastian Durbridge. Always so polite.'

He'd been checking up on me. How else would he

know my middle name? I never told anyone – and I mean *anyone* – my middle name. Dan didn't know it. Even Callie didn't know it. McAuley had been checking up on me, and what's more, he wanted me to know it. But that was OK. McAuley was watching me for my reaction. I met his gaze and didn't even blink. I had to convince him that I had nothing to hide. Byron, McAuley's bodyguard, stood at his side, making no attempt to hide the gun in his hand. Byron might've been a big bloke, but I didn't doubt that his reflexes would be viper-fast.

'So you want a job? I seem to remember that you weren't interested,' McAuley continued.

'I've changed my mind, sir. I need the money.'

'What's changed between now and last week?'

'Reality has set in.' I shrugged.

'Now why don't I believe you?' McAuley was a study in stillness as he scrutinized me.

I opened my mouth to argue, then decided against it. McAuley was no fool. The worst – and last – mistake I could make would be to underestimate him. I shrugged again.

'In your shoes, I wouldn't believe me either,' I said.

McAuley sat back and smiled. 'At last, something we both agree on.'

I nodded slowly. 'Fair enough, Mr McAuley. I just thought I'd offer my services. I'm sorry to have wasted your time.'

I turned and headed for the door.

'How's your girlfriend? What's her name again? Callie Rose?'

'She's not my girlfriend,' I replied, still heading for the door.

'Wait,' McAuley ordered.

I turned round to face him. He beckoned me over and pointed to the spot where I'd been standing next to Dan. I walked back to my previous position. I felt like a naughty school kid made to stand in front of the head. No doubt that was just what McAuley was aiming for.

'Why d'you need money?' he asked.

'To get out of this place,' I replied. 'Out of Meadowview.'

McAuley's eyes widened. I'd succeeding in surprising him.

'To get away from people like me?' he asked softly with the merest hint of a smile.

'Yes, sir,' I replied without hesitation.

There was no mistaking the horrified gasp that came from Dan beside me.

'You don't harbour any dreams of being just like me when you're older?'

'No, sir.'

McAuley leaned forward over his desk, his index fingers touching at the tips to form a peak which he then tapped against his lips. Several seconds passed.

'You don't like me very much, do you, Tobey?'

'No, sir.'

Dan was staring at me like I'd lost every bit of my mind.

'But you're willing to take my money?'

'To earn it, sir.'

McAuley started to laugh. 'I like you, Tobey Sebastian Durbridge.'

I said nothing.

'So what are you prepared to do for me?' he asked.

'Whatever will make me the most money in the shortest amount of time.'

'And why should I trust you?'

'Because I'm loyal, hardworking, I do as I'm told. And I know when to keep my mouth shut.'

'It appears that you do,' McAuley agreed. 'But loyalty is the most important thing to me.'

'I understand, sir.'

'I hope you do,' said McAuley. 'Because if I find out that you – or anyone else who works for me – is abusing my trust, there will be no second chances.'

I got the message, loud and clear.

'If you give me a chance, I won't let you down,' I replied.

McCauley looked up at Byron, who was still at his side, and nodded. Byron carefully placed his gun on the desk, then sauntered towards us. *Trouble.* I watched Byron approach, knowing that danger was only a couple of steps away – and counting down. McAuley hadn't believed a word I'd said and if I left this place in one whole, living piece it would be a bona fide miracle. Cold sweat pricked my back and my armpits. What was Byron going to do? Kill me where I stood? What did McAuley expect me to do? Fight? Beg? What?

'Mr McAuley, I can vouch for Tobey. He's a good guy,' Dan said quickly before Byron reached us.

It was a valiant try, but everyone in the room knew that Dan was wasting his breath. I turned to look at McAuley. If I was going down, it would be facing him like a man. Byron stepped behind Dan and me. I held my breath. But to my surprise, I wasn't Byron's target. Byron grabbed hold of Dan's arms and pulled them back. Dan cried out in surprise and more than a little fear. He struggled to get free, but he was wasting his time. He wasn't going anywhere. A couple of quick yanks on his arms were enough to make him yell out in pain, but it had the desired effect. Dan kept still, whilst Byron stood directly behind him, still pulling back his arms. I turned back to McAuley, who was watching me intently.

McAuley pointed to the gun Byron had left on his desk. 'Pick it up.'

I moved forward to do as I was told. The stock was warm where Byron had been holding it and the gun was unexpectedly heavy. I adjusted my grip, keeping my finger well away from the trigger.

'D'you know what kind of weapon that is?' McAuley asked me.

It was a M1911 Series 70, single action, semiautomatic handgun, with a single stacked magazine that took seven .45 calibre ACP bullets, plus one in the chamber – that's if the thing hadn't been modified to take more.

'It's a gun, sir,' I replied.

'You know your stuff!' said McAuley dryly. 'That particular gun happens to be a classic. I keep telling Byron that he should use a more modern firearm, but that gun is one of his favourites.'

Why was he telling me all this? Like I gave a damn which toys Byron liked to play with.

'That particular gun is loaded with point four five calibre, non-expanding, Teflon-coated ball ammunition,' McAuley told me. 'I have the bullets made especially for me.'

I went to lay the thing back down on the table.

'Tobey, do something for me,' said McAuley silkily. 'Point that gun at Dan and shoot him.'

I must've misheard. 'Pardon?'

'You heard me,' said McAuley.

He picked up his cup of mint tea and started sipping it. The gun sat awkwardly in my hand as I looked from Dan back to McAuley. 'You want me to . . . ?'

'Kill your friend.' McAuley's voice was soft and slick as melted butter.

Dan stared at McAuley, horror-stricken. He struggled against Byron's python grip in earnest now, but there was no way Byron was letting him go.

'Well, Tobey?' said McAuley.

'Mr McAuley, please,' Dan pleaded. 'I work for you. I'm a good worker.'

'You brought a stranger to my house unannounced and uninvited,' McAuley turned to snap at him. 'Into *my* house. You never, *ever* bring anyone here without my permission, Dan. For that alone, you need sorting.'

'I'm sorry, Mr McAuley. I messed up,' Dan cried out. 'Tobey's my friend. And you offered him a job. I didn't think it'd do any harm.'

'You didn't think – full stop. You're a fool, Dan, and that makes you a liability,' McAuley replied. 'Tobey, either shoot him or give me the gun so I can take care of business.'

Would I be included in his 'business'?

Probably.

I looked at Dan, who was shaking his head frantically at me. The gun in my hand was so heavy. My dad had taught me about guns, before he left. He used to buy all kinds of gun magazines and he'd sit me on his lap as we looked at the photos and read the specifications together. Before he took off. But Dad would never have dreamed of having a gun in our house or anywhere near it – not a real one. He had a couple of replicas, but he said it was to study the engineering behind them. The last time he disappeared, Mum put the replicas in the bin. That's when I knew he wasn't coming back. And now I had a real gun in my hand, loaded with real bullets.

Slowly I raised my hand, pointing the gun straight at Dan's head.

'Tobey, no. I'm begging you. Don't . . . *Please* . . .' Dan fought like a wild thing to get out of Byron's grasp, but it was futile.

Though his lips were a thin immovable slash across his face, I could tell Byron was enjoying himself by the gleam in his green eyes.

'Tobey . . . no . . .' Tears streamed down Dan's face. A dark stain began to spread across the crotch of his light-blue jeans.

Sorry, Dan. I lowered my gaze, trying to get it together. My arm fell to my side. The gun was heavy, so very heavy.

Stretch out my arm.

Hold the gun steady.

If I'm wrong, if I've got it wrong . . .

Take aim, Tobey.

I raised my arm to aim the gun directly at Dan's heart.

'TOBEY, NO!' Dan screamed out.

Legs slightly apart, body braced, I concentrated on just one face.

And I pulled the trigger.

Nothing happened. Just a click. It dry-fired. No bang. No boom. No gun recoil. Just a click. The loudest click in the world. I hardly heard it over the sound of my heart racing like a jet engine. Byron released Dan, who fell at his feet in a crumpled heap, still sobbing.

I turned to McAuley, turning the gun round to hand it back to him by the stock. The slide hadn't even gone back when I'd fired. 'This gun doesn't work.'

'That gun doesn't have any bullets in it,' McAuley informed me. He took the gun from me, placing it on the table. He took another sip of his tea, as we regarded each other over his cup.

'You definitely remind me of me,' said McAuley. 'I'll have to keep my eyes on you.'

'Do I get to work for you now, sir?' I asked.

McAuley took out a phone from the top drawer of his desk and handed it to me along with a charger. He turned to Dan, looking down on him with utter contempt. 'Dan, you're lucky you're still useful to me, but if you mess up again . . .' McAuley turned back to me. 'Keep that phone with you at all times. I'll be in touch. Now get out and take your friend with you.'

twenty-eight

McAuley wouldn't even let Dan use the bathroom first to tidy himself up. Byron saw to it that we were out of McAuley's house less than thirty seconds later. It was weird leaving the house, like stepping out of reality into a fantasy world full of sunshine and promises, a world that felt fake and insincere. A world of people who didn't know the likes of McAuley existed, mainly because they didn't want to know. Ignorance provided countless nights of uninterrupted sleep in a way that knowledge never did. Once the front door was shut behind us, I took a deep breath, then another, and another. I'd entered the lion's den and got out in one piece. This time . . . So why wasn't my heart battering its way out of my chest? Why wasn't I puking my guts out? Maybe because my mind was racing ahead, whilst my body and my heart were stuck in the Wasteland with Callie. God help me when they caught up with each other. But until then, I had things to do. I pulled off my T-shirt and handed it to Dan.

'You can tie that round your waist,' I told him. The front of his trousers around the zip was still conspicuously dark blue.

Dan smacked my hand away. I couldn't blame him. He wiped his hands over his face, but didn't look at me. With each step away from McAuley, Dan's fear cooled and his rage towards me grew ever hotter. I could feel it radiating from him. There was an eruption coming. I put my T-shirt back on as Dan didn't want it. We turned the corner of the street and the explosion happened.

Dan shoved me against a wall and pinned me there, his forearm against my throat. 'You rotten bastard. You tried to *kill* me.'

'No, I didn't,' I replied as calmly as I could. 'The gun wasn't loaded.'

Dan pushed down harder on my throat. 'You didn't know that.'

'Yes, I d–did.' It was hard to get the words out with his arm pressed against my larynx. 'I knew it was a t–test.' If he didn't move and soon, I'd have to move him. My throat was beginning to hurt.

Dan's arm relaxed on my throat, but only slightly. 'How did you know?' Though his arm had relaxed, his expression hadn't.

'Byron was standing right behind you.'

'So?' Dan hissed at me, his spit spraying my face.

'McAuley said the gun was loaded with point four five calibre, non–expanding, ball ammunition.'

'So what?'

'If I fired the M1911 at that range, that kind of ammo would've gone straight through your body and probably straight through Byron's too. McAuley might not care about your sorry arse, but he wouldn't risk losing his minder that way. I knew it had to be a bluff.'

Dan stared at me. He slowly let go of me and stood back. But he wasn't happy. Far from it.

'You could've warned me.'

'How? McAuley and that Byron guy were standing right there. I had no choice but to do what I was told.'

'Suppose you'd been wrong?' Dan snapped.

'But I wasn't.'

'But suppose you had been?'

'But I wasn't.'

'You could've killed me,' Dan said, his eyes boring into mine.

'But I didn't.'

Casting one last fulminating look in my direction, Dan carried on walking. I fell into step next to him. I buried my hands in my trouser pockets and kept my eyes straight ahead. I was very aware of the filthy looks Dan kept giving me.

'What happened to Callie wasn't my fault,' he said belligerently.

'I never said otherwise.'

'But you blame me.'

'Dan, this is pointless,' I sighed. 'It was just one of those unforeseen things, that's all.'

'I didn't know what was in that package you delivered to Louise Resnick,' said Dan. 'I swear I didn't.'

I didn't reply.

'I know you don't believe me, but it's the truth,' he insisted.

'What makes you think I don't believe you?' I frowned.

'The look in your eyes when you pulled that trigger . . .' Dan was looking at me like he'd never seen me before. His words made me start.

'Dan, you're wrong. Besides, no one forced me to deliver those packages. It was my idea.'

And though we fell back to walking beside each other, each step took us further apart.

'Dan, you've got to believe me,' I tried. 'I knew the gun was either not loaded or else it had blanks in it. Besides, if our positions were reversed, are you telling me you wouldn't have pulled the trigger?'

'Don't you dare turn this round on me,' Dan raged. 'The point is, our positions weren't reversed.'

'You're the one who said—' I bit back the rest. No good could come from finishing that sentence.

'What?'

'Nothing.'

Damn, this was so hard. In the space of a few minutes, everything had changed between us. In the space of a few days, everything had changed between us. But I still had to rely on his friendship. I had no choice.

'Dan, will you do something for me?' I asked at last.

'I want to do bugger all for you,' Dan retorted. 'Except maybe kick your head in.'

'But you'll do this for me anyway.' I smiled faintly.

'What is it?'

'If anything happens to me, make sure my mum and sister are safe. OK?'

Dan didn't reply. I risked a glance at him. He met my gaze. Neither of us was smiling. Not even close.

'D'you promise?' I asked.

'Yeah,' he said at last. 'I promise.'

Two Nought girls of about our age or maybe a bit older walked towards us. Dan sidestepped, to walk slightly behind me, still conscious of the state of his jeans. The girls looked Dan and me up and down as they passed before turning to each other and giggling. Why do girls do that? Is it meant to make them seem more interesting? Attractive? 'Cause if so, then it misses by several kilometres. It just made them seem like airheads. Once they'd passed, Dan fell into step next to me again, not saying a word. The normal Dan would never have let two fit girls pass by without trying to get their mobile phone digits at the very least. His hands hung with false nonchalance over the dark patch at his groin. We approached a small parade of shops when I had an idea.

'Wait here,' I said to Dan, before popping into the newsagent. I bought two big bottles of water. Outside the shop, I grinned at Dan as I showed him the bottles. He frowned at me. I handed one bottle to him before unscrewing the top of the other one. I splashed the water over Dan's shirt and jeans.

'What the hell are you playing at?' Dan hopped about like the water was boiling. He tried to snatch the bottle away from me, but I wouldn't let him.

'The best way to hide one stain is amongst many,' I said.

He stopped dancing about after that, having finally clicked what I was doing. He wasn't happy, but he let me carry on. Once one bottle was empty, we swapped and I doused him with the second one. I clamped my lips together as I poured water over his head. The next thing I knew, we were both howling with laughter. People walking by gave us a wide berth – no doubt they thought we were both barking. By the time I'd finished, Dan was dripping wet with barely a dry patch anywhere on his clothes. His dark-blond hair was now darker and plastered to his head like a swimming cap. We looked at each other, and our laughter faded to nothing. Dan walked to the side of the pavement, put his hands on his knees to steady himself and vomited up his last ten meals. I watched him and there was nothing I could do. When he'd finally finished, he used the last remaining drops of water in my bottle to rinse out his mouth before spitting the lot onto the pavement.

'All right now?' I asked.

Dan's expression gave me the answer to that one. 'Tell me something, Tobey,' he began quietly. 'What would you have done if you had known the gun had real bullets in it?'

Dan and I looked at each other. How could I possibly answer that question?

'I don't know,' I replied. And that was the truth.

Dan nodded slowly but said nothing.

We headed for the bus stop.

twenty-nine

'Naturally I deeply regret that my granddaughter was shot. I will of course be praying for her,' said Kamal Hadley.

'But will you be visiting her?' asked one of the forest of journalists standing around him.

'I would sincerely hope that this current government keeps its promise and tackles the growing problem of gun and knife crime on our streets. If my granddaughter can get caught up in this, then anyone's child could find themselves in a similar situation. This government lacks the will, the expertise and, quite frankly, the guts to do anything about this situation. The people of this country need to rise up and reclaim the streets from the scum blighting all our live . . .'

'Yes, but will you be visiting Callie Rose in hospital?' The same reporter repeated his question.

'I have nothing further to say at this time.' Kamal smiled apologetically. 'I need to be with my family. Thank you.'

Kamal Hadley slipped back into his house, leaving the journalists outside barking more questions at him. I turned off the TV, my expression set like concrete. What a scumbag. There was no way he was going to set foot in Mercy Community Hospital, but he was so slick he'd implied otherwise. No doubt he saw this as his way of getting back into the political arena, in spite of the fact that it was mainly thanks to him that his party had crashed so humiliatingly in the general election a few months before. Callie had told me all about her grandfather. About the way he threw Sephy out of his house when she was pregnant with Callie. And how he'd slammed the door in Callie's face the one and only time she had tried to see him.

But I must admit, watching Kamal Hadley had been instructive. The way he held himself, the way he met the gaze of everyone who spoke to him like he had nothing to hide, the way he lowered his tone when asked a difficult question to indicate the depth of his sincerity. Callie's granddad was a true master of fake sincerity and subtle manipulation. I could learn a lot, just by watching him.

thirty

'OK, Tobey, why should this establishment hire you?' Mr Thomas, the deputy manager, glanced down at his watch as he waited for my reply.

This establishment . . . Godsake! What was wrong with calling it TFTM like everyone else?

Mr Thomas was a slight man, bald as an egg and shorter than me by at least a head, neck and shoulders. He wasn't exactly skinny, more like wiry. His dark-brown dome glistened like it'd been rubbed with oil or something. And in the space of fifteen minutes, the man must've glanced at me twice — if that.

After what had happened with McAuley and Dan a few days ago, I'd spent every spare moment during the rest of the week on the Internet and at the library. I'd barely been at home — hardly even noticed Mum going to work and back, or Jess heading off to take her exams. I needed infor-mation — as much of it as I could get. And from what I could tell from my research (which included frying my brain by reading celebrity and gossip magazines), the best way to get close to the Dowds was via TFTM, one of the top three restaurants in the city.

So on Saturday, I'd headed into town and filled in an application form for a job at TFTM. On the same day, they'd asked me to take what they called 'proficiency' tests, which consisted of English, maths and general knowledge. The tests were multiple choice and each was supposed to take thirty minutes. I finished them in half that time, but I wasn't stupid enough to broadcast the fact. TFTM, or Thanks For The Memories, as those with time on their tongues called it, struck me as the kind of place which wanted its employees to be only just smart enough. Too smart would not be welcomed. That was two days ago. This morning, overcast and early, I'd been invited in for a final interview.

Mr Thomas glanced up to glare at me with impatience. What was his question again? Oh, yeah!

'Well, sir, I'm a fast learner, I'm reliable and I'm a hard worker. And I worked in a restaurant during the summer holidays last year so I do have some experience.'

Which was the truth, just not the whole truth. But he didn't need to know that all I did for that job was clear tables and mop floors.

Mr Thomas flicked through the papers on his desk and didn't even bother to look at me. He must've heard the same reply a thousand times before. Of course he had. This was TFTM, one of the most exclusive restaurants in town. It consisted of a restaurant on the ground floor and a club called The Club (very ingenious – someone put a lot of thought into that one) on the first floor, accessible via a separate entrance and rumoured to have its own secret exit, to ensure that its famous clientele didn't have to deal with hangers-on or the paparazzi. The only way to get to the Club from the restaurant was via the kitchens at the back of the building. What it boiled down to was that no one was getting into the Club without an invitation. TFTM actively promoted the feeling of not needing anyone's patronage, no matter how famous – which of course made it *the* place to be. Not that anyone had shown me around yet. What I knew, I'd learned from reading local authority planning permission requests and building reports, reviews, celebrity gossip and basically anything and everything I could find about the place.

TFTM definitely needed no one.

I definitely needed TFTM.

I needed a job in this place like I needed to breathe.

Mr Thomas still wasn't looking at me. I needed to do something, say something to get this man to remember my name. I continued, 'Mr Thomas, I'd be perfect for TFTM because I do my homework and I know how to keep my mouth shut.'

Mr Thomas's head snapped up at that, his expression speculative. For the first time since this whole excruciating interview began, I had his full attention. First McAuley, now him. They were all interested in workers who knew how to keep their lips glued together.

'What d'you mean – you do your homework?' asked Mr Thomas.

'I looked up TFTM on the Internet before I came for this interview.'

Mr Thomas sat back in his chair, looking distinctly unimpressed. 'And what was the most remarkable thing you found out about us on the Internet?'

'I knew your restaurant was one of the best – that's why I really want to work here – but I didn't realize that the restaurant had achieved its third Michelin star earlier this year. Only five restaurants in the entire country can boast three Michelin stars.' I cranked up the enthusiasm and the wide-eyed admiration, wondering if I was overdoing it.

Mr Thomas's expression visibly relaxed. 'Oh, I see. You have ambitions in that area yourself?'

I nodded vigorously. 'I'd like to own my own place one day. Oh, nothing as fancy as this, but maybe a little bistro or a bed and breakfast on the coast somewhere. Who knows?'

'Indeed. Who knows?' Mr Thomas couldn't hide his condescending smirk.

'So I reckon a number of years at TFTM will teach me everything I need to know about starting my own . . . establishment. Just give me a chance, Mr Thomas. I won't let you down.'

'Hmm . . .' Mr Thomas glanced down again at my application form and my test results. 'OK, Tobey, you've got the job. When can you start?'

A smile of pure relief split my face – and most of it was genuine. 'Is tomorrow night too soon?'

'Tomorrow will be fine. You will work from Tuesday to Saturday and have Sundays and Mondays off. Your hours will be from six p.m. till one in the morning with two breaks to be negotiated with your supervisor, Michelle. You'll need to wear black trousers and a long-sleeved white shirt which you'll have to provide yourself. They are to be neat and clean at all times. We will provide you with a bow tie and two waistcoats. You will be responsible for keeping your waistcoats clean. If you lose them, the cost of any replacements will be taken from your salary. Your pay will be minimum wage, but what you make in tips you get to keep. And if you do well, the tips are excellent. Any questions?'

Tons of them. Like where was Ross Resnick, the manager of TFTM? Nothing had been seen of him in over two weeks, or rather only his little finger had put in an appearance. The rest of Ross Resnick had disappeared into what was generally suspected to be a McAuley-manufactured black hole. And how about the Dowds? How did they feel about the disappearance of their manager? After all, it was common knowledge that the Dowds owned TFTM. What were they doing about ensuring Ross Resnick's safe return? Any questions? What a joke.

I shook my head.

'Arrive at five-thirty tomorrow for orientation. Ask for Michelle – she'll tell you everything you need to know.' Mr Thomas stood up, indicating that the interview was over. He stretched out his hand which I shook with zeal. All this for a frickin' job as a waiter. Still, it was worth it. I'd got the job. I was in – and one step closer to my goal.

I started at TFTM on Tuesday night, after assuring Mum that it was only a holiday job and certainly not permanent. By the end of my Saturday shift, I ached in places I didn't know I had places. Ankles, calves, thighs, bum, the soles of my feet, even between my fingers – they were all screaming with fatigue and pain. I spent my evenings whizzing round like I had a rocket up my backside, as did all the serving staff, but some of the punters still complained that the service wasn't fast enough. My mouth more than ached from smiling when some jackass or other threw a casual insult my way, or complained that their food was cold when they were the ones who sat talking and ignoring their food for twenty minutes before picking up their bloody cutlery to eat. Zara, a Nought waitress in her mid-twenties who'd taken me under her wing, had been at TFTM for almost three years. And she swore each day would be her last. But it never was, for one simple reason.

'The money is too good. So I bite my lip and dodge and weave every time some git makes a grab for my arse or my tits,' Zara told me during one of our fifteen-minute breaks. I watched as she took off her shoes and massaged the balls of her feet. And I listened. When I was in the restaurant serving, as well as during the breaks, I did more of that than anything else. I listened.

'Some of the regular punters think that T&A comes free with their dessert,' Zara had continued with disgust. 'That's why we girls call this place Thanks For The Mammaries. On my last day here, an awful lot of customers are going to get the face slapping they deserve.'

Mr Thomas had been right. The tips were excellent. I made about three times more at TFTM each night than I ever did selling phones. Not that that was the reason I was so keen to work there, but it certainly didn't hurt.

There were two sets of changing rooms, male and female, and all levels of staff shared the same changing areas, but the staff who worked in the club upstairs rarely deigned to speak to us lowly serving staff from the restaurant. And I couldn't help noticing that most of the serving staff downstairs were Noughts, whereas most of the Club staff were Crosses.

I pulled off my bow tie and rainbow-coloured waistcoat and was just hanging up the latter in my locker when

Michelle the supervisor entered the men's changing rooms unannounced. A couple of guys had to grab for their towels to cover their jewels, but they never said a word. Not one person protested. It was obviously a regular occurrence.

'Angelo, we're short-staffed in the Club tomorrow so you'll be upstairs along with . . .' Michelle had a quick look around. 'Keith, and you as well, Tobey.'

'But I don't work on Sundays,' I said.

'You do now,' said Michelle.

TFTM was closed on Sundays. What was going on?

'We have a private party going on in the club from ten tomorrow till late,' Michelle explained.

'But Sunday is—' I began my protest.

'You'll get triple time, if that's what you're worried about,' Michelle interrupted with irritation. 'Now is there still a problem?'

'Whose party is it?' I asked.

'Rebecca Dowd.'

My stomach tightened, like a hand was squeezing my insides. Rebecca Dowd . . . Wiping all expression off my face, I asked, 'Who's she?'

Michelle's eyes widened. And she wasn't the only one. I was getting significant looks from everyone who'd heard the question.

'Vanessa Dowd's daughter? The sister of Gideon and Owen Dowd? Do those names ring any bells?'

The blank look on my face was obviously convincing. Michelle's expression morphed into one of pity. 'Damn it, Tobey, don't you know anything?'

'I'm here to learn.' I shrugged.

'Just be here at nine-thirty tomorrow night,' Michelle ordered.

'How will I get home?' I asked.

'Not my problem.' Michelle headed out as Angelo shook his head and Keith looked particularly hacked off.

Me? I was ecstatic. A late-night party on Sunday night running into the early hours of Monday morning meant I'd have one hell of a job getting back home. If I couldn't catch a night bus back to Meadowview I was in for a two-and-a-half-hour walk. But I didn't care.

I was going to meet the Dowds.

thirty-one

'Callum, I need your help. Yours too, Mum. If either of you are out there, somewhere, please watch over Callie. Please don't let my daughter slip away. I know it isn't written anywhere that life is supposed to be fair, but please keep Callie safe. And here. Meggie has been through so much. So have I. Taking Callie away from me wouldn't be fair. I know I'm being selfish, but I don't care.

'Callum, bring our daughter back. Her body is still here, but not the rest of her. The doctors are baffled as to why she hasn't woken up yet. One doctor asked me if Callie is a fighter. I put her right on that one. Of course our daughter is a fighter. Callum, you mustn't let her forget that. Remind her of all the things she has waiting for her in this life. Remind her just how much I love her.

'Mum, I miss your humour and your practical advice. I miss you. I talk to Callie every day. I tell her all the news and talk about things gone and things to come. I don't even know if she can hear the things I say, but I say them anyway. But if she can't hear me, I know she'll hear you. Send her back to me, Mum.

'Please.

'*Please . . .*'

I leaned against the wall, my head bent as Sephy's words trailed away into tears. I'd thought that at this time on a Sunday afternoon, I'd get to see Callie with no interruptions. But her mum had beaten me to it. When I arrived, the nurse at the nurses' station buzzed me onto the ward, then promptly disappeared before the door had shut behind me. Heading towards Callie's room, I'd heard Sephy before I saw her – and before she saw me. Her words were quietly spoken, but the ICU was quieter, just the hum of machines and the regular beep of the monitor coming at me from the middle distance like so much background noise. Maybe I shouldn't have stood outside Callie's room and listened to her mum, but I did. Part of me wanted to head into the room and share how we were both feeling, but that was impossible. Two of the nurses were heading back to their station. Decision time. I closed my eyes briefly.

Until tomorrow, Callie.

Time to leave.

thirty-two

On Sunday evening, all us waiters (no waitresses, just Michelle supervising) were taken into the Club fifteen minutes before the first guests arrived. We were told the schedule for the night and assigned to different parts of the Club.

'Tobey, you'll be circulating around the leisure area with various drinks,' Michelle informed me. 'Anyone who wants a specific order will have to go to the bar. Make sure your tray is never empty. You can take one ten-minute break at midnight and that's it.'

I nodded, only vaguely aware of what she was saying. I was still trying to take in everything. This was my first chance to see the Club – and it was something else. I'd never seen anything like it. Statues in various states of undress adorned the alcoves around the main room and the ceiling was draped with red, orange and yellow silk. There was a huge dance floor lit up with multi-coloured underfloor lighting to the left. Opposite, on the other side of the room, was the bar and beyond that the small kitchen which served snacks – or, as they called them up here, canapés. Dotted around the dance floor were tables and chairs, with sofas hugging the walls around the rest of the room. It smelled of flowers though I couldn't see a flower in sight. I went to the bar to get my first tray of drinks.

'Man, I hope you're wearing your titanium underwear,' Angelo whispered to me.

'What d'you mean?' I frowned.

'You'll find out,' said Angelo grimly.

The first guests began to arrive and the party officially started. I got Angelo to point out Rebecca for me. She was shorter than I expected, about five feet three or four and not exactly skinny but sure heading that way. She wore her hair in thin locks down to her shoulders and her make-up looked a bit overdone, but what did I know? She was wearing a sleeveless red dress with matching red high-heeled sandals and she looked stunning. The dress had a V at the front and the back and the skirt flowed around her thighs every time she moved. Even from across the room, her diamond earrings twinkled, as did the rocks around her neck. Happy eighteenth birthday! I took in every aspect of her appearance, drinking in her face – her cat-like dark eyes set slightly too wide apart, her burgundy lips, her high forehead. A tall but stocky Cross guy walked over to Rebecca and put his arm around her shoulders. She smiled up at him in amusement. He smiled down at her with genuine affection, the creases around his eyes deepening. He had to be thirty? Maybe thirty-two.

'Who's the guy with his arm around her shoulder?' I asked Angelo.

'That's her brother, Gideon, and don't let him catch you staring at his sister,' Angelo warned me. 'And I'll tell you something else. Gideon is a mean one, but he's a teddy bear compared to his younger brother, Owen.'

'Why? What's Owen like?'

'Ambitious. Focused. Ruthless.'

'Where is he? Is he here tonight?'

'He's the one in the blue suit who just walked in.' Angelo pointed discreetly.

I tried to get a good look at Owen, but only caught a glimpse before Rebecca hugged him. The place was beginning to fill up so it was tricky to get more than a partial view. I walked a couple of steps forward to get a better look, memorizing his face before I headed back to the bar.

'Why the interest in Gideon and Owen?' Angelo asked.

'I don't want to get into trouble by stepping on the wrong toes,' I replied.

Apparently Vanessa Dowd wasn't going to be present. Angelo told me that she very rarely ventured out of her house. From what he said, Vanessa Dowd sounded like a puppet-master, working from on high and pulling everyone's strings, including those of her own family. Especially those of her own family. It was time to get to work. I turned back to the bar to retrieve my tray and headed for the crowd that was growing by the second.

By midnight, Rebecca Dowd's eighteenth birthday party was in full swing. The music was blaring, the Club was heaving and most of the guests were already off their heads. Canapés and finger foods were doing the rounds, but the food wasn't as popular as the drink. My job was to weave in and out of the crowd with a tray full of assorted drinks, allowing empty glasses to be swapped for full ones. Every time my tray contained more empty glasses than full ones, I had to head back to the bar for more drinks. No one had to pay for a thing. Food and drink were on the house – or rather, on the Dowds. Looking around, I figured there had to be close to one hundred people in the Club – mostly Crosses, but at least a fifth of those present were Noughts. I wondered how many of them were Rebecca Dowd's real friends. My guess was ten or less.

Within the space of an hour my bum had been pinched purple and there wasn't a centimetre of my body that hadn't been thoroughly groped. Now I understood Angelo's titanium underwear warning. But my pockets were also being stuffed with money – amongst other things, like a few phone numbers. I didn't feel the least bit guilty about the money. Way I saw it, I was earning it and then some. When at last midnight rolled around, my head was pounding and I was about ready to drop. It was my break time so it was now or never. I weaved through the crowds, seeking my quarry. At last I found him, leaning against a closed door. Taking a deep breath, I walked straight up to him.

'Mr Dowd, may I speak to you?' I had to really raise my voice to be heard.

'About what?' Owen Dowd frowned.

'Alex McAuley.'

That got his attention. 'What about him?'

'May I speak to you in private?'

Owen Dowd looked at me, really looked at me.

'It'll be worth five minutes of your time,' I said. 'I promise.'

Owen took a key out of his jacket pocket and unlocked the door behind him. Once the door was open, he waved me in ahead of him. He wasn't taking any chances. I walked in and spun round immediately. I wasn't taking any chances either. Owen switched on the light and shut the door behind him with an ominous click. The sounds of the Club stopped immediately, like a radio being switched off. The room had to be soundproofed. I glanced around. It was a tiny office, with a poster-sized window behind an undersized desk. The window was covered with a dark-grey vertical blind which was shut. On the desk were scattered a few sand-coloured folders and a desktop computer sat self-consciously on one side. The floor was carpeted, a navy-blue carpet which made the room look even smaller.

'Now then, what's your name?' asked Owen.

'Tobey Durbridge,' I replied.

'So what's all this about?' said Owen. 'And it'd better be good or you're going to find yourself out of a job.'

So without wasting any more time, I told him.

I only had five minutes left of my break. The restaurant was closed and I didn't fancy chatting to anyone in the changing rooms, so I headed up the stairs to the flat roof, hoping fervently that the door would be open. It was.

The moment I stepped outside, I breathed a huge sigh of relief. After the heated chaos of the Club and the atmosphere in the air there, up here was cool and fresh. The air-conditioning unit sat hulking in the middle of the roof, growling away like some great wounded animal. I walked to the nearest edge to peer over the side. Beneath my feet, I could feel the music thumping, vibrating through my body. I looked up. The stars were the furthest away they'd ever been. I looked down. Two storeys down to the ground. The longer I stared, the closer the pavement seemed to get. But I didn't want to look away. This was better than looking up and only seeing Callie looking down at me, blood spilling over her chest. Better this than closing my eyes and seeing Callie in the hospital as the nurses and doctors fought to bring her back to life.

'Are you going to jump?'

The woman's voice had me spinning round. It was Rebecca Dowd, standing beside the air-conditioning unit. How long had she been up here? I stared at her like I'd lost my mind. Rebecca smiled, amused at my goldfish impersonation. I snapped my lips together and tried to look like my IQ was greater than my shoe size.

'Sorry,' I said ruefully. 'You took me by surprise.'

'You're not going to jump, are you?' Rebecca sounded worried.

'The thought hadn't crossed my mind, no.'

'Good.' Rebecca breathed a huge sigh of relief. 'Because I'd have to try and talk you out of it and I'm useless at that kind of thing.'

'Fair enough.' I smiled, and looked up at the night sky again, drinking in the peace above before I had to head back down to the throng below.

'Are you OK?' asked Rebecca. 'You look . . . out of it.'

'I'm fine. Just a million kilometres away.'

'Nowhere pleasant by the look on your face.'

'I'm just missing my girlfriend,' I admitted.

'Oh? Where is she?'

How to answer that one? 'We're not together any more.'

'Oh. I'm sorry.'

I shrugged. Time to change the subject. 'So what brings you up here?'

Rebecca sighed, walking over to me. 'I came up a while ago for some peace and quiet.'

'Me too,' I said. 'But if I'm disturbing you I can leave.'

'No, that's OK. You can stay.'

I smiled. 'I'm Tobey.'

'Becks,' said Rebecca, holding out her hand.

I stepped forward to shake it.

'Hi, Becks. So what d'you think of the party then?'

'It's OK.' Rebecca's response was distinctly lukewarm. 'I'm not really a party person. What about you? What d'you think of it?'

'Well, I'm not exactly a guest,' I pointed out, indicating my waiter's uniform.

'All the better to get an objective opinion,' Rebecca replied.

I considered. 'I'm not really a party person either. I'd much rather see a good film and go for a meal afterwards.'

'Me too.'

Rebecca and I shared a smile.

'But as parties go, most of the people downstairs seem to be enjoying themselves. Mind you, in the morning they won't remember whether the party was good, bad or indifferent.'

'Yeah, so what's the point?' said Rebecca, antipathy in her voice.

'Excuse my asking, but aren't you Rebecca Dowd? Isn't it your birthday party?'

'It's supposed to be, but it's more for my mum's benefit than mine. My party will appear in all the right celebrity magazines and a tabloid or two, with photos of all the usual suspects, and Mum will deem my party a success.'

'The usual suspects?' I queried.

'All those people who would go to the opening of a fridge door as long as it got their faces in the papers and the gossip mags.'

I contemplated Rebecca. I'd thought she'd be some spoiled little princess who thought the sun revolved around her and who'd have nothing worse to bleat about than the merest wrinkle in her dress or a scuff mark on her shoes.

'What?' Rebecca ran her hand over her hair.

'Nothing. I just . . . you're not what I expected,' I said.

'Is that good or bad?'

'Definitely good.' I smiled.

We stood for a few moments looking out across the centre of town. The traffic, the lights from the buildings, the occasional siren, they were all just background, but vibrant background. I wanted to reach out my hand, snatch it all up and put it in my trouser pocket. But I deliberately turned my back on it to face Rebecca.

'So what did you get for your birthday?' I asked.

Rebecca's hand moved self-consciously to her neck. 'This necklace – amongst other things.'

'It's beautiful.'

'D'you really like it?' she asked doubtfully.

'Well, I wouldn't wear it,' I replied. 'But it looks good on you.'

'I thought it was a bit . . . ostentatious, but Mum insisted that I should wear it.'

'There are worse things to wear,' I said.

I deliberately took a step closer. Rebecca didn't back away. I lifted the necklace away from her neck for a better look. The metal beneath my fingers still held the warmth of her skin. The necklace was either white gold or platinum. I'd've put my money on the latter. It certainly wasn't mere silver. Adorning the chain was a cross set with at least nine diamonds and I reckoned each diamond had to be at least half a carat. Not that I'm into diamonds or anything like that, but I did occasionally glance in the odd jeweller's shop window with dreams about the watches I could buy myself and the everything else I would buy Callie if I ever had any money. Rebecca's necklace would've been dazzling around Callie's neck, complementing her beige skin.

'Tobey . . . ?'

I snapped out of my reverie and immediately released Rebecca's necklace. 'Sorry. I went offline.'

'Were you with your girlfriend again?'

I shrugged, not denying it.

'Did you love her?'

That was something . . . the one thing I couldn't lie about, couldn't even talk about.

'Like I said, it's over now.'

'Maybe you—'

'Tobey, what d'you think you're doing? Your break was over ten minutes ago.' Michelle looked about ready to fire my arse.

'Michelle, please don't blame Tobey. He was just being kind and keeping me company.'

'Oh, Miss Dowd. I'm so sorry. I didn't realize it was you.' Michelle did everything but curtsey.

'I do hope Tobey won't get into trouble because of me,' said Rebecca.

'Of course not,' Michelle hastened to reassure her. 'Tobey, take all the time you need.' She turned and headed for the door to go back downstairs.

'No, that's OK, Michelle. I'll get back to work,' I called out quickly. I wasn't ready to lose my job quite yet. I turned to Rebecca. 'It was nice to meet you, Becks.'

Michelle had already left the roof and was on her way back down to the Club. I guess it didn't pay to upset the Dowds, any of them.

'It's a shame we were interrupted. I was enjoying our chat,' said Rebecca.

Something in her voice made me stop. 'You make it sound like not a lot of people talk to you,' I said, surprised.

'They don't,' Rebecca replied. 'They talk at me or through me or around me. Very few people talk *to* me, and even less listen to what I have to say.'

'I like to listen,' I told her.

'I noticed that,' said Rebecca. 'Your girlfriend must be mad to dump you.'

I didn't bother to correct her.

'I'd better get back. I just hope I have the stamina to last until the party finishes.' I smiled to lighten my words, but more than meant them.

'Don't worry,' said Rebecca. 'I reckon this party only has another hour's life left in it – at most. Then you can go home.'

I sighed. 'Well, it'll take me nearly three hours to walk home from here, so that'll be something to look forward to.'

'Three hours? Why? Where d'you live?'

'Meadowview. But I didn't realize until I checked this afternoon that there are no night buses that run to where I live at this time on a Monday morning.'

'Oh, I see.'

'Anyway, enjoy the rest of your party, Becks.'

'I'll try,' Rebecca replied. 'It was nice talking to you.'

'You too,' I said. And I went back downstairs.

When I finally left the club it was nearly three in the morning. I'd be home long after dawn and all I wanted to do was crash into my bed now. My feet were killing me. What would they be like after a three-hour walk? Damn!

I'd even asked Michelle about kipping in the changing rooms until the buses started running again, but she shot that idea down in flames.

'You can't,' she told me. 'It's against health and safety regulations, plus you'd set off the alarms, plus Mr Dowd would never allow it.'

The fuss she made, I regretted ever asking her.

'Shouldn't've asked,' Angelo whispered to me. 'Should've just done it.'

Well, it was too late now.

After saying my goodbyes to the other waiters, I set off. The idea of sleeping in some doorway until my body, and especially my feet, recovered grew more and more appealing. I'd only been walking for a couple of minutes, though, when an executive saloon car pulled up beside me. The back window slid down.

'Hi, Tobey.' Rebecca leaned out to talk to me. 'Would you like a lift?'

I glanced past her to the Cross driver, who kept his eyes

facing forward. I looked up and down the sleek lines of the luxury vehicle. A lift in this car? Hell, yes!

'Thanks, Rebecca.' I grinned. 'I'd love one.'

Rebecca Dowd was taking me home. What a strange night.

thirty-three

Mum nagged and nagged until I gave in and let her make me some mid-morning breakfast.

'I know your job pays well,' she said, 'but I'm not happy about the hours you have to work. You're a growing boy. You need regular sleep and proper meals.'

'Mum, you're fussing,' I sighed. 'And the job is only until school starts again. Until then I'll survive. And anyway, I'm not back at work until tomorrow night.'

Though to tell the truth, I was still so tired, all I wanted to do was get myself something to eat, then fall back into bed. Jessica was at work and Mum had one of her rare days off. When Mum wasn't working at the local hospital, she did agency nursing to make extra money. Jessica's college fees and all the extras I needed for school meant that she spent every spare hour working. One day that'd all change. I'd be the one looking after her and buying her all the things she deserved.

'I want you to give up your job a week before school

starts. OK?' said Mum. 'You'll need to get back into the habit of sleeping at night and waking up at a reasonable hour each morning.'

'Yes, Mum,' I said.

It wasn't worth arguing. Besides, Mum needed to take her own advice more than I did. She was losing weight and was looking and acting distinctly brittle. Whilst Mum went off to make me something to eat, I had a quick shower.

After my wash, I put my pyjamas back on. Heading downstairs, I went into the living room. I switched on the TV and flicked from channel to channel, searching for something to watch. Mum walked in and handed me a plate with a fried egg toasted sandwich on it. She frowned at me.

'You do intend to have a shower sometime today, don't you?'

'I've already had one,' I replied smugly.

'And you put your pyjamas back on?' Mum's eyebrows were doing a disapproving dance.

'Yep!'

'How can you have a shower and put your jammies straight back on?' asked Mum.

'Like this, Mum,' I said, indicating my clothes. 'And what's more, I'm going back to bed after this.'

'All right for some,' Mum sniffed.

I took a bite out of my sandwich whilst using my other hand to change the TV channel again. I flicked onto a news bulletin and was about to keep flicking when Mum snatched the remote away from me.

'Leave it there,' she said quickly.

She sat down next to me to watch the news, sipping at the coffee she held in her other hand. I tucked into my food.

'. . . *Earlier this morning the Liberation Militia set off a car bomb outside the Department of Industry and Commerce in Silver Square, only two kilometres from the Houses of Parliament. A warning was phoned through one hour before the bomb was due to explode. The emergency services had to evacuate all the surrounding buildings in the area. The car bomb was detonated in a controlled explosion by the army. No one was injured. We can now talk to the Minister for Commerce, Pearl Emmanuel, who is in our Westminster studio. Tell me, Minister, what do you think—?*'

Mum pressed the button to switch off the TV.

'What on earth is wrong with those people?' She frowned.

'What d'you mean?' I asked, my half-eaten sandwich slowing on its way to my mouth. I looked at the blank screen. Why'd she turn it off? Even the news was better than nothing.

'The Liberation Militia,' said Mum, almost angry. 'The Equal Rights bill is about to be passed. Why don't they give the government a chance?'

'Maybe they want to make sure this government doesn't go back on its word?' I ventured. After all, it had happened before with the last lot.

'Of course they won't break their promises,' said Mum. 'This government would have to be stupid or suicidal to withdraw the Equal Rights bill now. The Liberation Militia are about to get what they're supposedly fighting for. So why're they still blowing up stuff?'

'Maybe they're trying to remind the government that they're still around and watching them?' I said, before taking another bite of my sandwich.

'If the L.M. aren't careful, they'll turn people against the bill. They're not helping our cause, not any more,' said Mum.

I took another bite of my sandwich.

'You know what this is?' she went on, eyes narrowed. 'It's the last gasp of a terrorist group who're about to become obsolete.'

'Maybe they have a job lot of explosives and need to use them up before the bill is passed,' I said flippantly.

Mum glared at me. 'It's not funny, Tobey.'

'I know,' I sighed. 'But it's not like the old days when they used to blow shit up with no warning whatsoever.'

'They shouldn't be blowing up anything at all. And stop swearing.'

'How is "whatsoever" swearing?'

'Ha bloody ha!' said Mum. She handed me the mug of coffee before getting to her feet. 'That's for you.'

I peered down inside the empty cup. 'You've drunk it all.'

'I know.' Mum grinned at me before ambling out the room.

'Ha bloody ha, Mum,' I called after her.

'Stop swearing!'

I washed my empty plate and Mum's empty mug before heading back to bed. I'd barely pulled up the duvet when my mobile started to ring. I checked to make sure it wasn't the phone McAuley had given me. It wasn't. It was my own personal phone. I decided to change the ring tone on

McAuley's phone so that when it rang I'd instantly know who was calling me.

'Hello?'

'It's me. I've been thinking about your proposal.'

Not even a hello. It didn't matter, I recognized Owen Dowd's voice at once. I sat up, waiting to hear his decision.

'The way I see it, I've got nothing to lose.'

'That's absolutely right, Mr Dowd,' I agreed. 'You don't.'

'And you seriously believe that you can deliver?'

'I know I can.'

'OK, I'll play. For now.'

'You won't regret it,' I said, my relief intense.

'No, but you might if you're playing some kind of game,' Owen warned. 'When you get me the information you promised, I'll take that as proof that you meant what you said last night.'

'Fair enough, Mr Dowd.'

'And if anything goes wrong . . .'

'I'm on my own. I know.'

Pause.

'Don't, under any circumstances, try to contact me. D'you understand?'

'Yes, sir.'

'I'll be in touch.'

He hung up. No hello. No goodbye. I didn't expect anything else.

I pressed the button to disconnect the call and let my mobile drop onto my bed. The previous evening hadn't gone quite as I'd planned, but that was OK. On the way back to my house, Rebecca and I hadn't stopped chatting. She was very easy to talk to, very easy to like. Too easy. I had to keep reminding myself that she was a Dowd. All the way home, I wondered if maybe I was reading too much into her offer of a lift. When we pulled up outside my house, we chatted for ages. I was the one who had to make my apologies, otherwise we would've been talking until the dawn broke over the car bonnet. And I'm sure that when I told her I had better head indoors, I hadn't imagined the disappointment on her face.

Rebecca's birthday party couldn't have come at a better time. What an unexpected bonus. I got to meet her brother faster than I would've done otherwise. I took it as a sign that out there, somewhere, someone was on my side.

thirty-four

Just before noon on Tuesday, the phone McAuley had given me started to ring. The unfamiliar ring tone threw me for a moment until I remembered. It took a few seconds to track down the phone, which was in the pocket of my denim jacket, hanging on the nail I'd hammered into the back of my bedroom door.

'Hello?'

'Good morning, Tobey. How are you?' asked McAuley.

I was instantly on my guard.

'I'm fine, thank you, Mr McAuley.'

'Sleeping OK?'

Pause. Now what did that mean? Some damage limitation was required.

'Sleeping just fine, sir. I've got some news actually. I wanted to phone you sooner, but I didn't know how to contact you as you didn't leave a number on this phone and I didn't want to turn up at your address unannounced.'

'It's a wise man who learns from the mistakes of others,' said McAuley, spouting the cliché like he'd only just made it up. How pathetic was that? 'What news d'you have for me?'

'I managed to get a job at TFTM.'

Silence.

'Mr McAuley?' I was the first to break the strained quiet between us.

'Why did you do that when you work for me?' McAuley asked softly.

'I thought it might be useful to you to have someone working in a place owned by the Dowds. I didn't mention it beforehand because I wasn't sure I'd get the job.'

Silence. Again.

'Just say the word, Mr McAuley, and I'll give up my job there straight away,' I said earnestly. 'I just thought it might be useful to you.'

'And it might be, Tobey. It just might be,' said McAuley. 'What exactly will you be doing at TFTM?'

'I've been employed as a waiter in the restaurant. I'm not up in the Club unfortunately, but that's what I'm aiming at.'

No need to tell him I'd already started working there. Let's put it this way – what he didn't know wouldn't hurt me.

'I see. I want you to report back to me regularly,' said McAuley.

'I don't have your phone number, sir.'

'I'll phone you,' said McAuley.

'Yes, sir.' I made sure to keep my sigh of relief inaudible. He'd bought it.

'And Tobey?'

'Yes, sir?'

'I do the thinking around here, not you. Understand?'

'Understood, sir.'

'Are you working there tonight?'

'Yes, sir. My hours are from six p.m. till one, Tuesdays to Saturdays.'

'Good,' said McAuley. 'Because I have a job for you before then. A delivery . . . no, actually, make that two deliveries, that need to be made before this evening. Can you do that?'

What kind of deliveries?

Ask no questions, hear no lies.

But no more body parts. Please.

'Yes, sir. Where and when?'

'Byron will meet you at the Wasteland in thirty minutes. He'll give you all the details.'

'Yes, sir.' But McAuley had already hung up. He didn't need to wait to hear that I would do as I was told. Besides, I would never have hung up on McAuley first. Little things like that meant a lot to him. The smaller the person, the smaller the things that mattered.

With a sigh I got dressed. So much for my lazy morning in bed. My lazy morning the day before had gone down a treat and I was so looking forward to another one. Ah, well.

Not surprisingly, the Wasteland didn't contain too many people and less than a handful of children. If I'd had kids, I wouldn't be taking any chances either, not after what had happened. I looked around, but there was no sign of McAuley's lieutenant. I wasn't exactly sure where I was supposed to meet Byron so I headed for the deserted football pitch, the first time I'd been there since . . . since. Just looking at it made my heart jump erratically. My eyes were drawn to the ground, the exact spot where Callie lay after she'd been shot. There was nothing to indicate she'd ever been there, not even the flowers that'd been brought to this place by friends and strangers alike after that day. Either a cleaning crew or the one day of rain we'd had since the shooting had washed away every trace of her blood. That was all it took – a shower of rain, the slam of a door, the thrust of a knife or a gunshot – and just like that, a person could be gone with nothing but the memories of others to show that they'd ever existed. Life was too fragile.

'Come with me, Tobey.'

Byron's voice in my ear made me jump. I hadn't even heard him approach. Already he was heading away from the football pitch and towards the road. He walked towards a black saloon car with tinted windows. Was this another set-up? Was the black car Byron's? Byron turned his head, impatience written all over his face. I followed him.

'Sit in the front,' he told me once we reached his vehicle.

I hesitated only momentarily, and I certainly didn't

argue. Byron headed around his car to get behind the wheel. The moment he was inside, he pressed a button to lock all the doors. The loud clunk made me flinch.

Tobey, take a deep breath and get it together.

I was altogether too jumpy. It made me look guilty of something. Byron turned in his seat to face me.

'Mr McAuley wants you to deliver a parcel and a letter. Can you do that?'

I nodded.

Byron produced a white envelope from his inside jacket pocket. He held it out for me to take. There was no address or name on the front, no markings of any kind.

'Who's this for?' I frowned.

'Vanessa Dowd.'

Vanessa . . . Was he joking? From the expression on his face, unfortunately not. Vanessa Dowd never came to TFTM. How on earth was I supposed to get the letter to her? I didn't know her home address and there was no way anyone at TFTM would just give that to me.

Was this some kind of trick to catch me out?

Godsake! I was being too paranoid. But being around people like McAuley and the Dowds could easily do that to you. I swallowed hard before taking the envelope and putting it in my inside jacket pocket.

'How am I supposed to get this to Vanessa Dowd?'

'You'll have to figure that out for yourself,' said Byron, totally unconcerned.

'Well, what's her address?' I asked.

Bryon shrugged. 'McAuley doesn't know. You'll have to figure that one out too. But my boss has every confidence in you. He knows you're a smart guy.'

There was no answer to that – and no mistaking the sneer in Byron's voice either.

'Oh, before I forget,' he said, handing me another envelope, much fatter than the last one.

'Who is this one for?'

'You,' said Byron. 'Payment for doing as you're told.'

I hesitated for a moment or two before taking the envelope and stuffing it into another pocket.

'Aren't you going to open it?'

'Later,' I replied. 'Could you thank Mr McAuley for me?'

Byron nodded, his eyes appraising me.

'What about this parcel I'm supposed to deliver?' I said.

'It's for Adam Eisner, Flat Eighteen, same address as before,' said Byron.

'What address would that be?' I asked without missing a beat.

Amusement lit Byron's green eyes. 'D'you really think my boss doesn't know that you delivered two of Dan's packages a while ago? One to Adam and one to . . . someone else.'

'Who told him that?'

Was it Dan or Adam Eisner himself? It seemed impossible to keep secrets from McAuley.

'You need to stop asking so many questions,' said Byron. 'It isn't healthy.'

A chill chased up my spine. Message received and understood. I looked around the car. The back seats were empty and Byron wasn't making any strenuous moves to hand me anything.

'Where's this parcel for Mr Eisner? Am I allowed to ask that at least?'

'It's in the boot. Get out and I'll pop the boot for you,' said Byron.

I did as directed, walking round to the back of the car. I had a good look around before I stepped up to it. The boot opened with a loud clunk, then rose to the sound of constant beeping. A package wrapped in brown paper and about the size of a car manual lay on the left. A supermarket carrier bag filled with food sat next to it. I lifted up the parcel. The moment I was clear, the boot descended. I looked through the back window. Byron was watching me via the interior mirror, no hint of a smile on his face. He drove off just as the boot clicked shut.

There I stood at the edge of the park, two unaddressed envelopes in my jacket pockets, an unaddressed parcel in my hands and the distinct feeling that I was being followed. The prickling of my nape left me in no doubt about that. I looked around nervously.

The question was, who was watching me?

thirty-five

I spent the next couple of hours hopping on buses and trains that took me all over Meadowview and beyond. A lot of the time, I didn't even know where I was. But when that happened, I just leaped on the nearest bus, getting off at the first place I vaguely recognized. I kept telling myself

I was being ridiculous, I wasn't in some spy novel. But I decided it would be better to waste a couple of hours by being over-cautious than to be nabbed by the police whilst carrying a parcel containing I-don't-know-what inside.

I could just see it now – 'Honestly, officer, I didn't know I was carrying two semiautomatic weapons . . .'

Yeah, right!

I took two trains into town and three back out again. I scanned the faces of my fellow passengers for those that were too familiar, those that I'd seen one too many times today. Only when I was convinced that I was no longer being watched or followed did I head for Adam Eisner's flat. Even as I climbed the stairs of his estate building, I couldn't help wondering what was inside the parcel I was delivering. If anyone had asked me, I would've sworn that my fingers were tingling just from touching it. It didn't matter whether the tingling was real or merely my mind playing tricks, I could still feel it. And it didn't feel right. I rang the bell. The front door opened almost immediately. Adam Eisner stood there, his black hair combed back off his face, his dark-blue eyes shooting poison darts.

'Where the hell have you been?' he roared at me.

There was no other word for it. It was a definite roar. He pulled me into his flat, slamming the front door behind me.

'I was expecting you over an hour ago,' he said, his face mere centimetres from mine.

'I'm sorry I'm late, Mr Eisner, but when I collected your parcel, I got the feeling someone was watching me, so I travelled around until I was certain I was no longer being followed,' I explained quickly.

Eisner backed off a bit, his expression wary. 'Who would be following you?'

I shrugged. 'I have no idea. Probably no one. Like I said, it was only a feeling, but I figured it was better to be safe than banged up.'

Eisner headed for his front door and opened it. He looked up and down the corridor outside his flat, before crossing it to peer down at the ground below. He scanned all around the block for a solid minute before returning to his flat, closing the door quietly behind him.

'You should've phoned someone to tell them what you were doing,' Eisner retorted.

Phoned who exactly? None of them were exactly on my speed-dial list. I held out his parcel to him.

'Bring it into the kitchen,' Eisner ordered.

I inhaled sharply. I just wanted to get out of there. I had an envelope which was burning through my jacket pocket and scorching my flesh. And I still hadn't figured out how I was going to pass it on to Vanessa Dowd.

I followed Eisner into the kitchen. Four Nought men sat around a farmhouse-style table, all stark naked. A number of small plastic bags covered the table, most empty, some half-filled with white powder.

'Put the package on the table,' said Eisner.

I couldn't wait to get rid of it. I dropped it like the thing was white-hot – which I now realized was exactly what it was. A set of electronic scales sat in the middle of the table along with a bigger bag of a dull-white powder. What was in the bigger bag? Flour? Sugar? Powdered baby milk? One of the men was weighing out exact amounts of the merchandise before carefully pouring it into the small bags, while the others were adding the same amount again from the bigger bag. They were cutting drugs. That's why they were all sitting around naked – it cut down the number of places they could hide the stuff for themselves.

Eisner picked up a small knife and cut a slit down the brown parcel like he was a surgeon making the first incision. White powder gently spilled out on either side of the cut. My heart was beating hard and heavy. Eisner turned to smile at me.

'I see McAuley was right about you. You have a smart head on your shoulders.' Eisner picked up one of the tiny bags filled with white powder which hadn't yet been added to and held it out to me. 'Take that for your trouble.'

I shook my head. Cocaine? No way.

'Take it,' said Eisner. 'You won't find better blow anywhere in Meadowview.'

I took the bag and stuffed it into my trouser pocket.

'I have more deliveries to make.' Was that really my voice playing back at me, so low and so calm? It had to be.

Eisner nodded and led the way out of his flat. I walked along the corridor towards the stairs, knowing that Eisner was watching every step. I headed away from his block and just kept going. Everything inside me was still, like my heart and my head and my very soul were all holding their breath.

As I turned some anonymous corner, a couple of bins came into view outside some local shops. I strode up to the nearest one and pulled the plastic bag out of my pocket, careful to keep the contents hidden in my hand. I stretched out my arm, my hand poised over the bin.

Let it go, Tobey. Before it's too late. Let it go.

But I couldn't. I just couldn't.

thirty-six

Hello, Callie. How are you feeling today? You look a little better. Your face isn't quite so ashen. They tried to suck the life out of you, didn't they? But you're strong, Callie Rose. Stronger than even you think. So hang in there. You don't have to wake up today or tomorrow or even this week. You'll come round in your own good time.

But you will come round.

And when you wake up, I want to be the first face you see. That's why I visit you every day, even if it's only for a few minutes. When you awake you'll see me smiling at you and nothing else will matter. My guess is that you've been through so much over the last few months that it all finally caught up with you and you're just dealing with it in your own way. Your mind is . . . resting, recharging. I'm not worried about you being in this place. I'm not worried about the fact that you haven't regained consciousness yet.

I think . . . I feel you're waiting for me. So don't wake up yet. I haven't finished what I need to do. Just sleep — and wait for me.

I had to see you today, Callie. I had to take that chance. You're the only one I can talk to. My pockets are full, Callie — and they're weighing me down so much I can hardly stand upright. I've got one jacket pocket filled with money. Blood money. Another pocket contains a letter that I'm afraid to deliver. And in my trouser pocket there's . . . there's . . . something that clings to my hand like superglue and no matter how hard I try, I can't shake it off my fingers, I can't get rid of it.

I'm scared, Callie.

There! I've admitted it. Just between you and me, I'm bloody terrified. But one thing keeps me going – you.

Just you.

Only you.

I'll hang onto that and do what I have to do. Whatever it takes, eh, babe?

So how am I doing? Well, the weekend was kinda strange. I met a girl. Her name is Rebecca, Rebecca Dowd. She's Vanessa Dowd's daughter. Yes, *the* Vanessa Dowd. I had to work on Sunday at TFTM. It was Rebecca's eighteenth birthday party. Private function. I got triple time plus tips so I made a whole heap of money. A few more weeks of this and I'll be able to buy you the birthday present I've been promising you for ages. Anyway, Rebecca gave me a lift home and we chatted and had a good laugh all the way back to my house. I think she likes me. I surprised her and that's a good thing. I don't know what she was expecting, but I kept up with her conversation and I even managed to tell her one or two things that she didn't know. And when she found out I was going to Heathcroft High . . . ? You should've seen the looks she kept giving me after that. My mum was right – that school is like a passport.

When we arrived outside my house, we sat in her car

for almost an hour, just talking. Reading between the lines, it sounds like she thinks most guys are more interested in getting to know her family's money than her. Of course I didn't ask for her phone number or for a date or anything. I think that surprised her too. I have to admit, though, Rebecca was all right. I think you'd like her. But enough of her. Besides, I'll probably never see her again.

Callie, I'll come and see you as often as I can. It's tricky because I can't let anyone know that I'm here. And I sure as hell can't let your Aunt Minerva, or worse still, your mum, find me here. Your mum is waiting for me to man up and tell the police what I know. And with every day that passes with my silence, I know she despises me more. But this is something I have to sort out for myself.

I'm going to make McAuley pay for what he did to you.

I'll get him.

Or die trying.

The trouble is, I can't do it without help – Owen Dowd's help. He's the only one with the money and the resources and the will to help me. I just wish I could get over this feeling that I'm crawling into bed with the devil to catch a demon. Crawling into bed metaphorically speaking, of course. I tell myself that it's the end result that counts, nothing else. Oh, I know what the end result needs to be, *has* to be. But it's the getting there that's tricky. Isn't it always? I have a vague plan and the will to succeed, but that's it. It will have to be enough. Trouble is, I feel like I'm stumbling through some improvised dance that I'm kinda making up as I go along. But that's OK, I'll survive. I hope.

Y-you have to live, you know that, don't you, Callie? I don't know what I'd do without you. I've . . . cared about you for so long, I don't know how to do anything else. I wouldn't tell this to anyone but you. Hell! I wouldn't even tell you if you were conscious enough to hear it and play it back to me.

But I do . . . care about you. Very much.

You force my heart to beat.

So don't ever scare me like that again.

When you got shot, it was as if . . . as if the bullet that got you had escaped your body to hit me right between the eyes. I survived, though, because you did. But when your heart stopped . . . When that happened, all hope inside me started to wind down like a broken toy. I guess everyone has their Achilles heel. Why should I be any different?

Hang in there, Callie. Remember, it's you and me against the world. I'll deal with McAuley, and when you wake up we'll go away together. Somewhere far away where Jude McGregor will never find us. You just sleep, Callie Rose. Sleep until it's all over. And don't fret about what happened to you. Trust me, Callie. I'm taking care of that. Whatever it takes.

And if it doesh't work, if I get jammed up, just know that it was worth it.

You were worth it.

thirty-seven

Vanessa,

I'm sure the last thing either of us wants or needs is a resumption of hostilities. The last turf war between us created casualties on both sides. But I will take out you and yours if your family try to muscle in on my patch. You need to rein in your sons. Once I have ALL my territory back, your manager will, I'm sure, find his way home.

And not before.

M.

thirty-eight

I arrived for my job at TFTM at least fifteen minutes too early, waiting for the opportune time to put my plan into action. Inside the restaurant, I saw a few very late-lunch diners with only a couple of staff visible through the tinted windows, but they were at the back of the restaurant and hadn't even noticed me – which was just the way I wanted it. I stood outside, glancing at my watch, tapping it periodically and holding it to my ear, strictly for the benefit of the person who was watching me. 'Cause I was now in no doubt that I was being followed. And I had a good idea who was acting as my shadow.

I looked up and down the street, waiting for the right moment. And I didn't have long to wait. A middle-aged Cross woman who reminded me a bit of Callie's aunt Minerva was walking towards me. The woman wore a dark-grey suit and a mustard-yellow blouse and she carried a laptop briefcase. Her braids were pulled back and styled elegantly on top of her head.

'Excuse me,' I asked, stepping in front of her.

'Yes,' asked the woman, slight suspicion in her voice. But at least she had stopped.

I took another small step towards her. 'I'm sorry, but my contact lenses are playing up,' I smiled. 'Could you tell me what address is on this letter please?'

With my back half towards the restaurant window, I pulled the envelope for Vanessa Dowd out of my inside jacket pocket and handed it to her. Sidestepping slowly, I watched as the woman looked down at the envelope. I had to make sure that she was seen with the letter first rather than me. She looked at the front of the envelope, then turned it over in her hand.

'There's no address on this letter.' The woman frowned.

'That explains why I can't read it then.' I grinned apologetically. 'I'm sorry to have troubled you.'

'That's OK.' She handed back the envelope, looking at me like my deck was short of more than a couple of playing cards.

'Thanks anyway,' I said.

The woman hurried on without another word. I looked down at the envelope and turned it over as the woman had done. Painting a frown on my face, I looked up, just as Michelle and Angelo arrived for work. The letter charade with the suited Cross woman had been for their benefit alone. I could only hope it'd worked.

'Oh, hi,' I said.

'You're early,' said Michelle.

'My watch is running fast.' I showed it to them so they could see for themselves, the letter still in my hand.

'Then for goodness' sake buy yourself a new watch,' Michelle snapped.

'What's that?' asked Angelo, nodding at the letter I was waving about.

'Oh, this. A woman just asked me to give it to Vanessa Dowd.' I pointed up the street in the direction of the woman who'd just left. 'I told her she doesn't work here, but she insisted that Mrs Dowd's son Gideon did. She wouldn't take no for an answer.'

'What is it?' asked Michelle.

I shrugged. 'Haven't a clue. Does Gideon Dowd work here then? Is there any way I can get this to Mr Dowd to give to his mum?'

Angelo held out his hand. I eagerly handed over the envelope. Fingerprints. I wanted the envelope to be covered in a whole database full of fingerprints. That way I could hide mine amongst many – just in case the Dowds had the means to check them out.

'I wonder what it is,' Angelo mused aloud before handing it back.

'So is Gideon Dowd coming here today?' I asked.

'As a matter of fact Gideon will be in later,' said Michelle cagily. 'He sometimes comes in to do business with Mr Thomas.'

'Oh, I see.'

'But how did that woman know?' Michelle looked worried.

I shrugged. 'Michelle, can I give this to you to pass on to Mr Dowd so he can give it to his mum?'

Michelle wasn't happy, but what could she say? She reluctantly took the letter from me. From what I'd heard, Gideon and Owen Dowd both kept small offices somewhere upstairs in the Club where I wasn't supposed to go without an explicit invitation or reason. I'd already seen Owen's office and I was in no hurry to see his brother's. Evidently Michelle wasn't happy about me delivering the letter to Gideon in person either. Rather her than me.

I left TFTM, shift over, in the early hours of Wednesday morning. At least, because it was a week day, the night buses were running so I could get fairly close to home. The bus would drop me about a fifteen-minute walk from my house, but that was better than having to walk the whole way. I was grateful for small mercies. The night was warm like a blanket around me. I looked up. The moon was a crescent and I could make out the odd star plus the lights of a plane flying high overhead. But there was too much city light pollution to see much more than that.

With a sigh, I started on my way. I'd taken five or six

steps when I heard, 'Get your filthy blanker hands off me.'

I spun round. Charles, a barman who worked up in the Club, was the one doing the shouting. The object of his wrath was a middle-aged Nought guy who sat cross-legged on the ground, a cup in his hand to collect the spare change of passers-by. On a piece of card in front of him, were the words: HOMELESS AND HUNGRY. PLEASE HELP. The homeless guy obviously wasn't doing very well if he was still asking for change at this time of night. But catching late-night revellers and staff heading for home must've seemed like a good ploy. The seated guy wore a woolly hat, despite the warm weather, with a plaid shirt and jeans, all assorted shades of grubby and dark.

'Sorry. I'm sorry.' The guy with the cup raised a placating hand.

What was he apologizing for? What had he done?

'Don't ever touch me again.' Charles carried on mouthing off, whilst brushing down the lower leg of his trousers. I couldn't see anything on them. Maybe he was trying to wipe off fingerprints. A number of TFTM employees had gathered around by now, wondering what all the commotion was about.

'Look at you,' Charles said scathingly. 'You're an embarrassment. Get off your arse and get a job, you worthless blanker.'

There were some gasps, but no one spoke.

'And what are you?' asked the homeless man, his gaze never leaving Charles.

I'd been wondering the same thing myself. Charles was as white as the homeless guy. As white as me.

'I'm not a blanker, I'm a Nought,' Charles announced.

Behind him, some of Charles's Cross colleagues started to snigger, a couple of them pressing their lips together real tight to stop themselves from laughing out loud. The seated guy stood up slowly, his cup still in his hand. He and Charles never took their eyes off each other. The homeless man slowly shook his head. Charles's eyes narrowed. He stepped forward. So did I.

'Here you are,' I said, handing the homeless guy a couple of notes from my trouser pocket. 'Go and get yourself a warm meal.'

The man took my money without a smile. I didn't expect anything else. Charles couldn't get to him without shoving me out of the way first, which he was probably prepared to do. And he had ten years and quite a number of kilos on me, but I wasn't going to budge – well, not without him body-charging me first. The homeless man ambled off like nothing was bothering him, which it most likely wasn't. I went to follow in his direction, but Charles grabbed my arm and spun me round to face him. He glared at me. I said nothing.

'Takes a blanker to know a blanker,' he said softly.

He let go of my arm and marched off. All the TFTM people who'd been watching the show faded away like a sigh. In mere moments, I was alone.

Noughts and daggers. Crosses and blankers. Noughts and blankers. Crosses and daggers. Circles within circles. Divisions and yet more divisions. No black. No white. Just myriad shades of grey, one shade for every person on the planet. I didn't like where my thoughts were leading me, but my mind was full of sharp things. Sharp words like blanker, sharp sounds like the Crosses laughing at Charles, sharp sights of Charles and the homeless guy regarding each other, and homeless smells and textures like needle points. Only with Callie could I be comfortable. I shook my head. Something about the encounter between Charles and the homeless guy had left me feeling... hollow. I needed Callie to fill all the empty spaces inside of me. But she wasn't here. At that moment, I felt incredibly lonely. I hadn't realized until this moment how loneliness could eat away at you so much that it actually hurt. I needed to get home. I'd barely taken ten steps away from the place when an unfamiliar silver sports car pulled up beside me.

'Fancy a lift?' Rebecca's voice reached me before the passenger window was even halfway down.

Poking my head through the open window, I grinned at her. 'Love one. Whose car is this?'

'Mine.' Rebecca smiled. 'An eighteenth birthday present. Check out the licence plate.'

I took a couple of steps back to do just that. The registration read BECKS 1.

'Very nice,' I said, wryly wondering what Mum would get me for my eighteenth birthday in a couple of weeks' time.

'Hop in then,' said Rebecca.

I did just that, grateful for the car and the company.

Once we were on our way, I asked, 'Not that I'm not grateful, but how come you're driving when you've only just had your eighteenth birthday?'

The government had recently changed the law so that you couldn't even take driving lessons until you were eighteen minimum. Yet Rebecca had been given a car for her eighteenth birthday and was happily driving around.

'Private lessons on private roads for the last year,' she said. 'I took my test on my birthday and passed. Mum said if I passed first time I could have a car, I just didn't expect to get one quite so quickly.'

Oh, the joys of having money. All together now. Everybody sing!

'So were you at the Club again tonight?' I wondered.

'Nope. I just happened to be driving past . . . Well, actually, that's a lie. I was waiting for you.'

I stared, stunned. 'Why?'

'I wanted to give you a lift home.'

'Are you thinking of starting up your own taxi service?'

Rebecca laughed. 'Not as such.'

'Why did you want to give me a lift then?'

'I wanted to talk to you again,' said Rebecca, looking straight ahead.

'About what?'

She shrugged. 'Whatever you like. I don't mind.'

Huh?

'Oh. I see,' I said embarrassed. Slow or what?

We exchanged a brief smile before Rebecca turned her attention back to the road. I sat back into my seat and relaxed. Wow! She really did like me.

'It's a shame you didn't come into the restaurant this evening,' I began. 'It must be International Have-A-Moan day 'cause we had them all in tonight. We had one guy who chose the woodland fruit strudel for dessert, then complained it was too dry. It came with a jug of apple and cognac custard and I came that close to pointing out that if he bothered to pour the custard on his strudel, it would be wet, so what was his problem?'

'I can imagine how that would've gone down,' said Rebecca wryly.

'Yeah, like a lead balloon,' I agreed. 'But it was so tempting!'

I spent the next thirty minutes telling her about some of the other restaurant customers I'd come across so far. It was very indiscreet, but what the hell. I was very good at impersonations and voices, and let's face it, TFTM provided some great material. At one point Rebecca was laughing so hard, we started to drift across the road. An angry beep from an oncoming car persuaded me to tone it down a bit. Finally we pulled up outside my house.

'Thanks for the lift, Rebecca. And the company. I appreciate it.'

'You're welcome.' She smiled.

I got out and headed for my front door. Giving her a wave, I went inside.

The next night, Rebecca was once again waiting for me outside TFTM. This time I held her hand as a thank you before I got out the car. When she dropped me home the night after that, I thanked her by kissing her cheek. The night after that she turned her head so that I ended up kissing her lips. It was brief, mainly because she surprised the hell out of me.

'What was that about?' I couldn't help asking.

'Tobey, for a bright guy you're surprisingly slow about some things,' Rebecca said, exasperated.

'OK, what am I missing?' I frowned.

She took a deep breath. 'Are you going to ask me out or not?'

I stared at her. 'D'you want me to?'

'Why don't you ask me and see?' Rebecca said patiently.

'Becks, I don't suppose you'd like to see a film or something with me some time?' I asked doubtfully.

'God! I thought you'd never ask.' She laughed. 'If the kiss hadn't worked, I was contemplating dancing naked on your doorstep tomorrow.'

'Damn! Now she tells me.' I grinned – then my smile faded. 'What about your brothers?'

'What about them? They're not invited,' Rebecca replied.

'What're they going to say about the two of us going out together?'

We both knew what I was asking.

'It doesn't matter what my brothers think, because it's my life and I'm the one going out with you, not them,' Rebecca said.

Question answered, but I decided to keep pushing.

'What would your brothers say if they could see us now?' I asked.

Rebecca took a deep breath. 'Quite frankly, it's none of Gideon's business and Owen couldn't care less if I dated the head of the Liberation Militia.'

'I'm sure Owen does care about you, in his own way.' Even I winced at that platitude.

Rebecca's brown eyes twinkled, though she did her best to hide the smile on her lips.

'OK, work with me here. I wasn't sure what else to say,' I said dryly.

Rebecca smiled. 'I appreciate the gesture. But Owen cares about Owen, no one else. He does love me and I love him; it's just that we don't like each other very much. Or at all. And as for Gideon, he's like Mum. He likes to run things, including my life.'

I nodded, without saying anything else.

'Tobey, you don't strike me as the kind of person who'd let anyone stop you from getting or doing what you really want. But if being with me is going to make you uncomfortable, just say and we'll forget all about it.'

'No, it's not that,' I rushed to reassure her. 'I'd like to go out with you. In fact, I'm glad I had the idea.'

Rebecca laughed and this time I joined in.

'So what would you like to see?' I said.

'Tell you what. Why don't we go to one of those multiplexes where they're showing lots of films and then we can decide.'

'OK. Sunday or Monday?' I asked.

'How about both?' Rebecca winked at me.

'Both it is,' I agreed with a grin.

I asked for her mobile number and she gave it to me without hesitation. I actually had Rebecca Dowd's digits! After one final kiss which lasted a bit longer this time, I got out of the car. I waved at her as she drove off, but the moment I turned to my front door, my smile vanished.

thirty-nine

Hi, Callie.

I bought these for you. Sorry they're a bit squashed and some of the petals have fallen off . . . well, a lot of the petals have fallen off, but I had them under my jacket. It's not that I'm ashamed of bringing you flowers or anything. It's just . . . I was keeping them safe inside my jacket in case the wind caught them before I could get to the hospital. Anyway, enough of the flowers. I'll leave them at your bedside and I'll ask one of the nurses to put them in a vase just before I leave. I know how much you like flowers.

So how are you today?

You're looking better. I know I always say that, but you really are. Was that a flicker of a smile I saw just then? Callie, I must admit, I sort of envy you. Nothing that's happening in the outside world can touch you now. You're above and beyond all that. I know when you wake up, it'll all be here waiting for you, but at least for now you don't have to worry about the world and everything going on in it.

Sometimes I look around and I wonder, 'Is this it? Is this all there is?'

But then I think of you. I remember the way you smile at me.

And my question is answered.

forty

'Rebecca, why don't you just come out and tell your mum that you want to be a teacher?'

'Because it wouldn't do any good,' Rebecca sighed.

She took a sip of her fizzy mineral water and looked around the Mexican restaurant. It was a bit on the loud side and probably not as upmarket as she was used to, but if I was paying half the bill for our meal – which I'd insisted on – then it'd have to do. We'd decided to dine today and go to the cinema the following day instead. And in all fairness, Rebecca had been enthusiastic about eating at Los Amigos. I was the one with doubts, which had proved to be unfounded. The restaurant was about one-third full. Not bad for a Sunday night.

'If you did go to university, what would you study?' I asked.

'History. Or maybe History and Politics. But what's the point of talking about it? It's never going to happen.'

'Why not?'

'Mum won't hear of it. As far as she's concerned, she and my brothers are working hard so that I'll never have to. She reckons I should – quote – find a good man, get married, produce grandchildren and enjoy myself – unquote. What d'you think of that?'

'Sounds like hell!' I replied truthfully.

Rebecca laughed. 'My sentiments exactly. Mum thinks that having money and having ambition are somehow mutually exclusive.'

'Have you tried to tell her otherwise?'

'Until I'm blue in the face,' she said. She took another sip of her mineral water, then sighed. 'I would've made a good teacher.'

'So you're going to give up? Just like that?'

'You don't know my mum.'

Was she kidding? Vanessa Dowd was a formidable woman and an implacable enemy. Everyone knew that. And her sons Gideon and especially Owen were cut from the same cloth. If you got in their way, they'd run you over and never spare you a first thought, never mind a second one.

'My mum always says that this life isn't a dress rehearsal,' I began carefully. 'Mum says that regret is an under-estimated emotion that can eat away at you just as much as jealousy or anger.'

'Your mum says a lot,' Rebecca said ruefully.

'Ain't that the truth!'

'You want something so you just . . .' She made a gesture with her hand like a rocket zooming upwards. 'You just go for it. It's that simple?'

'Yes, it is – if you want it to be,' I replied. 'I mean, look at you and me. To some people this is complicated. But not to me. What could be more simple than the two of us sitting here, enjoying a meal together? Mind you . . . Never mind.'

'Go on,' Rebecca prompted.

'I can't help wondering why you agreed to have dinner,' I admitted. 'After all, I am younger than you. Isn't that the kiss of death?'

'You're only younger by a few weeks. That's not much,' said Rebecca. 'Besides, you look much older than me.'

'Thanks,' I said dryly.

'No, I meant that as a compliment,' she rushed to explain. 'Some guys look younger than their age or they act all juvenile and silly, but you're much more mature. And I look younger than I really am, so you looking so much older than me works, don't you think?'

'Thanks. I think.'

'Oh hell, that didn't come out the way I wanted at all. What I mean is—'

'Tell you what,' I broke in. 'How about we change the subject?'

'I'd like that,' Rebecca agreed gratefully.

We grinned at each other. My smile faded first.

'Tobey, tell me more about your friends at—'

But she was interrupted by our first course arriving – a large bowl of guacamole sitting on a plate surrounded by mountains of nachos which we'd decided to share. I was so busy concentrating on the food being carefully placed between us that I almost missed Rebecca's gasp. I looked up immediately. She looked down, but not before I caught the expression on her face.

'What's wrong?' I frowned.

'Nothing.' The reply was terse, verging on a snap.

I looked around. There were people at the bar, Noughts and Crosses, mostly couples or small groups, but one or two people were drinking alone. More people were sitting down at tables, eating. No one was even looking at us. Nothing seemed out of the ordinary. I turned back to Rebecca. Something was still troubling her.

'Becks, I'm not a complete idiot, only half of one! So what's going on?'

'I'm so sorry, Tobey. This wasn't my idea, I promise you.'

'What?'

'We're being watched,' Rebecca admitted.

I only just managed to stop myself from spinning round. I took a deep breath, then another.

'Who's watching us?' I asked when I trusted myself to sound relatively calm.

'It doesn't matter,' she said, her head bowed.

'It does to me.'

'The man at the bar, the one wearing glasses. He works for my brother.'

'Which one?' I said sharply.

'I told you, the man wearing glasses . . .' Rebecca frowned.

'No, which brother does he work for?'

'Gideon. But what difference does it make?'

All the difference in the world.

'Why is your brother having us followed?'

'I don't know. I . . . I may have mentioned you, once or twice.' Rebecca was staring at her nachos like they were sprouting wings. 'Maybe more than twice. But I never thought he'd stoop so low as to have us followed.'

'What does he think I'm going to do to you? Kidnap you?'

'Look, I'm really sorry.' Rebecca still couldn't look me in the eye. 'If you want to bail on me, I'll understand. I would, in your shoes.'

Her expression was a cocktail of various emotions. Her lips kept twisting in a parody of a smile and she was blinking an awful lot. I realized with a start that she was on the verge of tears.

I forced a smile. 'I'm not going to bail, Rebecca. I like you. But this has to be the most original date I've ever been on.'

Rebecca's smile was more genuine than my own. 'Wait here. I'll be right back.'

She practically bounded from her chair and marched across to the bar. I swivelled in my chair and watched as she tapped the Cross guy wearing glasses on the shoulder. He turned, polite query on his face. Nice try! Rebecca's voice was too low for me to make out what she was saying, but her expressive face conveyed the conversation just as well as any words. Her words were flowing thick and fast, her expression thunderous. The guy tried to act innocent, but soon gave up on that when it became clear that Rebecca wasn't buying it. They had a heated discussion for a couple of minutes. Had this guy been following me when I met Byron? If it was him, then what had he seen? I'd lost him before reaching Adam Eisner's house, I was sure of it. And he couldn't've seen much through Byron's tinted car windows, but even so.

I stood up, wondering if I should join them. I dithered about for a few moments before making up my mind, but the moment I set foot in their direction, the guy headed for the exit. Rebecca walked back to me, her lips pursed together.

'Everything OK?' I asked as we both sat down again.

'It is now,' she replied.

'Does your brother do this every time you're on a date?' I asked.

'Not after today he won't. I'll make certain of that.'

'Can I ask you a question about your family?' I began tentatively.

'Go on then.'

'Now that your family are . . . successful, wouldn't it make more sense for them to give up all the . . . less legal stuff and go legit?'

'I regularly ask Mum that same question,' sighed Rebecca.

'And what does she say?'

'There's no guarantee that a legitimate business will succeed — too many external, uncontrollable variables. But there will always be a market for the illegal. That's as predictable as the sun rising each morning, plus it's a faster way to make money.'

'Is that you or your mum talking?' I frowned.

'My mum, of course,' said Rebecca sharply. 'With a bit of Gideon thrown in.'

A faster way to make money? For the likes of the Dowds and McAuley maybe. For the ones who worked for them, it was a faster way to end up rotting in prison — or rotting in a cemetery, more like.

'Besides, Mum's got some high-up Meadowview cop in her pocket, so we don't get troubled too much,' Rebecca added.

'You do stay away from that world, though, don't you?' I asked, anxiously.

'Of course. Nothing to do with me,' Rebecca said, suddenly looking concerned as though she realized she was saying too much. 'Besides, Mum wouldn't let me get involved, even if I wanted to.'

I could only admire the way Rebecca brushed off her family's business. Nothing to do with her – except that she dressed in it and drove it and ate it and slept on it and under it and every jewel she wore was paid for by it. I had to find out a few things before this went any further.

'How is Gideon going to react to you going out with one of his employees?' I asked, deliberately changing the subject.

'If it doesn't interfere with your work at TFTM, what difference does it make?' Rebecca frowned.

'The quality of my work will be irrelevant,' I pointed out. 'Your brother isn't going to like this.'

'Does that bother you?' Rebecca asked.

I shook my head. 'Not if it doesn't bother you.'

'It doesn't. I really like you, Tobey – in case you hadn't already noticed. And you're the first guy to treat me like Rebecca instead of Rebecca Dowd.'

'That means a lot to you, doesn't it?'

Rebecca nodded. 'Yes, it does.'

I lowered my gaze and bit into another nacho. She was with me because she thought her surname didn't matter to me. I was beginning to realize just how lonely Rebecca truly was.

'We should make this a regular thing,' I ventured. 'Our Sunday night dinner together.'

'I'd like that.' Rebecca grinned.

I grinned back. 'D'you wanna swap email and IM addresses?'

'Fine with me,' she said. 'If you give me your phone, I'll key in all my details.'

Once we'd swapped info, I checked my phone to make sure that all the information was saved. Rebecca had given me all her details, including her home address. I put my phone back in my inside jacket pocket.

I dipped a nacho into the guacamole and held it out to Rebecca. She grinned at me before opening her mouth. We fed each other until the guacamole bowl was empty. This dinner date had been more successful than I could've dared to imagine. The Dowds owned a copper – and not just a constable or a sergeant by the sound of it. I'd rapidly changed the subject when Rebecca mentioned it, especially as she looked so worried about what she'd revealed. The last thing I wanted was for her to think I'd latched onto what she'd said. But I'd taken it in and filed it away. My inner euphoria was fading somewhat, though. OK, so I knew at least one Meadowview copper was corrupt. One slight problem: I didn't know who. And until I did, I couldn't use the information to my advantage. And I sure as hell couldn't trust any of them. Should I risk trying to get a bit more information from Rebecca? Then I realized what I was contemplating and the direction of my thoughts startled me.

Don't do it, Tobey.

I needed the information, but part of me – a big part of me – was loath to use Rebecca like that. I didn't want her to think I was just like every other guy she knew.

I looked around the room, forcing myself to think of something else.

So Gideon was having us followed, was he?

Let him do his worst. I had plenty to hide, but neither Gideon nor any of his employees would ever find it.

forty-one

I'd only been home for ten minutes when my phone, or rather McAuley's phone, rang.

'Hello, Mr McAuley,' I said the moment I accepted the call.

'Hello, Tobey.' McAuley's oily voice sent a chill tap-dancing across my skin. 'You've been working at TFTM for long enough now. What've you got for me?'

Nothing.

Except . . .

'I've found out something interesting, sir,' I began.

'Oh yes?'

I took a deep breath. 'There's a crooked cop working at Meadowview police station, high up by all accounts, who's on the Dowd's payroll.'

'Who?' McAuley said eagerly.

'I haven't found that out yet,' I admitted.

'Why not?'

'My source didn't know the name of the bent copper.

Reb— I mean, er . . . regarding the bent cop, my source didn't have any other information.'

'I need a name, Tobey, and sooner rather than later, or your information is worse than useless,' McAuley snapped.

'Yes, sir. I'll see what I can do.'

'I want a name, Tobey,' he reiterated.

'Yes, sir.'

McAuley hung up. Damn it. Talk about providing the guy with steel-capped boots so he could give me a good kicking. What had I been thinking? Plus I'd almost given Rebecca away by saying her name. How stupid was that? McAuley wouldn't leave me alone now until I told him the name of the crooked cop who worked for the Dowds. I needed to find out who it was. And fast.

But how?

forty-two

Another Tuesday evening rolled around all too soon again. Tuesday evenings were beginning to feel just like Monday mornings used to. But at least my weekend had been OK. Dinner with Rebecca on Sunday and the cinema yesterday – some chick-flick she chose. The poster called it a 'romantic thriller', but it was thriller-lite as far as I was concerned. After the cinema we had a bite to eat and walked for a while, talking about anything and everything before Rebecca finally drove me home. The fifteen minutes we were parked outside my house were spent synchronizing lips rather than chatting. It was OK, I guess. Nothing like kissing Callie . . . but OK.

Until I got out of the car and saw Sephy watching me. We regarded each other silently. With a scornful toss of her head, she turned away first, dumping the bulging black bin liner in her hand into the wheelie bin for collection the following morning. She walked back into her house without saying a word to me. I stood on the pavement long after she'd gone indoors. I could see myself exactly as she saw me. It wasn't a pleasant picture.

So here I was back at TFTM, my mind full of questions and doubts and worries – and very few answers. I put on my multi-striped, multi-coloured waistcoat, trying not to take too many lingering looks at the thing before it brought on a migraine. Every time I saw my waistcoat I had to remind myself about all the money I was making. I was just fastening up my matching bow tie when Michelle came marching into the men's changing rooms. Luckily it was the beginning of the shift rather than the end, so most of us were dressed or heading that way. Michelle, however, had eyes for no one but me.

'Tobey, Gideon Dowd wants to see you in his office,' she told me.

'Now or after my shift?'

'Now.'

This was either about Rebecca or McAuley's letter to Vanessa Dowd. I knew which one I'd rather it was.

'Where's Gideon's office then?' I asked.

'That's Mr Dowd to you. Go upstairs to the Club. The office door is next to the upstairs kitchenette.'

I headed up to the Club via the back stairs and made my way to Gideon's office door. At the top of the stairs, I came to an abrupt halt. Someone was coming out of Gideon's office, someone I recognized. I only caught sight of his face for a second before he turned his back to me and strode towards the customer exit. He hadn't seen me — too busy scrutinizing the piece of paper in his hand. But it was him, I was sure of it. Frowning, I decided to keep what I'd seen to myself. At least until I could use it for my own purposes.

Now that I was back in the Club, I took another look around. The silk awnings had been removed, revealing the smooth white ceiling that hadn't been apparent before. All the statues in the alcoves had been replaced with huge potted plants. I shook my head. They shouldn't have bothered with the statues for Rebecca's party: she would've much preferred the plants. I guess the statues photographed better for all the glossy magazines. The Club was still relatively empty apart from a couple of guys taking an inventory behind the bar. I knocked twice on Dowd's door and waited to be invited in.

'Come!' came the gruff voice.

Entering the room, I closed the door quietly behind me. The smell of cigarettes and coffee instantly pummelled my nose. Godsake! Didn't the man believe in cracking a window to let in some fresh air? I turned round, taking in the tiny room at a glance. There were no windows. That explained a lot. How could Gideon stand to work in an office with no windows? The man himself was poring over some papers on his desk. He leaned back in his chair the moment he heard me move further into the room. Now I was close to him, I saw he had short black hair, carefully shaped around his face and ears like it had been measured using a ruler before being precision cut. His face and jaw were square, his lips thin like he was too mean to show any more than he had to. This was the closest I'd been to him. Too many other people had been in the way at Rebecca's party.

I stood. He stared. He stared. I stood.

'Have a seat, Tobey,' said Gideon, his eyes narrowing.

I sat.

'I'll get right to it,' he began.

No chance of a cup of coffee then?

'This thing between you and my sister has to stop.'

Or a chocolate biscuit or two? No? Oh well!

'Rebecca and I are just friends,' I began.

'I'm not interested in your view of your relationship,' Gideon interrupted. 'Rebecca is getting too attached to you and I won't have it.'

I sat back in my chair. 'Don't you think Rebecca is old enough to make her own decisions?' I asked.

'Of course not. Rebecca is totally naïve. She thinks everyone is who or what they say they are.'

Now just what did he mean by that?

'With me, what you see is what you get,' I replied.

'Tobey, this isn't a debate. You're to leave my sister alone. Quite frankly, she can do a lot better.'

'We're just having the odd meal together or trip to the cinema,' I tried. 'We're not doing any harm.'

'I don't want to hear it. I'm telling you to stay away from my sister.'

'And what does Rebecca say about all this?' I said.

Gideon looked me up and down, like he was seeing me for the very first time. 'Tobey, you don't want me as your enemy. You really don't. If you don't back off, you're out. And I can make it impossible for you to get any kind of job, anywhere – and that's just for starters.'

'I know that, Mr Dowd.'

'So what's it to be?'

I shrugged. 'No contest.'

Gideon smiled for the first time since I'd entered the room. 'I knew you'd make the right decision. You may go back to work now.'

Gideon bent his head, returning to his papers. I stood up and started to unbutton my waistcoat. It was only as I was pulling it off that Gideon noticed I was still in his office.

'What d'you think you're doing?' He frowned at me.

Saying goodbye to my university fund.

'You told me to choose between my job and Rebecca,' I said, laying my waistcoat on Gideon's desk. I took off my bow tie and placed it on top of the waistcoat. 'So I've chosen.'

Gideon's eyes narrowed. 'Tobey, you've just made the biggest mistake of your life,' he said softly.

No chance of a job reference then?

I left the room.

forty-three

Hi, Callie,

How're you feeling today? You look much better, babe, like you're only sleeping. A sleeping beauty. Godsake! I'm getting frickin' mushy. But at least most of the tubes going into your mouth and into your veins have now gone. That's a good sign – right? So you must be getting better. You're just not . . . waking up. Not yet. But you will. You have to.

I miss you so much, Callie. So much. I wish you were awake so I could tell you everything that's happened since you were . . . you were brought into hospital. I need to talk to you. You're the only one who'd understand what I've been going through, what I'm trying to do. Trouble is, I'm not sure who I am any more. I need you to remind me.

Now when I look in the mirror, a stranger stares back at me. I only feel like I'm me, the real me, when I'm in this room with you. I can't help wondering what you would say or do if you knew what I was up to. Would you try to stop me? Or would you urge me on? Six months ago, I would've said I knew the answer. Now I'm not so sure.

Your hand is warm in mine. We kind of fit together,

don't we, Callie? Like a two-piece jigsaw puzzle.

Oh my God! You squeezed my hand. I felt it. You definitely squeezed my hand. Open your eyes, babe. Please, just open your eyes and look at me.

Please.

OK then. Small steps. Maybe you're not ready to open your eyes yet, but you definitely squeezed my hand.

Small steps.

Promise me something, Callie. Promise me that when you do open your eyes, you'll recognize me. I couldn't bear it if you of all people didn't recognize me.

forty-four

The body of Ross Resnick, the manager of the well-known restaurant – Thanks For The Memories – was found in woodland this morning by two campers. Although Ross Resnick had been missing for over a month, initial forensic examinations revealed that he had only been dead for three or four days. The cause of death has not yet been established. Ross Resnick's wife, Louise, recently . . .

I switched off my phone. I didn't want to read any more news. I stared out of the bus window, watching the rest of the world pass by without a care in the world – at least that's how it felt. I was on my way home and I couldn't wait to get there. I just wanted to crawl into bed and hide away.

I no longer had a job at TFTM, but it didn't matter because the object of that exercise was to make contact with Owen Dowd. Working there and earning some extra money had just been a bonus. Meeting Rebecca had been a windfall. An innocuous date or two had turned into my sure-fire way of getting information about her family. I'd made a couple of deliveries for McAuley, but nothing I couldn't walk away from. At least that's what I'd told myself.

But now McAuley wanted more from me. He wanted to know the identity of the copper owned by the Dowds. I'd dangled that carrot in front of him because it was all I had. But all I'd gained was McAuley snapping at my heels for more. And I didn't have any more, nor the first clue how to rectify that.

And Ross Resnick was dead.

I didn't even know the man and yet somehow his death weighed heavily on me. Was he the one making all that noise in the upstairs room when Dan and I had visited McAuley's house? I'd suspected then, as I suspected now, that it had been him. And if Ross had been the one upstairs, he was probably bound and gagged and worse.

What else had they done to him before he died?

It didn't bear thinking about, but I couldn't get the question out of my head. I told myself all this was just guesswork on my part. I told myself a lot of things. But inside I *knew* Louise Resnick's husband had been alive and in the upstairs room when I heard the scraping noise.

Could I have prevented his death if I'd just phoned the police? Ross was no saint – he worked for the Dowds and they were just as bad as McAuley. But did anyone deserve to die the way he had – in pain and alone? Before Callie got shot, I'd've said an emphatic no.

Not any more.

And that scared me.

Once I got home, I headed straight for my room. I stripped off and crawled into bed, knowing that I'd have trouble sleeping. And I was right. Sleep and I remained strangers. I lay awake for the best part of the night, trying to see beyond my desire for retribution. Maybe Gideon was right about my making a mistake . . . And what about Rebecca? She was OK, much nicer than I expected her to be. What right did I have to drag her into the middle of all this? Especially as Callie was getting stronger every day. She'd squeezed my hand earlier, I was sure of it. If only I could clear my head of the image of Callie looking down at me, blood spilling out over her chest, then maybe I could let all this go. Maybe.

I had to find a way to walk away. I wanted to be around when Callie woke up. She needed me, almost as much as I needed her. I groaned inwardly as I thought of the day's events. Ross Resnick had lost his life. I'd lost my job. My problems were trivial by comparison. I'd quit my job at TFTM . . . Even now, part of me couldn't believe what I'd done. When I walked out of Gideon Dowd's office, I'd practically broken my arm trying to pat myself on the back. But now reality had set in. I mean, dramatic gestures were all very well, but what if Rebecca bowed to her brother's demands and decided not to see me again? Why did that thought bother me so much? It wasn't as if I was attracted to her or anything, but I liked her friendship. Or was it something more basic than that? Did I really like her friendship, or was it just useful? And if the answer was the latter, what did that make me? A man on a mission? Or a user like everyone else?

Rebecca always picked me up after work to drive me home so she had to be aware that I'd lost my job, but she hadn't tried to phone me. Maybe that was the end of that, but I didn't want to think so. She liked me, really liked me. That was flattering in itself. And I liked her company. So I'd give her a day and if I didn't hear anything, then I'd phone her for a chat. Perhaps I'd invite her out to dinner or maybe a film. No big deal.

And if she said no?

I'd dance across that bridge if and when I got to it.

I finally fell asleep, my head full of Rebecca, my heart full of Callie Rose.

I awoke the next morning far earlier than usual, and I still had no answers.

Let it go, Tobey.

Walk away from the Dowds and McAuley and that world – before it was too late. I headed straight for the shower to try and make sure I got my share of the hot water, but I needn't have bothered. Mum's bedroom door was open so she'd already left for the day. And there was no music or TV blasting so Jessica must've gone to college. Sweet! I had the house to myself, just the way I liked it.

I got myself a fresh towel from the airing cupboard and headed towards the bathroom. I glanced down at my pyjama bottoms doubtfully. Should I put them in the laundry basket or did they have another few days of wear left in them? I decided to keep wearing them. These ones were just moulding nicely to my body shape. I opened the bathroom door. Jessica was sitting on the floor, her back against the bath tub.

'Godsake, Jess. Suppose I'd walked in here naked? I thought you'd . . . gone . . .'

On the lowered toilet lid sat Mum's best teapot, plus a cook's blowtorch from one of the kitchen cupboards. A faint coil of smoke, like a dying mist, emerged from the teapot spout.

What the hell . . . ?

'Jessica . . . ?' My whisper of disbelief somehow got through to her. Her eyelids fluttered open and she looked at me, her pupils the size of pinpricks, her gaze unfocused.

Jessica opened her mouth to say something, but the words got lost somewhere in her head. She blinked twice like her eyelids weighed as much as her entire body, then she closed her eyes. She slumped over and would have hit the floor if I hadn't been there to catch her. Propping her up with one hand, I took the lid off the teapot with the other. A dark-brown stain coated the bottom of the pot. An unfamiliar smell wafted up to greet me. Vinegar . . . I looked at the cook's blowtorch and the teapot and my sister, and only then did I realize what I was seeing. And even then I still couldn't believe it.

What had she taken? From the look of it, Jess was smoking junk. But she couldn't, she wouldn't be that stupid. I looked round the base of the toilet then checked the bin. A crumpled piece of paper, like a waxed sweet wrapper, lay on top of all the other rubbish. She hadn't even tried to hide it. I picked up the wrapper and gingerly raised it to my nose. There was no smell to it. I guessed you had to burn the stuff to get the vinegary smell. I'm sure we were told at school that heroin gave off a sweet smell. Maybe it depended on the type. The inside of the wrapper was sticky, gummy beneath my tentative finger. What had Jessica mixed this stuff with? Crumpling up the wrapper, I dropped it back in the bin, vigorously wiping my fingers on the legs of my pyjamas.

Jessica was using. How long had she been doing this? And how had both Mum and I missed it? Should I phone for an ambulance? Was this a normal state for a drug-taker or had she overdosed? I tried to think back to the drugs education lessons we'd had when I was thirteen. Wasn't it harder to overdose by inhaling junk rather than injecting? Harder, yes, but by no means impossible. I hadn't paid much attention to the lessons at the time. I was sure I'd never be stupid enough to chase the dragon or inject or snort or any of that other stuff, so why bother listening? Now I wished I'd listened to each and every word the teacher had said. Was Jessica going to be OK? I had no way of knowing. The teapot sat there, mocking me. Me and my deliveries.

'Jess, open your eyes. Come on, Jess. Just open your eyes,' I begged.

I shook her and gently patted her face. Her eyelids fluttered open, a spark of recognition in her eyes. Without warning, she launched herself at the toilet bowl. The torch clattered to the floor and I only just caught the teapot as the toilet seat was pushed up out of the way before Jessica puked her guts out. Squatting down, stroking Jessica's back, I pulled her hair back off her face. She closed her eyes and slumped back against me. She was out of it again.

My sister was still breathing and her pulse seemed steady, but that was it. That did it. Time to phone for an ambulance. I couldn't take the chance of Jessica having a bad reaction to the stuff she'd inhaled – or vomiting again whilst she was unconscious. My thoughts must've communicated themselves to my sister, 'cause she opened her eyes. Coffee. Should I make some coffee? No, that was for hangovers. Godsake! Exactly what use would coffee be to my sister now? I wasn't thinking straight.

'Jess, listen. When did you use this stuff? Five minutes ago? An hour ago? When?'

I might as well be talking Martian for all the good it did me. It couldn't've been that long ago, not if the smoke was still coming out of the spout when I entered the room. I checked Jessica's arms. No needle marks. At least she wasn't shooting up. Yet.

Mum. Should I phone Mum? That's right, Tobey – this is all Mum needs to brighten her day. I wouldn't phone her unless it was absolutely necessary. But suppose Jess collapsed whilst I was dithering about desperately trying to make up my mind what I should do? Godsake, what did I know about drugs and all that stuff?

Don't shoot me, I'm only the delivery boy.

Just let my sister shoot up instead.

It was useless to say sorry and even more useless to think it, no matter how heartfelt. I looked at my sister and it was like every blood cell had turned into tiny shards of razor-sharp glass which were now dragging their way through my veins. Useless or not, I had to say it.

'Jess, I'm sorry.'

I checked her pulse and breathing again. Slow but steady.

'Jess, open your eyes,' I ordered when she tried to slump again. 'Jess, look at me.'

Godsake. How much of the stuff did she inhale?

I thought of all those half days in and full days off Jessica was always claiming to have. Is this what she'd been doing with all that time at home? Did she still have her job? Or did she just spend her days inhaling Meadowview Oblivion – or MO, as it was known around here? Two friends I'd known since primary school were addicted to MO, but I never for one second thought my sister had joined them. I still couldn't quite understand how I hadn't noticed what was going on. But then, what did I expect? I'd been so wrapped up in other things, I wouldn't've noticed if she'd sprouted another head in the last few weeks. Guiltily, I remembered that I hadn't even bothered to wish her luck in her exam – even though I'd known how important it was to her that she passed.

What should I do?

If I phoned for an ambulance, Mum would find out. But maybe that's what my sister needed – for Mum to find out and help her. My head was spinning. What to do for the best? Jess's eyes were open, she was looking at me.

'Jess, I'm going to phone Mum.'

Jess slowly shook her head. 'No,' she whispered. 'Please.'

'Jess, she needs to know.'

'No. Promise.'

I started to shake my head.

'Promise,' Jessica urged.

'OK,' I replied reluctantly.

'Promise.'

'I . . . I promise.'

'Y–you should . . . sh–should be asleep.' Jess's eyelids kept fluttering shut.

And I would've been if I'd still been working at TFTM. Getting home late from that job meant that I slept until past noon each day. Was that what Jessica had been relying on? She wasn't to know that I'd lost my job. Early to bed meant early to rise. Too early as far as my sister was concerned. I sat on the floor with her, cradling her in my arms as I waited for her to come out of it. There was nothing else I could do.

Deliveries.

forty-five

When my legs threatened to die under me from sitting on the cold bathroom floor for so long, I managed to stand up and half carry, half drag my sister to her bedroom. She was totally lethargic. Laying her on the bed, I covered her with the duvet. I sat down next to her and kept watch all morning. The house was so quiet, it didn't feel right. Jessica went from fitful sleep to long moments when she didn't appear to be breathing at all. I had to keep getting up to take her pulse or put my ear to her nose to feel her breath against my skin. It was only around midday that she finally started sleeping normally. I had to risk leaving her alone so I could have a shower and tidy up before Mum came home, but I popped into her room every few minutes to check on her.

I vacuumed the whole house, tidied the kitchen and the bathroom and scrubbed out the teapot. Mum only broke out this particular teapot once or twice a year, but I didn't fancy the idea of any of our elderly relatives getting high or, more likely, poisoned. A teapot . . . Godsake! Just what did my sister think she was doing? All I could do was hope that Jessica hadn't peed the bed or puked or done anything else that would be a dead giveaway. Whilst she was asleep, I searched through my sister's wardrobe, then her chest of drawers. In the right-hand corner of her bottom drawer, at the back, were two more wrappers. I opened one up. It contained a grey-brown lump, about the size of a chewy mint. Even though I'd heard all about the stuff – and who hadn't, living in Meadowview? – I'd never seen it up close and personal like this before. I tried to remember all I knew about this stuff, the different kinds manufactured around the world. It was sticky, highly addictive, extremely potent – that's about all that came to mind. The wrapper shook in my hands. I searched around for more paper wrappers in Jessica's bottom drawer, but there were no more. Heading for the bathroom, I emptied the contents of the two wrappers down the loo, dropping the wrappers in after them. I flushed the toilet, but whilst the contents disappeared, the wrappers didn't. It wasn't going to be that easy. A second flush, and then a third, and the waxy wrappers still wouldn't go down. They just floated on top of the water. I ended up having to stick my hand down into the toilet bowl to retrieve them before Mum came home and saw them. I washed my hands over and over for a good five minutes afterwards, but they still felt dirty. I sat on the toilet lid for ages, just trying to think straight.

I headed back to Jessica's room and sat at the foot of her bed.

'Jessica,' I said softly, not wanting to scare her into waking abruptly. 'Jess, wake up.'

My sister finally opened her eyes. For the first time in hours her gaze was focused and she knew who I was. I had my sister back. She sat up, then groaned, her hand flying to her head.

'What time is it?' she whispered.

'It's just after one.'

Her gaze grew watchful. Silence.

'Are you going to tell Mum?' she asked at last.

'No,' I replied.

Jess breathed a sigh of relief. The smile she turned on me was full of gratitude.

'But you are,' I told her.

Her smile vanished. She started to shake her head, but quickly stopped. She closed her eyes like she was in pain. 'I can't.'

'Yes, you can, Jess. 'Cause if you don't tell her, I will.'

'No, you mustn't. Please, Tobey.'

'I'm sorry, Jess. I'd keep quiet about most things, but not this. You need to get help before it's too late.'

Jessica's eyes narrowed. 'Stop looking at me like that. This is only the third time I've smoked the stuff,' she snapped. 'I can handle it.'

'That's what they all say,' I replied. 'Godsake, Jess. A teapot? Are you so desperate you had to use Mum's teapot?'

'He said it would be easier than trying to inhale the smoke off foil. He said the teapot would cool down the smoke and I could inhale it when it came out the spout.'

'Who's "he"?' I asked sharply.

Jessica turned away from me. 'I was just trying it,' she said, trying to defend herself. 'I'm not an addict. Addicts inject. I don't inject.'

'Smoking that crap leads to injecting, you know that. This is non-negotiable, Jess. You've got to tell Mum before it gets worse.'

'If you make me do this, I'll never forgive you.'

'That's up to you,' I replied. 'But I'm not going through another morning like this one. Never again, Jess.'

'You didn't need to spy on me. I didn't ask you to. Just sod off and mind your own business.' Jessica was getting more and more angry.

'You're my sister, so you are my business,' I told her. Ironic words, considering how much I resented them each time Jessica said them to me. I headed for the door before turning back, a frown biting into the corners of my mouth.

'Why did you do it? Godsake, Jessica. You know what that stuff does. Why put yourself through that?'

'You wouldn't understand.'

'Try me.'

Jessica shook her head. 'Just leave me alone.'

'Jess, how could you be so stupid?'

'That's right!' she screamed at me. 'I am stupid. Stupid Jessica who can't do anything right. Stupid Jessica who can't learn anything, can't be anything.'

I stared at her. 'Is this . . . is this about your hairdressing course?'

'Don't be stupid,' Jess dismissed. 'No . . . hang on . . . that's me, isn't it? I'm the brainless one in this family. I've spent my entire life running to catch up with you, Tobey.'

'So all this is my fault?'

'This isn't about you. Not everything is about you.' Her voice grew quieter. 'Tobey, just go away.'

I recognized that look on Jessica's face. She wasn't going to say anything else – nothing I wanted to hear at any rate. I headed for the door, but something else occurred to me.

'Jess, where did you get the gear from?'

'None of your business.' She lay down again, turning away from me.

I walked over to her, placing my hand on her shoulder and turning her round to face me. 'Who sold you that stuff?'

Jess sat up and glared at me. 'D'you really want me to tell you?'

In that moment, I knew – but I had to hear her say it.

Jess said one word, the one word I dreaded. 'Dan.'

Dan.

Icy fingers clutched at my stomach as I stared down at my sister. If my so-called friend had been standing in front of me right then and there, I'd've ripped his head off with my bare hands. Jessica staggered to her feet and headed for the bathroom. Moments later I heard the sound of the shower running. At least she was up and about now, making an effort before Mum arrived. But for how long? And she was going to seriously lose it when she discovered what I'd done to the rest of her junk. I still had the bag of cocaine Adam Eisner had given me, but that was hidden away where no one would find it. I sure as hell wasn't going to use it, but I hadn't thrown it away either. I had no such qualms about my sister's stuff.

And as for Dan . . . he was going to pay.

Him and McAuley.

They profited by biting huge chunks out of all of us in Meadowview. It was time for someone to bite back.

forty-six

The following morning brought cooler weather, which was welcome, and some unexpected visitors who were not so welcome. Two guests, to be precise. DI Boothe and Sergeant Kenwood. Like I didn't have more than enough on my plate already. Mum wasn't too thrilled, to say the very least. Not only did she get woken up early, but it was the police. Mum was always warning me that she didn't want the police knocking on our door for any reason. At least the police car outside our front door was unmarked. I was grateful for that, otherwise I would never have heard the end of it. I don't know why they sent the same two coppers who'd interviewed me at the hospital. Maybe their bosses thought we'd established some kind of a rapport!

'Would anyone like a cup of tea?' Mum asked, more out of politeness than anything else.

'I'd love one, Miss Durbridge,' said Sergeant Kenwood.

'It's Mrs,' Mum bristled.

'Mrs Durbridge,' he corrected with a false smile.

'I'd love a cup too,' said the detective. 'Two sugars. If you're sure you don't mind?'

'No trouble at all,' said Mum, her tone indicating otherwise. 'Tobey?'

I shook my head. Mum headed off.

Sergeant Kenwood sauntered over to shut the door. All my senses ratcheted up another gear, though I didn't turn round to watch him directly. The cups of tea were obviously a ploy to get my mum out of the room.

'We wondered if you'd had a chance to remember anything else?' asked the detective.

I shook my head. 'I've told you everything I know.'

'But I don't believe you,' he said.

Well, that was hardly my problem, but from the look on his face, the detective was about to change that.

'I think it would be best if—' He didn't get any further.

My sister Jess flung open the door and stalked into the room.

'Is Tobey in trouble?' she asked straight out.

'And you are . . . ?' asked Sergeant Kenwood, breaking out his notebook.

Jess walked over to him to stand at his side as he wrote. 'Tobey's sister, Jessica,' she said. 'That's J-e-s-s-i-c-a.' She peered over the sergeant's arm to make sure he spelled her name right. 'God, that's rubbish handwriting. Don't you have to rely on what you've written when you go to court? How can you even read that?'

And in spite of everything that had happened the previous day, I don't think I've ever felt closer to my sister than I did at that moment. I loved the way she refused to let Sergeant Kenwood intimidate her. Jessica smiled at me. It was uncertain, as was mine, but at least it was shared. We had our moment of connection which had been missing the day before.

'Paul, put your notebook away.' Detective Inspector Boothe sighed.

The sergeant reluctantly did as he was told, by which time Mum had come back in with two cups of tea. She handed them to the officers before turning to my sister.

'Jessica, this doesn't concern you. Could you go to your room, please?'

'Mum, don't send me to my room like I'm a child,' Jessica argued.

'Then go to the kitchen, go into the garden, go and sit on the roof if you want, but I don't want you in here,' said Mum.

Jess and I knew that tone of voice. Mum only brought it out a mere handful of times a year, so it was seldom used, but very effective. Pouting like a trout, Jess flounced out. Mum turned back to the coppers.

'Now then, is there a problem, officers?' she said, getting straight to it.

'Mrs Durbridge, we'd like your son to come down to the station to make a second formal statement,' said DI Boothe.

'Why does he need to do that?' asked Mum, clutching her dressing gown even more tightly around her. 'He's already told you everything he knows.'

'We need a new formal statement,' Sergeant Kenwood reiterated. He turned to me, his blue eyes cold as a winter sea. 'Tobey, you're the only witness we've got. Apparently, you and Callie Hadley were the only ones in the park at the time of the incident — apart from the shooters of course. Amazing, that. Saturday afternoon and only you and your girlfriend in the park. Who would've thought it?'

Sarcastic git. He made it sound like his lack of witnesses was my fault. But then wasn't I doing the same as everyone else when it came to not telling the police what had really happened?

'My son isn't going anywhere without me,' said Mum.

'Of course, Mrs Durbridge,' soothed the detective.

'If you could wait here please,' said Mum firmly. 'I have to get dressed.'

Without waiting for their reply, she headed back upstairs. No way was I going to stay in the living room with the two coppers. I bolted, mumbling something about getting my jacket. I went to my room and sat on my bed, waiting until I heard Mum head downstairs again. Formal statement, my eye. I wasn't going to say anything that I hadn't already said, so why drag me and my mum all the way down the police station? This was harassment. Or intimidation. Or both. But if they thought they were going to scare me into saying anything detrimental to my health, they were very much mistaken.

When we reached the police station, Sergeant Kenwood ushered me and Mum into an interview room and left us there. I waited for the explosion from Mum, but she didn't speak, not one word. In a way, that made it worse. I sat there with the weight of her disappointment pressing down hard upon me. We sat on one side of a table. Recording equipment had been set into the adjacent wall. A CCTV camera sat self-consciously in one corner of the room, attached to the ceiling like some great black beetle.

After about ten minutes, DI Boothe entered the room with some Cross woman I'd never seen before. She wore a black trouser suit with a light-blue shirt and lace-up black shoes with low heels. Her hair was cut ultra short and neat. And though her face was expertly made up, she was pretty average looking. If I'd passed her in the street, I wouldn't've looked at her twice. She and DI Boothe sat down and the woman pressed the record button before even looking at me. Mum and I exchanged a look.

'Interview room three, twelfth of August, the time is nine-fifteen a.m. Detective Chief Inspector Reid and Detective Inspector Boothe in attendance, interviewing Tobey Durbridge, aged seventeen. His mother Mrs Ann Durbridge is also in attendance.'

DCI Reid faced me and I immediately revised my opinion of her. The rest of her might've been nothing to write home about, but her eyes were ruthlessly sharp and shrewd and didn't miss anything.

'Tobey, could you tell me exactly what happened on the afternoon of the tenth of July when Callie Rose Hadley was shot.'

So once again, I told my story. And throughout the whole retelling DCI Reid kept checking her watch. If I didn't know any better, I'd've said she didn't have the slightest interest in what I was saying. The moment my statement was over and signed, DCI Reid thanked me and announced to the recording that DI Boothe was leaving the room. The detective stood up and did exactly that. DCI Reid stopped the recording and we all sat in silence. DCI Reid didn't take her eyes off me. Not once. What was going on? Less than a minute later, Detective Inspector Boothe was back. A quick nod of his head and a thank you from the DCI and we were escorted from the interview room.

The scratching claws in my stomach told me that something wasn't right here. What was all this about? Why drag Mum and me all the way down here to make a statement they already had and obviously didn't want again? They hadn't challenged me on anything I'd said. They hadn't tried to make me change my story. There was none of the usual stuff I'd seen on the TV.

So what was going on?

The claws in my stomach grew more vicious with each passing second. This just didn't feel right. And then I saw him coming towards me, flanked by two Cross coppers.

McAuley.

In handcuffs.

'I'm going to sue everyone here for wrongful arrest and malicious prosecution.' McAuley's voice held quiet menace as he spoke to one of the officers at his side. 'This is harassment, pure and simple. I haven't done anything so you have no right to arrest me.' He was so steaming mad, I'm surprised the paint didn't blister on the walls. He saw me and did a double take. Then he smiled slowly. One of his all-knowing little smiles. Recognizing him, Mum gave McAuley one of the filthiest looks she could muster, but he only had eyes for me. As we passed each other in the corridor, he didn't take his eyes off me, not for a second.

'Don't worry about the police, Tobey,' he said, low enough so that only I could hear. 'Once I'm out, I'll take care of you.'

My heart went into free fall.

I'd been set up.

'What did that animal say to you?' Mum asked angrily once McAuley was out of earshot.

'Nothing, Mum.'

'Don't give me that,' she argued. 'He clearly said something. You're as white as a white thing. Did he threaten you?'

I shook my head. 'He just recognized me as Dan's friend. That's all. Dan knows him.'

Mum didn't look entirely convinced, but she let it slide. And as for me? A potent cocktail of fear and fury had me shaking inside. All that crap about making a statement. The police just wanted to have McAuley and me in the same place at the same time to make McAuley think that I'd been telling tales. And if the expression on McAuley's face was anything to go by, it had worked.

forty-seven

When we got to the front desk, DI Boothe asked me, 'Are you ready to revise your statement now?'

'No,' I snapped.

DI Boothe took me to one side and lowered his voice as Mum signed the necessary paperwork at the desk. 'Tobey, we're the only ones who can protect you from McAuley. Tell us what really happened at the Wasteland. Be smart.'

DI Boothe and his colleagues had thrown me into the lion's den and were now telling me they could shield me? Yeah, right.

'I'll be fine,' I told him, knowing the words were a lie before they even left my mouth. I was a dead man walking.

DI Boothe shook his head pityingly.

'You want me to trust you? For all I know you could be the one working for the Dowds,' I said bitterly. 'Is that why you set me up? So McAuley can deal with me? Are you acting on Gideon Dowd's orders?'

The detective stared at me, genuinely shocked. It quickly morphed into anger. 'Are you suggesting I'm on the take?'

'It's well known that the Dowds own some high-up

copper at this station – no doubt someone who warns them about forthcoming raids and sting operations and undercover cops and the like. That's why the Dowds are untouchable. And then you wonder why no one in Meadowview will talk to you?'

DI Boothe was taking in everything I said like he'd never heard of such a thing before. He was either a great actor or he really had no idea there was at least one crooked copper, and probably more, on his patch.

He looked around quickly. Mum was still at the reception desk and no one else was close enough to hear our hushed conversation.

'Tobey, you can trust me,' said the detective. At my look of scepticism, he added, 'I know I would say that anyway, but it's the truth. All I want is to bring down Alex McAuley and the Dowds. We in Meadowview deserve better.'

'*We* in Meadowview?' My eyebrows were raised as high as they could go.

'Yes, *we*,' the detective emphasized. 'Because contrary to what you may think, I live here too. Tobey, talk to me. Tell me what you know.'

'All I know is, McAuley thinks I've been in here, singing my head off, thanks to you. Strange that, don't you think? Gideon Dowd warns me to stay away from his sister and when I refuse, the next thing I know I'm dragged in here for McAuley to see. What a great way for Gideon Dowd to make sure McAuley does his dirty work for him. And now I'm supposed to trust you to protect me? You're a bent copper in Gideon Dowd's pocket and we both know it.'

'I don't work for the Dowds or Alex McAuley,' DI Boothe denied vehemently. 'It wasn't even my idea to bring you in.'

'Then whose idea was it? 'Cause that person is probably working for Gideon Dowd,' I said.

Boothe didn't answer.

I glared at him, saying scornfully, 'And I'm supposed to trust you?'

'It's safer if you don't know who arranged to have you brought in. I'll look into it,' he said, his lips a determined slash across his face.

'You do that,' I said with scepticism. 'Oh, and are you having me followed?'

DI Boothe didn't reply.

'Is that a yes?' I asked, knowing full well it was. 'May I ask why?'

Boothe considered whether or not to answer my question. 'We needed to know who you were covering for – the Dowds or McAuley. We were hoping to catch you in conversation with one or the other.' He smiled without any real humour. 'But you like to fly with the birds and swim with the fishes at the same time, don't you? As far as those following you could tell, you were working with both.'

'Tell your officers to stop following me,' I said angrily. 'For one thing, they're not very good at it. And if you want to know who I'm working for, all you have to do is ask.'

'I'm asking,' said the detective.

I smiled. 'I'm working for myself. No one else.'

'And if I don't believe you?'

'That's your problem. In the meantime, I'm outta here.'

'Let us protect you,' Boothe tried again.

'Thanks, but no thanks.'

'I personally give you my word that no harm will come to you or your family.'

'I can take care of myself,' I replied.

DI Boothe shook his head. 'Tobey, you're a fool. Don't you realize I'm on your side? When you finally figure that out, give me a call – but don't leave it too long.'

He walked away just as Mum approached us and before I could say another word.

By the time we got back home, Mum was livid at the police for, as she put it, 'dragging us down to the station for no good reason'. I left her still ranting as I headed for my room. I couldn't forget the look on McAuley's face when he saw me. Surely he knew that I wouldn't blab? I wasn't stupid. Everyone was using me, and if the police didn't get me, McAuley or the Dowds would. I needed some insurance – not for me, but for my mum and sister. I wasn't going to let anything happen to them.

If it was just me, then I could tell them all to go to hell. But it wasn't just me. Anything I did to McAuley or the Dowds would be returned tenfold by those who worked for them. They'd make sure that it wouldn't just be me who suffered. My family, my close friends, they'd all be fair game too. That's why I had to tread so carefully. I wasn't ready or prepared to take on McAuley yet. So I had to get things straightened out with him. This thing with Rebecca had resulted in me taking my eye off the ball. It was time to remedy that.

I lay down on my bed, staring up at the ceiling. What had started off as a tentative saunter down this particular path had now turned into a roller-coaster ride over which I had absolutely no control. I'd known that if I started this, it would be very hard to stop, but no one had warned me it would be impossible.

Would that have stopped me from embarking on this course of action?

Probably not.

I lay still for almost an hour, just trying to gather my thoughts together into some semblance of order. What exactly was I letting myself in for? I was blundering into the unknown, but I wouldn't've turned back, even if I could.

The mobile McAuley had given me started to ring. I hadn't expected anything else. I knew the moment he got out of the police station, he'd be giving me a call. The moment I pressed the talk button, he launched in.

'I want to see you,' he said.

'Yes, sir.'

'I'll be outside your house in ten minutes.'

'Oh, but—' I began, thinking of the wobbly Mum would throw if she saw McAuley parked outside our house. He would be even less welcome than the police.

'Yes?' McAuley said brusquely.

'Nothing, sir. I'll be waiting.'

McAuley disconnected the call.

Ten minutes . . .

The countdown had begun.

forty-eight

I stopped outside Mum's closed bedroom door. She was probably fast asleep by now and wouldn't thank me for waking her up. Jessica had gone out somewhere. I so desperately needed to say goodbye to someone. Anyone. But there was no one. With a sigh, I headed downstairs, leaving Mum undisturbed. I headed out of the house, my hands deep in jacket pockets. I looked up at the blue sky, hoping . . .

But I didn't get my wish.

McAuley arrived right on time. I cast an anxious glance up at Mum's bedroom, but her curtains were closed against the daylight. Byron was the only other person in the car and he was driving. McAuley pointed to the seat next to him in the back. I got in. The door was only just shut when Byron drove off. And with each second, the hollow space inside me grew bigger and bigger.

'Mr McAuley, you have to believe me, I never said a word to the police,' I launched in immediately. 'They dragged Mum and me down to the station to make a statement, but I didn't tell them anything because I don't know anything. They're trying to set me up so that you'll think I've been telling tales.'

McAuley leaned back against the luxurious leather seat, his laptop on the seat between us, a newspaper on his lap as his gaze dissected me. Was it just me or was it uncomfortably hot in his car?

'Why would the police set you up?'

'To make you think I'm a danger to you. That way, with you after me, they reckoned I'd have no choice but to co-operate with them.'

'Co-operate?'

'The police think I know more about the shooting at the Wasteland than I'm saying. But I don't.' I looked McAuley in the eyes as I spoke, desperate for him to believe me. 'When the shooting started, I hit the ground and stayed there. I didn't see a thing.'

McAuley studied me for a long time. I didn't look away or flinch from his gaze. Not once. Because that would've been fatal. My heart was skipping like a boxer in training.

Don't throw up, Tobey. For God's sake don't throw up.

Especially not in McAuley's car.

Or worse still, over him.

At last McAuley's expression relaxed, although his eyes stayed hard as ever.

'How's your job at TFTM?'

What was he up to now? Were his unpredictable conversational leaps designed to catch me out? Careful, Tobey . . . Impatiently, I wiped my forehead with the palm of my hand. Would it kill him to turn on the air conditioning or to open the windows? But why should he? McAuley didn't have a single bead of sweat on him.

'I don't work there any more, sir.'

'Oh? Why not?'

I decided to keep my story as close to the truth as possible. 'Gideon Dowd fired me.'

'Why?'

'For going out with his sister.'

'Rebecca.'

'Yes, sir.'

'And you two are still together?'

'I don't know, sir. I haven't heard from her in a while.'

'D'you like her?'

I shrugged.

McAuley contemplated me. 'So you're sleeping with the enemy.'

I opened my mouth to deny it, only for my mouth to snap shut. Even if McAuley didn't mean literally, he meant figuratively. It was the same difference to him.

'Mr McAuley, if you tell me not to see her again, then I won't,' I said after a moment's pause. 'I'm only with her to try and find out the name of the bent copper in the Dowds' pocket. Rebecca was the one who gave me that information in the first place.'

'You still haven't found out who it is yet?'

'No, sir. But I will. I just need more time.'

'And you don't think you've had enough already?'

'I will get you the information, sir. I guarantee it.'

McAuley turned to his driver. 'What d'you think, Byron? Is Tobey a man of his word?'

Byron shrugged. 'I think he's too clever by half – or at least he thinks he is.'

McAuley smiled. And his smile sent a chill ricocheting around my body. Where were they taking me? What were they going to do? McAuley picked up his PC and placed it on his lap over the newspaper, before analysing the screen. His memory key was attached to one of the two USB ports at the side. Why did he need to carry his laptop around with him all the time? Was it just for effect? To make him look more businesslike? Or was there actually stuff on it that he needed at a moment's notice? I carried on watching him, but he completely ignored me. He appeared to be reading emails, but I couldn't exactly lean in for a closer look. Our conversation, such as it was, was over. At least for now.

I swallowed hard. Should I say something? Press my case? Did he believe what I'd said or not? I looked out of the window. I didn't recognize where we were and I didn't have a clue where we were going. After about twenty minutes of total silence in the car, I risked another glance at McAuley. His laptop was back on the seat between us and he was watching me. Sweat was dripping off my forehead.

'Too hot for you, Tobey?' asked McAuley.

'A little,' I admitted, taking off my jacket before I melted into a puddle on the floor. I put it on the seat between us.

'I like it hot,' said McAuley. 'I find I think better when the heat is on.'

I didn't doubt it. With a smile, McAuley picked up his newspaper and started reading.

Where the hell were we now? Somewhere countrified by the look of it. There were no houses now, just fields in various shades of green as far as the eye could see, and trees to my left, lining up on the horizon. Thoughts drummed in my head like rain on a corrugated roof. My intestines were tying themselves in knots. *Where were they taking me?*

Byron turned left onto a single-track road and we drove for another few minutes. More and more trees appeared all around us. Byron turned the car to the left and took us off-road. The suspension on the car must've been state of the art, because I did little more than bounce a couple of times.

'Bryon, stop here,' McAuley ordered, closing his newspaper and folding it neatly.

The car came to a smooth halt. Byron had stopped the car, but the engine was still running. We were in the middle of leafy nowhere. Trees surrounded us like sentinels, silent witnesses to whatever was about to go down. I couldn't even hear the odd bird chirping. I didn't recognize where we were at all. We'd only been travelling for slightly under an hour, but this might as well have been another planet.

This was it.

'Tobey, d'you know where we are?'

I shook my head.

'Neither does anyone else,' said McAuley, adding silkily, 'You do understand, don't you?'

Oh, yes.

'Mr McAuley, I work for you now,' I said quietly. 'There's no way I would ever betray you.'

'Loyalty means everything to me, Tobey. Everything. I've told you that before.'

'Yes, sir.'

'Maybe you should give him a test, Mr McAuley? See which side he's really on,' said Byron.

'Maybe I should at that,' McAuley agreed slowly.

I glanced between Byron and his boss. What kind of

test? Had I been granted a reprieve or set on the path to hell? Or was I already on my way?

'But maybe he just isn't worth it,' mused McAuley.

He smiled, enjoying the power he had over me. My life lay in his hands and he was making sure I knew it. And I did. He didn't have to bring me all the way out here to the arse end of nowhere to make his point.

'You're going to have to prove yourself to me, Tobey. I think that's only fair, don't you?'

'Yes, sir.'

The hollowness inside was gnawing away at me now. Godsake. What was McAuley going to make me do?

'First I want you to tell me everything, and I mean *everything* that happened at the police station earlier,' McAuley ordered. 'And take your damned jacket off my computer.'

'Sorry, sir.' I retrieved my jacket.

'That's a serious piece of kit and you just chuck your jacket over it?'

'I'm sorry, Mr McAuley.'

I slipped the object in my hand into my jacket pocket, trying to make my movements as unnoticeable as possible. If I never made it beyond this forest, at least . . . I was getting ahead of myself. One step at a time. I needed to survive. So whatever McAuley asked me to do, whatever test he gave me, I would do it.

No. Matter. What.

'Cause it had to be better than the alternative.

I told McAuley everything he wanted to know. I didn't leave out anything. He interjected with the occasional question, but that was it. When I finished, he scrutinized me some more.

'Well, Byron?' asked McAuley, never taking his eyes off me. 'Is he telling the truth?'

'I'd say so, sir,' Byron replied.

'You're still useful to me, Tobey – lucky for you.'

'Yes, Mr McAuley.' Very lucky.

'Take us back, Byron,' said McAuley.

And those words were like hard-rock music to my ears. Byron carefully turned the car round and headed back the way we'd come.

'Byron, I do enjoy my visits to the countryside, don't I?' said McAuley.

'That you do, sir.' I caught Byron's tiny smile in the driver's mirror.

The rest of the journey home was achieved in complete and utter silence. I looked out of the window, but had to wait over half an hour before I saw a landmark I recognized.

Once we arrived at my house, as I turned to open the car door, McAuley said, 'I've thought of a way you can prove yourself to me, Tobey.'

My hand froze on the door handle. 'Yes, sir?'

'When you've found out the identity of the crooked officer who works for the Dowds, I want you to make another delivery.' McAuley's smile held smug satisfaction. He was incredibly pleased with himself.

'Another package for Mr Eisner?'

'Not this time.' McAuley shook his head. 'I'll want you to make this delivery to me personally.'

'To you, sir?' My words were sharper than intended. What could I possibly bring him that he didn't already have?

'You have access to something that I can't get near. Rebecca Dowd, Tobey. I want you to bring me Rebecca Dowd.'

And just like that, the hollow, gnawing sensation deep inside me ceased. There was nothing left inside. I was now hollow all the way through.

Rebecca . . .

'Yes, Mr McAuley.'

'So you'll do it.' It wasn't a question.

'Yes, Mr McAuley. Anything you say.'

'I'll let you know where and when. Keep the phone I gave you with you at all times.'

'Yes, sir. I always do.'

McAuley turned away from me. I was dismissed. I got out of the car. Byron drove off the moment the door was shut. I watched the car until it turned the corner and was out of sight. And still I stared after it. Rebecca Dowd was now a package scheduled for delivery. And I was the one who had to deliver her. I couldn't jeopardize all my plans for Rebecca. I just couldn't. What about Callie? McAuley had to pay for what he did to Callie.

But could I really sacrifice Rebecca?

Yes.

No . . .

I didn't know. That was the scary thing. I really didn't know.

I entered my house, heading straight for my bedroom. Even with the door shut behind me, I couldn't relax. I flopped down on my bed, my head in my hands, willing the tension headache between my eyes to dissipate. Minutes passed before I stopped shaking. I emptied my pockets onto my bed. McAuley's memory key shone up at me, the one I'd swapped for my own. In his car, I'd really believed I wouldn't make it home again, at least not in one living piece. But if I was going to die, I wanted to make sure McAuley wouldn't get away with it. So using my jacket for cover, I'd switched his memory key for my own corrupt one. The fraught actions of a desperate man. And all the time I was swapping the memory keys, I expected to feel his hand around my wrist, followed by Byron's gun at my head. But I'd got away with it.

I wasn't even sure what I'd been thinking. Something about my body being found with McAuley's memory stick in my pocket. If that didn't directly incriminate him, then I'd hoped there would be something on it that the police could use to bring him down. Not exactly the way I originally had it planned, but I'd had to improvise.

So now what?

I had McAuley's memory stick.

And he had mine . . .

I sat bolt upright, staring a hole through my wall. Was there anything on that stick to link it back to me? I thought long and hard. My memory key was completely corrupt, totally unreadable. But what if McAuley found a way to retrieve data off it? Then he'd find my chemistry homework and the history presentation Callie and I had been working on. If he managed to retrieve just one file, I was screwed.

I forced myself to calm down. I'd tried every trick in the book to retrieve data off that stick and I was no slouch when it came to computing. If I couldn't do it, then surely he couldn't? I'd just have to hope I wasn't indulging in wishful thinking. I was safe. Was I safe? Until I heard otherwise, no news had to be good news. In the meantime, I maybe had something I could use against him. And I had to work fast before I was forced to do something monstrous.

My admittedly naïve initial plan had been to get close to McAuley. To follow orders – any orders – until I learned something I could use against him. I'd planned to become another Dan, with my eyes wide open and my mouth tight shut. But now I had the memory stick, I'd be stupid to pass up this opportunity.

My phone rang, just as I was about to switch on my computer.

'Hello, Dan,' I said coolly, after reading the caller ID.

'Tobey, can you be at my house in five minutes?'

'Why?'

'I need your help,' said Dan.

It only took me a moment to decide.

'I'll be there,' I told him.

He disconnected the call, like he expected nothing less.

forty-nine

Five minutes later, I was standing outside Dan's door. I hadn't forgotten Callie. Or my sister. I'd never forget the way Jess looked when I opened the bathroom door. It kept playing on repeat in my head, along with Callie being shot. Even now I was afraid I'd give myself away with every word I said to Dan and every look I gave him. Why would I even think about helping him? Friends close. Enemies closer.

'Hi, Dan,' I said, the moment he opened the door.

'Hi, Tobey.'

Dan shifted from foot to foot. I stood perfectly still. I'd never really noticed the way Dan fidgeted before. For the first time I wondered if he was sampling his own merchandise.

'So what's the problem?'

'Mr McAuley just phoned and gave me a job to do, but I can't do it alone,' said Dan.

'What's the job?'

'Some dagger, name of Boris Haddon. He owes Mr McAuley money and I'm being sent to collect it. Mr McAuley warned me this is my last chance. He told me if I screw this up, then I'd better crawl under a rock and stay there.'

'And you want me to help you strong-arm some guy into giving you money? I don't think so, Dan. That's called five to ten years in prison.'

'I just need some backup. I'll do all the talking and none of us will come to any harm. He'll hand over the money and we'll be on our way in less than a minute. But if I'm alone, Haddon might be tempted to try something stupid.'

'Who is this Boris Haddon?'

'He owns a bakery in North Meadowview. It's doing very well by all accounts.'

Hence a vulture like McAuley circling.

'Does Haddon know you're coming?'

''Course not,' Dan scoffed. 'At least . . . at least, I don't think so.'

'So are you supposed to go to his house or his shop or what?'

'Mr McAuley said Haddon would be in his shop till six this evening, but I thought we could go now before the lunch-time crowd hits the place.'

'Wouldn't McAuley have warned him to have the money ready to hand over?' I argued. 'In which case, Haddon does know you're coming.'

Dan considered. 'I suppose that makes sense,' he said grudgingly.

'Did McAuley tell you to ask for my help?' I frowned.

'No.' Dan looked puzzled. 'Why would he? I'm asking you as a friend.'

A friend . . .

'Are you going to help me then?' Dan asked. 'Please, Tobey.'

Pause.

'OK, I'll do it.' But my reasons weren't exactly altruistic. Not even close.

'Tobey, are you ready to get your hands dirty? 'Cause you're no use to me if you're not prepared to back me up.'

'I'll give you all the backup you'd give me,' I replied.

Dan's eyes narrowed. I forced a smile.

'We're cool,' I told him. 'So how do we get to Haddon's shop?'

Dan frowned. 'By bus. How d'you think?'

I only just managed to stop myself from creasing up. Two hard-guy wannabes getting heavy with one of McAuley's victims, then making good their escape on the local bus. Oh yeah, we were really threatening! If this Haddon guy managed to pick himself up from the floor when he'd finished howling with laughter, then he just might find the energy to boot Dan and me out of his shop.

'You'll need this,' said Dan, holding out a sheathed knife, its handle towards me.

And all at once, it wasn't so funny any more. I hesitated. Dan thrust it towards me. I took it.

'Am I likely to need it?' I asked.

'Probably,' said Dan. 'We have to show Haddon that we mean business.'

'And if he has a gun?'

'He wouldn't be that stupid, not when he knows that we work for Mr McAuley.'

Then why did we need knives? Dan sounded like he was one hundred per cent sure this Haddon guy wouldn't put up a fuss or a fight. But fear or desperation often drove people to do things that stupidity alone would never make them consider.

'Once you tell Haddon who you work for, surely you won't need any kind of hardware?' I pointed out.

'It's for protection, just in case.'

I stuck the knife in my jacket pocket.

'I'll get my jacket,' Dan said, heading into his house.

The moment his back was turned, the mask-like expression on my face slipped. My friend, Dan. The friend to all – if the price was right and it didn't cost him anything. And I had to hide my true feelings because I still needed him. Hiding my true feelings was so hard, but I was becoming a master at it. Dan grabbed his jacket off the banister and left his house, slamming the door shut behind him just as hard as he could. I was amazed the glass didn't fall out of it.

'Is your mum at home then?'

'Yeah, and fast asleep, but not alone.'

'Anyone you know?'

'Nope. She rolled in around three o'clock this morning, pissed as a newt with some guy in tow. I locked my door and left them to it.'

We walked in silence. In a world of changes, Dan's mum was a constant. She'd been that way for as long as I could remember. There'd been a time, before Dan started working for McAuley, when the only decent meals he got were round at my house. He used to bring his clothes to ours to be washed as well, before he made enough money to pay for a washer-dryer of his own.

My friend, Dan.

'Dan,' I began, 'what's your ambition?'

'What d'you mean?'

'I mean, what'll you be doing in five years' time, ten years, fifteen?'

'I don't know, do I?'

'Will you still be working for McAuley?'

'Hell, no,' Dan said vehemently. 'I'll have my own business by then. I'll be running things.'

'So you're not in McAuley's pocket?'

'I'm not in anyone's pocket. There's only three things in this world I care about – me, myself and I.'

That I could believe.

Less than fifteen minutes later, Dan and I hopped off the bus at the High Street. It was less than a minute's walk to Haddon's bakery. I was about to walk in, but Dan's hand on my arm stopped me.

'Tobey, are you OK with this?'

I nodded. 'Let's just get it over with before I come to my senses.'

We walked in. The smell of fresh bread and sticky cakes wafted enticingly around me. The shop was bright and airy and spotlessly clean. Behind the counter was a door, half wood, half frosted glass. Adjacent to the counter against one wall was a huge fridge filled with sandwiches and various drinks in bottles and cartons. Opposite, against the other wall, were bakery racks filled with different kinds of loaves, rolls and pastries, with tongs next to almost every item that wasn't already wrapped. The cream cakes were behind glass next to the counter and they looked good. I could see why the shop was so popular. A Cross man and a Nought woman were serving. Dan ambled about looking at the sandwiches and pies. I stood by the door as we'd agreed on the bus. When the last of the three customers in the shop finally paid for her cottage loaf and left, Dan nodded to me. I turned over the sign hanging on the door to indicate that the shop was now closed, just as a Cross man tried to enter the shop.

'Sorry, mate,' Dan called out. 'We're closing until we catch all the mice that are running around over the shop floor.'

The customer − ex-customer − looked horrified and hurried off. I stood in front of the door so that no one else could walk in uninvited.

'What d'you two think you're doing?' the Cross guy who I assumed was Boris Haddon exclaimed angrily.

'It's OK, Mr Haddon,' Dan said amicably. 'Mr McAuley sent us.'

Boris glanced uneasily at the Nought girl standing next to him.

'Sophie, take the rest of the day off,' he told her.

'But, Mr Haddon . . .'

'Just do as I say,' said Boris. 'OK?'

Sophie looked from her boss to Dan and me and back again. 'OK, Mr Haddon,' she replied nervously.

Boris gave her a studied look. Sophie pulled off her hat and her apron, throwing them beneath the counter, before bending to retrieve her jacket from the same place. Alarm bells started pealing, only the cacophony was inside my head, not in the shop. No employee kept their jacket beneath the serving counter if there was somewhere else to hang it up. Leaving personal possessions on the shop floor was a guaranteed way to get them nicked. And from the look of it, this shop had a private room behind the counter. I shifted my position to try and see through the frosted glass that led to the private room, but Boris moved almost imperceptibly in my way. Almost, but not quite.

'Who did you say you two worked for?' Boris asked.

'Mr McAuley sent us,' Dan began. 'You need to pay my boss what you owe—'

'Dan, I think we've got the wrong shop.'

Dan turned to me, frowning. 'What're you on about? Of course we haven't . . .'

I tried a different tack. 'Dan, your boss only asked you to request that the debt be paid within the next thirty days.' I turned to the shop owner. 'Mr Haddon, we're sorry to trouble you. We just wanted to politely request that you send a cheque to . . . that you send on a cheque at your earliest convenience.'

'Tobey, what the hell d'you think you're doing?' Dan rounded on me.

'It's time for us to go,' I told him.

'The hell it is. I'm not leaving here without the money this dagger owes Mr McAuley.' Dan's hand was already in his jacket pocket as he started behind the counter.

I raced across the shop to step in front of him. Furious, he tried to shove me out of the way. Eyes wide, mouth open, Haddon took a couple of steps back. Dan's hand was emerging from his jacket pocket, but his hand was no longer empty. So I hit him. Less than a second later, he fell to the ground, more from surprise than any other reason. I certainly hadn't hit him that hard. I squatted down beside him, holding out my hand to help him up, my other hand also busy as it moved over his jacket pocket. Dan scowled at me.

'Dan, I'm sorry about that . . .'

He pushed me aside as he struggled to get up under his own steam.

'I apologize for the disturbance, Mr Haddon,' I said. 'Dan, we should leave—'

'Is this what you call having my back?' Dan asked with contempt, shoving me backwards – hard.

He was starting towards me when the door behind Boris Haddon opened and a swarm of coppers flooded out.

'DOWN ON THE GROUND. NOW.'

'GET DOWN.'

The orders were coming from all directions. I dropped to the floor immediately. One copper knelt hard on my back as he wrenched my arms back to slap handcuffs on me. My head to one side, I glared at Dan. Slow or what?

Couldn't he pick up on what I'd been trying to tell him? Boris Haddon knew we were coming all right. And he'd set up a welcoming committee. There was only one reason for Sophie, Haddon's employee, to keep her jacket under the counter and that was because she didn't want to reveal who was in the back room by opening the door. If Dan had ever bothered to find himself an everyday, honest job he'd have been able to work that out for himself.

I groaned as I was pulled to my feet, but it wasn't so much the handcuffs or the pain in my back which made me cringe. It was something else entirely. I was heading back to the police station. Mum was going to do her nut! Both Dan and I were patted down. Apart from two mobile phones and some money, my pockets were empty. The copper patting down Dan quickly found two knives on him, one in each of his jacket pockets. Stunned, Dan stared at them. He turned to me, shocked. But we had no time to do more than exchange a look before we were both bundled out of the shop and into separate police cars.

fifty

I ended up with an official reprimand as apparently I wasn't old enough (by less than one month) to receive a formal caution. I had trouble working out exactly what the reprimand was for. As far as I could tell, the charge was affray – which was totally specious, not to mention bogus as far as I was concerned. What it did mean though was that I was fingerprinted and a swab was taken from my mouth to provide a DNA sample. I was told the records would be destroyed after five years if I stayed out of trouble, but I wasn't holding my breath on that one. Everyone knew the police were trying to build up a DNA database of all the Meadowview residents, especially us Noughts. It was only a matter of time before the DNA of everyone in the whole bloody country was held on some computer or other.

But I knew I should count myself lucky. Dan was charged with carrying offensive weapons and remanded on conditional bail. It could've been worse. He could've been charged with extortion or whatever the proper legal term for that is, but apparently he didn't say enough to make an extortion charge indisputable. He'd had a damn good try, though. I still couldn't believe how slow on the uptake he'd been. So the charge of carrying offensive weapons was the best the police could do. Dan was taken back to a cell to await the arrival of his mum. Knowing her, he'd be waiting an awfully long time.

And if Mum was angry before, she was spitting nails and breathing fire by the time she came to get me. One look at her face, and staying in a cell seemed almost preferable. She didn't waste a breath before she started.

'What did I say to you about not bringing the police to my door?' she stormed. 'And not just once but twice in one day. Are you aiming for some kind of record?'

'I'm sorry, Mum,' I mumbled.

'Sorry? *Sorry?*' That just made her even more angry. 'I

don't want to hear sorry. And what were you doing in a bakery in North Meadowview?'

'It was just a misunderstanding, Mum,' I said. 'Dan and I were just mucking around. Mr Haddon overreacted.'

'What were you doing with Dan in the first place?'

'Just hanging out. Mum, I didn't think it would do any harm—'

'And this is exactly how it starts.' Mum shook her head. 'Tobey, tell me something, does Dan work for McAuley?'

'I . . . I think so, but Mum, *I* don't. You've got to believe me, McAuley has got nothing that I want. Absolutely nothing,' I said quietly.

'I don't want you hanging round Dan. He's going nowhere fast and I don't want you tagging along for the ride.'

I looked around to make sure no one was within earshot. 'Mum, you're gonna have to trust me. Please, just trust me.' I don't know what it was – the expression on my face, some note in my voice – but something halted her tirade. She studied me long and hard.

'Tobey, what're you up to?'

I looked around again, nervous as a cat in a room full of rocking chairs.

'Nothing, Mum.'

'Don't give me that, Tobey. I know you. And I know when you're up to something,' said Mum.

'Mum, I—'

'Has all this got something to do with Callie getting shot?' she said slowly. 'Tobey, please tell me you're not—?'

'Mum, I'm not about to do anything stupid,'

I interrupted. 'Besides, I've got you to keep me on the straight and narrow.'

'Tobey, this isn't funny,' said Mum.

I sighed. 'I know. I'm sorry.'

'If I had any sense, I would ground you for the rest of the holiday.'

'Mum, I won't get into any more trouble, I promise.' At least, I promise I'll try not to. 'Besides, I want to visit Callie later. Please?'

'Hmmm . . .' Mum wasn't the least bit convinced, but she didn't follow through with her threat to ground me. I hadn't yet told her that I no longer worked at TFTM, which helped. I suspected that was the only reason she wasn't confining me to the house.

'So when you wake up later, if I'm not at home, that's where I am – OK?' I said, pushing my luck.

We took a couple of steps towards the door, but I couldn't go any further, much as I wanted to. And I really, *really* wanted to.

'Mum,' I began, 'I need a favour.'

Mum stared at me like one of us had lost our mind and she was trying to figure out which one. 'Tobey, I'm fighting a really powerful urge to explain all about the biological structure of nerves and their abundance in the human body.'

'Why would you want to tell me about nerves?' I frowned.

'So that when I tell you you're getting on every last one of mine, you'll appreciate just how serious that is,' she replied.

Godsake! Sometimes Mum was too much of a nurse. 'I really need this favour, Mum.'

'Tobey, you've got more cheek showing than a maternity ward. You drag me down here – twice – and you think you've got a favour coming?'

'It isn't for me, Mum. It's for Dan. He's still locked up in this place and you know what his mum is like. She'll let him rot in here.'

'And what has that got to do with me?' asked Mum testily.

'Mum, we've got to help him. He's in trouble.'

'He is trouble, never mind anything else,' she snapped.

'Mum, this is important. Please. He doesn't have anyone else.'

'Dan is not my concern. You are,' Mum argued.

McAuley had given Dan one last chance and Dan had messed up. For the life of me, I didn't understand why I should feel any anxiety for him. Rotting in a cell was no more than he deserved. But if I left him here, the only other person who'd bail him out was McAuley. And no matter what Dan had done, I couldn't leave him to McAuley's tender mercies. I had enough on my conscience already.

'Mum, we have to get Dan out of here.'

Mum frowned at me, her frown deepening as she scrutinized my face. 'Has this got something to do with Dan and McAuley?'

I nodded, albeit reluctantly.

'They're not going to release Dan into my custody. I'm not his mother.'

'Yes, they will,' I argued. 'The prisons and the police cells are already overcrowded so they're not going to keep anyone for longer than strictly necessary. As long as you say you'll take responsibility for him and sign the necessary paperwork, they'll let him go. Just tell them that if they don't release him into your custody, they'll be looking after him until his next birthday.'

'Take a seat,' said Mum after a few moments. 'I'll be back in a minute.'

'I'll come with you,' I said.

'No you won't. If you want me to help Dan, you'll do as I say. Sit down and stay put. I mean it, Tobey.'

'OK,' I agreed reluctantly.

I stayed put, but remained standing as I watched her head over to the reception desk. She and the woman behind the desk had a long and heated discussion which looked like it was veering dangerously close to an argument at times. Finally the officer called over one of her colleagues to help behind the desk whilst she headed off somewhere. Ten minutes later she emerged with Dan walking beside her, followed by DI Boothe, who barely glanced at me. The scowl on Dan's face when he saw me could've soured honey. He watched Mum sign the forms for his release, then we all left the police station together with Mum walking slightly ahead of us.

'Am I supposed to be grateful?' Dan asked belligerently.

'No,' I replied.

'Mr McAuley warned me not to screw this up,' he said, an edge to his voice. 'He already thinks I'm a liability. When he hears about this . . .'

'It's not your fault Haddon called in the police,' I said.

'Mr McAuley won't see it that way,' said Dan bitterly. 'So now I've got McAuley on my left and the cops on my right, thanks to that stunt you pulled. You had my back all right, just so you could stab me in it.'

The words I wanted – needed – to say were burning holes right through me. But I kept most of them inside. Forcing myself to stay calm, I said, 'Dan, since we're discussing backstabbers, explain to me why you felt the need to sell smack to my sister.'

Shocked, Dan took a half-step back. He put out his hands to ward me off even though I hadn't moved a muscle. 'Tobey, your sister came to me, not the other way round, I swear.'

'And that makes it OK, does it?'

'She said if I didn't sell her some gear she'd find someone else who would,' Dan rushed on. 'I thought if she got it from me, at least I could make sure she wasn't smoking something harmful . . .'

''Cause smack isn't harmful?'

'I told her she didn't want to start up with that stuff, but she wouldn't listen.'

'So you figured if someone was going to make some money from Jessica, it might as well be you?'

'No, you've got it all wrong. I was just trying to help.'

Help? Was he serious? My eyes narrowed.

'Tobey, listen. Please. Jess came to me.'

'When?'

'What?'

'When did she first come to you?' I said patiently. 'How long have you been selling that stuff to her?'

'I've only sold to her twice. The first time was four or five weeks ago. That's it.'

I studied Dan, my eyes never leaving his face. Did I ever really know him? He sure as hell didn't know me. Once again, all the words burning inside my head had to stay there. I couldn't even clench my fists. The definition of growing up – hiding what you truly feel, suppressing what you really want to do. Unless you were McAuley or the Dowds. I was beginning to see the attraction of their particular way of life. There was a definite appeal to living by your own set of rules. A very definite appeal.

'Dan, listen carefully 'cause I'm only going to say this once,' I said, once I trusted my voice to stay calm. 'Stay away from my sister.'

'OK, Tobey. OK,' Dan agreed.

He kept shifting from foot to foot. I stood like a statue, watching him. Ice was crystallizing in my veins and moving irrevocably through my body. Dan was nervous. I wasn't. We stood in thorny silence, regarding each other. And in that moment I knew that I'd lost him. No matter what happened now, we'd never go back to the way we once were; we'd never fully trust each other again. One day I might forgive him for what he'd done, but I'd never forget. He was probably feeling exactly the same way. In spite of the warmth of the day, that realization made me cold and sad.

We started walking again, though now we were way behind my mum.

'When did you slip the knife into my pocket?' asked Dan.

'When I was trying to help you up. I couldn't be caught with it,' I said, my voice edged with reluctant apology.

'And I could? Thanks a lot.'

There was nothing I could say to that. The silence between us continued to eat away at our friendship.

'Dan, I'm sorry.'

'No, you're not,' Dan shot back. 'Sorry implies that if

you could go back, you'd do things differently. We both know that you wouldn't change a thing.'

I didn't say anything because he was right. Dan looked at me, such a look that I stopped walking and reluctantly faced him to hear what he had to say.

'This isn't about your sister, though, is it?' Dan said quietly. 'Jessica added fuel to the fire, but what happened to Callie started it. I never realized till now just how much you hate me for what happened to Callie Rose.'

He had my full attention.

'I thought you blamed McAuley and the Dowds,' he continued. 'But you blame me as well. I was the one who asked you to deliver that package to Louise Resnick and there was no way the Dowds were going to let McAuley get away with the torture of one of their own.'

'We've already been through this—'

'Yes, but I'm seeing the real you now,' said Dan. 'McAuley's driven by greed and pride and the lust for power. With you it's different.'

'What d'you mean?'

Dan studied me like he'd just had a revelation. 'All this started because Callie was shot, and maybe you even managed to convince yourself for a while that she was the one you were doing all this for. But that's not true any more, is it?'

'I don't know what you're talking about.' I frowned. I wasn't sure I wanted to find out either.

'This has stopped being about Callie. It's not about Jessica. It's not even about me. You've moved on from that. This is now about you.'

'How sad are you?' I laughed derisively. 'Is this how

you manage to get through each day? By blaming everyone but yourself?'

'If this was about your sister, you would've taken me apart the moment you saw me earlier. If this was about Callie Rose, you would've come after me the moment you left the hospital after she was injured. That's what *I* would've done. But that wasn't enough for you. It still isn't.'

'Maybe I didn't come after you when Callie Rose was shot because I didn't blame you,' I ventured.

'But that's just my point,' said Dan. 'You *did* blame me. Not just me, but me included. And you were prepared to use me to get what you wanted. It was all about you and your revenge.'

Not true. This had nothing to do with me and everything to do with what had happened to Callie Rose. She was the one I cared about. She was the one I was doing this for . . .

'So because I didn't act the way you would've, I don't care about Callie and my sister? Is that it?' I said angrily. 'You're talking bollocks.'

Dan shook his head. 'You just don't get it, do you? You're getting too much . . . satisfaction out of all this. You've developed a taste for being the puppet-master and we're all – what's the word? – expendable. That's why you're so dangerous.' He gave a bitter laugh. 'McAuley doesn't know what he's in for.'

'Dan, you're wrong—' I began, but for the life of me, I couldn't think of anything else to say.

'Are we even now, Tobey?' asked Dan quietly. ''Cause if anyone but you had done this to me, I'd be back at my lockup getting ready to do some damage.'

'So what should I expect, Dan?'

Dan gave me a look. He opened his mouth to speak.

'Could you guys hurry up?' Mum called to us. 'I would like to try and get at least five minutes sleep before work today. Dan, I'll drop you home first.'

'There really is no need,' Dan replied. 'I can get the bus home.'

'Nonsense,' said Mum. 'Besides, I told the police I'd make sure you got home safely.'

Dan and I sat in the back of the car. Mum didn't even start the engine until she'd made sure we'd put on our seatbelts. Then we were on our way. And the entire journey back was achieved without Dan and I saying a single word to each other. I stared out of the window whilst Dan's words played round and round in my head like a song on repeat.

This wasn't about me. This was about Callie.

It was . . .

'Mum, can we stop off at our house first?' I asked as we got close to our road. 'I have something of Dan's that I need to give to him.'

'What?'

'Something,' I replied, reluctant to elaborate.

'As long as you hurry up,' said Mum.

When Mum stopped in front of our house, I was in and out in less than a minute. But now what? I didn't want to hand over what I'd retrieved in front of her. I got back in the car, doing up my seatbelt.

'Mum, could you drop both of us off at Dan's house?' I asked. 'And I promise I'll be home within fifteen minutes.'

I caught Mum's look in the driver's mirror. She didn't

need to speak, her expression said it all. If I wasn't home in fifteen minutes, she'd come looking for me and if she had to do that . . . I got the message. Less than five minutes later we were outside Dan's.

'Dan, you are going to stay out of trouble, aren't you?' asked Mum.

'I'll do my best.' Dan smiled faintly.

After one last warning look cast in my direction, Mum turned the car around and headed home.

The moment she was out of sight, I took out the envelope that Byron had given me, the one full of money, and placed it in Dan's hand. 'This is yours,' I said.

Dan's eyes narrowed. 'What's this?'

'McAuley gave it to me, but . . . but it's yours.'

Dan's fingers folded slowly around the envelope.

'OK?' I said.

'OK.' He turned abruptly and walked away, straight past his own front door.

Where was he going? To his lockup? What was he going to do?

'Dan,' I called after him.

He stopped, but he didn't turn round.

After a moment's thought, I said, 'We're even now.'

Dan carried on walking.

fifty-one

Back at home, I had to wait till Mum went back to bed before I could get down to what I really wanted to do. I connected up McAuley's memory stick and started scanning it. And what did it contain? Letters of complaint to the Inland Revenue and other government bodies about a shipment of rugs imported nearly a year ago and still being held by Customs. A spreadsheet comparing the price of rugs from around the world. More letters of complaint. An inventory of the contents of McAuley's warehouse. Godsake! The files contained stale, boring stuff that was of absolutely no use to me at all. And each file I checked after that was more of the same. They all contained import/export details of artefacts and luxury knick-knacks and other rubbish. It was beginning to look like swapping the memory sticks had been a complete waste of time. When I thought of the risk I'd taken, I felt sick. There were only three more files to check and from the file names, I didn't hold out much hope that they'd be useful.

The next file I opened was called *Schedule*. Only one problem – it was completely empty. Why on earth would McAuley keep an empty file? What a waste of disk space. I opened up the last two files. The first was more twaddle about misshapen figurines and sculptures. The second file contained the bank account details of McAuley's lieutenant, Byron Sweet. I couldn't believe that Byron, Mr Pit-bull himself, had the surname of Sweet. That was about the only interesting thing in the last file. I learned Byron's bank, his branch code and his bank account number – which were all worse than useless.

And that was it.

I slumped back in my chair. Now what? There was nothing in any of the files that was the least bit illegal, unless I was missing something. I listed all the files, in case there was one I'd missed and hadn't read yet. But there wasn't. I read them all again, every word, but there was nothing remotely worthwhile. I held my head in my hands and tried to think. There was no way I'd get another crack at McAuley's computer. I looked at the list of files on my screen, desperately willing them to turn into something I could use.

Something I could . . .

Something . . .

I leaned closer to the screen. *Schedule*, the file with nothing in it, was almost one hundred kilobytes big. Why would a file with nothing in it be so large? I opened the file again. It consisted of eight blank pages. I scrolled all the way down then back up again. The file was definitely empty. Or was it? A light bulb started flashing in my head. Mouth dry, heart thumping, I clicked the option to select everything in the file, then changed its colour to black. The file was immediately filled to overflowing with text and a grid that must've been from a spreadsheet.

Oh, yes!

'Very clever, McAuley,' I muttered.

I mean, credit where credit was due. The colour of the

words in the file had been changed to white. White words on a white background. No wonder the file looked blank. I tried not to get too excited, but this looked far more promising. I settled down in my chair and started reading. I read the file from top to bottom, then read it again to make sure I hadn't misread any of it.

According to the spreadsheet in the file, McAuley had invested every penny he had in three shipments coming into the country within the next few days. He'd euphemistically referred to his shipments as 'X'. The first shipment was due the day after tomorrow. Two more shipments were scheduled to arrive after that, each at intervals of three days. Each shipment was going to a different address, where they would be stored until McAuley arranged collection. He wasn't taking any chances. From the look of it, it seemed the Dowds had taken away more of McAuley's business than anyone suspected and he wasn't quite as loaded as we'd all assumed.

Why on earth hadn't he quit when he was ahead?

And then I realized. He couldn't quit. It wasn't just the money that McAuley craved, it was the sense of control and power it gave him. He was like a pathetic despot, looking out over the portion of his kingdom called 'half of Meadowview' and longing for it all. And the Dowds were exactly the same, two wings of the same bird. They targeted those who had little and made sure they ended up with less. And Dan's attitude to McAuley was 'at least he's one of our own'. I shook my head, wondering if he still felt the same way.

The file contained details of delivery addresses, times, the initials of a number of people who were going to pay for 'X' and the amounts of money involved. And I mean, large, eye-boggling amounts of money. I finally had something I could use. The question was, how? I could just tell the police, but there was no way to link the shipments to McAuley unless he was found with the stuff and McAuley was much too smart for that. After it was delivered, he'd have his minions do his dirty work for him. And even if there was some way to link the shipments to him, a smart lawyer could claim that McAuley didn't know what was being imported in his name or that it wasn't even his property. I could tell the police and they'd confiscate his shipments, but that wasn't enough. I admit it. It wasn't anywhere near enough. I wanted McAuley's world to unravel slowly but irrevocably. So I'd have to find some other way to use this information to his disadvantage.

It was time to make a phone call.

Phone call concluded, the next thing I had to do was protect the information I had. I printed off all the sheets, then placed them in an A5 envelope, which I addressed to Callie Rose. I took a second-class stamp from Mum's handbag and stuck that on the letter. This letter would be my insurance policy – just in case. I knew Sephy would never open her daughter's letters, and once Callie was out of hospital the letter would be easy enough to retrieve – if I got through this.

Once that was done, I tried to figure out my next move. I finally decided on a course of action. It wasn't smart and it sure as hell wasn't foolproof, but it was all I had.

I headed for my local library, memory stick hidden in the cuff of my jacket – just in case McAuley or the police decided they couldn't do without my company. At the library, I booked a computer for an hour and started working on my first letter. It would probably be the most significant one of my life. I decided to use a handwriting font that I didn't have on my computer at home. I couldn't take any chances. If the letter was ever traced back to me . . .

> To the Dowds,
>
> This letter contains information about Alex McAuley and his business interests that you will hopefully find useful. McAuley is expecting a shipment to be delivered to 3 Londridge Street, Meadowview on 14th August at 4.30 p.m. The shipment will arrive in a home food shopping delivery van. I don't know the route the van will take before it arrives at the above address. This delivery, one of the smaller ones scheduled to arrive in the next couple of weeks, is worth over three-quarters of a million pounds. How you decide to use this information is of course entirely up to you. If you do decide to act upon the information in this letter, I will supply you with the times, dates and venues of all McAuley's other consignments for the rest of the month – but only if you decide to act on the information contained herein.

I thought my use of the words 'consignment' and 'herein' was a good touch. No one ever used those kinds of words in real life. Hopefully those words and the way I'd phrased certain other sentences would make it seem like someone much older than me had written the letter. And possibly a woman? After a lot of deleting and rewriting, I decided the letter was ready – except for one thing. The Dowds would never believe the information I was giving them was genuine if I didn't ask for some kind of reward. As far as they were concerned, altruism – especially criminal altruism – didn't exist. So I added:

Once the above shipment is yours, I would expect payment of 10% of the gross worth of the product before I part with any further information about other future deliveries. I feel 10% is fair. I would expect this money in cash. I shall provide further instructions regarding the payment of my money once McAuley's goods are in your hands.

I had no intention of taking a penny from the Dowds, but they needed to believe I was just as avaricious as they were. I printed off the letter, making sure to hold it with a tissue so that my fingerprints wouldn't get on it. Folding it, I placed it in the envelope I'd brought with me. The question was, should I post it to Gideon Dowd at TFTM or should I post it to Vanessa Dowd? Thanks to Rebecca, I now had her home address. But I suspected I was one of a mere handful of people who knew it. If I posted the letter to Rebecca's mum, it might be easier to trace. Giving it to Owen wasn't part of the plan. Besides, I wanted as little as possible to do with him. TFTM it was then. I would just have to hope that Gideon Dowd would be at the Club the following day to receive the letter. I could've sent it as an email, but Gideon could trace the email back to this library and it was in my neighbourhood, plus it had twenty-four-hour CCTV. With Gideon's connections, he could easily get hold of the footage and discover that I'd been in the library around the time he received the email. No, far better to send it via snail mail. Slower but safer.

My second letter was far easier to write. I used the same font and took the same precautions to make sure that my fingerprints didn't appear anywhere on it. This letter was much simpler, though. This one gave details of McAuley's second shipment. What should I do about the third scheduled delivery? Tell the police? Tell the Dowds?

Tell no one?

I took the latter path. It would take expert timing, but maybe I could move the shipment, or at least part of it, to some place where no one but me would ever find it.

I mean, why not me?

Why not?

It's not that I fancied myself as another McAuley. Far from it. But I had to think ahead. I had to think. I had to look out for myself. No one else would.

I'd make no snap decisions about the third shipment. The answer would come to me. But one way or another, all this should start to hit McAuley where he would feel it the most. I wasn't finished with him yet.

Not even close.

fifty-two

Hello, Callie Rose.

I . . .

Today I . . .

I have nothing to say.

fifty-three

As I walked down the hospital steps, my whole body felt as if it was made of lead. I'd sat with Callie for over thirty minutes – and I couldn't think of anything to say. What was happening to me that I couldn't find anything to say to her? I pulled my T-shirt rapidly back and forth away from my sweaty chest. The sky was white-grey and the air was really humid and sticky. This damned weather was really getting to me. Time to head back home. My letters were posted and I'd managed to visit Callie again without getting caught. Mum must've set off for work by now, and as for Jessica . . . ? Well, I'd barely seen her recently. We'd been avoiding each other. But Jess wasn't uppermost in my mind. I had other matters to attend to. First a shower, then phone Rebecca to ask her for a date. I hadn't heard from her in a while and I needed to know where I stood now that her brother had banned us from being together.

Why couldn't I speak to Callie?

Head bent, I was lost in my own thoughts as I left the hospital grounds, so they saw me before I saw them. I only knew I had company when they appeared in front of me. Three sets of feet belonging to three morons – Lucas, Drew and Aaron. After a cursory glance at them, I tried to walk round them. I just wanted to be left alone. Drew deliberately stepped in front of me.

Godsake . . . I wasn't in the mood for this, I really wasn't.

'Hello, Durbrain.' Drew smiled.

That nickname was so old and tired it needed a walking stick. Was that really the best he could come up with? I tried to step past him, but he moved to block me again. OK, now he was officially pissing me off.

'Callie's not here to protect you,' Drew taunted.

I smiled faintly. He just didn't get it.

'Are you satisfied now?' Lucas asked, moving to stand directly in front of me.

My eyes narrowed. What was he on about? I took a half-step back so I could keep Drew and Aaron in sight as well.

'Thanks to you and your fellow blankers, Callie is in hospital,' said Lucas. 'I warned her that she'd end up getting hurt or worse hanging around you.'

'She could do better than you at the local pig farm. You're just about the same colour as a pig, aren't you.' Aaron turned to his mates, a stupid grin plastered over his face. He really thought he'd said something profound.

Lucas, however, never took his eyes off me. 'I told her not to trust you, that you were no good. And when she regains consciousness, she'll realize I was right all along and dump you like the steaming pile of dog—'

My fists shot out. Both of them hit their target – Lucas's stomach, followed by his face when he doubled over. He dropped like a stone. Aaron charged at me. I sidestepped him, then stuck out my foot to trip him. He hit the pavement like a felled tree. Not that he stayed there long. For a guy with such a big build he was surprisingly agile.

'Blanker, you'll pay for that,' Aaron hissed at me.

He came at me, arms up, fists clenched. So I kicked him where it'd do me the most good. This time he went down and stayed down. By which time Lucas was back on his feet, though holding his nose, which was bleeding. Aaron was still rolling on the ground.

'Who's next?' I asked quietly.

No one spoke. I stepped over Aaron and continued on my way. Maybe now Drew would realize it was never me Callie was protecting, even if he – and Callie – had thought otherwise.

Once I got home, I sat on my bed, rubbing my forehead with the palm of my left hand, trying to ease away the headache that was lurking behind my eyes. It was not the time for my phone to ring. I glanced down at the screen, checking the caller's ID, but it said 'Private'. At least it wasn't McAuley bothering me. I could guess who this was. Did I really want to speak to him? I had no choice. Even so, I let it ring seven or eight times before I answered.

'Hello?'

'I thought you weren't going to answer,' Owen Dowd said at once. 'It's far too late to have second thoughts.'

'No second thoughts. No third ones. I was in the bath-room washing my hands, that's all.'

'Did you do as we agreed?'

I sighed inwardly. This man certainly didn't believe in pleasantries.

'Yes, I did. And I made sure the letter was addressed to your brother as we discussed earlier.'

'Good. Excellent. Leave the rest to me.'

I had every intention of doing just that.

'Is there anything else you want to tell me?' Owen asked.

Like what?

'I don't think so,' I replied. 'It's all working out the way you wanted.'

'That doesn't mean that either of us can get complacent.'

'No, Mr Dowd.'

'You're sure there's nothing else you want to tell me?' he said.

'Nothing, sir.'

The existence and destination of my second letter, I intended to keep to myself. Or was this his subtle way of telling me that he already knew what I was up to? But he couldn't know anything about the second letter. I'd been very careful. Owen Dowd only knew about the first shipment. Unless I'd overlooked something . . .

Tobey, calm down, I told myself. *He's just fishing.*

I decided not to rise to his bait.

'What other information did you find?'

'Nothing of use. Lots of complaining letters to the tax office, I think. Oh, and Byron Sweet's bank account details. He's one of McAuley's minions. But there was no password information in the file or even how much money he has in the bank. It was just . . . just . . .'

And that's when it occurred to me. Ideas flowed one after the other like the tide coming in.

'I know a way we can use Byron's bank account to our advantage,' I said, trying to dampen down my excitement in case Owen didn't go for my plan.

'I'm listening,' he said.

'It will require quite a lot of money,' I warned.

'Doesn't it always?' he replied sourly.

So I told him what I had in mind. There was a significant pause when I'd finished.

'I'll think about it,' he said at last.

I released the breath I didn't even realize I'd been holding.

'Anything else?' he asked.

'When will I be paid?'

'Once I have what I want, you'll get your money.'

'I'll look forward to it,' I replied.

'You're going to be a very rich man, Tobey.'

'Yes, sir.'

'I'll send you a banker's cheque as we agreed. Don't spend it all at once!' Owen rang off, his laughter ringing in my ears.

It was lucky for both of us that he couldn't see my expression as I disconnected the call. Just listening to him made me want to go down to the kitchen and scrub out my ear with the saucepan scourer.

Rich people were so predictable. They reckoned everyone wanted money, that everyone had their price. And for rich people there was no such thing as 'rich enough' – at least not for people like the Dowds and McAuley. Too much was never enough. That was why I was going to succeed and they were going to fail. And there wasn't enough money on the planet to stop me now.

fifty-four

The whole of Meadowview was buzzing. McAuley's latest shipment had been hijacked by 'persons unknown'. The news was that, en route to its destination, a home shopping delivery van supposedly filled with food had been intercepted and relieved of all its contents. There was an awful lot of speculation as to what those contents might be. Some said drugs. Some said smuggled immigrants brought in as cheap labour. Some said dodgy electronic gear. All said illegal. None said food. The job was sweet (apparently), 'cause it wasn't as if McAuley could go bleating to the police about his lost merchandise. And the best thing of all was that everyone was having a really good laugh at his expense.

That, if nothing else, was enough to put McAuley on the warpath. He had to be asking himself some hard questions by now. Like how had the Dowds known about his shipment – for who else would have the brass nerve to take what belonged to McAuley? How did they know the route? Even I didn't know the answer to that question. I didn't have that information, so how did the Dowds get it? There was no way McAuley could let the hijacking of his goods stand. If he did, every minor-league, two-a-penny thug would try their luck against him. So once the laughter ceased, the whole of Meadowview would be holding their breath to see how McAuley would retaliate. He was going to declare war on the Dowds over this. Still, that wasn't my problem, at least not yet. I had a more pressing dilemma.

Like, did McAuley suspect me of any involvement in this? Well, I was still breathing and walking around on two working legs, so I guessed not. But surely it was only a matter of time . . . ? I'd tried to be careful and cover my tracks, but now was not the time to get complacent. If McAuley suspected me of being involved in the loss of his merchandise, then it would only be a matter of time before I got the Ross Resnick treatment.

fifty-five

Mum had the evening off, Jessica wasn't off to a party or to one of her friends' houses and I no longer had a job, so for once we all ate together. Mum made us spaghetti bolognese and we had a small bowl filled with grated cheddar cheese to sprinkle on top of it if we wanted. Mum reckoned she wasn't going to buy stinky cheese (as she called any cheese that originated in another country), just so she could sprinkle some on spag bol the once a fortnight we had it. We sat around the tiny table in one corner of our living room. Mum's eyes were trained on the TV in the opposite corner as she watched the early evening news. My eyes never left my sister. And it was getting on her nerves.

'What?' she silently mouthed at me, venom darting from her eyes and mouth.

'Are you OK?' I mouthed back.

Jessica glared at me and concentrated on her food. 'Mum, is there any orange juice?' she asked.

Mum turned back to the table. 'Didn't I put any out?' There were three non-matching glasses but no juice carton present. 'I'll just go and get some,' she said. She stood up and headed for the kitchen.

'Where's the rest of my stuff?' Jessica barely waited for Mum to leave the room before she started.

'What stuff?'

'Tobey, don't muck about. Where's my stuff?'

'I don't know what you're talking about?' I popped a forkful of spaghetti into my mouth.

'Tobey, I'm warning you.'

'Have you told Mum yet?' I asked.

Jessica drew back slightly. 'Not yet, but I will.'

'When?'

'When I'm ready.'

'You'll never be ready,' I said. 'If you don't tell her by this weekend, I will. I mean it, Jessica. You've had long enough.'

'Tobey, give me back my stuff. I need it.' Jessica's voice was half plea, half demand.

'Is this the same stuff that you only use occasionally and that you can handle?' I asked.

'I don't need a lecture from you,' said Jessica. 'Just give it back.'

'Can't do that,' I replied. 'I flushed it down the loo.'

She stared at me, then glared at me. Without warning, she launched herself across the table, knocking the glasses and her plate flying. My chair tipped backwards and I almost ended up on the floor. Jessica was on her feet and trying to pummel all bloody hell out of my body. All I could do was try to protect myself from her feet, hands and knees. I didn't want to hurt her by seriously trying to defend myself. Mum came running into the room and tried to separate us, but Jessica was like a wild animal. She was ready to knock Mum over just to get to me.

Mum grabbed my sister's arms and shook her violently. 'Jessica, what the hell is the matter with you? What's going on?'

'He . . . He . . .' The wild stare left Jessica's eyes and she slowly returned to normal, her breathing slowing down.

'Jessica?' Mum frowned. 'D'you want to tell me what's going on?'

'Yeah, Jessica. Why don't you do that?' I said, getting to my feet. I touched a tentative finger to my mouth. I was right. My lip was bleeding. Godsake! Jessica scowled at me like she hated me, which at that moment she probably did.

'I'm waiting, and this had better be good,' said Mum. 'Which one of you is going to tell me what this was all about?'

Silence.

'Tobey has started working for McAuley, delivering drugs,' Jessica said viciously. 'He's a drug dealer.'

Huh? I stared at Jessica like I'd never seen her before. I had to hand it to my sister. I hadn't seen that one coming. At all.

'Mum, that's not true,' I protested.

'It is true, Mum. Ask anyone around here,' Jess insisted. 'Ask Dan.'

Mum looked so shocked, my heart sank. She was already three-quarters of the way towards believing my sister.

'Is that why McAuley spoke to you at the police station?' asked Mum. 'Why the police arrested you?'

'The police didn't find a thing on me, Mum. You know they didn't,' I said. 'I'm not a drug dealer. Jessica's lying.'

'Why would your sister say something so outrageous?' asked Mum.

I looked at Jessica. She scowled at me, totally defiant. We both knew that if I now told Mum what Jess had been up to, Mum would never believe me. She'd think I was just trying to get my own back.

'Tobey, are you mixed up in drug dealing in any manner, shape or form?' asked Mum. 'And I want the truth.'

One package. One frickin' package with drugs inside. That's all I'd delivered. That didn't exactly make me a drugs baron. But it didn't make my hands squeaky clean either. Suppose something had happened to Jess? What if the first package I'd delivered to Adam Eisner had contained smack and she had overdosed on the stuff I'd ferried across Meadowview? How did I know that someone else out there hadn't, no matter what drug was in the package? I looked from Jessica to Mum, unable to say a word.

Mum burst into tears.

I don't know who was more shocked, me or my sister.

'Tobey, I've shown you how that stuff destroys lives.' Mum was so disappointed in me, her words came out choked and full of sorrow. 'After all my warnings, all the things I've told you about drugs? How could you?'

I tried to put my arm around Mum, but she shrugged me off and headed out of the room. She went upstairs, her steps slow, almost like she had to drag herself upward. I listened as she closed her bedroom door. Silence surrounded me like fingers pointing. I turned to my sister. All this because she didn't want Mum to know that she needed help. Jessica actually looked ashamed of herself, but so what?

'OK, Jess. You know what? You win,' I said. 'But do me a favour? When you move on to injecting junk instead of inhaling it, do it somewhere where Mum and I won't find you if . . . when it goes wrong.'

I went into the hall, grabbed my jacket and headed out of the door. At that moment, I needed to be as far away from my sister as I could get.

fifty-six

BLAZE DESTROYS TFTM

At around 3 a.m. this morning, a fire broke out in the well-known exclusive celebrity eatery – Thanks For The Memories. The restaurant's sprinkler system failed, leading to extensive damage of the restaurant and the famous Club above, but no one was injured as the building was empty at the time. Although local firefighters were at the scene within ten minutes, they still had to battle for over two hours to control the inferno. Police had to be called in to control the watching crowds.

'There is some water, smoke and fire damage to the furnishings and the décor, but the structure of the building remains mostly unaffected,' said Mr Thomas, TFTM's deputy manager. 'I'm looking forward to welcoming our regular customers and all newcomers to the new and improved TFTM. We shall return bigger and better than ever before.'

Mr Thomas stated that he expects his restaurant to be open for business within the next couple of months. The fire is being investigated by the police and the fire service. A spokeswoman for the Fire Department stated that because the fire took hold of the building and blazed so quickly, arson has not been ruled out.

It had begun.

fifty-seven

There was something I needed to sort out for Callie whilst I still had the chance. And if I could just find this out for her, then I'd have something to say the next time I visited her. Was that what Callie was waiting for? News as to whether or not she was safe from her uncle? Is that what she needed to wake up?

I didn't want to put it off any longer. I headed next door, even though the thought of being dissected by Sephy Hadley's penetrating gaze didn't appeal. At all. I could still remember her expression when she saw me kissing Rebecca. But it wasn't Callie's mum I needed to see. I took a deep breath and rang the doorbell, hoping against hope that Sephy wouldn't be the one to open the door. Surprise! Surprise! For once, good luck was running with me.

'Hi, Meggie.'

'Hello, Tobey.'

'I wondered if I could have a word with you in private.' I looked past Meggie up the stairs, then into the kitchen at the end of the hall.

'Sephy's at the hospital visiting Callie, if that's who you're looking for,' Meggie said, amused.

'No,' I denied quickly. 'It was you I wanted to speak to.'

Meggie looked surprised, but she ushered me into the

living room. After waiting for me to sit down, she sat opposite. It took her a bit longer than it took me. Once she was comfortable, she looked at me expectantly.

'Meggie, I need to ask you something.'

'Oh, yes?'

'It's about your son.'

Meggie's gaze was instantly watchful. 'Which one?' she asked.

'Jude.'

'What about him?'

There was no easy way to say this, so I'd just have to spit it out.

'Is Jude alive? Has he been in touch with you?'

Meggie sat back in her chair and regarded me long and hard. The silence scraped against my skin like a cheese grater.

'It's just . . . it's just that before Callie was injured, she thought that her uncle died alongside her Nana Jasmine,' I rushed to explain. 'Only then the news began talking about some guy called Robert Powers. Callie was terrified her uncle would come after her again.'

'Callie told you this, did she?'

'Yes, she did,' I replied. And in as many words. I looked at Meggie, waiting for her answer.

'When my granddaughter comes out the hospital then I will give her a direct answer to that question,' said Meggie.

'So is Jude alive then?' I asked.

'I'll discuss that with my granddaughter, not you.' Meggie's voice wasn't anywhere near a snap, but I still felt like I'd been firmly put in my place.

I wasn't poking and prying into Meggie's business for my own sake. I just wanted to have something to tell

Callie the next time I saw her. Hopefully something good. But Meggie was going to keep the subject of Jude as something only she and Callie would discuss.

I was excluded.

fifty-eight

Over the next couple of days, the tension at home was unbearable. I wasn't talking to Jessica, Mum wasn't talking to me. We might have been ghosts passing through each other for all the contact we made. I seriously thought about telling Mum to search through Jessica's room – as she probably had more 'supplies' by now – or to check her best teapot if she wanted to know the truth about who was using and who wasn't. I mean, I might've scrubbed the thing out, but surely there was some chemical or other that Mum could get from the hospital which could test for smack, no matter how little was left or how microscopic the residue? But then Jessica would accuse me of using as well as dealing, and what proof would I have that she was lying? That would just make a bad situation even worse. I couldn't do right for doing wrong, that was the trouble.

The only silver lining in a sky full of dark clouds was that Rebecca still wanted to see me, though it took some doing to persuade her that I didn't hold her responsible for losing my job at TFTM.

'That's why I haven't been in touch,' Rebecca admitted when I phoned her. 'I felt sure you'd blame me for what Gideon did.'

'Don't be daft. Of course I don't blame you,' I insisted. 'And to prove it, I'll buy you dinner.'

So it was all arranged.

We met in town and went for a pizza. In about half a minute, Rebecca scanned the menu, then closed it and put it down. Five minutes later, I still hadn't made up my mind.

'Are you OK, Tobey?' Rebecca asked. 'You seem preoccupied.'

'What? Oh, sorry. I've just got a lot on my mind at the moment,' I said.

'I'm really sorry about you losing your job,' she said quickly. 'I wish you'd let me help, at least until you find a new one.'

I shook my head. 'Rebecca, I'll be fine. I've some money saved and something will turn up. Besides, I wasn't thinking about my job, I was thinking about my sister, Jessica.'

'Is something wrong with her?'

'Yeah. And I'm still trying to figure out how to put it right.'

'Can I help?' Rebecca asked doubtfully.

I smiled. 'No. But thanks for the offer. I appreciate it.'

'If you need any money—'

'I don't,' I interrupted. 'It's not that kind of problem. And stop worrying. I'll find another job.'

'Gideon had no right to sack you,' Rebecca fumed.

'He didn't sack me. I quit,' I amended.

'OK, but he had no right to force you to quit,' she said.

'Rebecca, I promise it's OK,' I said. 'Besides, you're worth it.'

Rebecca switched on a smile bright as a lighthouse when I said that. I returned to my menu, focusing on the task at hand.

'Tobey, promise me something,' Rebecca began hesitantly.

'What?'

'Promise me you won't ever lie to me.'

Pause. 'I promise. What brought that on?'

Rebecca shrugged. 'I just need to know that you're being honest with me.'

'Fair enough,' I replied, studying my menu again so she couldn't see my eyes.

Rebecca waited until I'd ordered and was tucking into my garlic bread starter before she told me her news. For one hopeful moment I thought she was kidding, but her earnest expression indicated otherwise.

'You're serious! Your mum . . .' I coughed to clear the squeak in my voice. 'Your mum wants to meet *me*? But why?'

''Cause I told her all about you.'

'What on earth for?' I asked, aghast.

''Cause I like you.' Rebecca shrugged. 'You're the first guy since I was a kid to talk to me like a normal human being.'

'What about your brothers?'

'They don't count,' Rebecca dismissed. 'Besides, they don't talk to me. They dictate and command and argue.'

'What about your dad?'

'My dad and my uncle were killed when I was nine.' Rebecca's dark-brown eyes clouded over. At that moment, she so reminded me of Callie Rose. I turned away. I didn't want her to remind me of Callie or anyone else for that matter. This was already hard enough without thoughts like that making it harder.

I offered my sympathies. My reply was inadequate, but what else could I say? Rebecca's dad and uncle were the two Dowds that McAuley was rumoured to have taken care of. No wonder Vanessa Dowd and her family hated Alex McAuley so much.

'What about previous boyfriends?' I asked, to change the subject.

'I went to an all-girls school and whilst my friends were happy to come round to my house, very few of them ever invited me back. And as for the brothers of the few friends I had, well, I think my surname was either more than enough to put them off or the only reason they wanted to be with me in the first place.'

'More fool them then,' I said.

And I meant it. Rebecca was nothing like the rest of her family. Any idiot could see that. I knew she'd had at least one proper boyfriend and it hadn't ended happily, but I didn't want to push her any further into unhappy memories.

'Rebecca, do you—?' I began.

'Tobey! I thought it was you. How . . . er . . . how are you?'

My heart sank like a big stone in a small pond. 'Hi, Misty.'

'Are you . . . er . . . eating here too? Me and my friend Erik over there have just arrived.'

I glanced across at Erik, who was scowling at me. Erik was a Nought in our year, but in a different class.

'Misty, this is Rebecca. Rebecca, this is Misty. Misty

and I are in the same class at school.' I thought I'd better make some introductions. I didn't want Rebecca to get the wrong idea.

Which was what exactly?

Why was I so worried about what she might think? Misty didn't even bother to look at Rebecca. Her eyes were still trying to pin me to my chair.

'If you like pizza, maybe we could . . . you know . . . come here next weekend or something . . .' Misty began, adding a blatant wink. 'I'm still hoping to get you alone . . . on a date.'

'I . . . er . . . Well, I . . .' I began.

'Oh no, you didn't!' Rebecca couldn't believe her ears, her eyes or any of her other senses from the sound of it. 'You didn't just ask Tobey out when he's so obviously on a date with me?' She glared at Misty, and if looks could kill she'd've been banged up for life – Dowd family connections or not.

'Tobey's dating *you*?' Misty's eyebrows launched into the air at that news. 'I don't think so. Tobey wouldn't go out with a dagger.'

Rebecca jumped to her feet. 'Listen, bitch . . .'

I jumped up. We were attracting all kinds of attention, the last thing I wanted. I stepped between the two before the hair-pulling began.

'How about I kick your skinny arse?' Misty said, trying to duck round me.

Godsake!

Rebecca was about to hurl herself across the table. 'I'm going to bury my stiletto where the sun don't shine,' she said, pulling off her earrings.

Things were getting serious. When a girl pulls off her

earrings, then lightning and thunder are about to hit and hit hard. Anyone with a sister knew that.

'Tobey, you can do much better than this dagger skank,' Misty told me scathingly.

Whoa!

'Misty, enough. I *am* on a date actually,' I said firmly. 'And Erik's over there waiting for you, so maybe you should head back to him.'

'But, Tobey . . .'

'Bye, Misty.'

Misty frowned at me, then cast Rebecca a filthy look before taking the hint and heading back to her date.

I sat down. After a few seconds, so did Rebecca.

Silence reigned between us.

'I'm sorry about calling your friend a bitch,' said Rebecca quietly. 'It was inexcusable. I lost my temper. I guess I'm more sensitive than I realized.'

I shrugged. 'Forget it.'

'It was rude of me,' she went on unhappily. 'I really am sorry.'

'Rebecca, it's OK. Really it is.' I leaned across the table and brushed my lips against hers. 'Don't let Misty spoil our dinner. Besides, you were right. She is a bitch!'

Rebecca laughed as I'd wanted her to. I returned to my garlic bread. All that excitement had worked up quite an appetite. I couldn't believe Misty. She was on a date, I was with someone, and she still wanted to start some drama. Godsake!

'Tobey, you were about to ask me something, before we were interrupted,' Rebecca prompted.

I put down my bread half-eaten. 'Becks, d'you trust me?'

'Of course.'

'Why?'

The question took Rebecca by surprise. 'I just do.'

'But why?' I persisted.

'Because you didn't chase after me. If anything it was the other way round,' said Rebecca. 'You're quite happy to be seen with me in public and you don't try to hide me away like some shameful secret. You're the only guy who hasn't insisted that I pay for everything. Are those enough reasons to be going on with?'

'They'll do.' I smiled.

Poor Rebecca. She'd been so unlucky with the guys she'd met in the past. And her luck hadn't changed.

'So are you up for meeting my mum?'

'When?'

'How does tomorrow night sound?'

Like Hell on earth. I swallowed hard. 'Tomorrow night sounds fine.'

fifty-nine

Hi, Callie.

I'm sorry I haven't been to see you for a couple of days. Things have been a mess at home with Jessica and I couldn't get away. You're looking so much better, though. You really do look like you've just dozed off.

I've got some news for you. The police intercepted one of McAuley's shipments today. Apparently a little bird told them when, where and what to look for. There are little birds singing all over Meadowview! So that's the second shipment McAuley has lost. Once is bad luck, but twice is bad habits. Unfortunately there was nothing to tie the shipment to McAuley, but everyone – including the police – knows exactly who was running that delivery. By now McAuley is going to be a desperate man, and his desperation will make him even more dangerous than before. I'm definitely going to keep my head down.

I'm going on another date with Rebecca tonight. I'm off to meet her mum. And no doubt, Gideon and Owen will be present too. Gideon has already warned me off so I'd better wear full body armour and a box. Something tells me I'm going to need them. Rebecca is trying to make out that her mum can't wait to meet me, but I think—

'Tobey . . .'

The sound of Callie's voice made me jump out of my skin. I'd been looking down at her hand in mine as I spoke so I missed any signs that she was waking up. I could do nothing but stare as her eyelids fluttered open. She turned her head to focus her gaze on me.

'Callie!' I leaped to my feet and pulled her up to hug her just as hard as I could.

'Ow!' Callie croaked out her protest. 'Too tight.'

I loosened my grip, but no way was I going to let her go. My mouth was already beginning to ache from grinning so hard. I'd wanted my face to be the first one Callie saw when she woke up and I'd got my wish. I lay her back down on her pillows, then kissed her. I only shifted when she started pushing weakly against my shoulders. When I lifted my head, she gasped to drag some air back down into her lungs.

'What're you . . . doing? Are you' – Callie tried to swallow past the dryness in her throat – 'trying to kiss . . . me . . . until I pass out?'

I shook my head not yet trusting myself to speak.

'Besides' – Callie couldn't raise her voice above a whisper – 'my breath . . . is smelly.'

Godsake! Like I gave a damn!

'Water please,' she said. Her voice sounded deep and hoarse, but I've never heard anything so wonderful in my life.

I poured out half a tumbler full of water and held it to her lips to help her to drink. Callie took a few sips before collapsing back onto her pillows as if just sitting up and drinking had exhausted her. She reached for my hand and held it in her own.

'Tobey.' She breathed my name, like just saying it eased her pain.

Callie was looking at me like the last few weeks had never happened. I had what I'd been waiting for. To her I was the same. I was sane. I was safe.

'How're you feeling?' I asked. I really couldn't stop smiling.

'Got a headache.' Callie raised a hand to her temple.

The bandages had long since come off, but she still had a scar to show where the bullet had struck her skin. I bent to kiss it.

'You're very kissy all of a sudden.' Callie frowned.

I laughed. 'You'll be OK now, Callie Rose,' I said. 'Let me go get a doctor.'

Callie's grip on my hand tightened as she looked around her room. 'Tobey,' she said. 'Am I in hospital?'

My frown mirrored Callie's as I nodded.

'W-why am I here? And who's . . . who's Rebecca?'

sixty

I didn't want to be here. I wanted to be back at the hospital with Callie. When I explained about TFTM and meeting Rebecca Dowd, Callie had got more and more agitated. I backtracked and spoke about her getting injured. Just one problem. She didn't remember getting shot. She didn't remember even going to the Wasteland that day. She didn't remember anything that had happened in the days before the shooting either. It had all gone. When Callie found out how long she'd been unconscious, she started to freak. It'd taken two nurses and a doctor to calm her down and sedate her. After she succumbed to sleep, the doctor tried to reassure me that it was natural for those emerging from a coma to feel completely disorientated for a while. But I couldn't help looking at Callie and feeling that I'd just messed up. Again.

I really didn't want to be here with Rebecca. But I'd

started this thing so I had to see it through to the end. She'd picked me up from outside my house at six o'clock and at ten minutes past seven we were pulling up to an electronic gate with two CCTV cameras trained on it. Rebecca took out a small device like a mini remote control from the cup holder between our seats and pointed it at the gate, which then swung back like wings preparing for flight. We drove along a paved driveway before stopping outside her home. I looked up at it, impressed in spite of myself. It was only slightly smaller than Jasmine Hadley's old home, but then so were most public museums. Double-fronted and with copious windows on all three storeys, it looked like it could house half of my street.

I got out of the car, still looking up at the building.

'Ready?' asked Rebecca.

'As I'll ever be,' I replied.

She took my hand. 'Don't worry, you'll be fine.'

We'd see about that. The front door opened just as we reached it. A pocket-sized Cross woman wearing a lilac-coloured flowery dress stood in the doorway. I had to force myself not to pull my hand out of Rebecca's.

'Hi, Mum,' said Rebecca. 'This is Tobey.'

So this was *the* Vanessa Dowd, was it? She wasn't at all what I'd expected. Except maybe her eyes. Her dark-brown eyes were cold and calculating. She looked me up and down like she was appraising a piece of jewellery.

You'll know me next time, I thought. But I was careful to keep my expression neutral.

'Mum, stop that,' sighed Rebecca.

Her mum suddenly smiled. 'Well, so far he's lasted longer than most.'

'See! And Gideon couldn't intimidate him either.'

I was getting a bit tired of both of them talking about me as if I wasn't there. I stepped forward. 'Hello, Mrs Dowd. Pleased to meet you.'

Mrs Dowd shook my hand before stepping to one side. 'Come in, come in.'

Said the spider to the fly . . .

Rebecca and I waited till her mum had shut the door so that she could lead the way.

'Let's go into the drawing room,' said Mrs Dowd.

At home, it would've been called the front room! We entered a space as big as the whole of the downstairs of my house. It was amazing, with a fireplace big enough to walk into and two of the largest sofas I'd ever seen placed on either side of it. 'It's a lovely room,' I said sincerely.

'It does,' said Mrs Dowd.

It does indeed!

She indicated that I should take a seat. Once I sat down, Rebecca sat next to me and her mum sat on the sofa opposite.

'Tobey, how much—?' Mrs Dowd got no further.

Gideon and Owen came in. Gideon had a glass of something amber-coloured in his hand. Owen was on the phone.

'What's he doing here?' Gideon asked the moment he clapped eyes on me. 'I don't want him in my house.'

'Whose house?' Mrs Dowd asked quietly.

Gideon's lips tightened. 'He doesn't belong here.'

'For once I agree with my brother,' said Owen, his free hand clasped over his phone.

'I don't give a damn what you think, Owen,' Mrs Dowd rounded on him.

'Tell me something I don't know, Ma,' Owen said with sarcasm.

Owen was younger than Gideon but taller and more lean. I had to hand it to him. No one would ever guess that we'd met before.

'Owen and Gideon, you both promised me you'd behave. I live here too and Tobey is my guest,' said Rebecca. 'You two should have some manners.'

To my surprise, both Owen and Gideon looked suitably chastened. They really did dote on their little sister.

'I quite agree,' said Mrs Dowd evenly. 'Tobey, I apologize for my sons' distinct lack of class.'

I shrugged.

'Can I get you a drink?' Vanessa Dowd continued. 'Coffee? A soft drink? A glass of wine or lager perhaps?'

'No, thanks. I'm fine,' I replied.

Owen moved to stand over by the window so he could finish his conversation in relative privacy. Gideon sat at the other end of the same sofa as his mum.

'Now where was I? Ah yes . . .' Mrs Dowd smiled. 'Tobey, how much did McAuley pay you to deliver Ross Resnick's finger to Louise Resnick?'

Game, set and match to Vanessa Dowd. I hadn't even touched the ball.

Beside me, Rebecca gasped. 'Mum, what on earth . . . ?'

My blood began to run fast and hot through my body. Vanessa Dowd was a real piece of work. I turned to Rebecca and shook my head before turning back to her mum.

'Mrs Dowd, I delivered the package for a friend, not

McAuley. I didn't know what was in the parcel and it was the one and only delivery I made. Afterwards McAuley paid me three hundred pounds. I gave every penny away.'

I could feel Rebecca's eyes burning into me. I turned to face her, one of the hardest things I'd ever had to do.

'Y-you work for McAuley?' she asked. 'Ross . . . Ross was a friend of mine and you work for McAuley? How could you?'

Don't, Rebecca. Don't lump me in with all the other guys who lied to you and used you. I'm not like that . . .

Except that I am.

'No, I don't work for him. I did that one delivery and that was it,' I tried to explain. 'After the business with Ross Resnick and especially what he did to my sister, I made it clear I wanted nothing more to do with McAuley and I went looking for another way of making some money. That's when I started working at TFTM.'

And those were all true events – they just didn't happen with the motivation I'd implied. Rebecca drew away from me. It was only a slight movement, but it was enough. I looked from her to Mrs Dowd and back again. Nodding briefly, I stood up. Thank you and goodnight.

'I'm sorry you don't believe me, Rebecca. I've told you the truth, but I guess you have no way of knowing that.'

I turned back to Mrs Dowd. She watched me, a tiny smile of satisfaction on her face. She was slicker than Gideon, that was for sure. Where he used a sledgehammer, she used a razor-sharp stiletto. In a way I admired her. Here was an object lesson in how to get a job done.

'What . . . what did McAuley do to your sister?' asked Rebecca.

'Thanks to McAuley and one of my so-called friends, my sister Jessica is now doing heroin,' I said, adding bitterly, 'I have a lot to thank McAuley for.'

I looked around. Owen was off the phone and I had everyone's full attention.

'Tobey, I haven't figured out yet what your game is,' said Gideon. 'But don't worry, I will.'

'There's no game, no nefarious plans, no cards up my sleeve,' I told him. Gideon Dowd could sod off and die as far as I was concerned. I took a deep breath. 'It was nice meeting all of you,' I said, my tone implying the exact opposite. 'If you don't mind, I'll phone for a taxi and wait outside until it arrives.'

I started for the door.

'Tobey, have a seat,' ordered Mrs Dowd.

Like McAuley, she didn't need to shout. I stood for a moment or two, seriously thinking about defying her. But then I sat down again next to Rebecca, who didn't move away. What was going to happen now?

'Rebecca?' her mum prompted. 'Is your guest staying for dinner or not?'

I looked at Rebecca steadily. To look away would've been to appear worse than guilty.

'Would you like to stay?' she asked at last.

'Only if that's what you want,' I said.

'Then stay.'

'Very touching, I'm sure, but the blanker obviously can't be trusted,' said Gideon. 'And he worked for McAuley for goodness' sake. For all any of us know, he still does. Am I the only one in the room with any sense?'

'I worked for McAuley – past tense,' I said. 'And it was once and only once.'

'So you say,' Gideon dismissed.

'It's the truth.'

'Are you arguing with me?' he asked through narrowed eyes.

'Yes, I am,' I replied.

To my surprise, Mrs Dowd burst out laughing. 'Good for you, Tobey,' she approved.

Which was the last thing I'd expected from her. What on earth . . . ? I glanced at Gideon. His expression was very eloquent. If he could've punched through my chest and ripped out my heart to hand it, still beating, back to me, he would've done so – in a hot big city second.

'Mrs Dowd, dinner is served,' said a Cross man in a dark suit who seemed to appear from nowhere.

Who was this guy? He couldn't be a butler. I mean, Godsake! Who had a butler in this day and age? Ah! Apparently the Dowds did.

'Mum, I need to freshen up,' said Rebecca.

She looked fresh enough to me.

'Good idea. I'll join you,' said Vanessa Dowd. 'Morton, we'll be right there.'

'Yes, Mrs Dowd.' The butler headed out of the room, followed by Rebecca and her mum.

After giving me a filthy look, Gideon followed them. I stood up, unsure what I should do. I went to follow them, hoping to stumble across the dining room some time before morning but Owen blocked my way.

'Tobey, we need to talk,' he said.

Owen looked around to make sure we were truly alone, then he handed me a folded slip of paper. Frowning, I opened it and quickly read. I stared at him, completely shocked.

'Is this for real?'

Owen nodded. 'I had that amount deposited in Byron's account, just as you suggested. This had better work, Tobey. That's a lot of my money sitting in that blanker's account.'

Owen was such a tosser. He was talking to a Nought, but thought nothing of insulting us Noughts to my face. I looked down at the confirmation slip in my hand. Owen had transferred a mind-boggling amount of money to Byron's account, far more than I'd suggested.

'It'll work.' I nodded. 'Besides, you got McAuley's first shipment, didn't you? So that's your money back, plus interest.'

'I didn't get the shipment,' Owen dismissed. 'My brother did.'

'But you're poised to take over McAuley's entire operation,' I reminded him. 'And think how much money you'll make then.'

'I shall enjoy being out from under Gideon's shadow,' mused Owen. 'I have quite a few ideas of my own . . .'

I just bet he did.

Owen emerged from his reverie to tell me, 'I must admit, when you first came to me with this scheme, I thought you were either barking or a genius.'

'The jury's still out on that one,' I said, handing back the confirmation slip.

Owen smiled. 'Oh, before I forget, I need the name of

a straight career copper. Not a PC Plod, but not anyone too high up who'll be more interested in covering things up either.'

Surely he'd know more of the coppers in Meadowview than I did? Why was he asking me?

'It can't be anyone even vaguely connected with me. It can't be anyone I know,' explained Owen, taking another swift look around to ensure we were still alone. 'I've got to play this smart. Gideon is gonna go down and if Ma suspects I had a hand in bringing down her favourite son, I'm as good as dead.'

Happy families.

'I think Detective Inspector Boothe at Meadowview police station is straight,' I ventured.

'You're sure?'

'As sure as I can be. But it's not guaranteed.'

'DI Boothe, eh? Never heard of him, so he'll do.'

What was Owen planning? At that moment, I thanked God that I wasn't his brother.

'I like you, Tobey.' Owen grinned at me. 'I knew you and I could do business.'

'How did you know?' I couldn't help asking.

'Because I recognized you for who and what you are at once,' he replied.

'And what's that?'

'My mirror image.'

Inside my body, every drop of blood lost its heat. That was a damned lie. There was no way I was Owen's mirror image.

'I hear another shipment of McAuley's got . . . shall we say, diverted?' said Owen.

'Yeah, I heard that too,' I said. 'Something about the police getting it?'

'What a shame I didn't get to hear about it first,' said Owen, his eyes never leaving mine.

'Yeah, it is,' I agreed.

'You only got details of the one shipment in the file you retrieved from McAuley's memory key?'

'That's right,' I said. 'And I gave you all the information I had. Maybe the police bugged McAuley's house.'

'Maybe they did,' said Owen.

Silence.

'May I ask you something?' I began.

'Go ahead.'

'How did your family find out I delivered that package to Louise Resnick?' I asked.

Owen allowed himself a tiny smile. 'Whatever McAuley knows, sooner rather than later it finds its way to us as well.'

'Oh, I see.' That confirmed it. Someone in McAuley's employ was working for the Dowds. That question was answered. Wasn't there anyone in this whole crummy little world who could be trusted?

'So is that how you knew where and when to send your men on the day of the Wasteland shooting?' I asked. 'One of McAuley's men told you beforehand what he was planning?'

'It might've been,' said Owen. 'Tobey, I don't like a lot of questions.'

I had to bite back my response to that one.

'Fair enough. What are we talking about?'

Owen looked puzzled.

'We're not with the others. You obviously kept me

here to talk about something,' I said. 'Rebecca or your mum might want to know what.'

Owen studied me carefully before he said, 'Tell them I warned you that if you're lying and you really are working for McAuley, I will kill you myself.'

Silence.

Owen suddenly smiled and my blood ran like icy slush. He said, 'Now let's go eat.'

sixty-one

Dinner with the Dowds was excruciating. Owen completely ignored me. Rebecca was very quiet, only speaking when spoken to. Gideon spent the entire time either on his mobile or directing snide remarks my way. Only Vanessa Dowd seemed to be completely at ease and enjoying herself. The food reflected the ambience around the table. Shark's-fin soup was the starter, followed by the rarest steak I'd ever had. The thing was so rare I'm surprised it didn't moo on my plate. No one bothered to ask me how I wanted it cooked – I was definitely a well-done kind of guy. But I wasn't about to complain.

Rebecca's mother watched with amused interest as I chewed my first bloody mouthful. 'Tobey, I'm afraid it's one of the things I insist upon,' she said. 'Steak should be eaten very rare, otherwise it's ruined.'

'Rebecca, you like your meat rare too, don't you?' Gideon said pointedly, looking from Rebecca to me and back again.

Tosser.

'I'm a vegetarian, Gideon — as you very well know,' Rebecca replied.

I chewed on another mouthful. The steak was served with matchstick-thin chips and assorted vegetables. I cleared my plate. The dessert was lemon tart served with lime sorbet. It was foul, bitter and nasty. But I ate all of that too.

After dinner, Rebecca barely said five sentences to me. I gave it half an hour, but when she still wouldn't talk to me I decided I'd truly outstayed my welcome. I was quite prepared to phone for a taxi, but Rebecca insisted on driving me home. All the way home, she'd only speak to me when spoken to, so we quickly lapsed into an uncomfortable silence. Doubt had raised its ugly head and Rebecca was backing away from me.

As we pulled up outside my house, I tried one last time to get her to talk to me properly.

'Rebecca, would you like to come in and meet my mum and sister?' I asked.

She looked surprised, then pleased, but the light in her eyes soon faded. 'No, I . . . No, thanks. Better not.'

I sighed. 'Look, Rebecca, I never lied to you.'

'You never told me the truth either,' she replied. 'And you promised me, Tobey. Look, I have to go home. Mum's orders.'

'Can we meet up tomorrow? We need to talk.'

Rebecca started to shake her head.

'Please. I need to talk to you.'

'All right then,' she said reluctantly. 'When and where?'

'How about tomorrow outside Los Amigos at seven?'

'I'm not sure I want a meal.'

With me.

'Well, we can meet there and find a coffee shop nearby.'

'OK. I'll see you at seven.' At least it wasn't a straight-out no. Rebecca drove off the moment I was clear of her car.

I was getting the chilly treatment and, to be honest, I didn't blame her. I should've told her up front about McAuley. I'd thought about it, I really had, but had decided it would look too much like I was just trying to manipulate her. Big mistake.

I entered my house and went straight up to my room. Sitting on my bed, I thought through everything that had happened since Callie was injured. Before then, my life had seemed so neatly stitched together. It scared me just how easily everything fell to pieces.

There was a knock at my door. Before I could answer, Jessica walked into my room. Her typically unruly, spiked hair lay un-gelled and tamed in a pixie cut framing her face. And for once she wasn't wearing make-up. She smiled at me, albeit hesitantly. I was instantly on my guard.

'Have you come to get me into more trouble with Mum?' I asked with belligerence.

'Don't be like that . . .'

Was she serious?

'Jessica, what d'you want?'

'I want us back to the way we used to be,' she said.

'Then tell Mum the truth,' I replied.

Jessica looked me in the eye. 'I did. At least, part of it.'

'Jess, I'm not the one in this family who's into drugs,' I pointed out.

'No, you're just into money,' she said. 'And it's all right for you, 'cause you're smart. You have a real chance to make some and get out of this place. What're the rest of us supposed to do, Tobey?'

'I don't know. But you'll never find the answer in waxed paper wrappers.'

'I'm not looking for the answer.'

'Then what are you looking for?'

'A way to not mind so much about the question.'

'Jessica, that stuff will stop you minding about anything, except more junk,' I said.

'I know.'

'Then please stop taking it.'

'It's that easy, is it?'

'No. But Mum and I are here to help you.'

'I'll think about it.'

So much for that then. 'D'you want me to tell Mum for you?'

Jessica's eyes narrowed. 'Is that a threat?'

'No,' I said, exasperated. 'I'm trying to help. Can't you see that?'

'No, I can't,' said Jessica. 'You only want to help me your way, not my way.'

What was she on about? I really wasn't in the mood for a big argument so I let it slide.

I sighed. 'Are you still using?'

At first I thought she wasn't going to answer. 'Tobey,' she said at last, 'I'm not one of your maths problems. OK?'

'Meaning?'

'Meaning not every problem has a solution.'

'I know that.'

'No, you don't. That's the trouble. In your world A plus B equals C. It works for maths so you expect it to work for people too.'

'That's not true.'

'Isn't it?' asked Jessica. 'You assume you've got me all figured out. I bet you even think you know why I started on smack in the first place.'

'I thought maybe it had something to do with your course at college,' I admitted.

'You think I'm going to fail?'

I shrugged. It seemed logical.

'Tobey, I did my exam and submitted enough coursework to scrape a pass. My marks won't be setting any college records, but I did pass,' Jessica told me. 'So what does that do to your theory now?'

'All right then. Tell me why you started taking that stuff,' I challenged.

Sadly, she shook her head. 'Tobey, I did just tell you.'

'I don't understand.'

'I know,' said Jessica. 'And you never will until you experience the one thing that drunks and druggies and all the miserable, lonely, unhappy people in this world share.'

'And what's that?' I asked.

'Work it out.'

And she was gone.

sixty-two. Callie

How can I have slept for so long? It feels like I just nodded off, like I've been out of it for a day, maybe two max. I stopped. The world didn't. Time moved on without me. So did Tobey.

Who is Rebecca?

Just a girl? His girl friend? Or his girlfriend? I thought . . . Tobey and me . . . I thought . . . But I was wrong. He has someone else now. Rebecca. And what do I have? Uncle Jude and this hospital bed. I'm trying so hard to be glad for Tobey. I'm trying so desperately hard not to mind — or care. But though I've never met Rebecca, I hate her. I hate her for taking Tobey away from me, for being there when he needed someone.

I've woken up to find all the bad things in my life have been waiting patiently for me and all the good things have gone. Uncle Jude is out there, biding his time. I'm surprised he didn't visit me when I was unconscious and finish the job. Or maybe he wants me wide awake to fully appreciate when he takes his revenge. I still have to live with the fact that an innocent man is dead because of me. That hasn't gone away either. That fact has eaten an even bigger hole inside of me, because I'm still here, I've survived. And Robert Powers didn't. Is this karma? In the world of 'what goes around, comes around', maybe I'm getting what I deserve. I just wish someone would tell me when it'll stop hurting so much.

All I want is for Tobey to hold me tight and tell me that everything will be all right between us. Who am I trying to fool? All I want is Tobey.

But he's moved on.

And I'm stuck here.

And I've never felt so alone.

sixty-three

The following morning, me, Mum and Jess all sat down to have breakfast together again. Mum sipped at her orange juice. Jessica picked at her cereal. I stirred my coffee round and round. For once I didn't have much of an appetite. Every time I looked up, Jessica was looking at me. Should I say something to Mum? Should I try? I still hadn't worked out what my sister had been trying to tell me the night before. And I was desperate not to make things any worse.

'Mum, I lied to you about Tobey,' Jessica said unexpectedly.

Mum frowned at her. 'Pardon?'

'Tobey hasn't been dealing drugs. I only told you that because he threatened to tell you . . . to tell you that I'd been s-smoking . . . smack.'

'Jessica, please tell me you're joking,' Mum said, appalled.

Jessica bowed her head, unable to say a word.

'You've been taking drugs?' Mum whispered. 'Oh, Jessica.'

A tear followed in quick succession by a host of others fell from Jessica's eyes onto the table.

I looked from Mum to my sister, holding my breath.

'Oh, Jessica . . .' Mum got up and hugged Jess to her. Jess fell into her embrace and started to sob her heart out.

'Tobey, could you leave us alone for a while?' Mum asked.

I headed for the door, wondering what had happened to make Jess change her mind about telling Mum. Maybe she'd meant it about getting things back to the way they used to be. God knows that was all I wanted as well. But somehow it felt like those days were over, never to return.

Jessica and Mum were in the living room with the door shut for over an hour, almost two. I went up to my room and wrote an email to Callie. An email I knew I'd never send, but I had more than a few things to get off my chest. And it helped – a little. A very little.

I couldn't put it off any longer. It was time for another letter. I didn't have time to go to the library again so my own computer would just have to do. And this was just the sort of carelessness that could get me caught, but I had to do it now before I changed my mind.

Wearing a pair of my mum's rubber gloves this time to ensure I ended up with a sheet of fingerprint-free paper, I drafted my third and final letter. My brain must've been temporarily scrambled by a cosmic ray to believe I could use McAuley's last shipment for my own ends. Either that or scrambled by greed. But not any more.

I wanted no part of it.

My letter to the police was short and to the point, telling them everything I knew about McAuley's last drop-off. The man would be out of business, but it still didn't feel like enough. I was beginning to realize that nothing ever would. I placed the letter in a printed envelope addressed to DI Boothe. Time to get out of the house. Besides, I couldn't stand the silence any longer. Grabbing my jacket off the banister, I thought about just heading out the door without saying a word. But I couldn't do that to my mum. That was my dad's trick.

'Mum, I'm going to see Callie at the hospital,' I called through the still closed living-room door.

After a few seconds the door opened. Mum stood there, her eyes slightly red. She'd obviously been crying. And from where I stood in the hall, I couldn't see my sister.

'Are you OK, Mum?' I asked.

Mum nodded.

'If you want me to stay, I will.'

'No, that's OK. Say hello to Callie for me.'

'Is Jess OK?' I lowered my voice to ask.

'No. But she will be,' Mum said with determination. She looked up at me and stroked my cheek. 'I love you, Tobey. You know that, don't you?'

Whenever Mum told me she loved me, my response was invariably, 'I know.' As it was today. But today my usual response didn't feel like nearly enough.

'Mum, I . . . I . . . I have to go.'

She smiled at my discomfort, stroking my cheek again. 'Give Callie my love.'

'I will.' I practically sprinted out of the door.

I'd wanted to say it, I really had. But I'd never said those words to anyone in my life and I couldn't just start now. But Mum knew. She had to know. And now that she knew the truth about Jessica, everything would be OK. It had to be.

Now it was time to put things right between Callie and me.

sixty-four

Dropping my letter in the postbox outside the hospital, I headed into the building. Five minutes later, I took a deep breath and walked into Callie's room. Every cell in my body told me this was a bad idea, but I needed to see her. Her head was turned away from the door. She was looking out of the window towards the park beyond. I stood in the doorway, watching her, drinking in her stillness. Apart from the occasional blink, no other part of her body beneath the bedcovers moved.

'Hello, Callie,' I said softly.

'Hello, Tobey,' Callie replied without looking at me.

That hurt. I swallowed hard before I could trust myself to speak again.

'May I come in?'

Callie nodded.

I entered the room and sat in one of the chairs by her bed. She still wasn't looking at me.

'How're you feeling?' I asked. 'Have you remembered a bit more?'

Like the night we spent together?

Please remember being with me, Callie. Please remember making love with me. Otherwise I'll start to doubt my own memories. I'm already beginning to wonder. Maybe the whole thing was a dream, wishful thinking, nothing more than a fantasy.

Callie shrugged. How I wished she'd look at me.

'How's Rebecca?' she asked.

All kinds of explanations raced through my head. But that's where they stayed.

'She's fine,' I replied. 'We're having dinner once I leave here.'

Godsake! Why did I say that? To get a reaction? Because I have a big mouth? Or, God help me, to get back at Callie for not remembering our night together?

Callie turned to look at me. I had to force myself not to look away.

'Will I get to meet her?'

I shrugged. We regarded each other.

'My doctor says I can go home later today,' said Callie. 'Once I'm strong enough, maybe you, me and Rebecca can get together.'

'OK,' I agreed, knowing full well it'd never happen.

Rebecca wasn't stupid. One look at Callie and she'd know which way the wind was blowing. Head bent,

Callie laced her bedsheet in and out of her fingers. She wasn't the only one who was nervous.

'I've got most of my memory back now,' she said, looking at me again. 'I still don't remember the time around the shooting. But I remember everything else.'

'Oh.'

The time around the shooting? How did Callie quantify that? Two minutes before the shooting, or two hours or two days or two weeks before?

'Is that it?' she asked. 'Is that all you have to say?'

'What would you like me to say?' I asked.

Silence. The tension between us expanded like a balloon too full of air. An explosion was about to happen. I didn't have long to wait.

'Tobey,' My name burst from Callie's lips. 'Why did you—?'

Sephy and Meggie chose just that moment to walk in. Thank goodness for bad timing. Callie's look of frustration didn't go unnoticed. Sephy kissed her daughter's forehead before sitting down. Meggie did the same.

Sephy glared at me, her brown eyes giving me frostbite.

'Hello, Tobey,' said Meggie.

'Hello.' I wasn't sure what else to say.

I knew I should leave, but I didn't want to. Not now. Not yet. Meggie looked from Callie to me and back again. She sighed.

'Callie, I . . . I have something to tell you,' she began. 'And I don't want to put it off any longer.' She and Sephy exchanged a look before she continued. 'It's about . . . Jude.'

Callie flinched as if the word was a physical thing that had struck her.

'Tobey told me that you're . . . worried my son is alive and that he'll come after you.'

Though Callie didn't reply, Meggie had her full attention. I watched Callie avidly.

'Tobey, could you wait for us outside, please,' said Sephy. And it wasn't a request.

'No, Mum. I want Tobey to stay,' said Callie.

'But this is private family business,' Sephy began.

'I have no secrets from Tobey.' Callie looked at me as she spoke, her expression sombre. The words were said almost in a monotone, yet she still managed to make it sound like an accusation. Then she sighed. 'Will you stay, Tobey?'

I nodded. I wasn't going anywhere. Not whilst Callie needed me.

Meggie took a deep breath, closed her eyes momentarily, then spoke. 'Callie, love, Jude is dead. He died in the Isis Hotel bomb blast along with Jasmine.'

Callie shook her head. 'Uncle Jude isn't dead. The news said some man called Robert Powers . . .'

'Robert Powers was the alias Jude used. My son was infamous, notorious – and proud of it.' Bitterness hardened Meggie's voice. 'He knew that he wasn't going to die in bed of old age. He set up an alternate identity, complete with dental and doctor's records, a driver's licence, the works – and all under the name Robert Powers.'

'But how could he get an ID card and driver's licence?' asked Sephy. 'You have to produce a birth certificate to obtain those.'

'The real Robert Powers was born in the same year as

Jude and killed over fifteen years ago in a road accident. Apparently it's a well-known Liberation Militia tactic. Send off for the birth certificate of someone who has died and then use it to get all kinds of official documentation like passports,' said Meggie. 'So that's who Jude became and I was sworn to secrecy. He told me that if anything happened to him, his false ID would make sure that I wasn't hounded by the police and the press.'

'But the police must've had Uncle Jude's fingerprints.' It was as if Callie was afraid to let herself believe it. 'They had to be on a police database somewhere.'

'Callie, the explosion took out the top floor of the hotel. Jude's body was too badly damaged to identify using fingerprints. All the police had to work with were some teeth to match to dental records,' said Meggie. 'Please believe me, Callie, my son and Robert Powers are . . . were . . . one and the same person. I paid anonymously for Robert Powers's headstone. I even visit his grave occasionally to lay some flowers. Jude is dead.'

Meggie bowed her head. Sephy slipped an arm around her shoulder and whispered some words of comfort into her ear. I glanced across at Callie. Tears were flowing down her cheeks like a waterfall. I sprang up to go to her, but she shook her head, impatiently wiping the tears from her face.

'I'm OK,' she told me. 'I need to do this, before I bottle out.'

I knew what was coming. I moved to stand beside Callie's bed. Sephy looked from me to Callie, suspicion creeping into her eyes.

'Callie?' she prompted.

'Nana Meggie, you need to know something,' Callie began, fresh tears spilling onto her cheeks. 'The bomb that killed Uncle Jude and Nana Jasmine, I . . . I m–made it.'

Meggie stood up slowly and bent to kiss Callie's forehead. 'I know,' she said.

Callie stared at her. 'You . . . you know?'

'I've always known.'

'I don't understand.' Callie shook her head. 'Did Mum tell you? Why did you never say anything?'

'Your mum never said a word.' Meggie hastened to reassure her.

'Besides, what was there to say?' asked Sephy, as she moved to stand next to Meggie. 'I didn't realize what Mother was going to do until it was too late. I thought . . . Well, it doesn't matter what I thought.'

'Nana Meggie, how did you know if Mum didn't tell you?' asked Callie.

'Jasmine told me what my son was making you do,' said Meggie. 'She got in touch with me . . . and told me.'

'Do you know what happened that day?' Callie asked. 'Did Nana Jasmine decide to confront Uncle Jude? Did the bomb go off by accident?'

Callie turned to me, uncertainty written on her face, so she missed the swift look Sephy and Meggie exchanged. But I didn't. Callie's mum and grandma were both hiding something.

'Mum?' Callie prompted.

Sephy said gently, 'Love, I wasn't there. I was with you,

remember? But I'm sure it happened something like that. Callie, you mustn't blame yourself.'

Meggie added, 'It was an accident, love.'

'You think so?' Callie whispered. 'You really think it was an accident?'

Sephy and Meggie glanced at each other again. There was so much shared history between them that all they needed was a passing look to exchange volumes.

'Callie, we love you very much,' said Meggie. 'And Jasmine felt the same. She went to confront my son and . . . and the bomb went off. And the last person you should blame is yourself. I knew what my son was. So did Jasmine. He's responsible for what happened, not you.'

'But two people died . . .' Callie began.

'An accident. A tragic accident and not your fault,' Sephy insisted.

'Mum, did you know what Nana Jasmine was going to do when she left us in her house on my birthday?' asked Callie.

'Of course not. I would've stopped her,' Sephy said.

Callie was too busy looking at her mum to notice the look in Meggie's eyes at that question. With a start, I realized that even if Sephy hadn't known what Jasmine was up to, Meggie did. Meggie glanced at me. In that instant I knew the truth. And Meggie knew I knew. But I would never, ever tell Callie – and that was a fact.

'Mum, do you hate me?' Callie whispered.

'Oh, sweetheart, of course I don't hate you.' Sephy swept Callie into her arms. 'I told you before, there's nothing on this earth or beyond that could make me hate you.'

Callie and her mum hugged each other for a long time. When at last Callie let go, she turned to Meggie.

'Nana Meggie, I'm so sorry,' she said. 'I never meant for Uncle Jude or Nana Jasmine to get hurt. I was so lost and confused, I didn't know what I was doing.'

'I understand, dear,' said Meggie. 'All I want in this world is for you to stop blaming yourself.'

'Easier said than done,' Callie told her.

'But you've got to try,' said Meggie. 'Jude is dead, Callie. Don't let him ruin the rest of your life. You have to do what I did and let him go.'

Meggie looked down at the bed, but her gaze was somewhere in the past. An unhappy past. A couple of blinks later and she was back in the present, but her eyes still held a profound sorrow I was only just beginning to understand. Sephy stroked her daughter's hair. Meggie forced a smile. And though Callie tried to smile, it wobbled precariously on her face.

She turned to me, and the look in her eyes made my throat tighten so much I could hardly breathe. 'Tobey, you're going to be late for your dinner date,' she said quietly.

'I don't mind staying.'

'It's OK. I'm OK – or I will be. You should go.'

I knew a dismissal when I heard one. But even so, I couldn't help asking, 'Are you sure?'

Callie nodded. 'I'll see you . . . when I see you.'

And she turned away from me. Deliberately. Sephy watched me, a satisfied expression on her face.

I left Callie's room. Sephy followed me. Closing the door behind her, she walked a few paces along the corridor so that there was no chance of us being seen through Callie's window.

'As you can see, my daughter is now awake,' she said. 'So you needn't feel you have to visit her any more. I found out from one of the nurses that you've been here almost every day, in spite of what I told you.'

'How could I stay away? Callie is my best friend—'

'Oh, please,' Sephy scoffed.

'She is. I'd do anything for her.'

The look Sephy gave me was withering.

'It's true,' I insisted.

'Tobey, how stupid d'you think I am? D'you really think I'm going to stand idly by and watch you hurt my daughter?'

'I'd never do that—'

'But you did, Tobey. And you're still doing it. Don't forget, I saw you and your new girlfriend.'

'And you told Callie?'

Sephy's eyes narrowed. 'I didn't tell my daughter a damn thing. You did enough boasting about your new girlfriend on your own.'

'Rebecca isn't my girlfriend.'

'Tell that to her tongue and her tonsils,' Sephy replied with sarcasm. 'What is it with you? Off with the old and on with the new? Then keep the old as backup? Well, not where my daughter is concerned.'

'If you'd just let me explain . . .'

'Go on then.' Sephy folded her arms as she waited.

But I had nothing — at least nothing that was safe to share. No explanations. No excuses. No reasons. Nothing.

'That's what I thought.' Sephy's voice dripped with

contempt. 'Tobey, you obviously don't feel the same way about my daughter as she does about you. So do us all a favour and leave her alone.'

'That's not true,' I said. 'I . . . I do care about Callie.'

'Oh, spare me your lukewarm protestations.' Sephy raised both hands, her palms towards me as if she was warding me off. 'You know what, Tobey? I'm not getting into a debate with you. Callie doesn't need your guilt-inspired visits. I believe my daughter just made her feelings clear on that subject. I know I have.'

I closed my eyes briefly. The faster I ran towards Callie, the further away I got. Maybe I should just stop running.

'Miss Hadley, why are you doing this?'

'Because actions speak louder than words. When my daughter needed your help, when she needed you to tell the police what really happened, you turned your back on her. You let those responsible for harming her get away with it.'

Tell her, Tobey. Tell Sephy the truth . . .

'You walked away, Tobey. So keep walking. That's about all you're good for. Meggie and I have come to take Callie home. From this moment on, you leave her alone.'

And with one last look of pure disdain, Sephy headed back to her daughter.

sixty-five

Even though the sky was cloudy and rain threatened, I made my way back to the Wasteland. I had nowhere else to go. I glanced up at the darkening grey clouds. They filled the sky to overflowing. I sat on a park bench and watched the world pass me by. I was so close to getting everything I'd tried to achieve, and I'd never felt so far away from everything I believed in. It wasn't supposed to work that way.

I sat still for I don't know how long. Only the first fat splash of rain on my forehead roused me. I glanced at my watch. It was time to meet Rebecca. It was also time to draw a line under our relationship, such as it was. Maybe we could still at least be friends, though no doubt her brothers and her mum would do their best to make sure that didn't happen. But even if we couldn't stay friends, was it too much to hope we could part that way?

On my way to Los Amigos, the phone McAuley had given me started to vibrate in my pocket. Godsake! Much as I wanted to throw the mobile into the nearest bin, I couldn't. Instead, against my better judgment, I answered it.

'Hello, Mr McAuley.'

'Tobey, I'm deeply disappointed in you.'

Hello to you too. Had he finally figured out that I'd had a hand in the disappearance of his shipments?

'I don't know what you mean, sir,' I said cautiously.

'Tobey, don't make things worse by treating me like a fool. You were supposed to get me some information,' said McAuley. 'Where is it?'

It took me a second to catch up. He was talking about the bent cop on the Dowds' payroll. I was still safe. For now.

'I haven't been able to find out. I don't work at TFTM any more. Gideon got rid of me.'

'I'm not interested in your excuses. I'm very disappointed, Tobey. Now if you want to get back into my good books, you'll bring Rebecca Dowd to my warehouse on the industrial estate at ten o'clock tonight without fail. I can use her to get my shipments back from her family. Is that clear?'

Silence.

'Did you hear me, Tobey?'

'I'm sorry, Mr McAuley, but I can't do that,' I replied.

'Tobey, when you're in a hole you don't keep digging,' McAuley said silkily. 'You'll do as I say or you'll force me to show you what I do to those who let me down.'

'I'm sorry, Mr McAuley, but Rebecca has nothing to do with this and I think you should leave it that way. So I'm not doing it.' I disconnected the call before McAuley could make his threats more specific. I must be mad. This had to be the very definition of painting yourself into a corner. I dropped McAuley's phone on the pavement and ground it under my heel, enjoying the satisfying crunch it made as the plastic shattered. No more phone calls. No more orders. He was finished and I wanted nothing more to do with him or any of them. I knew what I had to do now. And I had to act fast. Time had just about run out.

sixty-six

At the coffee shop, Rebecca and I sat at a table by a window. Outside the rain was beginning to pelt down. Usually I loved the rain. It calmed me down. But not today. My brain felt hot-wired. My filter coffee sat untouched. Rebecca sipped at her skinny latte. She wore denim jeans, a red blouse and a denim jacket – and she looked the business. Her braids were tied back in a ponytail, but she seemed unaware or unconcerned about how pretty she looked. Conversation between us flowed like boulders travelling uphill. Neither of us had quite plucked up the courage to say why we were here. Rebecca took another sip of her coffee, then placed the tall glass down on the stained wooden table.

'Tobey, d'you like me? And please be honest,' she asked.

'I like you very much,' I replied at once.

'D'you love me?'

I thought of Callie. 'No,' I said.

'D'you think you could ever love me?'

All kinds of lines about not being able to tell the future and the like skipped into my head. But I couldn't lie to her. It wouldn't be fair.

'I don't think so,' I said. I took a deep breath and mustered up a straight answer rather than a prevarication. 'No.'

'I didn't think so,' Rebecca said. 'I'm your rebound girl.'

'My what?'

'You split up from your last girlfriend and I came along at the right time to stop you being lonely,' she explained.

'That's not true,' I protested. 'I mean, there was more to it than that.'

'Let's be honest, Tobey. You like me, but it'll never be more than that – and we both know it. I think it takes a lot for you to love someone, but once you do, that's it for you,' said Rebecca. 'Your ex-girlfriend doesn't know how lucky she was.'

'Rebecca, I didn't set out to use you,' I said at last. 'I want you to believe that.'

'Oh, I do,' she said. 'In fact, I want to thank you for helping me to realize that I'm more than just my mother's daughter.'

'You don't give yourself enough credit,' I told her. 'You can do anything, be anyone. The only person stopping you is you.'

'You really believe that? It's that simple?'

'Yeah,' I replied at once. 'When you get right down to it, it is that simple. And you're in a better position than most people. You don't have class or status or money holding you back. You just need to get out of your own way. Godsake! That sounds like something my sister would say!'

Rebecca laughed. I'd told her about Jessica's meditation and inner-peace phase. I just hadn't mentioned how much I missed it compared to Jess's latest kick.

'I love the way you have such faith in me,' said Rebecca.

'What's not to believe in?' I smiled.

'To be honest, I've already made enquiries about teacher training courses at university,' she said, almost shyly. 'I haven't told my family yet, though.'

'That's fantastic,' I said. 'You'll be a great teacher. You have a lot of patience.'

'Except with certain girls called Misty,' Rebecca laughed.

'You're not alone in that one,' I told her.

We both finished our coffees.

'I don't work for McAuley, Rebecca. I want you to know that. I detest the man.'

'I know. And I'm sorry about your sister.'

I licked my lips as I tried to frame what needed to be said next.

'I've heard that McAuley blames your family for the loss of some shipments he recently arranged. You need to be on your guard, Rebecca. McAuley's a filthy piece of work who'd roll a tank over his own mother if she got in his way. And his back is against the wall, which makes him even more dangerous.'

'Don't worry,' Rebecca said with a confident smile. 'Mum and I are off on holiday tomorrow so McAuley won't be able to get anywhere near me.'

I sighed, relieved. That was OK then. To my surprise, Rebecca leaned across the table and kissed me. It was short but sweet.

'So you and me, we're still friends?' I asked.

I guess I wanted to have it all, but I really did like her.

Rebecca placed her hand over mine on the table. 'Of course we are. Nothing's going to change that.'

'I'm glad.' I smiled. 'Fancy another coffee?'

She considered. 'Oh, go on then. But I can't stay long.'

'Fair enough,' I said, standing up. 'Want a cake to go with it?'

'Tobey, you're a bad influence,' she admonished with a smile.

I grinned at her. 'I know!'

Over the next thirty minutes, I told her about Jess and finding her on the floor in the bathroom at home. Rebecca told me about the long-running feud between her two brothers. Apparently they'd been at each other's throats since they were kids. Reading between the lines, it sounded like their antagonism towards each other had been fuelled and fanned by their mother, but I wasn't about to spoil the affability growing between us by saying so.

Rebecca glanced down at her watch. 'Tobey, I have to go now,' she said reluctantly. 'Mum's expecting me back home. I have to finish my packing.'

Which was a real shame because both of us were enjoying our time together.

I said, 'Make sure you send me a postcard, OK?'

'Every other day,' said Rebecca.

'One will do,' I replied. It was only when I caught the smile on her face that I realized she was teasing me.

I paid for our coffees. We walked to the exit and hugged.

'Want me to walk you to your car?' I asked.

'No, don't bother. I'm only a couple of minutes up the road. I managed to find a parking bay. It must be my lucky day,' Rebecca smiled. 'Tobey, can we meet up for another coffee when I get back?'

'I'd like that. Very much,' I replied truthfully.

Outside the coffee shop, Rebecca dug into her bag and pulled out an orange and yellow umbrella. The thing was up and over her head in two seconds flat. My sister didn't like her hair to get wet in the rain either. Another hug made a tad awkward by the brolly, then a wave and we set off in opposite directions. The rain was still pitching down, but after the heat wave we'd had I was now kind of enjoying it. I'd always liked the rain. I was actually smiling! My meeting with Rebecca had gone better than I deserved. When she got back from her holiday, I'd definitely take her out for a meal or something, rather than a measly coffee.

A black van drove past. It was only after about five more steps that I realized where I'd seen it before – outside McAuley's house. Was McAuley following me? I turned. The van was heading away from me. I was sure it was McAuley's, but in that case, why hadn't he stopped? Even with my hair plastered down and the rain falling like a barrage of arrows, he must've seen me.

Rebecca.

No . . .

I raced back to the coffee bar and saw Rebecca and her brolly about twenty metres ahead of me, heading back to her car.

'REBECCA,' I called out, trying to make my voice heard over the teeming rain and the roaring traffic.

'REBECCA, WAIT . . .' I sprinted towards her.

Rebecca spun round to face me, just as McAuley jumped out of the passenger side of his van.

'BECKS, LOOK OUT!' But I was still at least six metres away. And McAuley was right behind her. A slight movement of his arm was all it took. Rebecca didn't even have a chance to look surprised before she fell to the pavement. Her umbrella rolled away from her. She lay motionless on the ground as McAuley stood there, his arms at his side, a dripping knife held in his right hand. I skidded to an abrupt halt less than two metres away from him and stood stock still, unable to move. And even though the rain kept slanting into my eyes, I'll swear until my dying day that McAuley smiled at me. A brief, satisfied smile.

'You let me down, Tobey,' he said. 'My warehouse at ten tonight, or I'll come to your house – and through your family, if necessary – to get you.'

He climbed back into the van. It drove away at an unhurried pace. Those closest to Rebecca's prone body rushed to her aid, her discarded umbrella an indicator that something was very wrong. And still I couldn't move. Rebecca lay face down on the ground, her head to one side. Raindrops fell into her open, sightless eyes, but she didn't even flinch. She stared across the pavement and into the gutter. The world went very still, very quiet. Just for an instant, but it was enough. Cold sweat and warm rain drenched my body. My stomach began to fold in on itself. I tried to take a breath, but my body had forgotten how. It was only when my burning lungs were howling out for air that I managed a horrified gasp. Then all the sounds around me were amplified to such a degree that the noise was painful, deafening.

Through the drumming rain came cries for help, calls for an ambulance and pleas for witnesses. The crowd was getting bigger all the time. Most were still trying to figure out what had happened. One Cross man turned Rebecca over onto her back and tried to administer mouth to mouth and CPR. His actions were frantic, one breath away from pure panic. His face . . . the glasses he wore . . . familiar . . . he'd been in the coffee bar with us. Following us? I instinctively knew who he was. Rebecca's bodyguard – assigned by Gideon to keep his distance but protect. Too much distance.

He'd failed.

I'd failed.

My mistakes. Expensive mistakes. Costly. Priceless. I couldn't afford the price, so Rebecca paid. She was motionless. No blood . . . why was there no blood? The rain snatched it up and escaped away in every direction with it. I stared down at Rebecca and the world grew colder and quieter. It was only when a distant siren split the air that the blood started racing around my veins again.

My body shaking, I turned and walked away.

I was good at that.

I only made it halfway along the road before, without warning, my stomach erupted. I was sick all over my shoes and the pavement. I wanted to lie down and curl up in a ball until the image of Rebecca's unseeing eyes left my head. I wanted to lie down spread-eagled in the rain until I was washed clean again. But there wasn't enough water on the planet.

First Callie Rose. Now Rebecca.

Oh, God . . .

Rebecca.

No more. Please no more.

sixty-seven

My mobile started to ring. I answered it on auto–pilot, my hand trembling. My whole body was shaking. Breathe in, breathe out. Calm down, Tobey.

Rebecca . . .

Breathe out, breathe in.

Tobey, get it together.

Rebecca.

Rain washed over my hand and my phone, but I didn't care. Why couldn't I stop shaking? Keep walking, Tobey. Whatever else happens, keep walking.

'Tobey? This is Detective Inspector Boothe.'

'Yes, Inspector?' I said faintly.

'I have some good news for you.'

Good news for whom? Had he got to McAuley . . . before I could?

'Good news?' I prompted.

'We found our corrupt cop. She's been arrested, along with Gideon Dowd.'

'I don't understand.'

'Acting on an anonymous tip–off, we were able to place surveillance equipment and use undercover personnel from other regions to catch Gideon Dowd discussing future payoffs with DCI Reid. In return she gave him details of a raid on his house and one of his business premises planned for two days' time. DCI Reid was the one in the Dowds' pocket.'

DCI Reid . . . Where had I heard that name before?

'The woman who interviewed me at the police station?' I remembered.

'That's right,' said DI Boothe. 'I believed what you said, Tobey. And as it was DCI Reid's idea to bring you in, I went over her head to get permission to lay a trap for her. And she walked right into it.'

I shook my head, which felt like it was stuffed with cotton wool.

'I . . . I don't understand. You got an anonymous tip-off?'

'Yeah. Some public-spirited citizen provided us with chapter and verse. We know all about DCI Reid and her involvement with Gideon Dowd. We were sent files documenting meeting times and payoffs, offshore bank account details and all the operations she scuppered on Dowd's behalf. We also got information tying a whole ship-ment of hijacked drugs to Gideon. He was stupid enough to store them in the basement of his town house. With the data we were sent and the surveillance evidence, that piece of trash Reid and her scumbag lover Gideon will both be dining on prison food for twenty years minimum.'

'I see.'

'I did wonder if I have you to thank for the files I was sent?' Boothe enquired ingenuously.

'Nothing to do with me,' I replied slowly.

No, DI Boothe needed to thank Owen Dowd.

Gideon was out of the way. McAuley was on the ropes and busted. Owen Dowd now owned it all.

Meadowview was out of the frying pan – and into the fire.

Well done, Tobey.

What was my mantra? Whatever it takes?

All I had to do now was head up to the top of the tallest building in Meadowview and wait for one and all to thank me. With a psycho nut job like Owen Dowd now running things, the thanks would pour in.

'So are you prepared to talk to me now?' asked Boothe. 'Will you testify against McAuley?'

'Why would I do that?'

'Because we both know he's the one responsible for your girlfriend ending up in hospital. Testify against him and I can guarantee you and your family will be protected. We can even relocate you if necessary,' said DI Boothe.

'It's too late,' I replied.

'What d'you mean?' I could hear the frown in Boothe's voice.

'I mean, it's too late tonight. Ask me tomorrow.'

I disconnected the call.

sixty-eight

I tried phoning Dan, but his phone just rang continuously. There was only one thing left to do. I headed for his lockup. It was only on my second attempt that I accurately remembered the combination to his padlock. I went in, coughing against the smell of stale air and stale hopes and stale dreams. The single bulb didn't cast enough light to sweep the corners of the place. No matter. I knew what I needed. I found it in a box in the far corner of the room, a P99 military semiautomatic – the 9mm version. It had a green polymer frame – an eco-friendly colour, I told myself. I checked the magazine. It was fully loaded. Making sure the safety was on, I put the gun in my jacket pocket. I spun around and halted in mid–step. Dan stood at the entrance to the lockup, watching me.

'Dan, I need your help,' I launched in at once. 'McAuley killed Rebecca Dowd and now he is after me.'

'What d'you plan on doing about it?'

'It's me or him,' I said quietly.

'Finally gonna get your hands dirty?'

'Dan, please. Will you help me?'

The smile Dan gave then was a long way from friendly. 'Why don't you just call the police?'

''Cause then McAuley will find a way to make my whole family pay, not just me.'

'Why should I care about you or your family?' asked Dan.

'It's not about me, Dan. My mum and sister don't deserve what will happen if McAuley gets hold of them.'

'Says the man who started all this in the first place,' he said bitterly. 'You wound us all up like your little dancing dolls and now you're complaining because we're not dancing the way you want us to.'

What could I say to that? Nothing.

'Dan, please. McAuley's at his warehouse, but he's not alone. I can't do this by myself.'

'You're gonna have to.' Dan shrugged. 'This isn't my fight.'

'But McAuley's men will all be armed to the teeth.'

'Not my problem,' said Dan. 'And *now* we're even.'

So much for that then. The faint glimmer of hope I'd felt when I turned round and saw Dan standing there flickered and died. Only desperation had made me believe that he might help me. Far too much had passed between us.

'Can I take your P99?' I took the gun out of my pocket to show him.

'Are you going to bring it back?' he asked wryly.

Probably not.

'If I can.'

'Then go ahead. Take a couple of extra magazine clips, just in case.'

We could've been talking about comic books or sausages rather than guns. I took an extra magazine clip out of the box and headed for the exit.

'You won't change your mind and help me?' I tried one last time.

Dan shook his head, adding, 'You do know you won't get past Byron and the others packing a gun, don't you? It'll never happen.'

I looked down at the gun in my hand and shook my head. What did I think I was doing? I'd never fired a real gun in my life. Targets at a fairground and pellet guns with my dad were about my speed. What did I think was going to happen? I'd go in, guns blazing like some Cross cowboy in a film, and save the world from McAuley? Yeah, right.

I walked back to Dan's table and put down the P99 and the extra clip.

'Ah! Going to use a new technique against McAuley and his crew, are you? Gonna poke them in the eyes or swear at them? Or were you thinking of throwing the odd shoe?'

Dan was right – and I resented him for it.

I didn't stand a chance with a gun.

I didn't stand a chance without one.

'Welcome to the dance floor, Tobey,' Dan said with satisfaction. 'The song is called "Survival".'

And I was about to get crushed underfoot. I left the lockup and headed for McAuley's warehouse.

sixty-nine

As I walked, I tried not to think and I certainly didn't want to feel. It wasn't far, only thirty minutes from Dan's lockup, and at least the rain had eased off. I looked up at the sky, knowing I'd never enjoy rain again. I just wished I could've spoken to Callie one more time before seeing McAuley. Just one last time. I wasn't happy about the way things had been left between us, but then whose fault was that but my own? If I didn't know who or what I was any more, then what chance did she have of figuring it out.

At last I arrived at the warehouse. The industrial estate contained seven or eight units, most of which were empty and boarded up. At this time of night the place was deserted. The railway bridge beyond the estate was the only sign of irregular life in the whole place. Four or five street lamps had to illuminate the entire estate and were failing miserably. Two Nought security guards dressed in dark blue or black stood outside McAuley's warehouse, chatting. One wore a wool hat pulled tight down over his head, the other was smoking a cigarette. The guard wearing the hat was showing the smoker something on a mobile phone. I inhaled deeply, allowing the smell of tar and rubbish and traffic fumes to fill my lungs, then walked straight up to them.

'I need to see Mr McAuley. Could you tell him that Tobey Durbridge is here?'

The two guards exchanged a look. The smoker stubbed out his cigarette, grinding it under the toe of his thick-soled shoes. He looked me up, down and sideways as he broke out his walkie-talkie. Turning away from me, he spoke into it, his voice a low monotone. Thirty seconds later, he signed off and turned back to me.

'Turn left inside and head for the far end of the ware-house. The office is on your right. Mr McAuley is expecting you,' he told me ominously.

'Thanks,' I replied, though I had no idea why I was thanking him.

He opened one of the warehouse doors and left me to it. I followed his instructions, passing vast crates and boxes stacked on top of each other. The warehouse was dimly lit and eerily silent, a silence so deep it echoed back at me. The rest of McAuley's men had to be in his office already. I took out my phone, pressing the speed-dial icon to get through to DI Boothe. I was wasting my time. From within this warehouse, it was impossible to get a signal. Every nerve in my body screamed at me to turn back. There was no way I could take on the likes of McAuley. It was foolish to even try.

Don't think about that, Tobey. Just keep going.

Whatever it takes.

I knocked on the office door before I could change my mind. 'Mr McAuley, it's me – Tobey,' I called out. 'I have some news you need to hear.'

The door opened slowly. Byron stood in the doorway, gun in hand. He took a quick look around to make sure I was alone, then stepped aside to let me into the room. McAuley sat in the chair at his desk. My gaze zipped around his office like a pinball. Byron stood next to me at the door. Trevor, the guy from McAuley's house, and two other muscle-heads I'd never seen before were dotted around the room.

'So you came?' said McAuley. He turned to Byron. 'I told you he'd come. Search him.'

He stood up and sauntered towards me whilst Byron patted me down from head to toe, not missing a centimetre in between.

'Mr McAuley, I've got something to—'

McAuley threw his whole weight behind a punch to my stomach. It felt like a wrecking ball had hit my innards. I dropped to my knees, clutching my belly and coughing my guts out. Another punch to my head and I was down on the floor, seeing stars and the whole solar system whizzing round my head. My cheek was on fire. I could taste blood in my mouth. McAuley ambled back to his original position behind his desk.

'Byron, get rid of him.' McAuley's voice reached me through the ringing in my ears.

'No. W-wait. P-please. Wait.' My breathing came shallow and fast and sharp. Sweat coated every centimetre of my skin.

This is it, I thought. I tried to swallow, but nothing could move past the jagged rocks in my throat.

It's all over. I'm done.

Byron grabbed my arm and hauled me to my feet. I struggled to stay upright, holding my stomach, which still roared with pain. It felt like my stomach muscles or maybe my spleen had been split wide open. And my cheek was on fire.

'Mr McAuley, I f-found out s-something from Gideon Dowd.' I could hardly catch my breath to speak. But silence would kill me for sure, or maybe just sooner. 'Something you n-need to know.' I had to get the words out whilst I still had the chance.

'If it's the identity of the bent cop, I already know. It's been all over the late-night news,' said McAuley. 'You should've been the one to provide that information, Tobey, not a newsreader. You let me down on that score as well. And ignoring my instructions about Rebecca Dowd? Not smart, Tobey. Not smart.'

'I'm s-sorry about Rebecca, sir. I shouldn't have disobeyed you. It won't happen again.'

'That's right,' said McAuley softly. 'It won't.'

'But the information I have is something far more interesting than a bent cop, sir,' I rushed to assure him. I managed to stand upright to face him. Something was trickling down my cheek. I touched my fingers to my face. Blood. His punch had cut my cheek, inside and out. My hands dropped back to my side.

Silence.

'I'm listening,' McAuley said brusquely.

'It's private,' I said, deliberately looking at each of his squad in turn.

'I have no secrets from my men. I'd trust them with my life.'

'Would you really?' I asked carefully.

McAuley might've been a lot of things, but slow wasn't one of them. He glanced at Byron, who shook his head. I wasn't carrying any hardware, so I was no threat. It wasn't luck that had made me leave Dan's gun behind – it was a sense of self-preservation.

'Maybe you should get three of your men to guard the warehouse entrance, just in case?' I suggested. 'One of Dowds' men saw you – what you did to Rebecca. They'll come calling.'

McAuley stood up, his ice-blue, ice-cold eyes burning into me. 'Trevor, take Dave and Scott and go do as he says. And when you're outside, you'd better phone for some reinforcements.'

The three men left the room, albeit reluctantly. That was perfect. I hadn't had to engineer it so Byron was left behind.

'So what is it?' said McAuley.

This was it. The moment of truth, half-truths and downright lies.

'One of your men is working for the Dowds.'

'Bollocks!' McAuley didn't believe it for a second.

I remembered what he'd said about demanding the loyalty of the people who worked for him. He was like Rebecca that way. Loyalty was everything.

'I have proof,' I said.

'It'd better be watertight,' McAuley said silkily, the threat evident in his voice.

'Can you go online with that computer?' I asked, pointing to the one on his desk.

McAuley's eyes narrowed. 'Of course.'

'Ask Byron to log on and show you how much money he's got in his bank account.'

'What the . . . ?' Byron piped up. 'What is this?'

'Byron is working for the Dowds,' I explained. 'The proof is in his bank account. After today he was going to turn tail and run out on you.'

'I don't believe a word of it,' said McAuley.

'Then check his account. If I'm wrong, then you can hand me over to Byron.'

Byron marched over to me. 'I'm going to enjoy breaking your scrawny neck,' he hissed, spraying spit in my face.

I stepped back, wiping my face with the back of my hand.

'Just check, Mr McAuley. Unless of course you want Byron to get away with it.'

'Alex, you don't believe this bullshit, do you?' Byron turned to his boss.

'Of course not,' said McAuley.

My heart nose-dived. I was screwed.

'But it wouldn't hurt to check, would it?' McAuley continued. 'Log onto your bank account, Byron.'

Byron stared at his boss, unable to believe his ears.

'And once you've proved that Durbridge is lying, he's all yours,' McAuley added.

Byron gave me a look I'd never seen before, and if I lived to be two hundred I never want to see again. If Owen had been lying about putting the money into Byron's account, I was deader than a Sunday roast. Byron marched round the desk and started slamming his fingers down on the keys. I moved round the desk to see the computer screen along with him and McAuley.

Byron input the requested three digits from his four-digit pin code and the requested first, fifth and ninth characters from his password. They all came up as asterisks on the screen so I couldn't hope to learn or guess what his pin code and password might be. Not that it made much difference now. A new screen appeared, showing details of Byron Sweet's current account. It contained six figures, a very healthy six figures. Owen hadn't lied – thank goodness.

Behind Byron, McAuley straightened up.

'T-that can't be right,' Byron spluttered. He clicked on the refresh icon to redisplay the page. The amount of money in his bank account didn't change. He sprang to his feet. 'Alex, I don't know what's going on, but I have no idea how all that money got in my account. I really don't.'

I moved out from behind the desk. If things were about to kick off, I didn't want to get caught up in it.

'That's a lot of money, Byron,' said McAuley quietly.

'It's not mine. You've got to believe me, Alex,' Byron protested. He looked around as if searching for someone to back him up, but there was just him and McAuley – and me. He pointed at me. 'Tobey did it. He must've put it in my account.'

'Where would I get that kind of money from?' I scoffed.

'Boss, I—'

The gun blast made me jump. Byron's hands flew to his throat, but blood squirted out from between his fingers like a fountain. It splashed over McAuley's suit and sprayed his hair. Byron fell backwards like a felled tree. He was dead before he hit the floor. McAuley stared down at him, eyes wild. My mind was screaming. I didn't expect . . . I clamped my lips together so that no sound could spill out of my mouth.

Omigod . . .

McAuley was going to kill me next. I saw it in his eyes as he slowly turned to look at me, his gun still in his hand.

'I'm sorry, Mr McAuley, but I thought you should know,' I said quickly. 'I heard Gideon Dowd talking to one of your men on the phone when I worked at TFTM. Gideon called him by his surname, Sweet. But I only found out earlier today that Byron's surname is Sweet. I'm really sorry, Mr McAuley.'

Trevor, Scott and Dave burst into the room. McAuley was covered in blood, but Byron's body was behind his desk so they couldn't see it from the door. The three men looked me up and down, wondering how I was still standing, wondering where all the blood on their boss had come from. McAuley put his gun down on the desk so he could button up his bloodstained jacket, like he thought that would tidy him up.

'Get rid of the body,' he told them, still buttoning up his jacket.

The three men went round the desk. They stared down at Byron's body, shocked. Two of them bent down to pick him up. I saw it on the desk, my one and only chance. I snatched up McAuley's Glock 23 before any of them could make a move. I hadn't planned on this, but the gun was lying there just asking to be claimed. And I'd rather be at the stock end of it than the barrel end.

'All of you, just stay right there. And keep your hands where I can see them.' The gun was trained on McAuley and his men, who were standing together for the first time since I'd entered the warehouse. From what I could figure out, apart from McAuley and these three, there were just the two security guards at the warehouse entrance. But for how long? McAuley had sent for reinforcements. How long would it take them to get here? I didn't have much time.

We all stood like figures in an oil painting.

Now what?

'One at a time, I want all of you to take out your guns and place them on the table. Dave, you start.'

I watched as Dave withdrew a gun from beneath his jacket.

'You, the one with the red hair. What was your name again? Scott? Your turn.'

He reached round to pull the gun from the waistband at the back of his trousers. I would've thought keeping a gun there was a good way to blow your buttocks off, but what did I know?

'Now you, Trevor.'

Trevor took a gun out of his jacket and put it on the desk.

'Trevor, you'd better get lost,' I said. 'Unless you want to stay here and wait for McAuley to realize that you're the one who works for the Dowds, not Byron.'

'What the hell . . . ?' McAuley gasped.

'Oh, didn't I say?' I said. 'Byron didn't work for the Dowds. That money was put in his bank account by Owen Dowd to make you think otherwise. But when I worked at TFTM, I saw Trevor coming out of Gideon Dowd's office. And Gideon's brother Owen told me that one of your men was passing on information. So it has to be him.'

Trevor looked from me to McAuley like he didn't know what to do.

'Are you staying or going?' I asked impatiently.

Trevor took off like his shoes were on fire. Honour amongst thieves.

Three against one. Plus the two outside. Much better. I could breathe easy now!

I glanced down at Byron. There was a small pool of blood around his neck and head. One bullet and Byron's life was over. One thrust of a knife and Rebecca was gone. Life was too precious to be so fragile. Or maybe life was precious because it was so fragile.

'All of you.' I waved them out from around the table. 'Walk over to the door, please.'

McAuley stayed his men with one gesture of his hand. 'Suppose we stay where we are?' he said. 'Suppose I don't think you've got the balls to shoot anyone?'

He reached for one of the guns on the table. I aimed and squeezed the trigger in the space of less than a second. The gun McAuley had been reaching for shot off the table, propelled by the bullet from my gun. Splinters of wood flew off in all directions. McAuley and his mob flinched away from the ricocheting debris.

'Suppose the next bullet goes straight through your heart?' I told McAuley. I might not have shot a gun at living targets before, but that didn't mean I didn't know how to shoot. My dad had seen to that. 'Now all of you – move.'

I swept the rest of the gun hardware onto the floor with my arm. I certainly didn't need one of McAuley's men getting any bright ideas. If we all headed out of the warehouse, then I could get a signal, phone the police and we'd wait for them to arrive. And maybe, just maybe I might make it out of this in one piece. Scott and Dave led the way, followed by McAuley, with me following behind all three of them. The moment Scott and Dave were through the office door, they sprinted off in opposite directions. There was no way I could stop them. I ran in front of McAuley and slammed the door shut before he could pull the same stunt. Never taking my eyes off McAuley, I locked the door behind me.

McAuley's men were somewhere in the warehouse, just waiting to pounce once I left the office. They couldn't get in. We couldn't get out.

Now what?

'Half a million pounds to the one who kills Tobey Durbridge!' McAuley shouted out.

Bastard! What a time to raise his voice.

The slamming against the office door started almost at once.

'Sit down on the ground,' I ordered McAuley, my gun in his face.

He did as I said, a look of intense satisfaction on his face.

'You're dead, Durbridge. Deal with it. And when I get out of here, I'm going to take care of your girlfriend too.'

'You already took care of Rebecca,' I said bitterly.

'The Dowds needed to be taught a lesson.'

'Rebecca had nothing to do with her family's business,' I told him. 'She was innocent—'

'She was a Dowd,' McAuley dismissed. 'I had hoped to swap her for my merchandise, but you refused to play ball, so I had to opt for plan B – which was fine with me. And you made it so easy to get to Rebecca. Thank you, Tobey. I couldn't have done it without you.'

My index finger stroked over the gun trigger. Shooting McAuley would be a public service.

'But we both know Rebecca wasn't your girlfriend,' McAuley continued.

At my puzzled look, his smile broadened. 'No, I'm talking about Callie Rose Hadley. I was aiming at you that day at the Wasteland when she got in the way instead. But next time . . .'

I raised my fist and brought it down against McAuley's face. I forgot I was still holding his gun. Blood started gushing from his nose almost immediately. McAuley cried out in pain. The pounding on the office door grew more frantic. It didn't matter whether McAuley's minions were trying to save him or earn the reward money he'd promised, I'd be just as dead. I looked down at the gun I was holding. The Glock 23 felt heavy and seductively comfortable in my hand. The pearl stock, warmed by my body heat, fitted snugly against my palm. I now held McAuley's custom-made semiautomatic.

A real, honest-to-God gun in my hand.

A proper killing machine.

Or was that me?

'You're dead, Durbridge – and there's nothing you can do about it.'

seventy

I pulled Eisner's bag of white powder out of my trouser pocket and dangled it in front of McAuley's face.

'You know what this is?' It was a question that didn't need answering. Of course McAuley knew what I was holding. This stuff paid for his white suit and the blood all over it. It paid for the drug houses he had all over Meadowview, and for Ross Resnick's life and my sister's pain. McAuley revelled in the stuff I held in my hands. The harder life got in Meadowview, the more profit there was to be made. Simple economics.

McAuley's eyes narrowed. He spat blood out of his mouth and wiped the sleeve of his jacket across his nose before speaking.

'You want your cut?' he asked. 'Is that what this is all about? You want to go into business for yourself?'

I said nothing. McAuley took my silence to mean that I was listening to him.

'You're a smart guy, Tobey. I could use someone like you working for me. I could show you what it's all about.

In five years you'd be rich beyond your wildest dreams.' McAuley's voice flowed like warm honey. 'And whether you like it or not, you need me. Rebecca died after a meeting with you. What d'you think the Dowds are going to make of that? I'm the only one who can protect you.'

He really thought he had me. I walked around him, my gun still pointed at his head. The banging on his door was getting more insistent. I had about a minute, if that, before the door gave way. McAuley tried to twist his body to follow my movements. My gun against his temple soon persuaded him not to. But he wouldn't stop talking.

'You and me, Tobey, we live in the real world. We know the way things really work. Those that don't know, don't want to know. It's too much for them to take in. Life in Meadowview doesn't happen to them, so it doesn't happen at all. But we know different, don't we?'

Standing behind McAuley, I pulled the top of the small plastic bag apart. The top of the bag gaped open like a transparent mouth.

'It's that knowledge that has made me rich,' McAuley continued. 'And it will make you even richer than me, 'cause you're a smart guy, Tobey.'

'You don't get it, do you, Mr McAuley?' I said. 'This was never about money. This was about you. Why d'you think I did all this? I know you tried to kill me and Callie got hurt instead. All I cared about was bringing you down.'

'Then why didn't you just go to the police?'

'The police were my last resort. I didn't know how many of them were in your pocket. Besides, it's not exactly the Meadowview way, is it?'

'Seems to me that wouldn't've stopped you.'

'You're right. If there was no other way to get you then I would've taken my chances with the police.'

'Don't you see, Tobey,' said McAuley, 'you and I are the same. We go after what we want and we're ruthless about getting it.'

'In your dreams, McAuley. I'm nothing like you.'

'No?' He smiled. 'Look at yourself. Tell me that gun in your hand doesn't make you feel powerful. Tell me this situation isn't giving you the adrenalin rush of your life. Tell me otherwise and I won't believe you.'

I didn't want to hear any more. I couldn't think straight with his words dripping like poison into my ears. Time to shut him up.

'Open your mouth,' I ordered.

McAuley tilted back his head. 'What?'

'You heard,' I said. 'Open up.'

He slowly did as I'd asked. I tipped the whole bag of white powder into his mouth. He writhed on the ground, kicking frantically as he tried to spit it out, but I clamped my hand over his lips, forcing him to swallow.

'This stuff means so much to you?' I hissed. 'Choke on it.'

His eyes raged against mine, but I couldn't hear or feel a thing. I kept my hand against his mouth and my gun against his head. He was the one who'd tried to shoot me down in cold blood, only he'd hit Callie instead. He was the one who'd decided I was a danger to him because I'd unknowingly delivered Ross Resnick's finger to his wife Louise and the police had become involved. If he'd just left me alone, none of this would be happening.

The door was beginning to splinter. It was all over.

Outside the door there was a loud unexpected bang. Then another. And another. Gunshots. Each shot was loud as the devil's shout and reverberated right through me. Did McAuley's men have guns salted away throughout the warehouse? Maybe they'd got tired of banging on the door and were shooting out the lock. Another gunshot, louder than before . . . closer than before. I pressed my gun against McAuley's head, my finger on the trigger. He was coughing and retching. He could dish it out to anyone who wanted it and could pay, but he sure couldn't take it. The door burst open. I was ready. When I went down, so would McAuley.

Standing in the doorway was . . . Dan.

He had the P99 in his hand and two dead men at his feet.

'Get out of here, Tobey,' he said grimly. 'The police will be here any minute. The guards outside must've woken up by now.'

'Dan . . .' I stared at him. 'I thought . . .'

'I know what you thought. Go, before I change my mind.'

'But I can't just leave . . .'

'Yes, you can. You need to go,' Dan ordered.

'McAuley's got more men on their way.'

'The police will get here first.'

'Dan, I don't understand. What made you change your mind?' I couldn't help asking.

'I'm damned if I know,' he said. 'I owe you. You owe me. Everything is screwed up. Tobey, there are times, like now, when I hate your guts.'

'Then why?'

'The McAuleys of this world can't always win. Not all the time,' said Dan. 'And you and me, we were friends once.'

'We were friends,' I agreed. 'Once.'

Dan walked over to McAuley, watching with contempt as he vomited all over his suit, white powder smeared around his lips and frothing in his mouth.

'Dan, you don't have to stay here. Come with me,' I said.

He shook his head, adding with a defeated smile, 'Tobey, haven't you figured out by now, this is my proper place. But don't worry about me. McAuley and I have some business to take care of. Then it's every man for himself.'

I wanted to argue with him, but it would've been futile. I looked from Dan to McAuley, who was still retching. I didn't know if McAuley had brought it all up and I didn't care any more. I just wanted to be away from here. Away from all of them, including Dan. They made me heartsick. I went to walk past Dan, but he put out a hand to bar my way.

'Give me McAuley's gun,' he said.

We regarded each other. Laying the gun in Dan's open hand, I carried on walking. Would I feel the bullet tear into my back or hear the gun go off – which would be first? I looked straight ahead as I left the room. I could see nothing but Callie's warm, brown eyes smiling at me. I held onto her image. If Dan was going to kill me, then at least I'd die with her on my mind, at least I'd die happy.

I got McAuley for you, Callie, I thought with a grim smile. I got him.

Just as I'd promised her and myself when I'd cradled her in my arms at the Wasteland.

All this because of packages and deliveries and Ross Resnick and money. Thanks to my greedy impatience, I'd let myself get caught up in it. And thanks to my naïvety, so had Callie Rose. And because of me, Rebecca . . .

Rebecca.

Forgive me . . .

Who was I talking to? What was I hoping for? I was seeking absolution in a warehouse filled with blood. I blinked as I walked out of the building and into the moon-light. I was still standing. But only just. Behind me a single gunshot sounded. I flinched instinctively. The sound had come from inside the warehouse, from McAuley's office. Without turning round, I carried on walking away just as fast as I could. In the distance, I heard sirens approaching. I ran for cover, ducking out of sight behind some bins and staying there until the police cars had passed by.

I walked all the way home, my head down, my gaze turned inwards. I turned into my street, my whole body aching. But I didn't stop outside my house. Instead I went up to Callie's, intent on seeing her again. But I didn't knock and I didn't ring her bell. I just stood, staring at the closed door.

I did it for you, Callie.

But in doing so, I'd lost myself. I wasn't the same person as before and I couldn't bear to watch Callie turn away from the person I'd become. And she would turn away, maybe sooner, maybe later, but it would happen.

Slowly I trudged up the path to my house and went indoors.

The
Reckoning

seventy-one
===

'Tobey, Callie's here,' Mum called out from downstairs.

Five days had passed since McAuley had been shot. And my friend Dan Jeavons was wanted for his murder, as well as the murders of two other men who worked for McAuley. But Dan was still on the run and the police hadn't tracked him down. Yet. The DCI in charge of the case insisted that it was not a question of *if* Dan got caught but *when*. And all I could do was hope that Dan kept his head down and never stopped moving. And all I could do was wish he would stop running and give himself up, just to find some peace.

If it wasn't for him . . .

Dan and me. We were friends. Once.

Gideon Dowd and DCI Reid had both been arrested and charged on several different counts. I'd thought DCI Reid would be done for gross misconduct and kicked off the police force and that would be the end of that, but not so. The authorities wanted her skin, not to mention all her internal organs in a pickle jar. The deputy commissioner, no less, was at pains to assure the public that DCI Reid, if found guilty of the charges levelled against her, would be going to prison. The police were obviously on a roll. They'd even got Vanessa Dowd on a charge of tax evasion – not that she cared. She was still openly grieving over the death of her daughter Rebecca. The fatal stabbing had been all over the newspapers and the TV. Everyone seemed to be judging Rebecca and the circumstances of her death by the infamy of the rest of her family. She didn't deserve that. The press were still trying to establish a link between her death and the death of Alex McAuley as everyone knew about the enmity between the two factions. There was even speculation that Dan had been working for the Dowds.

My name hadn't been mentioned anywhere.

So Alex McAuley was out of the picture. And Owen Dowd now occupied the whole frame. Two days ago, I received a banker's cheque for a lot of money. Owen hadn't sent me a personal cheque – that'd be too easy to trace – but he'd sent me the money just as he had said he would. It arrived in an ordinary envelope with a first class stamp. And if the cheque had gone astray? Well, Owen had plenty more where that came from. Just touching the slip of paper made me feel unclean. I folded up the cheque just as small as I could, but I couldn't make it disappear. I went for a long walk to try and clear my head, dropping the cheque into the first charity collection box I came across. But I still felt contaminated.

Owen Dowd . . .

Not the outcome I would've hoped for as far as he was concerned. None of this was what I'd hoped for. I read a story once about a king who was greedy enough to wish that everything he touched turned to gold. Well, thanks to my desire for money and then revenge, everything I'd touched had turned to crap. I wasn't about to touch anyone I cared about ever again. Dan was right about me. So was Sephy. And Lucas. Everyone saw me more clearly than I saw myself.

I swung my legs off my bed to head downstairs. Too late. My door opened and Callie walked in. Her hair was loose, falling like a dark cloud around her face and shoulders and covering the scar on her temple. But in time, her scar would heal. She'd lost weight, but she was still the most beautiful thing I'd ever seen. She was wearing a white dress and white sandals and my insides started hiccupping at the sight of her. I remembered the last time Callie had been in my room. That'd been the first, last and only time in my entire life I'd been truly one hundred per cent happy. But that was another lifetime ago. And now I was broken inside.

Callie walked towards me and I froze. She reached out, her fingers brushing against the now permanent scar on my cheek, courtesy of McAuley. Her touch made my skin tingle.

'Your eye is a bit puffy and yellow,' she said softly. 'Does it hurt?'

I pulled away from her. 'I'll live.'

Callie's hand dropped to her side. 'Who did that to you?' she asked, indicating my face.

'Callie, I haven't got time to talk to you now. I was just on my way out.'

'Can I come?'

'No,' I said, pulling on my trainers. 'I have a date.'

'With who?'

'Misty.'

'I see,' said Callie. She studied my carpet as if she'd never seen it before.

'Why did you want to see me?' I prompted as I stood up. I had to get her out of my room. Seeing her like this was doing my head in.

'I came to tell you that Mum has invited you to come with us tomorrow to Bharadia and Hammond.'

'To who and what?' I frowned.

'Bharadia and Hammond. They're Nana Jasmine's solicitors,' Callie explained. 'We're going to hear Nana's will being read. Mum says you can share our car. We're leaving at two tomorrow afternoon.'

'Why do I need to be there?'

'You're mentioned in Nana's will,' said Callie.

I frowned at her. 'Why?'

She shrugged. 'No idea.'

Silence.

'Tobey, I was sorry to hear about what happened to your friend, Rebecca.'

I shrugged.

'Are the police any closer to finding out who did it?'

I shook my head. 'They'll never find out who's responsible.'

'You mustn't give up hope,' said Callie.

Hope? What was that? Every day was like standing at the gateway to hell. The knife McAuley had used on Rebecca hadn't been found on his body, so he'd obviously disposed of it before he got to his warehouse. They would never find it now. Rebecca's death would remain an unsolved mystery, at least officially.

'Callie, have you remembered anything about the day . . . the day you got shot?' I asked.

Callie shook her head. I waited for her to say more, but

she was silent. So she probably still didn't remember the night before the shooting either. She didn't remember the two of us together. I smiled bitterly. I didn't even have that to silently, secretly share with her. The memory was mine and mine alone.

'Tell me something,' I began. 'If you found out who shot you, what would you do?'

Callie flinched at my question, her gaze sharp. 'Tobey, d'you know who it was?'

I shrugged. 'It's just a hypothetical question.'

'Then my hypothetical answer is – I don't know,' Callie replied. 'I'd probably tell the police and get them arrested and sent to prison.'

'And if they were above the law?'

'No one is above the law.' Callie frowned.

I looked at her pityingly.

'OK, then. No one should be above the law.'

'What should be and what actually is are two completely different things,' I said with derision. 'The Equal Rights bill should've been made law decades ago, not a week ago. We shouldn't've had to wait for a bent copper in a gang-leader's pocket to be found out before the police started cracking down on the gangs taking over Meadowview.'

'Well, the law is man-made so of course it's going to be fallible,' said Callie. 'But there is such a thing as justice. Justice isn't the same as the law.'

'So what would you do to make sure you got justice, if you knew the person who'd shot you was above the law?' I persisted.

Callie shrugged. At my impatient look, she exclaimed,

'I really don't know, Tobey. I'd want revenge, of course I would. I'm human. But the desire for revenge is like hatred or anger, it eats away at you. And I should know.'

'And what if it was your mum or Meggie who got shot?' I asked.

Why was I doing this? Maybe I just needed to hear her say that what I'd done was not correct, but it was right, that it wasn't lawful, but it was justice and she would've done the same.

'I honestly don't know, Tobey,' Callie sighed. 'Why?'

I shrugged. 'I was only wondering, that's all. It doesn't matter.'

I tried to step past her, but she moved to stand in my way.

'Tobey, you and Misty? Is it serious?'

'Very,' I instantly replied.

'I see.'

This time she let me pass. I opened my bedroom door for her to leave first. As she walked past me, I inhaled deeply but discreetly. Callie didn't smell of my perfume any more.

'I'll see you tomorrow at two,' I confirmed.

Callie headed back downstairs with me following behind. I stretched out my hand towards the back of her head. Was her hair as soft as I remembered? I forced my hand back to my side.

'Oh, before I forget, I think this belongs to you,' Callie dug into one of the pockets on her dress and held out the letter I'd sent to her, the one with all the information about McAuley's shipments. 'Am I right? Is this yours?'

I nodded, wondering what she had made of the information on the sheets of paper. Had she read it? Did she believe I worked for McAuley? I wasn't about to ask.

'I'm afraid I opened it as it was addressed to me, but I stopped reading when I realized what it was,' she told me. 'I thought maybe it was sent to me for safe-keeping?'

I didn't answer.

'I take it you don't want me to hold onto it?'

'No. I'll take it,' I replied.

'Tobey, what happened when I was in hospital?'

'The Earth went round the sun. The tides ebbed and flowed. Life carried on,' I replied evenly.

Callie lowered her gaze momentarily. 'I'd better get back.'

'See you, Callie.'

'Bye, Tobey.'

Callie headed back to her house. I set off in the opposite direction. A conversation I'd had with my sister a while ago kept playing in my head. Jess told me that I'd never understand her until I experienced what all miserable, lonely, unhappy people shared. Only now had I finally figured out what she meant. Failure. I couldn't bear to look at myself in the mirror any more. I was someone I no longer recognized. I thought I could take my revenge on McAuley and emerge unscathed at the end of it. I had failed.

I thought about the stuff I'd poured down McAuley's throat and the gun I'd held against his temple. In that moment, I'd wanted so badly to hurt him. No, that's not true. I'd wanted to *kill* him. And if it had been anyone else but Dan who'd entered the office, by now I'd be a murderer. Who was I kidding? Rebecca was dead because of me, as was Byron. McAuley should've been dead because of me. The drugs I'd made him swallow would've done the job sooner rather than later. Dan had merely put him out of his misery.

Five people dead because of me. Rebecca. Byron. McAuley. The two guards Dan had shot . . .

I *was* a murderer. Now I truly knew who and what I was. No one should ever find out for certain exactly what they're capable of. It left you with no place to hide.

I walked around the block, then headed back home.

seventy-two

Mr Bharadia's conference room was truly impressive. The oval mahogany table was solid wood, not just mahogany veneer. At least I think it was, I'm no expert. I glanced under the table. The legs were carved like birds' claws on a stand. The ten chairs around the table all matched each other and had the same design on the front legs. The back legs were plain. The backs of each chair were also intricately carved . . .

Tobey, what're you doing?

I mentally shook my head. I knew exactly what I was up to. I was trying to take in everything in the room so that I wouldn't have to think about the one thing I was desperate to avoid. Callie Rose. She sat next to me, watching me with puzzled eyes. She was still trying to figure out what was wrong.

We all sat, waiting for Mr Bharadia to make an appearance. Minerva and Sephy were discussing Sephy's forthcoming wedding to Nathan, talking about the best places to buy a wedding dress. I wished Callie would join in their conversation. That way I wouldn't have to speak to her. Deciding to make myself scarce until the solicitor put in an appearance, I tried to stand up, but Callie's hand on my arm stopped me.

'Tobey, we need to talk,' she said softly.

Which was just what I was afraid of.

'How come I've hardly seen you since I've been home?' Callie's voice was barely above a whisper as she tried to keep the conversation strictly between us. Unlike Misty, she didn't believe in making a scene.

'I've been busy.'

'Too busy to even come round and say hello?'

'I've been busy.'

Callie looked at me, hurt clouding her eyes. 'Have I done something to upset you?'

''Course not.'

'Then why won't you even look at me?'

I turned to glare at her, my expression pure biting frost. She flinched. 'Tobey, what have I done? Why am I getting the treatment?'

'Godsake, Callie. Can we just get through the will reading without all this drama?'

'Tobey . . .'

'Callie, leave me alone. For God's sake, just leave me alone.'

The whole room went quiet. I jumped up and left the room before I did something incredibly stupid – like holding Callie and telling her the truth. I hid out in the men's loos until after the meeting was scheduled to start. It was the only way I could make sure that Callie and I didn't enter into the same conversation again. I went into the meeting room, grimly pleased to see that the solicitor had arrived and everyone else was waiting for me.

I sat down again, drawing my chair away from Callie as I did so. Callie kept looking at me, and I kept pretending I didn't see her. The solicitor started spouting some legalese which had me zoning out in seconds. I didn't even know what I was doing here. So Jasmine Hadley had mentioned me in her will. So what? She was probably using this opportunity to warn Callie off or something. This was a complete waste of time.

'Mr Bharadia, could you skip over all the legal jargon, please?' said Sephy, interrupting the solicitor's flow. 'I'm sure everyone here would rather just get to it.'

Apart from a slight tightening of his lips, Mr Bharadia's expression didn't change. He was too much of a professional for that. 'Very well, Miss Hadley. I'll get to the details of the will as you've requested.'

'How long before Mum died did she draw up this will?' asked Callie's aunt Minerva.

'Er, three . . . just a moment.' Mr Bharadia checked the top of the will and another document in the pile of papers before him. 'Yes, three weeks.'

The solicitor was obviously the kind of man who didn't yawn without confirming its date and validity first.

'Three weeks?' Minerva said slowly. 'So when she drafted this, she knew her cancer was terminal?'

Mr Bharadia frowned. 'I believe so.'

Terminal? I didn't know Jasmine Hadley's cancer had come back and was terminal.

'Minerva, what difference does it make?' Sephy asked her sister.

'I just wondered, that's all,' Minerva replied.

The solicitor turned to Minerva first and told her that she and her husband had been left a substantial six-figure sum and that half that sum again had been left in trust for their son Taj, which he would obtain when he was twenty-five years old. Minerva's husband was already a very rich man, but now they were richer. Taj was a lucky boy. How lovely to grow up knowing you had all that money waiting for you. I couldn't even begin to imagine what that would be like. Well, actually I could imagine. I could dream, just like everyone else. Minerva nodded at the solicitor, her face sombre.

Mr Bharadia turned to Meggie. 'Mrs Hadley wrote this letter one week before her death. She asked that it be read out to you before I tell you how much you've been left.'

Meggie nodded, but didn't speak.

Dear Meggie,

You and I were friends a long time ago, and giving up your friendship was one of the biggest mistakes of my life. I made a mistake and then lived in denial for years, blaming you instead of looking in the mirror for the real author of my misery. I really feel that we'd started to get back to the relationship we had when our children were young - as were we. I hope so. Please know that I think of you as probably the truest friend I ever had. No amount of money will ever make up for all the pain and suffering you've been forced to endure in your life. No amount of money will ever bring back what you lost, but I hope that the gift I leave you will at least ensure that the rest of your days are spent in some comfort.

Your friend, always,
Jasmine

Mr Bharadia stopped reading the letter and turned back to the will. When he announced how much money Meggie had been left, a collective gasp sounded through the room. She'd been bequeathed the same amount as Minerva. It was six figures and one hell of a lot. Enough to buy a new house outside Meadowview and still have enough to live life as she pleased. I regarded Meggie, but her expression didn't change. Was it more or less than she'd hoped for? Maybe she'd got past the stage of hoping for anything at all.

Mr Bharadia turned to Sephy. '*To my daughter, Sephy, I leave my two houses, all their contents and all attached lands to do with as she sees fit. I truly hope that Sephy will use this legacy to make her life easier — something she has never been particularly good at in the past.*'

Sephy smiled faintly at the last comment.

I knew for a fact that Jasmine's house by the beach was

worth a whole roomful of currency just by itself. I didn't know about her second home, but whatever it was worth, Sephy was a very rich woman.

'Sephy, will you be moving into Jasmine's house now?' asked Meggie quietly.

Sephy regarded Meggie, then smiled. 'Not without you,' she replied. 'I'm not living anywhere without you.'

The relief on Meggie's face was very evident. She looked far happier about that than about the money she'd been left.

The solicitor turned to Sarah Pike, Jasmine Hadley's personal secretary for years and the only other non-family member present. '*To my loyal personal assistant, Sarah Pike, I leave the sum of two hundred and fifty thousand pounds plus my black WMW which she has always admired.*' Sarah allowed herself a big smile, followed by a small sigh.

Well, apart from Callie and myself, everyone in the room had been taken care of. Had Callie's nana left her anything? None of us had to wait long to find out. Mr Bharadia turned to Callie. '*To my darling granddaughter, Callie Rose Hadley, I leave all my stocks, shares, bonds and other equity. The portfolio will be professionally maintained for her until she marries or reaches the age of twenty-five, whichever comes sooner. My fervent hope is that she will not let this money spoil her and will use it to do some good, but the choice is hers.*' Mr Bharadia looked around the table. All eyes were on him, but no one spoke. 'Oh, I beg your pardon!' He started flicking through the papers before him, whilst muttering to himself. 'Ah! Here it is. As of the close of the stock market yesterday, the portfolio is worth . . . two million. That's it. Two million pounds, give or take the odd thousand.'

What was the odd thousand between friends? I stared at Callie. Two million . . . Callie was super rich. She turned to me, shock written large on her face.

'Congratulations,' I said softly.

Someone had taken an acetylene torch to my insides. Callie was rich. I wasn't. And that was the end of that. I hung my head, trying to come to terms with the fact that I was going to lose the one person I cared most about in this world. What was I thinking? I'd lost her long before today, and ironically money had had nothing to do with it.

'*To Tobey Durbridge, I say this,*' Mr Bharadia continued.

My head shot up. Jasmine Hadley had left me a message?

'*Tobey, I know you'll think me an interfering old woman, but age brings certain busybody benefits. In fact, that's about the only positive thing that age does bring. I've decided to stick my nose into your life for my own selfish reasons. Call it my way of atoning for past mistakes if you will. Years ago I had the chance to help someone like you, and to my shame I stood back and did nothing. I'm determined not to let that happen again. Tobey, I want you to finish school and go to university. I want you to make something of your life. Never take no for an answer. Never let doors slammed in your face stop you from moving forward. Grasp life and every opportunity presented to you with both hands. I've watched you over the years and I know how much my granddaughter means to you. So I'll make you a deal. I've set up a savings*' *account in your name. You will be allowed to withdraw up to twenty-five thousand pounds each year whilst you are at school and university. On satisfactory completion of your education, any monies left in the savings account will be yours to save or spend as you wish.'*

I stared at Mr Bharadia, convinced his monotone voice had put me to sleep and I was now dreaming.

'Would you like to know the total amount in the savings account?' asked the solicitor.

I nodded, still stunned. Mr Bharadia flicked through some papers underneath the will he was reading. 'Let's see. Three hundred thousand pounds, plus interest.'

'Mum left Tobey three hundred thousand . . . ?' Minerva couldn't believe it. She wasn't the only one.

'Plus interest,' Mr Bharadia added.

Jasmine Hadley had left me all that money? All the things I'd been through in the last few weeks, all the things I'd done . . . And I had that kind of money waiting for me all this time.

'I don't want it. Any of it,' I said furiously. 'Give it to Callie. Split it between the lot of you. I don't want a penny.'

'Don't be silly, Tobey. That's your money,' said Callie. 'Nana Jasmine wanted you to have it.'

'Not interested. Excuse me.' I got up and headed for the door before anyone could stop me.

Once outside, I kept going. I headed out of the office and along the corridor towards the lift. I pressed the button.

'Tobey . . . Tobey, wait.' Callie came running after me.

Where the hell was the frickin' lift?

'Tobey, what's wrong?' Callie asked, laying her hand on my arm. The warmth of her hand singed my skin.

I drew away from her. 'You should get back in there,' I said.

'Not without you.'

'You belong in there with your family.'

'You're my family too.'

I couldn't take much more. The lift was taking for ever to arrive.

'Callie, go back where you belong,' I told her, heading for the stairs without looking back.

Even though we were fifteen storeys up, I just wanted to run down the stairs and out of the building and to keep going. I wanted to run and run until I left myself somewhere far behind.

'Tobey, wait,' Callie called out, coming down the stairs after me.

'Godsake, Callie. Can't you take a hint? I don't want you with me.'

'I don't believe you.'

I grabbed hold of her arms and pulled her hard towards me, her face only centimetres away from mine. 'I've got what I wanted from you and your family,' I said, adding viciously, 'You were an OK lay and your grandmother has left me a great deal of money. I don't need you or anyone else any more. So do me a favour and get lost. Or better still, run back to your mum and aunt and get them to contest the will.'

I released her and she stumbled backwards, rubbing at her arms where my fingers had bitten into her flesh. Her eyes were shimmering with tears, but none of them fell. I forced myself to look straight at her so she'd get the message. I clenched my fists, despising myself for hurting her. Just despising myself. And even though my insides were churning, even though my throat was so swollen I could hardly breathe and my heart was being squeezed by a merciless hand, I was careful to make sure that none of that showed on my face.

Callie took a halting step towards me, then another. My whole body froze with a wary stillness. What was she doing?

'You're trying to make me hate you,' she said softly. 'But it won't work, Tobey. I think you hate yourself enough for both of us.'

'Just go away, Callie.'

'D'you really mean that?'

'Yes.'

'Would you like me to go away for good?'

'*Yes!*' I shouted. I started down the stairs again.

'D'you wish I'd been killed?' Callie called after me. 'Is that what you're trying to say?'

Her words tripped me up so badly, I had to grab hold of the banister to stop myself from pitching forward. The breath caught in my throat. I couldn't move. My brain kept telling my feet to keep going. Go down the stairs, one step at a time. Run. But all signals seemed to stop at my heart. I heard Callie descending the stairs behind me. She moved to the step below mine so she could look up into my face.

'And if you really hate me so much, then why did you come to see me almost every day in the hospital – even if it was only for a few minutes?'

'How did you know that?' I whispered.

'You just confirmed what Mum told me,' said Callie.

I didn't answer. I watched her, unable to take my eyes off her face.

'Tobey, you may be my mender of broken things, but now it's my turn.'

'Callie Rose, you don't know who I am any more,' I whispered. 'You don't know the things I've done since you got shot.'

'So tell me,' said Callie.

'You'll hate me.'

'Never happen.'

But I couldn't take that chance. Maybe one day, but not today. I started to shake my head.

'Tobey, just tell me this,' said Callie. 'All the things you think I'll loathe you for, you did them for me, didn't you?'

I didn't reply. I sat down on the hard, cold concrete stair, too tired to even stand any more. Callie sat beside me, just as close as she could get.

'How was your date last night?' she asked.

'Fine.'

'Liar. You walked round the block and went back home.'

'How d'you know that?' I asked, stunned.

'I was in Mum's bedroom. I was looking up at the nearest star and wishing. And when I looked down you were just going back inside your house,' said Callie. 'So I got my wish.'

I closed my eyes. It didn't make any difference. I had to make her see that. I forced myself to look at her, bracing myself for her reaction to what I was about to say.

'Callie, because of me five people are dead, Dan is facing the rest of his life on the run or in prison, and you almost died.'

'But I didn't.' Callie took my face in her hands, her expression now sombre. But she hadn't looked away. Not once. 'Tobey, I didn't die. I'm right next to you. And as for the rest, we'll face that together.'

'No way. I'm in Hell and I'm not dragging you down with me. I have to do this alone.'

'No, you don't—'

'Five people, Callie Rose. Five people are dead because of my actions.' I pulled away from her. 'How do I get past that? How do I even try?'

'Tobey, look at me.'

But I wouldn't. I couldn't.

'Because of me, Nana Jasmine and Uncle Jude died,' said Callie softly. 'D'you hate me for that?'

My head snapped up. I shook my head. I could no more hate Callie than I could sprout wings and fly. Callie and I regarded each other, sharing something deeper and wider than the silence around us. She leaned forward to kiss me. Her lips were warm on mine, but I didn't respond.

'If you tell me to go away, I will,' she said, pulling back slightly. 'If you really don't want me any more, I'll leave. But if you do dump me, I'll just spend the rest of my life wishing that I hadn't come out of my coma.'

Callie's words ripped straight through me.

'Don't say that,' I said furiously. 'Don't ever say that again.'

'It's the truth. I couldn't bear to think that we'll never be together again,' she said, adding with a faint teasing note to her voice, 'Besides, you're my sexbot, no one else's. I saw you first.'

I stared at her. 'You remember? The two of us together, you remember?'

'I remembered the day after I woke up out of my coma. I still don't remember the day of the shooting. My doctor said that may never come back,' said Callie. 'But I remember the night before. I remember every detail. I remember you.'

There was a time when that was all I longed for.

'It's not enough. Not any more.' I started to turn away, but Callie's hand pulled my face back towards hers.

'Tobey, tell me the truth. D'you want me to go?'

Slowly, I shook my head.

'Why not?' asked Callie gently.

Somehow my hand found its way to her face. My fingers stroked against her cheek.

'Because I love you,' I whispered at last.

Everything else I'd known or believed in lay in ruins at my feet. Except for that. That was the only thing that hadn't changed. Callie hugged me, her arms tight around me like she'd never let me go.

She said softly, 'You and me, Tobey, against the world.'

My head on her shoulder, I did something I hadn't done in years and years. The one thing I thought I'd never do again.

I cried.

Epilogue

HEATHCROFT HIGH SCHOOL NEWSLETTER

Congratulations to the following students who have been accepted into university to read the subjects listed:

Student	Subject
Omar Ade	History
Solomon Ajuki	Medicine
Ella Cheshie	Medicine
Alex Donaldson	Modern Languages
Tobias Durbridge	Law
Jennifer Dyer	Geography
Samantha Eccles	Sports Therapy
Connor Freeman	English
Callie Rose Hadley	Law
Rachelle Holloway	Modern Languages
Misty Jackman	Popular Music
Bliss Lwammi	Communications Technology
David McVitie	Marketing
Gennipher Mardela	Maths & Economics
Maxine Mbunte	Physics

. . . continued on page 4

Other News

Our school is particularly proud to announce the opening of the Meadowview Shelter, set up and partially funded by one of our students, Tobey Durbridge. The shelter will provide support, help and information for those who seek drug and/or alcohol addiction rehabilitation.